Praise for Paul Genesse and THE GOLDEN CORD

"This is a story that's worth your time. It's almost like going back to that first fantasy novel that totally captivated you and you read it over and over again. HIGHLY RECOMMENDED."
—Russell Davis, author, editor, and President of the Science Fiction and Fantasy Writers of America.

"A good mix of action, angst, and romance. *The Golden Cord* has fine action sequences, like many a fantasy novel, but Paul Genesse takes the time to make the protagonist and his companions much more than hack and slashers. They have hopes, fears, doubts, secret motivations, and backstories that give the action gravitas. Plenty of swordplay and slaying for the action junkies, but also plenty of self-doubt and romance for those looking for a deeper story."
—Donald J. Bingle, author of *Forced Conversion*

"Paul Genesse's tale is elegantly written and filled with rich, believable heroes and villains. He transports you to a vibrant fantasy world that feels so real and complex you won't want to leave. It is irresistible."
—Jean Rabe, author of the *Finest Trilogy* from Tor Books

Praise for Paul Genesse and *The Dragon Hunters*

"Genesse stresses the necessity of trust between races and cultures and the perils of bias and dissention, and he keeps the plot moving quickly . . . "

—Publishers Weekly

"Paul Genesse is a talented writer with two rare gifts: the ability to create wonderful worlds, and the skill to share them with his readers. Through his deft handling of magic and mythic creatures, Paul Genesse transports us into a realm of wild imagining. Taut suspense and fantastic imagery make the The Dragon Hunters a tale no fantasy fan will want to miss."

—Michael A. Stackpole, *New York Times* bestselling author of The Star Wars novel *I, Jedi*

"With vivid world-building, Paul Genesse sets his characters on paths that wind and twist through the world as they try to reach their almost impossible goal—the death of the Dragon King. The characters are driven, each for their own reasons, united by their desire for honor, and vengeance for their kin. In the midst of a fantasy, Paul weaves in realistic themes of family and honor, prejudice and hate, love and redemption."

—Elizabeth Vaughan, USA Today bestselling author of *The Warlands trilogy*

The Secret Empire

Book Three of the
Iron Dragon Series

Paul Genesse

Paul Genesse

Hi Melody,

Find the secrets...

Paul Genesse

Published by Iron Dragon Books
Trade Paperback First Edition 2012

The Iron Dragon Series

Book One: The Golden Cord
Book Two: The Dragon Hunters
Book Three: The Secret Empire
Book Four: The Crystal Eye
Book Five: The Iron Brotherhood (the finale)

The Secret Empire
ISBN No. 978-0-9850038-0-7

For Patrick M. Tracy,
a dear friend and a great writer who
helped craft this book, and series from the very beginning.

Acknowledgements

I finished the first draft of what has become *The Secret Empire* in 2002. Ten years later the book is finally coming out, though this version bears little resemblance to the manuscript I wrote back then. The story is roughly the same, but I'm a much better writer now, though I know I still have a lot to learn. It took me years to become a good enough writer to break into publishing, and in 2006 I sold book one, *The Golden Cord,* to John Helfers at Five Star Books, which came out in 2008, followed by book two, *The Dragon Hunters* which released in October of 2009. There has been a two year and three month gap between book two and three coming out.

Traditional publishing is a rough business, and despite *The Golden Cord* becoming Five Star Books bestselling fantasy of all time, their fantasy/science-fiction line was not doing well overall, and they cut that whole segment of their business. The publisher tried to keep me alone, and finish the series, but upper management said no, as one book could not make enough money to keep an entire line open. So, I was orphaned in late 2009, with no publisher for the rest of the proposed five book series of which I had manuscripts already written, and plenty of fans who wanted to read them.

I soon learned that the major publishers will not touch orphaned series, and all the small presses I spoke with offered me very little aside from long wait times to hear back from them, which is normal, and awful contracts.

I went from being ecstatic after book one was so successful, my very first published novel, to very depressed when I heard my publisher was stopping all fantasy publications. It's been a rough three years for most everyone, (2009-2011) as the U.S. and world economy has taken a dive, and the worst I can say is that my 401K lost some money and I lost my publisher. Some people lost their house, or their lifesavings, and so I do not have a lot to complain about.

Fortunately for me, the paradigm of publishing has changed in the past couple of years. Electronic books are making huge gains, and print on demand services like CreateSpace by Amazon.com have become part of publishing that will never go away. I finally chose an outlet for the *Iron Dragon Series* and in late 2011 decided that I would put the rest of the books out myself, with the help of my published writer/editor friends and Amazon.com. The need to get the books out there became an obsession, and after years of little progress I was sprinting to get the manuscript I'd had for years, rewritten and edited.

I was fortunate to have the editorial help of Bradley P. Beaulieu, the acclaimed author of the *Lays of Anuskaya* series from Nightshade Books. Book one, *The Winds of Khalakovo,* and book two, *The Straits of Galahesh* are both incredible fantasy novels, and Brad is a far better writer than I will ever be. He helped me improve this book tremendously, and I know that Brad would be a fabulous editor for any major publisher. I'm fortunate to have him as a friend, and next time I promise I'll give him a lot longer to look at the manuscript, as I really wanted to get this book out there, and made him rush. His ideas were gold and I did my best to implement his thoughts in this final draft. The mistakes are mine alone, and the awesome ideas mostly come from Brad and the other big influence on this book, Pat.

Patrick M. Tracy, my college roommate and best friend, has been the most influential person on this book, my life as a writer, and the whole series in general. Pat suffered through this manuscript back in 2002 and earlier, and has helped me craft and shape this story more than any other. He and I have spent hundreds of hours talking about these books, and he's been patient and kind the whole way. I need a lot of hand holding sometimes and Pat is the best guy ever to brainstorm with. I come up with an idea and he makes it nastier. Pat and I have been going down this author path together for years and

I'm so impressed with his skill as a writer and poet. Find his short fiction and you'll see what I mean. Some of the best lines in this book are Pat's. He helped keep me going during those tough times after my books were orphaned and I could not ask for a better friend.

My loving and beautiful wife, Tammy has been extremely supportive as well, and allows me to write and keep crazy schedules. I read her all the proof pages out loud and she's put up with this story the longest out of anyone. We've been together since 1995 and soon after that I was thinking of the world of Ae'leron and the Dragon King. Tammy has been the most important person in my life, and I am blessed with a lot of great friends and family, but without Tam, nothing would be possible.

I also want to acknowledge the amazing cover artist, Ciruelo Cabral, whose images have graced the covers of the Iron Dragon Series. His yearly *Dragons* calendars are stunning, and please find them every year, as they are available in all the stores. He inspires me a lot and his work is perfect for the *Iron Dragon Series.*

I want to thank my amazing fans all over the world who pushed me to get this book out there, and especially my readers in Utah where I live. Thanks to Jordan Stephens, Jason and Natalie Wilson, Cheryl and Chris O'Malley, Katrina Miller, Glenn Lee, Barbara Webb, Seth Warn, Rebecca Shelley, Adam Davies, K.C. Anderson, Craig Lloyd, my parents, my friends at the hospital where I work as a cardiac nurse, and all the writers, librarians, and teachers who have inspired me to follow this dream.

Thank you all for your support and I hope you enjoy reading *The Secret Empire.*

Paul Genesse
January 8, 2012

Ae'leron

The misty Void,
an abyss of white
clouds, surrounds
the plateaus

Nexus Plateau

Nexus
City

Cliffton

Drobin
City

Kyrlune

Axos

Thor
For

Dark
Spire
Mts

Drobin
Plateau

Byford

Draemoor
Forest

Giergun
Lands

Thornclaw
Plateau

Valonia

Thorngrass
Plains

Wind
Walker
Mts

Cliffton

Khierson
City

Thornclaw
Forest

Arayden

Khoram
Desert

Far
Khoram

B.C. Hailes

N
W   E
S

= 200 Miles

Axos Plateau

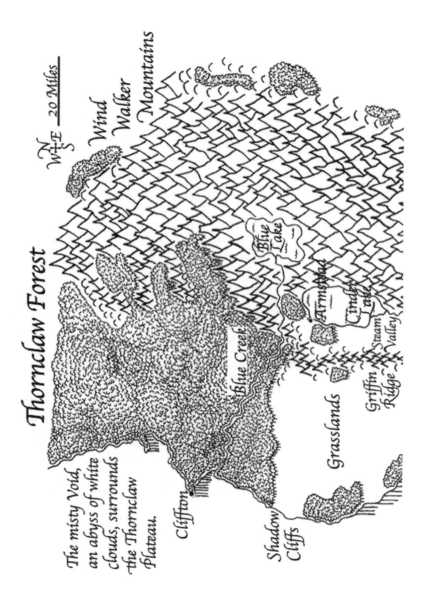

Thornclaw Forest

N W E S

20 Miles

Wind Walker Mountains

Blue Lake

Armstad

Cinder Lake

Blue Creek

Griffin Ridge

Steam Valley

Grasslands

Clifton

Shadow Cliffs

The misty Void, an abyss of white clouds, surrounds the Thornclaw Plateau.

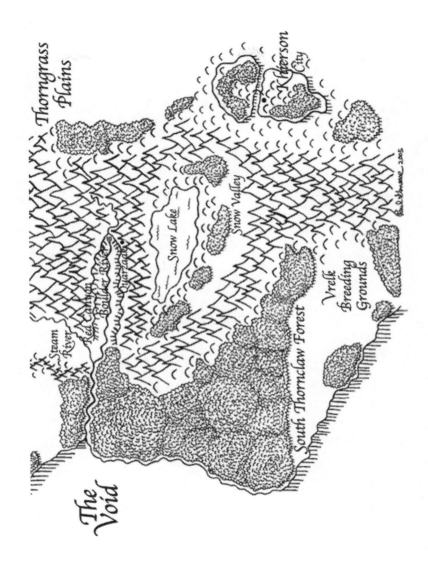

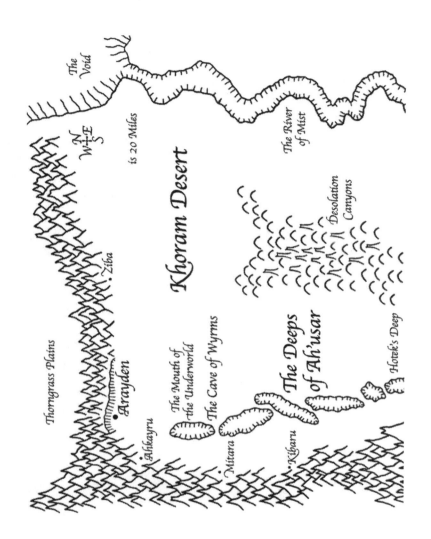

The Void

N
W + E
S

is 20 Miles

Khoram Desert

Thorngrass Plains

Ziba

Arayden

Ahkayru

The Mouth of
the Underworld

The Cave of Wyrms

Mitara

The Deeps
of Ah'usar

Kiharu

The River
of Mist

Desolation
Canyons

Hotek's Deep

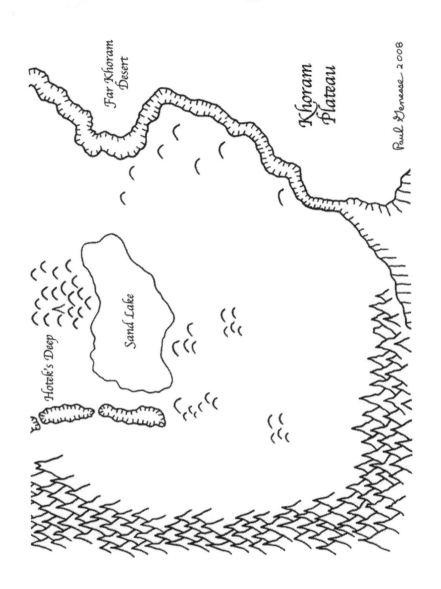

Far Khoram
Desert

Sand Lake

Hotek's Deep

Khoram
Plateau

Paul Genesse 2008

Part One

Shades of the Past

I

I will protect the Secret Land. I will not speak of it. Outsiders will
never hear of it from me. The desert will be barren to all outsiders.
A land of sand and death. To me, it will be a hidden garden of
plenty. My garden. My home. My land. My people. Unless the
Goddess Herself commands me, I will never leave the Secret Land.
May I be cursed, and exiled to the Underworld if I break my oath.
I vow in the name of Mother Amar'isis, that I will keep the secrets
of Mephitia, in this life, and the one beyond.

    —passage from the sacred oath of the Wings of Amar'isis

"Kill them quietly," Bree'alla whispered.

The words echoed in Drake's mind as she stared at him,
waiting until he agreed to the vicious order. Her face was calm,
as if killing the men creeping toward them meant nothing.

Drake forced himself to nod, his head barely moving.
Bree's green eyes narrowed in recognition, then she hid her
dagger against her forearm, shielding the blade from the massive bright moon that dominated the sky over the shadowy
landscape of the Khoram Desert.

How could she be so cold, so heartless?

It didn't matter. It had to be done. Their journey to find
the dragon hunters missing for forty years, and slay Draglûne
had taken many lives already. Killing a few more deluded men
who worshipped the Dragon King as a god would be a service
to the people of the plateaus. He had to believe it, or pulling the
triggers of his double crossbow would be even more difficult.

Bree had insisted they launch this surprise attack before
entering the southern Mephitian lands. Her words had been
clear. She would guide them no further until the cultist scouts
were dead. Their enemies had never been this close, and turning to attack now would serve as a final warning.

The footfalls of men walking along the edge of the shallow
wash made Drake's heart pound faster. The dragon cultists

were definitely following the tracks the companions' vorrels had left only minutes before. He rechecked his double cross-bow, feeling the tight cords and making certain the slender bolts lay perfectly in their tracks.

He caught a glimpse of his enemies now, and counted five, just as Bree had reported earlier when she returned from her own scouting mission. The men suddenly paused, scanning the dim horizon in all directions. Had they heard the companions lying in wait? Or perhaps the cultists were afraid of meeting the fierce Mephitian nomads that defended these lands? *Meh'fee'shuns*, Drake sounded out the foreign word in his mind.

The men pointed at the string of large pack animals, and the three dogs that Dabarius led across an area of flat desert just south of them, maintaining the ruse that the companions were unaware of their pursuers. The wizard had accepted the dangerous task, and had taken charge of the precious Sacred Scrolls of Amar'isis from Bree'alla. She had promised that if the scrolls were delivered to a safe place she would introduce them to someone who knew where Draglûne's lair was located, though she did not know herself.

Carrying the scrolls was a task that Dabarius accepted gladly, and Drake knew the wizard wanted to look at them, and see if there were spells or knowledge he could use. Dabarius acted unconcerned if he were caught alone by Mephitian raiders or the cultists themselves as he led the vorrels away. His overconfidence worried Drake, but Dabarius was probably right about being able to handle himself if he were attacked, and the rib injury he'd suffered at the Cave of Wyrms was almost healed now.

Drake could barely see the tall, four-legged, and three-humped vorrels tied together in a chain. The dragon cultists would not realize only one man led the train of animals. They would believe the companions were walking alongside the beasts concealed in their tall shadows, and giving the vorrels a

4

much-needed rest.

On the other side of Bree, Thor and Bellor kept their heads down, but Bellor made hand signs at Drake, asking how many enemies approached.

In reply, Drake raised five fingers, then signaled with his thumb and fingers slightly apart that they were very close.

Both of the broad-shouldered dwarves tensed up, ready to attack the cultists who had picked up their trail soon after the companions had departed from the Cave of Wyrms over ten days ago. Their enemies would not have caught up to them so rapidly if they hadn't paused to recover from their battle with Verkahna to allow Dabarius to heal.

Drake sank down as the crunching sounds of the men's footfalls grew louder. He slipped deeper into the shadows, remaining motionless and becoming the invisible hunter his father had taught him to be when he was a boy growing up in the Thornclaw Forest around Cliffton.

An irrational fear told him the cultists had seen him. There was no real cover here in the bleak and barren desert. He needed trees and brambles to hide himself in, not a dusty wash with faint shadows. The giant, cratered moon was far too bright and closer to the plateaus during this time of the year than at any other. The cultists would strike first before Bree gave the signal to attack. Had the ambush already gone horribly wrong?

The five men walked only an arms length away from Drake now. He could smell their stale sweat, the campfire smoke on their ragged desert robes.

Bree'alla exploded upward and slashed the back of a man's ankle with her dagger, sweeping his legs out from under him. He fell, and she punched him in the throat before dragging him into the wash. Drake, Bellor, and Thor struck at almost the same moment.

Drake lifted his crossbow and squeezed the triggers at point blank range. The slender wooden bolts coated with a thin layer of lamp oil penetrated the side of the men's ribcages at the level of their hearts, puncturing their lungs. The shafts passed all the way through the dying men, then sailed into the desert.

Bellor and Thor attacked the remaining pair of trackers, the moonlight revealing their stunned and exhausted expressions. Thor smashed one in the chest with his hammer, and Bellor hooked a man's leg with his axe using the reach of the long-handled weapon to pull him down. Thor finished both of them off with rapid blows to their skulls.

The small man Bree had dragged into the wash lay pinned under her. She pressed one hand against his mouth while holding her blade against his throat. She whispered to him ominously in the Mephitian tongue. The man's eyes filled with terror as the dust settled.

Drake wanted to help Bree by restraining the man himself. What if the cultist slipped free and stabbed her with a hidden blade? After all they'd been through, he couldn't risk losing her now. He would shield her with his own flesh, accept any wound, die for her if he must.

Thor held Drake in place with a firm hand, then motioned for him to reload. "She's got him. You keep watch."

"Ask him how many are following." Bellor let the prisoner see the moonlight glint off *Wyrmslayer*, the double-bitted axe the old *Dracken Viergur* War Priest had carried for over a hundred years.

The dwarves loomed over the captive while Drake reloaded, and searched the night for the main group of cultists. He glanced at the two men he had killed, trying not to think about who they were or who they had left behind. They followed the orders of Draglûne, like the men he had had to kill outside the Cave of Wyrms.

This just felt so different. He avoided looking at the bodies or at the two with crushed skulls that still oozed blood onto the thirsty sand. If they had wives or children, their families would

6

never know what happened to them. It would be the same if he died out here in the treeless desert, so far from home.

Bree'alla whispered one last warning before she removed her hand from the prisoner's mouth. He spoke to her with a pleading, quiet voice—probably begging for his life. She asked more questions and they spoke for a few moments until the man gave a one-word answer that made Bree blink with surprise.

"What did he say?" Thor's harsh expression fixed on the prisoner.

"There are about twenty men, and thirty vorrels behind us in the main group." Bree shook her head, as if disgusted with the prisoner.

"They're closer than we thought," Bellor said, "and there are far too many to face in the open."

"They're not planning an open attack," Bree said. "They'd sneak into our camp and try to cut our throats when we slept."

Drake trusted her prediction and felt rather relieved they wouldn't try an overt assault. With Jep, Temus and his new dog, the desert hound on guard, the assassins would never be able to approach their camp unnoticed. The dogs would smell or hear the cultists long before they got close. For an instant, he feared Jep and Temus would not obey Dabarius. He wished they were at his side—where they belonged—instead of guarding the wizard and the vorrels while maintaining the ruse.

"Is that what he said, that they are going to cut our throats when we sleep?" Thor glowered at the terrified man.

Bree glanced at Drake. "He told me they were going to kill us the next time we stopped to rest."

"Let them try," Thor said.

Drake eyed Bree'alla critically. "Bree, what else did he say?"

She hesitated. "He said the Iron Brothers who survived the battle outside the Cave of Wyrms fled toward the village of

Mitara. A cultist leader that I know of found them and rallied them. He leads them now."

"Who is this man who has led the chase after us?" Bellor asked.

"He's a high ranking member in the Iron Brotherhood," Bree said. "He'd been watching the villages in case we passed that way after we escaped from Arayden."

"Only one man?" Bellor asked.

"He had orders to kill us," Bree said.

"Humph." Thor scoffed and rolled his eyes.

"Since we killed the other leaders in Arayden and at the Cave of Wyrms," Bree said, "this vile man controls the Iron Brotherhood in the Khoram Desert now. He is called, Shai'keen." The loathing in Bree's voice made Drake wonder about the kind of atrocities Shai'keen had visited upon Bree'alla's people.

"Tell me about this man," Bellor said.

She released her hold on the prisoner and stood up. "Shai'keen is a heartless assassin."

Thor stared at her flatly. "Like you?"

She glared at the dwarf. "He's killed many of my order in Arayden. And their families. Shai'keen is the main reason why there are so few Wings of Amar'isis left in Arayden." Bree sheathed her dagger and rested her hand on the grip of her longsword. "He is nothing like me." She glared at Thor, her expression promising violence if he insulted her again. "Nothing."

"Now, now," Bellor said. "Thor, stop being rude to our guide. Accept our apologies, Bree'alla. Please."

She turned away. Drake wanted to believe Bree wasn't a killer like Shai'keen. She wasn't an assassin, was she? He thought of her more as a spy, and a swordswoman for the Wings of Amar'isis. Who the Wings actually served, he did not know, and Bree wouldn't say. Ever. There must be a High Priestess of Amar'isis that Bree reported to. He had long suspected that she was taking them to a hidden temple dedicated to the Winged Goddess.

"We'll be wary of this Shai'keen," Bellor said.

Thor snorted with disgust. "I have no doubt I've killed better men than him."

Bree stepped away from the prisoner, and tossed his short sword and knife into the center of a spiny bush. The man trembled as he clutched at the bleeding wound on the back of his ankle. She whispered to the others in case the man knew the Nexan tongue. "It's decided. There's too many of them to fight. We should catch up to Dabarius. We have to get through the gap between Zaratek's Deep and the Sand Lake before sunrise or the way will be closed to us. We can't be on this side of the gap after sunrise."

"Closed by what?" Drake whispered.

She turned away, her eyes fixed on the horizon outlined by the silvery moonlight.

"Go on ahead." Thor motioned to his friends as he looked over the prisoner. The dwarven warrior squeezed the handle of his blacksteel war hammer. "I'll take care of him."

"He's wounded," Drake said, his blood rising with disgust. "He's no threat to us now. They'll come after us no matter what we do. Leave him."

"No." Bellor spat out the word, surprising Drake with his angry tone. The old dwarf bypassed Drake and locked eyes his former apprentice, as if one hundred and fifty year old Thor Hargrim, full *Dracken Viergur* Priest and Champion of the Drobin Army had returned to being a lowly apprentice in need of correction. "Thor is right. We're not going anywhere until this man is taken care of. Thor, bind his wound and give him some of your water." Bellor said something else, this time in Drobin. The words hung in the air and Drake wished he'd paid better attention to the language lessons Bellor had given him in Khierson City.

The younger dwarf nodded, and reluctantly tore a strip of cloth from a dead man's robe, and tied it around the bleeding gash on the back of the cultist's ankle. Thor handed the Mephitian a small waterskin, and motioned for him to drink. Thor flashed a reassuring smile at the man, and Drake thought there might be hope for Thor yet.

The dragon cultist tipped his head back and gulped the water. After his third swig Thor bashed him on the back of the skull with a precise blow from the shaft of his hammer. The man collapsed and lay unmoving.

Drake gasped in shock.

Bellor turned away with a satisfied look as Bree shrugged, unconcerned.

Thor picked up the waterskin, wiped off the spout, and avoided Drake's gaze while he had a long drink.

"How could you do that?" Drake pulled the waterskin away from Thor and wondered if Bellor had told him to do that. Only callous Drobin soldiers bound for the Underworld would do such a thing. Thor and Bellor were different. Weren't they? If Dabarius had seen this he would probably kill Thor with some of his Lightning magic or choke him with one of his special battle holds.

Thor glanced up at Drake. "You've had too much sun. He's not dead. It was a stunning blow. Good soldiers follow orders, and I followed Master Bellor's. I made certain he won't be telling his fellows about us for a few hours. If he even remembers us."

"Lower your voices," Bree'alla whispered.

Drake knelt beside the Mephitian who was still breathing—although very slowly. The man would remember them, especially Bree. She was unforgettable.

"Don't worry about him," Bree said, "it would have been kinder if we'd killed him."

They all looked at her.

"Shai'keen will murder him?" Drake asked.

10

"No. He'll probably leave him behind," Bree said. "He'll be gone from this world soon enough. Didn't you see how pitiful they all looked? These trackers were half-dead already. They're too weak to face us. Shai'keen is sending them all to die. They don't have enough vorrels to carry supplies for that many men and trek this far into the Khoram and back out."

"And still they come after us," Bellor said. "Zealous fools."

"Verkahna was one of their gods," Bree said, "and Shai'keen cannot let her death go unavenged. No matter the cost or pain."

Drake remembered the excruciating journey from Arayden to the Cave of Wyrms without enough water or rations. That had only been a few days. He couldn't imagine a nearly two-week trek deep into the Khoram with limited supplies.

Movement to the north caught Drake's attention. A man rode a vorrel at the very limit of Drake's vision. The Clifftoner pointed and motioned for his friends to duck down. More riders slowly appeared in a column.

"It's Shai'keen," Bree whispered.

"Have they seen us?" Bellor asked.

"They have," Bree said, "we must run."

II

I shot the Giergun war chief in the chest from forty-five paces. His soldiers dragged his body into the trees and I ran for my life.

—Gavin Bloodstone, from the Bloodstone Chronicles.

Drake aimed at the riders in the distance. Hitting one of them from this range, just under fifty yards, would be extremely difficult, even though the Drobin made spring-steel crossbow arms of *Heartseeker* could easily cast a bolt that far. He tried to pick out the rider with the most confidence. If he could kill their leader, Shai'keen, what would the followers do?

"Killing one of them might not slow them down," Bellor said.

"What if I killed Shai'keen?" Drake whispered, thinking of a story his grandfather had once one told him. "Which one is he? The first rider or the second?" He considered switching out his bolts. He needed his best long-range shafts for this. He reached for the special quiver on his belt, which held his thorn bolt, the symbolic shaft every hunter from Cliffton earned when he became a man. He was surprised for an instant when his fingers touched the second bolt in the quiver. Ethan's thorn bolt. Though his deceased best friend had not earned it, Drake had made the shaft and carried it as a tribute to his friend.

"Forget it. I can't tell which one is Shai'keen," Bree said. "We have to go. Now keep your heads down, and stay in the wash."

The two thorn bolts stayed in Drake's quiver. A hunter only used them in the most dire of circumstances. This was not the time.

Bree'alla ran south along the wash, and Drake followed, watching her back and the approaching riders.

Thor gritted his teeth. Bellor took in a lungful of air, shook his head, and ran after Bree. Drake followed as Bellor and Thor struggled to keep up as they fled from Shai'keen and the riders. Their route wended its way toward Dabarius and the vorrels who had disappeared from view moments earlier. The riders followed, but at a slow pace. Perhaps they hadn't seen them after all?

A few paces beyond the wash, Bree came to an abrupt halt and knelt down. A bleached human skeleton lay on the ground. The skeleton's hands and foot bones were missing, and cut marks indicated the limbs had been severed by an axe or sword. Withered leather straps attached to stakes had once tied the person to the ground. No evidence of clothing remained.

Drake remembered what Bree and Dabarius had told them. The desert tribesmen would stake intruders under the sun. Their stripped bodies would be covered in oil that would cook them during the hottest part of the day. Their feet and hands would be severed, and then cauterized with torches. They would suffer a slow, agonizing death as the sun killed them.

Bellor and Thor caught up and stopped beside the skeleton. The two Drobin gazed into the desert using the bright moonlight, and their dwarven eyes unhindered by the night, to see further than Drake could. He paid close attention to Bellor, wondering if the War Priest sensed any restless spirits.

Thor motioned left and right. "There are more lying in a straight line in both directions. How far does it go?"

"From the Sand Lake to the edge of Zaratek's Deep," Bree'alla said.

Drake reeled at the distance, the sheer carnage. "How many?"

"Over a thousand, perhaps twice that," Bree said, "I don't really know."

"A final warning to turn back." Bellor tugged on his beard. "And yet I don't sense the spirits of any of these men lingering—and there are always those who don't pass to the other side."

"Will they do this to us if they catch us?" Drake asked.

She nodded her head. "The nomads will inflict this punishment upon all of us if they catch us. Anyone who crosses the border like we are planning will suffer the *Seh'ken'rah*."

"The what?" Bellor asked.

Bree'alla hesitated, her face grim. "The tribesmen call this death the *Seh'ken'rah*, the Embrace of the Sun."

Bellor ground his teeth, Thor cursed under his breath, and Drake looked for Shai'keen and the riders behind them.

"We cross this boundary if you want to find Draglûne's lair." Bree stood up. "I'm going to take us a secret way. With any luck, they won't be able to follow."

"Lead on," Bellor said, motioning for her to continue.

A short time later, covered in sweat despite the cool desert night, the breathless companions caught up to the wizard and the string of ten vorrels a half-mile south of the gruesome border.

The tall, dark-haired wizard lay on his belly at the crest of a low dune. He waved for them to crouch down as they approached. Bellor collapsed on the soft sand and tried to catch his breath while Bree, Drake and Thor crawled up to see what Dabarius was looking at.

Jep and Temus, Drake's two bullmastiff dogs who had been guarding Dabarius, wagged their tails and sniffed at them all. The dogs greeted Drake with dry noses, then ringed Bellor who appeared to need the most attention. The slender desert hound, a saluki that had once been owned by the cultists of the Cave of Wyrms, rubbed against Drake, his slender tail whipping about as it prodded him with his long snout. He patted the gentle dog. "I'm all right, Skinny. Now sit." The dog licked

Drake's hand. "Sit." The hound sat down, its sad brown eyes never leaving him as he joined his friends lying on the dune.

"The scouts are dead?" Dabarius asked.

Bree nodded. "Why'd you stop?"

Dabarius pointed straight ahead—due south.

A line of mounted vorrel riders in white robes and head coverings who carried slender lances waited at the crest of a dune ahead of them. Drake counted at least a dozen. They didn't look like Shai'keen's men.

"They've seen me and the vorrels," Dabarius said. "They've sent a rider galloping to the southwest."

"Nomads?" Bellor asked as he crawled up to join them, his breathing still ragged.

Bree didn't respond for a long moment. "We can't get past them without a fight and dozens more will be here by sunrise."

"We'll have to try," Bellor said.

"Impossible," Bree said. "Even if we eluded them tonight, they would find us in the morning."

Drake decided he wasn't going to become part of the skeletal boundary. He would go back and they would ambush the main group of cultists. They were numerous, but weakened. Maybe they could win.

"We can't go back," Bree said, reading his expression. "Shai'keen is in our way, and the chasm of Zaratek's Deep to the west bars our passage."

"What about East?" Drake asked.

"The Sand Lake lies there." Bree's eyes reflected the moonlight, and he saw hesitation—worry. "It's not far from here. I'd planned to skirt the edge of it to avoid being spotted by the nomads. Now we can't."

"What way can we go?" Bellor asked.

The moonlight hit Bree in the face, and her scant freckles stood out more as she paled. "We'll have to go *into* the Sand Lake."

15

The fear in Bree's face and the worry in her voice unsettled Drake even more. What was she so afraid of in the Sand Lake?

"The nomads won't follow us there," Bree said, her voice monotone, as she answered the question hanging in the air.

"Then what's the matter?" Bellor asked. "We're not going to stay here and end up mutilated and staked out under the sun."

"There are worse ways to die." Bree's words and expression were deadly serious.

"What are you not telling us?" Bellor asked.

"It would be better to leave that unsaid for now." Bree avoided looking at anyone. "Some things are drawn to you by the mere mention of them."

Bellor's golden-brown eyes looked haunted as he nodded in agreement.

"Ask nothing more for now," Bree said. "If we hurry, we can enter the Sand Lake just after the sun has risen. Then we trek south and get out before sunset."

"And if we don't get out before the sun sets?" Bellor asked.

Bree let out a long sigh. "We'll wish we had tried to fight our way past the nomads and risked the *Seh'ken'rah*."

III

Verkahna is dead in the Cave of Wyrms, but her servants follow us tirelessly, bent on revenge. I have no doubt they are sworn disciples of the Iron Brotherhood, but if they catch us, our resolve will prove stronger. They are slaves to Draglûne and his spawn. We are *Dracken Viergur*, servants to the True Fire.

—Bellor Fardelver, from the Desert Journal

Shai'keen's exhausted mount halted at the rim of the vast depression known as Sand Lake a short time after sunrise. Vorrel tracks led down the gargantuan hill of sand that had collected against the sheer cliffs of tan rock. The steep hill was the only route down he could see as the vertical sandstone escarpment extended north and south.

The master assassin knew the killers of the Divine Mother, Verkahna, had passed this way only moments before. They had waited until sunrise. They were afraid of entering in the darkness—as they should be. Their tracks snaked into the distance toward the gigantic dunes that filled the crater-like basin. He whipped his vorrel on the flank with his riding stick, but his mount rebelled by snorting and taking a step backward.

The bedraggled men of the Iron Brotherhood following Shai'keen stayed even further back, their vorrels refusing to approach the edge. The assassin dismounted without using his hands, his forty-years riding vorrels making the maneuver look effortless. He grabbed hold of the vorrel's halter to drag it with him and to show the others how to proceed. The foul-breathed beast protruded its long sticky tongue. Shai'keen whacked it across the eyes, and the vorrel dipped its head, letting out a muffled bellow. "Dismount," Shai'keen ordered, "we'll walk the vorrels down."

Only eighteen-year old Malek, the smooth-cheeked archer adept at shooting rabbits on the run came forward leading his vorrel. He was one of the survivors of the battle with the dragon hunters at the tombs of Ah'usar, and his heart burned for revenge. The rest of the nearly score of men stayed mounted with fearful expressions.

Shai'keen's eyes raked over the pitiful wretches he had forced to follow him into the deep desert for the past two weeks. Their emaciated, dirty bodies seemed only once removed from the ghosts they would soon become. "Given up at last?" Shai'keen asked them.

They said nothing as shame painted them all. Their silence was an insult to the Divine Father and the entire Brotherhood.

"*Cowards!*" Malek's fierce accusation hung in the air.

"Is this boy the only one who will face our enemies at my side?" Shai'keen asked.

"We can't go in there." One man gestured toward the Sand Lake.

"The killers must be punished," Malek said with the firm conviction and confidence of youth. "It's only superstition and lies that we've heard about this place." Malek glanced at Shai'keen for confirmation.

The assassin flashed a bleak smile and whispered, "Are you so sure of that?"

Malek shook his head. "No, Master."

"But you will follow me regardless?"

"I will follow you anywhere, Master."

Shai'keen studied Malek for a moment, knowing his stern gaze made him uncomfortable. He would take him along and perhaps someday, if Malek survived, Shai'keen would teach him the ways of the poisoned blade and needle. For the rest, it was time to cut them loose. There would be other desperate men who would fill the ranks once he returned to Arayden. "Malek, collect all the water bags and food. Put them on two vorrels."

The young man's eyes asked what he should do if the men resisted.

"If any try to stop you," Shai'keen said loud enough so that all could hear, "kill them."

"Yes, Master."

Malek marched over and took the few remaining water bags from the men and loaded them onto a pair of the strongest pack vorrels.

"Master Shai'keen," one of the men begged, "please leave us something."

"You won't need it," Shai'keen said.

The man blocked Malek from leading the pack vorrels away. Malek pulled the rider from his vorrel and plunged a knife into his back. He stabbed him three more times as the man screamed, Malek's blade finally landing in a lethal spot, though it took a while for the man to stop squirming and die.

Vorrels shied away, and the group of riders fought to keep the more skittish animals from bolting. Malek took the guide ropes in his bloody hands and pulled the pack animals toward Shai'keen.

The assassin glared at the men who were probably never fit to be in the Iron Brotherhood. They should have died defending the Divine Mother weeks ago, not out here. Failing to protect Verkahna, as well as Avner and Narouk was a stain on their manhood only death could erase. As the only senior leader left alive, Shai'keen was glad to finally leave the sniveling, weak-willed fools behind. He had pushed them to the sorry state they were in now—too afraid to fight a pair of men when they numbered twenty. Malek was right. Cowards indeed.

He glanced to the south. A line of at least five-dozen riders illuminated by the rising sun had assembled on a sandy ridge only a hundred paces away. Perfect timing. The riders would see him and Malek slip over the edge and enter the Sand Lake, but they would not pursue the two of them if the rumors were correct.

"Go back the way we came," Shai'keen ordered, "and you might outrun them." He gestured toward the growing number of lance- and bow-carrying men who appeared to be assembling for an overwhelming charge.

The men gasped and several whipped their vorrels, turning them north while Malek and Shai'keen forced their four animals to descend the treacherous slope of the sand hill. After they had reached the bottom and hid behind a dune, the screams of the cowards floated down to them on the wind. The Mephitian riders were taking them captive and soon they would all have the *Seh'ken'rah* inflicted upon them.

Shai'keen inspected the tracks leading deeper into the lake of fine grit. The wind and cascading sand had barely changed the vorrel tracks or the footprints of his quarry. After weeks of following them he was only minutes behind the four dragon hunters and the bitch Wing Guardian of Amar'isis who was leading them.

"Master?"

Shai'keen did not look up from the tracks. "There is doubt in your voice."

"I . . . don't know . . . I . . . "

"Don't waste words with me, boy. Speak up."

"I only wish to help." Malek's voice regained its strength.

"Help is not what I need from you."

Malek licked his cracked lips. "You never needed our help, Master. I knew that. I knew you had always planned to kill our enemies yourself."

"Then you are smarter than all the others." Shai'keen studied the young man. "Why did I bring you all along?"

"You brought us with you to punish us for what happened at the Cave of Wyrms. That's why we didn't bring enough supplies or water."

Shai'keen lunged at Malek and pushed him face down into the slope of dune, grinding his face into the sand as he lay on top of the helpless youth pinning him down with his hips. The master assassin had the tip of his blade against Malek's back.

"Please, Master! Spare me." Malek was limp and help-less, accepting whatever fate Shai'keen had planned. Perhaps Malek knew more than the Master assassin first suspected.

Shai'keen's dagger poked through Malek's thin shirt and drew a drop of blood. Then he found another section of his back and pricked him with his blade, then drew a third drop in a different spot.

"Please, Master!"

"*Quiet,*" Shai'keen whispered through clenched teeth as he pressed the young man into the sand. "The man you killed at the rim, you stabbed him three times. Here, here and here." Shai'keen touched the three dagger-pricks on Malek's back. "Next time, you put your hand on his shoulder for leverage." Shai'keen slapped his left hand on the young man's shoulder and grabbed on tight. "Then you stab him here as hard as you can." The assassin prodded the upper area of Malek's back with the handle of his dagger, and pushed it in hard enough to leave a bruise. "This is where his heart is located, behind this place. Your blade will puncture a lung and pierce his heart. One hard blow. Plunge it in fast and pull out hard. Will you remember this?"

"*Yes.*"

Shai'keen let his blade slide along one of Malek's cheeks, cutting off a few dark hairs. "If you cannot remember what I've taught you, boy, just cut the man's throat." Shai'keen jerked Malek's head out of the sand and put his dagger against the young man's windpipe. "Will you remember this?"

"Yes," Malek said, as the blade drew a drop of blood.

Shai'keen rolled off of the boy and up to his feet. When Malek did the same, Shai'keen studied him carefully. There was no trace of malice in his eyes, as he'd thought there would be. No, there was only joy. And blind faith.

Good, Shai'keen said to himself as he turned and sheathed his dagger. For if Malek had shown even one ounce of resent-ment because of the lesson, he would have killed him.

IV

Disaster does not wait for us to be ready. It comes on its own time, and as I lead the Dracken Viergur into danger I must make certain that when we are struck by it, we are ready to rise from whatever wreckage remains.

—Bölak Blackhammer, from the Khoram Journal

Drake's eardrums felt like they were going to rupture. The pressure built higher as if the weight of the entire sky was compressing his skull. The sharp pains had gotten worse the deeper into the Sand Lake they traveled. They had been going slightly downhill for over an hour as the heat of the day started to build.

Bree'alla kept them marching as fast as they could in the soft sand as she navigated through the maze of steep dunes that all seemed to be flowing in the same direction. The pace was wearing on him, and he fell to the rear of the string of ten vorrels. Bree'alla didn't seem to notice or care that he had left her alone near the front.

The dogs loped along on either side of Drake, their eyes sad and dry tongues lolling out of their mouths. The bullmastiff's stayed beside Drake as he trudged along with Bellor, Thor, and Dabarius in a valley between towering parallel ridges. Skinny pranced along beside Bree, his gait strong, as if the sand did not bother the desert-born hound.

Drake opened his mouth wide as he tried to relieve the pressure. "It's getting worse," he told Bellor.

"We are deep below the main surface of the Thornclaw Plateau," the War Priest said.

"*She* didn't say when we were going to stop or ride again, did she?" Thor asked.

Drake shook his head. "She said we're not going to stop again until we get out of here, sometime before sunset."

Thor's angry grimace was partially hidden by his dark brown beard. "We can't travel during the hottest parts of the day, and we have to stop sometime. Master Bellor can't keep this up."

"I'll make it," Bellor said. "We shouldn't stay here any longer than we have to. There is something wrong with this place. The vorrels sensed it when we entered. There was an invisible boundary at the rim of the escarpment."

"What kind of boundary?" Dabarius asked.

"I'm not certain," Bellor said. "It wasn't Warding magic, but something similar."

"Like it was keeping something in?" Dabarius asked. "That's what I thought it was."

Bellor shrugged.

"She knows." Thor stared at Bree'alla. "She won't ever tell us anything, and I don't mean about this place. It's not some vow of secrecy to her precious goddess like she wants us to believe. She could tell us where we're going if she wanted to."

"Could she?" Dabarius asked with a sharp tone. "I wouldn't wager on that."

The pain in Drake's ears intensified as his friends argued. The heat of the desert made it all worse. If only Thor and Dabarius would be quiet. It didn't help that his calves and thighs burned from hiking through the shifting sand. His nerves felt as frayed as a ten-year-old rope. A thick layer of branches should be there protecting him. It wasn't right for people to travel with no cover from winged predators—even if there were few griffins or other man-eaters in the Khoram. Three weeks in the blasted desert was too long, but no matter how long he spent under the open sky, he would never get used to it. With a growing lump in his throat he thought that Cliffton, Jaena, and the Thornclaw Forest would always be his home—though the farther south they went, the more he doubted he would ever see home again.

"I do wish you'd been there to hear them speaking," Bellor whispered to Dabarius, interrupting the argument between the dark-skinned wizard and Thor. "When she spoke in Mephitian to the prisoner you could have verified everything he said."

"Right," Thor lowered his voice. "What if she's lying to us? Am I the only one who sees what's happening? She won't say what's so dangerous in this sand pit, and what if her 'friend' doesn't know where Draglûne's lair is, or where my uncle Bölak and his *Dracken Viergur* really went? What if she's just using us again to kill another enemy of her precious order of Wing Guardians? They must be cultists just like the Iron Brotherhood, worshipping uncivilized gods and living in cursed places like this."

"Is there some reason you keep making the same accusations against the person who has kept us alive every step of the way?" Dabarius asked.

"If your ribs weren't almost mended," Thor pointed a meaty finger at Dabarius, "I'd crack one or two."

The wizard nearly smiled.

"Time to ride." Bree'alla interrupted them. She stood with an irritated look on her face. "Or do you *men* want to have a pissing contest and settle this?"

Thor's face turned an angry red as his Drobin pride flared up. The dwarf hated it when she referred to all of them as 'men.' Dabarius tried unsuccessfully to stifle a laugh and held his tender ribs protectively. Obviously, being crushed by Verkahna would take much longer than two weeks to heal—even with his own magic helping him.

"No," Thor said, "it's not time to ride. It's time for you to tell us why we're swift-marching through this sand. Are you afraid you're wrong about the nomads coming after us?"

"Get on your mounts," Bree ordered.

"After you tell us what's got you spooked," Thor said.

For a tense moment, Bree'alla regarded Thor with a seething disdain. "The Mephitians have a saying, little man. It loses something when spoken in Nexan, but even an uncouth brawler like you will understand."

Thor bristled as she paused to make her point.

"The spirits of the damned hear your thoughts as whispers," Bree said, "but when you speak of them aloud, you might as well be screaming their names."

The tone of Bree's voice sent a deep chill through Drake's body. He thought of Ethan. He sensed that Ethan's ghost was still with him, attached by the dark cord Jaena and her mother had told him to sever.

Bree walked away from Thor, and climbed into the saddle of the lead vorrel.

Thor's face wrinkled and he looked ready to spit something back at Bree, but Bellor talked over him. "She's right," he said. "We should cross this place as quickly as we can."

Drake helped Bellor, and then an irritated Thor, to mount the tall animals. Dabarius pulled himself into his saddle. They rode the swaying animals in silence, holding on tight as the unnaturally quiet vorrels ascended and descended steep dunes at a rapid pace. It was the most uncomfortable day in a long while, as dust filled the air, blown by a blistering wind that evaporated sweat before it could cool their bodies. Bree made them drink double their normal water ration, though it had little effect as the sun relentlessly tortured them. The companions rested only a half-hour during the peak temperature in the afternoon before continuing the brutal trek.

A couple of hours before sunset, the high wall of the escarpment that hemmed in the Sand Lake loomed before them. Fine dust blew everywhere by increasing gusts of wind. Bree'alla pushed the vorrels as the choking dust stung Drake's eyes and made him cough. It also obscured the low cliffs ahead of them. All he wanted was to get out of the dunes and collapse on hard packed ground where he could sleep.

When they arrived at the embankment, there was no route to the top. They might be able to scale the thirty-foot tall sandstone cliffs, but the vorrels would have no chance, and without them, neither would they.

For over an hour they trekked south in the meager shade of the escarpment searching for a suitable pathway to the top of the rim. Finally, Bree pointed to a steep slope of hard-packed dirt that reached upward to the lip. Some sand rested on the harder earth with one glaring hazard. A large triangular tunnel eroded by wind and time passed through the base of the hill against the cliff. The last third of the potential route up was a narrow land bridge supported by only a few feet of gravel-filled dirt.

Bree dismounted and Drake joined her as they inspected the hill. They looked back at the others. Skinny cowered behind the Vorrels, while Jep and Temus eagerly awaited a command from Drake.

Bellor's close-knit brows showed his reservations. "You don't have to be an Earth Priest to know this ground is too unstable. We should find another way."

"No time," Bree said, "we have to get out of here before sunset."

"So you say," Dabarius said.

Bree didn't answer, instead she began untying her vorrel from the front of their little caravan. "We'll each take one at a time. Hurry and untie them all."

"If we're going this way," Bellor said, "Thor and I will use the Earth magic to strengthen the ground."

"No," Bree said sharply, "don't use any magic here."

"Why?" Thor asked after she trailed off.

"I'll go first and test the route," Drake told Bree.

The Wing Guardian opened her mouth to protest.

"Nothing can happen to you," Drake said with a little grin. "You're the only one who knows where we're going."

"Nothing can happen to any of us." She smiled at him and her green eyes said, *especially you.*

It had become obvious over the past couple of weeks that she cared deeply for him. Something had changed between them ever since she had woken up in his arms after surviving being poisoned by Verkahna's dragonling who was still alive—somewhere near the Cave of Wyrms. Drake had prayed so hard for Bree to live, and that night his feelings for her had grown tremendously. It made him uncomfortable, especially when he thought of Jaena. He would never betray his woman in Cliffton. She was his soul mate, his best friend, the reason he risked his life to help slay Draglûne; but he could not deny his attraction to or his growing love for Bree'alla.

Drake watched as Bree took the cylindrical case containing the sacred scrolls of Amar'isis from her saddlebag. Her father had died defending them from Verkahna, and Bree always kept them close, protecting them until they reached a sanctuary in the south. He didn't know what was really on the scrolls, though Bree had said the ancient spells must never be lost.

Bree patted the neck of her vorrel and handed the guide rope to Drake. "Go slow, she will follow you."

He knew what she meant, but the way Bree's words came out made him wonder even more if she had the same feelings for him.

Jep and Temus bumped against Drake's legs. They needed to wait at the bottom until he knew it was safe. "Stay."

The bullmastiffs whined and Skinny lay down, averting his eyes.

"Stay. You can all come up soon."

Jep wagged his tail and pleaded with his eyes, while Temus sat down and watched Drake intently.

Bree's vorrel accompanied Drake without protest. They ascended the hill slowly, fighting the layer of cascading sand that fell in little avalanches after each step. He made it all the way to the narrow span near the top before the vorrel snorted and refused to go forward. Drake turned to coax the animal as the sun disappeared behind the mountains in the west. The red and orange sky darkened instantly.

Something appeared in the dunes back the way they had come. A man approached. Smoke trailed behind him like a black cloak. Or perhaps it *was* a cloak. Drake couldn't tell. The figure collapsed into dust as if he were made from this lake. Or perhaps was the very master of this place. Perhaps he'd made it long ago and summoned souls here so that he would not be so lost and forlorn. Drake opened his mouth to shout something when Bree's vorrel snorted and bucked. Drake held onto the guide rope as the ground at his feet became a sinkhole, swallowing him up to the knees and filling his boots with abrasive sand.

You are mine now.

The ominous male voice paralyzed Drake as a black robed figure appeared in his mind's eye. The sickly sweet scent of burned flesh irritated Drake's nostrils as burning cold fingers locked onto his legs and pulled him down. Sand filled his boots as he struggled not to slip into the pit opening beneath him. The vorrel's rope slipped out of Drake's hands as the land bridge broke apart. He flailed trying to keep himself from sinking, and clawed at the sand. The gritty taste of the dust choked him, suffocating him, then he was up to his chest and the weight of it pressed the air out of his lungs. He dropped suddenly, and was deep inside the hill as it collapsed. A mountain of sand crushed his body, and buried him alive.

V

I shall not leave behind anyone under my care. This I swear to
Father Lorak who sustains me every night and day.

—Bellor Fardelver, from the Desert Journal

Bree'alla stood in mute shock as a huge cloud of sand filled
the dusk after the land bridge collapsed and swallowed Drake.
Coughing on the dust and half-blind, Bree sprinted and then
crawled up what was left of the hill. Fear powered her aching
leg muscles and made her forget about the danger of climbing
on the unstable slope.

She slowed at the almost sheer drop-off where the hill had
caved in, then slid on her backside into the cavity where Drake
and her Vorrel had fallen. Smatterings of sand rained down
and she felt the hill rumble. With renewed fear she realized
the rest of it might crash down and bury her too. She dropped
to her knees and felt along the ground searching for any sign
of Drake or the vorrel. A gust of wind cleared the air for a
moment, but she had no idea where to start digging.

Two large shapes darted toward her. Jep and Temus had
come around the side of the hill and climbed onto the mound.
Skinny trailed after them. The three of them sniffed and pawed
at the sand. All three barked at the same spot and started
digging furiously. The bullmastiffs' large paws and powerful
shoulders scooped away the dirt while the lithe hound brushed
away as much as he could. Bree joined them, flinging the sand
away by the handful, praying to Amar'isis that Drake was still
alive.

For what felt like an eternity Bree and the dogs burrowed
into the hill. Temus barked and Bree spotted a hand. She
pulled hard on it, but he wouldn't budge. The dogs kept digging and the top of Drake's head appeared. She pushed the

dogs away and dug out the dirt from around his nose and mouth.

"Drake!" No response. He wasn't breathing.

Jep and Temus kept digging as Bree hooked her arms under his shoulders and heaved with all her might.

"Help me!" Bree yelled as she noticed Bellor and Thor standing at the base of the slope she'd slid down.

The dwarves had their hands on the wall of dirt and chanted something with their heads bowed as sand fell down the back of their necks.

"They're busy," Dabarius said as he appeared beside her.

The dogs whined and dug. Dabarius and Bree got his shoulders free, but his legs wouldn't come loose. It was as if something was holding him down.

"You've got to get him out of there," Bellor said. "We can't hold it much longer." A wave of dirt fell on them and more dust filled the air.

"He's stuck!" Bree shouted as she put her hands on Drake's face, willing him to start breathing. "Wake up. Come on." His skin was cold. "Bellor, something's wrong with him."

"What?" The War Priest asked as Thor continued the chant.

"He's cold," she said, trying to keep the panic out of her voice.

"I'll pull him out." Dabarius got behind Drake and wrapped his arms up and under his friend's shoulders and locked his hands together. The wizard's eyes glowed white for an instant as he heaved, his strength augmented by his magic. Pain from his injured ribs colored Dabarius's face as Drake started to come free.

Thank the Goddess, Bree thought with relief.

Drake was suddenly sucked back into the hole.

Bree and Dabarius fell away as if pushed by a gust of frigid wind.

30

Bellor stepped away from the unstable wall of earth and knelt in front of Drake as Bree realized what was stopping them from rescuing Drake.

Bellor put his hands on Drake's head. "In the holy name of Lorak, I bless this man and free him from darkness. I command you to release him!"

"Bellor," Thor said through gritted teeth, "I . . . can't . . . hold it."

"In the holy name of Lorak," Bellor repeated, "I bless this man and free him from darkness. Now, Dabarius!"

The wizard and Bree heaved with all their might, pulling Drake out of the hole. Dabarius and Bree dragged his body off the mound and away from the precarious hill. Bellor and the dogs followed behind as the slope collapsed with a *whump*, burying the spot where Drake had almost been entombed.

"Thor?!" Bellor shouted fearfully as they all coughed and wiped at their eyes.

The dwarf came out from the cloud of dust, brushing himself off as Bree attended to Drake. She put him on his side and slapped his back, trying to make him breathe as she prayed to Amar'isis.

He started to cough while Dabarius and Thor secured the remaining vorrels. He also shivered and Bree held him in her lap, leaning against him to lend her body heat.

"*Water*," Drake said, then tried to spit dirt from his dry mouth.

Bellor gave him a waterskin and no one said anything as Drake rinsed and spit the precious liquid onto the ground. He shivered even more and Bree hugged him closer as the three dogs crowded around, needing reassurance.

"Thank you," Drake said, managing a weak smile at his friends.

"What happened?" Thor asked. "What's going on here?"

"You've all got to climb out of here, up the cliff," Bree said, "right now."

"What are you saying?" Thor asked.

"We can't be here at night," Bree said. "I've already told you."

"Who was that spirit who held Drake's legs?" Bellor asked Bree. "No more secrets. It doesn't matter now. It knows we're here." He glanced around warily. "It's watching us."

Bree's eyes flashed with worry, then resignation. "It is known that the shade of an infamous Mephitian warrior haunts this place. He has for a very long time. The nomads call him the Black Ghost of the Desert. He is powerful only at night. The longer we stay, the more danger we're in. Please, all of you must climb the cliffs, wait for me on the rim. We'll haul up all the water and food. I'll stay with the vorrels and will lead them south until I find a way up. Maybe there's another route close by."

"Forget the vorrels," Drake said, "we're not leaving you down here."

"We can't leave our mounts," Bree said. "We can't carry enough water to make the final distance."

"To where?" Thor asked.

Bree'alla sighed and gave him a sideways glare. "I wish I could speak openly about our destination, but please, you must all get out of here."

"Why do you think you'll be safe alone?" Bellor asked. "Thor and I can protect us from spirits." Both dwarves touched the silver mountain-shaped medallions of Lorak, which they wore on stout chains around their necks.

"Do you really believe that?" Bree asked the old dwarf. "The sun had only been down a moment and you could barely free Drake from its grasp. As the night goes on the Black Ghost will get even stronger. Only I will be safe here, by the grace of Amar'isis." Bree touched the scarab beetle brooch, tucked into a hidden fold of her shirt. She hoped that it, and what she knew about the Black Ghost, would truly protect her. "You must all leave, and I'll stay and guard the vorrels. If we leave them here they won't last the night. The shade will kill them all. Then you'll never find out what happened to your Drobin kin or reach Draglûne's lair."

"Those cliffs look steep," Thor said. "A difficult climb for some of you."

"I can get up there in an instant," Dabarius said, alluding to his magic, "and drop a rope."

"Bree'alla, you are our guide," Bellor said, "and must be protected at all costs. Without you, we are lost and our sacred duty is finished."

"We're all staying," Drake said, as he sat up and stood beside Bree.

Of course you are. None of you will ever leave.

The companions faces all froze with shock as the icy voice assaulted their minds.

VI

The nights were the worst. The Giergun could see in the dark, and
we were blind and afraid, praying for dawn.

—Gavin Bloodstone, from the Bloodstone Chronicles

Shai'keen crawled toward the dragon hunters as the howling wind sucked the heat from his hands and feet. The sand
stinging his face felt like pieces of ice. He breathed downward so his breath would not turn into a white cloud and
alert his enemies. The foreigners and the half-Mephitian
traitor—Bree'alla—had taken refuge against the cliff edge of
the Sand Lake, arranging their vorrels, who sat on the ground,
to shield them from the fierce wind. The large animals had
tucked their heads down and no one—not even the three
dogs—appeared to be on guard while they waited out the unnaturally cold windstorm. Shai'keen had to get closer to use
his blowgun and the carefully prepared poisoned needles. At
twenty paces away, he was too far. In this wind, he'd have to get
five paces or less. He surveyed his route forward and noticed
a line of stones arranged in a half circle around the foreigner's
camp. Why had they done that? He would take a closer look
when he got to them.

The master assassin glanced to the north where he had positioned his lone servant. Malek's head, a vague shadow, was
slightly visible in the darkness. The young archer crouched
with a poisoned arrow on the string of his bow—in case any
of Verkahna's murderers tried to run. They wouldn't. First,
Shai'keen would shoot the dogs with poisoned needles, then
the Drobin, then the three humans. He would wait a few moments while the poison took effect, then would kill them all
with a silent blade—except perhaps the traitor woman. He
would save the Wing Guardian for last and take his time. He
would invite Malek to watch and learn how to exact revenge.

Bree'alla, daughter of Ben'syn, would die much slower than the others. Once she was awake he would give her the symbol of the Iron Brotherhood across her chest. He would carve the two wavy and parallel lines down to the bone, slicing slowly through the soft flesh of her breasts and grating against her ribs. She would be paralyzed, but would feel the burning agony of his blade—coated with fire ant venom. She would beg him with her eyes for the misery to end. And it would. When he was ready.

After years of hunting his foes and waging a brutal shadow war in the northern towns and Arayden, the only surviving member of the Wings of Amar'isis would soon be dead. Shai'keen allowed himself to feel joy as he slid a poisoned needle into his blowgun and crawled forward.

VII

Never bargain with the spirits of the Void. They will twist your words and steal from your soul.

—passage from the Goddess Scrolls of Amaryllis

Shivering, Bree'alla squeezed her eyelids shut as she huddled against Drake. She prayed for the warmth of the sunrise that seemed years away. Unable to stop worrying, her mind lingered in the place between sleep and wakefulness. Bellor and Thor's barrier had held the Black Ghost at bay so far, but there was no escaping the chill wind—or the dread that had tormented her since Drake had been attacked when he was almost buried alive.

The cold suddenly intensified, and the stinging pain in her arms and legs worsened. A heaviness fell across her, and for a heartbeat she felt utterly exhausted, her life drained away by a dread enveloping her in a viselike grip. She almost gave in, but then her mind shot wide awake, telling her to get up and draw her weapon. Bree reached for the handle of *Wingblade*, expecting to feel her father's sword in her calloused hand.

She felt nothing.

Her arm hadn't moved. She couldn't open her eyes or move any of her muscles. *No*, Bree told herself. *I will not give in to sleep or weariness.* Mustering every bit of willpower she had left, Bree'alla forced her eyes open.

Her four friends slept under blankets nearby. They seemed frozen in place—gray and lifeless, as if the cold had taken their blood and replaced it with ice. The vorrels had become partially covered by blowing sand. The dogs lay at her and Drake's feet. Only the small puffs of white mist coming out of their nostrils showed they were still alive.

Please, Amar'isis. Help me, Bree prayed as she tried to regain control of her body and throw off whatever curse was affecting her.

A black ghost wearing a tattered cloak moved beyond the circle of warding stones. Against her will, Bree's eyelids closed. She tried to open them, but felt like they were held shut by spider webs of frost. When her eyes popped open at last, Bree gasped in shock. Hundreds of ghostly black orbs and the figures of men with very thin limbs and narrow heads floated just outside the stones. They pressed in against the protective barrier. She could sense them draining the warmth from the air, sucking away all of the heat from the vorrels and her friends.

The gaunt figure of a teenage boy manifested beside Drake and challenged the robed figure. Who was this, some spirit guardian of Drake's? A dead brother? The ghostly boy swatted at the orbs and the other spirits, battling them furiously, though his blows had little effect. Bree realized the young man's palsied legs did not touch the ground as he retreated, but he would not move out of the way. The young man glanced toward her, his sad eyes finding Bree's—then he disappeared as the robed figure waved a hand dismissively, banishing the boy back to where he had come from.

The black orbs surrounded the specter as if he were a God King or an arch wizard, and the dark creatures were his thralls. The man's cobalt eyes flashed with an eerie light that bored into her. Bree could not look away as the scent of charred flesh and acrid smoke overwhelmed her senses. She knew who it was. The Black Ghost had come at last in the darkest hour when the forsaken ruled the night.

Bree dared hope that the Drobin magic would hold him back and spare their lives.

Nothing will hold me back now, Wing Guardian, his voice was like churning gravel as it echoed in her mind.

Please, don't harm my friends, Bree'alla spoke the words to herself, as her lips could only tremble.

Why have you guided these foreigners here?

Teeth chattering, Bree struggled to formulate her thoughts. *They are my friends and I have vowed to help them. Amar'isis herself asked me to do this.*

No. You have been deceived.

That's not possible. The Goddess came to me when I was poisoned. She saved me and told me I must help them.

It doesn't matter. Only you will leave here, Wing Guardian. These others will die in their sleep.

Please. We are taking the Sacred Scrolls of Amar'isis to a sanctuary. We mean no harm to you or this land.

The presence of the foreigners is forbidden. The Black Ghost raised his hand and pointed at Drake. *They will all be slain tonight.* The shade of the long dead man stepped past the barrier of stones as if they were nothing. The black orbs poured through the breach like a swarm of flying beetles and began clinging to the companions. The already-freezing temperature plummeted. The smell of burned human flesh and smoke overpowered Bree'alla. No matter how hard she tried, Bree still couldn't lift her arms.

The Black Ghost reached out toward Drake's neck.

I know who you are! Her mind screamed at the apparition. *You are Kan'yel, son of Hemett.*

The black spirit stopped and recoiled from her words, his cobalt eyes dimming as sadness and pain radiated from him. *Kan'yel is long destroyed, along with his faith in the gods of Mephitia.*

Yet you remain and are famous among the Priestesses who follow Amar'isis. Bree pressed on, *I know you are still an ally of Amar'isis and Ah'usar.*

None of this matters. In life and in death I have sworn to protect Mephitia from all foreigners. Those whom you have led here will not survive. You should have never brought them south, Servant of Amar'isis. You knew better.

Please, Kan'yel, Bree'alla pleaded, they must help me return the Sacred Scrolls to their rightful place. The wisdom cannot be lost and it is not safe for me to transport them alone. My friends and I are being hunted, even now, by enemies of Mephitia.

Your enemies are close. Kan'yel glanced into the dunes. I was almost robbed of my duty by one who is not unlike I was, so long ago, when I killed with a blade. He senses the kill now. Hungers for it, like I do.

Strike him down. Take him instead of my friends. Bree's gaze peered into the desert wondering if Shai'keen was on the rim of the cliff above them, or even in the Sand Lake itself.

Do not be so eager. You and the man who hunts you are not so different.

The truth of it made Bree's spine stiffen. She thought of all of the people she had killed for Amar'isis.

Know that I am not without regret for what I must do. The Black Ghost continued to look away, as if he were uncertain. *You will have to go on alone after I free the spirits of these foreigners from their mortal flesh. They will become my servants until the end of days and will join the Twice Damned—those who have suffered the Seh'ken'rah . . . and then me.*

The midnight black orbs and the gaunt spirits swarmed over Drake and the companions. *Please, Kan'yel, I beg you. Spare them.* She struggled against his power with every fiber of determination she had left. The scarab brooch on her tunic pulsed, its protective powers finally coming to life, and Bree lurched forward. She hugged Drake and turned her face to the ghost. *Can't you remember what it was like to lose those you love?*

Don't talk of love to me. I am denied love for eternity.

A cloud of freezing fog surrounded Bree and she began to shiver as she guarded Drake. She looked straight into what remained of Kan'yel's face. Even as a ghost his features were melted and burned, his eyes sockets black as the Deeps of Ah'usar. *You can remember love, can't you?*

No. I cannot. The Black Ghost grasped her by the shoulders. His freezing touch felt as solid as iron. He would throw her aside and kill Drake.

One last hope remained, a final gift of knowledge from her father. *Ti'yena! Do you remember her?*

The Black Ghost recoiled from Bree, as if touching her caused him terrible pain.

Your wife. Ti'yena was your wife. She was a Priestess of Amar'isis.

My wife. The words came as a faint whisper in Bree's mind.

Ti'yena, Bree leaned forward, *hers is an ancient name of great beauty. Her love for you changed everything. You cannot forget that.*

I shall not. The spirit's face twisted in pain again. *She made me see the evil in what I had done while in the service of Shenahr.*

The cold lessened as Kan'yel hesitated.

We all know what you did before the end, Bree said. *You regained your honor by turning away from Shenahr and becoming a champion of Amar'isis. The tale is well known to us all. Brave Kan'yel fought against the chaos of the Storm God and he cursed you. His Priests inflicted upon you the Seh'ken'rah and burned you in the desert, but they went too far and brought you back as a spirit to serve them.* Bree could move her whole body now and sat up straight.

Kan'yel's body became more transparent. *They should have let me pass on.*

Bree got on her knees and touched her Wing Guardian brooch for strength. *You killed them all. You took your revenge.*

Kan'yel glanced at the black orbs around him. *I killed them, but they had already slain Ti'yena . . . She was gone to the Underworld.*

Overwhelming sadness radiated from the dark spirit and Bree felt tears welling up inside her eyes.

They burned her in front of me! Kan'yel screamed.

Icy needles assaulted Bree's mind and she collapsed over Drake. *Please, Kan'yel, son of Hemett, husband of Ti'yena,*

Champion of Amar'isis. Don't inflict the pain of losing a man that I love. Don't take him and all my remaining friends. Please.

Kan'yel's face turned into a black void of hate. Will you reaffirm your Wing Guardian vow to me? *Will you do my work when the time comes?*

Bree nodded solemnly. *I vow to you . . . that if you let them live . . . I will kill them myself if they threaten the secrets of Mephitia. Now, please. I beg you. Let us go, for the love of Ti'yena.*

The Black Ghost stood tall and stared at her and Drake for a long while. The wind howled, sand stung Bree's eyes and the swarm of black orbs drained the heat from her friends more rapidly. Kan'yel's voice filled her mind once more. *You know what you will have to do.*

I know, Bree thought sadly.

It would have been easier for me to take their lives tonight. The longer they live, the more difficult it will be for you.

She sensed he would come back if she faltered now. *I swear in the name of the Goddess herself, I will keep my pledge as a Wing Guardian of Amar'isis.*

Then for my wife, Ti'yena, I will let your friends pass. Kan'yel left the half-circle of stones. The bitter cold began to relent and Bree'alla let out a sigh of relief. The Shade of the Desert flew into the dunes, and the orbs and the ghosts glided after him as if they were on a new hunt.

The figure of the boy who had tried to defend Drake appeared for an instant, standing protectively over him, and then disappearing. Bree wondered who he was and what had caused a spirit to attach itself to Drake.

Shaking her head, she took one final look at the dunes and thanked Ti'yena. Even in death, the love of the long dead Priestess had the power to save lives. When the ghosts had disappeared, Bree wondered if Kan'yel was right.

Drake's handsome face was starting to regain its color. Amar'isis had told her he was to be protected above all of them. How could she even consider putting a sword through his chest? The thought of it made her want to retch.

Bree shuddered and she knew that in a few short days—if they survived the final crossing—she would be asked to do just that.

VIII

The nomads speak of something perilous in the Sand Lake. They shudder in fear and draw their robes closer about them, but they will not tell us what is there when we ask. Perhaps it's better if we do not know.

—Bölak Blackhammer, from the Khoram Journal

I can't outrun the dead, Shai'keen thought as he sprinted along the base of the cliff. The wind and sand pushed him against the rock face at the edge of the Sand Lake. Malek lagged behind, the young man's strength fading from lack of proper food and water.

The dark spirit and his horde of black orbs and ghosts closed in and Shai'keen knew what had to be done. "Up the rock," he ordered Malek and made a foothold with his hands. Shai'keen boosted him up and the young man struggled to find handholds.

Malek frantically scraped his fingers against the rock. "I can't see a way up!"

"No matter." Shai'keen drew his dagger and slashed the back of one of Malek's knees, severing the tendons and muscles. The young man fell hard onto the ground, his confused eyes wide as he gritted his teeth in pain, held his wounded leg, and gasped for breath.

Shai'keen touched Malek's shoulder and gave him a single nod. "Fight them as long as you can. I'm counting on you."

"*Master,*" Malek's voice squeaked and he tried to get up, and he reached for Shai'keen, begging for help.

The assassin sprinted away as a figure in a billowing cloak appeared on the dune behind them. Frigid blue eyes flared in the darkness as a cloud of over a thousand black orbs descended upon the screaming young man.

"Master!" Malek screamed as he tried to crawl out of the cloud of angry spirits.

Shai'keen wondered if the fool even realized what had just happened. He would have made a poor apprentice. Better to end it now, assuring there would be no witnesses to the failed attempt on the dragon hunters.

The assassin ran as hard as he could and finally reached their vorrels, which had been hidden by the cliff. The four beasts lay sprawled on the dirt. Their mouths gaped open and their spittle had frozen solid.

Shai'keen grabbed two heavy waterskins and a sack of food. The skins felt like hard stones on his back as he climbed the cliff—following the route he had seen earlier. He was halfway up when the hungry ghosts attached themselves to his hands and feet. After a moment his breath came out in large white clouds. The pain in his numb hands made his grip falter. He had to force his hands to move, to grasp the rock, to hold on. He would not die here.

A foot slipped and he hung on by his fingertips as the ghosts drained away his body heat. He sensed someone was watching him and glanced downward.

The black robed figure stood watching, and the faint specter hung beside him. Shai'keen smiled as he met Malek's pitiless eyes. Perhaps he would have made the perfect apprentice.

IX

You shall guard this boundary from all outsiders who try to cross
into the Secret Land. In the Afterlife, you will be burned, handless,
and footless, but you will roam this desert until you are released
from the Embrace of the Sun.

—from the ritual of the Seh'ken'rah

Kan'yel, son of Hemett. Husband of Ti'yena. Fallen Champion of Shenahr and then of Amar'isis. The one cursed with eternal suffering. The Black Ghost of the Desert.

No. I am less than all of those things. My body has long faded and only my darkness remains. I am a shadow in the night.

The shade tried to forget who he had been, and still he felt never ending sadness. Ti'yena's death was more painful now than it had been in over a hundred years. The infinite grief and sorrow was as large as the lake of sand he was doomed to roam for eternity, but only during the night. He would never see the sun again. Warmth was forever denied him. When he tried to remember the heat from the day of his own death, there was nothing. Only Ti'yena's face, pleading for him to save her as the flames they had tied her over her crisped her flesh and made her long black hair shrivel and curl. His greatest failure was watching her die. She had endured a fate worse than the *Seh'ken'rah*.

The cold emanated stronger from his damned spirit as he watched the assassin struggling to climb the cliff. He could see the malignant aura surrounding his quarry. It reminded him of himself so many years in the past when he had served the Storm God. Still, he admired the stark pragmatism of his actions. Leaving the younger man wounded for the hungry ghosts to devour was as coldblooded as anything he had ever seen. Perhaps this ruthless killer was trying to add to his own collection of victims? Did he not realize that anyone who died

45

in or near the Sand Lake was doomed to be the thrall of the Black Ghost? The assassin was probably not even aware of the dozens of tiny ghosts—fragments of his many victims—that clung to his side. He used their life-force, or *kah*, as the old priests would call it, to make himself stronger and instill fear in those he met. The ghosts would cry out warnings to the assassin's victims; and though their ears would not hear the cries, the spirits of the living would hear them clearly. The warrior, Kan'yel had been the same. Many of those spirits were still with him now. Enemies he had killed as a young man had become part of his being.

This assassin was a man who had done much evil. But the shade hesitated, recalling his conversation with the Wing Guardian. She had stirred up bitter memories and he had granted mercy to her friends, in Ti'yena's name.

Ti'yena, how I miss you. He could see her face clearly tonight, and the sorrow crushed him like the road of endless time he was forced to walk. She had saved him on a night when he had questioned everything. He could almost remember the feel of her head on his chest after they had made love. "You can change, Kan'yel. Leave behind what you have done. There must be a way to atone for everything. Ask the gods for mercy."

Mercy, he thought. He did not deserve Ti'yena's mercy or her love. His soul was irredeemable, like the despicable murderer on the cliff or the Wing Guardian who claimed love for one of the foreigners—and pretended to help the others. None of them would find deliverance from their sins.

The shade's only salvation was to guard this uninhabitable region from trespassers and collect the souls of those killed by the *Seh'ken'rah* or his own cold touch if they strayed into the Sand Lake. Nothing would ever change. Ti'yena was dead. Kan'yel was dead. Hope did not exist.

"Please. Let me kill him!" The wrath-filled spirit of Malek brought Kan'yel back to the moment. The vengeful ghost of the young man begged to be unleashed upon his former master.

"Kill him then," the Black Ghost ordered. "Drag him down and he will join in our suffering."

Malek flew to the man called Shai'keen and locked his ghostly arms around his throat. The master assassin continued to climb and neared the top of the cliff. Kan'yel would not intervene, and was content to watch them struggling on the cliff. He would leave Shai'keen's fate in the hands of the boy he had betrayed.

X

I remember my mother first telling me of the Sacred Grove of Amaryllis when I was a little girl. She told me of her wonderful teachers there, especially Priestess Gwynedd, who taught her how to serve the Goddess and use the Tree magic. I often dreamed of traveling to the grove and learning from the women there, rather than at my mother's side as an apprentice. Now, the thought of going there fills me with dread.

—Priestess Jaena Whitestar, from her personal journal

Jaena entered the center of the blackened ring of dead sentinel trees alone. She held in her tears, and didn't want to believe that Drobin soldiers burned the two-thousand-year old sacred trees on purpose. It was beyond cruel to destroy them, and absolutely evil to have murdered the benevolent women who revered them.

The tree in the center of the circle had been charred worse than the others and only part of its trunk remained, as all of its upper branches had been destroyed. She approached it slowly and found the pile of stones at the base marking where the High Priestess of Amaryllis in the North, Gwynedd the Kind, had died. Bound to the tree by her enemies the old woman had perished in the flames while her students watched. Only bits of bone remained of her body for her few surviving followers to bury.

Would this be Jaena's fate if she took up the cause as Priestess Nayla had urged her? She knelt in front of the grave and prayed for the souls of all of the Priestesses of Amaryllis who had died practicing their religion and serving the Nexan people. How many lives had they saved before they were caught and killed?

Priestess Nayla and Emmit, her sworn Guardian, approached quietly and stood a respectful distance away, waiting for Jaena to acknowledge them. She wiped her eyes and looked back at them. Nayla stood in the bright sunlight, and Jaena imagined her long chestnut braid was the color of the tree trunk before it had been burned less than a year before. Emmit kept his eyes on the open sky. The other crossbowmen did the same from positions all around the grove. It was a risk being in the open, but if any aevian appeared it would be shot several times.

Nayla knelt beside Jaena and touched the grave reverently.

"You knew her?" Jaena asked.

"High Priestess Gwynedd was my teacher, and also your mother's," Nayla said. "She taught all of us the ways of the Goddess and Tree magic."

"Were you here when it happened?" Jaena asked.

"No, my grove was far west of Nexus City. I learned of this weeks after it happened."

Jaena stared at the grave. Who would teach the next generation now? If Nayla was right, there were no more Priestesses of Amaryllis in the north. Only those who lived in the distant villages like Cliffton had survived the purge carried out over the past months by the Lorakian Priesthood and their religious soldiers, the Father's Paladins, fiery zealots with no tolerance for Amaryllians. They had finally found the secret grove and slaughtered Gwynedd and her few followers after decades of searching for them.

"Do you know why I brought you here?" Nayla asked.

"You wanted me to understand what was at stake."

Nayla nodded. "I also want you to understand that kindness will not save you when your enemies come for blood."

The thought of armed resistance against the Drobin did not sit well with Jaena. There were a lot more Drobin than humans, and they were far more powerful. She wanted to help the Nexan people, but she did not want to be part of everything that Nayla wanted her to do. "Where will we go now?" Jaena asked.

"Further west. We will visit the villages on this side and north of Nexus City. The people need to know that there are still Priestesses of Amaryllis left alive. You will stay there and help them as best you can, while I go into the city and prepare things. You will teach them about the Goddess and will tell them about what you saw here."

The thought of Nayla leaving worried Jaena. She had already told her that she would take Blayne and some of the others with her to Nexus City. The young men of Cliffton and Armstead would become crossbow assassins. They would kill the king of the Nexan people, an old man, Alaric IV, who claimed dominion over every woman and man on the plateaus, but was no more than a minor lackey to the dwarven king in Drobin City, and the Lorakian High Priests in Nexus. Alaric had sat idly by while the Amaryllian faithful were savaged, their religion banned, and their Priestesses burned alive. Fear of being killed for her beliefs made Jaena worry incessantly, but if Drake could face Draglûne, the Dragon of Darkness who had haunted her dreams, she could face the danger before her.

She would not be by herself. Nayla wanted to take Blayne and all the others into the city, but not all of them would go. Blayne wouldn't leave Jaena. Ever since she'd healed him in Cliffton's shrine he'd been smitten with her. He was a handsome young man, strong and loyal. He didn't have the spark that Drake had, but perhaps someday she could grow to love him. Just knowing that he and Drake had dueled each other with Kierka knives in Armstead made her want to hate him, but she pitied him more. He'd lost more than a fight. He'd lost his village, the woman he wanted to marry, and his honor, in addition to the broken wrist she's healed. She would let him care for her. It made him feel like a man again. He would keep her safe or die defending her, and perhaps someday, she would marry him.

Jaena blinked her eyes. It was as if someone else's thoughts spoke inside her head. She found it hard to like this new voice within her. She had a deep foreboding about what was happening, and where she was goinsg . . . where they were all going.

"Are you ready?" Nayla asked.

Jaena nodded, and got up, bowing her head one last time to the grave, then walked beside Priestess Nayla. The woman was a little older than her mother, perhaps forty-five winters, but she was as wise as any elder and supremely confident. Blayne and the others gathered in the thick woods after Jaena, Nayla, and Emmit returned from the grove. Lyall and Holten from Armstead flanked Blayne, while Kraig and Rill from Cliffton waited opposite them. They'd all become friends on the long journey from Cliffton, but a rivalry for Jaena's favor threatened to divide them, though Kraig did not banter with them. She had always liked Kraig, but he was more of a little brother, and Rill was one of the bullies who had picked on Ethan. Drake had been in several fights with him, so Rill and Blayne got along quite well. Rill had matured since they were kids, but he was still a dolt, and no girl would marry him. He'd come along because Emmit and Nayla promised them all they'd get to kill Drobin, and the Nexan girls would be very grateful. The reason that Kraig had come was a mystery to her, though she suspected that her mother had sent him to keep an eye on her. He spoke seldom, and sometimes she could see the thoughts swirling behind his eyes, but they were as mysterious as what was below the clouds of the Void.

As they marched under a dense canopy, making their own trail through thick brush, Jaena wondered how the Drobin had finally found the Sacred Grove where generations of Priestesses of Amaryllis had trained in secret. Why had Gwynedd and her followers not run into the woods when the Drobin approached? They could have escaped, saved themselves from death and torture, though the trees may still have been burned.

Nayla turned and caught Jaena's eye. She often knew when Jaena had questions and could anticipate her thoughts. It was uncanny, and reinforced Jaena's respect for the woman who had convinced her to leave Cliffton and make a life for herself in the world away from the only place she ever knew.

They stood staring at each other, and the hunters paused, waiting for them patiently.

"Why didn't Priestess Gwynedd and the others run?" Jaena finally asked.

Nayla put her hands on Jaena's shoulders, then hugged her. "I wish I knew."

"They didn't have to die," Jaena said.

Nayla pulled away, but held firmly onto Jaena's shoulders. "When they come for you, and they will someday, you may have to run, but if you can, fight them with whatever followers you have around you. Show all the Drobin that Amaryllians will not go peacefully to the Afterworld. We will fight and die for our beliefs. We will kill them like they've killed us until there are more of us on the plateaus than there are of them."

Jaena could not blink, could not nod her head, could not look away from Priestess Nayla. She didn't want to die, and she didn't want to fight. She wanted to be a healer, not a killer. Her mother had always taught her that any conflict that lead to fighting and death was a tragedy, one in which everyone lost. Perhaps, in little Cliffton, they'd been too innocent.

"Do you understand?" Nayla asked.

She didn't know what to say, and finally she nodded. "I understand."

Nayla kissed her on the forehead. "When the time comes, I know you'll do what must be done."

Jaena fell into step behind the Priestess, but she did not know what must be done. She would help the people however she could, but she would not go against her beliefs. The Goddess Scrolls taught about peace and mercy, which was part of why the founders of Cliffton left the north and trekked so far

52

into the Thornclaw Forest. Rather than fight the Drobin for the right to worship as they wanted, they left to find a new place to build their homes. They had all had enough of wars and religious persecution.

When they made camp later that day, Jaena leaned against a tree, worried about what would come next. Rill and Holten laughed and argued about who was the better shot and who should be the one to shoot the Nexan king. They playfully ribbed each other and Jaena wished she could block out their voices. Kraig slipped in beside her, a thick root separating the two of them. His pale blue eyes met her bright sapphire ones. "We can go home anytime you want," he whispered. "I'll take you. Tonight if you want."

She looked away, and knew her mother had sent him like she suspected all along. Jaena thought about saying yes, but she had made a commitment to Priestess Nayla. The Nexan people needed her more than the folk of Cliffton. She couldn't live there anymore, not without Drake. He would not turn away from his duty, and she would not shy away from hers. He wasn't ever coming home and neither was she. "You go," Jaena whispered, and touched Kraig's arm.

He shook his head so subtly she could barely see it move.

Blayne glanced over at them, then playfully hopped into the hammock he had hung for Jaena. Rill tipped it over and dumped him out onto the soft ground. They all laughed, including Blayne.

Mildly amused, Emmit and Nayla sat stoking the small cook fire, and Jaena suddenly felt very angry at both of them. They wanted to turn Kraig, Rill, Lyall, Holten, and Blayne into murderers. She had known this all along, but it seemed so wrong for boys to be recruited to do such a vile thing. Jaena would do everything in her power to stop that from happening. The five men of Armstead and Cliffton were her responsibility now, and she would not let them out of her sight. Nayla and Emmit would have to commit the crimes on their own.

XI

We have found trees and open water in a small pool. The desert has given us our lives back once again. Even for the Viergur, it is sometimes difficult to remember that our enemy is the dragon, not this accursed land. We are weakened, and morale is as low as I have seen it.

—Bölak Blackhammer, from the Khoram Journal

Drake hid in the lush date palm grove, crouching behind the leafy bushes as he waited for Bree to return. He kept changing his position and could not hold still as the sunrise drew ever closer. The first faint rays of the sun colored the golden sky pink, and soon Bree's movements would not be covered by the early morning darkness. He tried to slow his breathing as he, Thor, Bellor, Dabarius and the dogs kept watch on the mud-brick complex of Mephitian houses atop the hill. She claimed she was going to speak with old friends that could shelter them for a few days and replenish their exhausted supplies.

She didn't say it, but they all knew it was a big risk trusting the Mephitians—even if they were Bree's friends. Drake kept his eyes and ears focused on the surrounding lands. Fields of wheat, barley and flax crisscrossed with irrigation ditches stretched as far as far as they could see to the north and south. The scant crops in the summer-scorched fields provided almost no cover. Drake recalled how Bree had used one of the larger dry ditches, sneaking like a thief in the early morning light as she approached the hillock, then climbed over the wall enclosing the half-dozen two- and three-story houses packed tightly together.

Only one dog barked, and judging by its sound, it had to be smaller than Skinny. Jep and Temus listened carefully to the frenetic barking, which stopped abruptly. Had she killed it? Either way, the little dog had done its job. Bree had failed to infiltrate the houses undetected. Drake glanced at Bellor, asking what they should do. The dwarven War Priest's weathered face betrayed no worry as he lowered an open hand, telling Drake to stay down and keep calm.

Bree was on her own.

Sighing, Drake knew he should have gone with her. Even if she was a skilled swordswoman, someone needed to watch her back.

Moments passed and no shouts of alarm came as more light shone from the horizon. Bree would be seen if she tried to rejoin them in the grove. The vorrels, hidden deeper in the trees, were saddled and ready in case they had to flee, but even if the companions had the strength to run, where would they go? Back through the series of palm groves and thickets they'd clawed their way through during the last two nights? Even if they weren't seen by laborers in the fields or the occasional group of men mounted on vorrels, then what? Trek back across the open desert in the shadow of the small white pyramid surrounded by a silent city of what Dabarius thought were tombs and funeral shrines. They would once again risk being seen by the processions of what could be mourners along the well-built road going straight as an arrow and running east and west from the Khoram Mountains.

The road had been packed with Mephitians of all ages walking or riding in carts pulled by vorrels. Most went west, toward the mountains as if they were abandoning the village outside the city of tombs, while other smaller groups marched in solemn processions toward the pyramid complex—escorting what looked like linen-wrapped bodies on wheeled carts. Near the pyramid the companions had almost been spotted twice and traveling back that way was a foolish risk.

Seven brutal days of travel since escaping the freezing night in the Sand Lake had finally landed them in the heart of the Mephitian nomad tribal lands; but there were no nomads. People lived everywhere in hilltop houses overlooking large farms. Even Drake, a hunter from the deep woods of the Thornclaw Forest knew that nomads didn't build roads, villages or cities for the dead around giant pyramids.

Bree'alla had said almost nothing during previous long discussions between Dabarius and the dwarves about what they were finding. She refused to comment or even acknowledge any of the structures. Her vow of secrecy was still binding even though the companions had begun to understand some of the secrets she kept about Mephitia—and possibly who the Wings of Amar'isis served.

The desert was not barren and uninhabited in the southern reaches as everyone in the Drobin Empire believed. Water flowed from the Khoram Mountains and canals spread it to the many fields and orchards in the foothills. The vorrels had finally been able to drink their fill and according to Bree, ingested at least forty gallons when they reached the first canal—impressively lined with mortared stone blocks. The starving animals had gorged on all the plants they could find with their long sticky tongues. The companions had enjoyed their first bath in weeks, and for the first time in longer than he could remember, Drake felt like he wasn't a shriveled piece of leather. If only the strength in his legs and arms would return. He needed real food. Meat. Not tasteless trail bread and dried dates that began to look more and more like desiccated beetles.

Weeks of travel had taken away almost all his stamina and his clothes were loose from all the weight he'd lost. Even Thor's prowess had been diminished and Bellor could barely stand without help. Bree had fared the best, though Drake noticed the weariness in her eyes and saw how slow she mounted her vorrel. Worse, she was getting more and more distant as they neared their destination. Something was terribly wrong and Drake admitted to himself that Thor's fears might have been justified.

Dabarius showed the fewest signs of doubt. He carried on

as if he had no worries at all. Like he knew that he would find his master, Oberon, alive and rescue him from Draglûne without any problems. Dabarius's broken ribs had improved and Drake suspected he used his wizardry to keep up his strength and resist the brutal might of the Khoram. Dabarius wouldn't talk about it, and the now deeply tanned sorcerer had become almost as quiet as Bree. What he was hiding? Drake had no idea.

Little had been said by anyone during the past two nights traveling through the palm groves. It was as if they were all afraid that at the end of their punishing journey they would not find Bölak, and the missing *Dracken Viergur* or any clue to the location of Draglûne's lair as Bree had promised. No one came out and said it, but Drake could tell they were all worried that trusting the half-Mephitian half-Nexan woman was going to be a fatal mistake.

Regardless, Drake had to do something while Bree'alla risked her life for them. Almost an hour had passed since she'd gone, and smoke from what had to be cooking fires had started to rise from the houses on the hill. Brief glimpses of figures walking past the tiny windows on the upper floors made Drake worry even more. "I need to go and see if she's needs help."

"No," Bellor whispered back, "we wait here. We carry on with the plan."

"And if she's captured?" Drake asked, trying to be calm.

Thor raised an eyebrow, incredulous. "She took her sword. There'd be a mob of bloody farmers running for their lives if they laid a hand on her. They wouldn't be cooking breakfast."

"Maybe Drake's right," Dabarius said. "But I should go. Not Drake. I speak Mephitian. I can pass for one of them, just as she can."

They all stared at the wizard. He did look Mephitian, much more than did Bree with her dark red hair, freckled skin and green eyes, which allowed her to roam among the Nexans in Arayden without arousing suspicion. However, Drake had sus-

57

pected since they left Arayden that at least one of Dabarius's parents may have been of the desert people. Master Oberon had adopted him at a young age, and Dabarius said his parents were unknown and long dead. They were probably Mephitian refugees killed while trying to reach the Khierson plateaus. Dabarius's almost-black hair, deep brown eyes, olive-hued skin that had become even more tan in the desert sun, and his absolute self-assurance would go a long way. If that failed, he could just kill a half-dozen of them with his lightning-infused fists.

"I'll find out what's going on," Dabarius said, "and I'll signal you if I need help."

"We're all staying here," Bellor commanded, "and no matter what happens, don't reveal to Bree'alla—or anyone—that you speak Mephitian. That is a secret we must keep from her for as long as we can."

Before Dabarius could argue the gate to the walled courtyard on the hill opened wide. The companions froze, hugging the ground. A bare-chested man opened the gates and was joined by at least ten more men and a few teenagers. They all carried long spears, javelins, and tall wicker body shields. Several of them looked up at the sky—reminding Drake that the aevian threat had returned. Bree had told them a few rogue griffins and other aevians prowled the land close to the mountains.

"If they come down here for us," Thor said, sliding his circular shield closer to him. "I'll get Master Bellor's and my armor from the vorrels."

The Drobin hadn't worn the thin chain mail shirts under their clothing since the night they ambushed Shai'keen's scouts, but the early morning temperature would permit it now—though Drake doubted the dwarves could fight for more than a moment before travel fatigue defeated them utterly, especially Bellor.

"If they come down here," the War Priest said, "we're in

no condition to fight, but if we have to . . . we'll take them in the trees. None must escape. There must be no survivors to speak of us. Understand?" He looked at Drake who felt his heart skip a beat. "If they attack, and then run, shoot them down."

XII

Even if we each killed ten of them before we fell, it would not be enough. After these many years of blood and sacrifice, going to Lorak with human blood on my hammer will feel like failure.

—Bölak Blackhammer, from the Khoram Journal

Drake touched the forward curved blade of the Kierka knife strapped to his thigh. The Mephitians gathered outside the gate on the hilltop, readying themselves for battle.

Thor gritted his teeth, itching for a fight as Drake prayed it wouldn't come to that.

"Ready the crossbows," Bellor ordered.

Thor spanned his and Bellor's smaller crossbows, while Drake began turning the ticking krannekin lever of *Heartseeker*, pulling back the four spring-steel arms of the double crossbow. Jep and Temus tensed while Skinny sprang to his feet, looking like he might run.

The armed Mephitians walked out from the gate and a handful more spearmen emerged with vorrels pulling four-wheeled carts. Large ceramic jars, bundles of fodder, and other smaller packages filled the carts to the brim. Twice as many women, most wearing sheer linen sheath dresses, and children in white kilts and sandals, marched after them and the spearmen dispersed into a protective ring. For a brief moment the Mephitians trundled along the ridge-top road, then unexpectedly disappeared down the far side of the hill. A short time later a few more Mephitian youths ran out of the gate carrying small baskets and spears.

"What are they doing now?" Thor asked.

"They're still leaving," Dabarius said.

Two old women and a short, burly man stood at the gate waving to the departing youths. One of the young men ran back and accepted another basket before sprinting after the others. When all the travelers had disappeared the three figures went inside, leaving the gate open.

"What does all this mean?" Thor asked.

"Bree succeeded," Dabarius said. "There's only a few left behind."

Bellor let out a long sigh as he tugged on his beard, obviously pondering what it all meant.

A lone figure came out the gate. A lithe woman with black hair walked, balancing a basket on her head. She turned off the road, still balancing the basket perfectly, and meandered down a trail that led into the fields in front of them, taking the route Drake thought the armed men would take. She wore a simple sheath dress of white linen and followed a path beside a canal that led toward the palm grove.

"It can't be . . ." Thor stared at the woman and shook his head.

The woman got closer and though she walked timidly—perhaps so she wouldn't spill the contents of the basket—and she didn't carry a sword, Drake knew it was Bree'alla. The rising sun illuminated her perfectly. The dress she wore was so transparent in the sunlight it revealed every part of her muscular body beneath. The form-fitting, ankle-length dress hung from below her breasts and two strips of the same see-through material went across her chest leaving little to the imagination. A black braided wig with locks of hair that went down past her shoulders completely covered her red hair. Her eyes were lined with kohl, and it flared boldly toward her ears, making her look more like some exotic beauty, not the dangerous fighter Drake knew so well.

Bree slipped into the palm grove right where the companions were hiding, and put the basket down. She stood over them and Drake's mouth gaped at her immodesty. She stood impatiently with her hands on her hips. Drake kept his eyes on the blue spiral tattoo that wrapped around her lower leg rather than at her private areas barely covered by her new clothing.

"I'll get the vorrels," Bree said, "then we're going up to the house. Now get dressed." She pointed to the basket.

"What are we supposed to wear?" Drake asked, deciding it would be embarrassing if he stood up.

"I am not wearing anything like that." Thor gestured toward Bree and scowled.

Bree shook her head. "Only women wear the *kalasiris*. You'll wear these." She took out a pair of pleated white linen kilts that went to the knees and a pair of thicker linen robes with cloth belts. She tossed one each to Drake and Dabarius. She also produced two short black wigs made of some kind of animal hair and scented with a pungent oil that reminded Drake of the myrrh he had smelled in the market in Arayden.

Thor glared at her. "I am not wearing any barbarian clothing."

Bree threw pairs of sandals to Dabarius and Drake, then handed Bellor a blanket and a scarf-like head covering. Thor let his fall on the ground.

"Just wear it until we get inside the house," Bree said. "Or you can wait here until sunset and then sneak to the house. If you go now we'll shield you and Bellor with the vorrels. These disguises will do little if you're seen up close, but from a distance they'll work. You all need to blend in as much as you can. If you're discovered here this will end badly."

"How badly?" Bellor asked.

She raised one eyebrow at him. "The innocents in the house who have offered to shelter us will pay with their lives."

Thor and Bellor agreed and Bree showed them how to wrap the head covering around their scalps, then down over their necks and beards. She put a robe over them as well.

"Why were you gone so long?" Dabarius asked. "What happened?"

"My friend, a woman named Zah'dah, sent her people away a few days early for a festival," Bree said. "We can trust only those who stayed."

"You are certain we can rely on them?" Bellor asked, his voice low and serious.

"I've already told them about you. They're old friends of my father. I trust them with my life."

"What about *our* lives?" Thor asked.

"Yours too." Bree picked up the bundle Thor had let fall and presented it to him.

"Very well," Bellor said, "we'll do what you ask . . . for now."

"We have to wear dresses?" Drake asked, his tone revealing his horror.

"They're not dresses," Bree grinned while shaking her head, "this is a *schenti*, a linen kilt. All the men wear them here."

Bree went to get the vorrels and the companions dressed in the odd clothing. Drake kept his smallclothes on underneath the kilt, then put on the longer robe, which was quite comfortable and hid his pale legs. He felt foolish and was glad no one from Cliffton could see him now—wearing a dress—a short one at that. He couldn't bring himself to put on the scented black wig. He busied himself figuring how to attach his Kierka knife to the back of his kilt. He also had trouble with the straps for the sandals. How was he supposed to wrap them around his ankles? He tied them in a way he was sure was incorrect. He missed his boots, especially the hunting knife hidden in the right one, though the sandals were much cooler.

The dwarves put the blankets over their clothing and wrapped the head scarves over their hair and beards. Bree returned moments later with the string of vorrels and smiled at Drake, who shifted uncomfortably in his *schenti* and robe, then put on the wig.

Bree'alla looked startled when she spotted Dabarius. He was the perfect image of a native Mephitian from the Sand Quarter in Arayden. He had even put on some kohl under his eyes, though Drake had no idea where he got it.

"You'll walk up front with me," Bree told the tall wizard. "We'll each lead a parallel line of vorrels. Bellor and Thor will be in the middle with the dogs, and Drake in the back. If we meet anyone, say nothing. I will speak for us."

"Won't it be odd if a woman does the talking?" Thor asked.

"No." She stared blankly at Thor, begging him to say different. "It won't."

Dabarius and Bree led the way across the field, two lines of vorrels hiding the dwarves. Bellor did his best to keep Thor from cursing too loudly while Drake ignored them and watched for any Mephitians. He wished he was carrying his crossbow rather than watching the sack he stashed it in sway on his vorrel. There were griffins here after all though no one seemed concerned except for him.

The disguised companions marched up the slope to the front gate of the hilltop complex and Drake was irritated that he couldn't see what was beyond the hill. The people had gone somewhere, probably to the looming mountains, though Bree would tell them nothing more.

Bree quickly led them into the courtyard, which smelled of vorrels, goats, chickens, plus baking bread and some sort of frying meat that may been lingering from breakfast. Drake's mouth watered at the thought of decent food. A small jackal-looking dog with perked up ears barked as they passed under the gate arch, then went silent as a woman shouted a curt command from inside the largest house.

All the companions waited outside the narrow doorway where the shout had come from. Two tiny old women dressed in slightly dirty robes, and a squat bare-chested man wearing a stained *schenti* stepped outside. The women had the dark honey colored skin of Mephitians and beamed with friendly smiles. The man, perhaps half the age of the women, had even darker skin. He grinned as well, but his face didn't seem right. His eyes were very close together and his head was too small with ears much lower on his skull than seemed right.

The oldest of the women smiled at the companions, bowing her head reverently at the dwarves. The women and the odd looking man seemed friendly enough, but they held the companions lives in their hands, and Drake wondered if they could be trusted.

The older woman whispered something to Bree, who replied in Mephitian, a more deliberate and slower language than Nexan. Drake heard his name and could tell Bree was introducing them all, though she spoke so slowly compared to how she rattled off her words in Nexan. The women nodded as Bree finished the introductions, then the oldest woman made a short speech, glancing at all of them.

"This is grandmother Zah'dah," Bree translated, saying her name with a pause in the middle, and accentuating each part carefully, distinctly. "She welcomes us to her home and her land. She is honored to have us and has already made an offering to the gods on our behalf that will keep us safe. She says while we are here, we are her children and very precious to her. She wants me to introduce her youngest sister, Em'wia," the other woman bowed, "and this is Em'wia's son, Te'tu."

Te'tu gave a generous grin, showing he was missing several of his teeth.

Jep let out a playful *wuf*, and Te'tu cringed, pressing his hands against his oddly shaped face. The three Mephitians recoiled in fear from the large bullmastiffs who sniffed the ground excitedly and wagged their tails. Skinny pranced over to Te'tu.

"Skinny, come," Drake ordered, upset the dog had left his side. Skinny didn't listen and poked Te'tu's crotch with his nose. Te'tu's dumb smile returned as he realized Skinny was very friendly, and he petted the dog.

Grandmother Zah'dah said something to her son and Te'tu hurriedly led the vorrels to a nearly empty stable with Skinny tagging along. Drake kept Jep and Temus beside him. At least they minded him. He would have to work on training Skinny to listen or the dog could not come with them. Undisciplined behavior could get them all killed.

To Drake's dismay, Zah'dah made him leave Jep, Temus, and Skinny outside on short leashes, then ushered the companions into the unlit mud brick house with a few slit-windows, each only a handbreadth wide. The air smelled of cooking food and odd, sharp spices. A shrine in a nook in the wall beside the doorway held several small humanoid figurines made of clay and Drake recognized the goddess, Amar'isis in the center with blue wings hanging from her spread arms. Without the wings, she would be his people's goddess, Amaryllis.

Zah'dah asked them to sit on a long rug against the plastered wall covered in painted scenes of verdant fields in the shadow of snowcapped mountains. The room had several small doorways leading into dark chambers and a shadowy staircase at the edge led upward.

Zah'dah sat on her knees as Em'wia brought rags and a ceramic basin filled with water.

"What's all this?" Thor asked.

"Custom," Bree said with a wry grin, "but poor Em'wia and Zah'dah."

"What?" Thor wrinkled his brows as Zah'dah struggled to remove his dusty boots. The strong odor from Thor's feet elicited no reaction from the old woman, though Bree appeared quite amused.

Em'wia and Zah'dah giggled at the way Drake had tied his sandals, and said something in Mephitian to him, then flashed happy grins that made him think of his own grandmother in Cliffton. The tiny old Mephitian women were nothing like his grandmother. A twinge of sadness made him scrunch up his face and he wanted to believe he would get back to Cliffton someday. He would marry Jaena and this trek would become a faded memory.

You're a stone-faced liar, Drake thought to himself, *but you can't fool me.*

He knew he would most likely never return to Cliffton. This road was too long and too dangerous, and even if he did one day return, Jaena might have moved on. He looked at Bree, who was smiling as Bellor tried to refuse the honor he was about to receive. He loved Bree's smile, and wished it would come more often.

Em'wia and Zah'dah began washing Thor and Bellor's wide feet after bowing low and averting their eyes. They massaged the dwarves' sore limbs with a lavender scented oil. The two old women continued their work, smiling as they cleaned, treated small injuries, and then massaged Drake and Dabarius's feet and legs. Drake almost fell asleep when they finished with him, then Zah'dah made a friendly sounding statement, bowed again, and went toward what had to be the kitchen area.

"What did she say?" Bellor asked.

"She says she will serve us a meal very soon, and that we should rest here." Bree pointed to the rugs and cushions on the floor nearby. "She also said we should stay away from the windows and doors, and to stay on the first floor."

"Why?" Thor asked.

"For our protection," Bree said. "No one must see us here. If we are seen, we jeopardize their lives as well as ours."

Drake watched Dabarius, wondering if Bree had embellished Zah'dah's words. It sounded like she had, and the wizard's almost imperceptibly irritated expression confirmed it.

"Don't think we're your prisoners," Thor pointed a finger at Bree. "You and two old women and that imbecile won't keep us here."

Bree spat something in Mephitian at Thor—definitely a curse—and followed after Zah'dah.

When Bree was gone, Dabarius stood. The annoyed look on his face lingered in the direction Bree had gone.

Bellor whispered to the wizard in Drobin. Drake thought the dwarf asked, "What did the woman say?"

Dabarius kept silent, motioning for Bellor to follow him up the stairs. Thor helped the gray-bearded dwarf off the bench and they both marched up the stone staircase in the rear of the house. Drake followed after them, not caring what Bree would say if she caught them.

"The old woman didn't bar us from anything." Dabarius made a dismissive gesture.

"What's she hiding?" Thor asked, his angry question directed at Drake.

Drake shrugged. "I'm just as tired of this as you are."

They followed the narrow stairs up past the second level and then to the top floor.

"Come back down here!" Bree yelled from downstairs.

Dabarius paid no attention and unbarred a stout door to a wide balcony facing west. The companions filed out and Drake kept an eye on the sky as the wind tousled his hair. A long valley filled with yellow and some green fields paralleled the gigantic Khoram Mountains, which were so close individual trees could be picked out on the slopes. A dark blue meandering river flowed south through the center of the valley. Tiny side canals directed the water to the desert, and dirt roads connected dozens of small complexes of walled houses, most of which were on the hilltops, with almost none in the flood plain beside the river.

Thor gestured to a large collection of several dozen houses atop a plateau two hours walk away where many roads intersected. "Look, a village."

"No," Dabarius said, "that's nothing. Look where the river comes out of the mountains."

Drake followed the ribbon of water upstream, and gazed at the beige hills and the similarly colored mountains where the river disappeared in one of two intersecting canyons. At first, he thought he was looking at a conglomeration of large boulders and hills, perhaps another two hours walk beyond the town. The morning sun shone straight into the canyons. His eyes focused and he gasped in shock.

A massive city blended in with the canyons and surrounding slopes. The walls, buildings, and houses were the same color as the landscape. If he hadn't been on a hilltop with the sun illuminating the area, Drake doubted he would have ever seen it.

The city lay hidden inside the mouth of two deep canyons, which came together at the edge of the mountains. Both rifts stretched out like the branches of a tree from the back of the city. The southwestern canyon was a rocky gorge with sheer walls where the river had been dammed and a lake had been created. The northwestern canyon was steeper as it snaked into the upper reaches of the Khoram peaks.

Blocking off the mouth of the canyons and abutting the cliffs on either flank sat a gigantic wall that looked like a natural ridgeline. Though he could barely see it, the river had been directed into a moat in front of the wall.

Inside the walls, sitting at the foot of a tall peak, a plateau sat at the point where the canyons diverged. Monolithic obelisks reached into the sky and cast shadows onto the cliff behind the plateau.

Bree'alla stepped onto the balcony. Only Drake glanced away from the impressive sight of the Mephitian city. Her lips were tight. Her fists were clenched at her side.

"That's our destination, isn't it?" Dabarius demanded.

"Forty years ago, my uncle Bölak and the *Viergur* went there," Thor challenged, "didn't they?"

Bellor stepped toward the half-Mephitian woman, his shoulders relaxed. "Please, Bree'alla, tell us now. We need to know."

She let out a breath. "In the morning I'll be leaving to deliver the Sacred Scrolls of Amar'isis to a safe place," her eyes flashed toward the city. "I am a Wing Guardian and only I can do this. You will all remain here and wait."

Thor shook his head, anger turning his face an angry red.

"I'll return as quickly as I can with all the answers you seek," Bree said.

"Not good enough." Thor shook his head. "No more of these stupid games."

"There's no game here, so let me make it clear: if you leave the safety of this house, or stand on this balcony or at a window, or outside the gate where anyone can see you, everyone in this house will be killed. Those old women are risking everything they have to shelter us. Understand? Now please get back inside."

"What will you do if I refuse?" Thor stepped toward her, his chest thrust forward.

Bellor pushed Thor toward the door. The Drobin warrior resisted at first, then stepped inside after cursing in his Father Tongue.

Dabarius had a satisfied grin as he glanced back at the city, then ducked through the doorway.

"You must hide as well." Bree'alla motioned at Drake with her chin.

He shut the door to the balcony and faced Bree. "This is the secret you've been keeping from us? This city, this place, all these people?"

"Just go inside."

"No. Tell me. What does it matter now?"

"I can't say anything more."

"Vrelkshit. You can. You just choose not to." Drake grasped her arms firmly and stood a hand span away from her face, their eyes locked together. "I've been patient. I've trusted you all this time. I've believed in you. How can you stand there after what we've seen just now and say nothing? This is not right."

She kept a stone visage, but didn't brush him away. "It's not that simple."

"Make me understand."

"I can't." A crack appeared in her defense and she blinked. He saw regret. Fear perhaps?

"Don't you trust me?" he asked.

Her eyes softened. "You, I do." She nodded slowly, moving closer to him. Bree's lips parted. She moved even closer. He could see her nakedness through the transparent dress, and feel her body heat on his skin. He didn't know if she was going to whisper the truth in his ear or kiss him on the mouth.

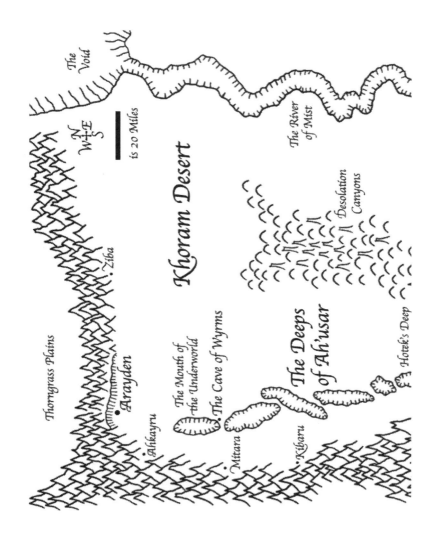

The Void

The River
of Mist

N
W + E
S

is 20 Miles

Khoram Desert

Desolation
Canyons

Thorngrass Plains

. Ziba

Arayden

. Ahkayru

The Mouth of
the Underworld

. The Cave of Wyrms

. Mitara

The Deeps
of Ah'usar

. Kibaru

Hotek's Deep

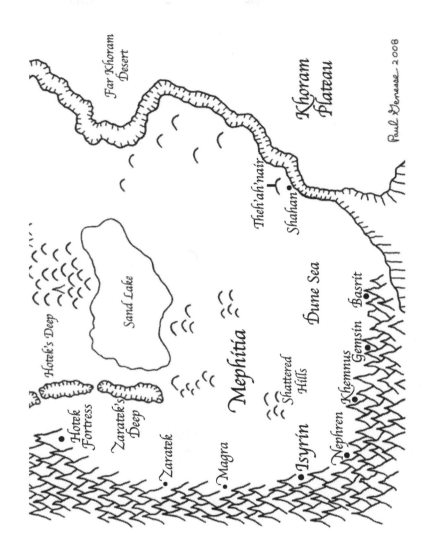

Far Khoram
Desert

Khoram
Plateau

Theh'ah'nair

Shaham

Dune Sea

Sand Lake

Hotek's Deep

Basrit

Gemsin

Mephitia

Khemnus

Shattered
Hills

Hotek
Fortress

Zaratek's
Deep

Nephren

Isyrin

Magra

Zaratek

Paul Genesse 2008

XIII

Today we entered a city that should not have existed. The scale of the deception perpetrated by the Mephitian people has no equal. With their guile, I could hide a mountain range.

—Bölak Blackhammer, from the Khoram Journal

Bree'alla leaned into Drake, hugging him as they stood on the balcony overlooking the Mephitian city hidden in the Khoram Mountains. "When I come back," she said, "I'll tell you everything."

He let out an angry sigh, and couldn't let her get away with this any longer. "When are you coming back?" he asked, wishing he would have screamed it at her.

"I don't know. Soon, I hope." Bree turned away and hesitated at the balcony door.

He stared at the blue tattoo of winged Amar'isis on her lower back, but refused to let it distract him. "Wait." He touched her shoulder.

Bree went rigid for a moment, then opened the door.

Dabarius stood there and must have been listening the whole time. She shouldered past him and descended the stairs. Drake tried to follow. The wizard put his hand against the wall making an arm bar and blocking Drake. "Is she lying?"

"I thought you knew *everything*."

"If anyone would know," Dabarius said, "it would be you."

"What?" Drake squinted at him. "Why?"

"Why? You ask me why?" Dabarius laughed. "She barely talks to anyone except you. Are you completely oblivious to the way she acts around you every day?"

No, he thought. He'd noticed, but he loved Jaena. Bree'alla was not going to come between them. If that were true, why did he feel ashamed already?

"If I was you," Dabarius cocked both eyebrows now, "I would lay with her. Once you do that, she'll tell you everything. That's how women are. You know I'm right." Dabarius strode away.

Drake's face flushed. He couldn't. He had to disregard the attraction he had for her. Acting on his foolish lust would be a titanic mistake. He would control how he felt about Bree.

More importantly at that moment: Why was Bree so afraid? Did she think that if she went by herself to the hidden city she would not be coming back? She promised she would tell him everything when she returned. This reminded him of the time she tried to abandon them after the Cave of Wyrms. Verkahna's dragonling had stung Bree's neck and she almost died. Even a swordswoman as skilled as she needed help. He decided right then he was going with her, no matter what.

No one else would have to know his plan, especially Bree, and he would not sleep with her either to get information. He would never stoop that low. That was not how he had been raised and he wouldn't do it.

As soon as Drake wiped the sleep from his eyes he realized the second meal in Zah'dah's house was going to be much larger than the first. He wondered what time of night it was as he sat in his own clothes in front of the wonderful smelling food piled high on the ceramic bowls and plates. Like him, the others had slept for most of the afternoon, just as they had during their trek across the Khoram, except this time each had their own private sleeping room. A clean, cool, dark, soft, and quiet space almost totally free of flies. He could have slept for twice as many hours, and was certain after this meal he might pass out for even longer.

But I can't, he thought. Bree could slip away in the night. He would have to stay up, or sleep beside her—like he had so many times during their journey through the desert.

Before his thoughts turned wicked, Zah'dah made a solemn speech, or maybe a prayer, her eyes filling with tears as she looked at Bree.

The Wing Guardian hugged the old woman as a single tear flowed down Bree's cheek.

"What did she say?" Bellor asked, after Bree wiped her eyes.

Bree'alla seemed lost in her thoughts. Drake thought he heard mention of Bree's father, Ben'syn. Had Zah'dah said something about her son? He had been slain by Verkahna only a few weeks before when the wyvern-dragon had raided Ahkayru and stolen the Sacred Scrolls of Amar'isis.

Bree's voice wavered a little as she began, "May Ah'usar be protected from the Dragon of Darkness as he travels through the Underworld. May He rise again in his fiery chariot and protect us all with His Holy Light."

"*Heh'en Ah'usar,*" Em'wia said.

"What else did she say?" Dabarius asked.

Bree pursed her lips and ignored Dabarius.

"Beautiful prayer," Bellor smiled at Zah'dah. "Now please tell her my words. May the Mountain god, Great Lorak, bless us with the strength of His mountains. May He bring peace and safety to this home."

"*Heh'en Kheb,*" Zah'dah replied to Bellor's prayer after Bree's translation.

"Praise the Mountain God," Bree said.

Following the custom the companions learned earlier, they all took a long draught from their personal cup of a warm, soupy alcoholic barley drink called *haunqt,* prepared only minutes before by Em'wia. This batch was even stronger than the first bowl and Drake realized some of his grogginess had been from the strong drink, similar to Drobin beer. Bellor and Thor, especially Thor, did not appear to mind the strength or the taste.

As Drake looked for some water to wash out the taste of the alcohol, Em'wia and Zah'dah served the companions generous helpings of flat oily bread, pieces of goat and chicken meat marinated in a salty reddish sauce, boiled beans mashed into a thick paste, and some kind of squash that was supposed to be dipped in a communal bowl filled with a sauce that mad his tongue positively burn.

Zah'dah chuckled as Drake struggled to pick up the pieces of meat on his bread. The lamps in the dim room provided enough light for him find the lost food on the floor and nothing was wasted. He smiled thinking that if Jep, Temus, and Skinny were there instead of being tied up outside, they would have gobbled the morsels up in an instant. "I should go out and feed the dogs," Drake said.

"Te'tu fed them earlier," Bree replied. "They ate the meat Grandmother didn't use from the goat."

"I should look in on them, though."

"No," Bree whispered, "it would be rude to leave dinner. Te'tu is on guard with them now. See them afterward."

He didn't like it one bit. The dogs should be beside him. Jep whined very loudly a short time later and Zah'dah shushed the bullmastiff with a loud shout, motioning for Drake to stay seated and eat. Ignoring the dogs made Drake lose some of his appetite.

The silence lengthened and the tension in the room increased.

Dabarius stopped eating and stared at Bree, waiting for her to meet his gaze. The wizard was the only one of the companions—besides Bree—who still wore the Mephitian clothing and he seemed perfectly comfortable in Zah'dah's house.

"Is there something wrong with you?" Bree set down her cup and finally looked at the wizard.

"I've been thinking," Dabarius said, "it's too dangerous for you to deliver the scrolls of Amar'isis alone. Someone should go with you." He glanced at Drake.

"No." Bree shook her head. "Don't start this. Honor grandmother Zah'dah, and listen carefully, I said everything that I'm going to say on the balcony."

"You still plan to leave in the morning?" Dabarius asked, "And we're all staying here? There's no other way?"

Bree nodded.

On the inside, Drake felt even stronger about going with her. "She'll be all right on her own," he said, hoping they would believe his lie.

"The scrolls of Amar'isis have spells on them, don't they?" Dabarius asked.

"It doesn't matter, you can't read them," Bree said.

"Then there's no danger if I look. Now tell me, why did Verkahna want them? Are they a weapon she could use against us?"

Bellor stopped eating, an intrigued expression on his face. Drake wondered if Dabarius already had seen them. He had the opportunity more than once to look.

"The scrolls are not for the unfaithful, especially foreigners or vile dragon kin who don't worship the Winged Goddess. I'm warning you,"—daggers shot from Bree's eyes—"keep away from them."

"What are you hiding in them?" Dabarius asked. "I know there's something in them about this place or dragons. Which is it?"

"You'll push me too far one day," Bree warned.

"And what will happen?" Dabarius asked.

"Shut up," Drake told Dabarius.

The wizard went back to eating with a smug grin on his face.

The old women kept filling the companions plates with food, trying to alleviate the tension with roasted goat smothered in a thick red bean sauce that made your mouth burn. Thor ate the most and per the thirsty dwarf's request, Zah'dah kept pouring more of the chunky beer into his cup.

Bree didn't say another word in Nexan, and spoke to the Mephitian women in soft tones. Em'wia and Zah'dah began to chatter at Bree after they finished their cups. The women made grand gestures with their hands and slapped the rug for emphasis. They both had big smiles, probably from the alcohol. After dinner, when the mood had shifted, they sang a quiet song, possibly a lullaby, that made Bree'alla grin. Though Drake couldn't understand a word, he thought of his grandmother singing him and his sister Tallia to sleep when they were little.

Bellor had fallen asleep before the singing had started, and he snored softly as he lay on the pillows Zah'dah had piled around him.

"Master Bellor needs to be put to bed. He's too old for beer, I'm afraid." Thor snorted as he tried to staunch his laugh.

The War Priest woke up enough to stagger off to his room—with help. When Thor and Drake returned from helping him find his private bedroom, Thor picked up Bellor's nearly empty cup of beer and finished it off. "Ah, my reward. Is there any more?"

Dabarius yawned. "You can have mine. I'm exhausted." The wizard put an almost-empty plate with a smear of bean paste in front of Thor.

"Not a friendly human," Thor said. "You never have been. I'd teach you some manners, except you're too thick to remember the lesson."

"Drobin manners?" Dabarius smirked. "I'm quite familiar with them from Khierson City."

The dogs were snoring when Drake managed to look in on them. He petted Jep, Temus, and Skinny for several minutes. He smelled beer on their breath and found empty bowls

79

nearby, as well as a few well-chewed bones. Who had given them beer?

Te'tu stood in a little enclosed guard post on the wall near the gate and waved at Drake whenever he looked over at him. Zah'dah's little gray-brown jackal-like dog pranced near the gate, looking out the cracks with its ears up. At least one dog was still on guard.

Skinny woke up and licked Drake's hand. The dog's belly bulged and Drake wondered how much he had eaten. A few days at Zah'dah's and they'd all gain back the weight they'd lost on the trail.

When Drake returned to the house, wishing he didn't have to leave his dogs tied up outside, Bree, Em'wia and Zah'dah were alone, engrossed in what appeared to be a very serious conversation. Bree said very little. Drake sat watching them while fighting off his fatigue.

Em'wia smiled at him and he wondered if she was asking Bree questions about him. He hated not knowing what they were saying. After what felt like at least two hours, the old women woke Drake, hugged him goodnight, then Bree proceeded to usher him down the hall toward their rooms. She held a tiny flickering lamp as she pushed him along.

Drake thought he saw a dim glow ahead that winked out quickly as they entered the hallway. Had it come from Bree's room? It was pitch dark in her little room when they looked past the curtain. Dabarius lay sprawled out on the sleeping matt, dead asleep. His room was one doorway further ahead, if Drake remembered correctly.

Bree scanned the chamber, first checking her bag that carried the scroll case containing the sacred text of Amar'isis. The scrolls were there, and she kicked Dabarius in the foot. "Get up, you're in the wrong room."

"Huh?" Dabarius squinted at the light.

Drake helped him stand and directed Dabarius to his room.

The wizard patted Drake on the shoulder as they parted. "Get some sleep." Dabarius winked, and for an instant he looked like he was wide awake.

Shaking his head, Drake went back to Bree's room and looked in. She lay on the soft matt, a blanket pulled up over her and the lamp up on a shelf. "Sleep well," she said.

"You too." Drake averted his eyes, nodded, and closed the curtain. He went down the hall, got a blanket, and returned a few moments later. He sat outside her room on the floor, the faint glow of the lamp in Bree's room providing the only light. He would stay there all night and would know if she tried to leave.

After a few minutes he heard Bree stirring inside. She made what could have been an impatient sigh.

"If you're going to stay there all night," Bree whispered, "why don't you come in."

Embarrassed, he peeked around the doorway. She patted the sleeping matt beside her and waved him in, a playful smile on her face. The dress she had been wearing lay beside the matt in a rumpled heap and her blanket covered only part of her chest.

He sat down beside her.

"Are you standing watch over me?" she asked.

"Something like that," he said.

"We're safe here, don't worry. We can relax for once." Bree touched his forearm, then sat up and leaned into him, resting her chin on his shoulder. He kept his eyes away from her bare chest as she pulled his shirt over his head. "Lay down. I know you're tired."

All traces of his fatigue disappeared as Bree's warm fingers touched his shoulder and the side of his chest. She gently coaxed him to stretch out beside her. Drake faced away from her, his heart pounding.

"You're worried about me, aren't you?" she asked, her breath tickling the back of his ear.

"You shouldn't go alone tomorrow," he said.

"It's the only way."

"What if you don't come back?" Drake turned a little toward her.

"I'll come back. If I'm delayed, I'll at least get a message to you with everything you need to know about what happened to Bölak and where you can find Draglûne's lair."

"So you don't know right now?"

"Not everything."

Drake smiled. She had actually told him the truth for once—even if it lacked substance.

"What is it?" Bree asked.

"Why don't you trust me?"

She pulled his shoulder down and he lay flat on his back. Propped on her side, Bree stared into his eyes, her dark red curls falling across her face. "The Goddess wants me to help you. She said *you* must survive. No matter the cost."

Drake blinked, a lump in his throat. He knew it wasn't the Goddess Amar'isis. It was Jaena traveling in her spirit body. The woman he loved in Cliffton had saved Bree'alla from the poison and brought them to this moment.

"I'm not going to let anything happen to you," Bree whispered, her lips coming closer to Drake's.

He felt the lust rising in his body, even as guilty feelings about Jaena filled his mind. What had Jaena done exactly? Had she abandoned him, given him over to Bree? Because that's what it felt like. He remembered a time when he and Jaena knew everything about the other, that they understood who they were and where they fit. The world was smaller then, simpler.

It didn't matter. He turned away from Bree. He would not betray the woman he loved like this.

Bree'alla draped an arm over his side and pushed into him, her soft breasts against his back, her hips rubbing slowly against him. She whispered, "I'm glad you're here tonight. I wanted you here with me."

He smelled the alcohol on her breath as her hand slid down his chest, down his stomach, going further in slow increments that nearly drove him mad with desire. He snatched Bree's hand, held it firmly against his chest as his breath came heavy and his throat inexplicably tightened. He clenched his teeth, having to fight his hardest against both the desolation of his journey and his body's need for comfort.

The lamp sputtered, sending wisps of aromatic smoke into the tiny room as they lay there in silence. When the light went out a moment later, Bree pulled up against him and whispered, "There is no other man in this world I trust as much as you."

Bree pulled the blanket over them and kissed him once on the lips, then waited for him to respond. He resisted the urge to kiss her back, and she relaxed beside him, snuggling against him. They lay there for a while, unmoving, and the passion he felt faded. Comforted by the brick walls, the thick roof, and Bree's presence, he fell fast asleep, the exhaustion of the journey across the Khoram finally winning out.

Drake woke face down in the darkness, his arms pinned behind his back. He was crushed to the floor. He smelled sweat as a wet rag soaked in something foul was thrust into his mouth and tied in place. His throat burned. He turned his head toward the direction where he thought Bree had been sleeping. Torchlight from the hall allowed him to catch a glimpse of her being restrained by a shadowy figure, then a musty sack was pulled over his head. A noose tightened around his neck and he fought for air. His lungs filled with the noxious substance coating the rag, and he thrashed and screamed as loud as he was able.

Chest burning, nauseated, and barely conscious, the fumes took hold of him and he stopped struggling. Moments later, bright pinpoints of light rose up and consumed him.

XIV

They ponder our fate. Either we live as the Sons of Kheb, or we die as foreign invaders.

—Bölak Blackhammer, from the Khoram Journal

Dabarius pulled against the bonds tying his hands behind his back. His whole body ached, and sharp pains from is recently broken ribs radiated across his chest. His hands were numb, and he realized he was lying on a cold stone floor. The rags were still stuffed in his mouth and a thick sack over his head blocked out everything except what had to be lamplight. The stifling heat and the foul vapors from the rags made him retch. He struggled to control his breathing, taking slow breaths through his nose. His wits returned to him in a rush of fear and rage.

That old woman, Zah'dah, or Bree'alla had betrayed them in the end. He squirmed about on the floor, realizing how futile his actions were. Was this what she meant if he pushed her too far?

The leather sole of a sandal or boot pressed against his neck.

"Be still." A man with a husky voice spoke in Mephitian. His sandal crushing down harder, choking off Dabarius's airway.

The wizard complied, and the pressure released. He would bide his time. Then his captors would pay a heavy price. The words to a lightning spell waited on the tip of his tongue, ready to be unleashed the instant the gag was removed, but he needed his hands to use it most effectively.

"They're ready for them." A different man said from across the room. His words echoed slightly off what had to be stone walls.

"I'll bring them in a moment. They're all starting to wake up."

All, Dabarius thought. His friends were there too, but which ones?

The man with the husky voice said, "Wake up," several times as he moved about the room. Judging by the groans, grunts, and muffled Drobin curses, the man began waking up Dabarius's companions. Thor was there, no doubt, but what about the others?

Two men lifted Dabarius by the arms sending a stabbing pain where his ribs had been broken. They forced him to march in between them and his bare feet slapped against a very smooth floor, possibly polished marble. There were many other bare-footed people following behind and in front of him. He heard the creak of a heavy door. Immediately the echoes of their movement became more pronounced, and a different sort of smell permeated the air. Waves of a sweet smelling incense tinged with lemon—Frankincense perhaps?—filled the air.

After taking another ten steps, the men on either side of him forced Dabarius to kneel. His knees crashed into the floor. The pain left him stunned as he was bent over in a bowing position. His throat was pressed against something hard, like a round wooden beam, and a scratchy noose was cinched around his neck and then tied down. The hood was jerked off and he stared down into a basket filled with crusty linen stained with old blood. He had been lashed to a raised log in a kneeling position perfect for beheading. He glanced to the left and right where two muscular Mephitian men stood with what he thought were curved khopesh swords, as their straight blades flared into a sickle at the end.

They were designed for chopping.

He eyed the basket under his head with a new sense of urgency.

Bree, Thor and Bellor were on his right, while Drake was

tied to the log to his left. Their hoods had been removed, and like him they were all still gagged. Bree'alla had a defeated, sorrowful expression and kept her eyes downcast, looking into the depths of the basket as if she believed her head would soon be in it.

Dabarius could not see the dwarves very well, though Thor grunted and the log wiggled as the dwarf struggled to get free. The two warriors behind Thor fell on him and held him still, then bowed their heads to someone in front of them.

Arching his neck revealed an impressive sight to Dabarius. The weathered execution log clashed with the magnificent chamber with its brightly painted pillars and walls decorated with expansive murals, Mephitian picture symbols, and gold accents.

The guards had apparently bowed to the tall young woman seated in the center of the room. She sat on a dais of white marble on a throne made of shining gold and decorated with vibrant lapis lazuli that reminded Dabarius of the bluest sky he had ever seen. Sunlight must have been directed downward through the ceiling by mirrors as the woman and the throne were bathed in light. Striking metallic wings painted blue extended from the throne and made the beautiful regal woman appear to be the goddess Amar'isis herself.

Except she was far too young. Perhaps seventeen or eighteen.

The young woman wore an elaborately embroidered and beaded *kalasiris* of the sheerest material imaginable. Atop her perfectly coiffed and jeweled black wig, a golden-winged crown adorned her head. A necklace and bracelets set with large green stones, glass beads that were all the colors of the rainbow, more lapis lazuli, and other shiny ornaments added to her impressive beauty.

A man twice as old as Dabarius—perhaps fifty—wearing many pieces of golden jewelry and a starkly white *schenti* and robe sat to her right on a lower throne. He eyed the companions with an expression of disgust. A mature woman, likely still in her childbearing years, and wearing a winged necklace of Amar'isis, sat at the young woman's left.

The older man motioned to one of the assorted bodyguards or servants beside the three thrones. A shirtless man carrying a piece of parchment came forward and began reading from a scroll. "The Goddess Queen Khelen'dara, Spirit of Amar'isis, Ruler of Isyrin, and Sovereign of New Mephitia condemns the Wing Watcher, Bree'alla, daughter of Ben'syn for her crimes against Mephitia. Bree'alla is guilty of breaking the vow of the Servants of Amar'isis, of bringing spies into the Sacred Lands, and revealing the secrets of our people. It is the judgment of the Goddess Queen and her advisors that Bree'alla, daughter of Ben'syn, and the spies she guided through the desert be executed. Their headless bodies will be buried in the desert and their souls will be banished by the Priestesses of Amar'isis to the Underworld for eternity."

The older man on the throne beside the Queen motioned to the guards flanking the companions. "Execute them."

"Wait." The Queen had a soft, feminine voice, but it carried a firmness, a confidence, that belied her years. "Before she dies, I wish to hear my Wing Watcher speak."

"She will speak only lies, Great Queen," the older man said. "I have learned all the important details already from the ones who were hiding them."

"General Reu'ven, your counsel is wise," Queen Khelen'dara said calmly to the man on the lower throne. "Regardless, I wish to hear her words myself and have them recorded by the royal scribe. I also wish to have the names of these foreigners and their fathers. High Priestess Mey'lahna informs me that if their souls are to be properly banished to the Underworld, we must write them down, assuring they will never escape from the Darkness of the Underworld."

A guard removed Bree's gag and the royal scribe stood ready. The fallen Wing Guardian coughed and took some deep breaths, avoiding looking at the companions before arching her neck toward the throne. "Great Queen, I have little to say." Bree's voice was weak, scratchy. "I thank you for giving me a chance to speak. I knew that my life would be forfeit for this terrible offense against our people. I am truly sorry and offer my soul to you freely. Take my life and banish my spirit.

"Forgive my boldness," Bree said, "but I humbly beg for the lives of my grandmother Zah'dah, Em'wia, and Te'tu who sheltered us. They are innocent and did not conspire to do anything against our people. Please, show mercy to them and punish me."

"They have been spared," the Queen said, and glanced at General Reu'ven.

"Queen Khelen'dara is merciful," Reu'ven said. "Those citizens and the one from their household who overheard you forcing them to allow the foreigners to stay with them have been banished to the Hotek Fortress where they will live out their days, learning the true cost of keeping our lands safe from the northern barbarians."

"Please, Great Queen," tears filled Bree'alla's eyes, "the women are old and will not survive the Hotek Fortress. I beg you, as a Wing Guardian of Amar'isis, in the name of my honorable father, Ben'syn a Wing Guardian of renown, and the only son of Zah'dah, please let them stay on their land. They will not speak of us, ever. I can assure you of this."

"No," General Reu'ven shook his head. "They are fortunate our Great Queen is merciful, or they would be dead already. Now tell us the names of your foreign friends here and we will give you all a quick death."

Bree stared into the basket of bloody rags. "I am not their friend. I mean no disrespect to our Great Queen, or you, honorable General Reu'ven. I know there is nothing I can say to spare my companions' lives. However, I wish to honor them before I die. I am not worthy to speak their names aloud, nor do I know the names of their fathers."

"Tell them to speak their given name to Ah'moz, the royal scribe," Reu'ven said, "and the name of their sire. Tell them if they do, they may be spared. If they do not, they will certainly die with you here."

She knew he was lying, but Bree'alla slowly turned her head toward Drake and whispered in Nexan. "I'm so sorry. I didn't mean for this to happen. You have to tell them your name, and your father's name. Do it and they will be merciful."

Reluctantly, Drake nodded. The dwarves' seemed unconvinced.

The guards removed the gag from Dabarius first—just as he had hoped. He resisted the urge to uncouthly spit the taste out of his mouth, or to lash out at Bree'alla for trying to give Drake the impression they would be spared if he spoke his father's name. Instead, he smiled and raised his head, already forming the Mephitian words in his mind.

"Great Queen of Isyrin, I am the wizard, Dabarius, adopted son of the master wizard Oberon, of Snow Valley. Who my real father is, I do not know." He spoke in perfect Mephitian, mimicking the accent the queen and her general had used, rather than the low-born accent of the Mephitian refugees which he was accustomed. It felt right to his tongue. Natural. The way he had learned the language as a boy, and the way he spoke with Oberon.

Murmurs of surprise rippled through the room as Dabarius paused. "No. We are not spies. We are allies of the Mephitian people."

"A wizard? Bah." Reu'ven waved him off dismissively. "Many speak our language in the north, especially spies and liars."

Dabarius whispered a spell that burned through the rope tying him to the log and the one around his hands. He then manifested a flash of white light and a puff of red smoke punctuated with a loud clap for effect. He stood up to his full height, ignoring the tiny burns from his spell on his neck and wrists. The guards regained their senses quickly and raised their swords to strike him down. He gracefully bowed low toward the queen, putting his head back on the log. "Bind me if you will, Great Queen, but I *am* a wizard."

Two guards held him down, and when the commotion ceased he continued. "I am one of the last wizards left alive on the northern plateaus. I would be killed by the Drobin authorities if I was ever discovered. Another reason they would kill me is that I am a commander for the Mephitian resistance in the city of Khierson, fighting for the rights of the refugees to worship the Winged Goddess and to break the leash of servitude to the Drobin Empire.

"These two sons of the Mountain God, Kheb, are Earth Priests. The elder is Bellor, humble son of Goren; and Thor, son of Karrick. They are heretics of the Drobin Empire, cast out by the Lorakian Priesthood. They would be killed or imprisoned if they ever returned to the north.

"And this man, Drake, a son of Cliffton, is a hunter from the Thornclaw Forest where his people live as renegades to Drobin law, worshipping the Goddess and venerating Her holy trees. No, he is not a spy. He is the deadliest crossbowman in all of the plateaus, and has killed many wingataur demons, griffins, wyverns, and the very daughter of the Dragon of Darkness, Draglûne's wyvern-dragon spawn known as Verkahna.

"We four are the last known members of an ancient order, the *Dracken Viergur*, dragon hunters. We are united by purpose and honor to kill the Dragon of Darkness, Draglûne himself. We are not spies of the Drobin Empire. We are its enemies. Most importantly, we are the sons of Amar'isis and the sons of Kheb who have joined together to bring order back into the world. That is why we accompanied your Wing Guardian, Bree'alla, across the desert, helping her to transport the Scrolls of Amar'isis to you, Great Queen—though

Bree'alla never spoke of our true location or of the wonders of your land. We have brought the scrolls of the Goddess as a gift to you and have come to offer ourselves as servants to the people of Mephitia."

Dabarius nearly smiled at the stunned look on the Queen's face. He held in his satisfaction as his words sunk in, though he did glance at Bree'alla, whose eyes were wide.

"The Sacred Scrolls of Amar'isis from Ahkayru?" Queen Khelen'dara looked at Reu'ven.

The General glared at the scribe who had read the judgment. "Forgive me, Great Queen, I had asked Ah'moz to give them to you."

The scribe, bowed. "An oversight, Great Queen." Ah'moz reached into the bag on his hip and presented the scroll case containing the holy relic Bree had been so concerned with—for good reason—Dabarius thought.

The High Priestess, Mey'lahna stood up, took the case, and carefully examined its contents.

"*You* speak Mephitian?" Bree whispered to Dabarius.

"Better than you," Dabarius said as he activated a spell that would make his hearing as keen as a watchkat's.

"These are indeed the scrolls hidden by the Servants of Amar'isis in the village of Ahkayru for so many years," Mey'lahna whispered. "What has happened there? Reu'ven's embarrassment has rushed this far too much. We must find out more, and especially about this man—this wizard—Dabarius."

Queen Khelen'dara waved the guards away from Dabarius. "You speak our language very well for someone adopted by a foreign man who lived in the North. I wish to hear more about what you have said."

"Great Queen, I wish to tell you more." Dabarius smiled broadly, then bowed his head again.

"What he has said must be verified." General Reu'ven pointed a bejeweled finger at Dabarius. "Do not be fooled by this sly-tongued trickster. I know of his kind."

"Perhaps we have been too hasty in our judgment." Queen Khelen'dara looked at Reu'ven. "In the twenty-five years you have been in command of the Hotek Fortress, no foreigners have ever breached the borders of our lands. We must learn how to better protect ourselves. To elude the desert rangers you trained yourself, General Reu'ven, they must be skilled indeed."

"Great Queen, I will learn everything about how this happened," Reu'ven tipped his head. "This will never happen again."

At the Queen's command, the companions were untied and their hands freed, though two guards stood beside them. The High Priestess and Reu'ven stood next to the Queen's throne and whispered to each other having in impromptu meeting. Dabarius focused on their words, the magic of his spell working perfectly.

"Make certain only the people in this room, and as few servants as possible, know they are in the palace," Mey'lahna said. "Their presence must be kept secret."

"I will personally make certain of it," Reu'ven said.

"Do you believe Bree'alla's words?" Mey'lahna asked the Queen.

"The magic of the Goddess within me said she did not lie," Khelen'dara whispered, "though there is much more to her story."

"She will tell us everything and she will be punished for breaking her vows." Reu'ven held up a colorful scarab beetle brooch. Dabarius recognized it as the one Bree had hidden in her lapel most of the time. The General had probably taken possession of all of their things, including his book of spells.

"Find out everything," Queen Khelen'dara ordered. "It can't be true that Bree'alla is the only Servant of Amar'isis left in the North."

"Why would she have lied to her own grandmother?" Mey'lahna asked.

"How can all of our spies except her be dead?" the Queen asked.

"They must have been infiltrated or betrayed," Reu'ven said. "I'll find out, personally."

"Find out if she is still loyal to us," Khelen'dara glanced at Bree, "and report to me as soon as you can. I will decide her punishment later."

Dabarius, Drake, Thor and Bellor were marched out of the throne room without another word from the Queen, while Bree'alla was taken a different way. Dabarius caught a glimpse of General Reu'ven trailing behind Bree'alla, and for an instant he was afraid his gambit had failed to save them all.

XV

Not while I live will another Queen of Isyrin fall prey to her enemies.

—the closing of every message written by High General Reu'ven,
Regent of Isyrin

Bree'alla pulled her knees up to her chest and shivered in the
dark corner of her tomb. The blackness felt solid now, like a
heavy weight crushing her down after hours without any light.
General Reu'ven had walled her in himself, laying the heavy
stone bricks and mortar with his own hands, somewhere deep
below the palace.

She sat there, watching the large bricks go higher and
higher as he worked with a blank expression. Her gag and
bonds had kept her from fighting or screaming at him. Now
they lay discarded on the floor after she had finally managed
to break free.

Why had Reu'ven done it? She had told him everything,
hiding no detail, and still he did this horrible thing, making
real her most terrible fear by burying her alive.

The words he had said to explain before he slid the last
brick in place was, "It's for the best."

When she had finally gotten loose of her bonds, Bree tried
to break through the wall. First with her shoulder, then lying
on her back she pushed with her legs. She tried every brick,
from the top down. Even with the mortar still fresh, it wouldn't
budge. Had he used magic?

Regardless, there was no escape.

She wanted to sleep, except the cold burned her nearly
naked body when she lay against the stone. Reu'ven's questions about what had happened in Arayden to the Wings of
Amar'isis haunted her. She had told him about the many assassinations by the Iron Brotherhood, and about how the leader

of the Wings, Master Sammuel, had betrayed them all. She had said all she knew about the four *Dracken Viergur*, who she had at first used to get revenge on Verkahna, and about the wingataur demon who had shapechanged into Bellor and stole back the Crystal Eye from them in the Cave of Wyrms.

Reu'ven listened quietly, almost never interrupting as she spoke about leaving her four friends in the middle of the night after Verkahna was slain in the Cave of Wyrms. The dragonling spawn of Verkahna had poisoned her with a sting as she fled, and Drake had found her barely alive. That night, Amar'isis herself had come to Bree and commanded her to help them, especially Drake. How could she disobey her Goddess?

"It wasn't Amar'isis." Reu'ven shook his head. "You are a fool. It was a trick of your dying mind."

No, Bree thought. *It had to be Her. I saw Her.*

"You should have listened to the Black Ghost in the Sand Lake," Reu'ven said. "If you had let them die there, you would not be in this trouble now. The spirit of Kan'yel was right."

"I couldn't let them be killed by him. I had to get them here. I promised to help them find their kin, the *Dracken Viergur* who came before, and I vowed to help them find the lair of Draglûne. I thought if they helped bring the Sacred Scrolls and the Queen found out what they'd done, she would want to help them."

"You shouldn't have promised those things. The stories of the Sons of Kheb are just stories the peasants tell. There is no truth to them. What is true is that you broke your vows. Queen Khelen'dara is very displeased. Your punishment will be severe."

"I am not important," Bree said, "my friends are. Please, spare them. Help them find our common enemy. I beg you."

Reu'ven shook his head. "The Dragon of Darkness is a God. Your paltry friends have no hope of defeating him."

"What danger is there of letting them try? Please."

"You know nothing of the past. There is terrible danger if we let them try. Your father would be ashamed of how stupid you really are." Reu'ven poked her chest. "Do not risk the anger of a God. If they attack him, he will direct his wrath against us. My duty is to protect our people, especially our Great Queen. Right now, I must defend her, and us, from you."

Bree pulled herself into a tighter ball of sadness on the cold floor of her tomb. She shivered as Reu'ven's words played within her mind over and over again, and she remembered the grating sound of the last brick being slid into place.

XVI

I fear that Bree'alla has sacrificed her life by bringing us here. If she is killed by her superiors, then I will have to believe that the followers of Amar'isis are as cruel and absurd as those of the Iron Brotherhood who follow Draglûne.

—Bellor Fardelver, from the Desert Journal

Drake paced around the opulent chamber where they had been sequestered after being escorted from the throne room. There was no way out. "What do we do now?"

"We wait. We pray," Bellor said as he lounged among several pillows on the floor. He had his feet propped up and looked very tired. "I'm sorry, lad. There's nothing else we can do for her for now."

"We have to do something." Drake turned to Dabarius. "Can you ask them—"

"Would you be quiet and sit down?" Dabarius spat. "They're not talking to us right now. They're talking to Bree."

Drake scowled at the wizard. "I thought you might have some idea—"

"No," Dabarius said, "I don't know what they'll do to her. I don't know where the dogs are. I don't know how long we'll be here. Stop pacing. Save your strength for when our moment comes."

Sulking, Drake sat down away from the others. What else could they discuss? Dabarius had explained everything he'd told the queen and what she had said to him. They were lucky to be alive, especially since Dabarius had stretched the truth about the dwarves worshipping Kheb, the Mephitian god of the mountains. Lorak and Kheb were not the same, just at Amaryllis and Amar'isis were not the same. They couldn't be the same and Drake had told Dabarius that. The wizard didn't care and brushed off any criticism of his explanations. It just wasn't possible for the gods to be the same being with different names and beliefs among the different peoples. Was it?

Dabarius had said what he thought and used the secret information he'd gleaned from the Scrolls of Amar'isis to help make his case. He had read the scrolls the night they had been captured at Zah'dah's. He said that Amar'isis and Amaryllis both encouraged their people to venerate trees and were both goddesses of the moon. Their teachings were quite similar in many respects, but Drake was unconvinced. Sneaking a look at the scrolls didn't make him an expert. Dabarius mentioned a few specifics, and said little else about what he had read—except to report that there were spells he could use against Draglûne. Ancient and powerful spells created by followers of Amar'isis long ago when the dragons ruled the plateaus.

The scrolls couldn't help them now and thoughts of escape seemed pointless as Drake worried about Bree and the dogs. The lone high window to their chamber was too narrow for a person to fit through, and the only door was solid and barred on the other side. They had no weapons of any kind, unless they broke up the small pieces of wooden furniture in the room. Even if they got out, what next? Fight their way through the entire palace guard, rescue Bree, find the dogs, take the queen hostage and force her to tell them about Bölak and Draglûne's lair?

Drake got up and started pacing again.

A few moments later the door opened. A large warrior pointed at Dabarius and said something in Mephitian.

Thor sat up, Bellor looked at the brown-skinned guard warily. Drake asked, "What does he want?" The Clifftoner thought about using one of the ceramic plates from their supper as a weapon.

"He says that General Reu'ven wishes to speak with me." Dabarius showed no fear as he went toward the door.

"Maybe you shouldn't go." Drake was suddenly worried for his friend.

"You want answers, don't you?" Dabarius smiled and walked out of the room.

When the locks and bars were put back in place, memories of his now-absent friends made Drake think of what he could have done to save them. First, Jep, Temus, Skinny; then Bree'alla, and now Dabarius. He leaned against the door and heard the guards outside snickering—probably making jokes about how pitiful he and his friends were.

Only three of us left, Drake thought as he glanced at the dwarves.

"When they come for me," Thor said in a gravelly tone, "I'll not go so quietly."

"Neither will I." Drake took an empty plate and broke it in two by smashing it against the floor. The edge was brittle, but sharp—good enough to cut a man's throat.

XVII

The intrigues of Isyrin's palace rival the petty plots and schemes of the so-called royal house of Alaric in Nexus City.

—Bölak Blackhammer, from the Khoram Journal

The stone-faced guards marched Dabarius through the darkened halls of the palace. They obviously took a circuitous route, avoiding the main passages and chambers. A handful of servants and warriors Dabarius recognized from the throne room were always ahead of the procession blocking off the way and making certain no one was there to watch him go by. They had made him wear a head covering and robe, though his height would give him away. Only a handful of the guards were even close to his size. The procession stopped in front of a wall covered with an intricate mural depicting what had to be a wedding between Amar'isis and a male god. Perhaps Ah'usar?

A hidden door in the wall opened inward and the royal scribe, Ah'moz who had read their judgment stood at the top of a shadowy staircase with a haughty expression on his face. "The General is eager to speak with you." The scribe's contemptuous tone made Dabarius consider missing his meeting with Reu'ven—though he didn't know if he could defeat all of the guards around him. Still, subterranean halls beneath palaces were no place to meet generals and answer questions. To delay them and give him a moment to reconsider his options, Dabarius summoned a gust of wind with a casual spin of his wrist that blew out both of the lamps the scribe was carrying.

Ah'moz eyed the wizard with some suspicion and sent a servant to get a lit lamp while the guards screened Dabarius from any prying eyes and blocked off the hallway on both ends. He wondered how many of them he could affect if he sent a bolt of forked lightning streaking down the passageway. He would have to run from the others and then hope to find a way out of the palace, preferably a cliff he could dive off. His magic would allow him to glide to the ground. Then he could certainly lose himself in the city of Isyrin and figure out a way to get back into the palace and save his friends. He couldn't abandon them, could he?

A woman carrying a lamp encased in glass ascended the stairs. It was the High Priestess, Mey'lahna. She wore a gold necklace with Amar'isis spreading her wings. "Bring him." Mey'lahna ordered the guards as she exited the stairs.

"General Reu'ven ordered us to bring him down—"

"Queen Khelen'dara wishes to speak with this man herself." The High Priestess proceeded down the hall and the guards followed obediently. Dabarius decided the power structure was: Queen Khelen'dara, High Priestess Mey'lahna, then General Reu'ven. Two women ahead of the general. Interesting.

A short time later, Dabarius was asked to sit on a comfortable padded bench and wait. Mey'lahna went through a door gilded with gold leaf while the guards waited with the wizard. A short time later, General Reu'ven stormed into the anteroom and waved the guards out of his way. He glanced at Dabarius with an angry expression, then threw open the doors to the Queen's chambers after waving off the guards. The startled warriors got out of his way, seemingly both afraid of letting him in, and equally frightened of trying to stop him. *Why*, Dabarius wondered, *were the General's hands so dirty? And why was his schenti stained with mud?* Dabarius struggled to hear anything inside with his magic heightened senses. At first he heard some commotion, raised voices, then a door slammed shut. Now, only silence. Were they fighting over him? Or were they arguing about his fate? Either way, he knew his life hung in the balance. In any case, fighting meant there was doubt, and doubt might just be a crack in the walls that held him.

XVIII

Trust is akin to madness here in Isyrin. I suspect that even the lowly maids and stable boys would see us strangled in our sleep if they could realize the smallest benefit.

—Bölak Blackhammer, from the Khoram Journal

"Please forgive my unannounced entrance, Great Queen," Reu'ven bowed in Khelen'dara private audience room, trying to suppress his rage from the prisoner being taken from him by Mey'lahna. "I must speak with you."

"I am unconcerned with protocol, General," Khelen'dara said, "when such important matters are before us."

"I have not been able to interrogate the man, Dabarius, because—"

"You mean, the wizard, Dabarius," Mey'lahna said, an edge in her voice.

"Yes, the self-proclaimed *wizard*," Reu'ven said, his anger making him spit out the word. "Perhaps there was some misunderstanding. It is my duty to interrogate him and report my findings to you. I have much experience in such matters."

"Your experience is vast," Khelen'dara said, "however, in this case I wished to speak with him directly. Mey'lahna has just been informing me of what you learned from Bree'alla."

That sly witch, Reu'ven thought. Mey'lahna had not been present when he questioned Bree. She must have been hiding in one of the hidden observation rooms, but she wouldn't have seen where he took the traitor afterward, and he would keep that hidden for some time.

"Do not be angry with Mey'lahna, General. I asked her to watch the questioning."

"Of course, there is no problem," Reu'ven said. "Perhaps you would both like to be present when I speak with . . . the wizard?"

"That won't be necessary," Khelen'dara said. "I will question him myself."

"Great Queen, I must protest. I am afraid he will influence you to make a rash decision, like allowing these foreigners to live. The more distance you have with them will make the final decision that much easier."

"I have already ordered their executions once, General, I do not intend to do it again until I am satisfied it is indeed the right decision."

"You cannot seriously be considering helping them." Reu'ven was astonished. "Remember what happened to your grandmother and to—"

"I have not forgotten." Khelen'dara stood up abruptly, a mask of calm over the anger hiding beneath her dignified façade. "Perhaps you have forgotten that you are not my regent any longer. Or perhaps you have forgotten that I remember *everything* that happened to my grandmother and mother?"

"Of course, Great Queen, I meant no disrespect."

Khelen'dara raised an eyebrow. "Then do not come into my chambers and insult me with your shortsighted arrogance. I am the Goddess Queen of Isyrin now. I have accepted the essence of the Amar'isis Herself. Perhaps it is *you* who have forgotten your place."

"Forgive me. Please." Reu'ven dropped to his knees and bowed his head. His wig fell off in a heap. "It is only that I care for you so deeply, and fear for your life. You are more precious to me than my own daughters and wives. Nothing must ever happen to you. If it did, I could not take such a failure. I would give my life a hundred times for you."

Khelen'dara walked slowly forward, her bare feet silent on the stone. He put his cheek on her foot and kissed her toes.

"Rise, General." She touched his bald head gently, and stroked his closely shorn scalp.

He stayed on his knees and she held his head in her hands as he looked up at her. "You have always protected me, ever since I was a child. A Queen, or a little girl, could not have a more devoted man in her life. Your counsel is always heard and given great weight. You must understand that I have no wish for history to repeat itself. I will not be killed like my mother and grandmother. The spirits of those women will not allow it. If the foreigners need to be executed, I will order it, but until then, you will follow my orders."

Reu'ven put his forehead against her abdomen and she touched his shoulders. He was so disappointed in her, and angry at himself. How could he be upset at her? Khelen'dara still looked like the little girl he had raised from a baby, and she was an exceptional person, but as he had feared, she had inherited the mercy of her grandmother. The fire of the Goddess had yet to take hold. Nothing could happen to Dara, even if he had to save his Queen from herself.

XIX

I pray that the glib tongue of Dabarius will save us from death. Of all of us, he is the most likely to survive this trial, and I believe it is not coincidence that has brought this young man who speaks their language like a native to this secret city deep in the desert.

—Bellor Fardelver, from the Desert Journal

The golden doorway into the Queen's chambers finally opened and the guards escorted Dabarius inside. General Reu'ven's arrival had no doubt delayed his meeting with Khelen'dara. What would be different now? He would soon find out.

The guards escorted him through the room and outside through beautifully carved white doors. The Queen waited on a covered balcony that jutted out to a point and overlooked the city of Isyrin. The pillars holding up the roof had been painted to look like trees, and as the sun dipped below the reddish-orange horizon in the west, Dabarius had the sense he was strolling through a giant forest. He could barely see the Queen past the guards' heads and focused on what he *could* see.

For the first time he got a good look at his surroundings. He realized he was indeed on the plateau in the middle of the twin canyons—right where he suspected. He caught a glimpse of a sharp peak soaring at the rear of the palace where a titanic obelisk rose against the cliff. He could not see the other obelisk that matched the first, but he knew it was there, located on the other side of the palace.

A reservoir filled much of the southern canyon and the northern one was packed with homes from slope to slope. Trees and gardens dotted the entire city, contrasting with Isyrin's uniform beige color, which blended in with the stone of the mountains. The gigantic wall that dammed the river and enclosed the city looked much more man-made from behind than it did from Zah'dah's house miles away. He could also see the series of levies and spillways that protected the lower parts of the city from the reservoir, and the river, in case it flooded. The engineering was a marvel and rivaled anything he had seen in Khierson or Arayden. There was no doubt. These Mephitians were not nomadic tribesmen. They were engineers and builders.

The guards parted and Khelen'dara stood before him at the promontory of the balcony with her back turned toward him. The tall, stunning woman stared at the sunset while High Priestess Mey'lahna waited beside her Queen, facing Dabarius.

Only Mey'lahna and a couple of the guards witnessed his hesitation as he blinked, awestruck by Khelen'dara's beauty. Her sheer linen gown blew in the breeze coming down from the mountain peaks. The dress outlined her body like a cloud of steam and revealed every bit of her honey-brown skin. A tattoo of Amar'isis graced the queen's lower back, just like Bree'alla's. The golden jewelry that adorned Khelen'dara's ankles, waist, wrists, neck, ears, and head shone in the fading light.

"Great Queen," Dabarius said, and bowed, despite the fact she was not looking at him.

"Come and stand with me." The young queen finally said, without turning to see him.

Dabarius walked forward, finally taking his eyes off her as he stared at the red, orange, and pink sunset painted across the horizon. "Great Queen, I am honored to be in your presence."

She gave a slight nod and grinned. He stood beside her, calm as he pretended to admire the sunset, when he was actually admiring her. She was quite tall, though her head came up just under his nose.

She finally said, "The city is beautiful in the evening."

He nodded. "Yes, very beautiful."

"Do you find your quarters . . . comfortable?"

"Yes, thank you very much, though the view is quite lacking."

She grinned and motioned subtly with her hand. All the guards, save one, backed away. Mey'lahna remained close by, listening. They must know he was a grave threat to the Queen. He could kill her with one magically charged blow to her head. Unless she could counter him, but he hadn't met someone yet who was his equal in magical and physical ability. Was Khelen'dara even proficient in magic? He couldn't imagine she been trained to defend herself with hand-to-hand fighting techniques as he had been by Oberon and Noah? He would certainly have to learn the answer to these questions—but not by attacking her.

"Do you know why I asked you here?" Her voice was teasing.

"No, Great Queen, though I have some notion."

"What notion?"

"You wished to enjoy the sunset with me." Dabarius flashed the smile that had gotten him into the hearts—and other more tender places—of many young women.

Khelen'dara laughed heartily and made eye contact at last. "Yes. That's it."

She laughed again, the sound was rich and genuine. He couldn't help but notice her full lips and her smoky eyes, outlined with kohl that flared into little whorls at the edges. She was young in appearance—though her eyes had the depth of a much older woman. Khelen'dara was no girl he could seduce. He would have to be very careful and use his charm perfectly.

Two Priestesses of Amar'isis approached Mey'lahna with jars of burning incense. The sweet aroma filled the air as Mey'lahna faced the sunset and raised one of the aromatic jars. All of the guards and the Queen turned to the sun as Mey'lahna prayed in what sounded like an archaic form of Mephitian, similar to what he read on the Scrolls of Amar'isis. Dabarius understood something about the journey of the god,

Ah'usar in his solar chariot, and heard bits of a spell protecting the sun god from the Dragon of Darkness who lived in the Underworld.

When the ritual was over, Dabarius faced the Queen with a questioning expression.

"You wish to ask me something? Please do," she said.

"Thank you, Great Queen. I was wondering, is that ceremony performed at every sunset?"

"Every household in Isyrin and all of these lands performs the ritual. We must."

"If you don't?"

She took on a solemn expression. "The Dragon of Darkness will be stronger, and if he succeeds in his nightly assault against Ah'usar's solar chariot, he will take away the dawn."

"The sun will not rise?" Dabarius asked.

"That is what the Priests say. They say the Dragon of Darkness will slay Ah'usar forever—not just for the night."

"Ah'usar dies each night?"

"And He is reborn every morning."

"That is an interesting way of looking at the sunrise," Dabarius said.

Khelen'dara slapped him hard across the face with the palm of her hand, then went calmly back to watching the sunset. His cheek stung, and he couldn't believe how fast she had slapped him. He could anticipate any blow meant for him and counter it, but this was too fast.

The guards moved closer, and Dabarius wondered if they were going to take him away. Khelen'dara seemed not to be angry, but he tried to comprehend what the slap had meant as they stared at the last crescent of the sun as it disappeared over the hills.

"Certainly you, Great Queen, are not afraid that the sun will not rise."

"I know it will, for we have great faith in the gods," Khelen'dara said, "and we do not insult the teachings passed down from our ancestors. Surely you Northerners understand that?"

"Some of us do," Dabarius said, "and I regret my words. Still, I shall remember and cherish the first touch of your hand as long as I live."

Khelen'dara grinned. "You are fortunate that General Reu'ven was not here when you spoke to me so impudently. He is not as forgiving as I am."

"Before I misspoke," Dabarius said, "you were trying to tell me something. If it pleases you, I do wish to hear you continue."

"The sun sets, and the Dragon of Darkness is real. He and his servants come at night, when Ah'usar is furthest from us. Amar'isis watches over us in the dark times, and protects Her people, but the night is a dangerous time."

"Great Queen, this is something my companions and I wish to do, protect your people, and ours from the Dragon of Darkness. We must find the wyrm we know as Draglûne, and slay him."

"You have all vowed to do this, yes?"

He realized she already knew the answer. "We have," he said with confidence. "We have all taken vows to the gods."

"In your master's tower, Draglûne spoke to you, did he not?" Khelen'dara asked.

"Yes, he did." Dabarius squeezed the railing, trying to remember what they had told Bree about the terrifying encounter with Draglûne. "Bree'alla has spoken of it then? She must have said what Draglûne promised to do to us."

"I wish to hear it from you."

"Of course, Great Queen. I am your servant." He bowed. Dabarius told her of the attack on Oberon's tower by Verkahna and her summoned griffins; of the arrival of Drake, Bellor, and Thor; and the subsequent use of the Crystal Eye to find Draglûne's lair—just as Bölak and the *Dracken Viergur* had done forty years previously. He spared no detail when recounting the Dragon King's words to each of the companions, and then described Draglûne's taking of Oberon into the Crystal Eye before the wingataurs came through the mist and attacked them.

When twilight descended Dabarius paused, then told her of how he struck a magically charged blow against the first wingataur who came into his master's tower, knocking it down with his fist and perhaps killing it. He stole a sideways glance at the guards and Mey'lahna to see if his words made them change their posture.

They hadn't moved at all.

"We should go inside," Khelen'dara said as the stars began twinkling in the sky and the bright moon rose over the city. The huge pockmarked disc, at least forty times larger than the sun when it was in the sky, dwarfed the titanic mountains behind Isyrin.

Inside her chambers, seated on comfortable couches across from each other, Dabarius and the queen continued their conversation. He told her about fleeing Oberon's tower, carrying Noah all night, going into Khierson City, the plight of the Mephitian refugees there, and all of the calamities that befell the companions in the city—especially what happened at Lorak's temple and the massacre on the streets. He omitted how he met Raina, but told the Queen of the girl's death and how he carried her body to Bellor, hoping the Earth Priest could save her with his Healing magic.

"She died in your arms?"

He remembered how Raina said she was sorry for deceiving him. A lump in his throat kept him silent as he searched for the words to tell of her passing.

"You loved her?"

"I would have come to love her even more . . . had she lived."

They watched the lamp light flicker for a moment and Dabarius knew by the longing expression that flashed across her face Khelen'dara was attracted to him. She wanted romance, and he would figure out a way to give it to her.

"Why have you come here?" Khelen'dara asked.

She surprised him with her directness. Was she trying to put some distance between them after a moment of weakness? He should answer truthfully and tell her it was for revenge. No, he wouldn't say that. "I want my Master Oberon back. I know he's alive and he must be freed."

"You are loyal to him. That is honorable."

"He is my father, since I never knew my real one."

"Your name, Dabarius, it means 'son of Barius.' Did you know that?"

"No, I didn't." He tried to hide his anticipation. Was his real father's name Barius? Was he Mephitian as he always suspected? Was Khelen'dara playing some game with him and had known all along who he was? "Do you know who my father was?"

"I have some suspicion."

"Please, Great Queen, tell me." He knew such a request was rude, but he couldn't stop himself.

"My scribes in the archives are searching for the answers as we speak. I will tell you everything we learn. The lineages of all of the wizards in our land are recorded."

"My deepest thanks, Great Queen."

"Now I wish to ask you about what happened when you left Khierson City."

Dabarius told of the alicorns carrying them to the mountain pass above Arayden and retold how the small herd had defended the tower against Verkahna, which caused her to summon griffins to attack them.

"You rode upon their backs?" Mey'lahna asked, interrupting their conversation for the first time. "Upon the backs of sacred alicorns?"

112

"High Priestess," Dabarius bowed his head to her, "they offered to carry my friends and I from the ledge where we were trapped. They are our allies against the Dragon of Darkness and know full well that he must be stopped."

The Queen and Mey'lahna exchanged shocked glances. Dabarius remembered they had avoided telling Bree of the alicorns. Riding upon aevians was an offense punishable by death in every corner of the Drobin Empire—and telling Bree hadn't been necessary, nor would it have been wise.

"Have you any proof of this?" Mey'lahna asked, irritation in her voice.

"I have gifts from the leader of their herd." Dabarius showed them the four long black feathers from the alicorns, which he had kept hidden in his robe.

Khelen'dara and Mey'lahna marveled at them, eyes wide. It was as if they were looking at the most amazing thing they had ever seen, holy objects more precious than jewels.

"May I hold them?" Khelen'dara asked.

"Of course, Great Queen," he said, handing them to her.

She held them and stroked the feathers reverently. "These are gifts that have no price."

"We were most honored to be given them," Dabarius said. "I would have used one of them to summon the alicorns and have them carry us all this way south, but they led me to believe that they will not come into the desert as long as Draglûne is alive."

"They stay away from here," Khelen'dara said. "That is true."

"They do live in the north," he said. "Several of the alicorns were slain outside my Master Oberon's tower."

"Sad news," Mey'lahna said, "There are so few of them left alive."

"In my belongings, which I assume you have somewhere, is one of their horns, hidden in my pack. I took it with the blessing of the Blackwind, their leader, from one of the dead mares. It is deadly against dragon kind and Blackwind wants the mare's horn to be used as a weapon."

"Do you know that the alicorns are the messengers and defenders of Amar'isis?" Khelen'dara handed him back the feathers.

"I do." He remembered the alicorns telling him just that.

"The Goddess has blessed you with these sacred gifts," Khelen'dara said.

"Some would disagree," Mey'lahna shook her head, "such as our esteemed General Reu'ven."

"And the entire Drobin Empire," Dabarius scoffed, "and practically every human on the northern plateaus. They're all slaves of the superstitions taught by the Lorakian Priests who want to keep them down."

"You hate them," Khelen'dara said.

"They hate me. They've killed scores of men and women who practiced wizardry. I grew up waiting for them to arrive at Master Oberon's tower and try to kill us. I believe it was divine providence that we were never discovered by the Drobin inquisitors."

"Divine providence?" Khelen'dara asked.

"When I went to sleep at night when I was a boy, I would pray to the Goddess that no one would ever find us."

"Do you claim to serve the Winged Goddess Amar'isis, Dabarius of Snow Valley?" Mey'lahna asked.

He could lie. He wanted to. "I wish I served Amar'isis more faithfully." Deep down, he knew his own desire for vengeance was what he served, not the Goddess that he prayed to so irregularly now. Curse the gods for all the evil they allowed in the world, and especially Draglûne. None of them could cross him now without incurring his fury. This Queen was gracious, but he wanted some answers. "Forgive me, Great Queen," Dabarius bowed his head, "I must ask of the whereabouts of my friend, Bree'alla, and also of the dogs that were with my friends and I when we were taken."

"No dogs were brought to the city," Khelen'dara said. "I do not know anything else of them. They may have been slain at the home of the woman, Zah'dah."

A chill went down Dabarius's spine. He couldn't tell Drake *that* news. "Please, will you send inquiries. My friends and I are quite worried."

"I'll find out," the Queen promised. "As for the Wing Guardian . . . " Khelen'dara glanced at Mey'lahna.

"She is still being questioned," Mey'lahna said. "Now, why don't you tell us what happened in Arayden? Describe to us as much as you can remember about your time there with Bree'alla."

"Of course." Dabarius recounted what happened in the city: how they met Bree when she rescued them from the Iron Brotherhood cultists pretending to be rug merchants; about their escape in the *khanat* tunnel and the ghost of the wingataur attacking them; the ambush outside the city; and their thirsty trip to the Cave of Wyrms. He also related Bree's story about what had happened to the Wings of Amar'isis in Arayden—betrayed by their Wing Master, and how she gained entrance to Verkahna's lair—pretending to be a traitor to Amar'isis—and the eventual death of Verkahna.

"What happened after the battle?" Khelen'dara asked.

"We were tricked. A wingataur took Bellor's form, though I have little memory of this, as I was wounded and nearly un-conscious. The demon seized Master Oberon's Crystal Eye and collapsed the tunnel, trying to kill my friends and I. Later, Bellor was found unconscious, and we escaped."

"You were brave to charge at Verkahna like you did," Khe-len'dara said.

"I did what I had to do. We all did." Dabarius felt such admiration for his friends just then, and felt a pang of guilt for thinking he might abandon them and escape the palace without them. "Bellor was going to give his life to heal me, and without Thor, Bree, and Drake, I would have died there.

If any of us had not done their part, we would have all been killed in that place."

Khelen'dara motioned toward his ribs. "Are you still hurt?"

"I'm all right."

"That night, do you remember what happened?" Mey'lahna asked.

"I was very tired after Bellor and Thor healed me, though I do know what happened. Bree left the camp in the middle of the night. She was going to leave us there and presumably come here . . . all alone with the Scrolls of Amar'isis. That's when Verkahna's dragonling stung her. If Drake hadn't found her she would have surely been killed by it after she fell unconscious from the poison."

"How did she survive?" Khelen'dara asked.

"My friends prayed for her all night, especially Drake. Bree was spared and in the morning she told us she had a vision from the Goddess. She said it was a miracle, and that Amar'isis had healed her, and that she was to help us find the Dragon of Darkness. Bree said she would take us south to where she spoke her original vows and became a servant of Amar'isis. She said she would bring us to the place where Master Bölak and his hunters traveled long ago. She said it was forbidden to say anything more, but when we arrived we would know why she was in Arayden."

"And now . . . do know why she was there?" Khelen'dara asked.

"She was serving you, Great Queen. The Wings of Amar'isis were protecting Isyrin, and the secrets of your people that have been kept for so long."

"Yes," Khelen'dara said, "and it has not been easy to hide from the Drobin Empire. The Gods and the Khoram Desert have protected us."

"My companions and I will never betray you. There is little chance any of us will survive this hunt."

116

"All of our lives are in the hands of the Gods," Mey'lahna said. "When mortals battle one as powerful as the Dragon of Darkness, death is the likely result. Then comes retribution. Unholy vengeance upon those who supported the mortals who dared to try an attack. The Queen's family has seen this before. You know nothing about that, do you?"

"I know that Draglûne is not a God." Dabarius shook his head, wondering what calamity had befallen Khelen'dara's ancestors.

"How can you be so certain?" Khelen'dara asked.

"Gods are immortal and Master Bellor struck the death blow that killed Draglûne's father many years ago in the Last Battle of the Drobin Pass. The former Dragon King, Mograwn died after a blow from Bellor's axe, and so will Draglûne. He is not immortal."

"You are only half-right," Khelen'dara said. "Draglûne's father may have died, and yet the ancient spirit of the first Dragon King is immortal. It found a new host . . . Draglûne, and if he is killed, the spirit will find another host for itself. And so it will be until all of his line are gone from our world. You see, the Dragon of Darkness is divine, and he does not forget. He will return as sure as the sun will rise in the morning."

"Not all of Mograwn's spirit could have gone to Draglûne," Dabarius said.

"What do you mean?" the Queen asked.

"Part of Mograwn's spirit is in Bellor's axe, *Wyrmslayer*. It wants revenge on his deceitful dragon son."

The two women exchanged surprised glances.

The shuffling of sandals drew Dabarius's attention away from the Queen. An old man with folds of skin hanging from his neck carried an armful of scrolls. He approached Khelen'dara and bowed. "Great Queen, may we speak privately?"

"Have you found what I asked for?" Khelen'dara motioned for him to rise.

"Yes, Great Queen, I have." The man glanced anxiously at Dabarius, and his gaze lingered on him an instant too long. He also clutched the scrolls tighter—like he was hiding something. Dabarius guessed the old man's report was about him, and judging by the scribe's nervousness . . . it was bad news.

XX

With each passing hour, I become more sure that the Mephitians will come to kill us. They will not find it an easy task. We cannot die here. My oath before Lorak, my Sacred Duty must not go undone.

—Bellor Fardelver, from the Desert Journal

The table leg with a broken floor-stone affixed to the end by threads from a rug didn't feel very reassuring in Drake's hand. It would probably only yield one good blow, but it would have to do, and he still had the brittle pottery shard knife in his belt, a far inferior weapon to his Kierka blade.

"Pour the rest of the lamp oil." Bellor pointed at the pile of pillows and rugs in the middle of the room. "Thor, get ready."

The younger dwarf hid in an alcove against the wall beside the doorway into their luxurious prison carrying a shield made from a tabletop and a similar weapon to Drake's. Bellor stood in the center of the room with a club in each hand. He was a master with his long-handled and double-bitted battleaxe, but the clubs would have to suffice.

The web of tripwires in front of the door would catch the first few guards by surprise as they rushed in to respond to the fire. Bellor, Thor and Drake would then battle their way out. The Clifftoner was going to fight harder than he ever had before, and his blood was pumping hard as he held the torch, ready to light the fire. He would take a sword from a guard as soon as he could, and then no one was going to stop them.

Thor and Drake shook forearms, and the dwarf had a madness in his eyes that Drake was starting to catch himself. He was not going to be led away and tortured like a criminal. He was going to fight and no one would keep him caged.

"They won't even know what hit them," Thor promised.

"We're getting out of here," Drake said.

"Light it," Bellor ordered. "We want as much smoke as we can get."

Drake lit the pile of pillows, rugs, and draperies on fire. The cloth smoldered and black smoke rose from the sputtering bonfire. The wet cloths tied in front of their mouths helped, though nothing could stop the smoke from stinging Drake's eyes.

"I hear something outside," Thor whispered as they waited for the smoke to fill the room.

"What?" Bellor asked.

"A lot of sandal-wearing men just came down the hallway," Thor said. "I think they're arguing with our guards outside."

A loud thump made the door shake and Drake flinched. Men's shouting filled the hallway as a melee had apparently broken out.

"What's going on?" Drake asked, raising his club and taking up his position in front of the trip wires where he and Bellor stood as bait.

The door burst open and slammed against the wall with a thunderous *crack!* Guards lay in the hallway bleeding. Several large bald men carrying war clubs stood over the defeated royal guards.

Drake raised his makeshift weapon, ready to kill whoever got in his way. Any fear that he had turned to rage as the large man who had flung open the door flashed a wicked grin at Drake. The brute sniffed the smoke with a nose that had obviously been broken multiple times. He pulled a thick iron dagger from his belt, and waved it at the thugs in the hallway. They drew their own daggers and stormed in with murder in their eyes.

XXI

If we all survive our stay as guests in this palace, I shall consider it a sign that we truly are the favored sons of Lorak.

—Bölak Blackhammer, from the Khoram Journal

"Captain Tal'mai," Mey'lahna commanded, "escort Dabarius from the room."

The large, royal guard with the bulging arms and broad shoulders nodded.

"Great Queen, may I please wait on the balcony?" Dabarius asked Queen Khelen'dara, then bowed humbly.

The old scribe carrying news of Dabarius's ancestry shuffled his feet and stared at the floor.

"Yes, of course." The Queen nodded to Tal'mai.

The four guards marched beside Dabarius as he exited onto the roofed balcony—pretending he was not worried at all about what the old scribe would say.

He stood outside the doorway between the pillars as a cool evening breeze swept down from the mountains. He whispered as spell under his breath heightening his hearing, and listened to what was happening inside. The old man said, "What you requested was in the archives of the royal viziers."

"The names, show them to me," Khelen'dara ordered.

Tal'mai touched Dabarius on the shoulder with the flat of his sickle-bladed sword. "Keep walking. We know what you are."

Dabarius strolled to the stone railing, and the sounds inside the Queen's chamber faded. He looked out into the city, listening to the high-pitched clicks of the bats hunting insects beside the cliff. Dogs barked down below, but none of them could be any larger than the desert hound, Skinny. Jep and Temus were probably the largest dogs in the whole of the Khoram Desert.

The sounds of Isyrin did not distract him from what was happening closer at hand. The royal bodyguards scrunched the leather handles of their swords with strong, nervous hands. They surrounded him, watching not only him, but the shadowy places created by the many pillars on the covered balcony.

He thought about his missing spell book and the alicorn horn, both most likely in the possession of General Reu'ven. He might not see his few belongings again, though he had memorized most of the spells while they traveled through the desert. It was Master Oberon's book, written by him over the course of sixty long years studying magic, that Dabarius did not want to leave it behind.

The alicorn horn was the worst thing to lose. Not that Bellor or any of them realized his plan for it. The horn would pierce Draglûne's black heart someday. For the horn, and his friends, Dabarius would come back into the palace. Now, he just had to plan his escape.

The drop from the balcony was two hundred feet to the structures below. The guards wouldn't see him when he landed in the darkness. They might think he had committed suicide. Maybe he could even distract them so none of them saw him jump. They would think he disappeared.

He would find a way back in to the palace and rescue the others. As much as he didn't want to admit it, he needed them. For now he would go—save himself and hide amongst the population.

The scrape and clop of many sandals against the stone made Dabarius look back. The royal scribe, Ah'moz, who had read their judgment in the throne room and then who had been at the top of the stairs behind the hidden door walked briskly toward them. Eight tanned, thuggish warriors carrying stout clubs accompanied the scribe. They seemed like they came from the streets rather than from the royal palace. Ah'moz avoided looking Dabarius in the eye and whispered into Captain Tal'mai's ear when he reached the four royal guards. "The

Queen wants him executed. These men and I are to take him into the tunnels and do it now." Ah'moz showed Tal'mai a piece of parchment. What had to be a royal seal caught the moonlight.

Dabarius smiled at Ah'moz. "Pleasant evening, is it not?"

The wily man nodded, his dark eyes filled with disdain.

"I couldn't help noticing the bats flying beneath this cliff," Dabarius said. "Do they live in caves beneath the palace?"

"What?" Ah'moz asked.

"I asked if a lot of vermin live beneath the palace, in the tunnels?" Dabarius stood to his full height. "Is that where you live?"

"The only vermin here is foreign in origin." Ah'moz didn't look away and met Dabarius's cold stare.

"Strange how you didn't come from the Queen's chambers," Dabarius said, "and yet you claim to carry the Queen's orders."

The scribe slowly swiveled his head to Tal'mai, locking his eyes on the leader of the royal guards. "You have your orders. Follow them now and step aside."

The eight warriors with Ah'moz dared Tal'mai and his three guards to get in their way.

"We're taking him with us," Ah'moz said, "step aside, Captain."

Tal'mai turned to Dabarius with a steely-eyed glare, and stepped away from the wizard, giving him over to Ah'moz and the eight men.

"I thought you were a man of honor," Dabarius said, shaking his head at the guard captain.

"I don't think you are," Tal'mai said, "and I don't approve the way you look at my Queen."

XXII

It is a pity that the Master Wizard Oberon refused to accompany us on our hunt for Draglûne. If we had a wizard in our troop we would be the most formidable group of *Dracken Viergur* assembled in over fifteen hundred years, the last known time when the wizards and the Drobin were last allies.

—Bölak Blackhammer, from the Khoram Journal

Ah'moz waved for his eight men to take Dabarius. One of them carried bronze manacles covered in sigils of power that were linked with a stout chain. The wizard's spine touched the stone railing behind him and he prepared to jump over the cliff and glide away. He gave Ah'moz a smug grin and put his hands on the railing.

Captain Tal'mai, standing by Ah'moz, caught the scribe in the throat with his forearm. The three other royal guards attacked Ah'moz's thugs as if they knew the exact moment when their leader was going to strike. Khelen'dara's guards punched and slashed into the other warriors with a vengeance.

The five remaining thugs pummeled Tal'mai and his men with their clubs. Outnumbered two to one, the Captain's men fell back and Dabarius leaped up onto the railing. Either he fled now or joined in the fray.

The butt of a club cracked a royal guard on the head and he fell senseless beside a fallen brother. Tal'mai and one guard stood between the thugs and Dabarius using sweeping sword slashes to keep the attackers at bay.

"There's no need for this," Dabarius said from atop the railing, wondering if he had suffered a blow to the head himself. "Captain, stop. I'll go with them."

"Lost your nerve to jump?" Tal'mai asked. "Perhaps you should end your life the way you want."

124

Dabarius hopped down from the railing and stepped between Tal'mai and the other royal guard, giving them a confident grin. He put out his hands, wrists together, so someone could put the manacles on them.

Ah'moz choked and coughed on the ground, then croaked, "Bind him."

One of the thugs retrieved the manacles. As he slipped the first onto Dabarius's wrist the man began to shake as if he were having a seizure. The smell of burned hair filled the air.

The others stood rooted in place by surprise as the wizard attacked with a surge of violence. He punched two thugs in the chest with his lightning charged fists, and wrapped the manacle chain around a third man's throat. Clutching at the iron links around his windpipe, the man fell to the ground writhing as electricity surged through his body. The two men Dabarius had punched in the chest fell like toppled trees and lay motionless.

Tal'mai and the royal guard attacked furiously, dropping the remaining pair of thugs just as a squad of guards ran toward them from the palace.

Dabarius thrust out his hand to Ah'moz, offering to help the scribe stand up.

"I'll not accept a hand from you," Ah'moz spat.

"Then you're not as dim-witted as I thought." Dabarius wheeled around and kicked the scribe in the side of his head, sending a painful jolt of electricity coursing through his enemy.

"You killed him?" Tal'mai asked with surprise and a touch of delight.

Dabarius shook his head as he dragged Ah'moz's body toward the stone railing. "He's not dead. We'll need him later, though we both know the Queen did not send them for me."

"I know who did," Tal'mai said, as he helped one of his injured men off the ground, and warned the hurt thugs to stay down. "These are some of Reu'ven's old soldiers from the streets."

"Of course they are." Dabarius attached a manacle to Ah'moz's ankle and the other to the stone railing. Then he grabbed one of the fallen thugs by the throat and sent a short electrical charge into him, which made the man clench his teeth and quiver in pain. "Did Reu'ven send more of you after my companions?"

The man nodded as the fresh squad of royal guards arrived.

"What were their orders?" Tal'mai asked the thug.

Blood leaked out of the man's mouth as he had bit his tongue.

"Answer me," Dabarius said, "or I'll send enough lightning into you so you'll never be able to hold your water or bowels again. You'll be a drooling pile of fly-covered flesh wishing you could die. Now, answer the question. What were your friends' orders?"

"To kill all the foreigners, take their bodies out of the palace, and bury them in the desert."

XXIII

Enemies who enter your circle must be pushed out.

 —Oberon, *Teha Khet* Master, and wizard of Snow Valley

The tripwires caught the charging thugs by surprise and half a dozen of them fell in front of Bellor and Drake. The man with the flat nose was the first one in, and he landed in the fiery pile of rugs and pillows. He rolled away from the flames, trying to peel off his burning linen kilt.

Bellor crushed his skull like it was a soft melon and the man fell back into the fire. The War Priest didn't pause for an instant. He attacked with a flurry of blows, striking the men on the floor with precise strikes to their heads with his pair of stone clubs.

Drake followed Bellor's example and didn't think about what he was doing, he just attacked. He fought for his life and struck the men on the ground before they could rise. He delivered several vicious blows before his club shattered as he smashed it against a man's jaw.

A dagger thrust toward his gut from a man on his knees. Drake sidestepped and slashed his ceramic dagger across the Mephitian's face, then kneed him in the chin.

Thor sprang from the alcove by the doorway and attacked without mercy, breaking knees and pummeling the warriors trying to get to Bellor and Drake. His sudden attack devastated the thugs who were caught totally by surprise.

Drake caught the wrist of a man trying to stab him in the chest. The attacker grabbed Drake's own wrist as the Clifftoner counterattacked and they tumbled to the ground. The thug ended up on top of Drake and pinned his knife arm against the floor.

Bellor had been forced back against a wall by a pair of brutes while Thor battled at least four in the center of the room, spinning and blocking the blows coming from all sides. Bellor's plan accounted for no more than six guards, not twice that.

One Mephitian head-butted Drake right between the eyes. Mind numbing pain made him go limp for an instant, then a sharp stab brought him back to the moment. The Mephitian's dagger point pierced the skin on Drake's chest, though he kept a hold on the man's wrist, not letting the blade penetrate too deeply. The bronze tip grated against his collarbone and slid further into him causing terrible pain.

Tears streamed from Drake's eyes as a result of the head butt. Almost blind, Drake grunted and pushed his enemy's arm back. The tip of the dagger slid out of his flesh and scratched down his chest. Drake rolled the sweaty man off him and came up slashing despite his blurry vision. His blade struck something solid—his opponent's dagger—and the ceramic knife shattered.

Drake wiped his eyes as the Mephitian bared his teeth in a feral grin. The man slashed and Drake tripped over a body. He landed on his backside and glanced at Bellor. The War Priest was cornered, his strength fading as two men slashed at him furiously. Thor bled from small cuts on his arms, and swung at his three remaining opponents who hemmed him in, trying to break through his defenses.

More warriors surged through the doorway, flooding the chamber and overwhelming Thor, who fell under a pile of Mephitians. Drake punched his distracted opponent in the face an instant before he was dragged down and pinned by several men.

Bellor shouted, "Lorak!" and swung with all his might as a surge of Mephitian warriors attacked and smashed him against the wall.

"TUU'AH!" A woman's deafening voice thundered into the room shaking the stone underfoot. In an instant all the fighting stopped. The Mephitian word reverberated in Drake's mind, stunning him completely. He felt like he was trapped at the bottom of a pool of water. His ears hurt and his eyes blurred even more. He lay there with everyone else in the room, helpless and immobile, part of the pile of living and dead.

Someone came to him. Hands pulled him up and held him in place though his legs tried to buckle. He blinked and tried to focus.

Dabarius stood there. His friend's lips moved. Drake heard nothing except the whooshing of an odd wind. What was Dabarius doing there? What was he saying?

A beautiful young Mephitian woman appeared at Dabarius's side. She had a stern expression on her face. He blinked as he realized it was the Queen of Isyrin. She touched Drake's shoulder and a warm feeling spread throughout his entire body.

"Are you all right?" Dabarius asked.

He nodded, his hearing back and the pain almost gone, though his body was numb. All around the room lay the men who had attacked them, and apparently the royal guards who had entered the fray. They were all motionless, dazed and staring at the ceiling.

The Queen moved toward Thor who was being hauled out from under a pile of stunned men. The dwarven warrior regained his senses almost immediately after Khelen'dara lay a hand on his head. She helped Bellor and all the companions were soon hustling down the hallway following the Queen, Dabarius, and a score of royal guards.

"It's all right," Dabarius said.

"What just happened?" Drake asked, feeling like he had just woken up in the middle of a nightmare.

"General Reu'ven hired some of his old soldiers to kill you," the wizard said, "and Khelen'dara's royal guard intervened."

"Why did she attack us with her magic?" Thor asked.

"She didn't want anyone else to die or get hurt," Dabarius said, "enough of her people were already wounded in the hallway."

"They attacked us!" Thor said.

"Not by her command," Dabarius said, "and not her guards."

"What are we doing now?" Bellor asked as he inspected the wound across Drake's chest and held a scarf against it. "I should stitch this up before we get too far."

"We're going to find Bree," Dabarius said. "Reu'ven's got her somewhere below the palace."

"Is she all right?" Drake asked. "What happened to her? What's happening?"

Dabarius translated the question to the Queen.

Khelen'dara said something and Drake heard the Queen mention Bree'alla's name.

"Well?" Drake asked.

Dabarius's face was ashen. "Come, Drake. We must hurry."

XXIV

There are tombs under the palace, and a city of the dead in the desert east of Isyrin. All of the Mephitians wish to be buried in one, and attach a great significance to their eternal life, and being interred in a proper tomb. I care not for their religion, but I admire the beautiful places where they bury their dead. Wulf has already explored the warren under the palace with one of our new Khebian friends, and if we must, we shall escape the palace through the tombs.

—Bölak Blackhammer, from the Khoram Journal

They left the sealed tombs alone as Drake and the search party scoured the tunnels beneath the palace of Isyrin hoping to find Bree'alla alive. Dust reflected the light from their lamps as their footsteps stirred up the fine grit that smelled and tasted of mold and decay. Drake jogged down the side tunnels, inspecting the tombs and calling out to Bree. He moved faster than anyone else, and his desperation only increased when he realized how vast the tunnels were.

The Queen, along with Captain Tal'mai, led from the front. Khelen'dara directed them in a methodical search. She knew every tunnel, every passage in the black maze, much better than all of her servants, and pointed out the dangers. The catacombs were filled with sudden drop-offs, and a large number of spiders and brightly colored scorpions skittered around on the floor. Dabarius had stationed himself at her side as if he were one of her bodyguards, though after Khelen'dara's display of magic, he thought she didn't need the protection.

The dwarves marched behind Drake, checking the walls and looking for any clue to Bree's whereabouts. Thor even called out to her, and the concern in his voice surprised Drake. Bellor had a tight-lipped expression and made certain they did not miss a hidden door or fail to explore a vault or side tunnel. The old dwarf expected an ambush, and wore his chain mail coat over his clothing, and like Thor, held his weapon ready. They had recovered all their equipment from a chamber near where Bree'alla had been interrogated by Reu'ven.

The only thing missing was the alicorn horn. Dabarius nearly tore a door off its hinges searching for the horn, and the Queen had to talk him down with soothing words as he was frightening all of her servants with his enraged demeanor. The wizard did not believe that the General had left the palace earlier in the evening—long before the attacks—telling the guards he was traveling to the Hotek Fortress per the Queen's orders. The scribe, Ah'moz had taken the blame for ordering the thugs to kill the companions and swore that the conveniently absent General Reu'ven had nothing to do with it.

"He's here," Dabarius said, "and when I find him he's going to wish we had all been killed at Zah'dah's house."

Captain Tal'mai reported to the Queen several times and said the palace was now safe. The men Ah'moz had let in had all been rounded up and accounted for. Not taking any chances, the Queen encouraged the companions to carry their weapons, though Drake left his crossbow slung over his back. The weight of the weapon pulled on the hasty stitches Bellor had sewn near his collarbone, but he didn't care about the pain. It was nothing, and he refused to acknowledge any of it until they found Bree. He felt so helpless, like it was his fault she had been taken away. How long had they been searching? It seemed like hours and with each passing moment he felt a sinking feeling taking hold of him. He could not lose her, not now, not ever.

"Dabarius," Thor called out, his deep voice echoing off the narrow tunnel, "I think we should question that scribe ourselves. He must know what Reu'ven did with her."

"Trust me," Dabarius shook his head, "he doesn't."

"Any fool knows he was lying," Thor said.

The wizard rolled his eyes. "Of course he was lying."

132

"Does the Queen think there is any chance Reu'ven might be down here?" Bellor asked.

"No." Dabarius said. "He was seen riding out of the palace, but I don't think he's gone."

"She sent him away?" Bellor asked.

"She told him she was going to," Dabarius said, "though she didn't tell him to leave so soon."

"You believe her?" Thor whispered.

Dabarius ignored the dwarf.

The Queen led them past the narrow tunnel and Drake felt a chill. Bellor stopped and stared down the passage, raising his lamp.

"What is it?" Drake asked. "Something down there?"

The War Priest shook his head. "No one . . . living."

Drake wondered how many ghosts Bellor had seen in the hours they'd been in the tunnels.

"Wait." Bellor's voice echoed down the passage. He inspected the floor and wiped his finger along the stone.

"What is it?" Dabarius asked.

"Fresh mortar," Bellor said, as the venerable Drobin Priest scanned the floor.

"Reu'ven's robe was smudged with something this same color when I saw him last," Dabarius said

Someone had brought wet mortar down here and a little had spilled on their way to wherever they were going. Bellor followed a few other drops on the ground, which led them down a passageway with three branches.

Thor went one way, Drake the other, and Talmai's scout down the middle while the others waited for a moment. Thor called them to follow him and showed them a narrow wheeled cart with four bricks on it and an empty bucket with freshly dried mortar coating the inside and a dirty trawl.

Bellor found more spots of mortar on the floor nearby, and they kept going down he tunnel. Drake called out Bree's name louder now and jogged ahead, expecting to see her tied up in a corner.

"Drake," Bellor said suddenly. The Earth Priest smelled a wall that looked very old, exactly like the hundreds of other walled-up alcoves they had passed. The floor was clean, and the mortar looked ancient. What was he doing? Time was wasting.

"These bricks were laid recently." Bellor indicated the bricks in a recessed niche not much taller than he was. "There's a hint of magic here. Someone wanted this to look old."

"They didn't clean the floor good enough." Thor wiped his hand on the ground, and came away with gray-brown grit coating his fingertips. Fresh mortar.

"The ruse wasn't meant to withstand Drobin scrutiny," Bellor said.

Khelen'dara inspected the bricks. She laid her hands on the wall and closed her eyes. She recoiled an instant later with a surprised look on her face.

Drake reached for his knife as he raised his lantern.

Khelen'dara said something in an urgent tone.

"We need to break down the wall," Dabarius said.

Thor stepped forward and raised his hammer in two hands, then turned it so the pointed claw side was facing the wall. Captain Tal'mai stepped between Thor and the Queen.

"If I wanted to split her lovely head," Thor said, "I would have done so before now."

"You can't even reach her head," Dabarius said.

Thor lowered his hammer and glared at Dabarius. "If I stood on your corpse I could. Now tell her royal ladyship and her guard to please get their asses out of my way."

Dabarius did so, politely by the sound of it, and Khelen'dara waved for Tal'mai to back down and let Thor do his work.

134

"Thank you." The dwarf smashed the wall and shattered a brick. He broke two more out and then peered into the hole he had made. "*Lorak's blessed beard.*"

The words made Drake's hair stand on end. "What is it?"

"She's in there. Walled inside," Thor said, then mumbled something in Drobin. His face darkened with rage.

"What?" Drake asked.

"The lonely death. A punishment we Drobin reserve for . . . only the most unspeakable crimes," the old *Viergur* answered. "Break it down, Thor."

Thor attacked the wall furiously. Shards of stone flew in every direction and the sound echoed down the hallway. There was only room for two to work, and Drake joined him and kicked and pushed at the loose bricks at the edge of the hole Thor was making, praying that they were about to rescue Bree . . . alive.

Bellor pulled Drake back. "No, your wound will start bleeding again. The stitches are too fresh."

Dabarius came forward to help. Drake pushed him back, handing him his crossbow to hold, and ignored Bellor's protests. The Clifftoner accepted Thor's small throwing axe and used the hammer side to break the mud bricks. He ignored the pain as at least one stitch tore loose. He swung so hard he thought he might break the head of the weapon off. When they had a hole large enough for Drake to crawl through, Bellor aimed his lantern into the black chamber.

Bree lay crumpled on the floor within the death cell. Her skin was gray and she was curled into the fetal position. Drake squeezed through the hole, a warm trickle of fresh blood leaking down his chest. His mouth felt like he had swallowed the driest dust in the entire Khoram Desert. He felt like it took forever to crawl over to her.

He touched her icy flesh. She was cold as the stone under her and wore only tiny smallclothes around her waist. Scabs on her shoulders, blood under her fingernails, rope burns on her

135

wrists and ankles made his heart feel like it was being squeezed by a thornclaw vine.

"*Bree?*" He pulled her to his chest, gasping at the sight of her bluish lips. What could he do?

They were too late.

She was . . .

Light shone from the entrance as Bree opened her eyes and squinted in the glare.

Thor let out a hearty laugh and yelled, "She's alive!"

A cheer erupted from everyone in the hallway and Drake hugged her close, lending her his body heat.

"You found me," Bree whispered and the corners of her mouth turned into the most beautiful smile Drake had ever seen. He could only nod and smile as his eyes misted over. Even amongst all the others, he wanted nothing more than to lie down and to hold Bree tight in his arms. He wanted to whisper in her ear and tell her that he loved her.

"Wrap her in this, lad." Bellor tossed his cloak into the frigid, claustrophobic tomb. Drake did as he was told as Bree'alla started to shiver.

"Take me out of here," she whispered.

Drake locked eyes with Thor. "Break down the wall. I'm going to carry her out."

Thor grinned and lifted his hammer.

XXV

Priestess Nayla has great confidence in me. She thinks that I will save so many lives, and restore the Amaryllian faith to the Nexan people. I will do as she asks, and hope that I will not disappoint her.

—Priestess Jaena Whitestar, from her personal journal

Jaena waited barefoot beside the young sentinel tree for the villagers to arrive. She tried to calm herself, but her stomach was in absolute knots. She hoped that the five hunters who guarded the perimeter did not notice her consternation. The daylight coming in from above provided enough light for them to see her, but she could not see any of them as they were concealed in the shadowy forest. She knew they all watched her, as they always did.

She felt safe under their protection, and the branches of the hundred foot tall tree added to her comfort. The dense canopy above her would keep even the strongest aevian at bay. The tree had been a refuge and a place of worship for years, as evidenced by the small shrine made of stones, and the well-worn path to the village only a short distance away.

The sound of a crying baby brought her attention back to the task at hand. She heard other voices too, murmuring quietly. Nayla and Emmit accompanied a group of over twenty into the space below the sentinel tree. They bowed to her, and Jaena felt so strange seeing so many faces that she didn't recognize. Young, old, and every age in between had come to her. Only a handful looked unwell, and Jaena assumed many had come to see if she was truly a Priestess of Amaryllis with the gift of Healing magic.

There were no doubters in Cliffton. She knew everyone in her home village, and some were less pious than others, but they were all her friends and she knew them well. These unfamiliar people made her nervous. Blayne had been the first stranger she ever healed, but there were so many now in front of her waiting to see if she was a fraud. She prayed to the Goddess for strength and waited for them all to file in and find a place to sit. The baby stopped crying, but an old woman said a little too loudly, "She's so young. How can she be a Priestess?"

Nayla motioned for Jaena to begin.

After taking a deep breath, Jaena raised her arms and looked up at the tree branches above them. All of the villagers followed her cue and raised their eyes. "Great Goddess, thank you for the clear sky today. Thank you for bringing me to Brearwood," her voice cracked and she tried to swallow her nerves, "so that you may help these folk. Thank you for all your blessings. May the sky be clear."

"May the sky be clear," all of the villagers repeated.

The first to come forward was a young woman with dark circles under her eyes, no older than sixteen, with very small baby, who had stopped crying, but began again as soon as the mother reached Jaena.

"How may I help her?" Jaena asked. She caressed the baby's cheek, wondering why the world was so cruel to make an innocent child suffer. The emaciated child, who had to be six months old, seemed far younger because of his small size.

"He's had a fever and he can't keep anything down for days. Not even my own milk."

Jaena nodded and placed her hand on the baby's stomach, and put one bare foot on a root of the tree. "Please, Amaryllis, bless this child with Your Light." Silently, Jaena asked Amaryllis to do Her will. She let go of her personal fears, and petty desires, trying to imagine that these folk were her friends from Cliffton. The magic coursed through her, like warm flowing water and a soft, golden-green glow emanated from Jaena's palms and into the child. The Healing magic flowed from the within the tree, through her foot, and out through her palms. She knew that the warm surges would overwhelm her—sap away her life—if she broke contact with the root. Time became irrelevant, and the forest disappeared. Jaena's skin tingled as magic flowed into the baby, bringing his sick stomach and bowels back into a perfect state of health.

The light faded, and Jaena opened her eyes before carefully withdrawing her hands from the now sleeping child. She realized the tree had aged more than a season to heal the little boy, who would not have lasted another week. Jaena rested her hands on the trunk. "Thank you, Great Tree. May we be worthy of your sacrifice."

The young mother hugged Jaena, and sat down with her son. The next to come forward was an old man led by his grandson. The grandfather's eyes had begun to fail him and he could barely see light and dark.

"Can you help me?" the old man asked.

"I will try," Jaena said.

In a few moments he was smiling and kissing Jaena's hands. "You are the most beautiful girl I've ever seen. Bless you and the Goddess. Curse the Drobin for what they did at the Sacred Grove."

The rest of the afternoon passed quickly as Jaena healed the villagers of all their ailments and injuries, succeeding with every one. Broken bones knitted together, digestive problems faded, rashes and boils disappeared, arthritic joints returned to their normal size and function, weak lungs became strong again, fevers went away, and those who were sick in their hearts or were worried about their loved ones serving in the human regiments of the Drobin army found hope and peace.

More came after hearing of her power, and by the end of the day the tree did look taller and older, as it had aged centuries as Jaena channeled the Healing magic though it. Thankfully, the sentinel didn't look weaker, but appeared stronger and wider at its base. The villagers who had come at first and returned later marveled at the transformation. Many who she had healed brought food and gifts for Jaena and her companions. She ate bread with butter, stayed in a warm house with a solid roof for the first time in weeks, and bathed in a wooden tub with hot water and washed with good soap that smelled of roses.

Priestess Nayla dried and braided Jaena's long blond hair afterward and told her how well she had done. The villagers of Brearwood begged her to stay, promising to protect her always from discovery by the Drobin marshals, but in the morning, Jaena and her companions prepared to depart, and thanked their hosts repeatedly.

The entire village gathered to see her off, and Priestess Nayla addressed the crowd of over four hundred as Jaena stood at her side.

"The blessings of the Goddess have been denied your people for too long." Nayla's tone was ominous and her voice boomed throughout the village. "The Drobin King and his man-servant, the so-called *king* Alaric, have left all of you to suffer unbearable diseases, and early deaths because there are no Priestesses to care for you and they do nothing. How many babies have died in this village in the past few years alone?"

"Too many!" a woman shouted, and others took up the call. They cursed the Drobin laws, faces filled with anger, fists raised. The hope Jaena had seen disappeared and a seething rage took hold of the villagers.

"The Drobin army, the Lorakian Priests, and the Father's Paladins have murdered every last Priestess of Amaryllis or driven them far away from the Nexan people," Nayla said. "Priestess Jaena has come here risking her life to help you good people of Brearwood."

The crowd cheered and called out their thanks to Jaena, who felt more and more uncomfortable standing beside Nayla.

"The Drobin are becoming more violent every day," Nayla said. "Their soldiers have slaughtered hundreds of unarmed men, women, and children in Khierson City only two months ago, but they will never admit this, and keep the news from spreading. The people of Khierson dared to ask for a larger share of the crops, and they were given the axe and hammer."

The people simmered with anger, shouting profanities.

"The Drobin will do the same here if you fail to meet their taxes," Nayla said, "but what do they give you? Sickness and the Great Father who does not answer your prayers."

"We want the Goddess!" a woman shouted.

"We want Priestess Jaena," another woman yelled.

"Priestess Jaena may never be able to come here again, for tomorrow this young woman may be arrested by the Drobin marshals."

"No!" the crowd shouted, and many cursed the Drobin.

"The threat of arrest and death will not stop her!" Nayla shouted over the clamor. "She will serve the people and the Goddess no matter what threat is upon her!"

The crowd cheered, and Nayla waited for them to quiet down.

"Someday, Priestess Jaena or I may call upon you to fight for the Goddess and her protection." Nayla nudged Jaena forward. "For your village, for your families, for your lives, will you answer her call?"

The villagers shouted, "Yes!" and made oaths to the Goddess.

"May the sky be clear!" Nayla shouted and the villagers echoed her words. Many of them begged Jaena and Nayla not to leave them. The crowed pressed in tightly and Jaena did not know what to do as she was jostled around. She was afraid of the grabbing hands and passionate faces all around her calling her name. The shouting made her head spin.

Nayla, Emmit, and Blayne led the way as they pressed through the throng and left the village with fresh supplies, mended clothes, and the sincere thanks of several hundred villagers whose loved ones would live without discomfort and disease, many for the first time in years.

Jaena and her escorts made it to the edge of the village and passed through the wooden wall. They quickly ducked off the main road and into the dense forest.

"Are you all right?" Blayne asked.

"Of course she is," Nayla said, and flashed a big smile.

Jaena nodded, though she didn't think she was all right. As they marched deeper into the trees, she began to understand that Brearwood was only the first of many villages they would visit. Nayla would make that same speech in all of them, and Jaena now knew exactly what seeds were being planted. There would be war against the Drobin if Nayla succeeded, and Jaena did not yet know how she would stop it.

XXVI

Queen Rama'dara of Isyrin must be the most powerful human I have ever met. I suspect that she knows the ancient wizardry, long eradicated and lost in the north, and she appears to have the favor of her Goddess Amar'isis, making her a Priestess of untold might. We shall not cross her, but will do our best to make her our ally, for we share the same enemy.

—Bölak Blackhammer, from the Khoram Journal

How had someone who appeared so young attained such tremendous power? Dabarius pondered this as he watched Queen Khelen'dara sitting regally on her throne of lacquered reddish wood in a windowless, secure room deep in the palace. Her knowledge of magic was far beyond his own, but more than anything, he wanted to know her secrets. All of them. To be able to stun so many men with a word. *One word.* That was truly powerful magic and he suspected she could have killed them if she'd wanted to.

"Dabarius, tell your companions what I'm saying. Make them understand."

"Yes, Great Queen." He bowed and found himself hoping she would soon answer the question about his lineage. There had been enough delays and now that Bree and his friends were safe, it seemed the right time.

"I am very sorry for what has happened tonight," Queen Khelen'dara said as Captain Tal'mai and Mey'lahna shifted on their feet beside her, looking embarrassed. The companions sat on soft couches facing her as several servants brought hot tea and plates of food.

Drake sat by Bree, who was wrapped in blankets. The dwarves had positioned their couch against the wall of the narrow chamber and eyed everyone who entered warily. The door into the room was guarded on the outside by squads of heavily armed soldiers with orders to keep the Queen and her guests undisturbed.

"The men responsible for these attacks will be punished," the Queen said, "as will the Royal Scribe, Ah'moz, and General Reu'ven, when his involvement in this is fully known."

Dabarius made certain his voice imitated the Queen's restrained ferocity.

"You will all be well protected." Khelen'dara spoke more calmly now, and bowed her head toward the companions. "Please, accept my apologies and I assure you, I will keep you safe as my guests."

Tal'mai and Mey'lahna's faces showed their surprise as the Queen bowed her head, her chin almost touching her chest.

Bellor bowed in return, much lower than the Queen had. "We graciously accept, and offer our thanks. Your protection is much appreciated. We are your humble servants."

"I should never have listened to General Reu'ven when you were brought to Isyrin. I let past events influence my judgment, when I should have listened to my heart from the beginning. You are as honorable as your kin who came in the time of my grandmother, Queen Rama'dara, the last of her name."

"Great Queen, you do know of our kin?" Bellor asked.

"They are known to me as the Ten Sons of Kheb. They were friends of my great house."

Dabarius translated her words as she spoke them, saying "great house" instead of "family."

"Your kin defended my people when few others would dare to oppose our enemies."

The dwarves sat forward in anticipation. "Pardon me, Great Queen," Bellor said, "when did the Ten Sons of Kheb defend your family in the past?"

"They arrived in the summer, almost four decades ago."

"Just as we thought," Thor said.

The Queen shifted in her throne. "The Ten Sons had been rescued from the desert and held in the Hotek Fortress for some weeks before they were brought here to Isyrin."

Thor grumbled under his breath about "prisoners" and Bellor shushed him.

"When Queen Rama'dara found out they were in the Hotek Fortress, she sent for them immediately. They repeated to her what they had told the desert rangers who captured them that they were searching for the King of the Dragons, the Dragon of Darkness, whom the Ten Sons of Kheb called Draglûne, as you do.

"My grandmother wished to hear what they had to say about the outside world, and learn as much as she could about the wars between the Sons of Kheb, the Northern Peoples, and the Dragon of Darkness. She learned how he used the Giergun tribes and abandoned them when their armies were stopped in the Battle of Drobin Pass."

"Great Queen," Bellor said, "I am very familiar with that event."

Dabarius quickly explained in detail how Bellor had been at the battle and was the one who dealt the deathblow that slew the former King of the Dragons, Mograwn. Khelen'dara raised her eyebrows and nodded at Bellor respectfully.

"The Ten Sons of Kheb came at a very difficult time for my grandmother. For many months prior to the arrival of your kin, Priests of Shenahr, the God of Storms, tried to convince Queen Rama'dara to send her armies north across the barrier desert and recapture the city of Arayden, and then march into the Drobin lands. It was soon revealed that the Priests were following a new prophet of the Storm God—a mystic from the desert who preached war and conquest. The mystic and his Priests had taken over a holy cavern dedicated to Kheb right behind the palace in the mountains. Every day they would come and beseech the Queen, asking her to come to the cavern and meet the Prophet of the Storm.

145

"Khebian Priests met him first, and one of them saw him for what he was, an agent of the Dragon of Darkness. He was a powerful shapeshifter wingataur in the guise of a man, and all of his attendant Priests were demons"

"We've met their kind more than once," Bellor said.

"Then you know how dangerous they are," Khelen'dara said.

"We do, Great Queen," Bellor said.

"Regardless of their threats, my grandmother refused to send her armies north. She would not reveal to the outside world the greatest secret of Mephitia, the secret the Goddess Amar'isis Herself asked the ancient Queens of Isyrin to keep. My grandmother would never send so many of her people to their deaths in the north. The Sons of Kheb are favored and Great Kheb Himself has given them dominion over the lands north of Arayden. It has been so since before the River of Mist separated the great house of the God King and the Goddess Queen.

Dabarius didn't know what she meant exactly, and decided he would ask her about this point at a later time.

"My grandmother and your kin became allies soon after they arrived in Isyrin. They offered to help her with her problem, as the wingataurs refused to leave the cave where they hid in the mountains behind the palace. Worse, they had threatened Isyrin itself with harm if Queen Rama'dara did not act. A dragon with iron dark scales had been seen flying in the mountain valley. The wingataurs said that the Dragon of Darkness himself had come to convince her to agree to send her armies north."

Thor interrupted when she paused, "My uncle Bölak attacked the dragon, didn't he?"

"Your kin marched to battle with the blessing of the Queen, and the help of the Khebian Priests, who were angered that a sacred cave of the Mountain God was being desecrated by beasts of the Underworld, wingataurs and a dragon. The Ten

146

Sons of Kheb and a handful of brave Khebian Priests entered the cavern." Khelen'dara looked down, her expression bleak. "There were terrible sounds of battle within. The mountain shook and boulders fell from the peak. Dust rose from within.

"A Khebian Priest volunteered to enter the mountain and see what had happened. He saw the bodies of the Ten Sons of Kheb and many wingataurs. All of them were slain. The Priest barely escaped before more of the mountain fell over the entrance."

Bellor's face became a mask of sorrow, and he let out a long sigh as his eyes filled with tears.

"What about the dragon?" Thor asked, more angry than sad.

"The iron dragon was not inside," Khelen'dara said. "No one knew where it had gone."

"What happened to the bodies of my kin?" Bellor asked.

"The cavern became their tomb. It was sealed by the avalanche soon after the Khebian Priest escaped."

"The High Priest of Kheb and Queen Rama'dara ordered the entrance to be undisturbed. The Ten Sons of Kheb were to be entombed for all eternity."

A long silence held as the news sunk in. Finally, Bellor said, "Bölak and the *Viergur's* trail ends here. We have found out their fate at long last." He bowed to Khelen'dara. "Thank you, Great Queen, for telling us this tale. We have harbored a brittle hope for two score years that our beloved kin still lived. How I wish there were a different ending."

"As do I," she said, "and you are welcome, though the tale is not over, and is far more tragic than you understand. Minions of the Dragon of Darkness returned on the day the tunnel was sealed. My grandmother, the Goddess Queen Rama'dara, who was the fifth and last to carry her name, was assassinated. She died inside the temple of Amar'isis, in front of the statue of the Goddess where she was praying for the souls of your kin and her dead Khebian Priests. We suspect it was a sorcerer wingataur of great power who took her life, for Queen Rama'dara was a Goddess Queen and possessed the power of Amar'isis Herself."

"I am so sorry, Great Queen," Bellor said. "We feel your suffering as all of us here have lost kin to the Dragon of Darkness."

"It may have been him who was responsible," Khelen'dara said, "but in my grandmother's mouth was found the royal seal of the Ra'menek, the God King of Old Mephitia. The new ruler in the homeland of my people has taken the name of the most powerful king they have ever had."

"Could Draglûne be the servant of Old Mephitia's God King?" Dabarius asked.

"I don't know," Khelen'dara said, and Bellor's expression showed his doubts.

"It would be the other way around," Bellor said. "Draglûne was likely in charge of the man. The wyrm has controlled the Giergun many times, and I know he could control a Mephitian king."

"Perhaps," Khelen'dara said, "or the royal seal was meant to confuse my grandmother's advisors."

"You may be right," Bellor said, "but regardless, there is likely an alliance between Draglûne and the God King of Old Mephitia, or at least the followers of this Storm God, Shenahr. Since a wingataur was involved, we must assume that."

"Yes, we must," the Queen said. "My mother did believe that there was an alliance between them as well." She hesitated, girding herself for a moment and then said, "My mother took the throne soon after my grandmother was buried. I remember my mother sitting on her throne, but when I was a small child she too was assassinated because she opposed the Priests of Shenahr, and their elusive Prophet of the Storm who had survived the battle inside the mountain."

"A wingataur shapeshifter is for certain this *prophet*?" Thor asked.

148

"Yes, or another shapeshifter demon who took on the same guise," Khelen'dara said. "None left the cavern, but wingataurs are often hard to see because of their Draconic magic."

All of the companions glanced at each other knowingly.

"Where is this Prophet of the Storm now?" Bellor asked.

"He hides in the desert. He is rarely seen these past years, and has few followers left. The Priests of Shenahr have no more temples, and few worshipers, since the Storm Revolt when the Shenahrian faithful tried to overthrow my mother. They killed a lot of her loyal followers," Khelen'dara glanced at Dabarius as if she wanted to tell him something, "but they were beaten in the end by General Reu'ven and his soldiers who slaughtered all who had sworn themselves to Shenahr. General Reu'ven protected my mother and me when the Shenahrian came for her. He was the savior of Isyrin.

"Then more than a year after the revolt was put down . . . " Khelen'dara hesitated, blinking rapidly, " . . . my mother was slain, by a sorcerer wingataur in a hallway of the palace. We found the royal seal of the God King Ra'menek in her mouth as well.

"Many think I too would have been killed had General Reu'ven not been such a staunch defender of my life. His skill as a wizard and a general, as well as the bravery of his soldiers, have protected me since I was a little girl. However, I do not condone what I believe he has orchestrated tonight, though I understand his concerns."

Bellor cleared his throat. "If you support us, he is rightly afraid the assassins will come for you too."

Khelen'dara nodded. "He believes that the Dragon of Darkness and his Shenahrian allies have left me alone because they think they can convince me to send my armies north. He has even let his information leak out of the palace, to protect me. I know that he would rather attack the north with our armies than see me die like my mother and grandmother."

149

"Please, Great Queen. Let us help you," Bellor said. "Let us avenge your family while we avenge ours. Help us find the Dragon of Darkness and we will eliminate his threat to you forever."

The Mephitian Queen stared at Bellor and the companions. Mey'lahna and Captain Tal'mai waited expectantly, holding their tongues though Dabarius knew they wanted to speak. Bree'alla let the blankets fall off her shoulders while Dabarius waited for Khelen'dara's next words, wishing she would just tell him about his own family.

The Queen stood. "I will not send you to your deaths. You will remain here in the palace under my protection."

"Great Queen, may I tell my companions for how long?" Dabarius asked.

"No, you may not, for I have not determined your fate as of yet. There are pressing matters I must deal with first."

"If we may be of any service," Dabarius said, "We would be honored to help if we knew what these pressing matters were."

Bellor looked at Thor and Drake, then stood up and said, "We would all be honored to help."

Tal'mai shook his head, ever so slightly, but Khelen'dara did not heed him and said, "I would like to hear your wisdom, for my former regent, who has been my best advisor and strongest defender, is now missing. My palace is not safe and is being searched room by room as we meet in the most secure chamber I possess. My spies in the north are all dead, save perhaps one Wing Guardian in the ruins of Ahkayru. I've been Queen for only a few months, and there is the problem of me not having an heir to the Winged Throne. The city cannot be without a Queen, and if I'm killed like my mother and grandmother, more than you know will slip away from my people forever.

"You all want to help me, but now is not the time to draw the ire of my most deadly enemy by sending you into the desert on a directionless hunt for a foe you have no chance of defeating. I protect my people from harm, and I am determined to protect all of you, as you are my subjects now, whether you approve of that or not. Understand that for quite some time, you shall all remain here and accept my hospitality. Do not be angry, there are far worse prisons than the palace of Isyrin."

Dabarius's friends looked at him with worried expressions as her tone had been severe, and he chose not to translate her last words.

XXVII

Draglûne is here. He hides in a cave behind the palace of Isyrin. His shapeshifter wingataurs have been bullying Queen Rama'dara to attack the north, but we shall deliver her final response. Tomorrow will be our greatest victory, and if any of us survive, we will live out our days in the Khoram Desert as honored guests. Thank you, Great Lorak, for delivering our foe to us at last.

—Bölak Blackhammer, from the Khoram Journal

"What did you say to anger her?" Thor pointed his stubby finger at Dabarius when the Queen, Mey'lahna, and Captain Tal'mai had left the room.

"Nothing." Dabarius was sick of translating, and was so irritated that the Queen had left without telling him what he wanted to know, in addition to her pronouncement that they would be kept prisoner for an indeterminate amount of time—perhaps forever.

"Nothing?" Thor asked. "Then why was she so angry?"

"She wasn't angry," Dabarius said. "She just said we're going to be staying here a while, and that she has more problems than giving us what we want."

"She said more than that." Bree'alla pulled the blankets over her shoulders again.

"What else?" Drake asked.

Bree'alla told them the rest of it, and Dabarius nodded to affirm her translation.

Thor cursed in Drobin, then started pacing around the room.

"Finally they know what I've suspected all along," Dabarius whispered to Bree in Mephitian. "Bölak is dead."

"I've known for weeks," Bree shook her head and replied in Mephitian, "though I could say nothing."

152

"Because of your vow, and something else, right?" Dabarius asked.

She glared silently at him.

"There's some Compulsion magic on you, isn't there? It stops you from revealing the secrets of Mephitia. It makes you follow your vows, doesn't it?"

"Leave me alone," Bree said.

"Who cast such a spell?" Dabarius ignored her request, and sat beside her. "Was it the Queen? Does that scarab you wear have anything to do with it?"

"Just because you're here,"—Bree gave him a condescending look—"doesn't mean I can tell you everything about the Wings of Amar'isis."

"Why not? Am I your enemy now?" Dabarius asked.

"Why didn't you reveal that you could speak Mephitian?" Bree countered.

He let out a sigh. "It was Bellor's idea, and it was a good one."

"Get away from me. I'm tired." She flicked her wrist to shoo him away as Drake looked on, wondering what they were saying.

"Do you know anything about my background?" Dabarius asked. "Do you know who my father or mother was?"

"I've heard a name like yours before. That's all." She lay down on some pillows. "And you speak with a noble's accent."

"That's all you know?" He didn't want to tell her he was copying the Queen's accent, though Oberon did teach him a higher form of Mephitian than he spoke with the refugee Mephitians in Khierson City.

"I'm tired," Bree said, and closed her eyes.

"Stop chattering at her," Drake said.

Dabarius took a lamp and found a place to sleep opposite where Thor and Bellor were grieving about the news of their dead kin. He listened to them praying until he fell deeply asleep. His last thought was the hope that he would dream about his real father, and the place where he was born.

For the next three days Dabarius wrote down everything he could remember from his quick reading of the Scrolls of Amar'isis. With the alicorn horn missing—damn General Reu'ven—they would need every advantage they could get to help defeat Draglûne. The spells in the sacred scrolls would help. He used ink and paper the Queen's servants had provided him and he tried to remember the words of power exactly right. The spells were wonderful and powerful, perfect for fighting wingataurs and especially dragons or their spawn. The Priestesses who had created them ages ago had learned much about how to defeat aevians, especially the draconic variety. He would tell his companions about them eventually, but not until he felt like he had mastered the intricacies of each spell—which would be difficult since he couldn't really practice casting them without drawing attention to what he was doing.

Lost in his thoughts, Dabarius lay on his belly on the floor of the niche he had claimed for his own, ignoring the sound of Drake endlessly shooting his double crossbow into the targets on the far wall of the chamber, and reloading as if his life depended on how quickly he could turn the krannekin and slip two bolts into the weapon. He admired Drake's dedication, but what he couldn't ignore any longer was the clang of Bree and Thor sparring—yet again—on their quest to drive him insane. "Will you two be still for once!"

"Why?" Bree kept Thor at bay with *Wingblade*, her longsword extended at the dwarf's face. "Haven't you rested enough?"

"It wouldn't hurt you to loosen your muscles, wizard," Thor said, "and show us if your fighting techniques can stand up to a real warrior like Bree'alla."

"Afraid to face me yourself, little man?" Dabarius asked.

"You would fall like a dead tree, you overgrown fool. I'm skilled in several forms of Kamarian wrestling and hand-to-hand fighting," Thor said. "I would break your long bones in several places before you could land one of those punches."

Dabarius rolled his eyes. If Thor was wearing his undershirt of chainmail a quick bolt of lighting would cook the dwarf in his own juices before he could ever land a blow.

Bree glanced over his shoulder. "What are you writing anyway?"

"Nothing that concerns you." Dabarius hid the pages from her prying eyes and knocked Bree's legs out from under her with a rapid reverse leg sweep. He sprang toward her and pinned her sword arm to the floor with a firm grip before she could react.

Bree pulled a short dagger and put it under his chin, but he brushed her arm aside and pinned it down as well. He smiled at her, feeling her small body trapped under his. "Try to get out of this."

Bree's withering look made him a little nervous. "Do you really want me to crush your balls with my knee and bite through your arm before I roll you head-first into that wall where you will crack open your skull?"

Dabarius stood up, careful not to press on her, and held his hands up in surrender.

"Smartest thing you've done all day," Drake said, nodding his approval, then shot a bolt into the center of the target once again from the crouching position he had been practicing from for hours.

Bellor chose not to look up from his prayers. Either that or he was asleep, Dabarius thought.

The far door opened a crack as Drake shot the second bolt from his crossbow at a target above the door's lintel. The guard knocked loudly, probably for the second time, and called out, "Friend," in heavily accented Nexan.

"Friend," Bellor said, as he roused himself. Thor helped his mentor stand and they faced the guard, who kept himself half-hidden behind the door until he knew it was safe to enter.

"What now?" Thor whispered. "It's not time to eat again, is it?

"Good morning," the guard said, using his two other Nexan words. It was definitely late afternoon, but Dabarius had little patience for teaching the helpful, but imbecilic palace guard any more words.

"What is it?" Dabarius asked in Mephitian.

"The Goddess Queen Khelen'dara requests that you, Dabarius, meet with her at this time."

"Finally, the little girl wants to talk?" Thor said, after hearing Bree's translation.

"She's the Queen of Isyrin," Bree said. "Speak of her respectfully or you'll feel the pain I was going to inflict on Dabarius."

The wizard put his scrolls away quickly and marched toward the open door.

Drake stopped him. "Ask her about the dogs."

"I will."

"Ask her about visiting the tomb of my kin," Bellor said.

"Ask her when we can leave this dungeon," Thor said.

"I may ask her about getting my own cell, Dabarius said over his shoulder, only half kidding.

Ignoring the coarse Drobin curse that Thor used as a retort, Dabarius nodded at Master Bellor before leaving the room, glad to be away from his opulent cell, and the annoying prisoners he was forced to share it with.

XXVIII

I shall keep the Crystal Eye safe for the rest of my years.
—binding pledge written on a scroll by, Master Wizard Oberon
of Snow Valley

Ancient columns of weathered tan stone rose toward the burning sun. Heat pushed down on Dabarius like a smothering blanket after spending days in the cool subterranean chamber beneath the palace. It took a moment for his eyes to adjust to the light. Then the green blurs turned into leafy vines snaking around the bases of the tall pillars. Sweet smelling plants with white and purple flowers grew in a great profusion in the rectangular courtyard where the guards had brought him. The space must have had a roof on it years in the past, but now it was a slightly wild garden.

"The Goddess Queen waits for you." Captain Tal'mai motioned with his chin toward a path through the bushes. "You'll find her by the pond. Just follow that path. My men will be watching."

The wizard ignored Tal'mai and walked confidently into the open space, sure that the archers he had spotted on the rooftops of the nearby buildings would shoot any aevian from the sky before it threatened anyone in the palace. Or maybe they would shoot him if he did anything stupid around the Queen. At least, they'd try. He was working on a spell that would throw off an archer's aim. Still, he would not to be stupid. He wanted too much from the queen to let himself foul it up.

He walked down the path, which led him through a forest of pillars and away from the center of the garden to the edge. He touched the dusty surface of a cracked wall with unique oval picture symbols encircled by thick lines. The framed glyphs looked like stylized Mephitian words. Names. They had to be, though he couldn't read them without detailed study.

A few steps later he found the Goddess Queen of all Mephitia completely alone and dipping her toes into a small circular pond. A trickle of water fell into the pool from a stone spout shaped like an open lotus blossom. White lotus grew from thick green lily pads that floated on the surface. Light blue tiles lined the bottom of the sparkling pool.

Queen Khelen'dara smiled as he approached. Her long, curly black hair, honey-brown skin, dark eyes, long legs, and beautiful body barely hidden by a transparent linen dress made his heart drum in his chest.

"Come sit with me." She motioned with her hand and the sun glinted off the golden rings encrusted with blue and red gems.

"Of course, Great Queen." He bowed, and then moved to sit down a respectful distance away.

She grasped his hand and guided him closer so he could down right beside her. "Take off your sandals and dip your feet in the water. It'll cool you off."

He did as he was told and felt the soothing relief as he dipped his feet into the water, which must have come from a stream on the mountain behind the palace.

"You seem uncomfortable. Would you have rather stayed below the palace to avoid this heat?"

"Oh, no Great Queen." He shook his head, and recovered some of his wit. "There is no other place I'd rather be, than here, beside you."

She brushed a stray curl away from her face and he saw playfulness in her eyes that he hadn't seen before. "Dabarius, when we are alone like this, I want you to call me Dara."

He grinned at her. "Dara. I like that very much." Then he wondered how often they would be alone together.

"How are you and your friends managing?"

158

"It's the finest prison we've ever been in. The food is excellent, especially the honey almond cakes, and the guards are courteous. Oddly, this is the only prison I know of that encourages weapons to be carried by the prisoners. Not that I carry any that the guards can take away."

She laughed loudly and Dabarius noticed one of the archers observing him carefully to see what was happening.

"Have you been in a lot of prisons?" She playfully grabbed a lily pad between her toes.

Dabarius raised an eyebrow. "No, have you?"

Khelen'dara laughed even louder and Dabarius saw true joy in her eyes for the first time since he'd met her. He wiggled his toes in the pond as he admired her long legs and perfect feet. Tiny rings adorned a few of her toes and intricate patterns had been painted on her ankles. "You need to laugh more," he said.

"I know I do." She wiggled her toes in return. "Things have calmed down now. The palace is safe again. I'm considering allowing you and your friends to move to a room with a window."

"A window? Splendid."

"Don't worry, it will be a small window. Not so big that anyone can get in, or you can get out."

"Why not a large window with very strong bars?"

"I'll consider that." She glanced up at one of the archers.

"Is that why we're almost alone together?" he asked.

"Reu'ven is still missing, though we have been hunting for him for days," she said. "That's very worrisome."

"No one knows where he's gone?"

"He may have gone to the Hotek Fortress, but my riders have not returned with him yet. They should have overtaken him by now." She sighed. "Something may have happened to him."

"You're worried about him. I'm sorry."

"He's like a father to me."

"A father is important." Dabarius hoped he would not offend her by his hint.

"Mine is a Khebian Priest. A good man."

"Where is he now?"

"Not in Isyrin. I see him on a few holy days, though he didn't come during the last festival. His duties keep him very busy."

"Was he ever king?"

"There is no king in Mephitia," she seemed rather amused. "The Goddess Queens rule here."

Dabarius felt chastised and remembered how little he really knew about the place. "Do you miss your father?"

"Sometimes. I wish he were here now. I could use his counsel. I may summon him to Isyrin."

Dabarius enjoyed the sparkling surface of the water for a moment until the silence made him uncomfortable. "I miss my adopted father, Oberon. You know about him of course, from Bree'alla."

She looked at him closely, her brows narrowing. "You have been very patient, Dabarius. I'm sorry I didn't tell you sooner about your own father. I do know his identity. I've known since we were interrupted a few days ago."

"I've suspected so."

"Don't be angry with me, please."

"I'm not, and I understand. Assassination attempts on palace guests do tend to cause delays. Sometimes permanent ones."

She stifled a giggle. "I had no idea you were so entertaining."

"I am full of hidden talents." He focused on one of the lotus flowers, the bloom was closed, as all of them were during the heat of the day. She stopped to watch him. He forced it to open with magic, saying the secrets words of power in his and spreading his fingers slowly apart. The flower opened and he made the lily pad float toward her. "A gift for you, beautiful

160

Dara." He bowed and she smelled the sweet scent of the white lotus.

"Thank you. It is very lovely."

"What else can I give a Queen on a hot day like this, save for a flower that only blooms at night?"

"I should give you something." Her tone changed. "If you are ready for it."

He wanted to make another joke, prolong hearing whatever it was she was going to say. He knew it was probably going to be bad, and they had been enjoying such a fine moment.

"My gift has none of the sweetness that yours had."

"At least we had a few moments of peace."

She took a deep breath. "First, I have a question. Where did you learn *Teha Khet*?"

"*Teha Khet*?" Then he wished he hadn't asked. He suddenly understood the archaic sounding Mephitian words. *Battle touch*. That was how Oberon described it in Nexan.

"Captain Tal'mai said he has only seen one other who has mastered *Teha Khet* as you have. The fight on the balcony with those ex-soldiers who tried to kill you sounded quite impressive. I would have liked to see it."

"I had two great teachers. My master Oberon and his lifelong companion, Noah."

"Neither of them were Mephitian wizards?"

"Noah was not. Oberon may have been."

"Where did they learn? Who taught them?"

"Mater Oberon would not say. He never called it *Teha Khet* or said who taught him. He did say that all wizards knew it, or a form of it. That's all I really know."

"Many wizards practice it in the North?" she asked.

"They may have. The Drobin slaughtered all of them. Master Oberon was the last, as far as we knew. If any others escaped, we never heard of them."

"I would be surprised if the wizards of the North knew it. *Teha Khet* is known only by Mephitians. How your Master Oberon learned it, I don't know. It has been passed down from the ancient sorcerers who served Amar'isis. The masters taught only their apprentices, and so on. There are few masters left now."

"Did Tal'mai say who the other man was who was as skilled as I am?"

"No, but I know who he meant."

"Who?"

She looked uncomfortable. "General Reu'ven, when he was much younger."

Dabarius's mouth tasted very sour all of a sudden.

"He was my teacher when I was a girl. He still is, though I rarely take lessons any more."

"Is that why you don't have any bodyguards?"

"Perhaps. Why? Would you like to give me a lesson?"

He shook his head. "Not with archers watching us. They would probably shoot me if I touched you."

"My style avoids touch." She grinned and waved her hand near his thigh. A strong and somewhat painful tingling sensation moved across his upper leg and toward his groin, then faded as she moved her hand away.

"Perhaps another time you can show me more." He hoped she would. In private. Without any archers watching them.

"Another time, yes," she said. "I hope we can have many talks like these in the future."

"I do as well."

They sat in silence for a time, and he sensed something had changed. She was more distant, holding something back. He finally asked, "Have I done something to offend you?"

"No," she said. "I was looking forward to this meeting, but not what I had to tell you. Forgive me for acting so informal in this meeting." She looked away from him, then met his gaze again. "When you sat down I entertained the notion of not telling you at all and just enjoying your company, but I have to tell you."

"You have bad news about my father and who I am."

"I have news, yes."

"Please, Dara, tell me."

"Your name is in the records my scribe found. Only landowners and their heirs are recorded at the Hall of Names. However, landowners who have the knowledge and talent for the ancient magic and practice *Teha Khet* are kept on a separate list entirely. It's a very small list. Mey'lahna and I have gone over it all and we agree with the scribes, and with the information gathered in the past days."

"You know who my father is?" He wanted a drink to soothe his now parched mouth.

"Your father is without a doubt the Mephitian nobleman, *Teha Khet* Master, and wizard known as Barius, son of Ibarius. Your family has the distinction of having been the caretakers of an artifact created during the beginning times of the Mephitian people."

"The Crystal Eye," he whispered.

She nodded.

"Your grandfather carried the rank of Guardian of the Crystal. Now, we know from Bree'alla that the Crystal Eye is in the possession of the Dragon of Darkness, who has been hunting for it for decades."

"How do you know this?"

"The disciples of Shenahr, the Storm God, have hunted for it since the time of your grandfather. It must have been Master Ibarius who carried it north and hid it with your Master Oberon."

"You knew of Oberon?"

"We know the history of your family."

"What history?"

"Members of your family have died protecting the Crystal Eye before."

"I have family who still lives here in Mephitia?" He spoke the words, but he already knew the answer from her eyes.

"You are the last living person in your family line," she said, "and have ownership of much of the land in the valley in front of the city of Isyrin. The Keeper of Names has been managing your land for twenty years, but it is yours now, as is all the wealth it yields, and has yielded. The Royal Treasurer informs me that a large sum is owed to you."

"There are no others who share my blood? What happened to them?"

"Some died in the Storm Revolt when you must have been four or five years old. The rest died later. Your cousins, your uncles, aunts, all those who had any blood tie to your father were taken and interrogated, and then killed by Shenahrian Priests."

Dabarius's wanted to be angry about the murdering of so many in his family line, but he did not know them, and felt only a vague sense of loss. He was more interested in knowing who had killed them, as they might come for him now. He wanted to know everything about the Shenahrians. Perhaps he would target them once Draglûne was dead. "Who are these Priests? Where are they now? You know for certain it was them?"

"We know that it was the Shenahrian Priests," the Queen said somberly, "and their followers, and perhaps wingataurs in disguise, who committed the atrocities against your family."

Atrocities? The indefinite sense of loss turned into a small fire that threatened to turn to a need for revenge.

"Your family members were asked where the Crystal Eye had been hidden. None of them knew, and they were all murdered."

Dabarius felt a chill go through his entire body.

"Your body had not been found among the slain, though the Name Keepers thought you were dead all this time."

He had so many questions, but he couldn't speak for some time. The queen didn't prod him. She merely sat in silence. Her index finger tapped slowly on her thigh. Dabarius didn't look at her, fearing he'd lose control of himself if he met anyone's eyes. "What happened to my immediate family?"

"Your grandfather, Master Ibarius, died about twenty years ago, before the revolt. Then you disappeared a short time after the fighting was thought to be over. Just before you disappeared the remaining followers of Shenahr went on a brutal campaign of murder and destruction. They swore to get revenge on anyone who supported my mother, and your father was very loyal, an obvious target.

"During the fighting, he led a regiment of my mother's soldiers, and defended a bridge near the home where you were born. It is known that Master Barius and the soldiers were outnumbered, but they drove the Priests of Shenahr and their followers back, because of your father's magic. The rebellion was eventually crushed after many faithful to my mother were slain. Much evil was sown in the land before it was all over. Mothers and children were not spared."

"What happened to my mother? Did I have brothers, sisters?"

Khelen'dara sighed. "A scribe at the Hall of Names told me that your mother and three sisters were killed after the rebellion. Now we know that your father somehow managed to save you, his only son. You were only a four-year-old boy. He must have been the one to take you north, where his father, Ibarius, had taken the Crystal Eye years before when the agents of the Dragon of Darkness began hunting for it."

"What happened to my father?"

"After your mother and sisters were killed, he disappeared. One of the scribes wrote that he was dead, but had to correct the entry some months later when Master Barius returned and took revenge on the Priests of Shenahr. He led a small group of men loyal to him and slew every last disciple of Shenahr that he could find. He chased them for years. Then after one last battle in the deep Khoram, your father was wounded quite badly. He died of a festering wound, and was buried near an oasis far to the east of Isyrin."

Dabarius wiped his face, though he held in his tears.

The Queen's hand on his shoulder made it easier. His father was dead. Oberon was gone. He was still alone with no one of his blood.

"Your father did much for our people," the Queen said. "He was a great hero of Amar'isis. Take comfort in that."

"I can't remember him." Dabarius choked on the words. "I can't remember anything about him, or even my mother. Why not?"

"You were made to forget," Dara said. "I can feel the spell lingering inside you. It's so old, and the edges of the magic are frayed now, almost broken."

"I want to remember," Dabarius said, after he wiped his face.

"You will," she tenderly touched his hand. "I will help you."

"Break the spell," he said, "please."

She squeezed his hand, her palm against his. "Are you ready?"

His chest shook as he took in a deep breath. "I am."

The heat started instantly, warming his palm, as magic flowed from her and into him.

"In your hand," she said, "is your cartouche. You must allow it to open. Then I can help you."

"My cartouche?"

"It is everything that you are. It is the frame around your soul. Like the lines around the names of the previous Goddess Queen's on the wall there."

He glanced at the glyphs on the wall, the pictures and letters inside the frame forming a unique name. Each symbol was the physical cartouche of a Queen.

Dabarius didn't ask her how to open his cartouche. He just willed it to happen. That was how the magic was. It obeyed.

166

The heat in his palm intensified, then shot up his arm and into his body. Something inside him surrendered, broken loose like a veil swept up in a wind storm. He closed his eyes as a wave of images and feelings flooded over him. The desert, a dark blue river, a tall man with dark eyes just like his own. Dabarius wanted to laugh and cry at the same time. The deluge of feelings and memories filled his mind. His real father, Barius, and his mother stood outside a house by a river. They wore soft linen clothing flowing in the wind. He remembered the feel of his mother's arms around him as she hugged him close. She wore lavender oil on her skin.

The image changed to a time by the river when his three sisters were running in the grass as he chased them with a reed he pretended was a sword. He chased them over a rise and caught them all. Why had they stopped? The whiff of smoke made him look past the older girls, at his family's large house.

Smoke came out of the windows in the distance. It was on fire! His sisters sprinted for the home and Dabarius dashed toward the river to get a bucket of water. The well would take too long. When he reached the bank he couldn't find any buckets. Where had he put them all? His mother would be so disappointed in him. *If only I could find the bucket I could put out the fire. It's going to be my fault that the house burned down.*

He stopped looking when he saw the body beside the bank. Blood oozed out of a hole in the man's back. It was one of their workers. The older man who would sing him funny songs about frogs and snakes.

His sisters screamed.

Men with spears rode out of the courtyard on vorrels toward the three girls, who stood motionless in the grass. A woman screamed from the roof of the house.

"*Run!*" she yelled.

Dabarius knew the men were bad. They must be the bad men father had been fighting in the desert.

The riders trampled over his sisters. Allaya's head exploded all red and pink. Why didn't she run?

"*Dabarius! The river!*" Momma screamed. Then she jumped off the roof, flames all over her dress.

The men came closer, their spear tips pointing at him. He jumped into the river, swimming out toward the center where he wasn't supposed to go. He let the current take him away like his parents had told him to do if bad men ever came to the house. He swam good and fast.

Arrows whistled by, and splashed into the water. Dabarius let his head sink beneath the surface and he hid from the world until his lungs almost burst. Then he swam with the current until he could barely stay afloat. He stopped in a marshy area that smelled like a dead animal was rotting somewhere in the reeds nearby. Crocodiles liked to let their food rot and he wondered if one of them was close by, listening to him swimming. He found a dry area on an old log and crawled on top of it getting as far out of the water as he could. The darkness came and he kept his feet and hands out of the river in case the crocodile or a sharp-toothed fish mistook his fingers or toes for worms.

The bad men came near his hiding place, riding their vorrels. He heard their voices at the edge of the marsh, but the night and the reeds kept him hidden. He stayed there, shivering as the bugs landed on him and bit him all night long.

The next day he heard the sound of many vorrels galloping along the bank. He feared the men with spears had found him, but he could see it was someone else. His father and some soldiers rode as fast as they could along the bank, speeding toward the bridge that would take them home.

Dabarius waded through the muck and struggled up the bank and onto the road. He waved frantically as the vorrels charged straight at him.

Father's vorrel stopped and a strong arm lifted him into the saddle. He was held tightly and was afraid to answer the

168

questions his father asked at first. Then he told him about the bad men and the fire. And about Allaya's head.

They rode to the house. It smelled like ash and something like burned meat. The house guards and momma were in the courtyard. Tears. Many tears. The pain made his chest hurt and he couldn't breathe. Father said his mother and sisters were gone forever. And he had to be strong. He had to be strong because someday he would have to take revenge.

Dabarius remembered riding with his father across the desert and traveling for several weeks—almost always at night—following the stars. He would doze in the saddle and they would sleep together on a rough blanket that smelled like vorrel hide.

Men with spears would come to their camp sometimes. He always thought they were bad men. Then father would show them the scarab brooch he wore on his robe, and the spear-men would give them food, water, and new vorrels. It took a long time before they crossed the desert. Then they climbed a steep mountain and rode through endless fields of green grass. Finally, they came to a mountain covered in strange trees with needles instead of leaves or palm fronds. He remembered climbing into a valley filled with yellow and blue flowers ringed with snow-capped peaks. There was a tower and two very kind men, who both reminded him of Grandfather Ibarius.

"These men will be your fathers now. Mind them and be a good boy. Learn the magic, and how to fight."

"Where are you going?"

"I'm going home now to fight the bad men, and if anything happens to me, you will finish what I'm going to start."

"Finish what, Father?"

"Vengeance. Do you understand? You remember what happened?"

"Yes, Father."

"Dabarius, you must forget me, and your life before today. Perhaps someday we will meet again, and your memories will be returned. Until then, I have much to do, and you must stay here and learn to be a great wizard like your grandfather."

"Yes, Father." Tears streamed down his cheeks as his father hugged him for the last time.

"I will always love you, Dabe." His father touched him on the forehead and a great blackness fell in front of the little boy's eyes.

Now he opened them as a man, pain like nothing he had ever felt burning inside him hotter than the sun. After struggling so long to remember his past, to know where he'd come from . . . It burned like heated iron against his soul.

Khelen'dara stared at him, tears in her eyes—somehow, she had seen everything. She squeezed his hand tighter. "I'm so sorry."

"Don't be sorry for me"—Dabarius slid closer to her—"just help me finish what my father started."

Dara slowly nodded her head. "The same ones responsible for killing your family murdered my mother when I was a little girl."

He took her other hand into his. "Dara, the time is right. We both need to take revenge."

XXIX

The customs of this land are scandalous at best, but they do have a joyous spirit that puts most of the Nexan and Drobin folk to shame. We of the north have lost the knack of being happy, I think.

—Bölak Blackhammer, from the Khoram Journal

Dabarius smiled as Khelen'dara danced. She had made him promise not tell anyone, especially Tal'mai or Mey'lahna, who would definitely not approve. Swearing the oath was easy, and he would not betray her trust. Enjoying the dance, he lay back on the plush cushions, captivated as Khelen'dara led three beautiful dancers, the Queen's best friends, girls of her same age whom she had grown up with in the sheltered palace. They mirrored her moves as she swayed her hips to the fast rhythm of the drums. Khelen'dara's exquisite jewelry and tall stature set her apart from the dancers, though she was obviously as skilled as they were. The five female musicians at the edge of the room played more furiously, increasing the tempo yet again. The flutes, a six-stringed lyre, a tambourine, and drums sent the dancers into frenetic spins on the marble floor of the luxurious royal suite.

A servant poured more wine into his cup. Dabarius reached for it, then decided he was already feeling lightheaded, and should refrain from more. He had enjoyed quite a lot of wine with the Queen over the past three days, but this was the first time she had ever danced for him.

Dara slipped away from the dancers and seductively sashayed toward the couch where he reclined. He wished that they were alone now, and was embarrassed because of the giggles and stares from the other dancers.

Khelen'dara paid them no heed as her body undulated, her hips moving in circles now as she approached him. The scent of jasmine incense wafting through the room was replaced by

171

her wonderful perfume—susinum—a blend of lily, myrrh, and cinnamon.

He sat up straighter, her every movement a feast of beauty.

Dara reached out her hand and he rose to meet her.

"Do you like the way I dance?" she asked.

"You put all the others to shame."

She smiled and kissing her was all he could think about.

"I have something to show you." Dara took his hand and led him up the white marble staircase to the large vaulted loft—her bedroom. Golden lamps with intricate glass shades lit the large room in a soft light. The opulence of the chamber barely registered as he watched the way her body moved beneath her clothing.

The musicians played on, and he knew the dancers kept dancing. He heard them giggling and calling out exuberantly to each other. Had Dara told them what she was planning? He didn't care. At last he and the Queen were free from prying eyes.

She made him sit on the bed while she danced in a circle, her long black hair cascading down her back, barely covering tattoo of winged Amar'isis. He wanted to run his fingers through her midnight hair and feel it tickling his skin. He was so pleased it was real and not a black wig like most of the Mephitians wore atop their shaved heads.

The dance was slower now, and her eyes burned with desire. He wanted to wrap his arms around her waist and pull her on top of him, but should he do such a thing to a Queen? He kept his hands on the bed and waited for her to make the first move. She touched his shoulders, smiled, and pushed him onto the bed.

He wanted her so badly and ached to touch her. She climbed on top of Dabarius, her breasts against his chest, and he put his arms around her feeling the heat of her body. He could tell she wanted to kiss him, but she held back, the hint of nervousness in her eyes.

172

Dabarius grinned. "Great Queen, may I kiss you?"

"You may do more than that."

He kissed her softly at first, then their passion grew, and their hunger for each other became an unquenchable need. They rolled on the bed, kissing and touching until little clothing remained.

"You will be my first," she whispered, as he caressed her body.

She took in a shuddering breath as her pulled her closer.

"I hope you are my last." He held her, the lust tempered with something he had never experienced with anyone.

She smiled and they kissed again, her lips sweeter than any wine.

Dara rested her head on Dabarius's chest long after the musicians and dancers had finally gone. She tickled his side with her fingertips and he felt as content as he ever had. Nothing could compare to the passion they had for each other.

"What are you thinking?" she asked.

He smiled and kissed her on the top of the head. "I'm thinking that against my best judgment, I've fallen for the most beautiful and powerful woman in the world."

"And I've fallen for the most handsome man."

"Flattery won't work with me," Dabarius said.

"Will this?" She kissed his chest.

"No. Not that either."

"This?" She gave him a lingering kiss on the lips.

"Yes. That will every time."

They laughed and embraced, getting comfortable beside each other with broad smiles on their faces.

173

"Are you tired?" Dara asked. "It's the middle of then night. Should we sleep?"

"How could I sleep with you beside me?"

She giggled. "You are such a man."

"I hoped you'd notice."

"I could get used to having you in my bed."

"For how long?" Dabarius asked, contemplating something he had never thought of before.

"How long do you want to stay?" She lifted up, her dark eyes filled with what he suspected to be much more than carnal infatuation. She loved him.

"If we were married," Dabarius said, "I would sleep beside you every night."

She averted her eyes, wilted a little.

"Forgive me," Dabarius said, feeling his cheeks flush. "I've been too presumptuous."

"No, though I have not been as forthcoming as I should have."

"About what?" he asked.

She hesitated, averting her eyes even more and pulling into herself. "I'm already married."

"What? You can't be."

"I am the Goddess Queen of Isyrin," her voice was deadly serious. "I am married to the God King, Ah'usar. After my coronation as Queen, he became my Immortal Husband."

Only a ceremonial marriage, he thought. His worry faded somewhat, but what shocked him was that he actually wanted to marry her. "Can you take a mortal husband?"

"The Queen of Isyrin can never marry a man who does not have the essence of Ah'usar inside him." She rested her head on his chest again.

"Is there such a man?" Dabarius asked.

"It doesn't matter. I can be with any man I wish, as long as he is of noble birth—like you."

"I'm glad you chose me."

174

"So am I." She snuggled against him. "One of our daughters will be the Queen of this city someday."

"How do you know we wouldn't have a son?" Dabarius asked, trying not to show his surprise at her statement.

"Amar'isis gives the Queen of Isyrin only daughters. It has always been so."

"Will you have a daughter because of tonight?" he asked.

Dara grinned seductively. "Perhaps we should make sure."

XXX

The Khebian Priests have told us there is but one entrance to the cave. Draglûne will have no way to escape unless he goes through us.

—Bölak Blackhammer, from the Khoram Journal

Drake leaned against a large boulder and watched the clouds pass over the crumbling mountain peak. The falcon he had seen earlier, which was strangely circling and watching them, was gone now. No other aevians were in sight, but he had a bad feeling, like they were being watched. He glanced back down the steep trail they had been climbing, his crossbow cocked and loaded.

Dabarius, Thor, Bellor and their supposed guide—more like a chaperone—the old Khebian Priest, Vhar'el, struggled along as Drake covered their ascent, waiting patiently. The half dozen guards from the palace struggled up the mountain with their bronze shields on their backs and long spears being used as walking sticks. Khelen'dara had insisted the warriors go along as bodyguards. More likely they were spies for the young Queen, who had stayed in the sprawling complex on the plateau below them.

The palace of Isyrin did look impressive from Drake's vantage point. He never would have guessed they painted the rooftops blue and red—though the ones in the city seemed to all be white or gray. He wondered how much Bree would like seeing this view. He tried to guess which building in the sprawling palace she was in now. Or maybe the Queen would meet with her in the Temple of Amar'isis located toward the front of the huge plateau where the palace and temple complexes sat, high above the city below.

His friends caught up and Vhar'el flopped down, panting heavily. Bellor fared better than the old man, and seemed invigorated by the hike. The mountain air was wonderful.

"How did you manage this?" Thor asked Dabarius. "Getting permission for us to come up here is the greatest bit of magic I've ever seen you do. Why don't you tell me how you convinced the Great Girl Goddess to let us come here?"

Dabarius picked up a fist sized rock, and offered it to Thor. "If you can put this in your mouth, I'll tell you."

Thor bellowed with laughter.

The guards appeared nervous and Vhar'el shushed them and said two harsh words. Drake knew what they meant immediately. Be quiet. Then he explained something in detail to Dabarius.

"What now?" Thor asked.

"Esteemed Vhar'el would like us to understand," Dabarius paused and raised his eyebrows at Thor, "that this is the holy mountain of Kheb. He reminds you—us—that we all promised to be quiet, to be respectful, and to follow his commands. Only Priests and Priestesses are allowed up here normally. We have special dispensation from Queen Khelen'dara herself and the High Priest of Kheb in Isyrin."

"Bah," Thor said, then grumbled in Drobin.

"Mind your manners, runt," Dabarius warned. "Priest Vhar'el can make us go back any time he wants. He also said you should stuff that rock in your mouth as I suggested." Dabarius spoke in Mephitian to Vhar'el. The Priest responded with a terse one-word answer. "He also said I could do it for you in case you needed help."

Bellor just shook his head.

"Say anything you want, Dabarius. Today, I will not be angry with your feeble insults."

Drake doubted that statement would prove to be correct. Though he didn't understand Thor's good mood. The dwarf had first said he was merely delighted that Dabarius had been absent from their quarters for much of the past three days. At first he had been gone during the day, and then, most inter-

estingly, at night. Bree seemed to know more, having slapped
Dabarius on the backside and said something in Mephitian
that had made the wizard's face darken. All Drake knew was
that his friend had taken to wearing scented oil that smelled a
little womanish to the Clifftoner's nose.

That morning Dabarius returned with an answer to Bellor's request. The Queen would indeed allow them to hike up
and see the final resting place of Bölak. Drake imagined this
would be a somber trek, then it dawned on him. Thor didn't
think his uncle was dead after all.

They hiked for a while longer along a fast-moving stream
that flowed out of a huge bowl at the base of the peak. The
source of the stream was a small shallow lake about a quarter-
mile from the cracked summit of Mount Kheb. House-sized
boulders filled a third of the light blue waters. A field of thousands upon thousands of large and small brownish boulders
stretched upward on an almost vertical slope around the far
side of the lake. A medium-sized waterfall poured out of a
short cliff and churned up the water sending ripples and waves
endlessly toward the rocky beaches.

Vhar'el and all of the guards got on their knees and prayed
toward the peak. Bellor knelt beside the Khebian Earth Priest
and motioned for Thor to join them. Dabarius seemed un-
interested and Drake kept an eye out for aevians. Someone
had to. There was always a chance a hungry rogue griffin or
something else would find them. All of this open sky made
him uneasy. Not a tree or any sort of real cover was in sight.
Drake's eyes kept going to the peak and walls of dark stone
that were peeling off the mountain. He sensed something up
there, watching him.

"Where was the entrance?" Bellor asked when the prayers
were over.

Dabarius translated the question and response. "The
Tomb of the Ten Sons of Kheb is there. On the other side of
the lake, to the right of the waterfall where the boulders have

filled part of the lake."

Vhar'el pointed to an area where gigantic boulders had come to rest. Drake looked up at the peak and the slabs of rock that were in the process of sloughing off the mountain. Sheets of brown stone could come down at any moment and he imagined that some did every year when the weather was wet. Vhar'el had warned them about avalanches before they began the hike to visit the site of Bölak and the other *Dracken Viergur's* deaths.

None of it mattered to the dwarves. They led the way and walked slowly along the shore passing several stone pylons with Mephitian symbols on them. They went toward the area Vhar'el had indicated—in spite of the Khebian's vociferous protests dutifully translated by Dabarius. It was too dangerous to go there. The rocks were unstable. An avalanche could happen at any moment. No one must make a sound. It was forbidden to go to the far side of the lake. The Queen authorized him to be in charge of this expedition. They must follow his commands. Kheb's wrath will be terrible. Go back now. Or else!

"Or else what?" Thor hopped onto a rock and went around Vhar'el. "Will you tell a Drobin the secrets of the stone? Pah! Every trek is filled with danger if you're a fool. All things are impossible until they are done by the brave and canny."

The Khebian Priest barked a command to the six palace guards. The soldiers glanced at each other, apparently questioning the order. The leader among them shook his head to Vhar'el.

Bellor looked at Dabarius.

"They won't stop us," the wizard said. "The Queen told them to protect us, not to get in our way."

"I'm sorry, my friend," Bellor told Vhar'el. "This is something we must do."

Bellor and Thor led the way to the far side of the lake and the defeated Mountain Priest followed them after saying several prayers directed at the mountain peak. The guards came along behind, all of them hopping from boulder to boulder until they stood in the shadows of the gargantuan rocks that had blocked the entrance since the avalanche forty years in the past.

"Wait here and do not move," Bellor said. Thor nodded and they all stood watching him as he put his palms on a large boulder and then rested his forehead there as well. He whispered something, as if speaking to the rock and waited for a several moments.

"What's he doing?" Drake asked Thor.

"He's an Earth Priest," Thor said with a wry grin, "he is speaking to the mountain."

Drake wondered what the mountain might say. As they waited, he got a very unsettled feeling when he looked up at the peak. The worry increased during the nearly quarter of an hour that passed before Bellor stepped away from the boulder. He bowed to the mountain and rejoined the mostly bored group of men. He and Thor spoke in Drobin for a moment, then with Dabarius's help, Bellor asked a few questions to Vhar'el regarding the precise location of the entrance to the holy cavern of Kheb. Dabarius relayed Vhar'el's words with disinterest, tired of the Mephitian Priest's warnings that an avalanche was about to happen at any moment.

Finally, Vhar'el threw up his hands and sat down, muttering under his breath. The palace guards pretended not to be paying attention.

"You wish you hadn't come along?" Drake whispered to Dabarius.

"Bellor insisted that somebody had to translate. Though I think even a backwoodsman like you would have figured out what Vhar'el was saying."

Drake and Dabarius exchanged grins. The wizard was a vrelk's ass most of the time, but Drake had finally taken a liking to like him. Especially since Dabarius had been spending so much time with the beautiful Queen. The wizard's mood had improved. Dramatically. Even if he did smell like a soft Mephitian.

"I think Lord Dabarius wishes he was back in the palace." Thor glanced back at the two young men. "The Girl Goddess has a different plaything today. Maybe she's getting tired of Too Tall there?" Thor looked at Drake for confirmation, who sighed and shook his head.

Dabarius directed a vague expression of loathing at Thor.

"Let's go back," Drake said. "This is enough." He scanned the boulder field high above them for any sign of a landslide.

Vhar'el looked even more disgusted and waved for them to start back to the safe side of the lake. Right now.

"We're not going anywhere," Thor told the old Khebian.

The two Drobin climbed higher into the avalanche site that had buried the entrance to the holy cavern of Kheb, now the tomb of Bölak and the *Viergur*.

"What are you fools doing?" Dabarius asked, possibly translating Vhar'el's irritated words.

The Drobin said nothing and kept climbing into the more unstable area of the boulder field. Vhar'el began an animated—though whispered—discussion with Dabarius. The wizard then climbed rapidly after the dwarves and Drake had a bad feeling about all of it. He climbed after them and caught up to Bellor.

"Maybe you better go back down, lad," the War Priest said.

"What's going on?" Drake put his hand on Bellor's shoulder.

"We're looking for a way into the cave," Bellor said.

"This is too dangerous," Drake said. "Even I can see that."

"You're right," Bellor said. "Take Dabarius, Vhar'el and the guards and go back a safe distance. Go to the other side of the lake. Maybe even go back to the palace. We might be here a long time."

"We can't stay here that long," Dabarius said. "Maybe I can get permission from Vhar'el to leave you two here."

Drake shook his head. "None of us are leaving the Drobin here."

"Fine," Dabarius said, and threw his hands in the air.

Vhar'el's expression had become a furious scowl. Dabarius engaged in another serious conversation with the Khebian. Drake climbed a little more and found a good place to keep watch. As he was looking at the lake and the sparkling waterfall he wished Jep, Temus, and even Skinny were there. Then he suspected that the three dogs would have probably run into the lake, urinated all over the place, barked so loudly that boulders would have come raining down, and given Vhar'el a whole new level of fury. Still, he missed them desperately, and Khelen'dara still had no information about what had happened to them.

The day wore on. All the guards save one lay down to nap beside the lake. The apocalyptic avalanche had not occurred in the two hours Bellor and Thor had been poking around the mountain.

Bellor had very confidently predicted that another avalanche would not occur until the winter snows fell again. Drake hoped he was right. Bellor also said he suspected there was still a way into the mountain. They just had to find it. Dabarius omitted telling Vhar'el that of course.

The Khebian Priest dozed against a rock and finally woke up when Thor called out excitedly and began motioning wildly for Bellor to climb up and join him. The dwarf had excavated a small patch of boulders where a stream exited the rock just to the right and on the same level where the tunnel entrance had been. Drake could barely see the small cave opening from his watch post.

Vhar'el started gesturing like a mad man when Thor crawled into the tight hole, a little over three feet high and wide. The Khebian scrambled up the boulders, hand-overhand, dragging Dabarius with him. Why Vhar'el thought his words would dissuade the Drobin now, Drake had no idea. The palace guards stayed at the lake's edge, watching the activity as they roused themselves from their afternoon nap.

A sharp, echoing sound made Drake stand up straight. It was like a crack of thunder. He scanned the clouds in the distance, then realized it came from high on the mountain.

Another crack. A boulder the size of an anvil skipped down the slope, each time it hit made an even louder echo. Vhar'el and Dabarius stopped as the rock crashed and tumbled until it finally splashed into the lake a dozen yards away from the palace guards, who had anxious expressions now. They all looked upward. A long, tedious moment passed. The sense of being watched that Drake had been experiencing the whole time intensified. He felt the blood pumping in his ears. He held his breath and looked up at the mountain, hoping nothing else was going to topple down on them.

Thor crawled out of the hole and waved for them to keep coming, uncaring or oblivious to the crack and the boulder.

Drake started climbing when Vhar'el pushed Thor away from the cave mouth and raised his hand as if to strike the Drobin warrior. Not the best idea, even if Vhar'el had been armed and was about forty years younger.

Dabarius grabbed the Khebian and Bellor stepped in front of Thor. Drake scurried up the rocks, his crossbow slung over his shoulder. The weapon was still cocked, but the bolts were in his hip quiver lest they fall out of their tracks. He finally arrived and peered into the muddy cave barely wide enough for Thor to crawl into. A trickle of water seeped out of the rock and disappeared under the innumerable boulders as it flowed toward the lake. The tunnel didn't seem to go back very far at all—though he couldn't be sure without more light.

"Priest Vhar'el says that he will not allow you to dig into this mountain," Dabarius told Thor. "We must go back now. Graves must never be opened."

"It's a dead-end, Thor," Bellor said. "Vhar'el is right. It's time for us to leave. There's no way in. We must accept Lorak's will."

A thunderous crack split the air as a gigantic slab of rock peeled away from the mountain peak. Dust and boulders slid down the nearly vertical slope gaining momentum and mass with every instant.

Drake pushed his friends toward the tiny cavern as the guards on the lake edge dropped their spears and ran for their lives. One man dove into the lake and started swimming. The avalanche was so wide the Mephitian soldiers had no hope of getting away.

Thor squeezed inside the cave. Bellor followed him. Vhar'el hesitated. Dabarius pushed the old Khebian forward, but Vhar'el couldn't get inside.

Drake, Dabarius, and Vhar'el's pressed against the tiny overhang, hands over their heads as the first of the house-sized boulders rolled over the top of them. In his heart, Drake knew this was no accident. Someone had just tried to kill them.

XXXI

Any who enter this holy place who are impure of heart will face judgment.

—inscription on a pylon outside the Holy Mountain of Kheb

General Reu'ven stood atop the mountain as the boulders bounced down the slope obliterating the foreigners, and covering their bodies forever. His hands tingled from the magic he had unleashed to cause the avalanche. Kheb's holy mountain had been desecrated, and he was the instrument of vengeance. What were the blasphemers thinking of doing? Were they going to try and enter the holy cavern? No one could fault what he had done. He was merely following the most ancient law of Mephitia set down by the God Kings of the old empire. Tomb robbers must be executed.

Pity that Vhar'el and the guards had to die. The old man was a good influence on Dara. She would be angry about his death. She *always* mourned when men in her service were killed. In the end, she would thank the Goddess—or more likely Kheb—for ridding her of the foreigners. It would all be considered an accident. They had tempted fate, trod on holy ground, and had been punished by the Mountain God. That's what everyone would say. He would figure out a way to return to the palace and assume his place alongside Dara once again, and she would never know what he had done to the foreigners.

Pity the Queen had found Bree'alla alive. He would find a way to be forgiven of that offense, and would send the Wing Guardian to her death eventually. She was too dangerous to remain alive, and would follow the foreigners he had killed to the Afterworld. All of their deaths were the best possible outcome for all of the Mephitian people. If the foreigners had been allowed to continue their suicidal and foolhardy journey to find the Dragon of Darkness, Isyrin would have another dead Queen due to the reprisals. Three generations of assassinated Queens. It made him sick to the core of his being.

Not while I live, Reu'ven thought. He spread his arms and leapt off the cliff. The air rushed around him as he plummeted toward the lake. He used the ancient magic of Amar'isis and turned into the falcon again. He pulled up just above the water and glided to the far side. Isyrin soon lay beneath him as he soared through the sky. He landed on an inaccessible tower of rock overlooking the city. There was an overhang nearby where he had spent time when he needed to think. He would wait until nightfall before sneaking back into the palace—coming in through one of the secret doors on the roof.

Perhaps tonight he would get rid of Bree'alla. Her loyalty was in question, and she had made a terrible decision guiding the foreigners into the heart of his homeland. No chances could be taken with the secrets of Mephitia. The half-Nexan bitch would die soon, or perhaps on some journey across the Khoram. He would arrange a suitable accident that no one would question.

Dara must never know. If he had to, he would stay away, an unseen hand that would steer her well and keep her safe. For her sake, and for the sake of Mephitia, he would sacrifice all that he was, all that he had accumulated over the years.

The Queen would never know about many things he had done to keep her safe for all those years after he failed to save her dear mother. A sharp spear of regret pierced his heart as he thought about seeing the corpse of the woman he loved carried away to be put in her tomb. Poor Lira. He should have been with her. He would have saved her life.

Reu'ven sprang from his perch on the tower of rock. He flew toward the palace roof. He couldn't stay away any longer. Dara needed him. He was the only one who really loved her. He was the only who could keep her safe. Reu'ven could sense in his heart that she missed him right now.

XXXII

We shall find a way into the mountain and find the bodies of our kin. If we must, we will make one.

—Bellor Fardelver, from the Desert Journal

Huge boulders pressed down on Drake as he gagged on rusty tasting dust and grit. His eyes burned as he squinted in the tiny pocket that had formed around him, Dabarius, and Vhar'el. The Khebian held his hands up, palms glowing red as he pressed against a series of boulders that held together like puzzle pieces stuck fast by a divine glue above their heads. The Khebian chanted under his breath and Drake realized that magic had saved them, but Vhar'el was weakening, his strength and the magic failing as the boulder pressed him down, shrinking the space where the three of them crouched.

"How long can he hold on?" Drake asked Dabarius.

The wizard spoke a few words to the Khebian who barked out a reply. "Not long. Crawl in there, you first."

"We can't leave him out here." Drake moved to help Vhar'el and pressed against the boulders.

"You can't help him, get in there!" Dabarius pushed Drake hard toward the tunnel opening as small rocks fell and Vhar'el grunted loudly, barely hanging on. Drake could barely see the entrance, but he felt the opening and slid inside on his belly. Cold water and mud soaked his shirt and the front of his pants as he squeezed inside. At least it was only a trickle of water, maybe half a finger deep.

"Get in there!" Dabarius pushed Drake's feet and the Clifftoner squirmed inside faster. He bumped his head, then used his crossbow to feel his way forward. The tunnel wasn't much wider than his shoulders, and if it got too tight, his crossbow wouldn't fit.

187

"Come here, lad," Bellor called in the darkness. "Thor and I are all right. Keep crawling."

Drake stopped a body length later when he hit Bellor's boots. Almost instantly, Dabarius caught up and pressed against Drake's ankles.

Boulders crashed down outside as Vhar'el screamed in pain.

A moment later Vhar'el's voice proved he was still alive.

"How bad is he hurt?" Drake asked.

"One of his feet is trapped outside," Dabarius said.

"Can you pull him in?" Drake asked.

"We're going to find out." The wizard strained, grunting and pulling. Vhar'el groaned and the words he said sounded like cursing. Large boulders crashed down behind them and more dust filled the tunnel.

Dabarius and Vhar'el had a short conversation, interrupted by moans of pain punctuated with harsh sounding words.

"Can we help him?" Bellor asked.

"He's in, but his foot is crushed. Maybe his leg is broken." Dabarius paused for a moment as the Mountain Priest whispered more.

"What is it?" Drake asked, when they had finished and a long silence began.

"There's no going back the way we came in," Dabarius said. "There's too much rock blocking the tunnel now. No digging out that way."

"Good," Thor said, "because we're digging in. I just have to unblock the rocks that are clogging this stream and we can reach the cavern inside the mountain."

"Then we'll just be trapped further in," Dabarius said. "We need to find a way to the outside, not the inside."

"Leave me be," Thor said. "I'm digging in so we'll at least have a dry place to die." The sharp ringing of a hammer chipping away at stone and digging through muck echoed in the narrow tunnel.

"Here, lads, this will help," Bellor said as a glowing golden light radiated from a glowstone he carried. After Drake's eyes got used to the brightness, he inspected the water-cut passage snaking into the mountain. He would bump his head if he raised it any more. At least he could see Thor working on the clog ahead of them. Thor passed back the pieces of fractured rock to Bellor who then slid them to Drake and he passed them on down the line.

The cold water started to numb Drake's forearms and his crotch as he waited, praying for some progress to be made. He rolled onto his side, but the rocks dug into his hip, so he rolled back onto his chest.

He lay there for perhaps an hour. Thor's hammering had slowed. They had made almost no progress. The faint hope Drake had was fading to a dim spark. He slipped into a state of lethargy and rested his head on some of the broken stones Bellor had passed back to him.

A long time later he woke up to an echoing voice. Thor spoke in Drobin—from far down the tunnel, though Bellor was still in front him with the glowstone.

"What's happening?" Drake couldn't move his arms. They were frozen in place, numb and rigid.

"He's through!" Bellor shouted. "Let's get moving."

Once Drake got his arms working again he could slither forward on his belly. He just kept following Bellor's light and knew Dabarius and Vhar'el were behind, because of the scraping sounds they made as the shimmied through the muck. Bellor waited ahead in a tiny smooth-walled cavern. The War Priest stood waist deep in a pool that slowly spilled over a lip of rock and ran down the tunnel the way they had come. A submerged tunnel led upstream out the other side.

"You'll have to trust me, lad," Bellor said. "I'll help push you through to the other side where Thor is waiting."

First, Bellor took Drake's crossbow and reached into the black tunnel where Thor took it.

"Ready?" Bellor asked.

Drake held his breath and nodded. The dwarf pushed him head first into the bitterly cold water and Thor pulled him out the other side. He came up in a shallow pool in a vaulted chamber lit by a glowstone sitting on top of a glistening rock nearby.

Thor heaved him toward a dry patch of rock where his crossbow sat waiting for him. The small cavern had a peaked ceiling, and the sound of water trickling down the rock was all around him. Dabarius came next and then they helped poor Vhar'el, who grunted every time he moved. His foot was crushed, and he they had to drag him up onto the dry shelf.

Bellor went to work putting a splint on Vhar'el's leg, while Thor scouted ahead, following the flowing water up a series of stepped waterfalls. Drake and Dabarius found a drier spot to rest and sat there shivering until Bellor took out his red rune stone with the black Drobin symbol on it.

"Feör." The War Priest spoke the command and the stone came life. The orange flames warmed their bedraggled group. "Wait here," Bellor said, "We'll be back as soon as we can."

The two Drobin spent a few hours scouting the cavern as cold and hunger gnawed at Drake. He couldn't rest in the freezing and shadowy cavern. He imagined them being trapped there for many days and a feeling of dread crept into his heart. He had to get up and look around, but Bellor told him to stay with the others and rest. "How can I rest? We need to get out of here."

"Drake, please go and sit down," Bellor said.

Vhar'el prayed, and Dabarius sulked as they waited, watching the fire stone until it lulled them into a fitful stupor. Despite the dire circumstances, the Drobin seemed cheerful.

He could do little else but try to sleep, and maintain his confidence that Bellor would get them out this. Either they would find a way out or the queen would come in and rescue them. She wouldn't leave Dabarius to die, would she? How long it all would take? Drake had no idea. He tried to get comfortable, though wet clothes and the dirt inside of them chafed his skin.

He was almost asleep when the heard the clicking sound of a two hoofed creature coming down the tunnel. He had heard the sound before, in Quarzaak, right before the wingataurs attacked them. Dabarius shot up at the sound and Drake lifted his crossbow.

A pair of red eyes glowed in the darkness as Drake reached into his quiver for a bolt to load into his crossbow. Something pierced his hand, the pain making him recoil as he looked down at the blood. The bolts had all turned to writhing black snakes, and one of the vipers had sunk its fangs deep into his skin.

XXXIII

The clouded eyes of the Night Serpent have fallen on you, trespasser. Look upon them and despair, for your soul is forfeit.

—curse written on the wall inside the Holy Cavern of Mount Kheb

The snake's fangs pierced the web of skin between Drake's thumb and first finger. He swung his hand trying to dislodge the viper and jumped away from his quiver, which was now full of black snakes instead of bolts. The serpents scattered into the pool of water on the cavern floor disappearing into the darkness as they swam toward his feet. The burning poison coursed through his hand before he flung the snake against a wall.

Dabarius assumed a fighting stance and blocked the advance of the wingataur. Red eyes loomed closer and the clatter of hooves echoed off the walls.

Vhar'el screamed and rolled off the dry shelf where he had been resting and splashed into the water. Drake leaped toward the injured Khebian and dragged him out of the water away from the snakes. Vhar'el shouted and grabbed his broken leg as Drake tried to pull him back onto the ledge.

The fire stone and glowstone dimmed as the air went ice cold. The wet smell of rotting leather filled the cavern as the wingataur demon loomed over Dabarius, tilting its bullish horns toward him. It reached for the wizard's throat, but he turned the attack aside, deftly parrying using both his arms. As the monster cocked its fists again, Drake noticed that its desiccated flesh clung tightly to its bones, as if almost all its flesh had wasted away. Despite its lack of muscle the bull demon flung Dabarius into the pool of water with the snakes.

"Get out of the water!" Drake shouted.

The wingataur ignored Dabarius, and leaped toward Drake. Sharp cloven hooves descended toward his chest, and Drake sprang out of the way, losing grip on his crossbow as he rolled. The monster crashed down right where he'd been and turned its head on a bony neck that didn't seem capable of supporting its large skeletal head.

Vhar'el tried to crawl away, but the monster grabbed him by his injured leg and lifted him into the air. The Khebian Priest's bloodcurdling scream filled the cavern. Drake wanted to run into the darkness. He would not stop until he couldn't hear the screaming. The demon would kill Vhar'el, then he and Dabarius would die. Bellor and Thor would find their bodies later, then they too would fall to this abomination.

"Put him down!" Dabarius yelled, as he stepped out of the water.

The wingataur shook Vhar'el, relishing in his agony, and grinned at Dabarius revealing sharp teeth and a withered black tongue.

Drake drew his heavy Kierka blade with his bleeding hand and stepped toward the wingataur's flank as Dabarius held its attention. The wizard shivered as he approached, perhaps from the freezing water, though Drake could feel it too. A palpable aura, like a swarm of buzzing insects emanating from the demon, and every small step made Drake's heart pound harder and faster.

With a clawed finger the wingataur beckoned Dabarius closer. The demon was larger now. Muscles bulged under its withered hide, where it had only been skin and bones before. With every scream from Vhar'el a surge of growth rippled through the wingataur's body. The demon was somehow feeding on his fear and pain.

Dabarius reached Vhar'el and the red-faced and convulsing Priest grabbed onto the wizard, trying to pull free of the wingataur's grasp, which only served to twist his broken leg to an even more unnatural angle. A wet, sickening sound cam from the broken limb, and Drake saw the white of bone erupt from the priest's flesh. The subsequent wail from Vhar'el stunned the demon as its body quivered and enlarged.

Drake found his courage and attacked. His blade bit deeply, slicing through the leathery hide and severing the wingataur's hand that held Vhar'el. Dabarius tried to cushion the Priest's fall, but he hit the ground hard.

Before Drake could strike again the wingataur knocked him backwards with the stump of his arm. As he flew through the air he realized that no blood flowed from the wound. Water broke his fall, then he remembered the snakes. He scrambled to get out as quickly as he could.

When he reached the edge, Thor and Bellor charged into the cavern screaming "Lorak!"

The wingataur faced their onslaught but did not notice Dabarius, who launched himself and struck the back of the demon's knees at the same moment Thor barreled into its groin with his shield. The wingataur lay on its back and Drake lunged forward and grabbed one of its sharp horns, holding its head down as Dabarius and Thor fiercely grappled with it.

Bellor arrived with *Wyrmslayer* raised high. He cut through the bone and sinew of the demon's neck, severing the skull from its body. The red eyes dimmed and black empty sockets remained as its eyeballs had rotted away to nothing.

Drake tossed the skull away, afraid that touching it would infect his wounded hand. He stood in shock, trembling. He stared at his bleeding hand, wondering how long he would live before the snake's poison killed him. Instead of two puncture wounds he saw one distinct injury, as if he had been pricked by something—a crossbow bolt perhaps? He scanned the pool where the snakes had been. His entire quiver of crossbow bolts floated in the water. No evidence of the serpents remained. It had to have been some trick of the demon to drive him mad with fear.

"Are you all right, lad?" Bellor asked Drake.

"I thought there were snakes in the water." Drake glanced at Dabarius.

"I didn't see any," the wizard said. "Just some trick of the demon."

The pain is his hand was nothing then, and he breathed a sigh of relief. Vhar'el whimpered and grunted as Dabarius and Bellor tried to stabilize his mangled leg.

Thor watched over the corpse of the demon, as if its headless body might rise up and attack them.

Bellor soon joined him, and inspected the remains. "Our work is not done yet."

Thor nodded.

"We must make sure it will not return," Bellor said.

"What is it?" Drake asked.

"*Grusslig boren,*" Bellor said. "That is what these things are called in the old stories. Horror born."

"Undead," Thor said.

"We brought it back by coming here," Bellor said. "The spirit of the demon returned to its body because of us. It fed on our fear and became stronger, but we can prevent it from ever coming back again."

"How?" Dabarius asked.

"Thor and I will break all connection the spirit has to its body," Bellor said, "before it gets a firm grasp in the physical world. The longer its spirit lingers inside its old body, the harder it will be to break the tie. We must sanctify the body with holy stones, water that has been blessed in Lorak's name, and we must use the old prayers."

"Holy water," Dabarius said. "This cavern is a holy place of Kheb."

"It was," Bellor said, "until a true dragon desecrated it some years ago. The water here may not work, even if we bless it."

"Then what will you do?" Dabarius asked.

Bellor produced a small waterskin he'd had on his belt. He and Thor prayed and blessed it in Lorak's name while Drake stood guard over the head and the body of the wingataur. He thought he saw the blackened nostrils flare. "Bellor, it moved."

The War Priest and his former apprentice said nothing, but kept praying as Bellor held the waterskin in his open hands. Then they stood on either side of the demon's remains and prayed in Drobin. Bellor put four small green crystal stones on the body that he said were green calcite and had been blessed in Lorak's Temple. He placed one on its forehead, throat, heart, and solar plexus. Bellor then dripped the water onto its head and torso. The water hissed and bubbled, as if it had been dripped onto a hot pan. It soon ate through the leathery flesh like strong acid and a musty odor wafted up from the corpse.

The Drobin prayed and made harsh gestures, burning the demon with drops of the blessed water and severing whatever tie it had to the remains. Holes covered its body when they were finished. Drake imagined that if they had more they could totally dissolve the wingataur's remains. Master Bellor finished by chopping off the limbs and scattering them around the cavern. Thor crushed the skull with his hammer. Drake was shocked at how thick the bone was.

"We will do same to all of the other bodies," Bellor said. "If this spirit crossed, others may follow."

"Others?" A lance of fear shot through Drake's spine.

"We found the skeletons of six wingataurs," Thor said, "not including this one."

"Six?" Drake was shocked.

"How did they die?" Dabarius asked.

"Five had crossbow bolt holes in their chests," Thor said. "Two had cracked skulls."

"Look here," Thor said, and he pointed to a hole in the chest wall of the wingataur they'd dismembered.

"They used bolts with wyrm killing magic," Bellor said.

The shafts in Drake's quiver would do the same. Each of them had been enchanted by Bellor and Thor who used wingataur blood at the temple of Lorak in Khierson City.

"The wooden shafts are gone," Thor said, "but we found two of the points." He held up two slightly rusted metal tips. "Drobin steel, still sharp."

"No sign of any dwarven remains, though," Bellor said.

"Maybe the water washed them away," Dabarius said, "or they were buried somewhere you haven't found yet."

"We've searched everywhere," Thor said. "We've explored this whole system."

Bellor gave him an incredulous glance.

"Well, almost everywhere." Thor seemed less sure of himself. "If my uncle and the *Viergur* were dead, we would have found their bodies near the wingataurs. Don't you understand? They weren't there."

"That's no proof they lived through this," Dabarius said. "The Queen would know if they escaped."

The Drobin left to do their Priestly work and Drake tried to dry out Vhar'el's clothes on the now brightly burning fire stone. They were all still wet and cold when Thor and Bellor returned a long while later. Vhar'el groaned, nearly unconscious from the pain, his tan skin gone sallow in the firelight.

"It's done," Bellor said, and sagged to the floor, thoroughly exhausted.

"What's down that tunnel?" Drake asked.

"This passage leads to a big cavern where the Khebian ceremonies were held," Bellor said. "We found the original entrance, blocked long ago, and a big slab that must have been an altar. There were Mephitian symbols all over it. We also found a place where a true dragon must have slept. I found two partial talon prints, claw marks on the stone, and the whole area was tainted with vileness of a wyrm, even after being absent for so long. Draglûne himself had to have been in this very cave."

Thor grinned like a fool. "That's not all we found."

197

"Did you find a way out of here or not?" Dabarius asked.

"A way out," Bellor whispered and sighed. "You'll have to judge for yourselves. We found a stream that goes into a hole. It might be a way out."

"We've got to get Vhar'el out of here," Dabarius said. "He'll die if we don't. As it is, I'm afraid he'll lose the leg."

"We're all going to freeze to death if we don't get dry," Drake said.

"We're just going to have to get wet again," Thor said. "We might as well go right now."

After a tortuous climb through the freezing stream, then a march through a cavernous chamber containing a slab of stone with Mephitian symbols carved and painted on it, they found a narrow ledge along a fast-moving river of frothy white water. The ledge and the tunnel went downhill, and Bellor directed them to take the slippery route. Dabarius and Drake took turns carrying Vhar'el, who seemed to be moving forward only through the providence of his earth god.

"There's the mark," Thor pointed to an etching on the cavern wall.

Drake could see it clearly. Bölak Blackhammer's personal mark, just like in the Quarzaak Journal. A hammer shape with a long handle. Beside it was another mountain shape with an oval around it—obviously done by a different hand, though with the same instrument.

"That's the cartouche of a Khebian," Dabarius said. Vhar'el squinted at the mark, then nodded. "A Khebian Priest made this mark next to Bölak's."

"They made the marks at the same time," Bellor said, "judging by the weathering and mineral deposits in the etchings." Then he pointed to a triangle pointing down and into the tunnel where the fast moving water flowed.

"It's a trail marker," Drake said, "isn't it?"

Bellor nodded. "My nephew is showing us the way, as we Drobin mark the road when we forge ahead. There is a ledge we can follow, but first . . . " He began to make his own mark with a small chisel. He etched a small axe with the rune mark for his name and clan.

While he worked on the mark, Drake and the others started walking on the ledge, which was a sometimes-one-foot-wide lip of slippery rock. It was difficult to navigate, especially for Vhar'el. They all helped him climb along the river's edge, taking turns with the Priest lashed to their backs until their limbs quivered with fatigue. Through the haze of exertion, Drake found himself praying the demon ghosts would not appear and attack them when they were so vulnerable.

Spray from the water was like icy needles into Drake's face. They followed its winding passage until the small but furious river ended in a wide cavern with an uneven dry area still tall enough for Dabarius to stand fully upright.

The water flowed to the far side of the chamber and disappeared in a swirling white vortex that sloshed and spit as is sucked everything down. A roaring sound echoed in the cavern as if the vortex were the mouth of a great beast.

Thor pointed to the wall beside the whirlpool. Three marks were etched in the rock. One appeared to be a Drobin symbol, the other a Mephitian cartouche, and the third was an arrow pointing down into a swirling symbol that had to mean the whirlpool.

"That is the symbol for 'faith,' in Drobin," Bellor shouted above the roar of the water.

Dabarius helped Vhar'el hobble over to the wall before conferring about the symbols. The wizard helped the Priest lay down, then said, "That cartouche is also the word for 'faith' in Mephitian."

"The arrow means they went down into that," Thor said. "I think it leads to the lake. Remember the waterfall we saw crashing into the lake from the small cliff?"

"How do you know this connects to that?" Dabarius asked.

Both the Drobin looked at him disdainfully.

"We haven't lost our sense of direction," Bellor said. "We're near the lake and that cliff with the waterfall. Of that fact, I am most certain."

"You want us to jump in there?" Dabarius asked.

"My uncle did," Thor said. "That's how he got out."

Vhar'el looked horrified after Dabarius filled him in on their conversation.

"They had to have faith to jump in there," Bellor said. "None of them could have known for certain if it would get them out, and the force of the water would be too strong to get out of once they dropped in."

The whirlpool became more turbulent and water splashed into the cavern where they stood, as if it was trying to spit at them.

"If this whirlpool got them out," Dabarius said, "the Queen would have known about it. She would have told me." His words lingered in the air.

A growling sound made Drake pull his Kierka knife and whirl around. His breath came out in clouds of steam as he faced the source of the inhuman noise.

Tremors wracked Vhar'el's body as he lay on the ground. The Khebian arched his spine and flung his head back, growling and screaming. His face had been twisted into a feral mask. Then his body went still. He stared at them with faintly glowing red eyes, his face placid.

"What's wrong with him?" Drake shouted.

Bellor knelt and looked into Vhar'el's face. "*Possession*," he whispered. "The demon can no longer go into its own body, so it has taken Vhar'el's."

"Do something," Dabarius said.

Bellor lifted the mountain shaped pendant of Lorak from under his shirt and pressed it to Vhar'el's forehead. "Leave this body now, demon!"

The Khebian went rigid, then convulsed, his entire body wracked with bone-bending spasms.

200

"It's killing him!" Dabarius shouted.

Bellor pressed the pendant harder into Vhar'el's skin. "Stop, demon, I command you with the power of the True Fire."

Vhar'el's face became placid again, then his eyes opened.

Bellor backed away, pushing Dabarius and Drake away.

"You cannot stop me from coming to this world, Priest," the demon said in perfect Nexan, though Vhar'el's voice was deeper and so different than before.

"We will stop you," Bellor promised.

"No, you will become my slaves," the demon said. "I will keep you here like all the other ghosts."

"We shall escape this place," Bellor said, "and you cannot hinder us."

Blood dripped from the corner of Vhar'el's mouth and a bleeding tongue licked his lips. "Yes, try to escape, go there now,"—he pointed at the vortex—"and you will drown as the *Dracken Viergur* drowned. Their bodies are lost under the mountain. Their bones splintered and cracked. Go now. Die like they did and no one will ever find your miserable corpses, but I will have what's left."

Vhar'el stood on his broken leg. The red marrow of the bone protruded from his skin and he leaned against the wall, grinning at them. His eyes burned with hatred.

"You will not possess this man's soul!" Bellor shouted. "Leave him now!"

"No," the demon ghost said, "I will not possess him. I will kill him." Vhar'el flung himself into the vortex of rushing water.

XXXIV

Demons of the Void have one weapon they use more than any other. Lies. Their edge is sharper than any dagger, and no shield or coat of armor can protect us from them.

—passage from the Goddess Scrolls of Amaryllis

The whirlpool spun the Khebian Priest around its edge and Vhar'el's eyes changed. The red glow disappeared and now they filled with fear as he screamed for help and splashed in the churning water.

Drake reached to help the old man leaning out and extending his crossbow so Vhar'el could grab onto it. The old man hooked an arm around the metal arms while Bellor and Thor grabbed Drake to hold him steady. An instant later Vhar'el jerked the crossbow out of Drake's grasp using the inhuman strength of a man who once again had demon eyes.

The creature grinned at Drake as the vortex sucked him down with *Heartseeker* clutched in its grasp. The voice of the monster shouted into Drake's mind, *You have failed like all of the rest. You will never kill our master!*

When Vhar'el was gone, Drake stood in shock, the demon's words and the loss of his crossbow having paralyzed him utterly.

Bellor gently ushered Drake away from the edge of the vortex and helped him sit down.

Dabarius stared at the whirlpool and when Thor tried to nudge him away the wizard shoved Thor backward.

"Lad, come away from the there now," Bellor said gently. "He's gone, and we must pray together. Please."

Dabarius shook his head. "I don't need prayers."

"We all do, especially now." Bellor extended his hand toward Dabarius. "Please. Stand with us here. We need you."

The wizard moved away from the pool. The four of them linked hands and Bellor said a long, solemn prayer in Drobin. The demons words immediately stopped echoing in Drake's mind when Bellor started praying. At first Bellor's hands were cold, then after a moment they had become warm and comforting. Bellor paused, then began speaking in Nexan, "Great Lorak. We four *Dracken Viergur* reaffirm the sacred vows of honor, courage"—he glanced at Thor—"commitment"— look toward Dabarius—"and determination." Finally, he stared at Drake. "I bless us all with the Sacred Earth magic and pray that it will always sustain us. May our will be like the strongest stone and our courage as tall as the highest mountain."

Drake felt the invisible rune of determination on his forehead flare to life and warm his entire body.

Bellor and Thor took their hands away from Drake and Dabarius.

The whirlpool seemed to slosh and spit more loudly.

"What do we do now?" Drake asked, noticing the cavern was warmer.

"We rest, and we pray," Bellor said. "We will make it through the night."

"In the morning?" Drake asked.

Bellor let out a long sigh. "We decide what to do."

Moments after Drake had finally fallen into a deep sleep some hours later he heard a scrape against the stone by his ear. Was it Bellor working on the protection barrier again? He opened one eye, and the glowstones revealed nothing by his head. Bellor slept near Dabarius against the wall of the cavern. They were all inside the circle of protection Bellor had drawn on the rock.

A heavy weight suddenly pressed against Drake's chest and large hands wrapped around his throat. He couldn't move, couldn't breath and couldn't make a sound as his life was being squeezed from his body by some invisible beast. The overwhelming feeling of hatred came from what had to be the demon ghost who was trying to kill him.

Unable to move, his panic turned to resignation that he would soon be dead. All Drake could think of was Jaena and his love for her. No matter what happened to him, he would always love her above all others. Their bond would never be broken.

The demon's grip loosened on his throat.

Drake felt a surge of energy in his body and he croaked out a word, "*Jaena.*"

The creature recoiled and Drake sat up choking and coughing.

"What's wrong?" Thor asked.

"It . . . was . . . here." Drake looked up to see his three friends huddled around him.

Bellor took out the silver mountain symbol of Lorak and pressed it to Drake's forehead. Then he started chanting in Drobin and walking around the cavern, casting out whatever foul spirit had gained entry.

"*Drown yourselves.*" A bestial whisper filtered from somewhere in the ceiling.

"Did you hear that?" Thor asked.

"It's taunting us," Bellor said.

"We can't stay here any longer," Dabarius said. "Let's go back up the tunnel, into the larger cavern. Maybe we can find a way out there."

"*Drown yourselves.*"

"Silence, demon!" Bellor shouted. "You will not frighten us."

"We should leave this chamber," Dabarius said. "We can't go out this way."

The wizard's voice sounded as anxious as Drake had ever heard. His own fear was still fresh, but what had happened to Dabarius?

A tremendous booming crash echoed from upstream, as if a pile of rocks had fallen.

"Can the demons cause a cave-in?" Drake asked.

"We must not underestimate anything they can do," Bellor said. "I suspect it was them who caused the avalanche outside."

Drake wondered, *Had the demons been watching them from the peak?*

"Look at the water," Thor said.

The flow of the rushing water lessened significantly and the level of the pool where the vortex swirled instantly dropped by almost a foot.

"They've have damned the river, why?" Thor asked.

"When the damn breaks," Dabarius said, "the water will rush down that tunnel and drown us all."

"It will carry pieces of rock with it as well," Bellor said. "We can't stay here."

"We have to go upstream," Dabarius said. "Right now."

Dabarius, Bellor, and Thor grabbed their gear. The frantic nature of their behavior made Drake shake his head. It all seemed so clear to him now. "No," he said. "Don't you realize what's happening? Demons of the Void do only one thing."

"They lie," Bellor said.

"What does it matter if they lie?" Dabarius said. "We have to back."

Thor looked at Bellor, who glanced at the slippery ledge they had come in on, considering what to do.

Drake pointed to the wall where Bölak Blackhammer had etched his personal symbol and a message to any who would follow. "The Dracken Viergur were here. They had faith. So should we. I'm not listening to any demon of the Void." Drake backed up to the edge of the cavern and picked up a glowstone.

"What are you doing, lad?" Bellor asked, fear in his voice. "Don't act rashly. We've got to get out of here. We're going upstream, not down there."

"Drake, don't be foolish," Dabarius said. "You can't go that way."

"Watch me." Drake took a lungful of breath, and leaped feet first into the center of the vortex.

XXXV

If you do nothing, you slip toward the darkness.

—passage from the Goddess Scrolls of Amaryllis

The cold water needled into every part of Drake's body as the whirlpool sucked him into the bowels of the mountain. The glowstone revealed a smooth tube through the rock that angled and snaked downward. He slid feet first, his small pack protecting his back from the stone.

The tunnel turned and the current flung him face first into the rock. His forehead banged against the stone and he dropped the glowstone. Some of his air escaped from his lungs as the pain made him go limp.

The blackness owned him then as the cold penetrated his bones. His faith wavered. The powerful current pushed him forward relentlessly and air hunger made his heart beat even faster. The burning in his lungs spread throughout his chest and he wanted to open his mouth, gulp for air.

The blackness dared him to lose focus. If he sucked in the icy water it would fill his lungs and kill him dead.

The tunnel kept going. There was no light, no waterfall. Had Bellor been right? The current smashed him against the wall again. He lost the rest of his air.

Fear made Drake gulp in some water and he choked. He grabbed at the stone, trying to slow his descent into the darkness. Nothing made sense to his air-starved brain. He knew at any moment that the tunnel would get tighter. His body would be wedged between the rocks. This was where he would die. No one would ever find his body. Jaena would never know what happened to him. He was never going home.

Light.

The pinpoint of light got closer. The roar of water filled his ears and he was falling in the air. He sucked in a breath and then slammed onto the surface of the lake.

Stunned, he sunk toward the bottom gulping water. Before he even realized what he was doing, he started clawing and kicking his way to the surface. His heart drummed against his ribs and a searing pain filled his lungs.

He gasped for air as he broke the surface and was nearly blinded by the sunlight. The roar of the waterfall behind him muffled the voices that were calling his name.

A woman with dark red hair dove off a rock and swam toward him. He wiped the water from his eyes to see her better and noticed the blood on his hand. His forehead ached and was bleeding from a painful wound.

"Drake, are you all right?"

It was Bree. She took him by the arm, pulling him toward the shallows where several men were standing. They lifted him out of the frigid lake and he took several breaths of air in the shadow of a huge boulder.

"Where are the others?" Bree hugged him as he caught his breath.

"They're in the mountain."

"Are they coming out like you did?" She glanced up at the waterfall.

"If they don't," he smiled at her, "they're cowards, and we'll have to go in after them."

Bree'alla grinned. "Thor will be coming next."

XXXVI

Down.

—Bölak Blackhammer's rune-mark on the wall in the Holy
Cavern of Kheb

Thor watched in horror as his friend jumped into the whirlpool
and disappeared. For a long moment, he couldn't believe what
he had just seen. Drake was gone.

Bellor sagged against the slick wall of the cavern as a groan
escaped his lips. Dabarius kept looking at the vortex of water
as if Drake would somehow return.

Thor looked at the wall where his uncle Bölak had etched
his personal symbol beside the one representing faith. He
touched the stone, feeling the grooves and lines of the wet
rock. Why were they so afraid of trusting their first impression? He and Bellor had thought from the beginning that this
was the way out. When had they changed their minds? It was
the demon in Vhar'el's body who convinced them not to go
that way. Why were they listening to a demon?

Thor secured his gear and faced his friends resolutely. "I'm
going after him." He pointed toward the whirlpool.

"You'll be lost. I can't allow that," Bellor said.

"I won't be lost. This leads to the lake. This is the way out.
We both knew it before the demon clouded our minds. Have
faith, go down. The message is clear."

"I'm not willing to bet my life on your assumption," Dabarius said.

"The demons have won," Bellor said.

Thor stared at him, defiant. "They haven't won."

"We are splintered. Confused. Fighting with each other."
Bellor tugged on his beard.

"The youngest of us has shown the way out. We should
follow Bölak's sign." Thor tapped the symbol on the stone.

"This is real. My uncle was here. He left this sign for us and this is the way he escaped."

"You can't know that," Dabarius said.

Thor pointed to the symbols on the wall once again and thought Drake was the bravest human he had ever met.

XXXVII

Draglûne has fled from us. He buried us in the mountain with his minions to die, but we killed them all and escaped. This Dragon King is a coward, hiding behind wingataur demons. He fears us more than we fear him, and now he thinks us dead. We will use this to our advantage and with Lorak's grace we shall track Draglûne to wherever he has gone. Blooded and victorious, the *Viergur* have regained their morale. The end, at last, is in sight.

—Bölak Blackhammer, from the Khoram Journal

Drake watched as Bree'alla dove into the freezing lake when Thor Hargrim crashed into the water at the base of the falls. Bree pulled him to the surface, but he waved off her help, trying to tread water on his own. Drake laughed when Thor sank almost immediately, his head slipping under.

The lone palace guard who had survived the avalanche that had trapped them inside the mountain, a strong swimmer named Jhe'oh, helped Bree'alla fish Thor out. After the dwarf had gotten out of the water, Drake locked forearms with him.

"I knew you'd come next," Bree'alla told Thor.

"I should have come first." Thor grinned at her and winked at Drake.

Arms flailing wildly, Bellor Fardelver splashed into the lake. The two soldiers waiting near the falls rescued him immediately.

Dabarius emerged next and knifed into the water, feet first, his body rigid. He popped right up and adeptly swam toward the shore, his long arms and strong kicks powering him forward. Drake helped him out of the water where the companions gathered. They all stood there, looking at each other for a long tense moment, then Thor began to laugh, then Drake, and the others followed. The dwarves and Drake hugged each and Thor slapped Drake on the back.

"You're not going first next time," Thor told him. "If anyone is going to do something stupid it's going to be me."

"As it should be," Dabarius said.

Thor and the wizard grinned, and cocked their fists at each other in jest.

The dozen smiling palace guards gathered around them and said prayers directed to the peak of Mount Kheb.

"What's all that?" Dabarius asked, looking at the lavish white tents, banners, servants, and soldiers arrayed on the far side of the lake.

"Queen Khelen'dara herself came to oversee the rescue," Bree'alla said. "She was quite worried when Jhe'oh told her what happened."

"Did any of the other soldiers survive?" Bellor asked.

Bree shook her head. "Jhe'oh was the only one who swam into the lake instead of running along the shore. When the boulders hit a wave carried him to the far side."

"Bless Lorak for that mercy." Bellor glanced at the not too distant shore of the small lake.

"We should escort you all to the Queen," Bree said.

"Wait," Bellor said. "Did you find . . . Vhar'el?"

"We found his body in the lake a while ago," Bree said. "What happened to him?"

Drake looked away. It was as he expected. The old Priest was dead.

"He showed us the way out," Bellor said. "He was a brave man."

"Why did he have—" Bree's words were cut short by the thunderous crack and boom from the mountain peak as a slab of rock tumbled toward them and caused the boulders on the slope to slide along with it.

Jhe'oh ran into the lake pulling Bellor along with him and waving for everyone to follow. Drake and Bree grabbed Thor and jumped in. A glance back revealed the entire mountainside sliding down toward them.

The fastest swimmers had not even reached a quarter of the way across before the avalanche hit the water's edge. Boulders skipped off the rocks at the shoreline and splashed around them. A man screamed and went under as a stone struck him between his shoulders.

Bree and Drake towed Thor through the water. "Swim faster!" Thor urged, kicking harder.

A swell of water pushed them all forward. Drake kept a hold of Thor as the wave sent them rapidly toward the distant shore. He stayed in front of the wave until the force of the water sucked him under. The next thing he knew he was banging into smooth stones and coughing as a series of waves crashed into him.

Soldiers and servants from the tents rushed to help. Drake looked for his friends and noticed they were all right. Jhe'oh stood beside Bellor and the old dwarf was thanking the Mephitian soldier for his quick thinking. A few other soldiers were helping an injured man who lay on the beach grimacing in pain.

The mountain had tried to kill them again. Drake eyed the slope, trying to see through the cloud of dust. It couldn't have been a coincidence this time. He had that feeling again that someone was watching them from the peak, and had caused the avalanche. Was it a demon?

The soldiers parted as Queen Khelen'dara ran toward Dabarius with her arms open. He swept her up in his embrace, hugged her close, then kissed her on the mouth. The sight of the beautiful Queen and Dabarius in such an intimate moment made everyone stop and stare—though some of the soldiers looked away. Drake finally put things together in his mind, and cursed himself for a fool. All that time, Dabarius hadn't just been talking to the queen. It had all been there for him to see, to smell, even. His father would have thumped him

213

on the head with a tree branch and sent him to the back of the hunter's file for such wood-headed thought.

Captain Tal'mai approached Drake and presented him with *Heartseeker*. The crossbow seemed in perfect condition, though the cord was still damp.

"You found it, thank you," Drake said, thankful and relieved beyond words.

Bree translated Tal'mai's response. "The lake was shallow. We saw it near the body of Vhar'el."

"Thank you very much." Drake squeezed Tal'mai's forearm. The Captain said something and motioned toward Bree'alla.

Drake looked at her as she wrung the water out of her long hair.

"He said that you should be thanking me. I was the one who found it."

He grinned like a fool.

Bree frowned and slapped him across the face, hard enough for the sting to overcome the residual numbness from the icy water.

"What was that for?" Drake held his reddened cheek.

Bree's face changed. Her stony façade cracked for an instant and he realized how worried she had been. Drake wrapped his arms around her and she hugged him back. She whispered, "When I saw your crossbow in the water, I thought you were dead. Hold onto it next time."

"I will. I promise."

She buried her face into the crook of his neck while Dabarius and Queen Khelen'dara walked arm and arm toward the large white tent.

Bree finally pulled away, took his hand. "We'll go to the Queen's tent."

"I am cold." Drake shivered, despite the heat and the burning sun. He thought about lying down on the warm rocks.

214

"We'll get out of these clothes and warm up." The playful look in Bree's eyes made Drake feel uncomfortable and excited all at the same time. She held his hand tighter and he wondered if his resolve to stay faithful to Jaena would be tested again.

Movement caught his eye near the peak of the mountain in the craggy rocks. Someone or something was up there. Was it the demons who had killed Vhar'el? Whatever or whoever it was had failed for the second time to kill him and his friends with an avalanche. He hoped there wouldn't be a third attempt.

A bird flew down from the upper reaches of the mountain and circled the lake. He couldn't look away from the tan and brown raptor as it streaked through the sky.

"It's just a falcon," Bree'alla said. "Don't worry about it."

Everyone else kept walking. Drake was rooted to the spot. He wanted to unlace his quiver of bolts and load his double crossbow.

"Falcons are sacred to my people," Bree said. "They're the sons of Amar'isis, guardians of Mephitia. They live in the mountains here. Now, come on." She tugged on his hand.

The falcon wheeled high above them and Drake thought about how different the Mephitians were from his own people. Birds were the least of all the aevian threats, but they were demons just the same. Spawn of the Void. Bree wouldn't believe his suspicions about the falcon, and reluctantly, he followed her toward the tents while the feeling of being watched was as strong as ever.

XXXVIII

Dead and buried Drobin are no threat.
> —Bölak Blackhammer, from the Khoram Journal

Smoke filtered out of the billowing white tent through a hole in the peaked ceiling of Queen Khelen'dara's tent. Dabarius stood with his friends around the fire pit in dry clothing. They all chased the chill from their bones while sipping hot tea and eating fried bread coated with honey. The wizard kept stealing glances at Dara, who observed the companions as she sat on a beautiful wicker throne with a high back. He kept thinking about their stolen moment when the Queen had helped him take off his wet clothes, and put on new ones. They had been alone in a screened-off area of the large tent for several lustful moments.

Mey'lahna had interrupted their passionate kiss, though he could still smell Dara's lotus blossom perfume on his hands, and taste her sweet lips. She promised that later that night they would once again be alone in the privacy of her chambers where they would be undisturbed all night long. If his friends or members of the court had any doubt about his relationship with the Queen, their kiss on the beach had dispelled any uncertainties. Of course he was in lust with her, and for the first time in his life, he thought it might be more. She was the most beautiful, intelligent, powerful, and dangerous woman he had ever met. He had the urge to tell someone about his feelings for Dara, but . . . he glanced at his companions and decided he would keep it all to himself.

Bree, the dwarves, and Drake stood beside the fire with him, wearing linen robes as their clothing dried outside. Khelen'dara had thought of everything and her servants had carried many baskets and bundles up the mountain to support the rescue. A larger number of people knew about the companions' presence now. Regardless, the information would have gotten out in the end no matter what precautions were taken.

The guards at the main entrance to the royal tent suddenly parted, and let pass a weathered old man with a shaved head. He had extensive kohl around his eyes and wore a tan griffin pelt over his white robe and *schenti*. The high-ranking Priest walked confidently toward the Queen. A large golden amulet in shape of a mountain hung from his neck, and Dabarius knew he was a High Priest of Kheb. He bowed toward Queen Khelen'dara, and she waved him forward, bidding him to take a seat on one of the stools in front of the throne. He kept looking at the dwarves with much interest and what could be . . . reverence?

Three more Khebian Priests came behind the high-ranking man. All three wore griffin pelts, though they appeared to be his assistants, as they were all younger than the first. One of the Priests, very tall and perhaps forty-years old, smiled broadly when he saw the Queen.

"Father!" Khelen'dara stood excitedly. For an instant, Dabarius saw the carefree expression of a little girl flash across her face. She regained her composure as he came forward and knelt in front of the throne. Dara extended her hand and he pressed it to his forehead. When he stood, she motioned for a servant to bring a stool for him to sit beside her. They engaged in a whispered conversation and she motioned with her chin toward the companions.

Her father stared right at Dabarius, his happy eyes turning cold. The wizard's first thought was that he must know what he and Dara had been doing behind closed doors. Should he be afraid of her father? Probably.

"Who's that man beside the Queen?" Bellor asked.

"Her father," Dabarius said.

"He's a Priest of Kheb, and a very famous architect," Bree'alla said. "His name is Sah'shem."

"And the older one?" Thor asked.

"He's the High Priest of Kheb in Isyrin," Bree'alla said. "His name is Ben'khar."

"Why are they wearing griffin skins?" Drake asked, a little horrified that they wore the pelts of aevian demons. He thought the Mephitians were much more civilized than this.

"To show that the earth has mastery over the sky," Bree said. "Why else?"

Her response seemed to bother the superstitious Drake.

Mey'lahna began to clear the room of all the unnecessary people as the Queen quietly informed the Priests of the companions escape from the mountain and their discoveries inside. Every guard except Tal'mai left, as did all of the servants. The four Khebian Priests remained, and Mey'lahna formally introduced High Priest Ben'khar and Khelen'dara's father, Sah'shem, then told them the names of the companions. Dabarius was the first to be introduced, as Lord Dabarius, son of Barius.

"We are honored to be in your presence," Dabarius said, then performed a bow with a flourish at the end, hoping his friends would follow his lead.

High Priest Ben'khar ignored him, his eyes on the Drobin. "Praise be to the Mountain God. You are the kin of the Ten Sons of Kheb. My brothers and I are honored to be in your presence."

Dabarius translated Ben'khar's words.

"Thank you, High Priest Ben'khar," Bellor bowed. "May I ask, have you personally met our kin who came some forty years ago?"

"When I was a novice at the temple, I was fortunate enough to see them."

"They didn't die in the mountain, did they?" Thor blurted. "They escaped. Someone from your order helped them. We found the mark of a Khebian. Please, tell us what you know."

High Priest Ben'khar blinked, though he kept a placid expression. "The Ten Sons of Kheb died in the mountain. The tale is well known."

His denial was hollow. Queen Khelen'dara raised one eyebrow. "Honorable Ben'khar," the Queen said, "if something has been kept from me, please tell me now."

"Forgive me, Divine Queen," Ben'khar said, "these are without a doubt the true sons of Kheb Himself, but they have not taken the vows. Only the Wing Guardian among them carries a trust scarab and has sworn to keep the secrets of Mephitia. Even if I knew more, I am bound by the laws of our land."

"You are right, Wise One," the Queen said. "They do not carry the binding scarabs of trust." She whispered to her father, then he whispered to High Priest Ben'khar. Dabarius used his magic to augment his hearing. He could barely make out their words.

Sah'shem said, "Honorable High Priest Ben'khar, the Divine Queen requests that you tell me all of what you know. I already have some knowledge of what happened at the end of her grandmother's reign. Please, Reu'ven is gone, and I want to give her the best counsel I can. She must know the full truth and learn of her grandmother's decisions."

"In another place I will say," Ben'khar said. "Not here when many could be listening." He glanced over his shoulder at Dabarius.

"Please," Sah'shem asked. "Tell me something. Confirm our suspicions at least."

"They did not die in the mountain," High Priest Ben'khar said. "They survived and escaped with help from Queen Rama'dara and the Khebian Priesthood after taking secrecy vows. That's all I'll say here. In private, I'll tell you or the Queen everything else I know."

"Wise One, thank you for your trust," Sah'shem bowed. "The Goddess Queen will be most grateful."

Khelen'dara's father whispered to his daughter for a while, then she faced the companions. "If your kin survived and escaped long ago, they would have been helped by my people.

They would have had to take vows to protect the secrets of this land. Are you all prepared to take similar oaths?"

"Great Queen, you know I am," Dabarius said.

"You and I have already spoken of this. Please tell your friends what it will mean to them if they say the vows, and what it means to submit to the power of Amar'isis."

He looked at his companions. Thor and Bellor were hanging on every word he translated. They would do anything to keep going and he could count on them to be very pragmatic. Drake was a different story. What would he do? Dabarius asked Bree in Mephitian. "Have you told him about the vows you took and the laws of this land?"

She shook her head.

"You know what'll happen if he takes them?" Dabarius asked her.

"I know what'll happen if he doesn't," she said. "Tell them to take the vows. You have to make them agree to take them."

If they were ever going to get out of Isyrin or find out what really happened to Bölak and the *Dracken Viergur* they had to swear the oaths. He addressed his friends in Nexan after pondering what to say. "The Queen asks if we will take vows of secrecy and swear allegiance to Amar'isis, similar to what Bree'alla did years ago. We will have to pledge to never speak of Mephitia and what we've seen here. If we don't, we'll never be allowed to leave Isyrin. We'll be sequestered here until the end of our days."

"Of course we'll take the vows," Thor said. "What choice do we have?"

Bellor nodded. "I will always serve Lorak, no matter what oaths I make now. Tell the Queen that Thor and I will honor Amar'isis and we will keep the secrets of Mephitia unto pain of death." He looked at Drake. "What about you, lad? I won't speak for you in this."

Drake studied Dabarius and Bree. "They're not telling us something, Bellor. What is it? What are you hiding? Haven't

220

we proved you can trust us after all of this?"

"If you say the oaths," Bree said, "there will be nothing hidden. We can speak freely at last."

Drake shook his head. "I wish I could believe that. Not even your Queen knows everything that has gone on here. Your people keep secrets from each other. What chance would a foreigner have of learning the truth?" With that, he walked out of the tent.

"What troubles your friend?" Queen Khelen'dara asked Dabarius.

"He is frustrated and still has hope that he will be able to go home someday," Dabarius said.

"He worries about the people he left behind," Bree'alla said, "and what's been kept from him here."

"Tell him . . ." Khelen'dara paused a moment, " . . . tell him that if he says the oaths tomorrow, he will have a new people,"—she glanced at Bree'alla—"and a new life."

"Great Queen, I brought him here," Bree'alla said, "and I knew the danger. It's my place to tell him about the oaths, and the life he might have. May I have your leave to speak with him now?"

"Make him understand," Khelen'dara said. "It's for the best."

Bree bowed and left the tent.

Dabarius wondered about the woman Drake had left behind in his village. Bree'alla obviously had feelings for him, and like a fool the stupid backwoodsman still resisted her overtures. Why couldn't he just seize the moment and follow his heart? After everything he'd seen and done, why did Drake think there was a chance of leaving? This was their home now. He should take what Mephitia had to offer.

The flapping of wings near the smoke hole of the tent drew Dabarius's eyes as a commotion outside occurred simultaneously. Drake and two guards rolled on the ground with Bree trying to break it up.

221

Tal'mai drew his sword and stepped closer to the Queen.

Bree'alla came back in almost immediately. "Forgive him, Great Queen. The guards stopped Drake from shooting at the sacred falcon who landed atop your tent."

"Atop the tent?" High Priest Ben'khar looked up. "A falcon would not land there."

"Agreed," the Queen said.

"The time has come for us all to return to the palace."

"Wing Guardian Bree'alla," Khelen'dara spoke loudly so all of her servants could hear. "Tell my guards that Drake shall not be stopped from shooting the falcon if he sees it again."

XXXIX

Comforted by the Wings of the Moon. Lifted by the Great Mountain of Life. I am blessed to serve the people of Amar'isis. I will be Her Wings.

—passage from the sacred oath of the Wings of Amar'isis

Drake hated Mephitia. Open skies. Few trees. The people worshipped accursed aevians. Worst of all, he was never going to see Jaena again. He had feared that very notion since the night after they had slain Verkahna at the Cave of Wyrms. Had Jaena really been there in her spirit body and healed Bree'alla? Now it all seemed like a dream. He still had the feeling that Jaena had said goodbye to him that night. Did she already know that he wasn't coming back?

Soon, after the upcoming binding ceremony in the temple of Amar'isis, there would be no doubt about the course of his life. Bree had made it plain to him, and all night he had dreamed about his fate. At least he had been given permission to shoot the falcon if he ever saw it again. The aevian had to be a spy sent by their enemies. Could it be a servant of the demons in the mountain, or Draglûne's Iron Brotherhood, perhaps Priests of Shenahr, or possibly even the missing General Reu'ven? A demon had possessed Priest Vhar'el, could it possess the falcon? They were surrounded by enemies, hemmed in on every side, exposed in this foreign country with its strange customs and barren terrain. The few things he'd always been sure of: Cliffton, family, Jaena—he was being asked to let go of those. In order to do the duty he'd sworn, he was being forced to break faith with every other touchstone in his life.

Tired and conflicted, Drake ascended the steps of the temple of Amar'isis with the morning sun at his back. The golden doors shone in the brightness, making his eyes hurt and aggravating his headache from lack of sleep. A mural of the goddess stood above the doorway. Her arms were spread wide and blue- feathered wings hung down from them. If the people of Cliffton could see him now they would think he had betrayed Amaryllis and everything he had ever learned. Was he really going to swear allegiance to a goddess with wings? Did they understand what they were asking him to do? They couldn't. His mouth tasted like corroded metal. His heartbeat thudded painfully behind his eyes. He would have approached a griffon's nest without his crossbow more readily than this.

The doors swung inward and Drake entered with Bellor, Thor, Dabarius, and their small escort of palace guards led by Captain Tal'mai.

Wide arches supported by vibrantly painted pillars lined the inner courtyard. Servants of Amar'isis, mostly Priestesses in white sheath dresses and black wigs, hustled about. The rectangular courtyard was larger than he imagined.

The fountain in the center drew his eye and he recognized the statues of winged, four-legged creatures standing on a rocky butte. Alicorns. Three of them reared up, wings spread as if they were about to take flight. Their black shiny horns glinted in the sunlight, contrasting with the white stone they had been carved from. Upon closer inspection it was plain to Drake that whoever had sculpted the statues was extremely familiar with the aevians. The bulging muscles and wide hooves were perfectly done. He remembered when he first met the alicorns outside Oberon's tower. He had been wrong about them. They couldn't be demons. The flight atop Starmane's back had proved it to him. Drake shook his head. If the people of Cliffton learned he had ridden an aevian he would be cast out into the unforgiving Thornclaw Forest. Or worse.

What did it matter now? He'd come too far, seen too much. Drake didn't think he was any wiser, but he was different now. Certainty had turned to doubt, innocence to hard-bitten reality. He wasn't going home for good reason. They wouldn't accept him. He barely accepted them before he left. Perhaps Drake needed the desert. He needed a new home. For the first time that morning he missed Bree'alla. She had stayed somewhere else last night. He hoped she would be at the ceremony. He needed to see her face.

Dabarius and Tal'mai spoke to each other when their group passed the fountain and the statues of the alicorns.

"What did he say?" Bellor asked.

"He said the alicorns are the messengers of Amar'isis," Dabarius said. "They are holy creatures. Blessed are those who have met them."

"You can you summon them again?" Bellor asked.

"I still have two feathers," Dabarius said. "Though Blackwind said he and his herd would not heed a call from the Khoram Desert unless a god summoned him."

"Good," Thor said. "We're not riding on one of those ever again. Right, Drake?"

"Right."

On the far side of the courtyard a tall door covered with gold paint opened wide for the companions, seemingly on its own, though Drake suspected some mechanical device operated by a hidden servant. Tal'mai led the way inside to the darkened chamber.

Dozens of towering pillars, like the trunks of perfectly straight ironbark trees, filled a grand chamber of immense proportions. He couldn't see the far side, except for a small point of lamplight. Hints of the sun seeped in at the edges of the gallery and Drake felt like he was in a petrified forest, though it smelled like dust, not rotting leaves. The pillars had even been painted to look like trees. The chirruping of small birds in the ceiling unnerved him and made the illusion of being in a forest even stronger. He should have expected the birds, considering the Mephitians love of aevians. Why would they chase precious birds out of a holy temple to a winged goddess?

Tal'mai guided them straight through the temple at a slow pace, muttering prayers under his breath and often glancing up at the ceiling. The smell of incense filled the air as they finally reached the far end of the hall. Eight Priestesses formed a corridor and stood holding incense burners and fans made of green and white feathers. The women wafted the sweet smelling smoke toward them with their fans and whispered prayers.

Tal'mai bid the companions to enter the small room beyond the hall. Warm light emanated from the chamber and was in stark contrast to the huge gallery. The little room housed the golden idol of a winged woman. The statue of Amar'isis stood on a simple altar of brown stone that was shaped like the mountain symbol of Kheb, a sharp peak with a split in the middle. Amar'isis stood upon Mount Kheb.

Queen Khelen'dara, flanked by High Priestess Mey'lahna and several others stood behind the altar. The incense made Drake feel lightheaded and he was glad to follow Mey'lahna's hand signal to kneel on the thick rug in front of the altar. Bellor, Thor and Dabarius joined him as Bree'alla emerged from the shadows behind them and also went to her knees. Bree nodded to them as Priestess Mey'lahna stepped forward carrying a wooden box decorated with Mephitian symbols. Mey'lahna opened the lid, displaying four scarab beetle shaped brooches made of dull bronze. They could easily fit in the palm of someone's hand and each had a strong double needle-pin on the back with sturdy clasps.

"Take one," Bree said. "Hold it in your left hand, and press it against the middle of your chest." She demonstrated with her own scarab brooch, which was the same size, except it had been painted blue, red, turquoise, white, green, and metallic gold.

"I will translate the words of the ceremony and the vows for you when it is time," Bree said. "You will repeat the words."

Drake nodded.

226

The Queen spoke in a firm voice that echoed in the chamber. She said what had to be a prayer that went on for some time. Finally, Bree spoke in Nexan, making eye contact and indicating for them to begin.

"From the Void I crawled. Through the forest I walked. Up the mountain I climbed. To the home of the gods. Mephitia. The Secret Land."

A dim glow emanated from their scarabs and Drake realized Dabarius was repeating the Mephitian words.

"Now, under the Eye of the Day."

The scarabs glowed brightly, turning their clasped hands red as the light bled through their flesh.

"Comforted by the Wings of the Moon. Lifted by the Great Mountain of Life. I am blessed to serve the people of Amar'isis. I will be Her Wings."

Golden-white light streamed out from the scarabs and Drake felt tingly magical energy entering his palm and going up his arm to his heart.

"I will protect the Secret Land."

The magic filled his chest like he had taken a lungful of air from an oven.

"I will not speak of it. Outsiders will never hear of it from me."

The magic was painful now, burning, as if it were giving a warning.

"The desert will be barren to all outsiders. A land of sand and death. To me, it will be a hidden garden of plenty. My garden. My home. My land. My people. Unless the Goddess Herself commands me, I will never leave the Secret Land. May I be cursed, and exiled to the Underworld if I break my oath. I vow in the name of Mother Amar'isis, that I will keep the secrets of Mephitia, in this life, and the one beyond."

The scarabs flashed with a brilliant light and the heat in Drake's chest relented.

227

Queen Khelen'dara stepped forward and extended her hand to Drake.

"Give her your brooch," Bree whispered.

He opened his hand the dull bronze brooch had been transformed. It looked like parts of the beetle had been colored blue, white, and green. The metal itself had changed color. It didn't look at all like it had before.

The Queen took the binding scarab and pinned it on Drake's chest. Bree translated Khelen'dara's words. "You are a servant of Amar'isis now. This is a symbol of Her trust."

The Queen repeated her words and actions with Bellor, Thor, and Dabarius. When the ceremony was over, Bree'alla led the four new servants of the Winged goddess out a side door.

In a small, shady courtyard at the rear of the temple of Amar'isis the companions sat on stone benches and examined their scarabs. Each brooch seemed a little different compared to the others.

"Do the colors have significance?" Dabarius asked Bree'alla. Hers was a lot more colorful, while two thirds of his was shiny bronze.

"They show rank, level of trust, and identify your family," Bree said.

"Rank?" Thor asked. "Are we Mephitian soldiers now?"

"In a way," Bree said.

"Who is the highest ranking among us, according to these?" Thor asked.

"I am," Bree said. "I am a Wing Guardian. Lord Dabarius is next."

"*Lord* Dabarius?" Thor grimaced.

"He is a son of a Mephitian nobleman," Bree said. "His father, Lord Barius was a wizard of great renown. Dabarius is the owner of much land in the valley outside Isyrin."

"What if I gave mine to Bellor?" Dabarius asked.

228

"The scarabs are bound to each of you specifically," Bree said. "In time, the colors would fade and it would become the dull piece of metal you saw before the ceremony began."

"If I lose it in the sand," Thor said, "it will fade?"

"Yes," Bree said, "and if you find it again, it will change back."

"What about our ranks?" Thor asked, pointing to himself and Bellor.

"Drake is ranked after Dabarius," Bree said.

"He's ahead of Master Bellor?" Thor shot an angry look at Bree. "Your religion is ridiculous."

"Lower your voice," Bree said. "We're still on holy ground."

"This doesn't make sense," Drake said, completely agreeing with Thor.

"Bellor and Thor are sons of Kheb," Bree explained. "They are considered to be true children of the Mountain God. They defy rank, and are above us all. We should defer to them, according to the trust scarabs."

Thor grinned. "Perhaps your religion is much more enlightened than I thought."

Bellor shook his head. "We have divine blood in us, but we are not free to leave Mephitia unless the Queen gives us permission?"

"Yes," Bree said. "If she gave you permission, your scarab would change. That would require her to perform another ceremony."

"Will she ever give us permission to leave and go back north?" Bellor asked.

"No," Bree answered quickly. "She would not endanger Mephitia like that."

"I said the vows," Drake said. "I wouldn't tell anyone anything."

"It's still too much of a risk," Bree said.

"Why go back north?" Dabarius said, shaking his head. "The Lorakian Priesthood would kill me if they knew I was a wizard. Bellor and Thor would be thrown into prison for the rest of their lives or executed, and if the Lorakians didn't imprison Drake, his own people would make him an outcast for everything he's done—riding aevians and such. We're all better off if we never go north again."

They sat in silence as blue birds and mountain jays chirruped on the rooftops above them.

"Could you go back to Arayden?" Drake asked Bree'alla.

"I'm known to the Queen's enemies in the north. It would be very dangerous. My time among the northerners is over. It's too late to bargain with the fates, Drake. We have to let go of what we were, what we wanted before, because we are all now feathers before the wind."

"I . . . " Drake looked down at his feet, jaw clenched.

"No one said this life would be easy," Bree said, her voice softer than her words. Drake gave the smallest nod, and Bree touched his shoulder for just a moment.

"Do you think the Queen still trusts you?" Dabarius asked the Wing Guardian.

"Since you spend so much time with her, I think I should be asking you, Lord Dabarius." Bree gave him a mocking bow.

"You were born in the north, weren't you?" Drake asked Bree'alla, regaining his voice, making himself think of what was now, not what might come in a future that would likely be short and painful. "Your mother was Nexan."

"She was, and my father was a Wing Guardian, a spy for Queen Rama'dara, then for General Reu'ven, before Khelen'dara took the throne a few months past."

"Did you know about who your father served?" Drake asked. "Did your mother know?"

"My mother never knew. She thought he was a merchant, a traveler in the desert who had many enemies. We were always very careful. When I was sixteen he left my mother for good.

That's when he took me to Isyrin for the first time. General Reu'ven had sent his approval for my journey south. My father wanted me to join the Servants of Amar'isis. I became a Wing Watcher when I was seventeen. Queen Rama'dara gave me a binding scarab in a ceremony like the one you participated in today. Then I went back north with my father. I could slip into the Nexan quarter, then back into the Mephitian district without anyone suspecting a thing. I became a merchant like my father, and we kept the watch on the caravans and traders, and anyone who wanted to explore the southern deserts. We fought the Iron Brotherhood. They were always stirring up trouble, convincing the poor people of Arayden to migrate north."

"Do the leaders of the Iron Brotherhood in the north know about Isyrin?" Drake asked.

"No," Bree said, "unless Draglûne himself, or his wingataurs told them."

"Would they?" Drake asked.

"I don't know," Bree said. "My father thought they might someday, to start a war between the Mephitian cities in the south and Drobin Empire."

"Cities?" Thor asked.

"There are several more, as large as Isyrin," Bree said.

"Finally, we hear the truth about this place," Thor said.

"When you were taking us here," Drake said, "couldn't you have said something? The scarab's don't really prevent you from speaking about Isyrin, do they?"

"You may feel something warm in your chest," Bree said, "before you speak about Mephitia to any outsider. It's a warning."

"A warning?" Thor said. "Surely this magic is not dangerous to us. It's not fatal, is it?"

Bree grinned at him.

"What would happen if we told the secrets of this land to someone who didn't already know them?" Drake asked.

231

"The words that you spoke during the ceremony would come true," Bree said. "Your spirit would be cursed and exiled to the Underworld upon the time of your death—which would be swift once the Servants of Amar'isis found out about the betrayal. If the secrets are told, Queen Khelen'dara will know right away, as the bond of trust was severed." She looked at them all very seriously. "None of you have to believe in our religion to be slain by our blades and cursed by our gods. Never forget that."

Drake sat pondering her ominous words in silence, and doubted they were true. He stared at his binding scarab—or trust scarab, depending on who was speaking about it. To him, you didn't need to threaten someone with the Underworld if you trusted them. The whole idea of a culture based on secrets, based on killing people who might harm you someday, was wrong. He'd agreed to their terms, but in his heart he would not keep the secrets just because of the vow. He would keep them because he'd come too far to quit, no matter the cost he had to pay. That didn't mean he had to like it. In the absence of trees, these Mephitians had all gone mad.

High Priestess Mey'lahna entered the courtyard. "The Queen is ready to speak with you now."

Bellor and Thor were the first to walk down the darkened hall into the large building beside the temple. Finally, they would hear the truth about what happened to Bölak and the *Dracken Viergur*. They'd finally get a step closer to their goal, though each step would now be taken under the shadow of an assassin's blade, and with the doom of the southern gods upon their heads.

XL

We have all said the vows in their temple. Even if some of us survive, there is no going home now. On days like this one, I find that I miss my kin nearly as much as I hate the dragon.

—Bölak Blackhammer, from the Khoram Journal

Smoky lamps and the scent of jasmine filled the dim audience hall Queen Khelen'dara had chosen for their meeting. She sat on a plush, high-backed chair with golden feather shapes sewn into the blue fabric. Her kohl-painted eyes fixed on Dabarius as Mey'lahna indicated the companions should sit on the soft couches arranged in front of the Queen, who wore a golden crown with white plumes.

High Priest Ben'khar sat on a simple wooden bench beside the young woman, pillows cast aside on the ground, as if he didn't indulge in such luxuries. Mey'lahna took up a standing position to the right of the Queen's makeshift throne. No guards were visible in the room, though Tal'mai and a few others stood outside the thick door that had been closed behind them.

Ben'khar and the Queen seemed to discuss that the companions now wore trust scarabs, as they both eyed the bronze brooches pinned to their chests.

Drake settled into the pillows beside Bree and listened to a brief exchange between the Queen and his friend, wishing once again he could speak the language.

"The Goddess Queen wishes for me to translate her words," Bree announced.

Dabarius seemed a little surprised.

Bree began her task with a somber voice, echoing the Queen's tone, though speaking in a slightly quieter voice. "High Priest Ben'khar has shared with me a secret kept by the Khebian order since the time of my grandmother, the Goddess Queen Rama'dara. He has confirmed your suspicions. The Ten Sons of Kheb did survive the battle inside Mount Kheb. They also escaped the same way you did."

"I knew it." Thor squeezed Bellor's shoulder and had an extremely satisfied look on his face.

"The Sons of Kheb returned to the palace with one surviving Khebian Priest under the cover of night. Queen Rama'dara and the High Priest of Kheb met with them and learned that a dragon had been inside the mountain, though the vile serpent had fled a short time before they entered. It is suspected that it was the Dragon of Darkness himself, but no one knew the truth of it. What is known is that wingataur demons ambushed the Ten Sons of Kheb inside the caverns. The demons were slain, but the Ten Sons of Kheb were trapped by an avalanche, likely caused by the Dragon of Darkness."

It all made sense to Drake. Draglûne had lured Bölak inside, then caused the rock fall himself. The Dragon King didn't care about a few wingataurs. They had been bait, nothing else. He glanced at Bellor and guessed the War Priest was thinking the same thing.

"My grandmother and the High Priest of Kheb decided what should be done next. They agreed with the leader of the Ten Sons of Kheb, Lord Bölak, Wielder of the Black Hammer. The Khebian Priesthood smuggled the dragon hunters out of the city and into the desert. This was done to fool the spies of the Dragon of Darkness in Isyrin, and give the Ten Sons of Kheb the chance to surprise the Dragon King. Everyone except for a handful of Khebians, and the Queen's advisors were told that the Drobin had died in the mountain.

"Until yesterday," the Queen said, "I believed the story that all of the Mephitian people believed—that the Sons of Kheb had died. My former regent, General Reu'ven, had not shared this secret with me. Though I am told that he knew the truth, and has known it for many years."

"Reu'ven knew and he still ordered us executed," Dabarius

said, so angry he wanted to break the general's fingers one at a time.

"He knew," Khelen'dara said. "My mother and grandmother were assassinated because they opposed the Dragon of Darkness. He did not want me to have the same fate."

"Great Queen," Bellor asked, "does High Priest Ben'khar know where the Ten Sons and the Earth Priests of Kheb traveled when they left Isyrin?"

"They went east, to find the lair of the Dragon of Darkness."

"Into the desert?" Bellor asked.

"Beyond the desert, to the plateau known as Far Khoram. Our people call it Old Mephitia."

"How did they travel there?" Dabarius asked. "Is there not a rift between this plateau and Far Khoram?"

"There is a rift. We call it the River of Mist. It is a wide canyon filled with a river of fog that flows north. For all of my life I believed there was no way across, but High Priest Ben'khar has informed me that there is a hidden bridge, below the mist. Khebians built the way across over a hundred years ago, and that's where the Ten Sons of Kheb, and the Khebian Priests, journeyed after leaving Isyrin."

"Great Queen, we must find this bridge," Bellor said. "Please help us."

She glanced at Dabarius. "I know you wish this," Khelen'dara hesitated, "and I will do as you ask. First, you must travel to the ruined city of Shahan. Beneath the cliffs of the city, find a staircase down, and a bridge is hidden below the clouds."

"In the Void?" Drake's curiosity was tempered with apprehension. It seemed to him that the quest would require him to commit every sin he'd been warned against. He needn't worry about Mephitian gods, his own would condemn him for his actions. The Void. He'd never hated Draglûne more.

235

"I know little of the River of Mist," Dabarius said, "but I thought there was no water and no settlements along the rift. Is that belief false, like so many others we are told in the north?"

"There were settlements," Khelen'dara said, "before the sundering of the Mephitian Empire when the Goddess Queen of Isyrin fought the God King of Mephitep."

"God King?" Thor asked, "I don't like the sound of that."

"The living vessels of Ah'usar and Amar'isis, husband and wife, made war on each other, to the shame of all the gods. Their armies met for the last time at Shahan where this plateau and the Far Khoram plateau were once connected by two bridges of stone. The bridges met on a large plateau of rock in the center of the River of Mist."

The Queen looked at High Priest Ben'khar and the old Khebian continued the tale. His voice was coarse and low. "Great Kheb, the Honored Father of Ah'usar and Amar'isis,"—Ben'khar spoke, and Bree'alla translated—"was angry at his children and punished them for their war. He sent an earthquake so strong that it broke the bridges of Shahan. He sent the island in the center of the River of Mist crashing down into the Underworld. The God King's entire army was slain, along with many of the Goddess Queen's men. She had remained on the west side of the bridge in her royal chariot and was spared.

"It is said that Great Kheb's Quake separated West and East Khoram from each other forever. After the Sundering, the wells for the cities along the River of Mist drained into the Underworld. All of the buildings had been destroyed and the people fled. The Spiteful Storm God, Shenahr, punished the folk of the New and Old Empire. He withheld the rains that had once come through the gap in the southern mountains. He annihilated the people on Far Khoram with drought and pestilence. All of the Gods turned on Old Mephitia, abandoning them for eternity. Since that time, nearly five hundred years ago, no sign has been seen of the God King's broken people. The desert has swallowed them all and only the Dragon of Darkness himself lives there now with his tribes of wingataur demons."

"The perfect hiding place for Draglûne," Bellor said.

The thought of a land filled with wingataurs and dragons made Drake more than a little nervous. He doubted all he was told, though. This could just be another, deeper level of secrets, lies, and misinformation. Just as the rest of the world didn't know about Mephitia, no one really knew about this Far Khoram place and what really went on there.

"What caused the war?" Dabarius asked.

The Queen and the High Priest exchanged a knowing glance. Khelen'dara spoke and Bree dutifully translated. "My ancestor, Queen Hetep'shya, the wife of the last God King who ruled over Isyrin, would not go to war with the Sons of Kheb." She gave a forlorn smile to Bellor and Thor. "For they had saved the lives of her people."

"Great Queen, I don't understand," Bellor said.

Khelen'dara glanced at the Khebian High Priest. "Tell them."

Ben'khar fixed his gaze on Thor and Bellor. "The prayers of the Khebian Priests brought your ancestors to the plateaus. We prayed, and the Drobin came from deep within the ground. The Sons of Kheb emerged on the plateau you call Nexus. From there, your people saved the Mephitians from their oppressors."

"How?" Bellor asked. "What oppressors?"

"From the dragons who ruled the plateaus," Khelen'dara said. "Like you, your ancestors were great hunters of dragons. Without the coming of the Drobin, the dragons would still be in control of all the plateaus. Now they dominate only one."

"One?" Thor asked.

"One." Bellor tugged on his beard.

Dabarius let out a tortured sigh and Drake knew exactly which plateau the Queen meant.

"Far Khoram," the Queen said, "the plateau where the Ten Sons of Kheb traveled forty years ago."

"Far Khoram is the domain of the Dragon of Darkness and all the surviving dragons who did not perish in the dragon wars long ago," High Priest Ben'khar said. "It is the place where he was spawned. It is the place where he has made his lair as all of the Dragon Kings have made theirs since the beginning times when the mountains were young."

The companions stood mute for a moment. All this time, they had known so little. Much had been lost through the long years, even without the layers of secrecy surrounding the desert. If the Khebians had summoned up the Drobin, where had they been before? From the look on Thor and Bellor's faces, Drake doubted they knew.

Khelen'dara said, "If you abandon your course now, you can still do the work of your gods. Defend and fortify the lands of Isyrin. Train my people in your ways of battling dragons. You will all be honored here and will do good works in the defense of my people. All of your knowledge will be preserved and if Draglûne comes here, you will have your chance to meet him in battle."

"Thank you, Great Queen," Bellor said, "for your generous offer. But he may never come here. With your permission, Far Khoram is the place where we will go, and where the Dragon King will die. Please, tell us all that you know of our enemy and where he hides."

"Many centuries ago," Khelen'dara said, "the dragons controlled all the plateaus, but now Far Khoram is their last stronghold. Draglûne may be the last of his kind."

"Great Queen," Bellor said, "my companions and I wish only to go there and find him. I formally ask for your blessing . . . as we will rid the plateaus forever of Draglûne."

"You have my blessing, and the blessing of Amar'isis," Khelen'dara said. "My mother and grandmother must be

238

avenged. This beast from the Underworld must be killed at last."

"My Beloved Queen," Dabarius glanced at the companions, suddenly aware of the immensity of his appellation, "we will do everything in our power to slay him."

"I know you will." She reached out to Dabarius for an instant, then rested her hand again on the arm of the chair.

"What more can you tell us of Far Khoram?" Dabarius asked.

"It was once the center of the Mephitian Empire," the Queen said. "The capital, Mephitep, was the home of the God King and his Solar Throne."

Meh-fee-tep, Drake thought, *Like Meh'fee'shun.*

"The Goddess Queen, Hetep'shya left her husband in Mephitep," Khelen'dara said, "and traveled here, to her home city. The history of the Sundering says that the Goddess Queen feared for her life, as she did not support an attack on the Drobin in the north. Then and now, an attack on the Drobin Empire would be pointless, and still there are those who want us to attack. The Wings of Amar'isis have traveled throughout the north. The Drobin have always been too strong. They killed scores of dragons. How could the armies of Mephitia hope to defeat them? Our only course is to keep our existence hidden. This would be the first city they found if they ever made it south.

"You must understand that Dragon Lords had been fighting with each other for centuries. They had claimed the richest territories and had pushed the Mephitian people out of the forested lands in the north. The Drobin Empire is built on the foundations that the ancient Mephitians left behind."

The Mephitians used to live in the north? Drake thought. *No wonder they worshipped trees in their temples. How ironic that they would be forced to inhabit a desert.* He also wondered if there was a connection was between Amaryllis and Amar'isis. They couldn't be the same goddess. Amaryllians hated aevians and Amar'isis had wings. It didn't make any sense.

Bree continued translating the Queen's story: "The servants of Kheb and Amar'isis had prayed for the destruction of the dragons who ruled the plateaus and enslaved the Mephitian people. Spawn of the first Dragon of Darkness fought over the land and the control of the people. My ancestors suffered terribly and were merely pawns of the dragons. There came a time when the abuse became too much for our people. Atrocities were committed by the dragons on what we call the Night of Fire. After that night the Mephitians, rich and poor, begged for help and gathered at all the temples to beg the gods for protection."

High Priest Ben'khar continued, "The Earth Priests of Kheb prayed to the Father of All Gods for deliverance. For one hundred days every novice and High Priest prayed every hour of the day and night. On the one-hundred and sixth day their prayers were answered. The Mountain God sent his children to strike at His enemies.

"The Sons of Kheb appeared inside the Quiet Mountain, the dormant volcano on what you call the Nexus plateau. To escape the mountain they had to defeat the dragons living inside the vast caverns. The Drobin slew many and crushed countless clutches of eggs. The Sons of Kheb fought the dragons with steel and magic that the serpents had never faced before. The Drobin hunted the dragon spawn in their underground lairs and killed them without mercy. At around the same time the Drobin arrived, it is said that the Giergun folk arrived on the plateaus. They too possessed steel and hunted the dragons, claiming their own lands on the western plateau."

Thor and Bellor glanced at each other, making Drake think the dwarves did not agree with High Priest Ben'khar's history. Drake thought the Giergun had been the allies of the dragons for all time. Could that be untrue?

"The dragons still fought each other,"—Ben'khar gestured

with his hands, poking his fingers together—"and in only a few centuries, the dragons were cleansed from most of the north. The Drobin Empire was blessed by Kheb. The Mountain God had given the northern lands to the Drobin and their Nexan allies. War between the Mephitian and Drobin would be wrong. A sin against the Mountain God."

"The God King Ra'menek of Mephitep thought otherwise," Khelen'dara said. "There were few dragons left, and some of those became the God King's allies. He wanted to expand the Mephitian Empire into the north, and was going to use the dragons to help him."

"Excuse me, Great Queen," Bellor said. "It is more likely that the dragons were using the God King."

"You may be right, Master Bellor," the Queen said. "The God King had already sent some of his warriors north and they had been turned back by Drobin soldiers. Some believe that the survivors of the God King's advance force became the founders of the Iron Brotherhood in the north, worshipping the Dragon of Darkness as if he were a god."

"My Queen, what do you think we'll find in Old Mephitia?" Dabarius asked.

"The Storm God withheld the rain," Khelen'dara said. "The people died. It is said to be a barren place now, except for along the mountains of the southern territory where Mephitep once stood."

"Does she know the location of Draglûne's lair?" Bellor asked.

"My ancient grandmother, Queen Hetep'shya, took the Goddess Scrolls of Amar'isis with her when she fled Mephitep. They contained spells to fight the Dragon of Darkness and they mentioned that he would always come from the south. His lair was in the Underworld near the southern edge of the plateau."

Dabarius questioned the Queen about any more specifics, but there were few things known, and even her knowledge about the "southern edge of the plateau" was not certain.

The best course of action appeared to be to avoid any servants of the God King once they crossed to Far Khoram. A letter of introduction and a peace treaty from Khelen'dara to the God King would be provided them, in case they could not avoid being taken, but they hoped to remain on their own and use their wits to find Bölak and the *Dracken Viergur*, then find the lair of the Dragon King, infiltrate it and slay him. Escape and returning to Isyrin wasn't even discussed.

If they had any allies in Old Mephitia, the Khebian Priests and any surviving *Dracken Viergur* were probably the only possibilities. Avoiding the servants of the Storm God, Shenahr, would be important as well.

No information was known about how many other dragons beside Draglûne might live in Far Khoram. Once there had been several, mostly the younger spawn and breeding females who consorted with the Dragon King. Currently, Queen Khelen'dara knew nothing of how many they might find, or precisely where Draglûne was lairing.

When they arrived, they would find a way to succeed. Bellor had faith, which was of little comfort to Drake. They might face multiple dragons, but at least in a wide open desert they would see them coming.

"I wish there were more I could tell you," Queen Khelen'dara said.

"Do not worry, Great Queen," Bellor said. "We'll make our way and we'll find your enemy."

"I trust that you will," the Queen said, "and I have no doubt that you will fight bravely." She sat forward in her chair. "There is one other gift I wish from you all."

"Name it, my Queen," Dabarius said.

"I want all of you to come back." Khelen'dara's lower lip trembled for an instant. "Return to Isyrin. This will be your new home, where your families will be raised." She stared at Dabarius and touched her belly.

The wizard's eyes opened wide. Bellor and Thor looked at the floor, and Bree smiled. Khelen'dara seemed so young and innocent at that moment, wishing for a family, but she was being overly optimistic. How could they go into the Void and find the lair of Draglûne and come out again? The alicorns would not fly down there and deliver them or rescue them afterward. Dabarius's magic could not get them out. Could they somehow ascend the miles-high cliffs of the Void and escape? The chances that all of them would survive the battle with Draglûne were slim. The Queen's wish for them all to return was more like a child's fanciful dream.

"Great Queen, first we must escape Isyrin and cross the desert," Bree'alla said. "As few people as possible must know of our route, and our task. It is better if we five travel alone."

Bellor and Thor approved.

"I will leave the planning to you, Wing Guardian," the Queen told Bree'alla. "High Priest Ben'khar will provide maps and vorrels."

"Great Queen,"—Drake found the sound of his voice odd, like it didn't belong in such a place—"will you please do all you can to find out what happened to my three dogs. Two of them are not from the desert. I would gladly go and look for them myself. Please, I am responsible for their lives, and must know what happened to them."

"Master hunter," Queen Khelen'dara smiled. "You have my promise. I will find out."

He wanted to believe her. She was a sincere person. He would give her a chance, but if she didn't bring Jep and Temus to him, or news of their fate, he was going to find them on his own. They were all he had left of home.

XLI

The Wing Guardians of Amar'isis live to serve the Goddess. At times She will demand sacrifices that shake the heart. It is in those moments that a Wing Guardian proves his worth.

—from the Sacred Scrolls of Amar'isis

Bree'alla stopped abruptly in the empty hallway of the palace. Her hand latched onto the dagger at her waist. All memories of the late-night meeting she just had with High Priest Ben'khar about the journey across the Dune Sea fled from her mind.

There was only now.

The shadowy figure beckoned her to enter the pitch-black room. Bree lifted her lantern and assumed a defensive posture, hand on her blade.

Queen Khelen'dara's peered out from the chamber, her smoky eyes shining in the lantern light. "In here," the Queen whispered and motioned with her head.

Bree hesitated, then followed. No guards. No attendants. The Queen was completely alone. Khelen'dara shut the stout door very quietly then turned to face the startled Wing Guardian. The serious look on her Khelen'dara's face spoke of ill news. Candles flared to life around the room after a flick of Khelen'dara's wrist. A marble statue of the goddess stood on an ornate table at the back of the small room.

The Queen knelt in front of the statue, her knees resting on a padded strip. "Pray with me."

Bree set down her lantern and knelt beside the Queen.

"Please Mother Amar'isis," Khelen'dara prayed, "let Bree'alla, daughter of Ben'syn have strength for the task ahead of her. Give her courage to do what is right for the people of Mephitia. Let her carry out Your will and forgive her for what she must do."

The Queen's prayer unnerved Bree. What must she do?

"Wing Guardian Bree'alla,"—the Queen said and Bree's back became a little straighter—"I must order that you perform a very difficult task. What I order will ensure the safety of Mephitia and all the people who live here. You have already sacrificed so much, and you will be rewarded for this service. First, I will have your family returned from the Hotek Fortress. Your grandmother will live out her days in the comfort of her own home. I am sorry for sending her away. It was a mistake. Forgive me."

"Great Queen, of course. Thank you for this mercy. My family will never tell of the foreigners. They are as loyal as—"

"—as you are? I know you are, and I know they won't."

The Queen bowed her head to Amar'isis. "Pray for our souls."

Bree'alla did, as a bead of sweat formed on her brow. She couldn't take the silence any longer. "Great Queen, what are your orders?"

Khelen'dara sighed, then her lips moved in a silent prayer before she spoke. "You will take the foreigners to Theh'ah'nair."

Bree's sweat turned cold. "Thunderstone?" Bree translated the ancient word. "High Priest Ben'khar said we must avoid that place above all others."

"You will take them and leave them at Thunderstone," Khelen'dara ordered. "Tell them they will find water there. Arrive just before sunset. Leave them as the sun goes down. You alone will depart."

The magnitude of the Queen's betrayal made Bree's entire body go numb. She could barely keep herself from falling to the floor.

"This must be done," Khelen'dara said firmly. "It is the will of the Goddess."

"Great Queen," Bree nearly choked on the words, "*why?*"

"It is a mercy," Khelen'dara said. "I have just learned that there is no secret bridge at the city of Shahan. There is no water there either. General Reu'ven had the bridge destroyed soon after my mother was assassinated."

"How can you be so sure of this?" Bree suspected Reu'ven had lied to the Queen.

"Earlier today I spoke with three of the Khebian Priests who carried out the task. High Priest Ben'khar was never informed of it. General Reu'ven worried that the bridge could be used by assassins who would come after me—so he destroyed the bridge."

"Please, tell my friends this. We will find another way." Bree's face scrunched together. The cold flush over her body was fading, though now she felt faint.

"They may find a way across the River of Mist. I cannot have them going to Old Mephitia."

"They have your letter of introduction and the peace treaty in case we meet the God King's servants. Dabarius showed them to me today, and the royal seals you gave him."

"The Khebians found a message on west side of the bridge when they arrived there twenty years ago. They found ten dwarven skulls, and six human ones. A message had been written on the stone beside the skulls."

Bree's body started to shake. She wanted to get out of there and pretend this had never happened. "What message?"

"Your assassins failed. Ours will not." The Queen put her hand on Bree's shoulder. "It was all a mistake for me to promise them my help. I've been praying about this for many hours. If I support them, my enemies will send assassins to kill me. Mey'lahna and Reu'ven are right. We must put our own selfish desires behind us. We must do this for our people. We cannot trust these Drobin or the others. They will betray us if they have to. They will do anything to slay the Dragon of Darkness, even if it means telling the secrets of Mephitia."

Bree shook her head. Drake would never do that. Dabarius would not either. Bellor and Thor, she could not say for sure.

"I am not asking you to kill them," the Queen said. "Take them to Thunderstone and leave them. I must have your vow."

How could this be happening? Queen Khelen'dara was in love with Dabarius and she was an honorable woman.

"You have already sworn to the Black Ghost of the desert to do what must be done. You knew this might happen if you brought them here. I am your Queen, and I must have your vow. If I do not have it, I will replace you for this task."

Her whole body felt like it was made of cold lead. She knew what she had to do. Bree had to convince the Queen that she would do the job. "No, my Queen, I will do my duty. If Amar'isis has command this, Her will shall be done. You have my vow to do your will."

"I knew I could trust you," the Queen said. "You are as strong as your father. I must bless you in the name of Amar'isis." Khelen'dara touched Bree's forehead with both of her hands. Pulsing waves of magical energy spread through Bree's body. The power of the spell stunned Bree'alla, who knelt helplessly as the enchantment penetrated every part of her.

The compulsion to lead her friends to Thunderstone and then abandon them there became Bree's only thought. She could think of nothing else as the Queen sent more magic into her body, rooting it to the core of her soul.

"It is a mercy to leave them at Thunderstone," the Queen whispered. "They would die if they reached Shahan. There is nothing there. No water. No food. No bridge. You will give your friend's mercy. It should be you. It has to be you." The Queen touched Bree's binding scarab and it flared with a golden glow. "You will not tell them what you have been ordered to do. You . . . will . . . not . . . tell them. When it is over, you know what to do."

A flash of light made Bree'alla go blind for a moment. Then Khelen'dara removed her hand from Bree's head. The Wing Guardian slumped over, catching herself at the last moment before she crashed into the floor. The Queen helped her sit up, but Bree hung her head in front of the statue of Amar'isis.

"Pray for forgiveness," the Queen said as she rose to her feet. "It must be done, for the sake of all the people of Mephitia. Leave them at Thunderstone."

The words echoed in Bree's mind as the Queen left the room.

Leave them at Thunderstone.

Over and over she heard the young Queen's voice telling her to murder her friends. To murder Drake. To betray them like the traitor they thought she was when they were in the north. It was driving her mad and she focused on the statue of Amar'isis, praying for forgiveness. The candles in the room had gone out when the Queen left, and finally Bree's lantern died, the oil burned. The Wing Guardian prayed in the darkness. The pain in her knees from kneeling for hours seemed like a minor punishment for the wrong she was going to commit. She was going to kill her friends, and the first man she thought she could really love.

XLII

She bids us farewell and we leave with her Priests of Kheb. Even if we succeed, she may be killed while we are away. Draglûne's assassins may visit her, or perhaps one of her own advisors will put a dagger in her back. My closest friend, Nalak, counsels that she is sending us off to die in the Khoram wasteland. I do not agree with him. Queen Rama'dara is our friend, and if we fail, she will not survive another year on her winged throne.

—Bölak Blackhammer, from the Khoram Journal

Bree'alla walked stiffly toward Drake, the dwarves, and the wagon that would take them secretly out of the palace in the predawn hours. The harsh stink of the four vorrels hitched to the wagon caused her exhausted and beaten mind to awaken a little more.

"You're bleeding." Drake noticed the blood on her knees and knelt to look at them. He gently held the back of her calf. "What happened? I was worried about you last night."

Her mouth felt like she had inhaled all the sand in the Khoram Desert. "I was . . . praying."

"On a floor with sharp stones?"

"I tripped . . . " It was true. She had fallen when she tried to walk out of the shrine room. After hours of being on her knees she could barely walk at first. Perhaps it would have been better to lie there and wait for someone to find her. She may have been able to delay the trip into the desert.

Bellor looked her up and down and had a very concerned expression. Thor just yawned and leaned against the wagon with one eyebrow raised.

Queen Khelen'dara embraced Dabarius in a dark corner of the stable. The sight of the backstabbing young woman sent a burst of energy into Bree'alla's exhausted body. "Where's my sword?"

"Here." Drake lifted her slender longsword, *Wingblade* out of the wagon. Bree buckled the belt around her waist, rested her hand on the pommel, and calculated her chances of killing the Goddess Queen of Isyrin. After she was dead, what would happen to Mephitia? Bree's life didn't matter, but if Khelen'dara was killed now her friends would never leave the palace. She had to stay her sword and do the bidding of her Queen.

Captain Tal'mai guarded the large doors of the royal stable. He was the only bodyguard present and he was too far away to stop Bree. He had dressed himself in a peasant's robe, and she assumed he would be driving them out of the city.

High Priestess Mey'lahna stood near the wagon and was no threat that far away. Dabarius and the Queen herself would be Bree's only obstacles.

Dabarius had his arm over the Khelen'dara's shoulder as they walked slowly toward the wagon. The young woman's expression was a mask of sorrow, and tears had smeared the kohl around her eyes. Khelen'dara suddenly stopped and hugged Dabarius, exposing her back to Bree'alla.

"Promise me again," the Queen sounded utterly devastated.

"I'm coming back, Dara. I swear to you. I am coming back."

They hugged each other again, and the Queen cried silently as she buried her face in his neck.

It made Bree'alla want to vomit the bitter acid in her stomach when she heard the Queen's lies.

Then something ran down Bree'alla's cheeks. She felt flushed and full of rage. All she had to do was draw her sword and cut Khelen'dara's head from her body. Not even Mey'lahna or Bellor could heal the royal bitch after that.

Drake wrapped his arms around Bree, hugging her and preventing her attack.

250

Let me go! Bree wanted to shout. Instead, she let Drake hold her. His arms gave her the only comfort she might ever feel again. Once he let go, she would attack Khelen'dara. Then she would be captured, tortured, and executed—her spirit banished for all time to the Underworld.

Dabarius whispered something to the Queen. She nodded her head as she stared up at his shiny eyes. Hand in hand, Khelen'dara and Dabarius walked right toward Bree. Drake let go, and the Queen hugged Bree'alla. The young woman's perfume was flowery sweet and made Bree sick.

"You are my best Wing Guardian," Khelen'dara said, as she held back tears and pulled away to make eye contact with Bree. "I have complete faith that you will do what you must."

The words hit Bree like a club. How could she kill this wretched creature? Khelen'dara's own guilt would be a much worse punishment. Bree could see it in her tear-filled eyes as she pulled away. Regret would grind Khelen'dara's heart into a fine powder that would blow away in the wind.

"Thank you for telling me about my dogs," Drake told the Queen, his voice filled with sadness. "I wish it would have been better news, but at least I know what happened to them."

"I am so sorry my desert rangers had such ill news," Khelen'dara said, after Dabarius translated.

Drake bowed to Khelen'dara, then helped Bree get into the covered room in the back of the wagon.

"Sit beside me, lass," Bellor patted the bench. The old dwarf and Drake sat to either side of her, while Thor and Dabarius sat on the opposite bench.

Bree sniffed the tears that had collected in her nose and wiped her face.

"Parting from those you love is always painful," Bellor told Bree. "No matter what happens now, the moments you've had together cannot be taken away. They will always be in your memory. Treasure them."

251

Or curse them, Bree thought, wishing she could forget the Queen's orders, and wondering why her friends had misread the whole situation. Did they not know her at all? Or rather the Queen was just too good at keeping things hidden.

Khelen'dara held onto Dabarius's hand, looking like a callow girl faced with a terrible loss, not the Goddess Queen of the entire Mephitian Empire. She finally pulled away and waved farewell as Captain Tal'mai shut the door.

Bree'alla decided then. That was the last time she would ever see the Queen or the city of Isyrin again. Her family had suffered enough serving Mephitia. The secrets and lies had torn apart her parents and now her father was dead—because of his service to Mephitia. Her grandmother would endure terribly because of her, even if the Queen kept her word and returned the old woman home.

This was all too much. Bree would carry out the Queen's vile order—how could she not?—then she would throw herself into the Void near Shahan. Her soul was already damned for all of the blood on her hands. She might as well jump and see the Underworld with her own eyes before her spirit would be imprisoned there until the end of time. The cold mist seemed to fly around her face, clouding her vision, even now. She was no more alive than the demonic ghost that Drake had told her of after his time within the tombs. One last, terrible task, and she would be gone, having never really loved, never really trusted. Her works were made of sand, meaning nothing, changing nothing. She'd caused nothing but pain. Bree'alla was glad that her father had not lived to see this day.

PART TWO

THE RIVER OF MIST

XLIII

We shall find Draglûne in Far Khoram or wherever he hides.

—Bölak Blackhammer, from the Khoram Journal

Vultures circled over a carcass in the distance, and Drake steeled himself against what he expected to find. Alone, except for a pair of vorrels he had strung together, he rode toward the scavengers, wishing and praying that whatever he found was not the missing dogs.

They had survived the soldiers who had taken him and his friends captive at Zah'dah's house, but how could they have survived this bleak place? The sun had baked him mercilessly for two days as he explored the flatlands ease of Isyrin, and just west of the Shattered Hills. He was well provisioned and had maps of where to find water, but the dogs had nothing. They had lived in the green places near the farms for a week, but they had been driven off by desert rangers and frightened farmers.

If Drake didn't find them, the Khoram would claim them for certain. His friends may have understood his reasons for coming, but he couldn't talk to them before he left. He had left a note, but Bellor would never have allowed him to go off alone if he had told him his intentions.

They would forgive him when he returned, Drake kept telling himself. He knew their proposed route, and had a map with all the places where they could replenish their water supplies on the way to Shahan.

This was only a short detour.

Another vulture descended and began feasting with the others at the site of the body, or bodies. He was still too far away to tell what they were eating. Drake prayed to Amaryllis that he would not find the dogs. This was probably a kill that the dogs had made, and the scavengers were cleaning the bones. Somewhere close by he would find all three dogs sleeping in some shade, and then he would catch up to his friends. They would follow the route through the deep desert and everything would work out well.

If only the dogs had stayed in the habitable areas in the south. According to the Queen, the rangers patrolling the area had responded to reports of doglike demons terrorizing farms, and killing livestock. Some thought they were lions—as there were no dogs as large or fierce as Jep and Temus in the Khoram Desert. There weren't supposed to be any lions left either, as they had been hunted to extinction or driven to the Thorngrass Plains north of Arayden. The superstitious Mephitians thought the large dogs were servants of Kheb, the god of earth and the dead. Dogs would devour the souls of the living—at least those who had lived wicked lives.

Superstitious vrelkshit, but the superstitious Mephitians had forced his dogs into this brutal patch of dirt to die of heat and thirst. He couldn't swallow the lump in his throat, and tried not to think about their big feet and droopy faces.

He pulled himself together and tapped his mount's flank, urging it onward toward the feeding aevians not far away now.

A few palm trees and some green plants hugged a wash near the place where the scavengers congregated. Bree'alla had told him about a dry oasis out here. This must be it.

Over a dozen vultures had landed on the ground, and feasted on three separate carcasses.

The lump in Drake's throat got a lot bigger.

He stood in his stirrups, trying to get a better look, and hoping he did not see the bodies of Jep or Temus. The vultures blocked his view, as some of them had spread their wings as they fought for a feeding position.

He rode closer.

Both his vorrels became agitated, snorting and trying to turn away from the kill site. The taps he delivered to his mount's flanks became more forceful and the animal reluctantly complied.

Drake thought about loading his crossbow and shooting a couple of the ugly pink headed birds. Their hooked beaks tore into flesh, then stared at him as they swallowed. If they were eating his dogs he would kill as many of them as he could before the rest flew away.

His vorrels snorted and balked when they got within a stone's throw. Drake dismounted and pulled the two animals forward, coaxing them with soft words, as Bree had taught him.

The vultures began hopping away from the carcasses, spreading their huge black wings and squawking at him. Drake got a good look at what they had been eating. He took in the horrible scene and vomit filled his throat.

XLIV

Friends, I'm going to find the dogs. I'm sorry to leave like this. I hope you'll understand. I'll search for them for two full days, then I'll catch up to you. My trust scarab will give me safe passage if I meet any Mephitian rangers. Don't worry. I know your route. I'm traveling light, so I'll see you in four days, maybe five. I will look for your tracks and for your fire in the night.

—Drake of Cliffton, note left behind on the back of a map

Bree'alla hoped that Drake would never find her. Two days had passed since Captain Tal'mai had delivered them to the waiting herd of vorrels in the desert east of Isyrin. They proceeded to ride into the hottest area of desert in all of New Mephitia. She picked routes in the sand where their tracks would be gone by the next day if the wind blew.

He was back there somewhere, but she saw no sign of the man she had grown to love. Either he was still searching for the dogs, or he was delayed in the Shattered Hills, following the route she had said she was going to take. Without the knowledge she had been given by High Priest Ben'khar, or detailed Khebian maps, Drake would wander aimlessly through the confusing canyons.

If her prayers to Amar'isis came true, he would not be with them when they reached Thunderstone. She had to hope. It was all that kept her from going mad. The order from the Queen and compulsion spell that cemented it combined and made her feel like her head was in a vice being slowly crushed. No matter how much she wanted to deviate from the command, her sense of duty to Mephitia and the Queen, coupled with the unyielding magic, prevented her from doing anything else.

Part of her had wanted to go after Drake on the morning they all learned he was gone, but she had resisted. The Khoram would claim him, she told herself, and she would fulfill her orders, which did not include hunting for anyone who left the caravan.

She would fulfill her orders and she guided Bellor, Thor, and Dabarius due east toward the Dune Sea. The terrain was so wide open that she was able to convince Bellor that Drake would easily be able to see them and catch up—especially at the pace they were going.

She was even able to truthfully say that she had gone over their route in detail with Drake. He knew exactly what their course would be. She said she had wondered why he had been insistent on learning the landmarks.

Now they all knew. He was planning to sneak off, then catch up once he found the dogs. At least that was what his note had said.

He would have been able to find them if she hadn't changed their entire route. Now he would die in the desert. That's what she told herself to placate the compulsion in her mind, even though she had a sliver of belief that he would survive.

How long the Drobin would allow their caravan of ten heavily burdened vorrels to continue ahead without their sharpshooting crossbowman, she had no idea. For now, she would just keep riding, and continue to ignore anything said to her. She would build a wall of silence between herself and the others, who she began to think of as her enemies.

It was better that way.

Leading your enemies to their deaths was much easier than leading your friends. Bree hated herself so much, and wanted more than anything to find a cobra and let it bite her on the leg.

XLV

The Khebians steer a straight course across the wasteland, using the stars at night, and the sun during the day. Somehow they have found the waterholes and oases. We all pray together when we find them, even if the water is dirty or tastes of salt. Wulf produced an ale cup from his pack and made a great show of drinking "Drobin Ale" at the side of a brackish pool. The Viergur spirit is still strong, though we are all parched as old leather.

—Bölak Blackhammer, from the Khoram Journal

Dabarius had little faith they would find enough water to cross the Dune Sea. Even if Bree'alla managed to find all the oases in the deep desert there were no assurances they would find water. Khelen'dara had warned him that some of the water-holes might be empty. If rain did not refill them they would dry out eventually, and rain did not fall for years sometimes in this burning place filled with scorpions and snakes.

No, he would prepare for the worst and that meant carrying extra water for himself and his friends. Khelen'dara had let him study the Sacred Scrolls of Amar'isis and one of those ancient spells would keep them all alive. He had practiced it once in the palace on the enchanted vessel she'd provided, and it had worked perfectly. He had managed to fill a small ceramic jug with twenty or more times its capacity, though it felt as if it only contained its usual weight in water. He'd enjoyed pouring it out over her body in the bath, as since she hadn't known he'd mastered the spell, Dara wasn't expecting how long it took for him to finish rinsing her off. They'd had a good laugh, and she'd supplied him with fourteen such vessels, specially enchanted by her personally for carrying extra water. Each of the small jugs—waterskins sadly couldn't hold the enchantment—were full and Dabarius would keep them in reserve.

He would have never told any of his friends about them, but as Thor unloaded a vorrel—doing Drake's usual job—one of the jugs slipped from the padded bag protecting it. If it had landed in the sand there wouldn't have been a problem, but it landed on a sharp rock and a crack formed across the base.

"Clumsy fool," Dabarius snatched up the damaged jug trying to think of a way to fix it.

"I'm a fool?" Thor shook his head. "Why do you insist on carrying stoneware pots? They're far too fragile and heavy. Water bags are the only sensible thing to carry out here."

Dabarius was about to start pouring the water into one of the empty bags when the crack expanded. A flash of bright light along the fracture preceded the jug exploding and showering at least a dozen gallons of water all over them both. The loud sound brought Bellor and Bree'alla running.

"What happened?" Bellor asked, stunned at the large muddy patch on the ground, and his dripping wet friends, luckily unhurt by the shards of pottery.

Dabarius was forced to explain, and Bellor chastised him quite soundly. The remaining eight jugs were soon wrapped with extra padding, and Dabarius would load and unload them for the rest of their trek. He would do so without complaint. Instead, he would think of the Queen of Isyrin. She was the most beautiful, intelligent, mysterious, and fascinating woman he'd ever known. Someday, he'd return to her, when he had personally eliminated the threat to her rule.

At the end of his journey he would free Master Oberon from Draglûne's clutches, or avenge him if he was indeed dead. The Dragon King would be killed, as they would find a way to slay him even if they didn't have the alicorn horn, which Dabarius had hoped to fashion into the tips of several crossbow bolts that would be lethal to any dragon. Pity General Reu'ven hadn't been found, and Dabarius wondered if Reu'ven knew how important that horn was to their mission to slay Draglûne.

261

Bellor was confident they could find a way to kill their enemy, and then Dabarius would be free to do whatever he wanted. He would never have to go into the north again. He would never see another dwarf, or worry about them coming for his head because of the magic he knew. He would live on his family's land outside Isyrin or in the palace with Dara, and he would take long baths with her, and never have to worry about running out of water.

XLVI

The Giergun stopped attacking so much at night when the dogs
became part of the regiment. They could hear or smell the enemy
coming long before we had any notion they were out there crawling through the brush with black-stained steel Kierka knives. In
skirmish warfare, a good dog is worth ten men.

—Gavin Bloodstone, from the Bloodstone Chronicles

The gaping empty eye sockets and punctured entrails made
Drake want to wretch. He forced himself to swallow the stream
of bitter vomit rising in his throat. Even in that moment of horror he knew the water and food was too precious to waste. He
turned away from the mostly eaten bodies of the three Mephitian men and took a slow breath. He took a swig from his waterskin to rinse the bad taste from his mouth. When he had
composed himself he turned back to the corpses. At least they
weren't the dogs, or his companions.

The vultures hopped away as he edged closer, eying him
suspiciously and squawking. Blood and bits of human flesh
coated their hooked beaks. The smell was atrocious and he
covered his nose and mouth with his dust scarf while keeping
a strong grip on the guide rope tied to the pair of vorrels.

As he inspected the bodies more closely he realized that all
three had more than one arrow sticking out of them. The long
shafted arrows had white and black fletchings. One man had
a wound across his neck, as if it had been cut by a blade, and
all of them had their hands bound behind their backs.

He instantly thought of Shai'keen, the Iron Brotherhood
assassin that had been following the companions south. This
was close to the border, and who else could have done this?
Who were these men? Vorrel herders? Desert rangers? He had
no idea.

An oval shaped piece of metal dangled from the torn clothing of one of the men. Drake used his Kierka knife to cut it free and turned it over in the dirt. It was a trust scarab, completely devoid of any color. The dull piece of metal kept its shape, that of a desert beetle, but it had lost all of the decoration he knew it must have had at one time. These men had been servants of Amar'isis, probably desert rangers.

He cleaned off his blade in the sand before sheathing it, and touched his own scarab, wondering how long it would take for it to lose color if he died.

The vultures called to each other, and a few flew over his head, making the vorrels nervous. He thought about burying the men. First, he would have to tie up his vorrels in the shade by the nearby palm trees.

The birds descended to feast on the corpses when he reached the trees. The scent of death faded and the vorrels suddenly dragged him forward through the bushes. A circular pool of clear water appeared as if by magic. The vorrels started drinking immediately and Drake decided to trust their noses and let them continue. Bree had told him they would know if the water was safe, though vorrels could stomach what humans never could. He tied them securely to the trunk of a palm tree with a long rope and took his small shovel off the pack vorrel. Once he buried the dead men, he would rest in the shade for a few hours, maybe have a bath, then he would find the dogs. This was his last day. Tomorrow morning he would have to keep his word to his friends and go after the others. First, he would deny the vultures their feast.

Digging graves in sandy ground took a lot longer than he expected, though he didn't need much of a hole to bury the scant remains. He covered what was left of the men with a mound of sand, then with stones carried from a nearby hill. The vultures had harassed him during the whole process, until he'd injured one by hitting it with a rock. They kept their distance after that. He was almost finished when he heard the vorrels hollering in alarm by the oasis.

He sprinted to the trees with his Kierka in one hand and shovel in the other. Both vorrels strained to break free of their tethers, frightened of something by the pool. *At least they're not dying from drinking bad water*, he thought as he leaped over a bush prepared to defend his mounts.

Standing in the water were three of the dirtiest, hungriest, and most beautiful dogs he had ever seen. Drake dropped his weapons and splashed into the water as Jep and Temus barked excitedly and charged toward him. Skinny ran in circles through the shallow water yipping as Drake hugged and patted the whining bullmastiffs. The dogs licked him and pressed against him as he knelt in the water laughing.

Furiously wagging tails swatted him, and splashed water as he patted all three dogs.

"*Good boys. Good boys.*" Tears of joy streamed down his cheeks as he forgot about the grisly burial. All he could do was hug the dogs and thank the gods for bringing them back to him. He let Jep knock him down, and Drake splashed into the water hoping to wash himself clean and start anew.

XLVII

Drake is a responsible and capable young man. I know that if those dogs are alive, he will find them. But I should not have let him go alone. Of course, my own fears and worries are the very reason that he chose to leave unannounced. I cannot shield my young Viergur from danger, no matter how hard I may try.

—Bellor Fardelver, from the Desert Journal

Bellor built the fire on the tallest hill he could find. Thor and Dabarius had been bringing him fuel for the blaze for half the night, gathering scrub brush, vorrel dung and whatever else they could find to augment the Rune stone that powered the flames. The old War Priest stood on the side of the rocky hill, never looking into the fire behind him, so he could preserve his night vision and keep watch for Drake. The young man would be looking for them now, and until he caught up, Bellor would not leave this spot.

They had made it to the edge of the Dune Sea, and no matter what Bree'alla said, he was going no further until Drake caught up. If the young man didn't appear by tomorrow night, they were going back to look for him. Bellor never should have allowed them to proceed without Drake. It had made sense at the time, when they read the note, to let Drake try to find the dogs on his own. Now, it seemed so foolish. Thor dropped another bundle of dead brush on the fire and stood beside Bellor. "What if he isn't coming this way?" Thor asked in Drobin. "He could've gotten lost?"

"Then we'll go back and find him."

"Bree said we don't have enough water to stay here. We have to keep going or we'll run out before we can replenish our supply."

"We're not leaving him behind," Bellor said. "I was wrong to have gone on without him."

"We all agreed he would cover more ground alone."

"Bree'alla steered us to that conclusion. Why?" Bellor shook his head.

"I thought she would be the first to want to go and find him," Thor said. "It's like she doesn't want him to find us."

"She may have changed our route. Remember when we veered north out of the canyons?"

"We had shade in there," Thor said wistfully.

Bellor pondered everything that had happened since they left Isyrin, and didn't understand what was wrong with Bree'alla. After all they'd been through together, he had come to trust her. He thought the burgeoning relationship between her and Drake would only make their group stronger. Now, he wasn't so certain. The Wing Guardian had been morose and distant since they had left the city. Bellor was too old to attempt to figure out the romantic hills and valleys of a young human couple, but something had happened to Bree'alla. Without Drake, they were at her mercy, and that made Bellor very uneasy.

"Come back to us, lad. Come back safe," he whispered.

XLVIII

We were ambushed more than once in the mountains. Men died before they knew what was happening. I've often thought a quick death when you didn't see the blow coming was a good way to go.
—Gavin Bloodstone, from the Bloodstone Chronicles

Something was following him. At first, Drake thought it was just a rabbit or some other small desert creature. Skinny could see it, and watched intently from the shade of a canyon at the entrance to the Shattered Hills. The desert hound could see so much better than Drake, or Jep and Temus. Skinny was always the first to see a rabbit hiding in the distant brush. The hound would usually wait for Drake's command—usually—then he would sprint after the animal until he caught it in his jaws. He often lost interest once he caught the creature and would let Jep or Temus kill and eat the wounded prey. Skinny much preferred the chase to the kill. But what did he see behind them?

Skinny whined, his long nose pointing west into the burning flatlands. His line of sight followed the way they had just come. Jep and Temus watched as well, though they didn't lick their lips like they often did before Skinny would sprint after some game.

Then Drake saw it. A small cloud of dust rose in the distance, though the shimmering heat obscured whatever it was. They all watched for several moments before Drake could see the two riders. Whoever they were, they rode their vorrels at a fast pace during the hottest part of the day.

They had to be following Drake's trail, or the trail of his friends who had passed this way several days before. It had been easy for Drake to see the tracks left by the large caravan of vorrels that Bree and his friends took into the Khoram. He knew they had entered the Shattered Hills right where he was now.

What if it's Shai'keen? Drake thought suddenly, his spine stiffening. It could have been the assassin who killed the three desert rangers at the oasis, and now he was tracking Drake and his friends.

The wide mouth of the canyon narrowed as it went east. That was where Drake would meet them.

The two Mephitians led their vorrels through the canyon, pulling them along with guide ropes. Each man wore white desert robes and covered his mouth with a dusty scarf—similar attire to what Drake was wearing. Powerful recurve hunting bows hung from their saddles, and each man carried a dagger on his belt, in addition to slashing swords that reminded Drake of his Kierka blade. The man in the lead was staring at the ground, apparently searching for tracks in the gravel-strewn canyon.

Drake watched them from his perch behind some boulders on the side of the canyon. He had scaled a rocky hill after hiding his pair of vorrels and the dogs in a side canyon deeper within the maze of hills.

As the men passed his hiding place he saw the quivers of arrows on the other side of their saddles. The long shafted arrows had white and black feathers on them. He recognized the arrows immediately. They were the same arrows that had killed the desert rangers he had buried at the oasis. These men were the ones who had bound the rangers, tortured them, and killed them. Then they left their bodies for the vultures.

Drake took aim at the back of the second man in line. This would be his best chance. Drake's mind started to spin with questions. What if these weren't the ones? What if they were desert rangers themselves? Could they be servants of Queen Khelen'dara?

No. They're not. Don't think about it. Just pull the trigger.

What would these men do if they found Bree'alla and his friends in the desert? Would they bind them and kill them too? Would they leave their bodies to feed scavenging aevians? What if this was Shai'keen and one of the dragon cultists? His intuition told him what he had to do.

Drake pulled the first trigger, then adjusted his aim in a split second and pulled the second. Both men fell off their vorrels, pierced by the streaking bolts.

The first man lay motionless on the ground while his vorrel galloped away. The second man fell off his mount behind a rock as his vorrel ran after the other scared animal. The vorrels soon disappeared behind a bend in the canyon, though Drake could still hear the sound of their feet digging into the gravel.

With his crossbow loaded, Drake made his way down from the rocks and marched toward the men. The first was dead, but he had to make sure about the second.

Drake took a wide approach, crossbow ready, so he could not be surprised. The wounded man was still breathing as he lay on his side, gasping for air. Blood leaked out of the hole in his back and the front of his left chest. The bolt had passed straight through his torso, but somehow had missed his heart. Bright red blood flecked the man's black and gray beard, and had soaked through his tattered clothing.

The dying man finally caught sight of him and the anger in his eyes flashed hot. Then the man pointed a bloody finger at Drake.

"*Seh'fekh Shenahr.*"

He had no idea what the words meant, though he knew it wasn't good.

"*Seh'fekh Shenahr.*"

270

"What are you saying?" Drake asked in Nexan. The few words in Mephitian he knew wouldn't help now.

"*Seh'fekh Shenahr!*" The man's eyes were wild with hatred as he coughed up more blood. A sucking sound coming from the hole in the man's chest made Drake shudder and turn away. Maybe he should pull the trigger and put him out of his misery? Why didn't the man die right away? Why didn't Drake ride away and try to lose them in the canyons? He never should have ambushed them like this. He was a hunter of dragons, not an assassin who shot men in the back.

"*Seh'fekh . . . Shenahr.*"

"Be quiet!" Drake was surprised at the sound of his voice, which echoed off the walls of the canyon.

The man lay still, perhaps chastened by Drake's words. The fire went out of his eyes as he lay down his head for the last time.

Drake backed away from the man with the feeling that there was a hole in his own chest. He was alive, but he had lost something precious today and he would never have it again.

XLIX

He did not arrive last night. We burned the last of the fuel, and I used the fire stone to make light until sunrise. Something has happened or he would have been here by now.

—Bellor Fardelver, from the Desert Journal

Shadows moved across the flat surface of the desert. Bellor saw them coming closer as he stood in front of the signal fire he had lit for the second straight night. He dared hope that it was Drake riding a vorrel, and called Thor to his side. "Do you see him?"

Thor scanned the moonlit desert of small scrub brush and blackened rocks. "No, Master. I don't see—wait . . . "

They both saw movement and craned their necks forward.

"What's going on up there?" Dabarius asked from the tent shelter Bree had built beside the hill.

"Someone's coming," Thor said.

For the first time since the sun had set many hours before, Bree'alla rose from her bedroll and marched up the hill. Her expression was calm, but Bellor saw worry in her eyes.

"Throw everything we've got left onto the fire," Bellor ordered.

Thor and Dabarius put the stacks of brush they had collected onto the blaze as Bellor hiked down the hill and out into the desert. Bree'alla went with him and they both stood under the giant moon, watching the shadows that had to be a pair of vorrels trotting across the landscape.

"It might not be him," Bree said.

"Who else would be out here?" Bellor asked.

She shrugged, her hand brushing the dagger on her belt.

"If he doesn't come tonight," Bellor glanced at her, "we're going back and we'll look until we find him."

They waited in silence for a long time as the shadows came closer. No one sat upon the two vorrels that ambled along, but they were still too far away to see any details.

When they came much closer, Bellor's dwarven eyes pierced the shadow cast by the lead vorrel. A man walked there. "Is that you, lad?" Bellor called out hopefully.

"Master Bellor?" Drake's voice replied.

All the worry on the old War Priest's face went away as the young man jogged forward with Jep, Temus, and the little desert hound trailing behind him. Drake looked unhurt, but judging by his eyes, there was a grim story waiting to be told.

"Bellor!" Drake said, as the old dwarf wrapped him in a bear hug.

"Lad!" Bellor said.

"I didn't think I'd find you until tomorrow night," Drake said, "or the next day. Did you stop?"

"We did," Bellor said as he pet Jep and Temus, "and we were going to start looking for you if you didn't show up soon." Both of the dogs whined as they rubbed against Bellor, tails wagging furiously.

"The dogs found your trail, though I lost it in the canyons."

"Good for you, boys." Bellor scratched behind Jep's big ears while Drake faced Bree.

She had been standing back, saying nothing. It was as if she were a statue. Her eyes were glassy and unblinking. Drake walked forward tentatively and wrapped his arms around her. She didn't move as he hugged her tightly. Her arms finally came up and she pressed her hands into the back of his shoulders.

Thor and Dabarius arrived a moment later. Drake stepped away from Bree, his expression confused. Bellor wondered what was wrong with her for the hundredth time since they left Isyrin. He thought she would be excited to see Drake and would return to her old self—although he had hoped she would be less secretive on this trip. Bellor suddenly got the feeling that Bree was unhappy that Drake had found them. But that didn't make any sense.

"You found those *stunken mutts*, did you?" Thor laughed while Jep licked his bearded cheeks and Temus whined loudly. "You missed me, didn't you boys?"

Dabarius looked Drake over, as if sizing him up. "Finally, you show up." The wizard's sarcastic expression had the hint of a grin.

"Thanks for lighting the fire," Drake said, wondering how they had managed to find so much wood.

As they walked back toward camp Bellor sensed something was wrong with Drake. "What happened out there?"

After a long pause, Drake recounted his tale about hunting for the dogs. He told of finding and burying the bodies of the men being eaten by the vultures. They had to be desert rangers—judging by the trust scarabs they wore—and then he spoke haltingly of ambushing the two Mephitians in the canyon.

Thor gave Drake an approving look.

"Did you find out who they were?" Bellor asked.

Drake shook his head. "They weren't friends. That's all I know. They were hunting us."

"Did you learn anything about them?" Bellor asked.

"One of them said something to me before he died."

"He spoke Nexan?" Dabarius asked.

"No. Something in Mephitian."

"What?" Dabarius asked.

"He said the same words to me a few times." Drake hesitated, as if he was wishing he could forget what the man said. "He said, *Seh'fekh Shenahr*."

"*Shenahr?*" Dabarius spoke the word as if it tasted bad.

"What does that mean?" Thor asked.

"It was a curse." Bree'alla's voice came as a whisper.

Everyone stared at her.

"He was wishing upon you the Eight Curses of Shenahr. He could have been a Priest of the Storm God if he invoked Shenahr's name as he died."

"What does that mean if he is a follower of Shenahr?" Bellor asked.

"Shenahr is the enemy of the Queen of Isyrin, and the ally of Draglûne," Bree said. "Remember that those who follow Shenahr have tried to kill her in the past. Shenahrians killed Dabarius's family during the last revolt."

Dabarius glared at her.

"Eight curses," Drake whispered to himself.

"You aren't one to believe in superstition," Thor said, clapping him on the shoulder. "Men often spew curses before they die. There's no power there. It's nothing."

"I know. It's just that I've been wondering about those words . . ." Drake looked back toward the Shattered Hills.

"Did you sense any foul magic when he spoke?" Bellor asked.

Drake's eyebrows scrunched together.

"Don't worry, you would know," Bellor said, wishing it were true.

"The eight curses of Shenahr are well known in Mephitia," Bree said. "The followers of the Storm God paint them on walls, scratch them onto copper tablets, and write them on anything they can. They even put the foul words of the curse onto the offering tables of the temples of Amar'isis with the Queen's name on them."

"Perhaps we do not want to hear what they are," Bellor said. "Sometimes the mind can manifest evils that would not otherwise be there."

"No, tell me," Drake said. "I need to know."

Bree'alla looked toward the moon. "Wind. Dust. Lightning. Heat. Thirst. Hunger. Madness. Death."

They all stood in silence as the fire burned atop the hill behind them. Drake looked worried, and even the dogs seemed anxious.

"Sounds like vrelkshit to me," Thor said, trying hard to sound convinced. "Right?" he looked at Drake.

The Clifftoner nodded.

"Break camp," Bellor ordered the others, "we're getting out of here tonight." Bellor had Bree take Drake's two vorrels and Thor took the dogs and gave them some food.

The War Priest and Drake stood alone. "Kneel down, lad. I shall pray to Lorak and give you His protection and blessings."

After Drake got on his knees, Bellor began the ceremony by laying his hands on the young man's head. He blessed Drake and also tried to sense if any magical curse had been placed upon his friend. After a moment of contemplation, in his mind's eye, Bellor saw a flash of lightning in a dark sky. Was it the storm god's curse? He looked deeper, and found no evidence of dark magic affecting Drake. It must have been his imagination when he saw the lightning.

Still, something haunted the young man. Bellor had sensed the spirit of the boy lingering nearby many times ever since Cliffton. But the ghost of Drake's childhood friend wasn't malevolent. He was lost, clinging to this world, when he could go so easily to the next. The spirit hid when Bellor tried to see him then. Only a dark cord connecting Drake was visible to Bellor's ghost eye as a black tendril disappeared in the spirit world. And what was in Drake's bolt quiver that tied him to the spirit? He had suspected Drake carried something before, but now it was so obvious. Drake had something of Ethan's. That was the boy's name. Ethan. Was it a bolt that he had? No matter. Drake wasn't ready for the boy to go. When the time was right, the two friends would break the bond trapping Ethan's spirit, and allow only a golden cord to remain.

Bellor stopped probing Drake's spirit and prayed for a clear sky. He surrounded the young man with the holy light of Lorak, and wrapped him in an invisible shield of protection. When he was finished, a few moments later, he inspected his work, making certain there were no holes or gaps in the barrier.

A faint distortion caught Bellor's attention. Something unnatural colored Drake's spirit. The War Priest summoned the light of Lorak, but nothing he did could clear it away. He realized that it also touched his own spirit body. He tried his best to look where it was coming from, and when he had failed for the third time he realized it was coming from the future.

Things were so different in the spirit world. The event, or whatever it was, could not be seen now—at least by him. Bellor was no seer, no oracle who could make accurate predictions. Whatever was going to happen had been reflected back, going opposite the timestream. The vague warning conjured only more questions for Bellor. He would have to spend hours in prayer and try to look ahead. What would he see? Not the death of more of his friends? Anything but that.

He did not know what it was exactly, but the shadow of something vile was on all of them. The Dragon of Darkness knew who they were. Draglûne was looking for them, perhaps as hard as they were looking for him, and someday soon, they would come face to face.

Bellor opened his eyes, and summoned a warm smile for Drake. "Be at peace, lad. There is no curse upon you. Bless Lorak."

"Thank you, Master Bellor. I do feel better."

As he had done so many times over the past two centuries since he had become a War Priest, Bellor nodded confidently to a nervous young warrior, and pretended everything was going to be all right.

L

Wind. Dust. Lightning. Heat. Thirst. Hunger. Madness. Death.
Seh'fekh Shenahr, the eight curses of the Storm God

"It doesn't smell like water," Thor said as he finished sliding the sandblasted capstone off the ancient well shaft. The dwarf wrinkled his nose at the odor coming from the circular opening, and stepped away.

Drake stayed by one of the dead palm trees that marked what once had been a small but verdant oasis at the base of some reddish hills. He wanted no part in this little adventure that Bree had already said was pointless. The vorrels didn't smell any water, and almost all of the three-dozen trees were dead.

Bellor dropped a leather bucket on a rope into the dark hole. Bree'alla didn't even get off her vorrel. She sat in the sun, her headgear and robes covering everything except her squinting eyes.

After working the bucket around for a moment at the bottom of the shaft, Bellor pulled up the load. He immediately dropped it on the sand and jumped back. Fist-sized bright yellow scorpions skittered out of the bucket and toward Bellor's feet. He got out of the way and the creatures went off in several directions, leaving sharp tracks and drag marks where their tail scraped against the sand. Drake held Jep by the collar, keeping him and the other two dogs as far away from the scorpions as he could.

Neither Thor nor Bellor admitted they had been wrong about the well. They just sulked around the dry oasis kicking at the scorpions and speaking in Drobin to each other.

"We need to get moving," Bree'alla said.

278

"What we need to do is find some water!" Thor put his hands on his hips. "You said we were going to find some out here."

"We'll reach Theh'ah'nair in a day or so," Bree'alla said.

"Will there be water?" Thor asked.

Bree sat up straighter in her saddle, saying nothing.

"You don't know," Thor said.

"I know the wells are dry," Bree said. "Only the gods know if the cistern beneath the obelisk will have water. I am just a lowly servant of the Queen of Isyrin."

"Well, thank you for telling us." Thor flourished and bowed low to the ground. "That's the most you've said in two days."

Drake raised a hand. "Stop it. We have enough water for several more days."

"We do," Dabarius said, and patted one of the enchanted ceramic jugs. Most were empty, but two still had something in them.

"She said we would find water," Thor fumed. "We've found nothing except dry wells. Whoever picked this route is trying to kill us."

Dabarius glared at Thor. "Get on your mount or I'll drop you in that well and seal it up."

"Did you just threaten me?" Thor asked, a slight grin on his face.

"No," Dabarius shook his head from atop his mount, "I made a promise, little man."

Thor's grim laugh was cut short when a scorpion crawled toward his boot. He crushed it into the sand and smiled at Dabarius, who wrapped his scarf over his mouth.

"We're going," Drake said, then began helping the two Drobin climb atop their tall mounts. Bree got her lead vor-rel, the largest of the entire group, moving and soon the chain of seventeen animals was walking slowly across the Dune Sea.

They headed east, like they had for the past twelve blistering days and shivering nights.

Aside from Thor's random outbursts, an uncomfortable silence had held sway once again. Even the vorrels had stopped their braying complaints. The group had splintered into tiny swaying islands, separated by the distance of one or two vorrels as they all rode during the day in the long chain of stinking beasts. The daylight meal was often a solitary one, eaten in the saddle. The almonds, figs, dates, hard trail bread, and raisins filled up their stomachs, but did not bring them together. At least every night they sat around a small fire eating a hot meal of fried flat bread, lentil stew with salted meat, and Mephitian tea sweetened with honey. The Queen had provided them with the best food possible.

Bellor would always offer his prayers of thanks before their meal, then after they ate they would all gaze into the fire until Bree'alla signaled they should get going. She would say almost nothing, though she expected everyone to help load and un- load the vorrels. Drake did a larger share of the work than he needed, and tried to make the trek as easy as he could for the dwarves, who did not fare well in the heat. Jep and Temus suf- fered tremendously, their paws bloody and sore, even though Drake wrapped their feet with cloth and leather. Skinny fared the best, and was the only one among them who seemed to thrive in the scorching climate.

They had started with plenty of water, and maintained a modest pace for vorrels of around twenty to thirty miles spread over ten or more hours of travel. They adjusted their speed depending on the terrain, which shifted from dunes to rocky stretches of sharp rock, and flat stretches of blowing white sand Bree'alla called salt plains. The pace wasn't difficult, but en- during the Khoram was the most difficult thing Drake had ever done.

At least the dogs weren't going hungry. Skinny supple- mented their food with rabbits, quail, large lizards, desert squirrels, a few flightless birds, and many large snakes. The sharp-eyed desert hound would discover the snakes and bark so loudly that everyone knew what he found. Drake would shoot the horned viper, or rattlesnake through the head as soon as he got close enough. He relished the practice with his crossbow, and was amazed at how many snakes lived in the Khoram. He rarely missed and started shooting from atop his vorrel when he could get the dogs safely out of the way.

The dogs had almost been bitten several times, and once in the middle of the night as they crossed some hills, Jep found a large gray snake with flaps of skin on the side of its head flared out like a hood. The snake hissed at him as it rose up to strike.

"What is that?" Drake asked Bree as he hurried to load his crossbow.

"Cobra," Bree said, "better get the dog away from—"

The snake spit venom into Jep's face.

Bellor, Thor and even Dabarius gasped, and the dog yelped before running off and rubbing his face into the sand. Drake shot the snake from a good distance, then spent precious water cleaning out poor Jep's eyes. The bullmastiff was half-blind for a few days and Drake kept a cool rag on the dog's eyes whenever he could. Three days later, Jep was back to his rowdy self, though he did not approach snakes so brazenly anymore.

Temus and Skinny took the lead with snakes, and without the dogs keeping watch, Drake suspected many would have infiltrated their camps, especially at night. The only thing they could not prevent from getting into their camp were the small black beetles that rushed headlong into the fire. They provided some extra fuel, but the stinking sharp smell they gave off was disgusting, especially when Drake was trying to eat. They were far worse than any curdle moss he had ever smelled in the Thornclaw Forest.

The whole journey was becoming a mind-numbing and painful nightmare made up of one uncomfortable stretch that bled into the next. The sun melted Drake's willpower day after searing day. If only he could get more than a couple of hours of decent sleep at a time, he knew things would be better.

"We're stopping," Bree'alla called a halt just before midday when the sun's rays felt heaviest on Drake's skull. She followed the same pattern since entering the desert, always stopping before noon, and resting during the hottest hours of the day. Drake pitched Master Bellor's shade tent, and then helped unload the vorrels. The smelly beasts lay their long necks down and rested. Some of them moaned, protesting that they hadn't had much water in nearly four days. Drake tried to ignore them and hoped he would get a few hours of sleep before they would start again just before sunset.

He set up his tent near Bree, hoping she would say something to him. She didn't even look at him and turned away. He watched the wind tousle her curly, dark red hair, which she would always put up in a bun, exposing the back of her neck.

As the afternoon went on, he felt like he was sitting too close to a campfire. No matter what he did, there was no escape from the heat. Even under the shade of the thick tents, the temperature was tremendously high. His skin felt so dry and any sweat instantly evaporated.

Temus whined, drawing Drake's attention. The big bull-mastiff rolled onto his back, the dog's legs moving like he was running after something. Jep, Temus, and Skinny had their own tent, pitched over the holes they always dug in the ground. The dogs knew instinctively to dig down to the cooler earth, then Drake would put a tent over them. He liked to be near them, but it was too hot to sleep anywhere near the dogs' warm bodies, except during the few times Bree allowed them all to actually sleep at night. Without fail, except during the one extended sandstorm, Bree kept them riding all night long, and navigated by the stars under the massive moon that provided more than adequate light.

Drake tried to sleep, and instead found himself once again watching Bree'alla. She tossed and turned a lot more on this trip than she had when they'd trekked from the Cave of Wyrms. He wanted to go and comfort her, but he held back. The few times he had tried, she had coldly told him to go back to his tent and rest. After he'd survived Mount Kheb, he thought she really cared about him. Now she was pushing him away.

Perhaps it was all for the best. Even if he was never going back to Cliffton, he should stay true to Jaena. He closed his eyes and remembered when they had climbed into the big cover tree in the village garden when they were twelve. They held hands until the sun went down and then he kissed her on the cheek after he walked her home. Someday, when he was in the Afterlife, they would be together again.

Groggy and exhausted, Drake sat astride his vorrel as the endless trek continued. Later, after hours of travel, he was thrilled to finally get off the irritable animal for a rest during the cool hours after midnight.

Thor and Bellor prepared the meal while Drake fed the vorrels the last of the grain they had brought along. From now on, the animals would have to live off their three humps of fat and whatever plants they found. He wasn't sure if he should give them any water and went to find Bree'alla. He'd learned a lot about taking care of vorrels, though he wanted her to make this decision.

She was nowhere around the camp, and after a quick search he spotted her footprints in the sand going over the swell of a dune. She was probably relieving herself and he kept himself busy for a few more minutes and watered the dogs,

283

letting them stick their faces into the watertight bags he had fashioned so they wouldn't waste a single drop of the precious liquid.

When Bree still didn't return he hiked up the dune following her tracks. Jep and Temus got up to follow him. "Stay. No. Stay." They did, their sad eyes looking away from him. Drake climbed over the dune, wondering what the strange long marks in the sand were beside her tracks on the way down the other side. He hiked over the next dune and realized the mark was from *Wingblade's* scabbard, which she usually kept on her vorrel.

Why was she carrying her sword?

He jogged up the next hill much faster, glad he was carrying his crossbow, then stopped dead when he reached the crest. Bree stood on a patch of rocky ground at the bottom of the dune. She walked around the stones holding her sword by the scabbard, her belt discarded behind her. What was she looking at?

Bree drew *Wingblade* and tossed the scabbard into the sand. The blade reflected the moonlight for an instant as she knelt down and set the handle firmly into the rocks, wedging it in deep, the tip pointing up at a steep angle. It didn't look like some religious ceremony, and had to be related to her strange mood since leaving Isyrin.

She stood again, hands on her hips, and seemed to admire her work. She tested how strongly the sword was set in the ground and Drake had a terrible thought. He could not look away as she held the sharp tip of the longsword, and pressed it under her sternum, aiming toward her heart. Bree appeared to be about to lean into the blade and impale herself.

No, she wouldn't do that.

Bree paused, and looked up at the moon. Her lips moved, but he could not hear her. By the gods, she was praying! She was going to kill herself.

He had to stop her.

"*Bree!*" Drake shouted as he slid and ran down the steep dune his heart in this throat.

She turned her sad face toward him. The pain in her eyes scared him more than seeing the sword about to pierce her body. He reached the bottom of the hill, two paces in front of her.

Bree's mouth moved as if she was going to say something. Only a tortured sound escaped her lips.

"What are you doing?" Drake reached out, stepping closer.

Her breath came through clenched teeth as she sucked in air. She wasn't going to stop. She was going to kill herself right in front of him.

He thought of Ethan. His best friend had let go of the cliff, and fallen into the Void. Drake could have saved him. If only he'd said the right thing, acted quicker. Instead, his adopted brother had died. Drake looked Bree in the eyes and spoke as strongly as he ever had, "You are *not* going to do this."

Bree slowly shook her head. Her body pressed a little more against the sword. A drop of blood ran down the channel that ran the length of the blade. "I have to."

"Tell me why," Drake demanded, stepping closer, his mind still tumbling down the dune and searching for answers.

"Because I love you," she said, and pulled away from the sword. For an instant he thought she was backing off, abandoning this madness.

Then he realized Bree was positioning herself to gain momentum before throwing herself onto the blade. Drake sprang toward her and kicked the handle of the weapon as hard as he could when she threw herself forward. Bree fell onto her belly, the sharp tip slicing along her rib cage.

He rolled onto her trembling body and pinned her wrists to the ground. She fought him and struggled with a primal ferocity, but he pulled her close and rocked her back and forth, whispering that she was going to be all right. After a moment she stopped and finally opened her eyes. She looked at him with a confused, and agonizingly sad expression.

Drake inspected the scratch across her abdomen, pressed his scarf against the wound. Tiny rivulets of blood ran down from it and he wiped them away.

"You should have let me die." Bree choked out the words.

"I would never let that happen." He hugged her close, and she wept silently, the tears coming slowly, like blood from a wound. Drake sat up and pressed her back against his chest, keeping his arms securely around her.

They lay there for a long time in the soft sand until the tears stopped.

"Are you going to tell me what's going on?" Drake wiped her cheeks.

"I . . . can't." Her face crumpled again. She shook her head from shoulder to shoulder.

Thunder rumbled in the distance. They both looked up. He thought of rain, though she reacted with concern, not hope.

"Bree, what's happening to you?"

"Leave me here. Go on alone."

"I don't know what's wrong, but I'm not going to leave you. I'm going to take you back to the others. We're going to sort this out. Bellor will know what to do." He pulled her to her feet and retrieved her sword, belt, and the scabbard. He carried the blade until they were on the dune beside the camp, then he stabbed it into the sand. He took her elbows in his hands. "Promise me that you will not harm yourself."

She shook her head.

"Listen." He made Bree look into his eyes. "I would rather be dead and gone than watch you do this to yourself. If I could take this pain for you, whatever it is, I would."

She shook her head again, her thin eyebrows coming together. "Why? Why do you have to say these things?"

286

"Because I love you." Drake's eyes softened and he let go of her arms. "Don't you understand me yet?" He wanted to say, *I would die for you.*

Her lips pressed together as she fought not to cry.

"Bree, promise me you will not hurt yourself."

She nodded. "Only if you will not tell them what happened."

He hesitated. Bellor should be told about this, but he had to agree with her for now. "All right. I won't."

She wiped her face and sniffed until her nose was clear, then they walked toward the camp. The smell of the frying bread and cooking stew permeated the air. She put *Wingblade* beside her saddle and sat down next to Drake by the fire. The other companions eyed Drake and Bree, obviously wondering what had happened. Surely they noticed the marks her tears had made on her face as they washed away the dust from her skin.

After a moment of terribly uncomfortable silence for Drake, Bellor asked, "Did you hear the thunder?"

Drake nodded, while Bree sipped some tea.

"Perhaps we'll have some rain?" Thor smiled, lifting a hand as if to feel falling drops.

Bree shook her head. "You won't feel any rain here."

"Where then?" Dabarius asked.

"Theh'ah'nair," she said.

Dabarius grinned. "Now you finally tell us something about this desert."

"What about the thunder?" Thor asked. "I heard some last night as well. There must be rain clouds if it's thundering."

"This desert was blighted by the spiteful Storm God, Shenahr long ago," Bree said. "It never rains here."

"But there is thunder," Bellor said.

"Yes," Bree nodded. "There is always thunder."

LI

The Khebians have steered us away from the black obelisk. They claim it poses a danger the likes of which we would have never imagined.

—Bölak Blackhammer, from the Khoram Journal

Dozens of gray carved stones as large as houses poked out of the sand of the Khoram. On top of each was a six-foot-tall obelisk of smooth black stone fused to the rock. If Bree'alla's description of was accurate, the obelisks were all smaller versions of Theh'ah'nair.

The significance of them was not obvious until Skinny found the first of the caves, carved into one of the large rocks by chisel. Drake killed the viper inside the entrance and Thor went in to investigate. The rock had been hollowed out, and a vast sand-filled basin lay beneath the upper chamber.

Thor began to dig and the three dogs helped him clear away some of the sand.

"Water was stored here," Bellor said, "It was a cistern."

"How can you tell?" Drake asked.

"There are water marks on the stone? See?" Bellor touched the white lines on the wall.

"Should we dig down?" Thor asked. "Maybe there's water at the bottom of this."

"The vorrels don't smell any here." Dabarius knelt at the entrance.

"He's right," Drake said. "We should keep going to Theh'ah'nair. There's a cistern there that will hopefully have water in it."

Thor shook his head. "According to Bree it will. I'll not believe that until I've drunk some of this water she's told you about."

Drake walked away from the cave and left Dabarius to help the dwarves mount their vorrels. He looked at her, sitting on the second vorrel in the chain with shoulders slumped forward.

"We found an old cistern," Drake said. "It's a good sign. We must be close to Theh'ah'nair." He smiled, but saw no reaction in Bree.

How could he lead them to Theh'ah'nair, then to Shahan? Following the same course Bree had laid out was his only solution. Two weeks ago she had showed him which stars to follow, and how to use the sun during the day, but he wasn't an expert on navigating in the desert.

He had been forced to take over the guiding duties as Bree would do nothing since the insanity at the dune. She had even refused to mount her vorrel. Drake finally had to physically put her on one of the most docile mounts, but she'd fallen off when the beast stood up. He had to tie the reigns to her wrists and supervise the next attempt, as she would not climb into the saddle. The others had watched them with shocked expressions.

Bellor made her drink extra water, and eat extra rations, saying she may have become dehydrated, and like all of them, overly sleep deprived. They all knew it wasn't either of those things. What had affected her, Bellor could not say for sure.

Drake had not betrayed her trust and revealed what had really happened. He prayed that whatever it was would pass, hopefully soon, and worried that if he did tell the others, Bree would do something drastic and he wouldn't be able to stop her. If she didn't improve in a day or so he would have to tell Bellor the truth. The kindly old Priest would find some way to help her. Perhaps Bree was realizing the futility of their mission? Trying to find a way to cross the Void and face the Dragon of Darkness on his home plateau was suicide, though no one would admit to that harsh reality. Better for them to focus on the next step in their journey; get water from the cistern at Theh'ah'nair as Bree had planned all along, though he wondered if she was lying about that. Was there water? There had to be, and they would find it then ride along the edge of the River of Mist and find Shahan, and the way across the Void.

Later that day, the companions stopped at another of the sand-filled cisterns carved into the black rock. They had passed many and Dabarius said that the land had not always been so barren. Rains had once been plentiful and great fields of wild wheat had grown there—according to the Queen Khelen'dara.

"What else did she tell you about this area when you were staying in her chambers?" Thor asked.

"Not much else," Dabarius said.

"Too busy to go over our route with her, were you?" Thor asked.

"She said she would not like to come out here, herself," Dabarius said, "and that we should be careful, as the gods had cursed this stretch of desert."

Drake got the string of vorrels and his friends moving as a warm wind began blowing from the east. They rode straight into it, and nearly blind, Drake hoped he was still going in the right direction. When the dust began to settle he caught a glimpse of a tower of shiny black stone. It had to be Theh'ah'nair, which looked to be quite close. Soon they would rest for an entire night and try to recover from the long crossing of the Dune Sea.

The distance was elusive, and after an hour of travel in the eye-scraping wind, they had not reached the obelisk. It was further and bigger than Drake had realized. It was massive. No matter how off course they had become, he still would have seen it. Perhaps this was why Bree had decided to let him lead.

Near sunset, the companions stopped on a dune to gaze at the base of the titanic monolith, well over two hundred feet tall. The four-sided needle jutted from a sharply sloped hill of rock and sand. The obelisk was much larger than those at the palace of Isyrin and Drake could hardly fathom how difficult it would have been to construct it, though there had to be more than one piece of rock fitted together to form the tower. How could anyone have cut it from a single piece of stone?

Once they had discovered the entrance to the obelisk and found the cistern, they would take a day or more to rest and recover. Bree would tell him what was wrong, or Bellor would be told the whole truth. That's how he would approach it. All he had to do now was get them to the top of the hill and find a nice cool place to rest for the night. Dividing up the larger things into little, reachable, understandable steps—it was the only way he knew to keep going. Otherwise, he'd be thinking of throwing himself on a sword, too. Maybe, if he could just talk to Bree about it, he could bring her out of her bleak mood. One step, then another. That was the only way.

The companions approached the obelisk after the sun had already started to dip below the ridge behind them. Bree was still tight-lipped, but she nodded her head when Drake asked if this was Theh'ah'nair.

The wind, which had never died away, blew with a fierce vengeance as the sunlight faded. Fine dust filled the air and low gray clouds blew toward them from the east where the River of Mist lay. With any luck, Drake thought, as he stared at the clouds, it would rain a lot.

The companions tied their scarves around their mouths and squinted to keep the dirt from their eyes. The dogs ran up the steep hill toward the tower and Drake urged the lead vorrel to follow. He got the animals moving and realized how much he wanted to reach the top of the hill. He had the feeling that when they reached the obelisk all of their problems would melt away. The fatigue in the vorrels seemed to be less as well, and they climbed with renewed vigor. *They must smell water.*

The light had changed and now Drake noticed there were large symbols carved into the surface of the shiny rock. The symbols were dull, not polished like the rest of the stone, and reminded Drake of the pictures inside the cartouches he'd seen in Isyrin. He would have to ask Dabarius if he could read them. The strangest thing he noticed was a metallic spear sticking out of the very tip of the spire.

Drake dismounted part way up, and signaled for everyone else to follow suit. Riding up the hill at such a steep angle would be difficult. He took Bree's hand and she slid off her mount after some coaxing. He caught her, and she held onto him, her face buried against his shoulder. He tried to pull away, but she held him in place.

"Please, Bree'alla. Enough of this. What's wrong?"

She shook her head, and finally released her hold.

"Come with me," Drake said. He took her hand, and with his other tugged the lead vorrel up the hill with the guide rope.

Bree stopped suddenly as the wind picked up. Everyone shielded their eyes. The wind moaned as it ripped around the obelisk.

"Talk to me," Drake said, blocking his face with his hand as Bree refused to keep going. She stood immobile for a long moment.

She squeezed his hand and he felt her nails digging into him. She wanted to tell him something and Drake got nose to nose with Bree. "What's so wrong that you'd rather kill yourself than tell me?"

She shied away, releasing her grip.

He grabbed her shoulders. "Talk to me, woman. There's no water here, is that it?"

Thor, Bellor, and Dabarius arrived at the front of the vorrel chain, and Drake backed away from Bree, who stared at the ground.

The companions ignored them and Dabarius said, "It'll be easier to find the entrance to the cistern in the daylight."

"Won't matter to me," Thor said. "We'll find a way in the dark." He nudged Bellor, whose golden brown eyes were unfocused as he passed his gaze back and forth over the obelisk and the surrounding area.

"We're not staying here tonight," the old Priest said.

"Why?" Drake asked.

Bellor turned away. "We have enough water to reach Shahan. We should keep going and avoid this place."

"We have no reserves," Dabarius said. "We're here. Let's just look for some water. We'll get it and leave in the morning."

"If Master Bellor says we go," Thor said. "We go."

The wind gusted, unbalancing all of them. The vorrels brayed in annoyance, shifting and testing the tethers that tied them all together.

"I'm going up there to look for water," Dabarius said. "Let's not waste any more time."

Now the vorrels fought as Drake led them up the hill. He sensed they were not just struggling against the steep grade. Unlike before, they didn't want to get close to the obelisk. Bree walked at his side, his hand firmly around hers while the others marched ahead. The dogs stayed behind him, ears and tails up, muscles tense, wishing he would let them run ahead with the others. Drake had to use every bit of his will to keep the dogs with him. Skinny tried to dart ahead, but Drake grabbed him by the scruff of his neck pulled him back.

Bellor stood back while Thor and Dabarius reached the base of the obelisk. Drake wanted to hurry and tie up the vorrels so he could investigate the spire as well. He watched while his friends inspected some of the half-buried inscriptions on the dark rock. The dogs finally broke away from him and began to sniff and dig in the sand a few paces from the obelisk. Bree gazed at the peak of the tower as she backed away from it.

"Look at this." Dabarius brushed away the sand to reveal more symbols and found a bronze chain attached to a stout ring in the stone.

"We found some too," Thor said, the wind muffling his words as he and Bellor lifted chains that the dogs had unburied. The chains were buried near the surface of the sand and were attached to the obelisk.

Gray clouds appeared overhead as the sunlight totally faded from view. Drake finished tying the lead vorrel to a block of cut stone.

Dabarius and the dwarves pulled on the chains. The dull bronze links slipped out of the sand as they snaked from the obelisk. Thor gave a hard tug and a desiccated human hand suddenly emerged from the ground. A manacle attached to the chain enclosed the wrist. The dogs each found a chain and began licking the metal links.

"Now I understand these glyphs." Dabarius touched the inscriptions again.

"What do they say?" Bellor asked.

"These men were sacrificed to bring back the rains," Dabarius said, "and lift the curse of Shenahr."

"They were chained here and left to appease the Storm God?" Bellor asked, inspecting the manacle that had once held a man's wrist.

Dabarius nodded. "It's as I thought. Theh'ah'nair. It's Old Mephitian. The word means Thunderstone. This place is dedicated to the Storm God."

Drake stopped struggling with the vorrels and stared at his three friends holding the metal chains. He very much wanted to find one himself, and knew there had to be more buried in the sand. If only he could start digging instead of battling with the vorrels.

A flash in the clouds drew his eyes toward the grim sky. The smell in air reminded him of what it was like in Cliffton before a storm. He thought of home. The spire was larger than most of the trees in the Thornclaw Forest. Would he ever see a tree again? Or would he become lost in this desert like Bölak and the *Dracken Viergur* who had gone before? He was so tired. The journey had been too long. Too painful.

No. What was he thinking? The Drobin rune of determination that had been imprinted on Drake's soul flared to life. He threw off the strange compulsion to give up hope and search for a chain.

The manacles his friends were holding snapped open, like the jaws of metallic beasts opening wide. Drake watched in horror as Thor, Bellor and Dabarius moved to put their wrists into the metal bonds.

"No! Let go! Now!" Drake shouted an instant before a pillar of lightning streaked from the clouds and struck the metal spear atop the obelisk. Bellor, Thor, and Dabarius went rigid, then flew backwards as the force of the electricity tore through their bodies.

LII

The Khebians claim that the obelisk was a blessing to this land long ago, bringing rainstorms to the fields and filling the cisterns, but after the Sundering of the Mephitian Empire, the rain stopped and the lightning storms began every night. Some of the people tried to appease the Storm God by chaining prisoners to the obelisk, but this only brought worse storms. I do not know if I believe these stories, but the Khebians believe it, and that is enough for me.

—Bölak Blackhammer, from the Khoram Journal

The odor of burnt hair filled the air as Drake crawled on the hot sand. Blind and deaf, he groped around not sure what he was searching for, and burned his fingers on scorched patches of ground. Everything was bright white as he fought off the daze affecting him. The last thing he could remember was seeing Bellor, Thor and Dabarius flying through the air as they were blasted backwards. They had each been holding a chain. Had they clamped them onto their wrists?

His hands found a body. He touched the face and felt the wide jaw and beard of Bellor. His eyesight began to return and he could make out the blurry face of the old dwarf.

Flashes of nearby lightning made Drake flinch, and a clap of almost simultaneous thunder rattled his skull. Vorrels screamed and several of the animals tied to the block of stone thumped to the ground. Little fires burned on the dying and dead animals' blackened hides.

Bellor moaned and relief washed over Drake. He didn't know what had happened to Bree or the dogs, but he prayed they had fled the hilltop. Nearby, Thor sat up and Dabarius crawled away from the obelisk as another bolt struck the top of the spire.

"Down the hill!" Drake shouted as he grabbed Bellor and dragged him to the edge of the steep decline as lightning struck the ground right where he had been.

Screaming vorrels broke loose from their dead brethren and ran down the hill in terror. Giant bolts of crackling electricity struck several of the animals as the lightning storm intensified.

Partially blinded again, Drake wrapped his arms around Bellor and rolled down like a log, taking the dwarf with him. They didn't roll for long before Bellor pushed him away, and began sliding and rolling down the hill by himself. The three dogs had already reached the bottom as Thor half slid and half ran down the sandy slope following a terrified and limping vorrel. Lightning struck and killed the poor animal and it fell a foot away from Thor. Dabarius deftly somersaulted down the slope, keeping as low as he could while controlling his rapid descent.

When they reached the bottom, they all lay in the dirt, gasping for breath as the wind howled. Thunder shook the ground. Drake looked into the cloudy vortex swirling above the obelisk and knew Bree had kept this from them. She had not wanted to lead them here because she knew what would happen. That's why she had acted so strangely. Why in the name of all the gods hadn't she told them?

Drake scanned the hillside for Bree, his eyes failing as flashes of light continued to blind him. He didn't care and kept looking into the storm. She would answer him right now for what she had done. Damn it all! Where was she? He called her name as the thunder muted his words. He started to crawl up the hillside to find her, then stopped as a trio of white-hot lightning bolts hit the smoldering bodies of the vorrels near the obelisk.

Dabarius grabbed him by the belt and held him back. "You can't go up there."

"I have to find her."

"If she's still there," Bellor said, "she won't be alive. I'll not see you die to recover her body, but when this is over, we'll find her together."

Several more bolts of lightning jumped out of the symbols on the obelisk and struck the vorrels, making a few of them jump and twitch. The lightning repeatedly shot out from the stone and hit the dead animals. The symbols glowed with a ghostly light, like the eyes of the misty Void, hungry to consume the newly dead.

Swallowing the lump in his throat, Drake gathered the frightened dogs to him, trying to soothe their frazzled nerves. Temus and Skinny whined and flinched as the teeth-rattling thunder rolled around them shaking the ground. Thor took Jep by the collar, and Bellor led them all away from Thunderstone and into the night.

Drake took one more glance at the hill. Small gray clouds rose from each of the bodies of the vorrels and circled the obelisk as they were drawn upward to the vortex. All the vorrels were dead, but he heard their spirits screaming.

Don't look. Ethan's voice pleaded in Drake's mind.

Don't look at what? Drake asked silently, as he turned away.

The storm.

Why? Drake wanted to look again.

It will see you, and it won't forget who you are.

The flashes continued, and Drake kept his face to the ground. He could sense his dead friend, Ethan, a cold spirit huddling against him.

LIII

The wind blows hard across the desert, covering the sun and stars. We cannot see, cannot breathe, cannot do anything except cover our eyes and wait for it to pass.

—Bölak Blackhammer, from the Khoram Journal

The abrasive sand lashed Bree'alla across the face as she ran through the dunes. Her lungs burned and with every indrawn breath she smelled smoldering vorrel hide. Still, she kept running. Instinct or perhaps the devious compulsion in her mind made her flee from the lightning storm, which rumbled in the distance, crisping the corpses of her dead friends. The vile Queen of Isyrin had won.

Bree'alla was a traitor to those who put their trust in her. A worthless and disgusting lump of the foulest dung. The Black Ghost had been right about her and he knew she would have to do this. She wished she had let him take them in the Sand Lake. At least then it would have been painless while they slept. Not like this, and after they had endured such pain crossing the desert.

How pathetic she was to let it all happen. In the two weeks since they left Isyrin she had been unable to overcome the Queen's charm, or her sense of duty to follow the orders of her sovereign.

Bree's legs ached and her pace slowed. She stopped and hung her head in shame, then spit out the burned taste in her mouth, which worsened and made her want to retch. Hands on her knees, her breaths came faster and faster. Her head spun and she stumbled, almost falling over as she thought about what the lightning was doing to Drake's body. His hair would burn, his skin would turn black and his eyes . . . would they burst as Shenahr's storm devoured him?

The Storm God would take their souls. Her friends were sacrifices. Nothing more. There would be no escape for Drake. He was gone now. Given time, or different circumstances, she would have taken him as her lover. No man had ever been kinder to her, and she repaid him with this? If only he had not stopped her from killing herself the night before. Perhaps none of this would have happened.

Something stirred ahead of her in the shadows, and Bree instinctively reached for her dagger. *Wingblade* would have been more comforting, but it was lost, left behind on one of the dead pack animals.

A tall creature walked tentatively toward her. The vorrel dipped its head and she recognized it as one of the more timid animals in their caravan. It had been Bellor's favorite mount. She wondered how many of them had survived, and if this vorrel had lived, perhaps some of her friends could have also?

A booming thunderclap made the animal shy away, and Bree's mind locked up like someone was choking off her air with two hands around her throat. The thought that her friends might be alive slipped away like the fragment of a dream remembered upon waking.

Her breathing came easier now.

The vorrel nudged her with its nose, and she rubbed its long snout. Tears welled up in her eyes as she climbed onto it.

"Let's get away from here."

Bree directed the vorrel into the desert. They would go to the edge of the Void, not far away now, and she would do what had to be done. An urgency to end the pain came over her. She slapped the vorrel on the haunches and made it gallop as fast as it could through wind and the darkness.

The vorrel ran at full speed and neither Bree, nor the mount, noticed the rut in the ground. The animal's front feet dropped suddenly and the vorrel pitched forward. Bree arms flailed as she sailed over the vorrel's head. Her legs were pointing almost straight when she hit ground, the back of her head struck first. A tearing pain exploded from her neck as a cracking sound filled her ears, and she blacked out.

Some time later, her eyes opened and Bree stared through the dust blocking out the stars. She couldn't feel the sand stinging her skin. A numb feeling had come over her entire body and she couldn't move her limbs. Every breath was a struggle and she only managed to take in small gasps of air. Her last thought before she lost consciousness again was that breaking your neck was not the way for a warrior to die. She deserved a much more painful end after what she had done to her friends.

After a short time, her breaths became much more shallow. Every time Bree closed her eyes she saw the image of her dead father in her mind. He stood over her, disappointed and shaking his head. She had disgraced him fully, though few would ever know of her betrayal of the foreigners. The one command she had been unable to disobey was the one that damned her.

Paralyzed, alone, and ashamed, Bree'alla tried to apologize to her father, but the words would not come. She forced her eyes to stay open so she wouldn't see him with her mind's eye, judging her. The sand blew more fiercely around her and she had to blink as the granules struck her face. When she could hold them open no longer, she looked toward her father's spirit in the darkness of her mind. She searched desperately for him now, but he was gone and there was only blackness.

Tears began washing the abrasive dust from Bree's eyes as she realized with a stab of soul wrenching pain that no one would guide her to the Afterworld. Even the ghosts of her dead loved ones had abandoned her. In the Underworld, she would be alone with her shame. It would be a fate well deserved.

LIV

The storms in the Dune Sea hate all life. Without any rain or snow
to deliver, they roil on and on, their only purpose to scour away at
those few fools and hardy creatures who brave this forsaken desert.

—Bölak Blackhammer, from the Khoram Journal

The dust blasted the four companions and the dogs all night
long, punishing them for surviving the lightning storm, which
stopped soon after midnight. The wind continued, and forced
the stinging sand into their mouths and eyes with a vengeance.
The howling wind blew for many hours and made it a miserable and sleepless night. All the while, Drake thought about
what he could have done to prevent the tragedy. He should
have told Bellor the night before. In trying to protect one
friend, he had nearly doomed them all. Even afterward, there
seemed to be no right answer. He was forced to lie there, stomach clenched, afraid he would find Bree up there on the blasted
hill, but was more afraid that he wouldn't.

The dust began to settle and the sky cleared by morning
and became vibrant blue. Drake was the first one to climb the
hill and inspect the carnage at Thunderstone. Most of the vorrels had been charred and blackened down to the bone. The
supplies were destroyed and their water almost totally evaporated or leaked into the ground.

Dabarius counted the bodies, and announced that out of
the seventeen vorrels, three had apparently escaped the lightning storm. There was no sign of Bree'alla. The wind had
wiped away any sign of her tracks, but that didn't stop him
from searching in the faint light of dawn as his friends scav-
enged supplies and equipment. He had the three dogs searching for her after he gave them what was left of her blanket
to smell. They had made a large loop around the base of the
obelisk and found nothing. The wind had erased her scent.

He returned to find his friends where they had brought the meager supplies not burned or spilled in the disaster.

Bellor stood, while the others sat inspecting their gear. The cord on Drake's metal crossbow had been burned away, and the wooden stock was scarred and blackened. The krannekin and metal parts were undamaged, and he replaced the cord with one of the spares he kept in his leg pocket. His quivers of bolts were singed, but had been thrown clear of the vorrel that had been carrying them. He lifted up *Wingblade*, shocked that Bree had left it behind. The scabbard was a little burned, but the sword was well oiled and in perfect condition. He would carry it until he found her again, and slipped it into the center of his pack.

"We need to march east," Bellor said. "Shahan is at least two days by vorrel. It might take us four days on foot, and there is little water left." Most of the bags had burned and the precious liquid had run into the sand. All of the remaining enchanted jugs had been shattered, as if the lightning had stuck them purposefully, the lightning attracted to the magic of Amar'isis.

Bellor and Thor had searched the obelisk for a doorway to a hidden cistern, but had found nothing after over an hour of searching and clearing away sand. Digging further down to find a buried door was discussed, but Bellor had prayed to Lorak and had no doubt that there was no water beneath the obelisk. Going to Thunderstone had been futile and pointless. It didn't rain there, and hadn't for many years. The whole place was a trap.

"We should find Bree," Drake said.

Bellor knelt down, and touched the young man's shoulder. "Lad, she's left us. If she had wanted to stay, she would have stayed close to this hill. We would have found her this morning."

"She knew what would happen up there," Thor said. "That's why she was acting so guilty since we left Isyrin." He shook his head and Drake could see the pain in Thor's expression. He'd lost a friend, a warrior comrade. It stung him badly, surprising Drake.

"Did she say anything to you?" Bellor asked Drake, who stared into the distance.

"Why didn't she warn us?" Dabarius asked, as he flung a blackened waterskin to the ground. "What in the world was she thinking, bringing us here?" He flexed his big hands so hard that the knuckles cracked.

Drake fixed his sad eyes on his friends. "She tried to fall on her sword the last time we made camp."

"What?" Bellor took a step back.

"I stopped her from killing herself." He told them the story of how he saved her and no one spoke for a long time afterward.

"Binding magic." Dabarius finally said, as he took off the binding scarab he had accepted in the temple of Amar'isis in Isyrin. "She was compelled to bring us here, and was prevented from saying anything. She was going to take her own life to stop us from going to Thunderstone."

"We should all pitch these into the Void." Thor touched his own scarab, affixed to his undershirt. "The word of these Mephitians isn't worth the breath that propels it. They've done nothing but hamper our progress and try to see us dead since we stepped foot onto their sands. I guess your young queen isn't as fond of you as we thought?"

The wizard scowled at Thor, balling up a fist. "That's it, you loud-mouthed, addle-brained oaf. I will—"

Bellor appeared between Thor and Dabarius, his face grave, his eyes flaring. "We still have a mission. You both swore an oath, and I won't see it broken. On the day that Draglûne lies in his death blood, you may take up old scores with each other, but until then, I will not allow you to tear this company apart with your bickering. Do you hear me?" The air shook with the old War Priest's words. Bellor must have used Lorakian magic on them. Whatever it was, it worked.

Thor ducked his head and muttered something in Drobin, stepping away, and releasing his grip on his hammer's haft. A moment of quiet stretched over the group while tempers calmed.

"Why didn't you say something to us after it happened?" Dabarius asked.

"I was going to. She made me promise not to or she would try to do it again."

"I knew something was wrong," Bellor said. "This is my fault. I had forebodings, but I was tired. Tired and hopeful for just one night's easy rest, and a little fresh water. I put my own comfort, and the frailty of these old bones before the mission."

"The queen must have ordered her to do this," Thor said, slapping his thigh. "It could be binding magic, but she had orders to betray us nonetheless. You come to know a warrior. Bree was loyal to her oaths. This had to be part of them, and though she didn't want to, she brought us here to die."

"Not possible," Dabarius said, "Khelen'dara wouldn't tell Bree to betray us. Never."

"I saw her tears at parting from you," Thor said, "but how can one know the heart of a monarch. She's seen her mother and grandmother killed for their part in helping us. Just because she may have tender feelings for you, that doesn't mean that she wasn't behind this."

"I know her heart, damn you. As well as I know my own. I tell you again, this was not her order," Dabarius yelled, his eyes glistening now with frustration more than anger.

"I'm tired of both of you fighting," Drake stood between them. "Whatever happened, Bree's missing now. She's our guide, and our friend. We have to find her."

"I'm sorry," Bellor said, "but we have to reach Shahan before the desert claims us. "Bree'alla is on her own now. She'll find us if she can. We must divide what's left, and we'll go as soon as we're ready."

"In her place, I would be too ashamed to show my face to those I'd damned to burn and be sacrificed to the Storm God," Thor spat. "She may not have a sword to fall on, but giving yourself to the desert isn't that hard."

"Thor!" Drake shouted.

The Drobin softened a little. "I'm sorry, my friend. I don't want to put a fire stick to your wounds. I know you have feelings for this woman. In the first book of Drobin lore the *Viergur* are made to read, it says this: 'a warrior is not judged on what he means to do, but upon what he does.' She brought us here to die. That is the truth. All else isn't important."

Drake just hung his head. There had been things he could have done. He just didn't know what they were.

"Pity we've lost the letter of introduction from Khelen'dara," Dabarius said. "Bree had it on her."

"We'll find a way to introduce ourselves," Bellor said. "We are the Sons of Kheb, after all."

"We should look for her," Drake said, "and for the three vorrels who escaped."

"On our way to Shahan, we will," Bellor promised.

There was little else Drake could do or say. She could have found them if she wanted to, and the vorrels were long gone. Perhaps in the time it would take to salvage and divide their gear, either Bree or one of the vorrels would show up? They began the task and soon everyone realized there was almost no food left unburned. They would have to eat charred vorrel meat, a poor idea especially since they had little water with them, and the inherently salty meat might make them ill. Vorrel flesh would actually accelerate the dehydration process—according to what Bree had told them. The sun would spoil the flesh after a short time anyway. Drake carved off as much as he could and fed it to the hungry dogs. They ate without much protest, but he knew that without enough water they might not be able to keep it down. He gave them some, and then had his companions take long swigs from their remaining water bags. They had enough water left for perhaps a day of travel, and that was if they drank half rations and gave almost nothing more to the dogs.

"We should go before the sun gets any higher," Dabarius said.

Shielding his face with his hand, Drake scanned the dunes for Bree one last time. She would have been there if she were coming back. He let out a sigh and nodded to the others, who began the march east toward Shahan. The dogs stayed at his side and Drake adjusted their makeshift saddlebags. Skinny kept trying to take his off, while Jep and Temus bore their burdens without complaint.

"Go," he commanded the dogs, who hesitated, then followed the others. Before going after them, Drake used the remains of their damaged gear to create an arrow on the ground pointing in the direction they went, just in case Bree returned. At least he had the dogs and the others. She was alone, with nothing.

LV

We are lost. Water gone. Only agony now. The Khoram is a dragon
. . . one too large for us to slay. We will die here, it seems.

—Bölak Blackhammer, from the Khoram Journal

A fiery ball burned into Bree's face. The heat lay on her like
a pile of smothering woolen blankets. She couldn't remember
what happened until the pain in her neck made her recall the
fall from the vorrel. Her mount had stumbled and thrown her.
Her eyes flickered open and the sun loomed high above her.
She squinted, and realized that by the position of the sun, it
had to be late afternoon—the hottest part of the day. She tried
to turn on her side and shield herself from the glare.

Her arms and legs wouldn't move.

Bree'alla lay paralyzed, and helpless as the sun beat down
on her limp body. Through parched lips and a dry throat she
whispered, "Drake." It was an apology, and a plea. He would
not hear her. He was dead. The last few people she could call
friends in all the world, and she had delivered them to the
Storm God's vengeance. Now, Ah'usar would deliver his fiery
kiss upon her brow, and she would be cast into oblivion.

She could barely lift her head off the ground, and the slight
movement caused her great pain in the back of her neck. Bree
glanced around, barely moving her head.

No one.

The broken Wing Guardian lay there for what had to be
an hour or more and decided the pain and apparent swelling
in her neck was the cause of her paralysis. The merciless sun
scorched her, and she kept her eyes closed. Baking to death in
the heat was a just way for her to die. If she had been killed by
the fall, it would have been too easy. This way she would suffer
slowly and painfully before finally dying. Things were as they
should be.

As Bree was becoming resigned to her fate, she felt something on her leg. It was the first time she had felt her leg since waking up. A dim hope came alive in her and she wanted to live. At the same time, she was tired, frightened to go on, knowing of her own sins. For a time, hope and self-hatred warred within her, but the desire to survive had not completely departed, regardless of her pain. She tried to move her lower extremities and felt them shift on the sand. The feeling was returning to her legs and she felt something moving up her thigh.

A black armored scorpion as large as her hand crawled up her body. Its many legs moving against her skin made her wish the feeling had not come back. The scorpion continued up her leg and stopped at the scabbed over the wound on her abdomen. Bree wondered how everything would have turned out if she had fallen on her sword. The scorpion's tail moved slightly and she thought it was going to sting her. The poison might kill her in this weakened state.

"Sting me." She could barely whisper.

The scorpion crawled up her chest and neared her neck. Would it sting her there like Verkahna's dragonling had? Bree wiggled the fingers on her left hand and her forearm moved a little. The insect paused at her neck and Bree froze, feeling it touch the soft skin below her chin with its pinchers.

A stark thought flashed through her mind. What if Drake and the others were still alive? She could go back and help them. The compulsion in her head seemed to be gone. Bree had carried out the betrayal and there was nothing but guilt left from carrying out the treacherous command.

She summoned every bit of willpower she could muster. In a burst of determination, she lifted her left arm off the ground and used it to swipe the scorpion off her neck.

The effort left her breathing hard, but she had broken some barrier within herself. She knew she could move. Bree spent the next half an hour rolling onto her side. Her legs were not responding very well, but her strength was slowly returning. Bree crawled along the sand dune, making her way up to the top of the ridge, where she hoped she could see Thunderstone.

After an agonizing climb, in which she practically dragged her legs behind her, she made it to the top of the dune. Bree gazed out over the desert and saw Thunderstone, perhaps two miles away. She also saw a vorrel and judging by its limp, knew it was the one that had stumbled and caused her fall.

Suddenly, Bree wondered how long she had been lying unconscious on the sand. Was it only one night? She guessed that it was. She could not have survived longer than that under the wrathful eye of the sun. The injured vorrel was standing in the sand only one dune away. It had not gone far from her and stopped to nibble at some hardy desert bushes growing by a rocky outcropping.

Bree struggled to reach the vorrel and when she crawled toward it, the animal came over and nudged her with its big snout. Using her years of experience with vorrels, she convinced the animal to kneel, so she could crawl on top of it. Getting onto its back took a tremendous effort, but she made it after a one failed attempt. The vorrel had belonged to Dabarius and she had adjusted the stirrups the night before, so they fit her legs perfectly.

The most important things on the vorrel were the three gallons of water she found safely secured. She drank a large amount from one of the sacks and didn't mind the taste of the hot, leather-flavored liquid. Her throat felt instantly better and her head began to clear. After a moment, she coaxed the vorrel toward Thunderstone. She had to see if her friends were dead or alive.

She arrived at the base of the hill and couldn't see Drake's, or anyone else's body. A wave of relief passed over her. They were alive, and couldn't be that far away, could they?

She saw their tracks and knew they had claimed whatever the lightning and subsequent fires had not destroyed. The shame at not resisting the binding magic came back full force. Would they be able to understand? If someone had betrayed her this way, no matter their reasons or excuses, she would have felt nothing but the desire to put a blade through their necks. Maybe Drake, with his soft heart . . .

Bree put those thoughts out of her mind when she saw the arrow constructed of arranged items on the ground. They pointed toward Shahan. The tracks around the message belonged to Drake. He had not given up hope that she would return and try to follow them. Her pulse quickened and a lump formed in her throat. She loved him and would not let him down again. She coaxed her limping vorrel to the east and wondered how much of a lead they had on her. The tracks had been made earlier in the day and she hoped to catch up to them soon, perhaps even before sunset.

Hope returned and she tried not to think about the lack of water that would surely kill them all. What she carried would not be enough to save them, but she wanted to see her friends one last time. She could explain, ask for forgiveness. Drake would give it to her. She had been pushing him away for many days and now all she wanted to do was draw him close, and tell him how sorry she was. She loved him and prayed to Amar'isis that she would live long enough to tell him at least once. Even if only anger and hate met here there, just seeing them, having a moment to apologize for all she'd done . . . that would be better than dying alone. At that moment, she knew that anything was better than that. "I've bent to your will, Goddess, even in the worst of all trials. Please, keep the man I love safe," she begged.

LVI

I am afraid of what Nayla is planning. She thinks that I do not understand, but I am not a fool. I will not let her start a war. In the end, the people will hear my voice, not hers.

—Priestess Jaena Whitestar, from her personal journal

The villages of the Nexus Plateau became a blur to Jaena as Priestess Nayla, and Emmit guided her to a different place every other night. They visited Coldwater, Thistlewood, Wardenvale, Gatewood, Littledale, Hillhouse, Trench, Wardenvale, and almost two-dozen more. They circled the dormant volcano, Mount Nexus, visiting the farming enclaves where most of the food for the Drobin Empire was grown in dark, rich soil. The large open spaces, almost entirely cleared of trees, unnerved Jaena at first, but few griffins or other large aevians hunted in the farming region after centuries of hard lessons taught by heavily armed human and Drobin soldiers. They saw few patrols on the roads, but mobs of vigilant watchkats lived everywhere, and large tree corridors connected every community.

Despite the safety, rarely did they travel outside of solid cover, though Jaena wanted to walk into the open just once to know what it was like. How would it be to look up and only see the blue sky with no trees at the edge of your vision? Drake knew. He had experienced such things. Where was he now? She shook her head when his face would appear in her mind. No. She had her own problems. Her mind and heart had to be her own. Drake was far away. He had . . . slipped away from her.

She had many strange thoughts in the four weeks that seemed like a lifetime. The woman who had been her inspiration, became her opponent. After the first few villages she refused to let Priestess Nayla have the last word and leave the people in an uproar. She was just a girl from Cliffton, but she would prevent war with the Drobin however she could. So, after Nayla's vitriolic speeches were done, Jaena would call the people to prayer, and would recite memorized passages or read from her copy of the Goddess Scrolls that promoted mercy, peace, and introspection, not hatred. She found her voice when she let the wisdom of the Amaryllis guide her tongue. Sometimes she would speak to the people during the marathon healing sessions that often started early in the morning and lasted late into the night.

She never turned anyone away, and though she could not heal everyone's physical afflictions, all who felt the power of the Goddess were full of hope when she finished with them. In most places she chose to see the youngest first, then the women, and last the adult men. Stragglers of all ages would always arrive during her sessions, and Jaena let some come forward spontaneously if their need was great. Many just came to watch, but if she had time she would bless them and try to heal what was wrong on the inside of their soul.

Blayne, Kraig, Rill, Lyall, and Holten managed the lines and watched for Drobin or human marshals, while Emmit and Nayla spoke to Elders and the leaders of the community, scheming and making plans, telling them what had happened to Priestess Gwynedd at the Sacred Grove. Jaena hated that she could not hear what they spoke about, but Kraig told her they were making discussing a future uprising.

Jaena could not stop what Nayla was doing, and had to focus on healing the people. She often asked Nayla to join her, as together they could heal twice as many, but the Priestess refused, and spent her time talking with village Elders who were almost all veterans of the last Giergun War. Most of the men had served in the army as well, and none had an abiding love for the Drobin King who used them as slave labor or fodder in the frontier regions of the Dark Spire Mountains where the Giergun still contested ground or raided outposts.

At least Jaena had succeeded in keeping Nayla and Emmit from taking any of her 'boys' into the city. She'd convinced Nayla that she needed all of them to help and protect her, especially when the Lord Marshal's agents began looking for them. Now they had to send scouts into each community the night before and find out if the Drobin were waiting for them. Emmit often led the scouting mission, but all of her boys were learning to fit in among the villagers. After all, these were their people, and every person in Cliffton or Armstead had descended from the folk who still called themselves Nexan.

The villagers welcomed them like long lost kin, and Jaena wrote down in her small journal the names of everywhere they went. Each day was a miracle as children returned from the brink of death, the lame walked for the first time in years, the blind saw, or the deaf heard Jaena's voice whispering their name, and those wracked with pain found comfort under the shade of a sacred tree. The Goddess worked through Jaena, and she knew that this was the right path for her life, despite her misgivings about Nayla's warmongering. Perhaps the balance of the natural world was seen through the two of them. Nature was always both gentle and destructive. Jaena held out hope that, in some way, Nayla's purpose in life was as vital to the Goddess as her own.

They argued sometimes, but Nayla would always convince Jaena that she did not want rebellion, but if it came time, the people had to be ready to rise up and fight.

However, the worst moment for Jaena was in Littledale when a woman brought her dead infant to be healed. The baby girl, little Halli, had died at least a day before, though the young mother, a girl named Minna who was perhaps eighteen, had walked alone all night through the woods to find Jaena, and had stopped in two other villages looking for 'The Priestess.' When she finally found her, Jaena could only try, but Halli's soul had gone to the Afterworld. They buried the tiny body behind the sacred tree, and Jaena held Minna as

Kraig covered little Halli with earth and round stones.

That night, in a small cabin outside Littledale, Jaena cried herself to sleep and wondered if she had prayed harder or longer, would the baby have come back? Despite what her mother had told her as an apprentice Priestess, of how the soul mustn't ever be coaxed back from beyond the threshold of death, she still felt as if she had failed.

The next morning they left after speaking to a large crowd who wanted to know where they were going next, so they could follow her, and hear her speak. Nayla would not tell them, but said that Jaena would visit all the villages if she could, though it would have been suicide to go too close to Nexus City, as local Drobin marshals would arrest her the moment she arrived.

Despite all their precautions, and after two weeks of traveling, they would often arrive at a village and find that hundreds had already gathered beside the sacred tree, usually a sentinel, rarely a cover tree. Word had spread and it became more dangerous for Jaena, as the Drobin marshals were on her trail, and they narrowly avoided them more than once. The villagers saved them and showed them secret ways to escape, twice delaying the marshals by leading them the wrong way.

Nayla was careful not to bring Jaena to villages with mixed Drobin and human enclaves, but soon those would be the only villages left. Masefield was the closest they'd come to Nexus City and after a month of visiting the hamlets on the Nexus Plateau, Jaena wanted to take no chances. After the sick people of Masefield and all the others had been cared for, Blayne and Kraig were sent ahead that night to scout their next destination. Early the following morning, Jaena awoke to find Nayla, Emmit, Lyall, Holten, and Rill had gone, and she was alone in the house they'd been given for the night. A scrap of paper sat on the table and Jaena read it with dread.

Jaena,

It is with a heavy heart that I write this. I have loved you like a daughter, and you have done more than I could have ever hoped for. The Goddess is strong in you, and I have great faith that you will bring her message to the people. You have your mission, and I have mine. The time has come for us to travel down separate paths.

I have taken Emmit, Holten, Rill, and Lyall to Nexus City. There was no point in discussing this any further. The Drobin High Priests, and king Alaric must be slain for their crimes. It will be justice. The revolution will start with their deaths, and I know you want no part in the violence ahead. Catch up to Blayne and Kraig, who have gone to Sherrington. You can continue your work in the villages, but the Drobin are after you now. Cover your tracks well and be strong in the times ahead.

May the sky be clear,

Priestess Nayla

Jaena crumpled the note and stuffed it in a pocket. She ran out the door moments later and did not take the trail to Sherrington. She ran the opposite way, toward Nexus City. She had to stop them. If she confronted them, her boys would not do it. They would come with her, and abandon Nayla and Emmit. She could convince them that they were men of the Thornclaw, hunters, warriors, not assassins.

The sunlight barely penetrated through the canopy over the muddy trail and Jaena did not see the three broad-shouldered Drobin in their grey-green cloaks until they stepped out in front of her. Three more appeared behind her, and many others closed in from the sides. All of them wore the crest of the Drobin king's marshals, a crown with a hammer under it.

"You are the one called Priestess Jaena," a dwarf with the air of leadership said.

She considered lying, but they knew who she was already. "I am Jaena."

"We've been looking for you for some weeks now," the same dwarf said.

She could see grins behind their beards, and sunk to her knees and prayed as they came closer. If this was to be the moment of her death, she would think of Drake, and her mother, and all those that she had healed. She would see her loved ones again in the Afterworld.

She was still praying when they manacled her hands behind her back, put a gag in her mouth and tied it in place, which pinched her hair in the back of her head.

Their apparent leader, the dwarf with a closely cropped brown beard stood over her. "If you come with us, quietly, and follow our orders, you will be well treated. If you try to run, or rally your kin to free you, I have the authority to execute you immediately." He lifted his war hammer and brushed the hair away from her frightened eyes. He rested the cold, steel claw side of the weapon against her cheek. "Do you understand?"

Jaena nodded, and held in her tears.

LVII

I do not remember Priestess Nayla from my time at the Sacred Grove. She preached to my people as if she never heard the wisdom of Priestess Gwynedd. Why have I let my daughter go off with such a questionable woman? I'm glad I sent Kraig with her, but he will not be able to convince her to come home. She will have to decide that on her own. I pray it is soon.

—Priestess Liana Whitestar, from her personal journal

The Shadow Wingataur, Nakarsh perched high in the branches of an ironwood tree, watching the small house where Jaena slept. Draconic magic kept him and his partner, Ehkuuz, invisible as they waited for her to awaken and find the note. They would watch her and relish the moment.

Nakarsh had taken great joy in writing the letter, and he knew the carefully crafted words would have the desired effect. The wingataur was very proud of himself. His role as the invented Priestess Nayla had been played to perfection once again. Ehkuuz had done admirably as usual. They had spent months during the last few seasons honing their performances as they visited the villages around Nexus City, getting to know the various elders and bearing the news of the destruction of the Sacred Grove and the death of High Priestess Gwynedd and her followers. The old woman's death had been exactly the grave news needed to make the Nexan villagers' blood boil, and prepared the way for Jaena, though Nakarsh did not conceive of bringing her to the villages until he visited Cliffton. The best plans evolved naturally, and this one had grown like a slow rot that eventually managed to topple even the oldest trees.

The wingataur King Priest, Zultaan, would be very pleased to know that his devious scheme to start a war between the Drobin and Nexans was coming to fruition, and Draglûne would be more than satisfied with Nakarsh's plan to use Jaena to stir the Nexans to violence. The Dragon King would have his revenge on the loved ones of the foolish human hunter who spied him, and Jaena's death at the hands of the Drobin would do much more than it would in the backwoods village where Nakarsh found her.

The door to the house burst open and Jaena ran toward Nexus City, just as Nakarsh had anticipated.

We'll follow her, Nakarsh projected his words to Ehkuuz.

The other wingataur sprang off the tree and the bowed branch sprang up as his weight lifted from it. Nakarsh spread his wings and used his magic to glide after his partner. They stayed behind her, skimming the underside of the canopy as they glided slowly along. Jaena's fear wafted from her aura like the sweet scent of death rising from a corpse.

How she did not see the Drobin ambush was a mystery to Nakarsh. He landed softly on a branch and Ehkuuz hung from the canopy near by, observing the moment of Jaena's capture. She was so pitiful when she surrendered to the dwarves. He had hoped that she would at least struggle a bit, and not go with them like a sheep to the slaughter. Her behavior was pathetic, and Nakarsh conceded that his talk to her of fighting them had been his only real failure.

He did want to see her struggle and scream for help. Perhaps some of the farmers in the fields not far away would have come to her rescue if she shouted. The Drobin would have had to kill the humans, and many would know the story of how the Drobin captured her and dragged her away kicking and screaming. Now Nakarsh and Ehkuuz would have to spread the story themselves, embellishing the details.

A few dead Nexan farmers near the trail would help. He and Ehkuuz would have to take care of that themselves. The other villagers would find the bodies, and the tracks, and know exactly what had happened.

The Drobin led Jaena off in manacles, and Nakarsh was satisfied that his plan would work perfectly.

Ehkuuz, we must kill a few of the locals and leave them here on the trail, Nakarsh said. *I'll summon them to us when the time is right.*

Ehkuuz grunted and found a more comfortable place in the tree to wait. Almost an hour later, when the Drobin were long gone, Nakarsh screamed using Jaena's voice, "Help! Help! Please help me!"

Five farmers from a nearby field came running. Nakarsh shapeshifted into a Drobin warrior and became visible on the trail, his booted feet blending in with the tracks the dwarven marshals had left. Ehkuuz followed his lead and they waited for the humans to arrive.

Nakarsh screamed again in Jaena's voice, and was pleased to hear the three men and two women running toward them call out Jaena's name. Right before they all arrived, Nakarsh created an illusion of Jaena in chains, being hauled off by a Drobin patrol further down the trail. He recreated the scene just as it had occurred less than an hour before. Ehkuuz and Nakarsh played the role of rear guards and sprang upon the farmers as they came out of the bushes and onto the path. The pair of Drobin marshals killed efficiently and quickly before the surprised humans knew what was happening. Four of them died before a woman past her child bearing years tried to run.

Ehkuuz leaped after her, his dwarven body flying through the air and closing the distance. He landed on her hard and crushed her to the ground. He bashed the side of her head with his fist knocking her unconscious. He wrapped his hands around her neck preparing to break it.

Let her live, Nakarsh said telepathically. *She will tell of what happened here.*

Ehkuuz hesitated, turned the woman to the side, then let her face fall into the mud.

"We go," Nakarsh said in a deep Drobin voice. "We must catch up to the other marshals."

Ehkuuz left tracks that showed him chasing the woman down, then he retreated with Nakarsh on the trail until their footprints meshed with the actual group of Drobin.

Nakarsh thought fondly of the morning as they flew in the clear blue sky a short time later unseen by any who looked upwards. They would meet up with the Thornclaw assassins and make their way to Nexus City. News of Jaena's capture would spread from Nexus itself to all of the villages she had visited and beyond. Priestess Nayla would put out the call to arms and thousands would answer her. The war would begin as soon as Jaena was executed, and according to the law, she would be killed in the public square. Tens of thousands would see her die and they would take their revenge on the Drobin until none remained alive in Nexus City.

LVIII

I pray for an end to our suffering. We must find Shahan or we will perish beside this River of Mist.

—Bölak Blackhammer, from the Khoram Journal

It felt like sand was grating inside Drake's eyeballs. It scraped away at him from the inside. He wondered how long it would be before he was totally blind. One more sand storm would do it. The storm on the day they had left Thunderstone had been the worst, blowing for most of the day and thundering all night long. The stars were blocked out and though they had made little progress, the companions had hiked for most of that first night. The second night of marching was better, but a few hours after sunrise they had a stark choice to make.

"This is the last of our water," Drake said, shaking the small amount of liquid in his waterskin.

"I've been waiting all night for a gulp of that," Thor said, then glanced at Bellor. "Or should we wait a little longer?"

Bellor glanced up at the hot sun. "We drink it now, or we might not make it through the day."

Drake volunteered to take the last drink, barely a half-swallow, but he did not complain.

Very early in the morning of the third day, both Bellor and Thor could barely walk—even after leaving some of their gear and their chain mail coats behind. They had kept all of their weapons and Thor would not leave his shield. He used it as shade when they made camp, propping it up with long-handled *Wyrmslayer*. Both of the dwarves would put their faces in the small patch and hide from the sun. It worked well, until Thor accidentally touched the metal and burned the tip of his nose.

Whatever sorcery augmented stamina Dabarius had used to keep going for the past two days was gone. The wizard hunched over, looking thin and weak. He wouldn't eat the vorrel meat, saying it would make his current condition worse. Drake knew he was right and did the same. The ache in his belly had gone away now, and the thought of eating the charred vorrel made him want to vomit. He recalled the awful sound of the dogs regurgitating the meat after the last time he had fed them. The poor dogs. They were the worst off. Their dry tongues hung from their mouths and the only reason they kept going was because of Drake staggering ahead of them. If not for him, he knew they would have lain down and waited for death.

The sun had not quite broken over the horizon in front of them, and at least it was still relatively cool. Soon, the glaring ball of fire would once again try to kill them with its scorching rays.

The only way to survive was to keep moving. Bree was not going to ride over the dune with vorrels and full bags of water. They were on their own.

Drake led them over one more dune. Then one more. Just before the sun rose, Drake fell to his knees at the top of a small ridge. In the pre-dawn light he beheld the black ribbon of a wide chasm stretching north and south like the body of a serpent. "The Void," he whispered. "We found the River of Mist."

The others crawled to the top of the sandy ridge and stared down at the gorge that separated the two desert plateaus, Khoram and Far Khoram. The gap was over two hundred yards wide and the terrain of Far Khoram was flat, but turned into hills and mountains further south. The dunes stopped well before the canyon, as if the wind had pushed them all west.

"Which way now?" Bellor asked, his voice hoarse and weak.

Shahan was either north or south. If they went the wrong direction, they would certainly die. Had the sand storm turned them north, or had they come too far south? He didn't know.

"North," Dabarius said firmly.

"No," Thor said. "We went too far north on the first night during the wind storm. The city is less than a day of walking to the south."

"If we walk north for a day,"—Dabarius said—"and don't find it, we won't have enough strength to turn around and come back."

Dabarius and Thor argued, and Bellor's expression told Drake the old dwarf had no idea which way to go.

"We've got one day left in us," Bellor said, staring at Drake. "Lad, you've studied the maps more closely than any of us. You've studied the stars. Bree told you how to get to Shahan."

He nodded.

"Then which way?" Bellor asked. "North or south?"

Drake gazed up at the gray dawn sky, filled with enough light that none of the stars shone through. "I need to see the sun," he said. "When I see where it is, I'll know."

His friends collapsed on the ridge, apparently mollified by his false confidence.

Moments later a wall of white fog stretching for miles north and south rose from the chasm separating the plateaus, and blew toward them on the faint wind. The fog rapidly covered the dunes, swallowing them whole, and Drake remembered how the mist would rise from the Void outside Cliffton just the same. The mist was soon upon them and began to coat the leaves of the small plants clinging to life. The dogs started licking the precious moisture off the plants and soon the companions did the same, finding that a lot more plants grew along the edge of the Void than in the deeper desert where they had come from. Each drop was precious and they stopped many times as they walked closer to the River of Mist to lick and drink the dew. The moisture sustained them and the fog cooled their skin until the sun burned it all away.

A ball of bright white pain peeked over the incredibly flat and barren desert to the east where only wisps of the fog now remained. Bridging the canyon seemed like the worst course they could take. It figured that Draglûne had decided to live on such a remote and forbidding plateau. Had Bölak truly made it across at Shahan, and if so, how did he find Draglûne's lair?

The sunlight blinded Drake and he shielded his face, wishing for the taste of the dew drops again. How odd that the Void mist itself had given them such a gift. If they could collect it better, could they survive this trek?

As the sun rose higher they reached the edge of the River of Mist and stopped for a rest. Drake hesitated, unsure about which way to go. North or south? He glanced back at the three dogs. Skinny was asleep, but Jep and Temus had their sad eyes open, as if they knew something important was about to happen and didn't want to miss it.

The temperature started to rise almost instantly and the last of the fog burned away. The sun had been slowly killing them over the past two days and now it might guide them to Shahan, and the water that had to exist there. *Which way?*Drake wracked his brain, thinking of all he had learned from Bree and the maps. Pity they had been on her person when she disappeared.

His mind felt like the shriveled pieces of vorrel meat they had been feeding the dogs. Just thinking of the salty meat made his parched lips and mouth feel even worse. With the back of his hand, Drake wiped the grit off his forehead. He kept his demeanor calm, hoping not to betray his inner turmoil or show his friends any sort of uncertainty.

The River of Mist wended its way north and south to the horizon and the sunlight revealed tiny wisps of fog clinging to the reddish and tan walls of the canyon.

"Which way to Shahan?" Thor asked.

Drake knelt in the dirt and used his and Ethan's thorn bolt to represent their course and the path of the sun. He scraped a little trench where he thought the River of Mist lay, then put a rock where he thought Thunderstone had been.

He used several more rocks to represent the last places in the sky where he'd seen the stars he was using for navigation. He imagined Bree'alla's map and realized where they had gone wrong. "We've come too far north," Drake said. "We have to go south now." He spoke as confidently as he could. None of his friends questioned him, though Dabarius looked north for a while.

They started walking south a short time later. All Drake could think about was that if he had chosen the wrong direction, the dogs, and his friends would die a miserable death at the edge of the Void.

LIX

Some of the Khebians have said they will jump into the shady canyon, rather than die in the heat of the desert.

—Bölak Blackhammer, from the Khoram Journal

This is a good place to die, Bree'alla thought as she stood on the lip of the cliff staring straight down into the River of Mist. The midday sun had forced the white clouds to retreat hundreds of feet into the deep canyon where they flowed swiftly north. The wind currents that moved the clouds blew through her hair, whipping it around her face as she watched the little wisps of fog that would swirl up along the sheer walls and then disappear.

Her vorrel snorted and Bree glanced over her shoulder. The animal put one of its soft hooves onto the worn saddle and bridle laying on the rock, as if puzzled about why she had taken them off.

"You are free," she whispered. "Go." Bree thought the vorrel would head north, to Shahan. There might be water there, but she didn't care anymore. Her friends were dead and their bodies were being covered by the sands of the Khoram. She had searched for them for almost three days now, pushing her vorrel to the limit of its endurance. She had found their trail once, early in her search, but they had gone the wrong way, into the nothingness. She had searched, but found only the dwarves discarded chain mail coats gleaming atop a pile of rocks. It proved they had traveled off course, and she found no other clues. The wind had erased their trail and they were lost to all but the gods. Bree had even searched the edge of the River of Mist going north to the edge of Shahan and south as far as they could have gone, but there was no sign of them. If they hadn't reached the chasm by now, they wouldn't.

Her neck ached and she felt like the fog in the canyon was in her head. She had drunk the last of her water and now was the time to end her journey. Her friends were dead, and Bree wished to join them in the Afterworld. She was a traitor to her father, her friends, her goddess, and her own soul. Only the vile Queen Khelen'dara would be pleased.

End it now. The compulsion in her head told her, even more insistently.

Bree spread her arms. She would dive into the rift and see the Underworld as a living woman before she was condemned to stay there as a dead one.

The vorrel snorted behind her, but she refused to look at the animal, preferring to remember Drake's face as her last memory before she plummeted to her death. *He said that he loved me.*

Bree took a deep breath, it would be her last before she jumped.

"*Sister.*" A woman's voice stopped Bree the instant before she leapt off the cliff. "Sister," softer now, "you have no wings, and cannot fly."

LX

Does blind faith makes all things possible? Or are we fools to believe? Doubts plague me as they never have before. We are as steel left too long in the forge, denied the relief of the quenching trough until all that is hard and unbending begins to sag as the heat slowly unmakes us.

—Bölak Blackhammer, from the Khoram Journal

Jep licked the stone at the lip of the cliff, then whined as he looked up at Drake with profoundly sad eyes. "Sorry, boy," Drake said, roughing his coat and scratching behind his ears.

Jep's tail wagged for a moment. Only a moment.

There was no moisture left on the rock. The dew that they had found early that morning coating the plants and the stone on the edge of the gorge was long gone.

Drake shepherded Jep away from the cliff and toward the spindly bushes growing near the dunes where the others were resting. He scraped away the hot surface sand and fell to the ground. The oppressive heat had drained away all his energy, but despite his exhaustion he couldn't sleep. The decision to walk south haunted him and he knew that if they didn't find water by that night, they would be too weak to keep going. Should they have gone north?

In the late afternoon, after what felt like an eternity in an oven, Drake roused his friends, and helped them all stand. Jep and Temus were still panting so rapidly that he didn't know if they would be able to continue. Skinny, who had fared the best of all of them at first, tried to get to his feet. He barked weakly at a small lizard that skittered under a bush. He clearly wanted to chase it, but couldn't so much as make it to his feet to do so.

"Here, boy." Drake lifted the thin dog in his arms, and patted him on the belly, holding him up. "You can do it." Skinny

329

kept an eye on the lizard for a moment, then fell over.

The dog tried to get up, and Drake said, "We have to get going now. Come on."

Temus licked Skinny's face and let out a plaintive *wuffling* sound.

Skinny closed his eyes, his panting slowing down as he lay there.

The companions stood there for some time. No one wanted to say anything.

Bellor put a hand on Drake's shoulder. "Sorry lad, we'll have to leave him."

Drake shook his head. "Skinny, get up. Come on." Drake rubbed the dog's neck. Jep and Temus looked on, their blunt faces even more scrunched up.

"He's done all he can do," Thor said. "He's finished. We'll all be like him in a few more hours."

"I'm not leaving him." Drake picked up the dog and draped him around his neck, holding his front and back feet against his chest. Skinny whined a little, but didn't struggle. "I'm ready."

"Of course you are." Bellor smiled.

The companions stumbled along the edge of the Void keeping as straight a course as they could while the canyon snaked its way south. Dabarius took over carrying Skinny after a while, while Thor kept Bellor from falling down. Jep and Temus barely kept up, and their panting became so rapid that Drake thought they would collapse at any moment.

Drake took Skinny back from Dabarius a short time later when they reached a very steep and rocky hill that abutted the River of Mist. The wizard nearly toppled over when he passed the dog to Drake.

"He wasn't that heavy," Drake said, his voice a whisper. "I thought you were a lot stronger than that."

"Shut up," Dabarius said, the words barely escaping his throat, "let me sit down, just for . . . "

330

"No, you can't sit down," Drake said. They had just stopped a few moments before and if they sat down again, they might not get back up. "We're almost there. I know it. We can probably see it from the top of this hill."

Thor shook his head. "You've said that twice before."

Skinny squirmed out of Drake's grasp and fell, tangling himself in Dabarius's legs.

"Stupid dog," the wizard pushed the desert hound away.

Thor eased Bellor down before sitting beside him. Jep and Temus instantly collapsed. At least they were all in some shade. The sun was nearing the horizon in the west and the hill blocked it out entirely.

Skinny sniffed the air and began climbing the rise.

"Look at that. If he can climb, so can we," Drake said.

"We've been carrying him for an hour," Dabarius said, "of course he can."

The hound reached the top of the hill, and stared into the distance, ears up. Skinny barked. Three times.

"Probably another lizard, maybe a rabbit," Thor said.

"Shahan," Drake said. *It has to be.*

Thor rolled his eyes.

It took Drake some time to crawl to the top of the hill, but when he got there his mouth gaped open. The ruins of Shahan spread out for miles at the edge of the River of Mist. Most of the walls were toppled, as were the large buildings and blocky houses, though their outlines poked out of the shifting sands. In every direction around the city, land had been cordoned off in rectangular patterns by low walls made of deteriorating beige stone. Sand-filled ditches that must have been canals connected the fields, and what had to be an elevated road supported by arches on the far side of the city ran due south toward the distant mountains. He could hardly believe what he was seeing, and the fact so many people once lived in this place boggled his mind.

He was so happy to see the color green. Several palm trees and a few other varieties of trees poked up here or there, but a long line of thick palms grew toward the center of the city forming a verdant line that seemed to follow the course of a river way or canal. There had to be water there for so many trees to grow.

His attention was drawn to the bottom of the hill in front of him. A small animal walked through the branches of a thorny tree. He waited, rubbing his eyes and making certain he was not hallucinating. Skinny's eyes never left the tree and the feline form that crouched on a branch. The tan cat with white stripes watched them intently. Drake hugged the dog tight as his laughter came out as wheezes.

"What is it?" Bellor asked.

Smiling, Drake pointed to the city. "There's a cat. In a tree."

The dwarves glanced at each other incredulously.

"Come back down here," Bellor said. "You need to rest a bit."

"No. It's Shahan. I see it."

They all lay there, disbelieving, while Drake watched the desert cat leap from the tree. Tawny falcon wings suddenly extended from its body. It glided for a long while before landing softly on the ground. The wings folded up and tucked against its body as it turned to look back once, then scurried toward the ruins.

"It flew," Drake said. The small creature was spawn of the Void.

"What flew?" Bellor asked.

"The cat."

"Come back down here, lad," Bellor said, "and take a rest. You're seeing things that aren't there."

LXI

The city is empty of people. Only their ghosts remain in this forsaken place. We shall not linger here.

—Bölak Blackhammer, from the Khoram Journal

"I don't see any cat," Thor crossed his arms. "I think the heat's
turned you dunder-headed."

Drake could still hardly believe his eyes as he surveyed the
ruins from the ridge with his friends. He'd finally gotten them
to come and see after repeated pleading and a few insults. "I'll
show you the tracks," Drake promised.

"Find the water," Bellor said. "It has to be where those
trees are."

"Is that an elevated road?" Thor motioned to the narrow
wall with an endless number of arches supporting it that ran
from the opposite side of the city toward the mountains to the
south. Most of it had been buried by the shifting sands.

Dabarius shook his head. "That's not a road. It's an aqueduct. See the channel running down the center of it?"

"The people here brought water all the way from the
mountains," Bellor raised his eyebrows. "There must not have
been enough water here already."

"The mountains have to be forty miles." Thor squinted at
the tiny bluish peaks south of them.

Whatever it was, the only thing it carried now was sand
and rubble. The roof over most of the aqueduct had fallen in,
and all the apparent canals the aqueduct had fed around the
city had been covered over.

To the east, at the edge of the now narrow gorge, the remains of a huge stone bridge thrust out from Shahan into the
River of Mist. The armies of Far Khoram and Isyrin had met
on the plateau that used to sit in the center of the canyon. The
small plateau was gone now, destroyed by the earthquake that

had killed the God King of Far Khoram. Only the nub of the bridge on the far side remained and the vague outline of a road that went southeast along the rift.

"This is where my uncle came and crossed the Void." Thor gazed into the flat desert. "We will follow him."

"Not unless we find something to drink and eat," Dabarius said, nudging them to get moving.

The companions slid down the hill and Drake's fuzzy mind cleared a bit. He focused on the tracks left by the cat, which started extremely far away from the thorn tree. The feline had glided through the air like a griffin. Bellor inspected the tracks for a moment, but there was no discussion of what Drake said he saw. They were all too preoccupied with putting one foot in front of another.

Skinny had regained his will to live and led them forward, following the cat's trail, which led them to a partially intact bridge that spanned a sand-filled ditch. One at a time, they crossed, avoiding the gaps in the crumbling and ancient construction. Bellor and Thor inspected the bas-relief statues on the walls of the gate to the city. The sandblasted raised carvings were of dragons in flight and two huge dragon heads poked out from the columns beside the gates, their mouths opened wide.

"What in the name of Lorak's Holy Blood is this about?" Thor asked. "I thought the Mephitians hated dragons."

"Not all of them," Dabarius said. "The old Mephitian empire fell apart a few hundred years ago because the God King of Far Khoram sided with the dragons. Weren't you paying attention in Isyrin?"

"Bah," Thor shook his head. "Human religion never has made any sense. The True Fire is the only God any man or dwarf would ever need." He looked at Bellor for confirmation.

The old War Priest let out an exasperated sigh and walked through the archway into the city and onto an avenue of flat road stones. The cat's trail disappeared, but Drake had seen where the trees were, and headed in that direction.

"It must be difficult on morale . . . so many unnecessary gods and goddesses just hanging around," Dabarius said in Drake's ear.

"Huh?" Drake said, his brain having a hard time processing anything other than cat tracks and getting his depleted body to move.

The wizard quirked his lip and huffed. "Never mind." He looked out into the abandoned ruins. "The louts and bumpkins I'm forced to travel with . . . "

Dozens of seated lion statues lined the roadway that led into the heart of Shahan. Quite a number of the lions were missing their heads. Had they been vandalized by conquering soldiers during the long ago war?

The road of lions led them through a vast plaza and directly toward the grove of trees. They shambled down a dusty avenue toward a tall structure that appeared to be the gateway into an expansive walled temple complex. Two rectangular towers—Bree had called them pylons at the temple of Amar'isis—rose like a pair of notched hills and the front of them, which was elaborately decorated, faced the east. The pylons flanked a grand doorway into an inner courtyard, which was where the trees and the water had to be.

Everything in the city had been drab, and tan colored, but above the gateway in the very center was a bright red sun disk. The symbol of Ah'usar, the long lost husband of Amar'isis seemed freshly painted.

Movement in the shadows on either side of them and the sounds of sandaled feet coming toward them from the front made them all react with alarm. Drake slipped his crossbow off his back and started to crank his krannekin to load the upper bow. Bellor tried to get *Wyrmslayer* off his back sling, but fell to one knee.

A small animal on a rooftop caught Drake's eye. As he turned, he became dizzy and nearly fell over. The animal, definitely a feline cat, stared down with intense, slitted eyes, its ears back and teeth bared. All three dogs started wagging their tails at the beige cat with brown stripes running across its short fur. It looked like the cat from the thorn tree, but it had no wings. He must have been delirious and imagined them.

The sandals stopped in front of them. Four dark-skinned Mephitian women stood in the doorway of the temple grounds. Two of them held small cats, who scrambled out of their arms and ran off at the sight of the dogs, who barked weakly before Drake silenced them.

The women frowned at the dogs, and Drake took a hold of both bullmastiffs' collars. "Sorry," he said in Nexan, forgetting the Mephitian word.

"*Moh'kem eh'sair,*" the oldest of them called out the Mephitian word for welcome. She appeared to be in her thirties, but the other three were at least ten years younger. All were very short of stature and had very large eyes accentuated with kohl. They wore rough linen *kalasiris* dresses, and long corn-rolled wigs with diadems that prominently displayed golden sun discs above their foreheads.

"*Mu'aat, eh'tair,*" Dabarius said. *Water, please.*

The little women motioned at the dogs with worried expressions, and Drake herded Skinny, Jep and Temus into a small shady building and leashed them to a bench. With the dogs secured, the women rushed over and helped the companions.

The eldest woman eyed the dogs and said something to Dabarius about them, making gestures with her delicate hands.

"They want to help us," Dabarius said, "but no dogs on temple grounds, even if they are the guardians of Ah'usar, and the Takers of Souls to the Afterworld."

"What?" Drake asked.

"I'll tell you later," the wizard said.

"Who are they?" Thor asked.

Dabarius spoke a few words and the oldest replied with a great smile on her face. After a moment she grinned at the dwarves.

"They are Priestesses of the Sun God, Ah'usar," Dabarius said.

A young woman much smaller than Drake took his pack, Bree's sword, and his crossbow. She smiled and he looked at her white teeth to avoid staring at her body, which was barely obscured by the sheer linen dress. The other two women helped Bellor. Drake smelled the sweet scented oils that coated the women's bodies.

The Priestesses helped them through the gate and into a palm tree-shaded courtyard. A small rectangular lake of clear water beckoned them.

The oldest Priestess gave Bellor, Thor and Dabarius their own small jug of water they had just dipped into what Dabarius referred to as the "Sacred Lake." Drake received his and poured half of it down his parched throat and the rest over his head. It was the best tasting water he'd ever had, and knew that no matter how long he lived beyond that moment, he would never forget the feeling or take for granted having enough water again. Grinning, he got some more and brought it to the dogs outside the temple, filling their water bags full, then letting them stick their heads in them and lap it up.

When he returned a short time later two of the younger Priestesses were undressing Dabarius. They led him like some Mephitian prince by the hands into the shallow pool, one on each side of him. The tall wizard sunk below the surface then floated on his back. The women began undressing Thor next, who was so exhausted he barely put up a fight. The dwarven warrior didn't wait for his boots to come off and stepped into the lake with them still on. Bellor followed without complaint and the women came for Drake next. He left on his smallclothes, despite their protests, and went into the pool. Merely touching the water was like waking from a terrible dream, and he drank several swallows after submerging himself. The sweat and grime from the past two weeks of travel melted off him.

The trio of younger women slipped off their kalasiris and entered the pool where they proceeded to sponge off the companions with rags. Slightly horrified, but mostly relieved, Drake wondered why the Mephitian people had no sense of modesty. He had little energy to fight, but he escaped from them eventually, and they moved on to Dabarius, who stood still while they washed his dark hair.

After a few moments, the older Priestess had a conversation with Dabarius, while Drake and the others waited for a translation. Drake wasn't sure how long it took—he'd lost all sense of time since arriving in this city—but Dabarius eventually finished his conversation. "She is Elder Priestess Kasiya," he said, "the Keeper of the Flame, Devoted One to Ah'usar." Dabarius let the other two scrub his legs and feet. "They are her acolytes, Faydra, Maralla, and Laris. We are their welcome guests."

"Obviously," Thor said as he floated against the side.

Dabarius nodded to Kasiya and thanked her. She bowed her head and hustled away into an adjacent building.

"What now?" Thor asked.

"Elder Priestess says they have food for us and she will prepare a place for us to sleep."

A short time later, the young women tied linen kilts around the companions and led them down some stairs into a building beside the pool. A wide, but very small waterfall dripped down one wall of the room, which cooled the air tremendously. Waiting for them were reed sleeping mats atop grass stuffed mattresses, rolled blankets, soft pillows, bowls of roasted almonds, plates of soft flat bread, goat cheese, and ceramic jugs of cold water. Drake left and fed and watered the dogs again.

He returned and ate a few bites himself before he fell asleep with the trickling sound of the waterfall in the background.

He awoke once during the night. A shadowy woman stood at the top of the stairs to their room. Her long hair fell loosely about her shoulders and he thought he recognized her profile. Bree'alla? He rubbed the gritty sleep from his eyes. But when he looked again, she was gone. He shook his head at the vivid dream, then lay down, letting the exhaustion claim him. He missed her so much, but Bree was gone. He had to accept it. As he drifted off to sleep, Drake wrapped his hand around *Wingblade's* scabbard lying beside him and pulled it close.

LXII

We have found water at last, though it is but a trickle of what it must once have been.
> —Bölak Blackhammer, from the Khoram Journal

Cool fog from the River of Mist shrouded the vast temple complex of Ah'usar early in the morning. Broken rooftops were hidden as the mist passed through the fallen arches of tan stone, obscuring the ruins of a once-great city. Drake kept Jep, Temus, and Skinny on leashes as he walked them to a place more appropriate to see to their needs, then returned, and tied them up in accordance with the rules set by the Daughters of the Sun. He kept the dogs inside the roofed building near the gate to the temple. He fed them, pet them, and scratched their bellies, then returned to the temple's holy ground, which was overrun with dozens of small cats—none of them with wings. Drake thought that he must have been dunder-headed at the time, as Thor said.

The shortest Priestess, Faydra, watched as he returned, then she slipped into an archway and disappeared. He sat on a stone bench looking at the narrow rectangular lake in the courtyard as the mist drifted across the still water.

The sound of sandals moving slowly over the ground from the archway where Faydra disappeared drew his attention. A woman walked hesitantly toward him. He stood and blinked as the pale fog swirled around her, making her dark red hair even darker in the faint morning light. Strands fell across her face, her hair unkempt so different from the tight warrior braid she usually kept.

Drake ran to her and wrapped his arms around Bree. She trembled as she buried her face in his shoulder. She felt strong and alive, but somehow defeated.

"I thought you were dead," he finally whispered.

She pulled away, her face scrunched up. Guilt and sadness radiated from her. "I'm so sorry. I was not myself."

"What happened?"

She cupped his face gently with her hands, as if praying to him for forgiveness. The pain in her made his heart ache, and she sunk down as if she were on the verge of collapsing in shame. He tried to keep her on her feet, but she fell to her knees and stared up at him with glassy eyes. "Forgive me, please, and know that I didn't want to do it. I had to. I'm so sorry."

Several figures approached in the fog from the waterfall house. Bellor, Thor, and Dabarius came with severe expressions fixed on Bree. She got down on her knees, her eyes wide and full of remorse.

Thor muttered Drobin curses. Bellor and Dabarius stared at her, full of judgment.

"It would have been better if you'd stayed dead," Thor said at last.

She reacted with a nod, prepared for whatever pronouncement that might come.

Bellor stood in front of her, shaking his head and dangling the mountain symbol medallion of Lorak in his hand. "You nearly led us to our deaths. Explain yourself and hide nothing. I will know if you lie." He held the medallion perfectly still at the level of her mouth.

She nodded earnestly, and looked at the venerable dwarf. "Master Bellor, forgive me. I should have taken my own life in the Dune Sea. That would have been the only way to prevent what happened." She glanced up at Drake. "He stopped me."

"He told us what happened," Bellor said, "but it doesn't explain what you did."

"I tried to stop us from going to Thunderstone," Bree said, "but I couldn't."

"Why?" Thor asked.

"Queen Khelen'dara," Bree said.

341

The medallion did not stir.

"It was not Khelen'dara," Dabarius said, full on condemnation.

"She used binding magic on me," Bree said. "She forced me to bring you there and then commanded me to leave you all at the obelisk after sunset. I was to flee into the desert afterward . . . and I was to take my own life. There was a compulsion in my mind that I could not resist . . . or break by force of will. I couldn't tell you about it. I tried many times after we left Isyrin, but the magic prevented me, and I had made a vow in the Sand Lake on that very cold night when we crossed the border."

"What vow?" Drake asked, "What are you talking about?"

"The Black Ghost of the Desert, who guards the land there came to our camp that night when we couldn't get the vorrels out," Bree said. "The Drobin wards did not stop him."

"You should have woken us," Bellor said. "We would have fought him."

"We all would have died," she said, "but I couldn't have woken you if I wanted to. He had us in his power. The only way to save your lives then was to promise him that I would kill you all with my own hands if you betrayed the secrets of Mephitia—the secrets I had vowed to keep as a Wing Guardian. The Queen used that knowledge of my vow to the Black Ghost and as a Wing Guardian to further bind and compel me."

She rocked slowly back and forth and Drake wanted to reach out to her, but she shied away when he did.

"Now that the task I was given is over," Bree said, "and I have been purified here in the Sacred Lake of Ah'usar, I can finally speak of these things. I couldn't before, no matter how hard I tried. The Queen put the spell into my mind on our last night in Isyrin."

"That's why you were acting so strangely ever since we left," Drake said.

Bree nodded. "I was weak. I couldn't fight it. It tortured me ever since we left the city. It was different than the binding scarab magic. Stronger."

"What happened after Thunderstone?" Bellor asked.

"I was thrown from the vorrel I was riding, and was knocked unconscious all night and most of the next day. Then I searched for you for days, but the storm continued . . . and I couldn't find you, though I found the chain shirts and the supplies you left behind, and I thought . . . I was sure you were dead. Then I was at the River of Mist south of Shahan." She looked up at Drake. "I was going to jump into the canyon, fulfill the final command of my Queen."

Drake put his hand on her shoulder. To him, it made sense now. He felt so relieved, and ashamed for not knowing what was wrong.

"Elder Priestess Kasiya stopped me," Bree said. "She'd seen me riding as I looked for you around Shahan. If not for her . . ." Bree slowly hung her head.

"It wasn't Queen Khelen'dara," Dabarius said.

"Bree'alla did not lie," Bellor said, as he put the medallion back around his neck. "I am certain of this."

"I swear, Dabarius," Bree pleaded, "it was her."

"No," Dabarius said, "you *believed* the Queen put binding magic on you, but she couldn't have."

They all waited for him to continue as he considered his next words.

"Khelen'dara could not have come to you the night before we left Isyrin," Dabarius said.

"She did, in the darkness, after my last meeting with her advisors," Bree said.

"It wasn't her," Dabarius said. "I was with her every moment that day and night."

"Then who was it that came to me?" Bree asked.

"Don't you know? Who else has enough magic to assume another person's shape? Who else knew all the details you told

343

the Queen? Use your mind for once, damn you!" Dabarius commanded, his face dark with anger.

"A wingataur," Thor said.

Bree looked startled. "No. It was General Reu'ven . . . "

Dabarius nodded. "I found out from Khelen'dara that he was a powerful wizard, and I don't think he truly left the city as we all suspected. I believe it was him who caused the avalanche that buried us in the mountain, then he tried to kill us again when we escaped from the second avalanche and had to swim across the lake. Do you remember the falcon?"

Drake did, and knew he should have shot that damned aevian when he had the chance. If only Khelen'dara's guards hadn't stopped him.

"The falcon could have been Reu'ven himself or one of his spies," Dabarius said. "He knows such shapeshifting magic, and it was Reu'ven who took the form of the Queen, and put the binding magic into Bree's mind. I'm certain of it."

"He disobeyed his sovereign's orders," Bellor said, and shook his head.

"Yes," Dabarius said, "and he's very clever. No one would ever know what happened if Bree succeeded and ended her own life. There would be no evidence against him and all of us would be gone."

"Is he in league with our enemies?" Bellor asked. "Is our course known to Draglûne and his followers?"

"I don't think so," Dabarius said. "Reu'ven is loyal to Isyrin and his Queen, in his own way. He raised her since she was an infant. He loves her as much as his own children. Her mother—a woman he loved—and her grandmother, were both assassinated for opposing Draglûne, and he did not want Khelen'dara to suffer the same fate."

"There's more," Bree said. "I was told that there is no secret bridge here and no water either. I was told that General Reu'ven had the bridge destroyed soon after Khelen'dara's mother was assassinated, and that High Priest Ben'khar was never informed. I was led to believe that General Reu'ven worried that the bridge could be used by assassins who would come after the queen—so he destroyed the bridge."

Thor grumbled and Bellor let out a low whistle.

"Also," Bree said, "I was told that the Khebian Priests found a message on west side of the bridge when they arrived here twenty years ago. They found six human skulls and ten dwarven ones. A message had been etched on the stone beside the skulls."

"All lies," Dabarius said. "Believe none of it."

"They may be lies," Bellor said, "but tell us everything as there may be something worth considering in all of it. Now what did the message say?"

"Your assassins failed. Ours will not," Bree said. "Queen Khelen'dara's mother did fall to assassins."

"Reu'ven uses some truths to mask his lies," Dabarius said. "That's all." The struggle to sound sure of himself began to show.

"What else?" Bellor asked Bree.

"I was told that sending us after Draglûne was too much of a risk for all of Mephitia. I should have known my Queen wouldn't do or say such things." Bree looked both relieved and sickened. "I've cursed her name every day since we left Isyrin."

"Reu'ven will pay for this in the end," Dabarius said. "Once Draglûne is dead, I'm going back to Isyrin and the Queen will know the truth, and he will not be able to hide from me."

"When we've done what we set out to do," Bree said, "I'll go with you."

"Then you are going with us to finish this?" Bellor said, extending his hand to her. "For your Queen?"

Bree put her hand in Bellor's and stood up, then hooked her arm around Drake's, and smiled at the young man. "Not just for her."

345

LXIII

I was like Jaena when I was a young. I wanted more than anything to leave Cliffton and see the world outside the Thornclaw. The Elders gave me my wish and sent me to the Sacred Grove to learn. They were good years, but Priestess Gwynedd did not only teach us how to be Priestesses. She showed us how the Drobin ruled. We walked the streets of Nexus City. We saw. Now I have failed my own daughter, for she has to see these things for herself.

—Priestess Liana Whitestar, from her personal journal

The patrol of Drobin marshals marched Jaena through the woods on a narrow trail, avoiding the main roads and all of the farmers in the fields, until they arrived at a stone fort with a tall tower soaring above the treetops. Two enormous vroxen tethered to a prison wagon waited outside the gates. The six-legged beasts snorted when the patrol approached. Their horns pointed up at the sky and she imagined that griffins would have to be careful if they were going to take one of them down.

The marshals and the wagon driver exchanged words when they arrived, and though Jaena knew little of the Drobin language, she thought the wagon driver, a dwarf with very bushy eyebrows said, "You're early."

The lead marshal grinned, and Jaena wondered, not for the first time, if they had known she was going to be on the trail that morning. Was another patrol on the path to Sherrington, in case she had gone that way? Had the marshals already captured Blayne and Kraig? Had they told the Drobin where she was? Not likely, but why was a wagon waiting for her if her capture had been by chance? Unless one of the people from Masefield had turned her in. Not likely, but Priestess Nayla had told her she was naïve and far too trusting.

346

The wagon driver climbed into the back of the iron cage, then lifted her up after him. At five-and-a-half feet, she was taller than him by a foot, but he picked her up like she was a child. His hands seemed twice as big as hers and if he had wanted she thought he could have crushed her rib cage. He unchained her wrists from behind her back, then chained her left wrist to the wall.

"Is the Priestess comfortable?" he asked in accented Nexan.

She narrowed her gaze at him and touched the gag in her mouth.

He removed it gently and asked, "Care for a drink?" He took a swig from a waterskin before passing it to her.

She accepted it and he winked.

"Keep it," he said.

Two of the marshals got in the back of the wagon with her. One was the leader and he had a sack that contained all of her personal belongings, including her journal and the note from Nayla. He did not look through them and kept his gaze on her, studying her every move.

Before they got underway a fitted canvas covering was placed over the iron cage that blocked the exit as well. No one would see her on the road. The driver whipped the vroxen and they bellowed, then pulled the wagon forward down the bumpy roadway.

"If you speak," the lead marshal said, "I'll have to replace this gag."

Jaena hated the gag and agreed to follow the rules by nodding and bowing humbly.

The bumpy road made her full bladder want to burst. She hadn't emptied it before she ran out of the house that morning. The marshal realized her problem and told her to go in the hole in the center of the wagon. Her wrist chain reached just far enough and she could see the stone road passing beneath them. She relieved herself while the two guards turned their heads. None of the Drobin looked at her with hatred. They seemed to simply be doing their jobs, without any outward emotion. On the dark nights when she'd worried that she'd be captured, she had imagined that they'd be rough, brutal, sneering. They were not. It didn't matter, though. She was still captured, and she knew what happened to Amaryllian Priestesses at the hands of the Drobin Empire.

Over two hours later they left the cool and shady forest and entered a bright and sunny place. The smell of sewage wafted up from the ground as the wagon passed over a wooden bridge and onto more cobblestone streets. She heard the voices of men and dwarves in the street and knew she had arrived in Nexus City. Charcoal smoke, unwashed bodies, vroxen droppings, and a myriad of other scents entered the wagon. Jaena had such a sudden pang of longing to see Cliffton that she had to push one fist against her mouth to keep from crying out. She would never see her village again, never see her family. She would never see Drake, never know whether he would fulfill his promise to return.

"Not long now," a marshal told her.

Not long before I arrive at a prison, she thought. When she was young, Jaena, Ethan, and Drake had talked about seeing Nexus City, and now she was there, but could see nothing. She tried not to dwell on it and focused on being strong. She would not break down in front of her guards.

They put a musty hood over her head and took her out of the wagon and down a long, twisting dark hallway, through several doors and down many stairs. She heard men, and perhaps one woman shouting, and dwarven voices telling them to be silent. She stumbled several times, but the two marshals kept her from falling. The terror she felt made her shake and the lump in her throat made her constantly clear her throat. The guards finally removed her hood and the manacles on her wrists when they deposited her in a dank, black cell that radiated cold.

The marshal sat her on a thick folded blanket and patted her head before he walked to the doorway with the lantern.

"You are a good girl," he said. "Do what is asked of you and this will be over soon."

She touched her lips, asking him if she could speak.

"You may speak," he said.

"Thank you for taking care of me," she said.

He looked at her for a long time, and his eyes softened. "The High Marshall knows that you're here. He'll speak with you soon."

"Thank you."

He closed the door and walked away, leaving her in the blackness. The darkness robbed her of the resolve she had remaining, but she held in the tears that threatened to pour from her eyes. She curled into a ball, holding her knees against her chest. She would die here alone in the dark. Drake would never know and she would never get to see him again in this world.

She heard footsteps coming back to her cell. The marshal hung the lantern outside the tiny window, and a little of the light entered her cell.

"Wrap the blanket around yourself, girl," he whispered and then was gone.

The small mercy of light and the blanket kept her from falling into despair.

The door to Jaena's cell opened as the lantern began to burn low. The lead marshal stood with a lantern so bright that it hurt her eyes. She was surprised to see him, and was very glad, for in his face, in his eyes, there was a decency—or at least a mercy—she hadn't expected. He carried a large sack of items

349

and placed them on the floor inside the cell, then walked inside.

"Forgive my lateness," he said. "I am never late, but matters kept me occupied, and I wanted to personally deliver these items to you. He opened the sack and brought out warm sheepskin blankets, a pillow, packages of food, a full waterskin, a chamber pot, a golden glowstone that shed an amazing amount of soft light, and a fire stone from which a flickering red flame danced. He kept the burning stone in a ceramic tube and left it on the floor in front of her. The stone immediately began heating the cold room, but he warned her not to catch anything on fire with it. She promised she wouldn't, and as if to reward her answer he handed her a copy of the Goddess Scrolls.

"Thank you very much," she said, wondering why he was being so generous to a prisoner who would soon be executed. Did he have a conscience that needed to be appeased?

"I do wish to make you comfortable, and if you answer my questions, I shall move you to a more pleasant room. You have my word of honor."

"I shall answer all of your questions truthfully," she said, and meant it. Lying had never come naturally to her, and she couldn't imagine that any story she might make up would help her now. She would stand by all she had said, all that she had done. If she faced this next trial with a brave heart, she would have nothing to be ashamed of.

He sat on a padded wooden stool he had brought, and stared at her silently for some time. His eyes flashed from pity to wonder, to frustration all at once. "You never should have come here," he said, shaking his head.

"I had to come," she replied with a whisper.

"Why?"

"There was nothing left for me at home. I was needed here. The Nexan people needed a healer, and I came."

"There are Drobin healers," he said.

"Pardon me, but the Drobin do not heal like we Amaryllian Priestesses do. Your folk are fine physics and surgeons if the fee can be paid, but none of you have the gifts that the Goddess bestows upon us."

"The Goddess has no place here. Only the True Father."

"I respectfully disagree."

"You know what the penalty is for practicing Tree magic."

"Yes."

"Yet you came, practiced it many times in the villages around Nexus City, risking your own death?"

"I had to."

He looked at her for a while, his eyes narrowing. "Why were you running toward Nexus City?"

"I had to find my friends and stop them from committing a terrible crime and starting a revolt against your people," she said.

"What crime?" he asked.

"I know of a plot to assassinate King Alaric and the Lorakian High Priests. This must not happen. Please, I'm begging you, help me. I have to stop this or so many of your people and mine will die in what is to follow."

"Why do you want to stop this? You and your religious zealots have been preaching war for weeks now, and long before that, and now you want to stop it?"

"I never preached war. I'm a healer, and if there is war, I will have failed."

"Tell me of the woman, Priestess Nayla, with whom you traveled."

Jaena did. She held nothing back, telling him everything about her first meeting with Nayla, their trip to the Nexus Plateau and the burned Sacred Grove, the speeches and the healing sessions, and even the note, which he undoubtedly read as he had taken it from her pocket. He may have even had time to read her journal. She was determined to be as honest as she could. She had no one to protect, save perhaps Blayne and Kraig who might still be free. She would not reveal the location of Cliffton, though he might be able to find it from the clues in her journal. Why had she written so much down?

"How will your friends try to assassinate king Alaric and the High Priests? Which High Priests will be targeted?"

"I don't know which ones. Names were never mentioned to me, but my friends are all expert marksmen with crossbows. That's why Nayla sought them out."

"Crossbows are illegal in the city unless they are carried by a soldier or marshal. How would they hide them from the watch marshals?"

"I don't know, but they will get them into the city. Please, have no doubt of that. Protect your leaders. Help me stop this."

"Why have you told me so much?" he asked.

"I don't want war. You must believe that."

He didn't hesitate. "I *do* believe you."

"I only want to help, and may I please ask you one question?"

He nodded and gave her a flourish of his hand.

"I wondered if you knew what happened to High Priestess Gwynedd and the Sacred Grove of Amaryllis?"

"You may not believe me," he said.

"I will listen with an open mind, like you have with me."

He let out a sigh. "I did know that the grove had been burned and the Priestesses killed. I learned that from a young Amaryllian woman, a student of Gwynedd's, who fled the grove. She said that a handful of Drobin soldiers surrounded them and captured Gwynedd and the others. Except for this young woman, and one other who escaped, all were killed. The witness that I spoke to saw Drobin warriors the night she fled." The dwarf paused and his spine stiffened. "I can assure you that none of my kin participated in such an attack. To this day we do not know the location of the grove, though we trust the reports and believe that it is indeed burned."

Jaena wanted to believe him, but she couldn't. "Forgive me for suggesting this, but is there any chance that you were not told of this by your superiors?"

He shook his head. "I have served the Drobin King for over a hundred and thirty-five years, and before that I was being trained to do so. I have held many ranks and offices and know the details of all military and marshal activities going back over seven hundred years."

His words seemed genuine, but she still had doubts. Why would he admit to such a brutal massacre? It would not serve the Drobin at all, except perhaps to make the Nexan people more afraid than they already were.

"You have been to the grove," he said, "tell me more about what you saw there."

She told him in detail everything she remembered, but not its location, though she doubted she could find it again herself as it was so deep at the northern edge of the Thornclaw Forest.

"You say the central sentinel tree was burned down to the trunk, but none of the other trees were destroyed so much as that?"

"Yes, it was by far the worst damaged," she said, "like a candle burned down to the base."

He asked several more pointed questions about the grove, and she answered all his inquiries with specificity. He seemed pleased with her candor, and she trusted him more. She wondered if perhaps the dwarves who destroyed the grove could have been vigilantes, separate from the Drobin hierarchy.

"Thank you, Jaena. I shall move you to a more agreeable place now."

"I thank you for your kindness."

"I do not wish you to suffer needlessly. You are my prisoner, but you are no base criminal who deserves little consideration. Though we both know what the law proclaims as punishment for what you've done, I shall not see you endure unnecessary pain before the end."

"I have already made my peace with my Goddess. Take my life if you must."

"How can you be so unafraid?"

"I am afraid of pain and the trials of the flesh, but I know what happens beyond this life, and it gives me solace. In the last weeks, through the Goddess's bounty, I have brought comfort to the sick, easy steps to the lame, health to babes who would have otherwise perished. I have done more good than I could have accomplished in twenty years in my own home. If my life is the cost, so be it."

The dwarf nodded, pondering her words. "Many of my people believe that the magic you wield is not a blessing, but a curse your folk cannot wield without destroying yourselves, and we Drobin along with you."

"The Goddess will bless your folk as well," Jaena said. "Your Earth Priests do not need to sacrifice years of their lives to heal the sick or injured. The trees will accept the price and become stronger for it."

"What happens when the Nexan people turn away from the Earth Father and look to Amaryllis?" he asked.

"Our people can still be allies," Jaena said.

"Many of the High Priests of Lorak have a very different view," he said. "They say the Nexans will seek even more freedom and there would be war between us, and someday war amongst the humans, as your kind cannot keep a lasting peace if left without the guidance of the Drobin. The histories point to a time when Amaryllis was not among your kin, and there was peace on the plateaus between the Nexan and Drobin who were united by one god. Your goddess has brought chaos and violence."

"Sir, I am a young woman, and I know of only the blessings of Amaryllis. She allows me to heal and save lives. The magic is not evil. It comes from a place of light and hope. I do not regret what I have done, and if I must be punished for breaking the Drobin law, I will accept my fate. I am just so sorry to have caused any discord. It was not my intent, and please forgive me for causing you this trouble."

He studied her for a long moment. "It is an honor to know you, Jaena Whitestar, Priestess of Cliffton. I thank you for your example. Few in your position behave with this much courage. After I heard of your deeds in the villages, I wanted to know for myself if it was all true. You are far stronger, and look far younger, than I imagined, but your soul is as old as mine, and I wish for you to know my name."

He sat up straighter, and she tensed, wondering who this dwarf could be. He was not some village patrol marshal as she first thought. He was of a much higher rank, which she had suspected for some time.

"I am Lord Marshal Gunther Krohgstaad of Clan King-shield. I am the first son of Geurik and Uhlda, and first cousin to the king of the Drobin Empire."

She was stunned into open-mouthed silence. He was one of the highest ranking Drobin on all of the plateaus, and he had power, perhaps enough to pardon her. "Lord Marshal, I only wish we could have met under better circumstances."

It was not the response he anticipated, and his glum expression told her much, but left her questioning what might happen next.

"I shall have you moved immediately and we shall speak again." He walked to the open door and paused. "I am still honored to know you, but I wish we had never met, for the law is clear and I must do my duty. You have defied the laws of the king. You have stirred up the Nexan people, whether you wished to or not. You should have stayed in your home village, waited for your young man to return."

He had read her journal as she thought. He knew everything she'd written, that's what had delayed him, and now Jaena had to ask. "Lord Marshall, is there no hope for me to live? Am I condemned to death?"

"There will be no trial," he said eventually. "You will be executed, though it will not be by bonfire, as the Lorakian Priests will demand. You will die quickly, as painlessly as I can manage. This I promise you."

She believed him and though it was agony to hear his words, it was a relief to know her fate at last.

LXIV

The temples of Shahan go untended, and will soon crumble to ruins or be swallowed by the desert. I am saddened by this, for the exquisite stone will be buried forever.

—Bölak Blackhammer, from the Khoram Journal

It took three days of sleeping late, eating well, and doing little for Drake to feel like himself again. His feet and eyes finally recovered, and in the tolerable heat of the evening he left the temple complex of Ah'usar, made up of a dozen large walled courtyards filled with wild gardens and abandoned buildings. Dabarius and the dwarves stayed behind and spoke with Kasiya and the other Priestesses while he hunted in the vast ruin of Shahan with Bree at his side. She wore her father's sword, *Wingblade* strapped to her belt. Drake could see that having her father's sword in her possession again had given Bree her confidence back. She was a warrior again, her mind free and unburdened, unlike how she had been during their trip to Isyrin, and then to Shahan.

Drake had brought her longsword all the way from Thunderstone, and she had carried the discarded chain mail shirts of the Drobin on her vorrel for days while she searched for them. The surprising exchange of gifts had helped mend the rift between Bree and the others, and a friendly camaraderie had begun to blossom between all of them—though Thor and Dabarius constantly traded insults in Drobin, Nexan, and now a smattering of Mephitian—the profane words supplied to Thor by Bree'alla. They were all hunters again, united by a common purpose. Drake felt so good now that the Dune Sea was behind him, and he felt like soon they would reach the end of their long trek, one way or another.

In a wild garden, in the shadow of a pair of tall towers and a ruined palace complex, Drake shot four quail, and three desert sparrows with blunted bolts. He fed most of the aevians to his dogs, who stayed on his heels unless he released them to run. He missed once, his first shot of the day, but Skinny retrieved the errant shaft. The little dog was learning. All three dogs had recovered somewhat, but they still looked thin, and were all more tentative than usual as they explored the ruins. Shahan was a somber, dead place, abandoned for more than a century and buried by the desert.

The ruins, mostly one level hovels without ceilings, spread out for some distance as sand blew idly down the weed-choked avenues and alleys. The quiet was enforced by towering pillars and walls etched with picture symbols that Bree could not read. The dogs often hesitated and did not bark, as if they sensed it was not safe.

The Daughters of the Sun had told them the only dangers were snakes, scorpions, vorrel spiders, collapsing buildings, and perhaps a misstep at the sheer cliffs on the edge of the River of Mist. No predators lived in or near the city, and they assured Drake that nothing flew out of the Void here—except for the morning mist.

As a son of Cliffton, his nature did not allow himself to take chances, and he always watched the open sky wherever they went, though Bree and Drake avoided the eastern edge of the city where the chasm lay and instead went west, following the green strip of trees, shrubs, and grasses that followed the underground stream that supplied the pools in the sun god's temple.

One of the tawny temple cats followed them, always keeping well away from the dogs and usually out of sight. It seemed odd to Drake, but he tried not to let it bother him, though he couldn't forget what he had imagined when he first saw the first cat outside the city. The idea of a winged cat seemed ridiculous now. This one was just hoping for scraps from one of his bird kills. If the dogs left anything, the cat was welcome to it.

Near the edge of the city they found the small herd of scrawny goats the Daughters of the Sun allowed to roam and graze in the ruins. One wuffling bark from Jep sent the skittish animals running for the lives. Some of them climbed atop narrow walls and half a dozen took refuge in a squat tree, perching on narrow branches that sagged under their weight.

Jep, Temus, and Skinny whined and begged to be allowed to go after them and up the tree. Skinny nearly broke free of Drake's grasp when a goat fell off a branch and tried unsuccessfully to rescale the trunk. It was the first time he and Bree'alla laughed heartily in what felt like years, though they had only known each other less than three months.

They left the terrified goats in their tree and walked back to the temple complex smiling. Drake presented three of the quail to Kasiya, and she gratefully accepted them. Not long after sunset, the five guests and Kasiya sat on the floor of a cool and dimly lit chamber where the young attendants served a simple meal of fresh—but still sour—cheese curds, flat bread, bitter greens, and small pieces of quail meat.

Everyone laughed when Bree told the tale in Nexan, then Mephitian of the dogs chasing the goats into the tree, though Kasiya warned Drake to keep his dogs from harming her precious animals. The goats were their main source of food and were all they had, aside from Bree's lone vorrel penned in a large courtyard nearby.

"How did they get here without vorrels?" Drake asked. It seemed impossible.

"They had some, but let them go three years ago after the four of them reached the city," Dabarius said, "because of lack of food here." They could let the goats graze on the plants around the city, or the vorrels, not both. Dabarius had learned a lot about the four women in the past days and explained about how Kasiya was called to reclaim the temple in Shahan in the name of the Sun God, Ah'usar by her order in a sanctuary along the southern mountains. Someday perhaps, her order, The Daughters of the Sun, would send more devoted followers and they would rebuild the city. Coming to Shahan was her mission and she greatly respected anyone who followed a path determined by their patron god, as Bellor and Thor did especially. They were very pleased to serve those who carried the trust scarabs of the Queen of Isyrin, and would do anything they could to help, though they knew of no way to cross the River of Mist, and had never heard of anyone crossing at Shahan since before the bridge was broken and Old and New Mephitia were separated forever.

Dabarius conceded in whispered Nexan that he'd been casually deflecting questions about their purpose in crossing to Far Khoram, though he had admitted they carried a letter from the queen of Isyrin for the God King of Old Mephitia. Kasiya also had many questions about the two Drobin, whom she called the "Sons of Kheb" and held in great esteem. Kasiya did not disguise her hunger for news from the outside world, and especially word from the forbidden north, where only those Mephitians with sanction from the Queen and trust scarabs could travel. Drake and the dwarves were obviously from the north and this elicited an unending line of questions translated by Dabarius when he felt it important for Bellor to actually hear the question.

At the end of the evening meal, Kasiya surprised them with a dessert of tiny green grapes that were quite sweet, and then she produced a jug of wine, carefully pouring a clay cupful for everyone. It was strong, barely watered down, and Drake found it quite tasty, though his head was spinning after one cup. Bellor abstained from more than a sip, but Dabarius gladly accepted their wine, and Thor had two cups.

At the end of the meal, Kasiya called for entertainment. Laris began to play a small four-stringed instrument similar to a lute, plucking strings with her tiny fingers, while Kasiya played a hide drum and sang. Short Faydra and tall Maralla danced and clapped their hands, moving their hips and swaying to the rhythm as the Drobin and Dabarius clapped along.

Drake's eyes lingered on the young women's bodies, barely covered by their sheer dresses. Nothing like this display would ever happen in Cliffton, and he found himself stealing glances at Bree more than the dancers. She was far more beautiful than any of the small-statured and thin Mephitian women.

Well into the second dance as the music built to a fevered pitch, Bree suddenly took Drake by the hand and led him outside then into a neighboring courtyard where she pushed him against a wall. Hiding in the shadows created by the bright moonlight, Bree pressed her lips against his and he tasted the wine on her breath. The warm night became hot as they explored each other, caressing, touching, and kissing. The wine had bent his will, but it hadn't broken it. He pushed her gently away when she tried to unbuckle his belt.

"What's wrong?" she asked.

"I can't do this."

"Why?" Her eyes flashed with confusion and dullness from the wine.

What could he say? She knew a little about Jaena already, but Bree had never mentioned her to him. Now he had to tell her. He'd let things go to far with Bree and felt terrible about it. He composed his thoughts and let out a long sigh. "There's a woman, back home. I'm promised to her. I love her. If there's a way, I'm going back to Cliffton when this is over."

"Stupid man. You're not going home." She pressed the trust scarab pinned to his shirt painfully into his chest. "You can't go home. Ever."

"Sometimes I don't know if I believe that." He tried to muster his defenses, but his head was spinning.

She seized his hesitation and kissed him, hard. "Believe what's right in front of you." She stepped into the moonlight and nudged the dress off her shoulders. She traced the scab on her side where her sword had cut her skin, then put her fingers under her sternum between her breasts. "In the desert, before

Thunderstone, my sword point was here. You saved me. You said you loved me."

He nodded. He meant everything he'd said, and cared for her even more now.

"Then love me," she said.

"I want to, so badly." He ached for her and it took all his will not to take her in his arms.

"Men and women often lay together in temples to bless their union. There's nothing stopping us." She came closer to him, rubbed a hand across his chest.

"Yes there is," he said.

"What are you talking about?"

"I can't do this."

"You're a man, I know you can." She touched the front of his pants, and he pulled away.

"This is not the way of either of our peoples," he said.

"What worries you so much?"

"I might still find a way to go home, but if we lay together . . . and I put a child in you . . . "

"You think I'm trying to trap you here with a baby?"

"No, but if I lay with you . . . " he couldn't believe what he was about to say, "I would first ask you to become my wife."

That surprised her. "Are you asking to be my husband?"

"Not yet."

She kissed him softly and smiled, her green eyes sparkled. "Perhaps we should bind ourselves together in this temple before the Sun God in the morning when it is proper to seal a bond. Only the gods know what the future will bring and now we have peace. Don't you agree? We may not live much longer. This could be our only chance at some happiness before the end."

He thought for a long moment, perfectly sober now. Dying in the desert or trying to slay Draglûne was a real possibility, but he knew the true answer, and why he couldn't be with her. "What if this lasts for longer than we think? What if I took you as my wife and lay with you tonight, and in many months we still hadn't reached the end of our duty . . . but you were heavy with child?"

She smiled. "No matter what condition I was in, I would never let you go without me."

"And I will not bring my pregnant wife against the Dragon King. This mission is more important than any of us, or what we might want. I swore an oath when I became a *Dracken Vier-gur*. I intend to keep it. Maybe I'll never go home, but I won't deprive our cause of a great warrior, just because I have . . . yearnings."

Bree wrapped her arms tenderly around him. "There are no men like you among my people."

"Perhaps someday, there will be one."

LXV

I shall never see the Temple of Lorak in Nexus City again. Nor will I have to endure the righteous Priests of the High Council who would rather hide in their courts than face what has happened to them. The 'Benevolent Fathers' of the Nexan folk have become 'Tyrant Kings' and their laws do not account for the freedom that every soul craves.

—Bölak Blackhammer, from the Quarzaak Journal

Lord Marshal Gunther Krohgstaad was true to his word. He had Jaena moved immediately to a large and comfortable room in a tower in what she learned was the Marshal's Keep, a sprawling fortress on the slope of Mount Nexus. She had two windows to look out over the vast city and her last days would be spent in a place of warmth and light. The narrow windows were too small for her to fit her body through if she decided to jump before her execution, but they gave her the sun, moon, and wind to soothe the stifling heat of summer, and a view of an amazing place she had always wanted to see. She thought that if she did manage to escape the tower she should know the streets well enough to determine the way to run.

The keep was high enough above the city that she got a perfect view of the guard stations and Drobin neighborhoods, which she would have to avoid on her way to the green forest beyond the walls. Though she could not imagine a way over the walls. Jaena imagined that, even if they had the skill at stonework, it would take every person in Cliffton many years just to build one guard tower along the Nexus walls.

Thinking about it, she understood that Drobin were people who didn't plan in seasons or years, but in decades, in centuries. The warriors who guarded her probably had boots older than she was. Sighing, she stood at the narrow window and studied the view. She could almost smell the leaves on the wind, and she needed something of nature to look at if she was going to get into the right frame of mind to slip into a trance and escape at least with her mind.

The green domes of all manner of trees ran in long lines throughout Nexus City and she wished she could touch the bark of just one of them. The tall buildings with red and white rooftops out numbered the trees. Most buildings had three or four floors that stretched out to the giant walls topped with guard towers and ballistae. Wing catcher ropes crisscrossed the spaces between buildings, shielding the foot traffic below on the narrow streets. The people were protected from the rare aevian that would come this far into the center of the plateau attracted by the noise and the smell of so many people.

All day her only distraction was marveling at the Drobin architecture, engineering, and the Nexan labor. The whole city filled her with awe, but none so much as the gigantic Temple of Lorak on the mountain's slope beside the Marshal's Keep. They had carved an entire ridge of gray stone to look like the head of Lorak himself staring out over the cityscape. If Old Man Laetham's stories were true it had taken them two hundred years to finish the carving, which had stood for over five hundred years or more by now as the modern city took shape beneath it.

The streets were orderly and in a mostly grid pattern, except for the hilly sections where fortress-like houses of palatial sizes rose from the plain. She was amazed at all the walls and wondered where so much stone had come from, but her restricted view limited her, and she could not see the towering peak of the dormant volcano behind her where some quarries had to exist.

Some sections of the city had walls that were fifty feet thick and had giant trees and grass atop them. Windmills and canals, reservoirs and avenues, bridges and gleaming monuments stretched out for several miles from the Keep and the temple. She would need a Master Scholar to teach her all of the landmarks and streets, but she would never walk them until perhaps the end of her life, which was rapidly approaching. She suspected her execution would take place in the large square in front of the Temple of Lorak not far from the Keep. She tried not to spend too much time guessing where it would happen and instead focused on the distant places and strained her eyes to study the details.

One section of the city seemed to be a wild and overgrown forest, hemmed in by tall and crumbling walls. She focused on it, her eyes getting lost in the treetops and small meadows. She learned from Lord Gunther that it was a place of graveyards and tombs where the first Drobin and Nexans who settled there were buried. Now it was a place apart where wild animals roamed free, and no one but poachers dared hunt for the penalty was death.

Thousands upon thousands of Drobin and Nexans mixed on the streets before going back to their segregated neighborhoods at night when the sun finally set the summer heat lessened in her tower room. Lights in the windows twinkled all over the city and she even saw boats navigating the canals with lanterns on their prows.

The moon had welcomed her during her first night in the tower and finally Jaena felt ready to slip into a trance and meet the Goddess. The moon dominated the sky and cast its silvery glow over the city. She wanted to embrace the light, and go into her spirit body, escape the confines of the tower. Jaena had purposefully avoided any astral travel since she left Cliffton since Priestess Nayla had warned her against it. The Dragon of Darkness could attack her if she was not careful. Nayla had been very intrigued by Jaena's stories about meeting Draglûne as she tried to reach Drake, and counseled her against any further attempts to find him or go into the spirit realm. It was too dangerous and she had to focus on her future, not finding a man from her past.

What did Nayla's warnings matter now? Jaena prayed to

the Goddess, and let herself go into a dream trance. After she had done the breathing exercises, her inner eye opened. She flew across a vast desert following the golden cord that connected her to Drake. She found him in a ruined desert city whose streets were prowled by demons with yellow eyes and ivory fangs. She knew what would come to pass the instant she saw the city. The demons would attack him, kill him if they could, striking when he least expected it. She had to warn him of the danger lurking in the shadows.

Her vision showed him helpless as a dark dragon stared at him, and feral demons waited to tear out his throat. She tried to reach him, but as it had once before, a bank of black clouds in the astral, a storm of infinite size created by the Dragon of Darkness, Draglûne himself, threatened to consume her if she tried to reach Drake's side. She did not accept this boundary and made her way to a higher plane of light and love where Draglûne could not stop her.

She broke through to Drake and her spirit floated in the place where the past and future collided, then she pushed through to the desert city of ghosts and forgotten memories following the glowing cord that would connect them forever.

He was with Bree'alla. They kissed passionately in a shadowy courtyard as feral cats watched them from the shadows. Jaena could not rise above the hurt and jealousy growing inside her. She needed to warn him about the danger coming so close now in his future, but she couldn't stand to see him in the arms of another.

Bree was his future in this life. She had no right to him. Besides, her mortal thread would end soon enough. She sent him her warning, and hoped he understood the message that would play in the back of his mind.

Then in an instant, she left the desert and was back inside her own body in the Marshal's Keep, a prisoner of the flesh, and the stone tower once again. She awoke, shaking and feeling more alone than she ever had before.

LXVI

The Khebians have shown us a way across the gap.
—Bölak Blackhammer, from the Khoram Journal

The morning fog had already burned away when Drake finally dragged himself from the soft bedding where he and Bree had spent the night wrapped in each other's arms. It had been almost impossible not to do more than kiss her, but if he was going to live with himself, he had to resist the temptation. He dozed for a while, but did not get out of bed until he heard her get up. When he followed, he found her in the Sacred Lake with all four of the Daughters of the Sun. The women laughed and frolicked in the water wearing only smiles, and he avoided staring at them as he made his way inconspicuously to the shadowed sleeping place of his friends in the waterfall house, wondering what they would think of his absence last night.

The Drobin weren't there. They'd left before dawn, taking all three dogs into the ruins to search for a way across the Void, which he learned from Dabarius when he appeared a while later as Drake ate a breakfast of goat's milk and dates.

"Does your head hurt like mine?" Dabarius asked, rubbing his forehead.

"I didn't have as much wine as you," Drake said.

"What *did* you have?" Dabarius asked, a sly grin on his face.

Drake stared at him with contempt.

"Well, I had a very good evening," Dabarius said. "Maralla and Faydra were very entertaining. They never tire of me, and I'm afraid they'll be sad to see me go as they're quite starved for a man's attention. At least they were."

"How can you stand yourself?" Drake asked. "Women are not playthings."

"And neither are they statues to merely look upon. I'm human, and so are they. What's the harm in recognizing it?"

"I have a woman back home."

"So what?" Dabarius opened his eyes for a moment and stared at Drake before closing them once more. "Oh. I forgot. You're Nexan."

"I'm not Nexan."

"You 'backwoods Clifftoners' then," the wizard said.

Drake wanted to remind his friend how harmless his dalliance with Raina had been in Khierson City, but instead he said, "I'm going to find the dwarves." He prepared to leave through the back way, so he wouldn't be embarrassed seeing the nude women in the pool in the main courtyard. He wanted to see Bree, but in private, not in full view of the four Priestesses. Why didn't they understand that there was nothing wrong with modesty or shyness? The desert folk should know that.

"Maybe I'll go for a swim with our hospitable hostesses and your woman," Dabarius called after him, then laughed devilishly. "If you're too bound up in your own morality, perhaps I can rise to the occasion in your stead."

Drake stormed away wondering if Bree really was his woman. He loved her, no doubt about that. He would give his life for her if he had to, but Jaena would always be his first love and he would return to her and his family in Cliffton if he could. Bree seemed to accept that, but he knew she didn't like being second to anyone. He suspected she was just humoring him. He'd taken the vows in Isyrin, and he knew it was unlikely that he would ever be allowed to leave Mephitia, but he had some hope. Bree said he should come to accept the fact that he was never leaving the desert.

Maybe someday he would. But not today.

A cat stalked a bird on the wall in front of him. He watched as it crept toward its prey and a disturbing thought came to mind. The cats of Shahan had been watching him and Bree

369

last night in the courtyard. Then in his mind's eye he saw fangs flashing in the dark. They waited to sink their teeth into his neck, as if he were about to be ambushed.

Despite the heat of the day, he was chilled and tried to shake off the foreboding image prominent in his mind. He was worried, and found Thor, Bellor and the three dogs near the green strip of land that ran toward the cliff. He wanted to tell them about his premonition, but he rationalized it was just his imagination after the stress of the journey.

He joined the dwarves as they methodically searched for a way across the chasm. The oppressive heat baked them like they were in a clay oven. They needed to find a way down into the earth, as the secret bridge they'd learned of had to exist below the fog, hidden from view and it would be accessed by a hidden stair or tunnel that went down to the canyon wall.

No stairs could be found along the cliff edge and instead they searched in the strip of trees and shrubs that ran through the city. Bellor thought the river would cut a passage downward and he wanted to find a way to access it.

The mostly underground river came up to the surface is several places in addition to the lake at the temple of Ah'usar. There were a few small ponds, and covered conduits—tiny canals—that fed water to wild gardens and thick orchards of date palm trees that the Priestesses tended.

Bellor and Thor did learn that the hidden river followed the contour of the land and dropped down as the elevation of the plateau did as it neared the terminus of the cliff. However, there was no waterfall at the sheer precipice and no evidence as to where the river went. The green strip stopped over a hundred paces from the barren and dusty drop-off into the canyon, but no evidence of where the river went could be found.

At an elevated lookout perched on the cliff, the three companions rested while the dogs slept in the shade of a wall. Drake watched the fog in the canyon flow northward, snaking through the canyon. The top level of the mist lay over two hundred feet below them, mostly in shadows, and it never parted to reveal a hidden bridge or the bottom of the Void. He could sit here for days looking and waiting, with the hope of seeing the bottom, but it was too dark down there, and would be pointless. Still, he wondered. The morning fog was fascinating and it smelled similar to the morning fog in Cliffton, but it was cleaner here, less polluted with whatever lay at the base of the titanic cliffs outside his forest home.

To the south of them, Drake marveled at the remains of the Shahan bridge, which had once spanned the wide canyon. If the old story was true, a plateau, more like a round butte of flat-topped stone had existed in the center of the canyon here at Shahan, and a bridge had come from either side of it. Now, the island in the center of the River of Mist was gone, fallen during the earthquake that separated eastern Khoram and the western Khoram Desert forever. Only the beginning of the wide arched bridge clung to the Shahan side now. On the far side, not exactly opposite the Shahan bridge, the foundation of another arch bridge jutted out over the canyon then broke away to nothing. Crumbling obelisks flanked the nubs of bridges on either side.

Bellor studied everything, searching for a clue to how to get across. He scanned the red and striated walls of the canyon, lying on his belly, head over the cliff. His eyes went from the upper layers of tan rock, down to the white, red, and gray layers until the clouds hid the rest. How far did it go down? A mile? Five? No one knew, though Bellor said he suspected the bottom was closer here than in Cliffton. They had come down a long way in elevation since leaving the verdant grasslands outside of Khierson City.

"The Mephitian story of the collapse here is true," Bellor announced suddenly and stood up. "There was a plateau in the center and it fell northward into the Void as we were told. Look closely and you can see the marks it left, mirroring each other on both sides of the canyon. See the wide grooves in the canyon arcing down?"

Drake did see the scars of the fall, smooth cuts in the rock that started partway down and disappeared below the mist.

"That's where the bridge may be," Bellor said, pointing to where the central plateau fell. "The canyon narrows as it goes deeper. The rock may have lodged there."

Thor nodded in agreement. "But how do we get down there? I see no trail, and it's too far to climb down a rope."

"There must be a passage of some kind that starts in the city," Bellor said. "Your uncle and Khebians found it, and so can we."

Hours later, when the heat finally started to yield and the horizon was red brushed with burnt yellow, Thor found a carved well shaft two hundred yards from the cliff edge and near the green strip of trees. He shouted excitedly for Bellor to come and look.

"What is it?" Bellor asked.

A smile beaming from behind his beard, Thor pointed below the lip of the stone shaft only a hand-width down. The markings were tiny and hidden from view unless you looked directly at them. They blended into the rock and Drake wouldn't have seen them unless Thor pointed them out, but Drobin eyes knew rock and earth.

"Drobin rune letters," Drake said, as he inspected the carvings in the beige stone.

"My uncle was here!" Thor said, slapping the rock. "This is the rune for Bölak of clan Blackhammer and you can see the symbol for 'down' beneath it. He left his marker so we could follow him."

"He went into the well," Drake said.

"He followed the water as I thought he would," Bellor said. "There's a passage that goes to the Void and leads to the bridge. There must be."

"We need rope," Drake said. "Bree had some on her vorrel. I don't know if it'll be long enough."

"Well find out tomorrow," Bellor said, and clapped Thor on the shoulder, his own smile broad and victorious. Bellor carved his own mark beside Bellor's, an axe with the rune for his name and clan.

They walked back to the temple of Ah'usar. Drake wondered what they would do when they reached the other side of the canyon. How would they cross the desert? They knew approximately where the city of Mephitep was along the southern mountains, but the distance was far, and would require many days of travel. Their lone surviving vorrel wasn't going to fit down a tiny well shaft. Was there another way down besides the well? Regardless, how would they carry enough water and supplies across the vast desert on the other side? They didn't even know where they would go. What had the company of *Dracken Viergur* before them done?

He tried not think about it too much as he tied up the dogs outside the temple where he sequestered them safely away from what he had found out were "holy cats" of the Sun God.

Then he saw Bree'alla standing with the four Priestesses wearing the revealing dress they had given her, her hair braided beautifully and kohl accentuating her eyes and protecting her from the glare of the setting sun. They said prayers as it went down between the pylons of the western facing gatehouse. He watched them praying and when Bree'alla smiled at him, he let go of most of his fears.

When the ceremony was over, all of them met and sat by the lake, some of them dipping their toes into the water.

"Tell them," Bellor said.

"What?" Bree asked.

"We think we found a way to the secret bridge," Drake said. "There's a carved well shaft with Bölak's mark."

Bree translated the news, and the Priestesses looked somewhat surprised and a little sad. Kasiya eventually said something and Bree translated. "Priestess Kasiya has enjoyed our company very much, and she doesn't want us to leave. While you were out she has asked me to join her order and become a Daughter of the Sun, and she wants Dabarius to become a Priest of Ah'usar and stay here as well."

"What did you tell her?" Bellor asked Dabarius and Bree.

"I said we would think about it," Dabarius said, then he splashed Maralla and Faydra who giggled and splashed him back. "I'm a wizard, a Mephitian lord, consort to the Goddess Queen . . . I imagine that becoming a Priest would not be all that difficult."

Thor rolled his eyes.

"This place has its charms, but it's far too quiet for my taste, in point of fact. I didn't want to be rude," Dabarius whispered, his grin never leaving his face.

Kasiya looked expectantly for some kind of answer, as did Maralla, Faydra and Laris.

"Tell her we must go on," Bellor said. "Thank them for all they've done for us."

Dabarius translated. It was clear from the number of words he used that his version was far less direct than Bellor's had been. Kasiya looked somber and said, "Please, do not go. There is nothing but pain if you leave Shahan. You cannot cross the River of Mist and you cannot return and cross the Dune Sea now. The season is too hot. Stay at least until the end of the summer before you decide where to go. Another two months and the rains will come."

"We cannot stay so long," Bellor said. "We must leave as soon as we can."

"Stay and make a life with us," Kasiya urged. "Live out the rest of your days in peace with us. Stop your wandering and make a home here."

"We are thankful for your offer," Bellor said. "I wish I could leave these three young folk with you, and go ahead with only Thor, but Drake, Bree, and Dabarius would not let us go alone. Our journey must continue, and we shall depart as soon as we can. We mean no offense and are grateful for everything you have done for us."

Kasiya nodded, accepting the words sorrowfully. "Then we shall honor you tonight, and pray for your journey to be safe. Rest now, and we shall prepare a feast to celebrate your discovery."

The Priestesses departed and Bellor asked Dabarius, "Did they really think we might stay here with them?"

"We're the cure for their boredom," Dabarius said. "Without us, all they have is their blind faith and these ruins in the middle of nowhere. Being in the presence of such a startlingly handsome man as I am tends to make a woman lose all sense of herself."

"A Drobin female would likely have a strong impulse to punch you in the groin, tree-legs," Thor grumbled.

Bellor shook his head. "Perhaps we will have the opportunity to render aid to these women when our Sacred Duty is done. They have been our saviors, but we must leave them behind now."

At least they have peace, Drake thought, as he walked with his friends back to their quarters. He hoped that coming to Shahan would not cause the Priestesses any trouble in the future. What if Draglûne or his enemies tracked them here? Or if Reu'ven sent agents to verify their deaths and find their bones? What would happen to the four Daughters of Sun then?

LXVII

How will we face the desert in Far Khoram? The vorrels must remain on this side of the canyon. If the desert beyond is as desolate and cursed as we have been told, crossing it on foot will be nearly impossible.

—Bölak Blackhammer, from the Khoram Journal

When the heat of the evening had lessened and the moon had come out, Kasiya and her three Priestesses served large bowls of salty soup flavored with bitter greens—leaves from the weeds that grew in the ruins no doubt—and bits of stringy meat Drake did not question. He suspected it was aevian, as the temple's cats often brought dead rodents, lizards, and birds to the Priestesses. He hated eating aevians, but he didn't want to insult the Mephitian women and thought of the meat as desert squirrel. The main course was a plate of roasted white meat, already boned and spiced with something that smelled like thyme. He hoped it was goat, and it wasn't bad.

They ate and sipped a vaguely minty tea, while Bellor and Thor discussed what they'd need to descend into the well shaft while Dabarius told a story in Mephitian to Maralla and Faydra, who didn't laugh as much as usual when he spoke to them.

Near the end of the subdued feast, Drake was feeling rather tired and could barely keep his eyes open. He leaned closer to Bree, who had become very quiet and was staring at a blue and green pattern painted on wall and restored by Laris years ago when she arrived at the temple. He didn't think much of it, but Bree was apparently fascinated by it that evening.

"Bree," he said, but she didn't hear him. He suddenly became very dizzy, and fell forward, catching himself with one arm. The sound in the room was muffled and he heard Kasiya saying something, giving a command perhaps. Laris helped Drake sit up and Dabarius also looked a little lightheaded.

"What's wrong?" Drake asked Bree, as she wobbled and fell over. He tried to reach for her and noticed the dwarves slumped against each other on the floor, their eyes rolling back in their heads and mouths gaping open.

Kasiya put a large platter of food in front of Drake with a blood stained cloth covering it. Laris held him up, holding him by the hair and aiming his face toward the plate. Kasiya removed the covering and revealed the cooked and furless head and carcass that could only be one of his dogs. She tore a piece of flesh from the cheek and put it into Drake's gaping mouth.

He recoiled in horror and the taste made him want to retch as he realized the meat they had all been eating was from one of his dogs. The room was spinning and Drake could see the Priestesses of Ah'usar glaring at him. Then half a dozen small feline creatures came from the shadows and began tearing the flesh from the dog's head and carcass. His last memory before passing out was of a demonic winged cat with yellow eyes entering the room. It gnawed on the dog's face, then tore the tongue out of its mouth. He threw up on himself and blacked out.

LXVIII

Wulf found more statues and paintings of dragons in one of the temples. The Khebians try to answer our questions as rational men would, but I know the truth of it. The folk who lived in Shahan were mad. Why else would they venerate a race as foul as the dragons?

—Bölak Blackhammer, from the Khoram Journal

The sound of slow drumming echoed in Drake's ears as the nightmare continued. It must be a dream, he thought, but he could feel the vibration of the drum in his chest and taste the dog meat and bile in his mouth. He could even smell burning meat in the air now.

It had all happened, but why couldn't he open his eyes?

Something was in the food. A poison of some kind. The Priestesses had poisoned him and his friends. Why? What was happening? He raged inside as he thought about what they'd done to his dogs. All of them must be dead, not just . . . poor Skinny, such a good dog.

Drake's eyelids fluttered open. His arms and wrists were numb, and he realized he was tied to a stone pillar, his arms tightly lashed behind him. Treelike columns rose up to a dark ceiling and he guessed he was in the temple of Ah'usar somewhere, but in a long hall he hadn't seen before, one of the many sacred spaces he and his companions were barred from entering.

Three of the Daughters of Ah'usar, Maralla, Faydra and Laris danced slowly in unison at the end of the room, while Kasiya played a drum. They all wore lioness-faced demonic masks as they swayed in front a giant wall painting. A burning copper brazier lit up the image and Drake recognized it instantly, a dragon with iron gray scales painted with metallic paint, and red eyes that must be rubies. A black aura radiated from around the beast and storm clouds gathered behind him. He'd seen this monster before, in the Crystal Eye in Oberon's tower when Draglûne looked at each of them and promised vengeance.

The Priestesses were in league with their greatest enemy and Drake knew he had to escape right now or his life was forfeit. He came fully awake and looked around frantically. Dabarius, Bellor and Thor were tied to individual pillars and sat flanking him in a line facing the painting of the Iron Dragon King. All three were half-awake, groggy and obviously still under the effects of the toxic substance they'd all ingested.

Bree lay in front of him, just behind the dancing women on a small pile of pillows. She stared blankly and looked as if she were lost in a trance as she faced the dragon image. She was not bound, but whatever they had given her held sway.

"*Bree*," Drake whispered.

She didn't react.

Kasiya turned her head toward him. She kept playing her drum, but her catlike eyes lingered on him, measured him.

Thor grunted as he tried to burst his thick bonds. The dwarf's thick forearms bulged, his cheeks turning dark with effort, but to no avail. Kasiya shook her head at him, then glanced back at Drake. He heard her voice in his mind, speaking to him like a wingataur demon would. *You are not the first to come hunting for our master, but you will suffer the same fate as the others.*

"What others?" Thor shouted in Nexan, and Drake realized he wasn't the only one who could hear her words in his mind.

The Ten Sons of Kheb, she replied, though her lips did not move. *They failed and so have you.*

"You should kill me now," Thor said, "for when I get free you will wish you had."

"In good time," Kasiya said in Nexan, her perfect northern accent like a blow to Drake's face. "Our master will be most

379

pleased when we offer your blood and souls to him tonight. We will be rewarded for killing you."

"Bree!" Drake shouted as he struggled and pulled against the rope. She didn't stir at all and he couldn't get loose.

"Do not worry for her," Kasiya said. "She will be our sister for some time. She will become one of us, as she is the only one fit to remain alive. We will know everything she knows, and will finally be relieved of our tedious duty here. Others will have to guard this place, perhaps Bree'alla and the ghosts she carries with her, and we will be unleashed to hunt at last in Western Mephitia. Perhaps we will be the ones chosen to kill Queen Khelen'dara in Isyrin. We know so much about her now, thanks to Dabarius, and soon our master shall know all that she has done."

Dabarius struggled and tried to shout, but a gag muffled his wizard's voice.

"If you let us go," Bellor said "we will depart."

"After we kill you and all of your precious cats," Thor said.

Kasiya stopped drumming and the three women stopped dancing. The eldest Priestess motioned with her chin and Faydra slinked toward Thor. The small woman raised her hand, which now ended in curved bony yellow claws. She cocked it back, ready to tear out his throat.

"No," Drake said, "don't do it."

"You wish to be first?" Faydra asked him, though she made no sound.

"I will be first," Bellor said.

Faydra shook her head at him and walked to Drake. "It has already been decided," she glanced at Kasiya. "First it was your foul dogs, then it will be you, then Dabarius, the young dwarf, and last, the older one, who will watch all of you die."

"Tonight shall be our feast," Kasiya said, "as we feed on your anguish and your lives."

Drake struggled against his bonds, not giving up. The dogs were dead and soon he and friends would all suffer the same fate, but he was not going to give up.

Faydra saw him struggling and raked a long claw across his bare chest. Burning pain made him grit his teeth as the woman-demon licked the blood off the claws extending from her fingers. Her tongue was thin and longer than it should have been, and her teeth were sharp and pointed like a cat's.

Blood oozed from Drake's wounds and Faydra collected some of it in her cupped hand, then proceeded to drip it onto the burning brazier in front of the painting of the Dragon King.

The coppery odor of singed blood filled the room and Kasiya played her drum again. She chanted something in Mephitian, then struck the drum hard one time and stopped. The demon women removed their masks and bowed down, sharp claws extended toward Draglûne's image. Then they stood and breathed in the burnt blood smoke from the brazier. Their once-pretty faces began to twist and contort into those of lioness demons. Long-fanged teeth, more like a lioness than a feline cat's, grew in their mouths. Feathery griffin-like wings sprouted from their backs and their eyes glowed with amber fire.

LXIX

Amaryllis wants us to listen to Her voice speaking within us. We must learn to always listen, even if her message is not what we had hoped to hear. The most profound wisdoms can sear our souls like an unchecked fire in the thorn trees.

　　　　　—passage from the Goddess Scrolls of Amaryllis

Jaena tossed and turned on the bed in her tower cell, sweat pouring from her body. She couldn't stand the guilt anymore, and felt terrible for not warning Drake about the danger he would soon face. Was it too late? Had her jealousy doomed him? She had sent him into Bree'alla's arms, but seeing them together had hurt more than she would have ever imagined. She had to go to him now and warn him in whatever way she could. This would likely be the last time she could ever prove that, despite the events that had ripped them apart, the decisions they had both made, she was still true to him and the promise they'd made to each other.

She slowed her breathing and stilled her mind, going into the trance that would bring her into her spirit body. She lifted out of the Drobin prison and rose above the city, entering the world of spirits. Jaena followed the golden cord connecting her to Drake and went to the higher plane. In an instant she arrived in a ruined city inhabited by scores of ancient ghosts, and four very dark entities of the Void. She also sensed many young demonic spirits that had possessed small animals and were trying to evolve.

Drake and his companions were bound to large stone pillars, while lion-headed demon women writhed as their bodies changed in front of the image of the Iron Dragon King. When their transformation was complete they would brutally murder Drake and his friends. The lioness demons had already poisoned them and now they would sacrifice them to Draglûne and bind their spirits, trapping them in this dark temple. Their spirits would be consumed and would not live on in the After-life.

It was her vision come to pass.

Jaena could not counter what had already been done. She was too late and guilt wracked her soul. Her pain attracted one of the demons and the creature's yellowish-brown eyes peered through the veil of the material world and fixed on Jaena's spirit-body.

"Who are you?" the demon asked.

She avoided the lioness woman's glare and flew toward Drake, determined to do something to save him, or at least comfort him when the end came, and escort him into the next world. As she approached him she noticed the confused and lost spirit of Bree'alla floating outside her body. Bree did not see Jaena and was watching the demon women change into their bestial forms.

Bree already knew she would soon become what they were, a half-human demon creature under the control of the Dragon King. That's why she had been given a different poison than the others. It made her more susceptible to the bite that would change her forever into a creature of evil. Her spirit had been cast out of her body so her will could not fight what was com-ing. She would be helpless as her soul would forever be cast into a dark future.

There was nothing Jaena could do to purge the substance from Bree's body and pull her spirit back inside. Only time could do such a thing, but Jaena realized she could do some-thing else. She could take control of Bree's unattended phys-ical form and try to save Drake's life. She didn't fully under-stand the risks or the consequences of her decision, but there was nothing else she could do. Jaena was already doomed to die, so what difference would it make? She would rather die here, doing all she could to help a good cause, than await a crushed skull beneath a Drobin hammer.

383

The bestial women were still changing forms, and Jaena quickly slid into Bree's strong physical body, possessing her entirely, which felt invigorating, but completely wrong. She was instantly assaulted by a mind-altering toxin that she sensed was crafted with dark magic. The magically augmented poison coursed through Bree's veins, and tried to separate Jaena from Bree's flesh, cast her aside like a leaf on the wind.

Summoning every bit of mental fortitude she could muster and touching a place of light in the astral plane where the Goddess was strong, Jaena took control. She made her consciousness immune to the effects of the toxin. It was difficult for Jaena to make Bree's sluggish muscles move at first, then she let go of herself and became Bree'alla, swordswoman and Wing Guardian of Amar'isis.

She looked at Drake and their eyes met. She wanted to tell him what was happening, tell him she loved him, tell him she was going to be executed outside a Drobin prison in Nexus City, but she said nothing, and just stared at the man she would be with in the next life when his soul left this mortal realm.

"Bree, cut us loose," Drake urged, "there's a knife in my boot."

Jaena crawled to him and found the razor-sharp blade. She sliced through his bonds quickly and Drake took the knife from her and cut the others loose.

The writhing demon women finished transforming. They were now lion-headed with long fangs, claws on their feet and hands, and leonine tails. Their small, lithe bodies had become frames bulging with thick, corded muscle. Burning amber eyes stared straight at Jaena as she led the freed companions into the hallway at the rear of the chamber.

"Run!" Dabarius shouted, and pushed his friends down the corridor behind them, which appeared to be the only way out of the room. Drake lingered at Dabarius's side holding the small knife from his boot, refusing to flee.

Jaena grabbed onto Drake, trying to get him to run down the hall. The dwarves clenched their fists and prepared for a fight to the death as well.

"I said run!" Dabarius shouted, "I'll hold them off."

The four lion-headed women spread out and moved methodically toward the companions using the pillars in the room as cover.

The dwarves tried to pull Jaena with them down the hall. She couldn't leave Drake and struggled to remain as the insanity of the moment struck her like a blow to the gut. Then he relented and went with her leaving the wizard alone with the four demons.

Dabarius cocked his arms in a fighting stance. He shook his head, trying to focus and fight the effects of the poison. He let out a breath, and golden sparks of electricity shot from his fingertips.

The lion women stopped advancing and hid behind the pillars, shielding themselves from the power coursing through him. They knew to hide and kept behind cover as they closed in, preparing to pounce all at once.

"Dabarius," Drake said, "come on!"

The wizard nodded as the demons made it to the line of pillars right in front of him. They would attack from both sides at once.

Crackling light streamed and then rushed out of Dabarius. The magic formed a sparking wall of golden-white energy that sealed off the arched doorway.

Dabarius gestured rudely to the lion women and dared them to touch the wall, then turned and walked calmly away.

"How long will it last?" Drake asked as they both started running.

"If I cast it as Master Oberon taught me," the wizard said, "we'll be far away from here when they escape their cage."

"Well done," Drake said.

"I should have stayed and killed them," Dabarius said.

"You're not so dumb to face them alone," Drake said, "are you?"

Dabarius ignored him and they found their way out and into a previously off-limits courtyard, then back to their quarters in a building near the entrance to the temple complex. As the men quickly gathered up their things, Jaena came up behind Drake, put her arms around his waist, and rested her head against his back.

He turned, hugged her and asked, "Are you all right?"

She wanted to tell him what she'd done, but time was short. Instead, she said, "Let's get far away from here." Jaena hugged him again and enjoyed the warmth of his body that she had been denied for too many months. She didn't know how long her spirit would stay inside Bree, and she hoped it would be long enough to speak to him as Jaena.

Bellor, Thor, and Dabarius raided one of the storage areas and gathered all the food and empty water bags they could carry, plus the only coil of rope they could find. It was dry and frayed, but it might serve their purpose.

"Ready?" Bellor asked them all.

Jaena nodded first, and they stared at her, questioning and surprised.

"They gave her something different than the rest of us," Bellor said.

"I'm all right," Jaena said. "We can go."

"What about *Wingblade*?" Drake asked her.

She stared at him blankly, and realized she had no idea what *Wingblade* was, though it sounded like a weapon. She looked around the dark room and saw a sword and snatched it up, then didn't know what to with it, or how to hold it. Should she draw it from the scabbard? She didn't even know how to hold it.

They looked at her with concern as she fumbled with the sword.

"Watch over her until the poison wears off," Bellor told Drake, who helped Jaena strap the weapon around her waist. Then he put a pack over her shoulder and escorted her outside.

He stopped on the steps and aimed his loaded crossbow into the shadows around the courtyard. Drake whispered back at her, "Stay close to me."

She did, gladly, and they navigated out of the temple complex with Thor in the lead, shield raised. They exited the main archway of the complex and still no attack came, though a slender tawny cat watched them from the top of a wall as the moon shone brightly down upon them.

"Should I shoot it?" Drake asked as he aimed at the cat.

"No," Bellor said, "wait for the demon cat with wings."

"You saw it too?" Drake asked.

"Aye, lad," Bellor said, "at the feast before I passed out, and I should have believed you saw one when you first spied the city. This place had an ill feel to it from the start. I let myself believe they were our friends."

"We all did." Dabarius let out a deep sigh and shook his head. "Some of us were bigger fools than the rest."

"How much did you tell them, wizard?" Thor asked the guilt ridden young man.

"Nothing vital," he said, "but they know we serve the Queen of Isyrin. It would be best if we kill all four of them before we leave. That way there's no chance they'll tell Draglûne anything."

"Yes, let's find them," Thor said. "Dabarius is right and I made them a promise I intend to keep."

The tall, dark haired man, and the stout dwarf seemed surprised at each other, then exchanged a determined look and clasped forearms.

"I knew I saw that cat," Drake said.

"Let's set up an ambush," Thor said. "We'll take them when they come out of their dark temple."

Bellor hesitated, looked at Bree, then said, "No, we're in no condition to fight them here. The poison lingers, dulls my senses, as it does us all. We leave the city tonight if we can."

The nearly three-hundred-year-old War Priest accepted no discussion. They made their way hastily into the ruins, Thor leading with Drake covering them. Jaena kept behind him with Dabarius and Bellor as their rear guards. Drake told Thor which way to go when they got lost in a labyrinth of dusty alleys with desiccated thorny weeds. Eventually, they found their way through the ruins to a wide street that followed a line of trees and shrubs. It surprised Jaena that Drake allowed them to stay in the open, but this place was so different than the Thornclaw Forest.

Moments later they arrived at a small well with a circular black shaft going into the ground. Jaena was quite confused about where they were going now, but deep underground seemed safer than in the streets with winged lioness demons after them.

Thor affixed the rope securely and dropped it into the darkness. "I'll climb down and investigate. Then you can follow." He rigged a harness around himself and dropped fearlessly into the well with no source of light.

She envied his Drobin eyes, and scanned the shadowy trees and ruins nearby as they all took up defensive positions around the shaft.

Thor's echoing voice announced, "There's a stream and a pool of water behind a low manmade dam at the bottom. There's also a carved tunnel going toward the River of Mist and another going the opposite way along the stream."

"Can we follow the way toward the canyon?" Bellor called down.

"We can," Thor said, "but Dabarius will have to duck his useless but thick head."

"Stay alert," Bellor said. "We'll drop the supplies down first."

When they'd finished that task, Drake suggested that Bree go down next with a glowstone tied around her neck.

She was about to argue when loud barking echoed from somewhere in the distance of the city.

Jaena instantly recognized the sounds of two agitated bull-mastiffs.

"Jep and Temus are alive," Drake said, and squeezed Jaena's hand.

She'd wondered where the dogs were. Now it made sense. He thought they were dead.

The barking was coming from nearby. They seemed quite angry, and Drake called to them loudly. He also whistled several times, not caring if the lion women could hear any of it.

They waited a few moments, but the barking did not come any closer.

"They want us to hear the dogs," Dabarius said. "They want us to go to them."

"The dogs are bait for a trap," Bellor said.

"Doesn't matter," Drake said.

"I know," Bellor said, then turned to the well and called to Thor, "Climb back up."

"Why?" Thor asked, "It's nearly thirty feet free hand on that rope."

"We're going back to your first plan," Bellor said. "Jep and Temus are alive."

They all helped Thor by pulling him most of the way up. The rope held together, though it was becoming more frayed after Thor's calloused hands had assaulted it on the way up.

Jaena couldn't sit still as she listened to the men planning how they would kill the four demon women and free Jep and Temus. The odds were five to four if Bree was able to fight.

"Can we count on you and your sword?" Bellor asked her.

Her eyes widened. What should she say?

"Can you fight?" Drake asked.

389

She knew that if she did fight she would have to be prepared to kill. Even if she had Bree'alla's abilities as a swordswoman, and she did not, would she do it? She would rather flee down the well shaft, but in this case, yes, she would do it. The dogs had saved Drake's life many times. How could she fail to return that favor?

Jaena would help save them. She could not let herself be afraid of killing these creatures of darkness that had taken human form. Her thoughts must have shown on her face.

Drake and the others were extremely worried. They were counting on Bree, and Jaena knew that she wasn't the confident swordswoman at all.

"Well, can you?" Thor asked.

Jaena clenched her fists, and knew she had to keep up the illusion for now and remain Bree'alla. She nodded slowly. "I'll fight."

LXX

The demons of the Void who serve Draglûne must have some draconic blood within them. Why else would they serve him? They are his children.

—Bölak Blackhammer, from the Khoram Journal

Drake followed the sounds of Jep and Temus barking. He avoided a direct route in case the demons had set up an ambush along the way. He circled around, and closed in from behind. The area was not that familiar to him, but he had hunted birds nearby in the days before, and had a good idea where the dogs were being kept.

"It must have been a palace," Drake whispered as they spied on the walled complex with a gatehouse and two flanking towers, which were the tallest structures in the whole city. They overlooked everything, including the gardens and groves of palm trees.

"The dogs are inside the main structure," Dabarius said as the sporadic deep-throated barking echoed in the night. "An easy place for an ambush in a building we do not know."

"They want to draw us in," Thor said, "hem us into their trap and kill us."

"Then we should draw them out," Drake said. "I can climb into one of those towers, then I'll be able to see any move they make above the buildings."

"Above?" Thor asked.

"They are winged demons," Drake said. "If they are like the wingataurs they'll use their wings to move about, but they won't be able to fly much inside the palace. They'll have to use the open air to move. If they do, there's enough light for me to shoot them." He didn't bring up or suggest they might be able to turn invisible like the wingataurs could.

"I like this idea," Dabarius said.

"Are you certain you can see well enough?" Thor asked Drake.

"The moon is bright tonight," Bree'alla said, and Drake looked at her twice. Her voice sounded different compared to normal. Softer, more tentative and had a different quality he could not quite identify. Whatever they put into her food must have still been affecting her mind. Even her eyes, usually quick, hard and sharp, were filled with something . . . he had no time to figure it out now.

"I'll draw them up and out for you, crossbowman," Dabarius said. "Just don't miss."

***

Drake and Bree waited for Bellor, Thor and Dabarius to go to the opposite side of the palace complex and enter through the overgrown garden and palm grove, which would have been their route if they'd come directly from the well shaft. The three of them would draw the eyes and ears of the demons, and give Bree and Drake time to get into position. Bellor opposed separating, but agreed the risk was worth it in this case, though he insisted that Drake not go alone. Someone needed to watch his back, and Bree volunteered.

The pair of them waited in silence, leaning against the stone of a dark alcove inside a building with a partial roof. She bandaged the claw wound on his chest, and he was surprised at her skill and gentleness. Thankfully, it wasn't deep, though it stung whenever he moved wrong. They had said little, though he wanted to talk to her.

Instead of talking they kept silent, as he was content to hold her hand and let her lean against him as they waited for the signal. It was longer coming than Drake expected, but Thor's shout echoed loudly through the ruins. He yelled in Drobin mostly, and though the sound was far off, it startled Bree'alla. Drake only smiled as he recognized some of the more profane words in three languages. The shouting continued and they waited for a few minutes, just as they had planned, then Drake whispered, "We'll go now."

Bree kissed him before they stood up, which caught him by surprise. He stared at her and wondered what she was thinking. They made their way silently into the gatehouse and found the winding stone staircase that led up to the top of the northern tower, which was more intact than the southern one. Drake led the way slowly through the moonlight and shadows, his crossbow aimed ahead in case one of the demon women happened to be lurking inside, while Bree carried Thor and Bellor's crossbows, plus their extra bolts.

They stopped climbing on the tallest floor on the tower, a small square room with rectangular windows facing each direction. It wasn't the top, as the highest level had partially collapsed and left a gaping hole in the ceiling, which Drake did not like. He did manage to stay out of the light and away from the window, then crawled into position on his belly.

The view was perfect, and he could see across the broken palace to the garden where his friends made their distraction. Thor stood in front of a distant bonfire and shouted, challenging Kasiya, Faydra, Maralla, and Laris to a fight. He banged on his shield with his hammer and yelled at the top of his lungs, his deep voice carrying far and wide.

Jep and Temus barked only occasionally now, though they had barked more when Thor began shouting. At least Drake knew they were still alive. The demons couldn't fake those sounds, could they?

He didn't want to think about that and instead measured the distance across to the garden, which was too far for him to be very accurate. However, and most importantly, the range to the crumbling roof of the main palace building was within his ability with *Heartseeker*. He hadn't shot Thor and Bellor's smaller crossbows very often, but hoped he could shoot them effectively if need be. They weren't as powerful as his own spring-steel weapon, but were Drobin crafted, and accurate nonetheless. He'd just have to aim a hand's length higher to account for their trajectory. *Aim for the chin, and you'll hit the heart.*

That's what he told himself as he loaded them all with wyrm-killing bolts, and showed Bree how to use the krannekin to cock back *Heartseeker's* matched set of metal arms. He didn't know if the enchanted shafts would be as lethal to the lioness demon women as they were to wingataurs, but Bellor had said they might be. Dragon magic had created these creatures, and dragon blood was in them. If the shafts could kill wingataurs, they could kill these demons too—according to Master Bellor. He just had to do his part. He went through the shot sequence in his mind. *Stock to shoulder, cheek to the wood, settle the sight, let out half your breath, squeeze the trigger.* His mind's eye showed him the bolt's path, the arc to the target, the moment when the front edge of the feathers slammed to a stop and were bloodied. Drake swallowed, wiping his hands on his shirt. *This is why I'm here. I can do this. No doubts. They killed Skinny. They would have sacrificed us to the Iron King.*

Thor's shouting and the bonfire died out suddenly—Dabarius's doing he hoped—and Drake whispered to Bree. "It's time."

She nodded and prepared herself as Bellor, Thor, and Dabarius moved toward the palace. He lost sight of them and wished he could see their exact moment of entry. The three of them had the most dangerous task, while Bree would guard Drake's back, hand him loaded crossbows, and cock them if need be. He had four shots, exactly enough.

Not long after his three friends must have entered, Jep and Temus began barking very loudly once again, from somewhere near the center of the ruin. Drake scanned the rooftops, waiting for any sign of movement. His fingers wanted to press the trigger so badly, but no target appeared.

He kept his attention on the rooftop, but he was distracted by Bree's fidgeting with one of the spare bolts. Her nerves had gotten the better of her, and Drake found it so odd that she was acting like this. Bree was so calm usually, and could sit for long stretches without moving, even during the most intense moments.

"What's wrong?" Drake whispered.

She let out a sigh and looked down at him. "I have to tell you something."

"What?" he asked, very worried about what she was going to say, but he didn't take his eyes off the palace.

"It's going to be a shock to you, and I don't know how to—"

"Wait," he said. Movement on the rooftop drew his attention and he aimed very carefully at the figure that flew up through a hole in the palace roof.

LXXI

A well-executed feint will leave your enemies vulnerable to a telling blow. Compared to wit, strength is as nothing.

—Oberon, *Teha Khet* Master, and wizard of Snow Valley

Dabarius walked behind Thor as they entered the dilapidated palace of Shahan's long-dead rulers. He followed the sound of the barking bullmastiffs, which were very close now. Bellor marched behind him as they made their way through several empty rooms and then to a hallway lined with faded frescoes, dimly illuminated by the glowstone Bellor carried. For some reason he had yet to unravel, being near Bellor's axe when a battle with wyrm-kin approached put the wizard's hair on end. The axe . . . scared him a little, and not just because he'd seen the old Priest cut a man nearly in two with it.

Though he kept most of his attention on hiding places where the demon women might leap from, Dabarius did steal glances at the painted walls. The most interesting image depicted a dragon sitting proudly on the long-destroyed plateau that once stood in the River of Mist that connected Shahan to Far Khoram. The people of Shahan bowed to the huge dragon and sent a line of chained men and women across the bridge toward the seated wyrm. Dabarius wondered what the dragon did with the human offerings? Did he enslave them or consume them? A mystery he would ponder again.

"Keep going," Bellor whispered as Dabarius slowed his pace.

They soon entered a hallway filled with debris from the mostly fallen ceiling. The stars and moon peeked in from above, which was perfect for Dabarius's plan. He stopped the dwarves with a hand signal.

"Elder Priestess Kasiya," Dabarius called out in Mephitian. "I wish to speak with you."

After only a brief pause Kasiya's voice echoed down the hallway ahead of them. "You should not have delayed coming here, Dabarius, son of Barius," she said in Mephitian.

"My Drobin companions are cowards," Dabarius said. "They had to gird their courage with a fire and strong words before they could enter this dark place, but I wish only to talk with you. I have information that the Dragon King will want to have."

"You think to trade the hounds lives for your words?" Kasiya asked.

"No, I care not for them," Dabarius said.

"Then what do you want?" she asked.

"I wish to save my life, and give you the lives of my boorish companions. Also, I could care less for those smelly dogs," Dabarius said. "And if you wish to know where Bree'alla and Drake have gone, I will tell you that too . . . if you meet with me."

"I will speak with you here, now," Kasiya said.

"No, I wish to be away from these suspicious little men. If we speak much longer they will know something is amiss."

"Where and when shall we meet?" Kasiya asked.

"On the roof of this place," Dabarius said. "I will give you the information and you will determine what it is worth. I'll meet you there right now."

"Very well," Kasiya said.

"What did she say?" Bellor asked.

"She will meet with me," Dabarius said in Nexan, "so wait here for my return." He nodded to Bellor, then put his palms together and invoked the secret words of power under his breath, just as Master Oberon had taught him. Dabarius rose in the air, slowly levitating up through the hole in the ceiling. When he had cleared the roof he stepped forward and found his footing on a stone archway. He walked away from where the dwarves were below and found a stable place to stand. He waited only a few moments.

Kasiya, Faydra, and Maralla climbed out of different openings in the rooftop. He suspected Laris was with the dogs. The women's demonic lion faces grinned as they unfurled their wings and leaped forward, gliding and then landing within a claw's reach from him, Faydra and Maralla behind him.

"Tell us then," Kasiya said, "what must our king know?"

Dabarius bowed at the waist and got on his knees. He held the bow for a long breath, head down.

Nothing happened.

He smiled stiffly as he looked up at Kasiya. "I'm pleased that you decided to meet with me."

The bloody point of a crossbow bolt erupted from Faydra's chest. Another sprouted from Maralla's an instant later.

Dabarius wished Drake had taken the shot at Kasiya when he bowed so low, but his friend had decided not to shoot a bolt right over him. If his shot went low Dabarius might be dead himself.

Kasiya folded her wings and dove for cover crashing through a small hole in the rooftop. She disappeared before Drake could get off another shaft or Dabarius could strike at her with his lightning magic.

He wanted to jump after her, and levitate to the ground below, but he decided on a different strategy. He ran across the roof to the place where he heard the dogs. He would bypass the maze of rooms in the palace and get right to them.

As he picked his way across the interconnected stone supports one of the dog's barks changed. The sound was pained, strangled, and high-pitched, as if Jep or Temus were being choked to death. He ran to the sound and shouted to Thor and Bellor in Drobin, "Over here!"

Then he found a hole in the ceiling and through the gloom saw Temus tied to a stone block. Jep hung dying in the air beside him, dangling by his neck, but wriggling and growling ferociously.

A large winged cat crouched on the floor in front of them, teeth bared and watching as the dog jerked and struggled on the end of the rope. The cat glanced over its shoulder then fled the room.

Bellor and Thor charged in, running straight for the dogs. They must have kept moving through the palace when he levitated up to the roof, which was not part of the original plan. Jep hung, still struggling, but too far up for them to reach.

"We can't get to him!" Thor shouted as he looked up at Jep.

Then he was knocked down as Kasiya tackled Thor from behind. Laris crashed into Bellor's back and flattened him as well, pinning him down.

Dabarius had only an instant to save his friends as the demons locked their claws around the dwarves' throats. He willed a scorching hot fire to erupt inside the ropes that held the dogs.

Jep fell almost on top of Bellor and Kasiya, and managed to knock her off the old dwarf. Temus lunged forward and locked his jaws around Laris's arm and dragged her off Thor.

Laris grabbed Temus by his collar and dug her claws into him, but Thor came up swinging and crushed her skull with his hammer.

Kasiya hissed, and bared her pointed teeth as Bellor swung *Wyrmslayer* at her. She dodged the axe, which glowed faintly red, and backed away as Thor, Bellor, Jep and Temus confronted her. All four of them growled like crazed dogs and attacked. In the light of the axe, Bellor's eyes were wild with hatred, and he moved with the speed of a dwarf half his age.

LXXII

Our spirits are intertwined in this world and the next.
— passage from the Goddess Scrolls of Amaryllis

The bodies of the pair of lioness demons on the rooftop of the palace had not moved since they'd collapsed an instant after he shot them, but Drake kept his crossbow trained on them just in case. Dabarius had given him an encouraging signal before disappearing inside a hole in the roof, but what had happened since? The dogs had stopped barking, but were they free or dead now?

They were all supposed to gather at the base of the tower after it was over, but his friends hadn't appeared yet and Drake feared the worst.

"I have to tell you something," Bree said again.

The events on the roof had stalled her for a while, but she wanted to speak now. He didn't want to hear anything shocking until he knew if his friends were all right. He shouldn't be distracted now. "Later, when this is over," he said.

"I don't know if I'll be able to tell you later."

"What do you mean?"

The entire floor collapsed and Drake fell straight down on his belly. He landed hard amid chunks of stone and a cloud of dust. Clawed hands grabbed onto his shoulders and flipped him over. Stunned and out of breath he stared up at a demon woman with burning yellow-orange eyes.

Kasiya.

Her voice assaulted his mind. *For my sisters I will tear out your heart.* She wrapped one clawed hand around his throat and cocked her other hand as she was about to plunge it into his chest.

"You!" Bree'alla shouted from one floor above. She hung onto the wall with one hand, her feet perching on a slim ledge.

400

The demon looked up as Bree's other arm came forward holding Thor's crossbow. As their gazes met, Bree pulled the trigger. The bolt entered Kasiya's left eye and the shaft poked out the back of her head.

The demon fell onto Drake, still choking him. His strength faded, but just before the light went out of his eyes, Bree smashed a rock against Kasiya's skull. Then struck it over and over again, before finally dragging the demon off him.

"Are you all right?" Bree asked frantically, her hands under his head. She asked him over and over to say something.

"I'm all right," me managed at last once he got a good breath. "Help me sit up, I'll be fine."

She did and started to calm down as he reassured her several times. The look in her eyes was unbelievable. She was shaken to the core, but why? Was it the poison in her body? It was a close call, but Bree had been through much worse than this and come up smiling.

The sounds of booted feet coming rapidly up the stairs drew their attention.

"You all right up there?" Bellor shouted from far below, his deep voice echoing in the stairwell of the tower.

Drake coughed on the dust filling the room, then shouted back, "We're fine."

"What happened?" Thor yelled.

"Bree killed Kasiya," Drake said.

"Then it's over," Thor said. "Now get down here and take care of these stinking mutts."

Later that night, near the well shaft, Drake and Bree sat under the stars on a soft hill of sand overlooking the camp. The bright moon filled the sky above them while the others slept around a low fire. Drake had made the dogs stay near the others while he walked away with Bree for some privacy. Now he would face whatever she had to tell him.

She looked at him, then closed her eyes, holding them shut for some time. When she opened them again, her eyes were sapphire blue, when they should be green.

"What magic is this?" Drake whispered, thinking instantly of Jaena.

"This is the color of my eyes," she said.

"Those are not your eyes."

Bree turned away and caressed the soft sand said with her fingers. "I wish we were sitting on shade clover."

"How do you know about shade clover?" He hadn't told her about it and thought either she was going mad, or he was.

"Remember the last time you were on shade clover outside Cliffton?" she asked.

He nodded. He would never forget.

"Your ankle was injured, remember?" she asked.

Jaena had used the Healing magic for the very first time. She had healed him, allowing him to leave the next day with Bellor and Thor, to guide them to Armstead so his father wouldn't have had to do it. Only Jaena had known about his injury, so what was happening? Had she seen his memories? Had he spoken out in his sleep?

"I've been trying to tell you," she said. "Something happened last night. I knew you were in danger and I came to warn you in my spirit body, but it was too late. I found you tied up, those demon women about to kill you. I had no choice."

He knew and it was like time stopped all around him.

"I've come to you, Drake," she said. "It's me."

He looked into her blue eyes and he believed. This was not a demon masquerading as his woman, and this was not Bree's voice. It was Jaena. "How?"

"Bree's soul was out of her body when I arrived. The poison they gave her separated her spirit from her physical self.

The only way I could save you was to join with her body, possess it and control it. Please, don't be angry with me for what I've done."

"I'm not," he said, holding her close and remembering the flowery smell of her hair and the many times they shared growing up together.

"You know that I would do anything for you," she said. "I love you more than any other."

"I love you too," he said, "but I thought I'd never speak to you again. I thought I'd lost you and home forever."

"You can never lose me, I'm always with you," she said. "We may never see each other again in this life, but in the next, we will be together."

"In the next?" he asked.

"This life is temporary. Our spirits are immortal. Even if you or I die, we will go on. I don't know what will happen in the days ahead, but no matter what, as spirits, or in the flesh, we will see each other again."

"What should I do?" he asked, suddenly lost.

"Do what you must. Finish your journey, and I will finish mine."

"Yours? What's happened to you?" he asked, suddenly very worried about her. Hadn't she stayed in Cliffton where it was safe? Had Draglûne followed through with his threat and attacked the village? Where was she now?

He could tell she didn't want to answer him. He could see that in her beautiful eyes. Instead she said, "Be true to what you've sworn to do, to your friends, to Bree. I give you my blessing to be the man she needs you to be. She loves you, and she's not the only one. Don't withhold what she needs, Drake. Don't deny her the comfort of your arms. Not for my sake."

Jaena kissed him passionately, and for a moment he had returned to Cliffton, sitting on the shade clover under the protective branches of a cover tree by the Lily Pad rocks. He and Jaena were together, saying goodbye.

403

At that time, only a few months ago, he felt like he was going home and would see her again. This time he did not. This was the end for them. He thought he wouldn't see her in this life ever again.

He tasted Jaena's salty tears as his own mixed with hers in his mouth, and he held her, not wanting to let go, but he felt her slipping slowly away.

LXXIII

The spirits around us may be hidden, but they do exist, and are a part of our lives whether we are aware of it or not.

—passage from the Goddess Scrolls of Amaryllis

Bree floated above her body, terrified and powerless to help her friends. Kasiya had poisoned her, and she assumed that soon she would be dead. There was no pain, only a loneliness and a helplessness as she watched Drake and the others struggle to break free from the ropes which secured them to tall stone pillars. She could not hear them speaking, but she could feel their fear and rage, and understand some of their thoughts. Her poor friends would die tonight and she would have to watch them being brutally murdered.

Why had Kasiya done this? It had made no sense until Bree saw the four Priestesses' dark auras. They were not women at all, they were demons who had taken female forms, and now they were changing into beasts, taking on the aspects of lions, and also growing wings like griffins.

Kasiya and the others served the Dragon of Darkness himself. She saw his image on the wall. They worshipped him with their dance, and offered Drake's blood to him, burning it in a brazier. Soon they would offer Drake's organs, one at a time. This she knew.

These vile creatures were the secret gatekeepers of Shahan and Far Khoram, watching and waiting for anyone who arrived in the city from either route, protecting Draglûne from his enemies trying to come or go.

Bree wondered how much had they learned from Dabarius, and from her? Queen Khelen'dara was in danger now, but Bree could do little to help, except pray for a miracle. She beseeched all the gods of Mephitia, especially her patroness, the Goddess Amar'isis. The Winged Goddess was her only hope now, as all Bree could do was hover over her immobile body and wait.

Kasiya made a vile pledge to kill Drake first, and Bree could not bear it any longer. She hid herself, trying to block out the emotions from her friends and the demons that flooded her spirit-mind. All she could do was pray. She did pray a thousand times to the Winged Goddess. Time moved so differently here and she felt like she had spent an entire night in front of an altar, but almost no time had passed in material world. The very core of her being prayed for help. It was like she was waiting for a sunrise, and it came brighter than she could have ever imagined.

A brilliant, blinding golden light suddenly filled the space as a radiant being emerged from the spirit world in answer to her prayers. A true miracle! Bree recognized the beautiful spirit of her Goddess and rejoiced. She looked the same as when she had healed Bree near the Deeps of Ah'usar. Strangely, Amar'isis had the gray colors of distress in her aura. Bree wanted to tell her not to worry, but that was ridiculous. How could she comfort a deity, so she stayed distant, bowing and pleading respectfully for help to save her friends' lives.

Amar'isis seemed to pay her no attention. She glided toward Bree's physical body and the Winged Goddess melded with Bree's flesh.

Yes, this was what Bree wanted. *Use me, Goddess. I am your servant in all things.*

Amar'isis took control, directing Bree's body to free Drake and the others. The four demonic Priestesses finished changing into lion women, but they were too late and Dabarius used his magic to trap them in their secret worship chamber with the painting of Draglûne.

Bree wanted to follow her friends, go with them, but she was trapped too, not by Dabarius's magic, but by the spell Kasiya had cast upon her, and was banished from her body by the poison she had ingested. She was trapped in this unholy place consecrated to the Dragon of Darkness. And he watched her from the wall, seeing her for what she was and coveting her soul. He would take her essence into his, and know all that she knew once the ceremony was complete. Once Kasiya and the others returned, they would summon a creature from the Void and they would bite her flesh, opening a way for the demon to become part of her. She would change and become like Kasiya, a half-human demon who hunted as a lioness, and fed on flesh and fear.

The lion women eventually escaped the worship hall of Draglûne, but Bree remained, trapped by Kasiya's spell. The Dragon of Darkness eyed her and she hid in the corner of the room, waiting for her soul's destruction, and praying for the lives of her friends many thousands of times

Time passed, but she had no conception of it, though the darkness outside the hall changed to light, as the sun rose over Shahan. The power of Draglûne faded with the sunrise, and the spell Kasiya had used to trap her spirit in the hall shattered like a ceramic jug dropped on the floor. The shards of it were still sharp and dangerous, so she avoided them and fled into the light of day.

The God of the Sun, Ah'usar, held dominion now as He entered the sky in His solar chariot. The bright light of the sunrise revealed to Bree a golden cord trailing off from her spirit. She knew it lead to her physical body. There were other cords too, leading from her spirit to the people that she had met and loved. So many of the cords led to the spirit world.

Bree followed the cord that led to her body and in an instant she was floating over her physical form. Joy filled her being as Drake cradled her in his arms. He was alive and so were all the companions, including Jep and Temus, but not poor Skinny.

Bree moved closer and the radiant spirit of the Goddess Amar'isis rose up to meet her. Bree bowed, offering her love and devotion to her patroness.

"Sister," the spirit replied, "Please forgive me for possessing your body,"—Bree instantly knew everything that had happened while Jaena controlled her. "Please forgive me for allowing you to believe that I was a goddess. I am not Amar'isis. I am the woman, Jaena of Cliffton."

"Jaena? You healed me at the Deep of Ah'usar. You told me to protect Drake, to help him. You gave him to me, but you are the woman he loves and wants to return to. Why would you do all of this? Why would you give him up?"

"Because your love might save him," Jaena said. "I am far away, and my envy does no one any good. You are there, and he needs you. I think you need him, too."

Bree did love him, and Jaena understood. Bree would die for him if she had to. Jaena knew this. She had manipulated her in a way, but it felt right, natural. Drake was a good man, and he deserved her love more than she deserved his. If he knew the things she had done to protect the secrets of Mephitia, he would not love her.

"He does love you," Jaena said. "It is painful for me to see it, but it cannot be denied. Love is a shield for you both. Use it and survive this journey. Help him let go of Ethan's ghost, and let go of the ones that you carry with you. Cut the dark cords that hold both of you back, then you can be truly together in the times ahead, not weighed down by the past."

"You know for certain that he will not return to you when this is over?" Bree asked.

"He and I will always be connected," Jaena said, "our spirits will find each other again. He will not see me again in the flesh."

"Will he die?" Bree asked.

"I do not know how or when his life will end," Jaena said, "and I have my own journey, which is near an end."

"You will die?" Bree asked, surprised at how much this thought disturbed her. She should despise his woman, but she cared for her, loved her for her kindness and for her gentle

408

spirit. She said what Drake would say. "Tell me that you are all right. That you are safe. It must be so."

"That is not to be. I have been sentenced to death," Jaena said, "but it will not be the end for my spirit. Death is not the end."

Bree knew she spoke the truth.

"We must part now," Jaena said, "as sisters, as women who love the same man, and care more for his life than our own. Do not tell him that I am in danger. It will not help him, or you."

"Why did you tell me this?" Bree asked.

"Forgive me for burdening you," Jaena said, "but someday, if the time is right, you may want to tell him my words to comfort him. It will not be easy for him to stay away from his home in the forest, and away from me. For now, I want you to know that he is yours, and you should love him with all your heart."

"I will." Bree embraced Jaena's spirit, and then watched her fade away, a sad smile on the blue-eyed woman's face. She was not Amar'isis, but Bree felt the Goddess inside Jaena, working through her. She may have been a young woman in this life, but her soul was wise and ancient. She had served Amar'isis countless times in the past. Bree would keep Jaena's confidence, and she would love Drake.

Then Bree entered her body and instantly awoke, the feel of her body so foreign and heavy compared to the form she had just been in. She felt the warmth of the morning and the wind tickled her skin, blowing across her ear. She opened her eyes and the sun peeked over the horizon. She was blinded, but it was nothing compared to Jaena's inner light.

She tried to comprehend what had just happened as a torrent of emotions flooded her mind. She was in Drake's arms and it felt so good to be close to him. She loved him more deeply than ever before and wondered if some residual feeling had been left behind from Jaena. There was an attachment to him much greater than she had experienced before. Had these feelings been inside her all along? Bree didn't know or care, and wrapped her arms and legs around him as he dozed beside her. He woke quickly and stared into her eyes, carefully examining them.

"Bree?" he asked.

She nodded, and kissed him, then rested her head on his chest.

"Do you know what happened?" he asked.

"I know it was Jaena who healed me at the Deep of Ah'usar after the dragonling stung me. I spoke to her."

"You did?" he asked, then waited, his entire body tense.

"You were right to love her, and to tell me that you might go back to her. She is a good woman, and I am nothing compared to her. She serves the Goddess in a way that I could never hope to. She—"

"You are a good woman," he said, hugging Bree.

"Perhaps someday I will be," she said. "Perhaps someday I will be cleansed of all that I've done after we finish this. If that time ever comes perhaps you will choose to stay here with me. It will be a gift that I may not deserve, but I will accept it with open arms. I will not force you, but I will be here, and if you do stay, I will love you, as I love you now."

LXXIV

I would like to see the bottom of this canyon. It's the closest I've ever come to setting foot in the Underworld.

—Bölak Blackhammer, from the Khoram Journal

The water-cut tunnel under the well shaft led east toward the cliff at the edge of Shahan. The underground river was more like a medium-sized stream that could easily be leaped across. It flowed down the center of the smooth passage, gurgling quietly. Drake thought the tiny river seemed incapable of having hollowed out so much rock, but Bellor said it had been much larger in the distant past and was older than any of them could fathom.

The slippery bank was wide enough for the companions to walk five abreast on either side of the water, and the cavern was twice as tall as most men, but Drake, Jep and Temus followed behind Thor, Bellor and Dabarius in a single file line, while Bree served as the companions' rear guard, sword drawn. It was strange. She had smiled more in this one morning than in the months they'd traveled together combined. Then again, Jaena had been there. It seemed that she'd healed Bree'alla's spirit somehow, just by her presence. Drake was so confused. He loved both women more than he ever had.

The dogs remained wary as their nails clicked sharply on the stone and added to the dull slapping steps of the others, which made a significant echo in the humid passage. They would not surprise anyone, but with the four Priestesses dead, burned, and buried, the only ones listening to them in the city were the many feline cats and the lone winged cat they had seen. Since the battle with the demon women all of the cats had all given them a wide berth, hissing at them. Still, they took no chances, and Drake aimed his crossbow ahead, using the light from Bellor's glowstone to scan for threats as they explored the river cave. This had to be the way down to the bridge that spanned the River of Mist, supposedly hidden in the canyon below the abandoned city.

They did not travel far before the hazy light of a fog-shrouded morning beckoned them onward. An oval-shaped window wider than the passage itself looked out onto the striated layers of the canyon, mostly hidden by the morning fog. The mist clung to the canyon walls and rose upward from the depths of the Void before slipping over the lip of the plateau over a hundred feet above them.

The river died without a roar after being collected in a wide, shallow pool. It spilled over a swath of reddish rock then flowed into at least six natural channels, which trickled down the backward sloping canyon and disappeared. Above them, a broad overhang of pitted whitish rock hid the cave from anyone looking down from Shahan, though from the opposite side of the canyon, it would be visible as long as the mist was low enough.

Drake thought of Cliffton as he watched giant clouds rise and obscure their lookout as they drifted upwards toward the rim. It was the same in his village almost every day, though the mist here was not as moist as the massive fog banks, which rose every day and cloaked the edges of the Thornclaw Forest.

"Over here," Bellor said from the north side of the cavern where he and Thor were exploring. The others backtracked, and jumped across the channel to join them.

"Man-carved steps," Thor said, indicating the narrow trail leading out of the cave and along a cliff ledge that had been widened and shaped by chisels perhaps centuries ago. A knee-high and deteriorated wall made of chunks of rock that had been chipped off the canyon wall was the only thing separating the trail from a sheer drop into the Void.

Dabarius, Bellor, and Bree'alla examined the Mephitian glyphs etched into the wall at the entrance to the trail. Drops of water ran down the stone as the wizard brushed his large hands over them.

"Well," Thor said, as he kept watch on the tunnel behind them, "can you read them?"

"These are wardings," Dabarius said, "meant to keep the spirits of the dead and the demons of the Underworld from entering here, and coming into the city."

"Worthless," Thor said, shaking his head. "The only thing that I'll trust against my enemies, be they man or monster, is good steel."

"Khebian Priests carved them," Bree said, pointing to the mountain symbol on the rock, which was not that different from the split-peaked mountain medallions Bellor and Thor wore around their necks.

Drake looked past his friends at the slick trail of carved and mortared steps, partially shrouded in fog that descended into the canyon. How far down did they go? All the way to the Underworld at the bottom of the River of Mist?

The superstitious beliefs of his people and his own fascination with seeing the Underworld clashed in his mind. He didn't care what the elders of Cliffton or anyone thought. He wanted to see where his friend Ethan had fallen. He wanted to know what was down there, more even than he wanted to find a way across. His mind wandered as his friends looked at the glyphs and his eyes began to lose focus as he stared at the trail. He sensed something moving in the mist, and his eyes locked onto it.

The ghostly outline of a scrawny young man appeared on the steps and beckoned Drake to follow as he floated down the trail. Drake could hear Ethan's voice in his mind, *Come on. I'll show you the way.*

None of the others had seen Ethan, and he didn't want them to.

Without a word to his companions, Drake went after his dead friend. Surprised, the others followed without comment. The steep steps hugged the natural contour of the ledge as they angled downward around a bend, then stopped at a landing where all of them could gather without crowding each other. A rectangular altar with the etched symbols of the Ah'usar, a sun disk, and Kheb, a mountain, faced into the canyon.

More steps continued from the landing, and descended into a thick bank of mist swirling below them. Drake did not want to stop, but Dabarius bid them halt while he examined the picture glyphs on the canyon wall again. The wizard said they were from the time after the bridge to Far Khoram fell and the God King and Queen were separated 'by the will of the gods.' The High Priest of Kheb in Shahan had the new steps built and dedicated them to the Mountain God, and his 'Hidden Blessings.'

Bellor confirmed that the steps were a much newer construction than the landing and the trail leading to it, but asked, "What does 'Hidden Blessings' mean?"

"Let's find out," Thor said, and Drake took his cue and led the way into the wall of mist. His legs touched first, and he paused as it flowed around him, swallowing his boots.

Don't be afraid, Ethan said again, and Drake thought he could see his friend's face in the mist for the briefest of moments.

The fog was oppressive and breathing was harder in the hot humid air. He could barely see the end of his crossbow or even his feet as they carefully found the slick steps, coated with a thin layer of moisture. He took one step after another on the increasingly narrow stairs as the heat increased, as if he were descending into a Drobin sauna.

After descending for only a short time the fog blocked out the sky and the canyon above, which became a dull white glow. The fear of stepping down and not finding a step, but instead empty air, needled him, then made his body tremble as the worry grew. He leaned backwards, waiting until he could feel each step below before he settled his weight on it. He couldn't see anything and decided his crossbow was useless for now.

414

He unloaded, uncocked, and slung it over his shoulder to free his hands. He touched the handle of his Kierka knife on his belt for reassurance, and felt the side of the canyon to steady himself, using it to guide him downward.

The dogs followed him closely, hesitating often. Temus would whine sometimes, and the sound came out muffled and strange, but far too loud for his liking. He reassured the dog with pats and a few quiet words. The others said little and Drake was glad. Who knew what their voices might attract down here?

Drake's toe hit something solid and he lost his balance for an instant as he pitched forward. His heart pounded so loud his friends must have heard it as he tried to calm himself. He thought the stairs ended, but it was a landing and he'd hit a low wall with his boot. The path switched backwards and went down the other way still deeper into the Void.

"This way," he whispered to his friends, calling them to him. He could hear each of them, and knew the sound of their steps. Both dwarves' heavy boots were obvious, while Bree's light step was the quietest. Dabarius had the longest strides, taking two steps at a time, and moved with an assured gait. They followed him closely and the agonizing descent continued until Drake's thighs trembled as he had been holding his legs up and setting them down carefully on the stone steps, testing each one with his partial weight before committing fully.

The stress of not knowing what lay ahead was worse than the physical effort, and it took a toll on his mind. He didn't want to fall and when the stairs became steeper, it became harder and harder to step down carefully. Finally, he decided to sit and stretch down toward the next step with one foot. It took a lot longer and was very tedious, but his friends did not push him to go faster or complain even once. They just kept following, helping the dogs when he could not.

Time seemed to drag on forever and little annoyances began to bother him. He felt like he was cooking in a steam pot and his hands were wet from touching the stone. His clothes clung to him, chafing his skin as he slid his backside from step to step. The air was so thick that it was hard to breathe. His eyes ached from trying to pierce the fog. He no longer cared about finding the bottom of the Void. He just wanted to get back on top of the plateaus. Any plateau would do.

An hour passed, perhaps more, and the path continued down into the heat of the Underworld . . . until Drake found where the steps ended. He stretched and reached with one foot, but he could find nothing solid to stand upon. The fog was too thick to see more than an arm's length ahead, but he waited, hoping for it to clear.

It didn't, and Bellor whispered, "What is it, lad?"

"I can't find the next step," Drake said.

After some discussion about what to do, Dabarius handed Drake a short length of rope with a small, weighted leather pouch tied to the end. He dangled it into the mist and struck a surface almost immediately, perhaps six feet below him. It was very narrow and sloped sharply on either side.

"I'm going to have to climb down and look at it," Drake said. "I can't see anything."

Bree joined him on the last step, her lips tight together.

Bellor crowded in behind them and touched Drake on the shoulder. "We'll tie a rope around you," he said, then wrapped a short length of frayed rope around Drake, creating a harness, Drobin fashion, and secured the other end to a small steel spike Thor hammered into a crevice.

With his heart fluttering, Drake dropped the rope over the edge and prepared to repel down.

"Careful now," Bellor warned, "it might be slippery."

Drake nodded.

Bree squeezed his hand and wouldn't let go for a long moment.

"I'll be all right," he said. "It's not far." Then he climbed backwards over the edge, his feet against the cliff as he walked down. He reached the rock below and found himself on a peaked ridge of stone that looked like the blade of a titanic stone sword, notched and crumbling, but pointing straight across to the other side of the canyon. Drops of water collected along the reddish surface and dripped down on either side, sliding into the nothingness of the mist.

"*Drake?*" The worry in Bree's voice made him hang on extra tightly to his handholds and squeeze the rock with his thighs.

"I'm fine. I think I found the bridge." He paused for a moment and inspected the tan rock he straddled. It was colored exactly like the top of the canyon, not the grayish and red stone where he had climbed down from. Could this be the remains of the plateau that had once been in the middle of the gorge and was now wedged between the opposite sides of the canyon walls as Bellor suspected? Was this like some gigantic boulder caught in between the walls of a crevasse?

He couldn't tell, but had to find out if the sword edge went all the way across. "I'm going to explore," he said, then explained what he found.

"Be careful," Bellor said. "Thor will be ready to come down if you need help."

Straddling the wet rock he slid forward until his short rope ran out. "I have to untie myself to go forward," he shouted through the mist.

"Call to us if you need help," Bellor said. "Don't take any unnecessary risks."

It took him a moment to untie himself, then he kept going, his legs pressed against the rock tighter than he had when he'd ridden a vorrel at full gallop. If he slid off either way from the peaked rock, he didn't know if he could hang on. How far he would slide before the rock ran out? He didn't know, but he knew he was still high above the bottom of the Void.

417

A faint scent filtered up from the depths below. He had smelled nothing like it before, though the closest memory he had was of decaying marshland in a swampy area in the Thorn-claw Forest. Was this part of the Underworld a swamp? He couldn't be sure and didn't want to think for a moment of what creatures might live in such a terrible place.

Trying not to worry about what might be down there, Drake slid forward for a long while. The oppressive heat made his skin hot and damp as the fog rose up toward the sky. He considered resting for a moment, but then the bridge of stone ended at a sheer face of rock. The cliff went straight up to the glowing white sky hidden by the mist. He searched for a moment and then found the carved steps, this time starting within easy reach. He climbed up them for a moment, then decided he should go back.

The return trip was faster, and less stressful until Ethan's voice screamed in his mind, *Watch out!*

He turned his head as something dove toward him from above gliding on outstretched wings. Drake ducked and slipped to one side of the bridge, holding on with both hands as his body dangled down the steeply sloped rock as he tried to take cover.

Burning pain in one hand forced him to let go and he pulled it back, seeing the blood leaking from his torn flesh. The aevian disappeared before he could see what it was.

"Drake!" Bree'alla shouted. "What is it?"

"I don't know, aevian of some kind!" he shouted, realizing he was very close to his friends now. Jep and Temus barked ferociously.

"Are you hurt?" Bellor asked.

"Not badly," he said as blood gushed from his left hand. He didn't have any footholds on the smooth rock, and wanted to pull himself up and try to mount the peaked bridge, then he heard the rumbling high-pitched growl. The sound made his hair stand on end and he knew it was on the other side of the rock now. He felt its breath on the trigger finger of his right hand and imagined what it was about to do.

But if he let go, he would slip down the rock face, fall into the Underworld and join Ethan as a restless ghost. If he didn't let go the thing would mangle his right hand anyway.

Ignoring the pain, he put his bloody left hand back on the peaked rock, offering it to the aevian. He braced himself for more pain as the creature's yellow green cat's eyes locked on him through the wisps of thick mist. Its face was more draconic than feline, twisted and stretched, like tanned leather with bits of fur still attached. The winged cat had grown much larger, and was as big as his bullmastiffs. Tan- and black-striped draconic wings, perfect for blending into the desert spread wide above it and blocked out the hazy light from above. The rumbling growl came again as black lips peeled away revealing long teeth as the demon's eyes flashed toward Drake's bloody hand and locked on.

He wiggled his fingers like fish lures to keep the demon's attention, then pulled himself forward as fast as he could. He used the pain in his hand to fuel a chop from his forward curved Kierka blade. He drove the steel into the center of the demon's skull and split it open.

As the aevian reeled, stunned and bleeding, he straddled the stone ridge and used an overhand swing. His blow fell on the back of its neck as a great blast of wind drove away all of the fog around him.

The bloody head of the demon rolled down the rock and disappeared into the whiteness below as its body slid down the opposite slope. Drake's anxious friends stood on the stairs nearby. Dabarius held out his arms in a grand gesture as if he were directing the gust of wind, which kept the fog away, as Thor repelled down to the bridge in one quick jump.

Bree did not wait her turn on the rope and sprang over Thor. She landed deftly on the narrow bridge of stone, slightly wider than the width of her foot. She came fast, not hesitating

419

at all.

Bellor aimed *Heartseeker*, ready to release a bolt, then let out a sigh of relief when he saw Drake victorious over the creature's body.

A moment later, Bree reached him. She urgently examined the back of his left hand, which had two deep claw marks that exposed muscles and tendons. It hurt terribly and he could barely control his fingers. Pulling himself up to strike the feline demon had made the wound worse and the blood was gushing down his wrist and staining the rock.

Using her scarf, Bree tried to staunch the flow, painfully tying off the wound. Drake sucked his breath through his teeth as she increased the pressure.

"It's not that bad," she said then gave him a wry grin, "at least you've still got your hand."

"One hand," he said, and he tried and failed to move his fingers.

"Move out of the way," Thor said to Bree as he arrived at last. "I best look at that."

Bree explained what she'd seen under the bandage, urging Thor to leave the scarf in place. The Drobin made his own inquiries and carefully inspected what he could see of the wound.

"How bad is he hurt?" Bellor asked Thor.

"Master Bellor," Thor said, ominously using a formal title and avoiding Drake's gaze, "I've seen wounds like this before. He'll be crippled forever if we leave him like this."

Drake didn't want to believe Thor's words, but they still hit him hard. He wouldn't be able to crank back his crossbow with one hand, among another hundred things.

"Is the ground there tainted?" Bellor asked his former apprentice.

Thor closed his eyes and concentrated, touching the bridge with both hands. If the area was tainted somehow by the Void, no healing would be possible. It would be the same if they entered the lair of Draglûne or his kin, as Verkahna's lair in the desert had been irrevocably tainted stopping Bellor and Thor from using the Healing magic.

"No, Master," Thor said, his eyes still closed.

"Very well," Bellor said, "Then Thor, you know what to do." The air of command was heavy in the old dwarf's voice, though he did not ask for such a sacrifice lightly.

"Let us not delay any longer," Thor said. "I'm going to use the Healing magic."

"Thank you," Drake said, relieved, and so thankful he would not have to face the time ahead with one hand. The pain was also going to go away, as would an unknown amount of time from Thor's life. Thankfully, it would be months, or even weeks perhaps, not years. The wound was fresh, and reversing the flow of the time stream—the *zeitströmen*—and going back to the moment before he was injured would not be that difficult, would it?

Thor touched the tan rock of the bridge with one hand, connecting with the magic of the Earth Father, Lorak, while Bree kept watch and Dabarius held off the mist, creating a pocket around them. How much longer could the wizard keep the fog away? The strain on his face was evident, but he kept up the magic as Thor began to pray. It seemed important to keep the Void mist away now.

Beneath the landing where Dabarius, Bellor and the anxious dogs watched them, Drake noticed that there had once been steps leading all the way down to the bridge. Evidence of mortared stones, and a foundation remained, though almost everything had been broken away. Was this what Reu'ven meant when he said he had had the bridge destroyed? The stone span could not be sundered, but breaking a few steps were within the powers a few men with chisels and hammers. They may have even embellished their tale to Reu'ven, or perhaps he wanted to keep the bridge accessible?

Pain from his wound surged up Drake's arm as Thor

pressed one hand over the bloody scarf. A golden glow emanated from the dwarf's palm as he bowed his head and mumbled prayers in Drobin, invoking the "True Fire of Lorak." There were many more words, but Drake understood few, as his language lessons from the temple in Khierson City faded from his memory.

Silent now, Thor prayed, his whole body trembling and shaking as he exerted a tremendous amount of effort to keep his hand over the wound. It was as if the timestream were trying to pull him or knock him off the stone bridge and into the Void. Bree'alla grabbed Thor, and held his shoulders down as the force of the magic coursed through him.

The full body shaking stopped suddenly and the dwarf opened his eyes, and nodded at Drake.

"It's done," Thor said.

Drake unwound Bree's scarf and found his skin still covered in blood, but no evidence of the deep scratches remained on the back of his hand, which he could move perfectly. "Thank you very much, Thor. I'm sorry for what you had to sacrifice for me."

The dwarf smiled, "It doesn't matter. I won't live to be an old dwarf. I'm going to die the instant after I smash a hole in Draglûne's skull, and you can all say grand words about me after you bury what's left."

"You don't think he'd swallow you whole?" Drake asked playfully.

"Even Draglûne is not so stupid," Thor said. "Even in death I would stick in his throat."

PART THREE

THE DRAGON OF DARKNESS

LXXV

Water hides in the ground under this infernal desert, but we are
Earth Priests, and we know where to look.

— Bölak Blackhammer, from the Khoram Journal

The burning pain in Drake's arms and shoulders forced him
to put down the heavy water bags. Bellor, Thor, and Bree
followed his example, sighing with relief, eager to rest before
they hiked up the long and gradual incline before them. Only
Dabarius protested them stopping again, but Drake thought it
was just a show.

"We'll go another mile today," Bellor said, then he slumped
down.

A mile would have been nothing if they had sturdy vorrels,
but acting as their own beasts of burden and carrying so much
water was torture. They moved at a fraction of the speed they
had crossed the Dune Sea, and Drake wasn't so sure that Bellor's plan would work. The old dwarf said they would march
ahead and drop off water bags, then return and get more water from the little spring in the side of the cliff opposite Shahan. They would repeat the process many times until they had
enough stashed ahead of them along their path so they would
have plenty to reach a new source in the distant mountains.
At least the return trip to get more water bags would be made
without heavy burdens on their backs.

Jep and Temus flopped onto the ground and panted loudly
after Drake told them to sit. They had been hitched to a drag
sled loaded with water and supplies. Drake pet Jep on the head,
and thought about giving him something to drink.

"Poor dogs," Bree said, as she loosened the harness on
Temus as he tried to rest.

At least the companions were able to follow the mostly
sand-covered and obstacle-free road built by the God King

Ra'menek. According to a weathered stele they had found the ancient Mephitian ruler had built it as a gift to the people of Shahan. The road meandered along the edge of the eastern side of the River of Mist at the base of some hills. The desert had reclaimed large sections, but the roadbed was easily seen most of the time, often marked with half-buried stele that indicated the distance to Shahan.

"I wish we had some shade," Thor said as he rested his head on a water bag, and used his shield to block out the sun.

"I can put up the shade tents," Drake said.

"We won't be stopping that long," Dabarius said, "will we, Bellor?"

Bellor ignored his question as he crawled rapidly through the spindly bushes and yellow grass, heading for the lip of the cliff not far from the road.

"What're you doing?" Dabarius asked.

The War Priest stopped at a patch of brownish rocks and started running his hands over them. "Thor, come over here."

The urgency in Bellor's voice made Drake sit up, as did they all, except for the dogs who tried to sleep despite the glaring sun.

"What is it?" Thor asked as he arrived at Bellor's side his boots skidding as he stopped.

"Look at the pattern," Bellor said.

Drake was on his feet and looking over the dwarves' shoulders. All he saw were a bunch of head-sized rocks placed randomly on the ground.

"It's a Drobin marker," Thor said, astounded. He shuffled to the far side of the rock patch and found more, buried by sand, then made his way forward and found four stones arranged in a roughly diamond pattern, though they were at least three full paces apart. He and Bellor made lines in the dirt between the four stones and where they crossed Bellor began to dig through the dirt and gravel.

"Bölak's mark," Bellor announced in awe after he turned over a flat stone.

Drake saw the hammer with the long handle, but he had to touch it, rub his fingers over the etched mark. Even then he couldn't believe it.

Bellor laughed and dug with renewed enthusiasm, brushing away loose rocks and dirt.

"They buried something here?" Bree asked.

"We'll find out," Thor said, as he helped clear away the sand.

The dwarves uncovered a circular flat stone as wide as a man's shoulders.

"It's a cap stone," Bellor said.

Mephitian picture glyphs covered the surface of it.

"Can you read this?" Thor asked Dabarius.

"It's archaic," Dabarius said, "but I can read it. There's a royal seal, the symbol of the sun, and it says, 'This gift is from the God King Ra'menek, Son of Ah'usar, Eternal Father of the People, Ruler of the Empire of Mephitia, Head of the Great House of Lesh'heb.'"

Drake had thought Bölak left something buried under sand, but he had only marked it. Bellor and Thor managed to pry up the lid and Drake immediately felt a draft of moist air and he smelled water inside. Thor explored the shaft, going down a steep staircase that led to a long and narrow water trough that paralleled a similarly long window in the cliff. A cave had been carved out of solid rock, and mist from the Void entered through the window high above the clouds of the River of Mist. Every morning the clouds would rise up to the rim and moisture would form on the walls of the cave. The drops would trickle into the cavern and were funneled into large water traps that held hundreds of gallons, perhaps even more.

"We have all the water we can drink!" Thor said, then handed Drake an old ceramic cup filled to the brim with

427

clear water. A faded golden sun disk had been painted on the cup, which was undoubtedly another gift from the God King. Drake swallowed a mouthful, and passed the rest of it to Bree.

He savored the water and thought the Void mist tasted a little sandy and with a hint of minerals. He didn't care. It was cool and he was parched.

Dabarius found a Mephitian stele buried in the hillside. It had been uprooted from somewhere, and purposefully covered, though the tip had been exposed by erosion.

"Who buried this?" Dabarius asked.

"Not Bölak," Bellor said. "My nephew marked this place, though its location has obviously been hidden."

"Why?" Dabarius asked.

"The marker in the hill has been there a long time," Bellor said. "It was buried there long before Bölak came this way."

"The God King of Mephitep could have hidden the caches," Dabarius said, "to keep anyone from going to Shahan, or from coming from there."

"Another barrier to crossing the desert," Drake said.

"How did Bölak find this?" Dabarius asked.

"All of the dwarves with him were Earth Priests," Bellor said, "and so were the Khebians. They must have used magic."

"Do you and Thor know of such magic?" Dabarius asked.

"We do," Bellor said, "but it would take a long time and we would have to stop and probe the ground almost every step of the way. Dousing rods would be helpful, but we don't have any of those."

"Let's just enjoy what we found," Thor said, passing cups of cool water to his friends.

"I think they knew the mist traps were here before they crossed the bridge at Shahan," Bree said.

Everyone looked at her.

"I think water traps like these exist on the western side as well," she said. "The Khebian High Priest Ben'khar told me there were water caches there, but they had been hidden long ago, their markers removed."

"What else haven't you told us?" Thor asked.

"Mephitian rangers have looked for them in the past," Bree said, "but they never found them."

"So there are many of them?" Drake asked.

"If we can find the mist traps on the western side with Bellor and Thor's Earth magic," Dabarius said, "we'll have a way back, even if we don't have any vorrels."

"Do you think you could find them?" Drake asked Bellor.

"We could find them," the old dwarf said, as he chiseled his own mark into the rock next to Bölak's marker.

The somber tone of Bellor's voice made Drake think that the dwarf didn't think he was going to be alive on the return journey. His urgency to put his own mark on the rock made Drake wonder if Bellor thought another group would someday follow their trail to Far Khoram.

"What else do you know about these water caches?" Dabarius asked Bree.

"They are evenly spaced apart," she said.

"How far apart?" Dabarius asked.

"No one in Isyrin claimed to know," she said.

"How will we find them?" Drake asked.

"We'll find them," Dabarius said. "Bölak probably marked them all."

The wizard was right. They found the next mist trap three miles further south on the road, marked with the hard to spot—unless you were a Drobin—stone markers. They had covered the distance with only a small amount of water on their backs, as Bellor agreed that a scouting trip was more important now. Thor noticed the markers first, and they followed them to the buried mist trap, which was filled with water.

Every few miles they found another cache, and they had all the water they needed. The Ten Sons of Kheb did not leave obvious piles of rocks that anyone would find and scatter or toss over the cliff. They left a pattern of ten stones that blended into the desert, but showed the way. Sand had covered a few, but most of the rocks were easy to see and pointed to a camouflaged and capped tunnel that led down to the cave where the mist gathered every morning.

Drinking the mist of the Void had never crossed Drake's mind, but after three days of walking south along the cliff in Far Khoram it seemed as natural as walking under the gigantic sky without worrying about aevians. Nothing larger than hawks and falcons hunted along the ancient roadway.

They would reach the Mountains of Kheb in less than a day now, which was where the people of Old Mephitia were reported to live. The entire northern part of the Far Khoram plateau beyond the Mountains of Kheb was thought to be uninhabitable desert, and Drake agreed after what he'd seen of it. As they endured the brutally hot temperatures, his greatest wish was to sit under the canopy of a tree—just one tree—and not feel the sun burning his now-tanned skin.

He dreamed of cover trees and home as the purple mountains in the distance became closer, turning brown and gray as they neared them. The land rose steadily in elevation and they hiked slowly up the incline. The plants grew more abundantly, and Drake shot a few birds for the dogs, always on the lookout for perfect feathers that he could use as fletchings for his bolts. He also shot ground squirrels and small rabbits for himself and his friends. The food they had taken from the temple of Ah'usar in Shahan and carried down the steps and across the bridge was conserved as much as possible, as they did not know how long it would take to reach their destination—as none of them knew where they were actually going. They had only the vague information that Draglûne's lair lay somewhere on the southern edge of the Far Khoram plateau, south of the Mountains of Kheb. They had a very basic map, copied from an ancient scroll that showed the shape of the plateaus, but they had no real knowledge of where to look or how to get there.

For the first time in a long while, Drake felt like he was on a hunt instead of a marathon trek, and his quarry was very close now. He wondered if the people of Far Khoram would defend Draglûne. Would they act like the Iron Brotherhood in the North? If they did, they would have to die? With that in mind he kept his eyes focused on the horizon, looking for movement or the dust from people or animals walking. "Bellor," he asked, "what do we do if we meet Mephitians on this road?"

"First, we avoid them," Bellor said. "We keep our presence unknown as long as we can."

"Then we better start traveling more at night," Drake said. "If our enemies are ahead in the mountains, they'll see us coming because of our dust."

"You're right, lad," Bellor said. "We'll stop as soon as we find the next mist trap, then we'll rest until sunset."

They found it a short time later and made camp. "What do you think the people here are like?" Drake asked Bree.

"I don't know," she said. "They've been isolated for so long who knows what's happened to them? They won't be friends of Amar'isis, that I do know."

"Then you think we'll have to fight," Drake said.

She nodded her head, and he wondered how many Mephitians he would have to kill to reach Draglûne.

LXXVI

We shall entice Draglûne with bait that plays to his bad temper and arrogance.

—Bellor Fardelver, from the Desert Journal

As the sun slipped toward the horizon in a pink and red sky, Bellor called the companions to a meeting. Drake woke up the dogs and said, "Guard."

Jep and Temus stood up and patrolled the edge of the camp, while he joined his friends and sat in front of Bellor.

"We are getting close to inhabitable land now," the old dwarf said, "and must do all we can to avoid the God King's servants, especially the servants of the Storm God. We must keep our presence unknown to all, and strike Draglûne's lair by surprise. We will never be able to surprise him once we enter his lair, but simply arriving there unexpected might be enough to cause him to make a fatal mistake. He will come for us, and Drake will pierce his heart with a pair of bolts.

"We don't have a large group of *Dracken Viergur* to fend off his minions, and I doubt we shall find Bölak and his warriors, so we must be prepared to handle the dragon ourselves. We will draw Draglûne in close and kill him swiftly, for if the battle lasts more than a moment . . . he will kill us all."

"What do you propose we do?" Dabarius asked.

"Dabarius, you will use your wizardry to kill or incapacitate his guardians," Bellor said. "Eliminating his servants will be of utmost importance, as we cannot fight them and him at the same time."

"I'll take care of however many he does not," Thor said.

"You'll guard Dabarius," Bellor told Thor.

Dabarius and Thor opened their mouths to protest, but Bellor cut them off. "No arguments from either of you. You'll both watch each other's backs."

432

"If I must," Thor said.

"And expect the fight to be mostly in darkness," Bellor said. "We'll be underground."

"Gauging distance will be more difficult in the dark," Drake said. "How far away do you want me to shoot?"

"He'll be right on top of us," Bellor said. "The distance will be close."

"Tell them about the dragon's fire," Thor said.

"What about it?" Dabarius asked. "We'll be protected from it with your magic."

"Yes," Bellor said, "but we must all close our eyes before the dragon breathes. The firelight will still blind us and ruin our night eyes. We have to keep our eyes shut until most of the flames have dissipated. Also, a deep breath before the fire will help, as the air will be consumed by the flames."

"What if we're in a fight with his servants at that moment?" Bree'alla asked. "We can't shut our eyes then. We'd be killed."

"Do your best to not be engaged with any guardians he might have when he arrives to fight us," Bellor said. "That is the best advice I can give, though with just the seven of us, that may not be possible. Draglûne and his father had armies around them in the Giergun Wars to guard their flanks, and always there are guards watching the entrances to their lairs. We must eliminate all threats as quickly as we can."

"That's what I do best," Thor said.

"We shall see, little man," Dabarius quipped.

"All of you, listen carefully," Bellor said. "We have never been to a place as dangerous as this. We have little knowledge of what we might face here, but it is Draglûne's home territory and I expect the worst. From now on I want all of you to be vigilant and on your guard at all times. We've been lulled into complacency marching in this heat. No more. We cannot afford any mistakes now, and I do not want to lose any of you.

"None of you must take any foolish risks." Bellor glanced at Thor. "All of us must stay alive, but I want to make certain

433

that Drake is unhurt before we face Draglûne. He carries our most powerful weapon, and must not risk himself unnecessarily in the battles before Draglûne arrives. I know he would sacrifice himself to save any of you, but he must not. Never forget that *Heartseeker* and Drake will kill Draglûne. With Dabarius's magic we have a chance against his minions, but at all costs, we must protect Drake until the Dragon King arrives to face us. We shall all do our parts, so Drake can land the telling blow."

Drake felt a heavy weight settle on him for a moment as they all sat in silence.

"What shall I do?" Bree'alla asked.

"You must guard Drake," Bellor told her. "That will be your assignment. Keep him alive, for he must be ready to strike when Draglûne arrives. Then Thor and I will draw Draglûne's attention. When the dragon prepares to engage us, Drake will shoot."

They went over the plan in more detail and Dabarius mentioned some of the magic he would use, as did Bellor. Drake hoped that the enchantments on his bolts would indeed be as powerful as they promised. When the meeting was over, Bellor sent Bree to scout ahead and look over the hill in front of them. Then he spoke to Drake alone.

"Draglûne will try to read our thoughts to know what we will do when we get close to him," Bellor said while he and Drake walked ahead of the others. "The fact that we are *Dracken Viergur* will save us. We four will be protected from his mental probing by the rune of power that we have chosen for our spirits."

"What about Bree?" Drake asked. "She doesn't have the rune. Will you have her join the order and say the vows as we did in Khierson City?"

"No," Bellor said. "Draglûne will read her thoughts and there is nothing I can do about that. I don't know if she could serve more than one god, and besides that, we would need a temple of Lorak to complete the ritual."

434

"You can't leave her unprotected," Drake said.

"Her thoughts will be known to him," Bellor said, "and that's the way I want it. She will not know everything about our plan to slay him, but she will do her part, and Draglûne will believe everything she is thinking."

"What else will you have her do?" Drake asked.

"No more than I've already told her," Bellor said. "She will protect you, and her only assignment will be to keep you alive. Your part will be simple as well. Stand your ground. That is difficult when a dragon charges. Just be ready to shoot. Nothing else matters."

"What do you mean, stand my ground?" Drake asked.

Bellor explained the full plan, and swore him to secrecy. Bree could not know everything, and Drake felt terrible about what he was going to have to do. It was so devious, but Master Bellor was in charge, and Drake would follow his orders, even if he hated them.

LXXVII

Dedication without passion is a flower without a scent.
> —passage from the Goddess Scrolls of Amaryllis

Drake had been thinking about how he would shoot Draglûne through the heart ever since they had left Snow Valley. With Bellor's plan fresh in his mind he was thankful that *Heart-seeker* was in perfect working order. He had meticulously cared for the spring-steel double crossbow every day, and now he practiced by shooting tiny ground squirrel-like rodents off the branches of spiny bushes at almost fifty paces away. The dogs enjoyed them more than birds. He also killed two huge venom-spitting cobras, piercing one through the mouth as it reared up to strike at Temus, while Jep kept a good distance away letting his brother face the threat alone. Drake shot the other cobra a day later as it slithered toward their campsite. One of the cooked snakes was enough to feed the dogs for an entire day. He also shot scaly lizards of various colors and sizes. He rarely missed any of his quarry in the daytime, but at night it was much more difficult, even with the bright moon.

Bellor's words, and the huge responsibility he had given Drake, helped the young man focus whenever he shot his crossbow. He would let go of everything on his mind and would aim with his intuition more than his eyes, willing the bolts to fly straight and strike true. He would have practiced more at night, but he had a limited number of bolts, and if he missed, he could lose one—and he had lost three already. Jep and Temus would fetch the game and the shaft most of the time, but they weren't as good as Skinny had been. He missed the little dog and cursed the demonic Lion Women for what they had done.

Trusting anyone they met in the future would be a challenge. He would be much more wary in the days ahead, es-

436

pecially since they had arrived at the foothills of the barren Mountains of Kheb. The peaks were a brownish black wall of crumbling stone with sharply carved gullies, and dark cliffs. Even taller mountains in the distance had tiny patches of dingy snow clinging to their north faces. The peaks with snow blocked the way ahead. They could find a way through if given enough time, but would they have enough food and water? Drake could only find so much game and the dogs ate a lot of meat as they regained the strength they had lost crossing the desert.

The last mist trap was at least four hours march behind them now, and they had not seen another Drobin marker. They could only carry a small amount of water, which was still extremely heavy. Their food would last perhaps eight days, even if Drake fed the dogs entirely from hunting. He would shoot as many game animals as he could and feed his friends, but how long would it take them to find Draglûne's lair? Would their supplies run out?

"Which way now?" Drake asked, as they reached the base of the mountains. They had two apparent choices. Go east toward the city of Mephitep and follow the road, or south and try to cross the mountains. No longer could they follow the River of Mist. The vast canyon cut a path through dark cliffs of black and red rock that soared almost as high as the peaks. There appeared to be no way to travel along the edge any longer unless they all sprouted wings.

"We'll try to find a way through the mountains," Bellor said.

Later, they all discussed their route and rested in the sweltering afternoon and part of the stifling evening.

"Drake and I should scout ahead," Bree said.

Just the thought of being alone with Bree made Drake's pulse quicken. He wondered if Bellor noticed his eagerness. "We'll be careful," Drake said.

"Don't take any chances," Bellor said. "If you see any

437

Mephitians or signs of them, return immediately. If the four of you aren't back by sunrise, the rest of us are coming after you."

"We'll be back," Bree said.

"Don't worry," Drake said.

"Very well then," Bellor said after some more discussion. He sent the dogs along with Drake and Bree to investigate the foothills. They were the fastest and most stealthy among the group, and it would give Bellor a chance to recover from the march. It had hurt him the most out of all of them.

Right before they left, Master Bellor spoke to Bree alone for a moment.

Once they had gone over the first hill, Drake asked, "What'd he say?"

"He told me to keep an eye on you," Bree said, then she winked.

"That's all?" he asked as she took off ahead of him.

He was hoping for a private moment alone with her, but she did not relax for one minute as they explored the hills. She took the lead much of the time, and they kept to the shadow sides of the hills and traveled in gullies, avoiding the bright patches of desert illuminated by the moon. He took over after a while as they looked for signs of human settlements or camps of nomads. Finding a new source of water was vital as well, since none of them wanted to hike back to the last mist trap.

No fires drew them and they found no Mephitian villages or waterholes after an entire night of searching. Before they returned to camp, somewhat exhausted, they did find a sheltered place to look out over the territory they had just searched. During the day they would go over it again with the others to make sure they didn't miss anything.

"Before we go back . . ." Bree said, then spun him around and kissed him passionately.

It was the best surprise of the night. He responded eagerly and they embraced, kissing and touching as they pressed into each other. It felt wrong, but he couldn't help himself tonight. For days they had been eyeing each other and sleeping close together when the temperature wasn't too hot. He had resisted every urge, but he couldn't now. He wanted to kiss her, and feel every part of her beautiful body with his hands and lips. Her skin tasted salty, and she responded with a moan to his hungry attention. Desperately, he wanted to be with her as a husband was with a wife.

She helped him resist the primal need they both felt with her own attention to him. They kissed and touched each other until the sun was nearly up, finally disentangling their limbs only because they didn't want their companions to worry.

They returned to camp as the horizon turned reddish with golden streaks. Drake was almost unable to hide the grin on his face, though Bree was able to wipe away her smile masterfully, and replace it with a placid and mildly tired expression. When the others weren't looking she beamed at Drake and winked, then returned to her unemotional look when she turned back to the others. He laughed once when she smiled at him, but she gave a perfect performance, and he had no doubt she had been a master spy when she was in Arayden serving the Wings of Amar'isis.

When he lay down to rest, Dabarius asked with a sly grin, "See anything . . . good?"

"I'm just glad I didn't have to look at your ugly face all night," Drake said, and turned over, wondering if Dabarius could see him blushing.

Later that day all of the companions climbed and hiked up the same canyons Drake and Bree had explored trying to find a way through the mountains. No path aside from routes that would take them up several sheer cliffs covered with slippery scree were found. The only choice was east, toward Mephitep, and Drake sensed only dread if they went there. He told himself he would explore every gully until they found a pass across the mountains.

439

Once again, the next night, Drake, Bree, and the dogs scouted ahead going more east looking for Mephitians, water holes, campfires or smoke. They found nothing except a comfortable place in some soft sand where they could sit with each other and kiss and caress, satisfying themselves as much as they dared while keeping their clothing on. Was it wrong to enjoy the moment? Drake had convoluted feelings; guilt about what he would tell Jaena if he ever saw her again, but the idea of rejecting Bree's kisses felt wrong. How many more moments would they have together before they reached Draglûne's lair?

The next night they found what remained of farmers' fields that hadn't seen water in years. The only reason they knew they were old fields was because of the partially buried irrigation ditches. Nearby they discovered a small—and long abandoned—village of dilapidated mud brick hovels perched on the side of a hill and overlooking a dry stream bed. They watched for a long time and were totally certain no one lived in the place. Neither of the dogs smelled or heard anything either. The empty riverbed in front of the canyon also looked promising as a route into and hopefully over the mountains.

"We better get back," Drake said, disappointed they had spent so much of the night scouting and observing when all he had thought about was kissing her. They probably shouldn't now, and needed to tell the others what they had found.

"Another night, then," she said with regret, "we'll find a moment." She kissed him quickly and they marched back to camp under cover of darkness. Later that morning all the companions inspected what was left of the farmers' fields at the base of the hills. The fields themselves were barren except for tenacious scrub bushes and dead yellow grass.

The hovels in the village were still standing, all clumped together on a ridge and utterly abandoned.

"No one has lived here in at least one human generation," Bellor said.

"What happened here?" Drake asked.

"Drought, pestilence, I'm not certain," Bellor said, "but we need to find water today or we're going back to the last mist trap."

They followed the dry streambed into the foothills. No sign of animal or human presence could be found. Even the birds and squirrels avoided the place. After a short hike up the canyon, they found a broken man-made earth and stone dam, which had once held a lot of water. Now it was dry as baked clay. The source of the stream was not far up in the valley. Bellor examined the water stains on the rock and said that a natural spring had once bubbled out of the ground at the foot of the tall mountain. Now it was empty save for smooth rocks and sand.

"No water here," Dabarius said. "We should get moving. We might find something further up the valley."

"Give us a moment," Bellor said, as he motioned for Thor to join him in the shallow basin where the water had once collected. They both touched the ground, palms flat on the rocks and bowed their heads.

After a while Bellor said, "There is water here."

"It's deep," Thor said. "Something is blocking the flow to the surface."

"Thor and I can try to change that," Bellor said.

Dabarius raised an eyebrow.

"Do something useful," Thor said to Dabarius, "and keep watch while we work."

They worked for three hours and working appeared to be them praying silently while touching the ground while kneeling. The dogs and Drake watched the sky and the valley below them carefully. Bree watched his back and the upper slopes of the mountain, and Dabarius took a nap.

Thor's laugh startled all of them.

"What is it?" Dabarius asked, "I was just having a very good dream."

Bellor joined Thor in laughing and they both backed away from where they had been kneeling. A faint pop sounded at their feet and then the ground turned dark and became muddy.

The bullmastiffs bounded over and started licking the mud and Thor tugged on Jep's tail. "Wait a minute for it to clear up, you mongrel."

Jep didn't wait, but Temus backed away.

"How?" Drake asked Master Bellor.

"It was not an easy thing," Bellor said, "to reverse what an earthquake has done so long ago, but with enough faith—"

"—and enough time," Thor said with a grin.

"—many things are possible," Bellor finished, "if Father Lorak hears your prayers and blesses you with His gifts."

The dogs frolicked in the muddy water and Drake thanked Lorak silently and put his arm over Bree's shoulder. She smiled and he got her to laugh when the pretended to jump in the mud with the dogs.

The water cleared up and four hours later the pool was half-full. Shortly after that the water cascaded down the mountain past the broken dam, partially filling the parched streambed that ran toward the village.

After sunset, Drake shot a tan and white antelope with three long curly black horns from over fifty paces away as it drank from the stream. It made one bounding leap, its six legs powering it up a bank, before collapsing in a heap. Dabarius cooked it inside an overhanging cave, making sure the smoke would not be visible for anyone who might be in the area. The next day, with meat in their bellies, the companions explored the mountains, looking for a pass, but returned to their camp and the clear water spring that night.

On the third day after exhausting searches up treacherous and steep mountain goat trails, they returned to their shadowy camp by the spring, still without finding a way over the mountains and totally exhausted.

442

Jep and Temus entered the campsite and a moment later growled menacingly at something downstream that moved toward them in the gloom of evening.

Bellor and Thor brandished their weapons as Bree'alla stood near Drake and drew her sword. He turned the krannekin of his crossbow, the ticking sound of the metal as fast as his pounding heart. He loaded two bolts as Bree stepped closer to him, sword raised in both hands in the high guard position.

Dabarius stood ready, in a defensive stance, watching and waiting.

"It's too late to run," Bellor said.

"*Tari'shaam ut Kheb!*" The Mephitian words echoed from the steep trail just downstream of the pool. A lone man shouted the phrase and Drake pulled the stock of his crossbow against his shoulder, taking aim and trying to find the man in the blurry twilight.

"*Tari'shaam ut Kheb!*" Dozens of eager voices repeated the words.

They had blundered back into camp and right into a trap.

"We must go," Bellor said. "There are too many to fight."

A large group of shadowy figures marched up the streambed toward them.

"*Tari'shaam ut Kheb!*" The Mephitians chanted as they surged forward.

LXXVIII

The griffins of this land are smaller and not as tasty as the northern ones. I shall not complain too much, we have full bellies and many new friends.

     —Bölak Blackhammer, from the Khoram Journal

A group of at least three-dozen Mephitians in threadbare peasant robes streamed toward the companions. The group was chanting the phrase, *"Tari'shaam ut Kheb!"*

Drake let his fear melt away. They'd come too far and endured too much pain to fail now. He would shoot the first pair he saw, then reload and drop two more if he had time. When the Mephitians got close he would draw his Kierka blade and fight with his boot knife in the other hand. He would stand shoulder to shoulder with Bree and no one would touch him or her without feeling their steel. Those who attacked their flanks would feel the fury of Jep and Temus. Bellor and Thor would fell many before they were overwhelmed and Drake wondered if Dabarius would slay the most with his lightning magic. This was not going to be the end.

The first man appeared and Drake aimed at his chest, then raised his aim to his throat. The bolt might go through his neck and kill the man behind him at this close range.

"Stop!" Dabarius shouted to his friends, and Drake withdrew his finger from the trigger, sparing the life of at least one man.

Jep and Temus came out of the shadows and barked savagely, ready to attack. The Mephitians had apparently not seen the companions or the dogs until that moment, and froze in place, utterly shocked and obviously terrified of the dogs. Some of them ran away, while others got on their knees and begged for their lives.

444

Drake let the murderous thought simmer in his mind. They still might have to fight.

"Stand your ground," Dabarius said. "Bellor, Thor, step forward. Lower your weapons."

"What are they saying?" Bellor asked. "What do they want?"

"They're saying it's a miracle," Dabarius said.

"What's a miracle?" Thor asked.

"The water," Dabarius said.

"A miracle of Kheb," Bree'alla said, sheathing her sword. "They were going to the spring, not to attack us."

"Drake, calm the dogs," Dabarius said as he walked closer. "They're frightening these poor folk."

He called Temus and Jep to his side and made them sit. Jep did after Drake put his hand on the dog's neck and squeezed.

"Go forward, Bellor, Thor," Dabarius said. "Let them see you. Stand on those rocks. Look like the sons of the Earth God. Important, proud."

Both Drobin presented themselves, and the Mephitians bowed reverently, whispering of Kheb to each other. That much Drake understood.

When the people were silent, Dabarius made a grand introduction of Bellor and Thor, then went on for a time making a heartfelt speech. He translated nothing and Bree did not either, despite Drake's whispered requests. Finally, Dabarius arranged for Bellor and Thor to bless all of the people, who claimed to be from "the tribe of Jeriah." Their oldest member, and the one who they had heard first shouting about the miracle, claimed to be Jeriah himself, and received the first blessing.

Thor dipped water out of the pool with a clay cup, blessed it—in Lorak's name—though Kheb was mentioned per Dabarius's request—then Jeriah drank. Bellor repeated the ritual on the old man, touching his forehead at the end and saying a prayer in Drobin. The rest of the men followed their

445

chief, and after a time the elders and many of the warriors of the tribe of Jeriah agreed to help the Two Sons of Kheb in any way they could.

The old village nearby, abandoned when Jeriah was a boy, could be rebuilt and the fields replanted. Their tribe could be strong again, instead of having to scratch out a living in the bleak hills, always wandering to new pastures. Too many of their infants had died because of their nomadic lifestyle and far too many of their families starved when the rains failed to make it over the mountains. Now the Mayesh'tah spring was flowing, and the love of Kheb had returned because of the arrival of the Earth God's sons.

Dabarius paused for a moment in his translation and asked Jeriah, a man with dark, weathered skin, a sparse white beard, and tired eyes, some very pointed questions.

"What's he saying now?" Bellor asked Dabarius.

"He's asking where you and Thor have been these past years," Dabarius said. "He thinks he's met you before and wonders where the other sons of Kheb are?"

"He's met my Uncle Bölak?" Thor asked.

"I believe he has," Dabarius said, "though he does not use that name. He thinks he met you when you came to the village when he was a young boy. He claims that you slew the rogue griffin that hunted their animals and killed their people. He says the griffin was killed with one of those,"—Dabarius pointed to Drake's crossbow—"and then 'Bölak' fed the meat to the entire village. It was a big feast."

"They ate griffin meat?" Thor asked, wrinkling his nose.

"We should tell Jeriah the truth," Bellor said.

"Should we?" Thor asked.

"I don't think it will change things," Dabarius said.

"Then tell him," Bellor ordered.

Jeriah soon apologized for his mistake and bowed, pressing his forehead to the ground, genuinely afraid for his life.

446

Bellor raised him up and said a few reassuring words in Mephitian, which calmed him. The old man, who could not have been more than fifty-five, but looked twenty years older than that, smiled, showing his stained yellow teeth. Bellor said, "Ask him to tell you everything he remembers about when Bölak came here long ago."

Dabarius and Jeriah spoke for a while, with Bree listening in but staying close to Drake, and the rest of the tribe sitting as close as they could, while the dogs sat at the edge of the camp. The simple folk feared that if Jep or Temus barked too close to them the dogs would send their souls to the Underworld and leave their bodies alive, but without a spirit, and doomed to eternal damnation in the Afterworld. Never before had such large dogs been seen by Jeriah's folk, but they had to be the ones from the old stories. The only dogs in Far Khoram apparently guarded the royal tombs and assisted the Khebian Priests who prepared the bodies of the dead for burial. Dogs as large as mastiffs required more food and water than even a big man each day, and Drake doubted that they had ever been kept in this sparse desert land.

Bellor and Thor waited patiently as Dabarius translated Jeriah's story and told them what he had learned. The Ten Sons of Kheb had come from the northern desert and found this same village as they did. The villagers welcomed them and sheltered them. To repay Jeriah's father, also called Jeriah, Thor's uncle led a hunt into the mountains and killed a griffin that had been preying upon their people for months. Word of this never went east, as griffins are sacred and are not allowed to be slain, except by the Priests of Shenahr after the proper rituals are performed. The village was not deemed important enough for Shenahrian Priests to travel so far and sanction a hunt for the griffin, so it was allowed to remain.

"Sacred? A griffin?" Drake asked. These folk were mad.

"It's one of their ancient laws," Dabarius said. "Jeriah was specific about that."

447

"What about my uncle?" Thor asked.

The companions learned that the Ten Sons of Kheb and the human Priests of Kheb with them had tried to cross the mountains and go south without permission, but the soldiers of the God King of Mephitep stopped them near the Lesh'heb road and brought them north to the capital. Jeriah did not know what happened to them after that, but he assumed they did not survive. The chief would not say much more, but something dramatic had happened in Old Mephitia, that changed everything, especially regarding the Priests of Kheb. Punishments and new laws were carried out by the Solar Priests of Ah'usar and the Storm Priests of Shenahr. The Khebians were much diminished and the common people suffered, as the Earth Priests main task seemed to be caring for the peasant class. They also worked with the dead, ensuring their immortality in the Afterlife.

"Ask him about these laws and punishments," Bellor said.

Jeriah would not speak of them, but it was plain he hated and feared the God King named Ahken'ra of Mephitep, and all those who directly served him. Jeriah did speak of the old laws given by one of the first God Kings who swore an oath to venerate and appease the favored creatures of the Dragon King, namely griffins, and all manner of dragon kind.

"You haven't told him why we've come, have you?" Bellor asked.

Dabarius glared at him. "I'm not an imbecile."

The wizard spoke at length and learned that the Khebian Mountains formed a border between the Lands of Men, the Mephitian lands in the north, and the Lands of the Gods, the territory of the dragons in the south, a place forbidden to the common folk of Mephitia. Only Priests and their special servants were allowed to travel or live there, and only in one place, Lesh'heb, the city of tombs where the royal and noble families had buried their dead for more than a thousand years.

"Does more than one dragon live south of the mountains?" Thor asked.

"Jeriah doesn't know," Dabarius said, "but there are griffins and wyverns on the far side of this range. It's been that way forever, according to Jeriah."

"What does he know of Draglûne?" Drake asked.

Jeriah would not speak of the Dragon of Darkness, and said it was not his place to speak of the gods. He was definitely afraid.

"Gods?" Thor asked. "He thinks Draglûne is a god like those other fools of the Iron Brotherhood in the North?"

"He has no doubt," Dabarius said.

"Then who *will* speak of the Dragon of Darkness?" Bellor asked.

"Only holy men have the right to do so," Dabarius said. "Priests of Ah'usar, Shenahr, or Kheb can speak of the gods. It's the law given by the God King Ra'menek, Son of Ah'usar, Eternal Father of the People."

"I don't care about their ancient laws," Thor said. "Does he know any trustworthy Priests of Kheb we could speak with?"

Jeriah said all of the Priests of Kheb were trustworthy, though there were very few of them left.

"He believes that all of them are honest men?" Thor asked.

"I think so," Dabarius said, "but he would never say otherwise. These folk fear all the gods and all their Priests, who control everything here."

"Why are there so few Priests of Kheb left?" Drake asked, guessing they had been purged for helping the *Dracken Viergur* forty years in the past.

The chief would not speak for a moment, then explained that very few men of the Priest caste were called to serve Kheb now, as only a small number were brave enough to endure the tests of the faithful.

"What's he talking about now?" Thor asked.

"He won't say more on this," Dabarius said. "Common folk are not supposed to speak of such things."

Moments later, Jeriah agreed to go himself and summon "the very best of all the Khebian Priests" in the morning, but per Dabarius's request he would not tell him why, only that the Mayesh'tah spring was flowing and their village needed a blessing before he moved his people back there.

"Tell him that if he betrays us we'll make the water stop," Thor said.

Dabarius looked at Bellor.

"Do it diplomatically," Bellor said, "though we will do no such thing."

"No," Thor said. "Warn him. I don't trust these simpletons. They might betray us for the price of a vorrel for all we know."

"I will tell him that the blessings of the Earth Father will remain as long as he keeps our presence here secret," Dabarius said.

"Agreed," Bellor said, and Dabarius spoke to the chief.

Jeriah threw himself on the ground and swore on the names of all his dead relatives in the Afterworld, and promised that if he broke his vow he would go willingly to the Underworld after feeding his own heart to a ravenous beast for the terrible sin of betraying their trust. He also forbade the other men to leave the area or speak of any of this to any outside their group, and made them swear the same vow. He assured Dabarius that all his men would stay and work on their village for a few days, while he retrieved the Khebian Priest and told the rest of the tribe about the flowing spring. They would only come to the village of Mayesh'tah after the Priest of Kheb had blessed the site. To come there sooner might anger the gods.

"Do you trust him?" Bellor asked. "Will he betray us to the Priests of Shenahr or the God King's Solar Priests?"

"No," Dabarius said. "He hates them."

"Why?" Bellor asked.

450

"His older brother is the Khebian Priest he's going to bring here," Dabarius said. "I think his brother was punished for helping Bölak, and Jeriah has never forgiven the God King or the other Priests for what they did to his family."

"What did they do?" Bellor asked.

"He won't say," Dabarius said, "but I can tell that Jeriah wants us here, and he wants revenge."

"Good," Thor said, "so do I."

LXXIX

Our Khebian companions have found their brothers who follow Kheb here on this isolated plateau. They smooth the way and we are in good stead with these folk. I hope that our presence does not bring harm upon them when their God King finds out why we are here.

—Bölak Blackhammer, from the Khoram Journal

Jeriah's brother, the Khebian Priest Ranab, arrived late the next day riding atop the sickliest vorrel Drake had ever seen. The beast was tiny compared to the vorrels they'd ridden, and its back sagged under the weight of one very short and emaciated old man. The venerable Priest of Kheb had a shaved head and beard. A similarly shaved teenage boy, with limbs as thin as reeds, led the vorrel slowly along as it struggled to climb the path to the Mayesh'tah spring. Jeriah walked proudly beside Ranab as if he were escorting royalty.

When they arrived beside the spring, Jeriah and two other men helped Ranab dismount from the vorrel, and that's when Drake noticed the old Priest was missing his hands. Brown stumps with ugly scars started where his wrist bones ended. He was also blind. Milky white eyeballs, sunken and vacant, made him appear closer to death than life. And he did not blink.

The teenage boy guided Ranab toward the spring, and helped the old man remove his shabby robe, which had been held in place with a tan belt that looked suspiciously like griffin hide. Prominent ribs, a sunken stomach and far too many scars on Ranab's body made Drake wince as Jeriah and the young man waded into the water taking Ranab between them. The old man knelt down and tears of joy streamed from his dead eyes as he felt the cool water. He sobbed and his brother comforted him for some time. Drake put his back to the scene,

452

feeling as if he were intruding upon something. The thought of Ranab's torments made him profoundly sorry for the man, especially because they had surely been inflicted to punish him for helping the *Viergur.*

After his brother had mastered his emotions, Jeriah dipped a cup into the spring, and put it to Ranab's lips. He swallowed slowly, then raised his arms joyfully. The men of Jeriah's tribe cheered about the miracle again, pumping their fists to the sky.

The shouts continued, and after Jeriah's brother enjoyed the water for a moment, he was escorted into the warmth of the afternoon sunlight. He then sat on a blanket cross-legged in front of the companions, his robe, and a belt that was definitely made of griffin hide, draped over his shoulders.

Jeriah dismissed all of the others, sending the men to work in the village, as they were not to hear this conversation. Then he introduced the companions to his brother with reverence.

Ranab bowed his head once, then strange clicking, choking, and gasping sounds, and few intelligible words came from his mouth. The old man's tongue was gone. It must have been torn or cut out.

Drake and the companions looked at each other, aghast. Now was not the time for questions, and so they held their silence and waited.

The young man attending Ranab, to whom Jeriah introduced simply as Gurion, spoke for the Khebian Priest. Astonishingly, he understood most of his words, though Jeriah helped when needed. It took a lot longer than most conversations, but eventually, the words and the story of Ranab came out.

Dabarius explained to the companions that the humble Priest begged their patience and forgiveness for his "condition," though he said nothing more about it. Then he thanked them for the miracle of the spring, wishing prosperity and health to their families, and endless blessings to all of their ancestors in the Afterworld. He said that the coming of the Two

Sons of Kheb and return of the water was a sign from Mighty
Earth Father. Ranab had been praying for this moment every
day since the water stopped flowing from the spring over thirty
years ago, forcing them to abandon their village. He thanked
them profusely and more tears leaked from his eyes, which
Gurion wiped gently away with his slender fingers.

Ranab soon regained his composure, and Bellor asked if he
had personally known the Ten Sons of Kheb, and if he knew
where to find them or the Dragon of Darkness.

The old man had indeed known them, as he said he was
the assistant to an Elder Priest who had shown the dwarves the
way over the mountains and to the road to Lesh'heb where the
Dragon of Darkness has lived for centuries.

"He knows where Draglûne's lair is?" Bellor asked.

Ranab said the dragon lived in the Tombs of Lesh'heb, a
vast complex of burial vaults inside a giant cavern at the edge
of the plateau. Bree'alla put out a map and Gurion pointed to
a spot south of the city of Mephitep on the edge of the Void.

"Now we know," Drake said, relief, excitement, and fear all
mingling in his mind. Their enemy wasn't very far away now.
After all this time, the reality of their mission came home to
him. They would face Draglûne. He would stand his ground
before him and take the shot that would probably be his last.
They would either slay the dragon or all die in the attempt.
Shivers went across his shoulders.

"What about my Uncle?" Thor asked. "What happened to
him?"

The Khebian explained that he and the Elder Priest had
parted company with the Ten Sons of Kheb on the road to
Lesh'heb, but learned later that the soldiers of Ahken'ra, the
"Mortal King of Mephitep" had captured them and brought
them secretly to the Sun Palace in the capital city. None of the
common folk were supposed to know this.

"Mortal King?" Bellor asked Dabarius. "Why did he call
him that and not the God King?"

Dabarius asked and Ranab made a strange clicking sound and threw his head back.

Drake realized he was laughing. The sound was chilling. Then he explained with his broken voice that Ahken'ra, the vile man sitting on the Solar Throne in Mephitep was not a God King who carried the essence of a deity within him. Ranab went on for several moments, shaking his arms and speaking with great passion. Gurion didn't seem enthusiastic to translate the words. In the end, he told them that Ranab took a dim view of the Mortal King and all his works.

Khelen'dara carried something of Amar'isis, but apparently not this man if Ranab was right.

Dabarius translated the next words as Gurion said them. "He is a man, like all others. The *real* God King of Mephitia is in Lesh'heb, and has been since before the Empire of Mephitia was broken apart by Mighty Kheb's Earthquake."

Jeriah became very nervous after hearing that, and got up and left, disappearing down the path to the village and leaving Gurion to interpret Ranab's words.

"I don't understand?" Bellor asked. "He's not saying Draglûne is the God King, is he?"

Dabarius squinted his eyes as Gurion's subdued, but high-pitched voice continued. "No, not Draglûne," the wizard said. "Ranab is saying that the Eternal King Ra'menek, Son of Ah'usar, Eternal Father of the People, Ruler of the Empire of Mephitia, Head of the Great House of Lesh'heb is the true ruler of this land."

"We saw the name of the God King Ra'menek in the mist traps," Bree'alla said. "He's long dead. He was the one who presided over the sundering of the Mephitian Empire. Ranab surely must mean another ruler of the same name."

Dabarius questioned Ranab for a long while, and the old man grinned and laughed again. The clicking unnerved Drake and he found it difficult to look at him, as his disfigurement made him think of a fate in which he was deprived of his hands and eyes, so that he was a burden to those around him, unable to hunt or work. It was a terrible fate. Without his hands, without his eyes, what would Drake amount to? Could he retain his sanity, his purpose? He thought that this emaciated Priest had a stronger spirit than he would ever have.

"Ranab says that the Eternal King Ra'menek, was interred in the Tombs of Lesh'heb five hundred years ago," Dabarius said. "But he did not give up his throne or his life."

"Is he a ghost, a restless spirit?" Bellor asked, and Drake almost hoped for this to be true. Bellor could deal with ghosts, couldn't he?

Ranab smiled and shook his head before explaining more.

"The Eternal King Ra'menek is in truth a corpse, a creature of the world of the dead," Dabarius said. "His body remains because the divine essence of the sun god, Ah'usar is still inside of him, bound there by unholy magic. He did not let it go to his heir when he breathed his last breath. Instead, he rose from his tomb after his mummified body was interred. Some say he purposefully drank poison and killed himself, others that he was assassinated and returned to take his revenge."

"He is undead," Bellor said. "Much more powerful than any ghost if he inhabits flesh and bone. What more does Ranab know?"

"Much has been learned over the centuries and we Khebian Priests know the secrets," Dabarius translated. "We were the caretakers of the tombs of Lesh'heb and it is known that the Eternal King Ra'menek's body slowly rots when he goes out into the night, exposing himself to the light of Amar'isis, but during the day in the sun, he looks to be the man he was during the prime of his life.

"He lives inside the tomb complex of his ancestors, built along the edge of the cliffs of the Underworld, now served by the Priests of Shenahr and Ah'usar who write down everything he says to them. They store the scrolls and tablets in vast libraries collecting his wisdom for his mortal heirs and

456

the Priests to study. He insists they all come to study under him and learn by his side for a number of years. The Khebians watched it all for centuries as we cared for the tombs and the dead, but my order has been banished from his service, punished for what we did."

"I have some suspicion what they did," Bellor said.

So did Drake.

Ranab let out a sad sigh before going on, and it took a long time for Gurion to understand everything the old man said. Finally, Dabarius explained that the Khebians and the Mortal King Ahken'ra, who is most recent heir to Ra'menek, were trying to get rid of him. Ahken'ra used the Ten Sons of Kheb as assassins. He wanted them to destroy Ra'menek and Draglûne both."

"What?" Bellor asked. "They're allies?"

"They both live in the tombs of Lesh'heb," Dabarius said, then he didn't seem to understand or believe what Gurion was saying.

"What?" Thor asked. "Tell us."

Dabarius shook his head and wiped his forehead.

Bree'alla translated, "He said 'the brother gods live together' in the tombs and the Ten Sons of Kheb were to destroy them both."

"That doesn't make any sense," Thor said.

Dabarius continued at last, "Ranab says that Draglûne has the essence of the Storm God, Shenahr, inside him, making him the divine brother of Ra'menek. The Sun God is the elder and the Storm God serves him. For this service, Ra'menek teaches him the ancient magic entrusted to the God Kings of Mephitep by the first of the Dragon Kings."

"Draglûne serves no one but himself," Bellor said.

Ranab disagreed.

"That is not what the people and the Priests of this land believe," Dabarius said. "They believe that the Dragon of Darkness is their protector against all their enemies and that he will return to them the power they once had."

"Have all of these people gone mad?" Bellor asked.

"Ask him what the Khebians did," Thor said. "What happened to this man and my Uncle Bölak?"

Time moved slowly as Ranab told the story to Gurion, and Dabarius spoke the words in Nexan to the companions. "The Khebians and King Ahken'ra sent the Ten Sons of Kheb into the Tombs of Lesh'heb. The Sons of Kheb failed to kill either of the gods and all the dwarves, and their Khebian allies, perished. The Priests who served Kheb in Mephitep and Lesh'heb were punished severely. Many were killed, and many more were maimed like Ranab. All those who had seen or spoken to the Sons of Kheb were blinded and had their tongues cut out."

It was true. The *Viergur* who had come before had caused all of this.

The old man lifted his stumps to show them the scars, and slowly Ranab explained that for centuries the Khebians had been architects, scribes, caretakers of the dead, and healers of the living. They would use their hands to administer to the sick, perform surgeries, to write down words that needed to be preserved and many more important duties. As punishment for trying to rid Mephitia of the Eternal King Ra'menek, and the Dragon of Darkness, every last Khebian Priest had his hands removed. No longer would they be able to do their work, and now all who wished to enter into the Khebian Priesthood had to have their hands severed.

Anger made Drake clench his fists and look at his fingers. He wanted revenge for what had been done to this man and so many others. He had thought he imagined what it was like to live beneath the boot heel of an oppressive empire, but the Drobin, on their worst day, would have never stooped to something so barbaric.

"There will be no Khebians left soon," Dabarius trans-

458

lated, "as few men will endure such a test of their faith and become an Earth Priest. For as long as the Dragon of Darkness serves the Immortal God King, their power is unchallenged, and they are unconquerable. They are both the night and the day, the sun that nurtures the crops and the storm that savages the peoples of the land, and withholds the rain as a punishment."

All that he had just learned buzzed like a swarm of wasps inside Drake's mind. He thought of all of it and wondered what information he could use to help defeat their enemies. What would they do now? His friends, even Bellor, seemed to be at a loss. They all sat quietly and pondered the new knowledge. Was it all true? Two gods? They'd heard of Bölak's death before and it was a lie. Could this be one again? Was Ranab just a deluded and senile old man who believed the rumors that circulated on this backwards and isolated plateau?

Gurion asked a question for his master.

"Ranab wants to know if we will go to the tombs of Lesh'heb," Dabarius said.

"Of course we're going," Bellor said, "and you can tell him that. We have taught ourselves to endure any ill tiding, and this changes nothing. We won't stop until the dragon lies dead."

Ranab smiled and nodded, then touched Gurion on the shoulder with one of his stumps as he spoke.

Gurion sat up a little straighter and explained that he—Gurion—would personally guide them to Lesh'heb, as his master was too weak to make the journey.

"This boy knows the way?" Drake asked.

"He does," Dabarius said after a short explanation. "Gurion will take us there and we will meet with a man in Lesh'heb who will help us. Ranab has hoped all these years that the Sons of Kheb would return and bring the fight to the tyrants of this land. He says that if we slay Ra'menek and Draglûne, their people will be free again to follow the true Gods, and not these unholy monsters. Draglûne's ancestors stole the essence of the Storm God long ago, and that wrong must be set right."

"It will be set right," Bellor promised in Mephitian.

Ranab kissed Bellor's hands.

"But Draglûne does not have all of this essence," Bellor said, as he held his axe, *Wyrmslayer.* "When I slew Mograwn, some part of his essence, his soul . . . was trapped in my axe."

Dabarius studied Bellor for a moment, then nodded, as if he had just received the answer to a question he'd been working on for a long time. "Then he is but half a god," the wizard said. "Nothing to worry about."

Ranab laughed again and when the old man had gone away with Gurion, Drake could hold his question no longer. He asked Bellor, "How will we defeat Draglûne *and* this undead King?"

"One at a time," Bellor said with a grim smile. "One at a time."

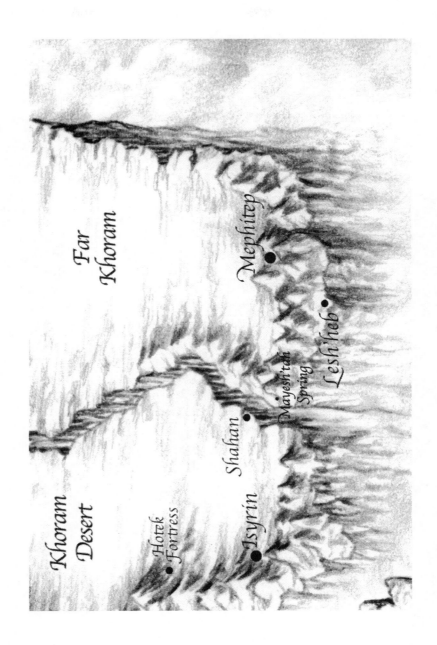

Far
Khoram

Khoram
Desert

Mephitep

Lesh'heb

Mayeshtah
Spring

Shahan

Hotek
Fortress

Asyrin

461

LXXX

Old Mephitia is very different from where we have just been. The people here are not under threat of invasion from the north, but they live in a constant state of fear, and do so with good reason. This place has long since gone insane and begun to rot from the inside out.

—Bölak Blackhammer, from the Khoram Journal

The young man, Gurion, and three of Jeriah's kin had led them through the tall mountains along secret trails known only to Jeriah's tribe. For almost two weeks they had hiked east, always keeping at least one ridge of peaks to the south of them. The Land of the Gods on south side of the mountains was too dangerous to travel through for so long. Fortunately, the aevian predators preferred the heat of the lowland forests to the cool high-altitude slopes and valleys.

Despite the reassurances from the shepherds who had accompanied them, Drake kept watch on the brooding sky. Dark clouds from the south blew toward the north most days, and spent themselves by dropping rain before reaching the parched lands where all of the Mephitian people lived.

Compared to the furnace-like conditions of the Khoram Desert, the rain, and the often-muddy trails were a dream and reminded Drake of home. The cold and windy nights in camps made on the sloping ground were tolerable, especially since Drake and Bree had slept beside each other under heavy blankets.

Leaving the blankets in the morning had proved to be a daunting task, partly because of the brisk air, but mostly because it was the only time they both felt free of the doom they were approaching. The moments huddled together in the night and early morning hours gave Drake solace, and he knew Bree felt the same way. Their bond was strengthening, and the moments in each other's arms gave him the courage to face the day as they neared the end.

He would miss those mornings.

Everything felt like it was going to change as he looked at the thick forest beneath the mountains. Rain and stifling moist heat would assault them once they descended into the Land of the Gods, a place where the three shepherds would not travel. They departed that morning, carrying all the blankets with them.

Gurion would lead them the rest of the way. He didn't know the trails in the mountains very well, but he knew the way to Lesh'heb, and the secret path to get inside avoiding the warriors of Shenahr who guarded the town.

"How did you learn the way?" Dabarius had asked the night after Jeriah's kin had left.

The pensive young man did not answer right away, but just stared into the fire that warmed them.

"I lived there for five years," Gurion said. "From when I was ten years old until the last summer. I studied in the great library school with all the other sons of Priests."

"Your father is a Priest?" Dabarius asked.

"He is one of the few Priests of Kheb left in Mephitep. He took the vows and suffered the amputation of both his hands."

"Will you do the same when you are old enough?" Dabarius asked.

"I was going to," Gurion said softly, "until the school masters said that I would not survive losing my hands. None of those who accept the penalty survive now."

"What does that mean?" Bellor asked.

"They would let me bleed to death," Gurion said. "Master Ranab did not want to tell you, but there will be no more Priests of Kheb in a generation. All of the sons born into the Priest class are being forced to join the ranks of the other two Priesthoods, Shenahr or Ah'usar."

"Who ordered this?" Bellor asked.

"The Eternal Father, Ra'menek," Gurion said. "If I had stayed in Lesh'heb I would have been forced serve the Sun or the Storm god, or I would have been killed. Many are, at least one out of three are not found worthy."

"So you left?" Dabarius asked.

"The man I will bring you to in Lesh'heb helped me escape. He sent me north on the God King's road to Mephitep. My father could not keep me there, so I was taken along the mountains to live in a village several days away from the city, but the Priests of Shenahr found out. The tribe sent me west to the edge of the plateau to live with Jeriah's people and serve Master Ranab. My father does not know where they sent me."

"Do you wish you would have stayed there with Jeriah's people?" Bellor asked.

Gurion did not speak for some time as the fire crackled and danced on the mountainside. "Master Ranab is a kind old man, but I never felt like I belonged there."

"Where, then?" Thor asked. "Lesh'heb?"

Gurion shook his head, fear in his eyes.

"He belongs with his own family," Dabarius said, "with his father in Mephitep."

"Boy, are you afraid to return to this place?" Thor asked.

Gurion nodded. "They will kill me if they find me there, and it will not be a good death."

"We won't let anything happen to you," Bellor said.

Gurion said nothing, but Drake could tell that the young man did not believe Bellor could keep his promise. Many people across the plateaus had paid a high price for helping in the effort to destroy Draglûne, despite any efforts they made to prevent it. Anyone who helped them brought the dragon's ire, and as much as Drake wanted to believe it wasn't so, there was little they could do to protect their friends and allies once they had gone on their way.

LXXXI

Our young guide, Gurion, is a good lad. He is smart and hard working, but he has a look in his eyes that tells me he has endured much pain and suffering in his short life. I do not want to ask him what was done to him at the Priest school in Lesh'heb. It is only out of great need that I ask him to go back there. I have put so many in harm's way over the years, all for the sake of my Sacred Duty. Once more, I am forced to ask the highest sacrifice of those I count as friends.

—Bellor Fardelver, from the Desert Journal

Drake watched the large wyvern with burnt orange scales glide high above the lush green treetops that stretched from the slopes of the Mountains of Kheb all the way to the edge of the plateau a dozen or so miles further south. The drop-off where the endless white clouds began formed a jagged line to the south where the plateau of Far Khoram ended and the Underworld began, but Drake was more interested in the aevian. The dark orange-brown color of it reminded him of the wyvern that had tracked Bellor and Thor to Cliffton's gate. Was this place where the demon had come from?

The aevian's draconic head focused downward—scanning for prey—and used its long stinger-tipped tail like a rudder to navigate the wind. Something caught its eye and it flapped its leathery wings, which sprouted from the front of its serpentine body to at least a forty-foot span where a true dragon's front arms would be. It flew hard and fast in the direction of the Void, then dove into the forest, tucking its wings close to its body. Before it disappeared under the canopy the wyvern reached forward with its claws and extended its stinger as it prepared to strike its prey.

Drake signaled his friends, using a hand-sign—fingers splayed wide and held motionless over his head—which told them the sky was clear. Bellor, Thor, Bree, Dabarius, Jep and Temus crouched low on the mountain hiding under the short trees with fluttering leaves. Their guide, Gurion, was just ahead of them, taking refuge behind a boulder covered with thick yellowish lichen. He saw Drake's signal, but did not know what it meant. When he could, Drake would explain some important hand signs to him as they had days left before they reached Lesh'heb. Sky wariness was not as well engrained for the Mephitians as it was for a northerner.

The wyvern did not rise into the sky after a moment, and Drake knew it was feasting on some hapless creature. The time was right. He and his companions hurried down the exposed grassy mountainside. When they reached the cover of the forest his friends breathed easier, but Drake knew the danger was still close at hand and kept alert, his eyes skyward. He told his friends to whisper, and to move as quietly as they could from now on. Voices carried, and despite their efforts, as a group they were unable to move even as quietly as any group of seven-year-old children born in Cliffton. At least they were learning. Bree'alla had taught them how to survive in the desert, but he would teach them about the forest.

The direction Gurion led them was east, which suited Drake. The wyvern was south and west of them. At least it had been . . .

Gurion guided them straight to the God King's road. Drake had never seen anything like it. The structure cut through the forest like a wall.

"This took decades to build," Gurion whispered, "and cost the lives of many slaves."

The roadway—more like a bridge—was elevated twenty feet above the forest floor and sat on a series of interconnected giant stone arches with supporting square columns, which were encased in smooth gray stucco. A peaked roof of pitted stone covered anyone who traveled on it from rain or attack, and thousands of vertical windows and drains at road level, all small enough to keep griffins out, lined the sides. Vines and moss crept up the pillars, and many treetops sat at the height of the road or above it, though their branches seldom reached into the shadows inside.

"Ambitious design," Thor said, his eyebrows raised. It took a lot to impress a Drobin, who always seemed to build things twice as strong as needed.

Gurion kept to the plan of following the road south, walking far enough away so they would not be seen, and parallel with it so they would not get lost in the forest. It would lead them straight to Lesh'heb, which was nine miles south of the foothills where the road started. Master Ranab also said that predators didn't hunt near it as frequently as in other, wilder places, but Drake did not believe him. He suspected that griffins, and perhaps even wyverns like the one they had seen, liked to lounge atop it, despite the sharp peaked rooftop. They would wait and watch for prey then would swoop down and attack.

He kept his eyes wide open and his crossbow ready, as this was not a forest that offered good protection from above. The trees were mostly tiny in girth, with few exceptions, and most were shorter than the giants in the Thornclaw Forest. The canopy was sporadic, and not enough to keep a large aevian out.

Most worrisome were the marshy clearings where few trees could grow. Instead, verdant grass and reeds sprouted from leech-infested pools that smelled of rotting plants. The companions avoided those at all costs and Drake imagined that the wyvern they had seen earlier in the day had attacked some grazer as it wandered into a clearing to nibble on the soft swamp grass.

To keep them from being seen by potential travelers on the road, Gurion kept them in the trees at all times. The young man picked his way through the brush, but kept the road in sight. Drake soon took over the duty of finding the path, as he was much more at home in the forest than poor Gurion,

467

who had trouble pushing through the undergrowth with his skinny arms. The plants were dense, and often prickly, but they weren't as tough as the Thornclaw. The bushes were softer here, more pliable, and didn't have as many painful defenses. Drake could press past the fronds and undergrowth easily, and he almost never had to use his Kierka knife. On the few times he did, Gurion seemed unduly impressed with the tool's ability to clear a path, chopping through limbs thicker than a Drobin thumb with ease. He actually stopped Drake at one point and felt his upper arm. The young man whispered excitedly to Dabarius, but the wizard just laughed and showed his own burly arm, even larger than Drake's.

The dogs were overwhelmed with all the new sights and musty smells of the forest. Their ears were constantly pricked up at the colorful lizards scurrying up and down the trees. He didn't like that his bullmastiffs were constantly on alert, but after a while they would learn what was a threat and what was not. He worried they would eat one of the brightly colored lizards, or the frogs he had seen, as they were most likely poisonous, just as their cousins in the North were.

Until the dogs calmed down, he would rely on the insects and the shrieking birds. He listened for the birds to stop or change their sharp calls and the insects to halt their buzzing. He didn't know the alarm calls like he did back home, but he would pay close attention and learn. Every person from his village knew that the sounds of the forest were the most important signs of danger. Leaves and tree trunks blocked sight past a few paces here and in the Thornclaw, and the hunter who stayed alive listened to the forest.

Not having the sun burning down on him was such a relief, but by early afternoon the oppressive heat made taking a deep breath feel like a chore. This forest was much hotter than the Thornclaw and the heat frayed nerves and made tempers short.

Drake and Bellor told Thor and Dabarius to stop arguing with each other several times, but finally Thor lost his composure and his biting retort echoed in the trees. The bird sounds stopped instantly. Before Dabarius could respond Drake stopped the wizard by grabbing hold of his friend's shoulder and gripping it tightly. Drake knelt down and Dabarius followed his lead. The others did as well. The Clifftoner stared warily up at the sparse canopy, his eyes wide, pretending that he saw something. He put a finger to his lips when Thor glanced at him, shield and hammer ready. For a moment they all hunkered down . . . waiting, breathing quietly until the forest sounds all returned.

"*It's gone.*" Drake mouthed the words a short time later, not uttering the sound, and making the 'sky is clear' hand sign. He waved for his friends to quietly follow him and he led them into a thicker part of the forest.

No one spoke or argued, and they all walked as quietly as they ever had since entering the trees. A short time later, when they stopped to drink from a fast-moving stream, Thor asked what he had seen.

"Not sure," Drake whispered, "but it was big."

Thor raised both eyebrows. "Dragon?"

Drake shrugged. "Maybe the wyvern. I need you to help me keep watch."

Thor nodded and took up a position where he could keep his eyes on the sky while they rested.

Bellor whispered, "Well done, lad. That'll keep him quiet for the rest of the day."

Dabarius grinned and almost laughed, but Drake stopped him with a very fierce look.

In the late afternoon a torrential rain pounded the forest. The fat drops pummeled the leaves and the thunderous din blocked out all other sounds. They marched for a while, but the ground turned to a sticky reddish mud, slowing their already-ponderous advance tremendously. At least the bugs trying to suck their blood had been driven away by the rain.

After their wet slog, his friends needed a rest, and the dogs limped along, totally exhausted.

After unsuccessfully trying to find a dry place to sit for a while, Drake guided his friends under the elevated roadway, which was over fifteen-feet wide and provided good shelter. The ground was mostly dry and the rain could not get them there. His clothing was soaked and it would never dry out in the humid air unless he exposed it to the sun for a few hours, and that was not going to happen. He leaned against a foundation pillar, sitting on a lip of stone as the dogs napped at his feet. Bree'alla inspected the rough markings chiseled into the huge block. Six lines had been cut into the surface.

"What are those?" he asked Bree.

She asked Gurion, who was scratching the insect bites on his shaved head. He looked at the pillar and replied somberly, speaking for quite some time, then stepped away, nearly going into the rain.

"What is it?" Drake asked, keeping his words hushed.

"He said that six slaves died while building this particular pillar," Bree said.

"*Six*," Bellor said. "That they were slaves makes it even worse."

"The strong always enslave the weak," Dabarius said. "It's worked for the Drobin."

Thor held his tongue for once as Bree explained, "Gurion told me that one of his teachers in Lesh'heb said that two men died for each pillar built along this road."

"That would mean . . . over three thousand of them died," Bellor said.

"Because of the aevians?" Drake asked.

"There were more griffins in the past, among other things," Gurion said, "but most of them died of fevers and gut rot."

"Gut rot?" Thor asked.

"There's worm larva in the water here," Dabarius said, "and they get inside you and eat through your bowels."

470

Thor dumped out his waterskin and tried to catch the rain running out of a drain hole in the road above them with his shield.

Drake also worried about catching the sickness, but hoped the fast-moving stream they drank from had been safe.

The rain stopped over an hour later and Drake led his friends back into the forest on the eastern side of the road, picking their way along with sodden boots and necks sore from constantly glancing skyward. They traveled for some time until a stinking swamp halted their advance. Their only recourse was to cross under the roadway and go to the western side. Drake followed their only route, an animal trail that led along the edge of the marshy ground and went under the God King's road.

None of them heard any traffic passing on the road as it loomed above them. The elevated structure was hemmed in by thick bushy trees and was covered with vines, the plant life clinging to every crack in the stone. Drake stopped them for a moment, frowning at the way forward.

Dabarius gave him a questioning look. "What?" he mouthed.

Drake glanced around once more, then shrugged, motioning them to continue.

After giving them the 'quiet steps', and 'open eyes' hand sign, Drake led his friends under the archway. As he reached the far side with Jep and Temus he heard a terrible crash behind him. He whirled about and saw that a large draconic tail with burnt orange scales had just batted Bellor, Dabarius, and Thor—the last three in line—against the stone column.

Drake shoved Gurion away as the wyvern's tail snaked up, then struck at Bree. She dodged, but the wicked stinger missed her shoulder by a handbreadth. The wyvern clung to the side of the raised roadway. Only its hardened tail—covered with scars and iron-strong scales—was clearly visible. Drake didn't have a shot at anything vital—though two bolts lay in his cocked crossbow and he almost pulled the triggers to keep the poisoned stinger away from his fallen friends.

Bree drew her sword and put herself between the tail and Drake. If she was stung, she'd be dead in a hundred heartbeats.

Thor grunted, trying to get up, and the stinger instantly stabbed toward him. The dwarf barely managed to deflect the arm-long barb with his shield, which was dented and smeared with viscous black poison.

Bellor began to stir and the stinger rapidly stung at the area where he, Dabarius, and Thor had been knocked down. The wizard lay facedown and apparently unconscious as blood streamed out of a cut in his scalp.

Bellor dove on top of Dabarius, shielding him with his body. The stinger stabbed the dwarf in the back, penetrating his pack, and injecting its venom into his belongings. Only his chain mail shirt turned the hooked spike aside.

Thor sprang up and swung his hammer, but his blow glanced off the wyvern, who augured the sharp stinger into Bellor, trying to drill through his armor. The old dwarf groaned in pain and hung on to Dabarius's prone body.

Drake kept Jep and Temus away as they barked ferociously, but Bree'alla attacked. She managed to cut through the scales and open a small wound, which caused the tail to recoil to the entrance of the archway. It was poised to whip forward as a grimacing Bellor tried to roll Dabarius's body away from the danger. Thor helped him as Bree warded off the wyvern's next thrusting attack using *Wingblade* to turn aside the tip of the bony lance.

The tail surged forward again, and Bree had to fall back just as the dwarves pulled Dabarius clear. The tail swung back and forth like a clapper inside a bell striking both sides of the column and rattling the entire archway. Then it hit the ground, sending and dust and dead leaves into the air. Old animal bones scattered as the beast stirred up the leaf litter. It had used his ambush before, and they had walked right into it.

The wyvern roared and flailed about, but the companions were just beyond its reach. Drake silenced the dogs, then wiped his slick palms against his shirt. As calmly as he could, he switched out the bolts he had in his crossbow and replaced them with a pair of wyrm-killing shafts Bellor and Thor had prepared for Verkahna. He knew what he had to do if he was going to get in position for a killing shot. "Thor, draw the stinger to you when I say."

Thor raised his shield, glancing at Drake with a furrowed brow.

Bellor had a similarly worried expression as he lifted *Wyrmslayer* while wincing and clenching his teeth.

Drake dropped his pack and waterskin.

A glob of black poison oozed out the tip of the wyvern's tail.

Gurion whimpered and the stinger aimed at the boy who crouched against the column. Bree put a hand over his mouth.

The dogs tensed, and Drake pointed to the ground. "Down." He had to repeat the command and push against Jep's shoulders, but they lay down as they'd been trained. "Stay," he commanded with a deep voice.

Jep stared up at him, but Temus kept his eyes on the wyvern's tail.

"Lad, I don't . . . " Bellor began.

"Trust me," Drake said, then shouted "Thor, now!"

Thor banged his hammer against his shield and took a step forward. The stinger went right for him and dented the steel disk. Thor rebounded from the blow, his feet skidding before catching grip again. Bellor swung his axe, but the tail undulated like a slithering serpent and knocked *Wyrmslayer* from the dwarf's grasp. The old War Priest spun awkwardly and winced, holding his knee. Bree leaped forward and slashed. Her sword scraped against the stinger and chipped off a small fragment. The raw, painful noise of her blade echoed in the short-tunnel.

Drake sprinted toward the forest the way they had come. The wyvern must have sensed him and withdrew from striking at Thor. It tried to crush Drake against the wall with the side of its tail. He dove out from under the roadway as the tree-trunk-sized appendage cracked the bricks and stucco.

Drake rolled into the bushes at the edge of marsh, spun around and came up aiming his crossbow. The wyvern clung to the side of the enclosed road with its rear claws, dangling its tail downward. It used its teeth to hold on to the edge of the rooftop as it had no front legs, which told Drake it was a true wyvern despite its great size, not a wyvern-dragon like Verkahna. The creature also used its expansive dark orange wings with brown veins to hold onto the tree branches and perch above the tunnel passing under the road.

The first bolt *thunked* as it struck the back of the wyvern's neck, penetrating all the way to the fletching. The monster scrambled onto and over the peaked rooftop pulling its tail behind and waving it in the air as if to ward off Drake's next missile. Just for a moment, he saw one of its yellow-orange eyes, filled with hatred.

He held the second bolt, as he didn't have a kill shot from this angle.

Suddenly the creature disappeared from view.

"This way!" Drake shouted.

Bellor and Bree yanked Dabarius to the middle of the arch-way as the wyvern's tail shot into the tunnel from the far side, narrowly missing Bree's head. She parried the tip of the stinger with her sword just before it sunk into her flesh.

Drake slung his crossbow over his shoulder and clambered up the tree beside the path—hand over hand, foot over foot, practically running, just like he used to do in the Thornclaw almost every day. He heard the wyvern smashing its tail inside the archway and roaring as his friends backed away.

When Drake reached the level of the road he perched on a branch, leaned far out, and nearly lost his balance before he found what he was looking for. He could see straight through a small window in the road. A pair of one-foot-wide openings that allowed rain to drain out at road level gave him a view of the wyvern on the far side.

He pulled the crossbow up to his shoulder.

Took aim.

The wyvern moved, and Drake couldn't tell what part of it was in his sight. He pulled the trigger and the bolt streaked forward, passing just over the surface of the road and exited the drain hole on the opposite side.

The wyvern screeched in pain and Drake turned the krannekin as fast as he could, hoping for another chance. The aevian launched itself from its perch and took to the sky, its wings buffeting the treetops as it tried to gain altitude, hampered by its new belly wound. With two strong flaps it was over the first line of trees and disappeared from his view before he could reload. The wyvern winged away, wounded but very much alive.

Drake dropped out of the tree and ran to his friends. Bellor held a scarf against Dabarius's bleeding head, and the was wizard still unconscious. The *Dracken Viergur* Master locked his wide-eyes with Drake as the whooshing sound of wyvern's wings faded in the distance. Thor, Bree and Gurion looked at him as well. They all knew what this meant. The wyvern might die, but Drake knew it wouldn't. The aevian would reach Draglûne's lair and the Dragon King would know. He would know they were coming.

The sound of wings were gone now, and Drake felt the icy cold claws of fear scraping down his back as wondered how long they had before Draglûne came for them.

LXXXII

The land south of the mountains in Far Khoram is filled with trees, rich game, good soil, and plentiful water. The few humans in Lesh'heb are the only people who live here, by decree of the false gods. It is wrong that the Mephitians are forced to scrape by on the north side of the mountains in the desert. When Draglûne is dead, perhaps they will settle this land, and prosper for the first time in centuries. If enough of us *Vierugur* survive, we shall linger here and rid them of all the wyverns who hunt in the forest.

—Bölak Blackhammer, from the Khoram Journal

Drake kept watch from the middle branches of a tree above where Bellor stitched closed the gash on Dabarius's head. The wizard had awakened right after the wyvern escaped and refused any healing magic, saying he was all right, except for his aching head and the ringing in his ears. He had no memory of what had happened and Drake listened as Bellor filled him in.

"The wyvern must have been one of Draglûne's territory guards, and she will tell him about us. We have lost the surprise I had hoped for."

"It was a 'she'?" Bree asked.

"Male wyvern's don't grow that large," Bellor said, as he finished the stitches.

"Then we best get moving," Thor said, "before Draglûne or another of his servants turn up. You ready to go, Lord Dabarius?"

The wizard sat there, a slightly puzzled look on his face.

"Did you hear me?" Thor asked.

"Of course I heard you," Dabarius said.

The others prepared to leave, but Dabarius remained in a daze, a vacant and confused look on his face, as he touched the stitches on his head and looked at the blood on his fingers.

Bree and the dwarves exchanged worried glances. Even from up in the tree, Drake knew something was wrong. It was like a different person sat before them. Little Gurion just looked lost and afraid as he crouched by the dogs.

Bellor made Dabarius look him in the face. "The blow to your head . . . "

"What about it?" Dabarius asked, annoyed.

"Forgive me," Bellor said, "but I have to see how much this injury has hurt you."

Dabarius glanced around at the trees and the elevated road nearby. "I don't like this place."

"You know this place?" Bellor asked.

"Of course."

"Can you recall exactly where we are?" Bellor asked.

He hesitated. "A forest south of . . . in Far Khoram."

"Where are we going?" Bellor asked.

Dabarius ignored him, and touched his wound. "What happened to my head?"

"You don't remember what I just told you?" Bellor asked.

"Let's just go," Dabarius said, and got up, but he was instantly dizzy and nearly fell over. Bree and Thor steadied him. "I'm fine." He pushed them away, and wobbled again.

Bellor got in his way. "We're counting on you, Dabarius. We may have another fight today. The final fight."

"Fight?" Dabarius asked, holding Thor's shoulder to keep his balance.

"I can heal him," Thor said. "It hasn't been that long. The price won't be high."

"No," Dabarius said. "I'm all right, a little dazed. Stop pestering me."

Bellor studied him for a while. "He just needs time to recover. Maybe walking will do him good."

The tall wizard could not find his balance for a while, and Thor kept him upright. His memory was off and in his current state Drake doubted there was any way he could use his magic. Their chances of defeating Draglûne and his servants was almost nothing without Dabarius, and the whole group was worried, even Thor, who guided his injured friend without throwing one insult.

The companions sped away from the ambush site under the roadway as fast as they could, and Drake took them off the animal trail. They would not use any more trails and he blamed himself for the attack. He found a stream and they followed it for a short time going south walking on the rocky bottom but leaving a few tracks, then he had them double back and went down a different branch of the same stream flowing more southeast. Drake walked last and tried to remove all evidence of their new trail through the water, smoothing out the bottom and wiping away any disturbed mud or stones. It was the best he could do before they entered the thickest area of forest he could find, once again disguising their trail as they left the waterway.

Dabarius had to stop and vomit once they entered the woods, and Drake buried the evidence very carefully in a deep hole, hoping that would be enough. If only he had some curdle moss, but none of the sour milk smelling plant grew in this southern forest. They marched until the sun went down and the pain in Dabarius's head got worse. The wizard fell asleep in a hammock Drake constructed out of his shade tent, and the others had a whispered meeting several steps away, leaving Gurion to watch him.

"How hurt is he?" Drake asked.

"It's too soon to know," Bellor said. "Maybe in a day he'll be well."

"We might not have that much time," Drake said. "The forest is not thick enough to keep Draglûne or a wyvern off us."

"We'll go to Lesh'heb," Bellor said. "We're not staying out in these woods any longer than we have to."

"Draglûne will know we're coming," Drake said.

"They'll be waiting for us," Bree said. "Maybe we should stay out here a while."

478

"No," Bellor said. "We go to Lesh'heb as soon as we can, enter the secret way Gurion knows of while Draglûne has his minions searching the forest for us."

"You don't think he'll look for us himself?" Drake asked.

"Not after he sees the wounds Drake inflicted on his pet," Thor said.

"Terrible as he is, Draglûne has always been gripped with cowardice," Bellor said. "He'll want others to deal with us. He's run from *Dracken Viergur* before. Remember, there is a good reason why there are so few dragons left alive today."

"Because of us," Thor said, "and those *Viergur* who've come before."

"Then we go to Lesh'heb," Drake said, "at first light."

The companions reached the outside of Lesh'heb in the late afternoon the next day after a fierce rainstorm finally slowed to an annoying drizzle. Drake kept them in the dense forest taking a winding course south that eventually led them to their destination. No sign of pursuit had been noticed during their very tense day.

Dabarius had been irritable and did not seem himself, but when they spied the elevated road from a distance, he seemed focused again, his eyes sharp. They observed that the covered road had finally become a true bridge as it followed the center channel of a river swollen with summer runoff. The enclosed bridge crossed over a small lake that was held in check by a fifty-foot-tall dam built in the mouth of a tall canyon. The river filled the lake in front of the dam with dirty red-brown water and then changed course and flowed west along the base of an escarpment of knife-edged towers of gray stone. Gurion directed them to walk parallel to the lake, though they kept far inside the trees moving slowly and silently.

"Will someone find our tracks here?" Drake whispered to Gurion through Bree'alla.

"No, sir," Gurion said. "No one who lives in Lesh'heb travels outside . . . except the Dragon of Darkness."

It made sense, as the God King's road had no staircases down because only the gods were fit to walk upon land here, according to Gurion. The bridge went right to the top of the dam, and though someone could drop a small boat and get down to the lake perhaps, it seemed unlikely. Still, Drake didn't like leaving their tracks so close to their destination, and brought the companions even deeper into the forest and tried to smooth away the prints they had left where they observed the entrance to Lesh'heb. He refused to take chances now when the dragon was so close, and Bellor approved.

The rain stopped when they reached far eastern edge of the lake, and Drake got a good look at the mass of jagged spires of scalloped rock that formed the labyrinth known as the Lesh'heb Fortress. It went on as far as he could see, an endless mass of giant limestone skewers pointed at the sky.

"How far does it go?" Drake asked Gurion through Bree.

"For miles in each direction," Gurion replied, "and all the way to the edge of the plateau, at least two miles south of here."

"Where are you taking us now?" Bellor asked.

"There's a way through the maze that leads to Lesh'heb village," Gurion said.

It took their guide some time to find the correct slot canyon, no wider than Drake's shoulders and screened by trees. Gurion entered three incorrect canyons before he found the right one, then led the companions deep inside. Drake lingered behind and erased their trail as best he could, leaving one false trail into the first canyon they'd all entered. He hoped that the rain would wash away their scent and cover their tracks by the next day. For now, his efforts would have to do.

Gurion led the way now with Bellor right behind him as they stepped further into the maze. The towers of serrated stone rose two-hundred-fifty feet on either side, and the vertical walls pressed in close.

"We call these kind of canyons grykes back home," Bellor whispered. "It does not surprise me that Draglûne would want to lair in a place like this. There's a similar limestone formation southeast of Drobin City. I was with Bölak and his *Dracken Viergur* a long time ago, and we spent six months searching for the lair Draglûne kept there."

"You didn't find him?" Drake asked.

"He left when we got close," Bellor said. "He will run again if we muck this up."

"It'll be different this time," Thor said.

Drake hoped Thor was right, but Draglûne knew they were coming now and he might attack them in the grykes when they had nowhere to hide. He didn't want to spend six hours, let alone six months like Bölak had, in the musty canyons climbing over sharp rocks. He should have felt protected so far down inside the gryke with only a ribbon of sky above him, but he felt trapped.

He would make certain he knew the way out as they pressed on, astonished at the trees which grew on the walls of the canyon, sending down cable-like roots to the ground far below where tiny rust colored crabs skittered through the dead leaves.

One of the crabs pinched Jep's nose, and the dog bit and chewed it up, then spit it out. Temus kept his distance from the crabs and Drake wondered what else was in the maze with them. A wyvern was small enough to get down among them or reach around a blind corner with a poisoned tail.

481

Hours later, close to midnight, Gurion climbed up the canyon wall in the moonlight. He froze when the emerald green snake slithered down the thick root toward him, flicking its tongue at the air. Drake reached up and cut off the serpent's head, carefully avoiding clanging his Kierka blade against the rock. He sheathed his weapon, then grabbed the still-writhing serpent and flung it down to the hungry dogs waiting on the wide ledge below them with the others.

"Thank you," Gurion whispered.

"You're welcome," Drake replied in Mephitian. The language was beginning to make sense to him now, though he had a hard time replicating the slow and drawn-out pronunciation of some words.

The young man climbed up to the top of the jagged spire, avoiding the spiny plants clinging there, and Drake joined him on the stone fence that seemed to be topped with broken glass. Avoiding being cut by the rock was difficult, and there was no comfortable place to sit or even stand. Bree'alla came up next, then Dabarius, who still complained of a raging headache and vertigo when he climbed.

The dwarves and Drake hoisted up the dogs after they finished eating the snake. Temus spit up most of what he ate of the serpent, and Drake berated himself for not skinning the thing first. That might have helped the dog keep it down and now they would leave evidence behind.

Once they had all assembled they moved to a lookout point and stared into the distance. All around them, illuminated by the moonlight, for miles south, east, and west they were surrounded by endless ridges of scalloped, pointed, gray rocks.

Gurion led them across a barely walkable path, and over

an arch of stone that connected two ridges. They crept to the cliff and stared down three hundred feet to the gorge below.

Lesh'heb village had been built at the entrance of a winding canyon less than a hundred paces wide. The dam kept the river, and the lake, from entering the canyon as the water had before the construction of the forty-foot thick dam topped with three towers. Now the Lesh'heb River flowed west and eventually found its way around the natural stone fortress and poured into the Void.

The town itself was quite small, dotted with tall trees, and according to Gurion perhaps four hundred people were in residence here. The rest lived in the library school further in. Everything was quiet on the streets and no lights were seen. The only movement was from two guards passing in front of the window of the central tower that connected the God King's bridge-road to the top of the dam. If Draglûne knew they were coming, no evidence could be seen in the town.

"Gurion," Bree whispered, "how do we get down?"

"There is a way further south. Follow me."

They backed away from the cliff and Drake wanted to get off this exposed rock as soon as possible. Draglûne would crush them up here and he wondered how difficult it would be to climb down the sheer and sharp limestone rock without rope. Gurion led them a short distance and they skirted the edge, far enough away so that no one in the canyon could see them silhouetted by the moon.

Gurion led them down a slanted ridge and they descended several steep drops that required Drake and Thor to lower the dogs in their makeshift harnesses.

At another vertical face they peered into a vast stone quarry, apparently in use for centuries, judging by the amount of stone missing from the many large 'steps' cut into the walls. The entire town and the dam had probably been made from limestone cut from here. Lesh'heb was not far away, but was out of sight, as the quarry was in a large box canyon in the side of the gorge.

Gurion pointed to an ornate and impressive three-level stone house made with huge blocks at the level of the canyon below them. The house sat near the entrance to the quarry, a hundred paces away, but very far down. A covered well sat in a square garden courtyard in the middle of the house. "That's where we are going."

"The man we are to meet lives in that house?" Bellor asked.

"Yes," Gurion said. "That is quarry master Ben'ahmi's house."

"Where are all the tombs?" Dabarius asked.

Gurion pointed south where tall towers of rock blocked their view of the Void. "Further down in the main canyon and in the side branches are the tombs of royals, and the nobles. There are tombs everywhere, but the God Kings of old, and the Eternal King Ra'menek, and his brother, the Dragon of Darkness, live in the Tunnel of Tombs. Once, before the river was dammed, only by boat could you reach the tombs there. Now there is a road and a gate."

Gurion showed them the route to climb down and the dogs were able to go most of the way. In the end, they all stood on the flat ground where the stone had been cut away.

As silently as they could, they approached the quarry master's house. Gurion walked up the steps in front of the hardwood door, while the others hid in the shadows beside the stairs. Bree and Drake's shoulder's touched as Gurion knocked on the door.

"Relax," Bree whispered, a wry grin on her face.

He tried to smile, but was sure he'd failed miserably. He wanted to be with her. He wanted to do more than just stare into her green eyes.

"Who's there?" a man inside called out and opened a tiny window on the door.

"Master," Gurion said, "it's me."

484

"Gurion?" The man opened the door and pulled the boy in without revealing himself and shut the door quietly.

Bree whispered to Drake what she heard inside. The quarry master was quite upset and shocked.

"What're you doing here? Did you bring a message from Mephitep? Why did they send you back?" the quarry master asked.

"Master, I brought others with me. I knew the way, so I was sent."

"What others?"

"They're outside. Please, Master, let them in."

"Who are they?"

"Friends from far away," Gurion said. "Two Sons of Kheb are with them."

The door opened, and a very tall and muscular man with a cleanly shaven head came out. He had to be in his late fifties, but appeared to have the strength of a much younger man. He wore only a simple linen kilt around his waist and no sandals. He was much taller than any Mephitian they'd met so far and he towered over Gurion, who appeared at his side and pointed into the shadows. The handsome man's eyes went wide with surprise and he waved the companions inside, and scanned the area for prying eyes.

After the dogs were in, he bolted the door shut. They stood in the darkness with only a sliver of moonlight coming in through a crack in the door. In a rare display of his magic, Dabarius touched an oil lamp on a table and it sputtered to life.

"Mighty Gods," the quarry master said when he looked at all of them.

"Hello," Bellor said in Mephitian, smiled and bowed.

Drake looked deeper into the dark house, wondering if there were others present. The dogs seemed relaxed at least.

"This is the man," Gurion said. "This is Master Ben'ahmi. He will help us."

485

Ben'ahmi stared at the companions warily, first at the dogs, who wagged their tails and lay down on the cool tile floor at Drake's command. His gaze lingered on Bree, Drake's crossbow, then on both dwarves. Then his brows scrunched together as he made eye contact with Dabarius, who was slightly taller than he was.

"Who are you?" Ben'ahmi asked and Bree translated quietly.

"I am Dabarius, emissary of—"

"*What* is your name?" Ben'ahmi interrupted.

"Dabarius," the wizard repeated.

"*Dabarius*," Ben'ahmi said, his gaze narrowing.

Ben'ahmi studied the young wizard intensely. "Where are you from?"

"I am an emissary of Queen Khelen'dara of Isyrin."

"No, where were you born?" Ben'ahmi asked. "Do not lie to me."

"Near the city of Isyrin."

"Do you carry a trust scarab?" Ben'ahmi asked.

"Yes," Dabarius said, and removed the golden scarab from a hidden pocket inside his robe, and displayed the intricately painted brooch.

The quarry master's eyes locked on it, studied it carefully. "Do you all carry them?" he asked.

"We do," Dabarius said, and he indicated for everyone to show the man.

They did and he studied each of them for a moment in the flickering light.

"Wait here," Ben'ahmi said, and disappeared with the lamp into a small room by the door.

Bellor raised his bushy brows at Dabarius meaningfully.

Dabarius merely shrugged, as much at a loss as everyone else was.

Ben'ahmi returned a moment later with a golden scarab beetle brooch of his own held in his palm.

486

"That's a binding scarab from the Queen of Isyrin," Bree said. "This man is a follower of Amar'isis, a Wing Guardian and . . ."

"Ask him where he got it," Bellor said. She did.

Ben'ahmi ignored her question and locked his gaze once more on Dabarius. "Where did you grow up?"

"In a place far north of Mephitia," Dabarius said, voice trembling. "A place called Snow Valley. I was raised by a man. A wizard." Dabarius stared into Ben'ahmi's dark piercing eyes, which were filling with tears.

"Oberon," Ben'ahmi whispered the name.

Drake was stunned. They all were.

"Oberon," Dabarius confirmed, utterly shocked.

"You found me," Ben'ahmi's said. He put a hand over his mouth, his eyes wide and amazed. "All these years, and the many miles . . . "

"How do you know about Oberon?" Dabarius asked. "No one knows of this. It is a secret that I have kept from all."

"I brought you to him," the quarry master said. "I am Barius, your father."

LXXXIII

Many generations of dwarves and men have come to the same conclusion, Draglûne must be slain. They have simply lacked the knowledge and fortitude to do it. No more. Before another moon wanes, we will give him the doom he so richly deserves.

—Bölak Blackhammer, from the Khoram Journal

The revelation left Dabarius speechless. He could only stare at the tall man in front of him. He thought he recognized the quarry master's face when they entered, but he did not remember from where, and his shaved head confused him. Now he looked upon a face remarkably similar to his own and he remembered. Khelen'dara had helped him recall what had been blocked out by magic so long ago, but many of the memories were hazy and distant, and his head still pounded from when the wyvern had thrown him against the column. But when he looked at this man he felt like the five-year-old boy his father had left in Snow Valley. He recognized him, and held in his tears. "Father," he said, his voice pinched.

"Dabe," Barius said.

Dabarius hugged him and knew without a doubt this man was his father. The facts were unassailable. Their physical resemblance, the same family marks on both their binding scarabs, the fact that Ben'ahmi knew about Oberon proved it, but how? A thousand questions came to his mind. "I was told you were dead."

"Son," Barius said. "I never dreamed I'd ever see you again."

"I don't understand," Dabarius said. "Tell me what happened."

"I will."

Barius invited them into his home, poured them lemon-flavored water, and urged them to lounge on rugs and pillows in a comfortable meeting room. The tale came out quickly, and Dabarius was barely aware that Bree'alla was translating the words to the others. He'd forgotten they were even there as all he could focus on was the man sitting in front of him.

"My enemies would never have stopped if I hadn't left Isyrin," Barius said. "My presence would only have caused more misery for those I cared about."

"The Queen of Isyrin thinks you died in the desert, killed by Shenahrians."

"Just as I hoped. I staged my own death to fool everyone," Barius said. "I learned how powerful staging one's death was from the Ten Sons of Kheb. Then I left New Mephitia forever. The Shenahrians had to believe I was killed and there are spies in Isyrin who would find out my plan. It was my only way to escape their suspicion and cause them to forget about me."

"But what are you doing here? Of all the places in the world you could be, why here?" Dabarius held in his own tears. "Why didn't you come north and find me?"

"I made a vow, my son," Barius explained, "after they murdered your mother and sisters . . . almost twenty years ago, I swore to hunt the Shenahrians until no more of them remained."

"You could have left word with Oberon," Dabarius said.

"I could have, but I barely knew him. He was a friend of your grandfather and I didn't know what I was going to do, I'm sorry. I wanted you to have a good life, more than I could give you. With the plans that were forming in my head, even then, I had no reason to hope that I would live this long.

"I knew that as long as you were in New Mephitia you would be in danger. You were all I had left. I had to protect you and sending you away gave you the best chance to survive, so I took you as far away as I could, knowing Oberon would keep you safe and train you in the ways of wizardry and battle touch. I knew he would not tell you of your ancestry, because your grandfather had used binding magic on him years before and given him a trust scarab."

"It has to do with the Crystal Eye, doesn't it?" Dabarius asked.

"Yes, your grandfather gave the Crystal Eye to him to keep it safe and keep it away from the Shenahrians, who were searching for it tirelessly. Oberon had kept it safe for decades already. I knew he would keep you safe as well. I never imagined you would ever come south, but you followed me, how?"

"Father, I didn't follow your trail. I never knew about you until I arrived in Isyrin. By then, my feet were already on the path."

Barius was perplexed, then he glanced at Bellor and Thor and the glint of understanding appeared in his face.

"I will tell you everything," Dabarius said, "but please, first tell me how you came to be here and why?"

"This place, *Lesh'heb*"—anger flashed across Barius's face—"is the root of everything, my son. This is where the Shenahrians take their orders. This is where they train, and study, and scheme to overthrow the Queen of Isyrin, and the Drobin Empire too. For eleven years I have been masquerading as the quarry master, saying my prayers to Ah'usar and Shenahr, fooling them all as I study my enemies from an arm's length away. I have seen the Shenahrians' leader and the sight of him is an insult to all the Mephitian people and the true gods.

"He is not a man or a god. He is a serpent of the Underworld. The Shenahrians believe that the Dragon of Darkness has the essence of Shenahr within him, and all of their Priests and the common people of this putrefying land and beyond believe it. The Dragon of Darkness is no god, only the offspring of a line of thieves who stole the mantle of divinity in the distant past. This newest King of the Dragons is the same as his line has been for over five hundred years, a hammer in the hand of the Eternal King, Ra'menek.

490

"This dragon that the Drobin hunters who came here called Draglûne is an enforcer, a killer, a dullard, who is in total reliance on the counsel of others. He learns the ancient Draconic magic from Ra'menek, as the line of dragons has forgotten their old ways, and must now rely on an unholy abomination to teach him. He wishes to be rid of Ra'menek, but he cannot break free."

"Draglûne is under the command of Ra'menek?" Dabarius asked.

"Not entirely. Draglûne controls the Priests of Shenahr, as a wingataur demon in man form is their High Priest in Mephitep. It is through this imposter that Draglûne directs the Shenahrian worshipers in New Mephitia, and the so-called Iron Brotherhood in the northern lands. They all sow chaos and destruction, as they prepare for the rise of the Mephitian Empire once again."

Barius raised his trust scarab and pointed to the tiny blue feathers painted on it. "Those who follow Amar'isis are in the way. We are an inconvenient obstacle. We must all be subjugated or slain before armies from Mephitia can strike the north and regain the lost lands once again. If you had any doubt before, let it go now, for all of the rebellions in New Mephitia have been planned here in Lesh'heb, by this unholy alliance. Draglûne and his demon High Priest of Shenahr ordered the revolt in Isyrin twenty years ago. After all this time of searching and spying I know it is Draglûne who is responsible for the deaths of your mother and sisters. He delights in exterminating the families of his enemies to wipe out the line forever like the line of dragons was destroyed so long ago."

Dabarius did not doubt his father, and he had suspected the same thing all along. The Dragon King was behind it all. The confirmation only reaffirmed his resolve.

"Son, for years I've been biding my time, making plans, and praying for retribution. I've learned so much, but killing a creature of Draglûne's strength or the undead King Ra'menek is beyond the power of a single wizard like me. I've been forced to wait and plan for a time when the moment to strike was right, but the weapon has never been forged. You never should have come here."

They locked eyes. "Father," Dabarius said, "the time to strike is now. I stand before you today not only a wizard, but a *Dracken Viergur*."

LXXXIV

To know one's father is a blessing that cannot be measured. I wish mine had survived the Eighth Giergun War, so I could have joined him on campaign. I remember our years together very well, and I know of his deeds in battle, but I wish I could have served under him in his regiment. When the *Viergur* sit in the firelight and reminisce on the iron smelted and stone broken while studying at their fathers' shoulder, I can't help but feel as if my own was taken away too soon.

—Bölak Blackhammer, from the Quarzaak Journal

Late into the night, despite his exhaustion, Dabarius spoke with his father, proud of what this lone man had accomplished, but upset about all the years he was never told about him. What would life have been like if Barius had stayed near Isyrin and raised him there? He had been denied his real father and believed he was some unwanted orphan all these years. He was so pleased to have found him, but this man had given him up and left him behind forever. Dabarius sensed there was guilt in his father, and he did not want him here, the most dangerous place on the plateaus.

"Draglûne knows we're coming here," Dabarius said, and told his father about the wyvern.

"None have seen a wyvern, and no alarm has been raised," Barius said. "The Shenahrians have not alerted the guards or increased the patrols."

"Perhaps it did die," Thor said.

"Not possible," Bellor said.

"Perhaps you are below the worry of the Dragon of Darkness," Barius said. "That is his way. Only Ra'menek is equal to him."

Dabarius wondered, but they still had to assume the worst. For now, they would speak of other things as they had a lifetime to catch up on and they seemed safe in Barius's house, as he was not under suspicion as being a traitor to the Priests of Lesh'heb.

The others listened and asked their own questions, but father and son spoke as if no one else was in the room. Dabarius told of growing up with Oberon and Noah, learning from them, and the fateful day when Bellor, Thor and Drake had arrived at the tower. The story of how they traveled to Khierson City, fled and rode on the backs of alicorns to near Arayden impressed Barius greatly. How they escaped the desert city, and killed Draglûne's daughter, Verkahna made him even more proud and convinced Barius that they might actually have a chance against Draglûne.

Barius described spending almost two years hunting the Shenahrians in the Khoram Desert and in the cities of New Mephitia. He also told of finding Shahan empty, and crossing the bridge below the mist and coming to Mephitep in disguise, where he stayed for eight years in the capital, eventually becoming an ally and spy for the Priests of Kheb who had the support of the common people.

"Does you father know anything about Bölak?" Bellor asked, unable to hold his tongue any longer.

Barius did, and had read an account of the Ten Sons of Kheb. It was a copy of a scroll written by a Khebian Priest, the only man who survived the battle inside the Tunnel of Tombs when the Drobin had come to Lesh'heb with the God King in Mephitep's blessing some forty years prior.

"Where is this scroll?" Bellor asked.

"Not far from here, hidden in the locked vaults of the great library of the Eternal King," Barius said. "Do not worry, I remember it well, though you will not like to know what it says."

"Regardless, Thor and I must know the fate of our kin," Bellor said, and he took out his journal to write down what was said.

494

"I remember this tale very well," Barius said. "I grew up hearing whispered stories of the Ten Sons of Kheb, and when I found out what they did here, I was even more impressed, but quite saddened."

"I shall write down what you say," Bellor said.

"I will try to recite the scroll as it was written, but I may not get it exactly right."

"Please, proceed," Bellor said.

Barius cleared his throat. "In the four hundred and sixty-seventh year of the reign of the Eternal King, Ra'menek, The Ten Sons of Kheb entered the House of Lesh'heb with the blessing of the God King Ahken'ra of Mephitep. The Great Earth Father, Kheb, sent his Sons to slay the Dragon of Darkness and reestablish balance in the world. The Ten Sons of Kheb and their Khebian allies entered the Tunnel of Tombs. They all wore the griffin robes of Khebian Priests and were allowed to pass by the Eternal King's servants as it was night and the Eternal Lord rested in his tomb. They met the Dragon of Darkness near the end of the tunnel and mortally wounded him, but his divine essence saved his life. He fled the tombs, but at a great cost to the Ten Sons of Kheb. All perished, save for me, a humble man of Mephitep dedicated to the Earth Father, who spared my life. I buried what remained of them where they died and made a marker with their names upon it." Barius let out a sad sigh. "It was signed, Hezekiah, Priest of Kheb."

"I do not believe this," Thor said. "If Draglûne was driven away, how could all of the *Dracken Viergur* be dead? This is a trick, another ruse left by my Uncle and his Khebian allies. Pretending he was dead to throw off his pursuers."

"They were never seen again after they entered the Tunnel of Tombs," Barius said. "No one disputes that, and Draglûne, as you call him, has been seen many times. It is said that the Dragon of Darkness appeared the next day, and though the tombs were still rank with puddles of his dark blood, he bore not the slightest scar or infirmity, but was as glistening and potent as ever. In the next week, three villages on the far outskirts of the empire were destroyed. Every man, woman, dog and goat was devoured or burned. Dragon-sign was clear on the ground in each place. Each village was loyal to Kheb, of course. Such was his anger, and such was the hunger that awakened in him."

"What happened to this Priest, Hezekiah?" Bellor asked.

"He was taken back to Mephitep and told the same account to the God King Ahken'ra before he escaped and went into hiding. Ahken'ra blamed the Khebians and said they were lying, that he did not give his blessing for this attack. Ra'menek knew the truth and he took action. He had his Solar Priests and the Storm Priests work together. They purged the Khebian Priesthood and made sure that they would never have power again in Old Mephitia. No longer would the Khebians have any control over Lesh'heb either. Everything changed after the Ten Sons of Kheb came here and tried to kill the Dragon God. Two great powers were enraged, and each took their vengeance, though Ra'menek's was far more potent."

"What will happen after we succeed?" Thor asked.

Barius laughed. "I do not know what will happen, my new and confident friend, but how to destroy Ra'menek is always the question."

"We know how to kill Draglûne," Bellor said, "but the other, this undead King, worries me."

"As well he should, friend," Barius said. "In his darkened shrines, Ra'menek is eternal and nearly indestructible. He truly is a god walking upon the land."

"That is the axe that darkened Mograwn's eyes," Dabarius said, pointing to Bellor's weapon. "We just need a similarly effective weapon for this misbegotten God King."

"How will we end him?" Thor asked. "I assume he does not bleed."

496

"He does not during the night," Barius said, "nor does he burn. He has the power of the sun god, Ah'usar within him."

"Dragon fire does not harm him then," Bellor said.

"No," Barius said. "Only the light of the moon seems to weaken him. The Goddess Amar'isis is his opposite, and her magic has power over him. In the moonlight his young face of handsome flesh begins to rot away and he is shown to be what he truly is, a walking corpse, dead for over five centuries."

"You have seen him, seen his flesh rot?" Dabarius asked.

"No," Barius said. "None who still live have seen that. I read it in one of the scrolls in the great library, though I have seen him in the great library school, and heard him speak. He avoids going out at night unless he wears a burial mask of gold to hide his decaying flesh."

"I know magic of the Goddess," Dabarius said, "for I have read the Sacred Goddess Scrolls of Amar'isis and the spells written on them will help kill him. Moonlight can be harnessed." He thought about a way to put out any fire, especially unholy ones. If Bellor could lend his aide to the spell Dabarius had in mind, they might have the weapon they needed.

"We should do what my nephew did," Bellor said, "and avoid Ra'menek if we can. One fight at a time, remember?"

"I agree," Dabarius said, "but we must plan for the worst. Father, don't you agree?"

"Yes, you may not be able to avoid him," Barius said. "He rules the entrance to the Tunnel of Tombs and you must pass there to reach the lair of Draglûne, for he lives at the very end of the tunnel, where it meets the Void, and he will surely see you coming."

"You are certain of that?" Bellor asked.

"Yes," Barius said, "for he is in possession of the Crystal Eye of Ah'usar."

"He will see us enter?" Bellor asked.

"If he is looking," Barius said.

"You know for certain that he has a Crystal Eye?" Dabarius asked.

"I know for certain that Ra'menek has one," Barius said, "and that Draglûne has two."

"Two?" Bellor asked.

"The one Oberon guarded in Snow Valley, the Crystal Eye of Amar'isis, was brought here some time ago," Barius said, "and he already had the Crystal Eye of Shenahr."

"How do you know the one from Snow Valley is here?" Dabarius asked, as he thought about poor Oberon trapped inside the crystal sphere as he must be. Dabarius had to find it, and free him. He was so close now.

"The Priests of Shenahr have been searching for the Crystal Eye of Amar'isis for decades and when it was brought here some weeks ago there was much celebrating, though it was a very sad day when I learned of this, for I thought you and Oberon were likely dead."

"Oberon is alive," Dabarius said. "I believe he is trapped inside Draglûne's Crystal Eye, but why does Draglûne want two?"

"They are rare and powerful. There are only three," Barius said. "The Queen of Isyrin had one, and Rama'dara had hers sent to Snow Valley by my father. The God King in Mephitep had one, but after he became the Eternal King five hundred years ago he had it brought here. The third has been in possession of the Dragon Kings for at least two thousand years, maybe longer. Draglûne has been intent on finding the missing Crystal Eye for a long time. He wants it very badly and he wants the Crystal Eye that Ra'menek has."

"Why?" Dabarius asked, dreading the answer.

"The three together are said to create an artifact of tremendous power," Barius said, "though no scroll I've read or of Priest of Shenahr I've spoken with knows what the three might do if brought together, though they can be linked in some way. After hearing of how wingataur demons traveled from

Draglûne's Crystal Eye to the one in Oberon's tower, I fear what else they might be able to do."

"Aren't the three together now?" Dabarius asked.

"No," Barius shook his head. "Ra'menek will never allow Draglûne to have his favorite tool. Though Draglûne has promised him anything to have it, according to the tablets in the library. Ra'menek's Crystal Eye is what brought Draglûne here in the first place so he could learn to use his father's Crystal Eye, after he slew Mograwn and became king."

"Mograwn," Bellor said, unconsciously gripping the haft of his axe, his jaw clenching.

"Yes, Draglûne wanted to learn how to use the Crystal Eye he inherited from his dead sire," Barius said.

"How do you know all of this?" Bellor asked.

"I've spoken to many Priests of Shenahr and read the tablets that have been kept for centuries," Barius said. "Ra'menek wants everything written down, preserved forever. The library is extensive."

"Why have the Priests of Shenahr told you all of this and let you read the scrolls?" Dabarius asked, the side of his throbbing again.

"They trust me," Barius said with a sly grin, "for I am one of them. A fortress does little good when your enemy is already within the walls."

LXXXV

The plans we have made with the Khebian Priests of Mephitep and Lesh'heb are strong. We have the sanction of the God King Ahken'ra, For whatever that may be worth. He is a young man I trust less than Draglûne. I fear his conviction will fade, especially if we fail. He cannot hope to keep the Priests of the Storm God under control if Draglûne survives. To us, of course, none of those concerns will matter. There is nothing beyond the goal.

—Bölak Blackhammer, from the Khoram Journal

"Father, *you* are a Priest of Shenahr?" Dabarius asked, utterly amazed and in awe of what his father had done to infiltrate the very heart of his enemies.

"I am a Storm Priest, and have sworn their vows," Barius said. "They trust me, and I've seen the inner sanctum of their temple attached to the Library School. I've spent years studying them and have been planning an attack, but in all that time the plan has been incomplete. Neither I nor the Khebian Priests in Mephitep have ever devised a sure way of defeating Ra'menek or Draglûne. We can get his guardian Priests in the school out of the way, but even if every Shenahrian were killed, their order would rise again unless the Dragon of Darkness was slain. The Eternal King Ra'menek himself would rebuild them, for they are the might behind his Solar Priests. The Brother Gods must both be slain or whatever we do will all be for nothing."

"Father, we can do it," Dabarius said without any hesitation. He still had some doubt about his plan to defeat Ra'menek, but they would make it work, and then Draglûne would be next.

"I want to believe you," Barius said, "but before I risk the lives of the people of Lesh'heb who will fight against the Priests, I must know how you will defeat the Brother Gods."

Bellor explained roughly how they would slay Draglûne.

"What about the Eternal King Ra'menek?" Barius asked.

"There is a spell I studied in the Scrolls of Amar'isis," Dabarius said. "It can harness the power of moonlight and infuse the light in water. If the water was also blessed by Bellor and Thor . . . " Then Dabarius explained the parts Drake and Thor might play.

"I don't like it," Thor said.

"Neither do I," Drake said.

"I'll keep him occupied," Dabarius told them "and you'll both have your chances."

"What if it doesn't work?" Drake asked.

"Then we'll retreat," Bellor said.

"Regroup outside the Tunnel of Tombs?" Barius asked.

"No," Bellor said, "we'll retreat forward and attack Draglûne. Surely Dabarius can goad this 'divine being' to allow Draglûne to face us himself. Why should the Eternal God King Ra'menek serve as guardian for his younger brother god?"

"That does cater to his nature," Barius said.

Dabarius thought about using that approach right from the start. Draglûne was their target, and if Ra'menek did not have his strongest weapon, the Dragon King, perhaps they would stop Ra'menek's plan to re-establish the Mephitian Empire after all?

"We shall prepare as best we can," Bellor said, "we shall pray for guidance. I wish to know more about how we will get into the Tunnel of Tombs. Is it guarded?"

"Yes," Barius said, "hundreds of Priests of Shenahr live beside the path to the tombs, though only a few watch the gateway. Still, they will have to be defeated before you attack the Brother Gods."

"Have you allies who will help us?" Bellor asked.

"The people of Lesh'heb are tomb builders, and many work at the Library School," Barius said. "Almost all of them have been ill-treated by the Priests of Shenahr over the years. They are my people, and they will fight."

"What is your plan?" Bellor asked.

"We must get as many Priests of Shenahr out of Lesh'heb before we attack," Barius said. "They control the only ground approach to the Tunnel of Tombs, and there are over four hundred men in the Library School. Only three hundred and fifty are of an age who will fight."

"They are warriors?" Bellor asked.

"The Priests of Shenahr are spies, assassins, and warriors," Barius said. "They are the enforcers who come in the night and crush all dissent in Mephitep, and in the tribal lands. All of them who swear the vows to Shenahr come here for training, both in the library, tended by the Solar Priests, and the fighting school, administered by the Storm Priests. Those men who fomented the past rebellions in New Mephitia, and carried out the assassinations there were trained in this place. Some of them may have even gone north into Arayden and beyond, organizing the Iron Brotherhood there."

It gave Dabarius pause when he thought of three hundred and fifty trained assassins living beside the approach to the Tunnel of Tombs.

"How will we defeat so many?" Bellor asked.

"First we must get as many of the Priests of Shenahr out of Lesh'heb," Barius said. "I will summon them north to Mephitep, to put down a Khebian revolt."

"You can arrange a rebellion?" Dabarius asked.

"The threat of one," Barius said, "but by the time they reach Mephitep to position themselves to crush the revolt they will have been on the road for over three days. Even if they turn around and come back straight away, they'll be gone almost a week, and by then it will be too late for them to save their precious Brother Gods, and we will have many hostages."

"Hostages?" Bellor asked.

"We will capture the youngest sons of the nobles of Mephitep who are studying in the school," Barius said.

"Is there no other way?" Bellor asked. "I do not want to threaten the lives of children."

"We will not hurt them," Barius said, "but we will keep them here, and use them to stop any attack on Lesh'heb."

"The Priests of Shenahr will be stopped by this threat?" Dabarius asked.

"The Mortal King of Mephitep will not dare attack us," Barius said, "for we will hold his only son as a hostage."

"I do not like this hostage-taking plan," Bellor said.

"The God King of Mephitep will not risk the life of his last remaining heir," Barius said. "Ra'menek has killed the first three after finding them all unsuitable to be the next ruler in Mephitep, but this final young boy, Ahken'mose is favored by him."

"How difficult will it be to capture the library school?" Dabarius asked.

"There will be hard fighting," Barius said, "but we must take it, for if we want to open the Tunnel of Tombs we will need the key to open the gate there. The key is actually a bronze staff, approximately six feet in length. It is inserted into a deep keyhole in huge bronze gates, which block the entrance to the cavern where the ancient God Kings are buried, and where the Brother Gods make their home."

"Is there no other way to enter this place?" Bellor asked.

"There are entrances atop the highest peaks of jagged stone," Barius said, "where Ra'menek has built places where he can watch the sunrise, but they are unreachable, protected by cliffs and endless rows of jagged rocks. The Dragon of Darkness comes and goes at the place where the river once poured into the Underworld. That way cannot be reached either and it is guarded by wingataurs trained by the wingataur King Priest Zultaan, a powerful demon who advises Draglûne."

503

"Then we must have the key," Bellor said,

"It is kept in the inner sanctum of the Temple of Shenahr," Barius said, "where all the greatest treasures are held. We will have to fight our way in to get it. There is no other way."

"What treasures?" Thor asked.

Dabarius glared at him disapprovingly.

"I have only seen the treasury of Shenahr once," Barius said. "The whole Priesthood is funded by the dead God Kings."

Bree'alla shook her head as if it were a most heinous crime.

"They've looted them since Draglûne has made his lair here. This is how they have gained such influence over Mephitia and beyond. Ra'menek and his Solar Priests have done the same, though they have never told the Mephitian people. Stealing from the dead is one of the worst crimes. These Priests have made a mockery of our religion."

"I can think of many worse crimes than stealing from moldy corpses," Thor said, "but what is actually in this place?"

"Golden treasures, jewels of God Kings and Queens, the original tablets of containing the holy writings of Shenahr, other relics, and weapons blessed by the Storm God."

"What relics?" Dabarius asked.

"The Vessel of the Night," Barius said. "A stone decanter that contains a gift from the Dragon of Darkness himself. The Priests of Shenahr use drops of what's inside for their most powerful spells."

"Dragon's blood," Bellor said as he sprang to his feet.

"Yes," Barius said. "The blood of the Dragon King."

"We must have it," Thor said.

"If we have his own blood," Bellor said, "we can use it to create wyrm killing bolts that will slay Draglûne."

Even Drake smiled at this, and Dabarius wanted to hug his father.

"I will make the preparations," Barius said. "It will not take long."

LXXXVI

I wonder if the spirits of all the Dracken Viergur who have died are carried inside of us, urging we few to keep going. Only Lorak knows, but I feel my fallen brothers giving me strength when I am weak.

—Bölak Blackhammer, from the Khoram Journal

Hundreds of armed men marched outside the quarry master's house on the road. Drake could hear the warriors' feet crunching on the gravel and sometimes heard muffled shouting.

Instead of worrying, he methodically went about his work and prepared his crossbow bolts for the next day. Behind a locked door in the large, windowless cellar filled with spider webs with a few oil lamps providing light, Drake made sure every single crossbow bolt was in perfect working order. He glued loose fletchings, replacing some with the feathers he'd been gathering from the aevians he'd shot over the past weeks, straightened the shafts as best he could, and sharpened the points with a small whetstone.

Thor pressed his ear against the outside wall, listening carefully. He gripped his hammer and muttered curses.

Drake ignored the marching sounds outside and his anxious Drobin friend inside.

Bellor nodded at Drake, admiring how calmly he went about his tasks, and watched as he coated a few of the shafts with a thin film of thickened lamp oil, making them extra deadly as they would slide through anything they hit. Lastly, he put a dollop of wax on the tips of the bolts he was planning on shooting at Draglûne. The wax would give them extra sticking power, and they wouldn't slip off the scales, or any shields they might hit.

As he worked, Jep and Temus sat at his feet, their ears pricked up as the assassin Priests of Shenahr, the Solar Priests of Ah'usar, and their older students, made their way toward the God King's road.

Bree'alla sat up from her nap on the floor just behind him as a man shouted right outside, while Bellor and Thor leaned against the exterior wall, listening carefully, as if they could somehow gauge the number of men passing. Gurion sat beside them, his eyes wide when he was not praying silently or rocking back and forth, his terror barely concealed.

Dabarius worked beside Drake, taking each bolt that Drake had finished with, and whispering words from Oberon's small book of spells for several moments before putting the shaft in the completed pile.

"No matter where they hit," Dabarius promised, "they will burrow in like they are the tip of a drill, and if you think about where you want them to hit, that will help them find their mark."

"If my aim was off by the length of my arm," Drake asked, "would it adjust in flight and hit?"

"No, not that far," Dabarius said. "Maybe a hand-length or less. It'll help, but this magic will fade on the second sunrise from now."

"This will be over long before that," Thor whispered.

They planned to attack in the morning. After the next sunrise they would face Draglûne. Drake was amazed at the speed everything was happening. Dabarius's father had not exaggerated when he said the preparations would not take long. The very next day a runner arrived from Mephitep, as one did every three days. The courier stopped at the quarry master's home, as they always did, to drop off any correspondence, wash themselves, and change into clean clothes before running the last quarter-mile to the Library School and presenting their bundle of messages to the Priests there. As the exhausted courier bathed, dumping water over his head and shaving his scalp, Dabarius's father opened the man's satchel and put the forged message inside. The courier had been none the wiser.

Dabarius had told the companions what his note said, something about a serious uprising in Mephitep that had to be dealt with immediately before it was launched. All able bodied men of fighting age—fifteen and up—were to march toward the capital. Older Priests who were fit to march were asked to accompany the warriors and direct them in battle, which would leave only a few elderly teachers and many young boys behind. Only a handful of warrior Priests would be tasked to protect the school from the unlikely attack of some rogue aevian, and of course to regulate the slaves and workers there. When the force arrived in Mephitep, the God King Ahken'ra would give them orders and they would be tasked to kill every last rebel, mostly Khebian sympathizers and other criminals. The note had been signed by the notoriously stern and uncompromising First Minister Min'kar. The God King's seal completed the ruse.

Barius had also arranged for two runners of his own to go north that very day, and intercept anyone coming south on the road, or any messengers sent from Lesh'heb. The two loyal men would kill and then dispose of the body of anyone who could cast doubt on what was in the forged message. They would also deliver a coded letter to the rebels in Mephitep that the time to strike would soon be at hand. A rough list of the hostages would also be provided, and when the time was right, the God King would learn that his last remaining heir, young Ahken'mose was in the hands of rebels in Lesh'heb.

The plan that Barius and the Khebians in Mephitep had been planning for years to get the Priests out of Lesh'heb was about to be set in motion as they finally had the weapon to defeat the Brother Gods. Now, only five hours after the fake message had been delivered to the Library School, hundreds of men marched north as "Priest Ben'ahmi" supervised the work in the quarry, saying nothing to his loyal men there. No one in Lesh'heb would know of tomorrow's attack until late that night when the Storm and Solar Priests were hours away,

507

in case a traitor attempted to betray them.

The plan would work. It had to, and Drake didn't dwell on what would happen if it all failed. Instead, he inspected Ethan's thorn bolt. It was the only shaft left that he hadn't prepared. The perfectly straight and long thorn had grown from the sikatha tree on the furthest Lily Pad Rock outside Cliffton. It had been only just under four months since he had used the thorn to puncture his skin and make an offering to the Void in the name of his dead best friend, but it felt like a lifetime. Since then, the thorn had gotten harder, drying out in the desert climate. The point felt very sharp as well, but it needed a metal tip.

Drake hesitated, then decided that he had to get it ready. His supply of shafts was limited, and Ethan would want him to use thorn bolt if he had to. With that in mind, Drake affixed a point from a broken shaft, using a wyrm-kin slaying broadhead that he'd been saving since the battle at the Mouth of the Underworld. The glue would be dry by the next day, but Drake would not use it unless all his other bolts were gone and his life was in danger. Thorn bolts would often be good for only one shot, but they were stiffer and heavier than wood, and would punch deeper when it counted.

The last two bolts that Dabarius enchanted were Drake's and Ethan's thorn bolts, and each of them had been fixed with wyrm-kin slaying heads that would kill a wingataur almost on contact. If Bellor and Thor were able to get the dragon's blood from the temple of Shenahr, Drake had no doubt that Draglûne would die. Since General Reu'ven had stolen the alicorn horn, which would have been carved into several deadly crossbow tips that were lethal to dragons, this was the best plan they had. If they survived all this, the General would receive a visit. For what he'd done to Bree, to all of them, Reu'ven's chest would grow a set of feathers one day. Drake remembered a time when he could not have so calmly decided to kill a man. That seemed so long ago.

The front door of the house banged against the wall as it was flung open, and men shouted at each other inside Barius's front hallway. All of the companions paused and listened. Drake pulled his Kierka knife Dabarius listened at the small door to the cellar, putting his ear against the wood as feet stomped across the floor above them.

"It's my father," he whispered. "He's arguing with someone of high rank."

The raised voices continued and Dabarius listened, refusing to say anything else as he focused all his attention on the sounds. More men entered the house and their sandaled feet could be heard right above them. At least four or five men were there.

Jep and Temus let out low rumbling growls. Drake shushed them and the dogs quieted down, but still looked up with ears raised.

"If they find us here," Bellor whispered, "we fight our way out right away before they can trap us here. We run for the canyon wall and climb back into the grykes the way we came in here."

Bellor put a steadying hand on Gurion, who was trembling with fear.

The companions gathered their belongings in preparation to make a fighting exit from the house, leaving Dabarius to listen at the door while they packed.

A loud voice just beyond the cellar made all of them stop moving and hold perfectly still.

Drake thought it might be Barius. A whisper came through he door, only a few Mephitian words.

Then all of the sounds faded as the men left the house.

"What happened?" Bellor whispered.

Dabarius slid down to the floor, his expression filled with anger and frustration. "An elder Priest of Shenahr made my father go with him to Mephitep."

The companions were all too stunned to speak. The plan had unraveled. How they would be able to succeed without Dabarius's father?

"What else?" Bellor asked. "He gave us a message didn't he?"

Dabarius nodded. "He pretended he was getting supplies and complaining about having to go, then he whispered that he would try to return by tonight and that we should wait here and keep hidden."

"If he doesn't come back?" Drake asked.

"Gurion, you know my father's most trusted men?" Dabarius said in Mephitian and Bree translated.

The boy nodded.

"Good," Dabarius said. "Tonight you will go and bring them back here if my father doesn't return."

Gurion appeared as if he was going to faint.

"I'll speak to the men," Dabarius said, "and convince them I'll lead the attack. My father told me everything. We can do this without him."

Drake had a bad feeling about this, and he thought he heard someone upstairs in the house.

LXXXVII

Be vigilant against all spawn of the Void, for they are the spies of the Underworld.

—passage from the Goddess Scrolls of Amaryllis

Drake motioned for his friends to be quiet as the person upstairs walked around the house. Was it a Shenahrian spy going through Barius's things? Whoever they were, they were there a half hour before they shut the front door and left.

"Who was that?" Thor asked.

"I hope a servant," Bellor said. "Dabarius, who do you think it was?"

Dabarius shrugged and kept a perpetual scowl on his face, which had been there since his father was taken away. Now that the person was gone from upstairs he cursed and grumbled under his breath.

Drake tried not to pay any attention to the wizard and finished the maintenance on his crossbow, then sharpened his Kierka knife. Long slow strokes curving with the blade. Bree sat beside him and sharpened *Wingblade* while Thor and Bellor whispered to each other in Drobin.

After the marching sounds outside were long gone, Master Bellor crouched in front of Dabarius. "Do you think that little boy can bring the men we need here tonight?"

"He'll do it," Dabarius said confidently.

Gurion looked more like he had gut rot than courage when they stared at him.

"Look at him," Thor said. "He's going to wet himself."

"Even if these men come," Bellor said, "they don't know you. They won't do this."

"I'll make them do it," Dabarius said. "We need to open the gates to the tombs and the key is in the temple of Shenahr, sitting next to a jug of dragon's blood."

"This is rash," Bellor said. "Perhaps we should wait for a few days until your father returns. Our enemies will never look for us here and we are shielded by Earth magic from being seen by the Crystal Eyes of our enemies."

"No, we should proceed tonight," Dabarius said. "All of the Storm Priests might return in a few days. We have to strike now while they're gone. It's our only chance. Gurion is going to bring my father's captains here and in the morning we're going to take the wall of Lesh'heb and attack the library school."

"Master Bellor decides what we're going to do," Thor said, "or have your forgotten because of that bump on your head?"

Temus whined, interrupting the staring contest Thor and Dabarius had begun.

"We're going to wait here until tonight," Bellor said. "Then we'll decide what to do. If Barius returns, the plan will go ahead if it's still possible. If he doesn't come back, we'll consider what Dabarius is proposing. I want to talk to Gurion about all this and we need to think through anything we do. If we take one wrong step now, we fail . . . and we cannot fail."

Dabarius sulked in a corner after that. He made Gurion sit beside him for a while and whispered to the boy. Bree had helped Bellor speak with Gurion earlier and the young Mephitian did know who to talk to. A man named Oved, a quarry boss who could gather the rest of the rebels in Lesh'heb. Gurion knew where he lived.

Drake kept out of it and when he had finished his work, tried to sleep, but all he could think about was the wounded wyvern flying away and leading his friends into the ambush under the roadway. If only he could have killed the aevian everything might be different. Draglûne would not know they were coming.

Bree put her arm over him and his mind relaxed. When he awakened sometime later he watched Dabarius working a spell on some painted urns that his father had provided. Four of them were short and thin and had once held flower offerings in

512

Lesh'heb's temple of Kheb, which had long been closed down. The wizard was trying to make the incredible water-carrying urns that had been destroyed at Thunderstone.

Khelen'dara had made them in the Temple of Amar'isis and Dabarius said he could not do it when they were out in the desert, but now he was confident since he had sacred vessels from a temple. Their plan hinged on making the urns and they had no chance against the Eternal God King, Ra'menek if he failed. Dabarius's infrequent outbursts of frustration did not bode well, and Drake wondered how badly his friend's memory had been damaged.

The night came after many tedious hours in the cellar. The dwarves prayed a lot while Drake lay next to Bree, wishing he could be alone with her instead of being stuck in a veritable jail cell the others. They tried to rest, and ate the dry food Barius had left for them. The dogs were the only ones who had no trouble sleeping and snored louder than Drake had heard in a long time.

"It's getting late," Dabarius finally said, the first words anyone had spoken above a whisper in a long while. The dogs both woke up and licked their lips.

"Your father still might come," Bellor said.

"We must act," Dabarius said. "Gurion needs to find Oved and bring him here."

Drake could tell from Thor's conflicted expression that he wanted to support Dabarius in this. He wanted action, not more waiting, but he would do what his master commanded.

"I have been praying about this," Bellor said. "I will consent to let Gurion try and bring Oved here. You can speak with him, and what we learn from him will determine what we do. If Oved is in favor of this attack, we will move forward. If he is not, we will wait for your father, no matter how long it takes."

"Can Oved be trusted not to betray us if we wait here for days?" Thor asked.

513

"Gurion thinks so," Bellor said, "and I do trust this boy, and don't want him captured."

With that, Dabarius sent little Gurion to the village of Lesh'heb two hours to midnight. He returned quickly with a short stocky man in his mid thirties with thick black eyebrows that linked over his nose.

Dabarius greeted Oved in the center room of Barius's house, while the companions waited in an adjoining hallway keeping hidden, but peeking through a curtain. Bree translated some, but it appeared that Dabarius won the man over after half an hour of talking. Oved appeared to trust Gurion and the boy helped a lot. From Bree's whispered translation, little Gurion wanted to see the Storm Priest destroyed as much as Barius.

"Come in here," Dabarius said at last, "all of you, and meet our new friend."

Bellor and Thor entered first, then Drake, Bree and dogs following behind.

Oved bowed to the dwarves, and regarded Drake's spring-steel double crossbow with fascination.

"Oved has agreed to bring the other two leaders, Ja'den and Gha'brel, here tonight for a meeting," Dabarius said. "They might agree to help us and launch the attack."

Oved departed to summon Ja'den and Gha'brel, and Gurion remained behind, as there was no need for him to risk his life again tonight.

"That's not what it sounded like to me," Bree said. "Oved doesn't like their leader not being here."

"He knows he'll return," Dabarius said, "and this is their chance while most of the Priests are gone. This may never happen again and they have to take advantage. If the other two agree, I will serve in my father's place and lead the attacks."

"You don't know how to command men in war," Thor said. "Master Bellor has led men and dwarves into battle for almost two centuries. He should be the one."

514

"I don't question Master Bellor's experience," Dabarius said, "but he doesn't speak the language, and my father told me his plan."

"Let us see what these other two men have to say," Bellor said, "before you two go at each others throats any more."

A soft knock sounded on the door and the companions tensed, reaching for their weapons. It was too soon for Oved to have returned.

"*Khem'ruu*," a man outside the main door said. It was the secret word Barius had taught them and it meant 'all is at peace.'

Dabarius unbolted the door after peeking through the tiny window. His father entered wearing a bright white linen kilt and a golden medallion of a swirling storm around his neck. The dark kohl under his eyes made his furious expression even more fearsome. The two argued and Barius pushed his son and pointed a finger at him accusingly.

"No need to translate," Thor told Bree, "Lord Dabarius is in trouble for overstepping himself. I think Barius met Oved outside, and found out what was going on."

"Sending Gurion out could have ruined everything," Bree said, "and he's angry Dabarius didn't wait for him like he was told."

The two tall men argued for some time until finally Dabarius backed down, and though Drake did not understand the words, he thought his friend might have apologized.

The two eventually recused themselves to the kitchen and spoke quietly while the companions waited. Oved returned a short while later with two other men, but Dabarius and the companions were kept away and did not meet Gha'brel or Ja'den.

"What's the news?" Bellor asked the chastened wizard.

"My father slipped away, and we attack tomorrow."

"Anything else?" Thor asked sarcastically.

"My father has a short temper," Dabarius said.

"What about the person who went through the house after he left?" Bellor asked.

"He doesn't know," Dabarius said. "It might have been his housekeeper."

"Is there other news?" Bellor asked

"He said that over four-hundred and fifty Priests and their attendants went north today," Dabarius said. "More than he'd hoped. Only a few men remain in the gatehouse in Lesh'heb, and a very small number of fighting men guard the children and the Mortal King's son at the library school."

"It's a miracle that your brashness hasn't ruined everything," Thor said.

Barius suddenly entered the room where the companions had gathered. Father and son regarded each other sternly.

"Tomorrow we attack," Barius said, his son translating.

"Master Barius," Bellor asked, "do you have any knowledge that Draglûne knows we are here? He may be anticipating our attack."

"The Storm Priests did not seek his counsel before leaving today," Barius said. "Revolts in Mephitep are below his notice."

"Perhaps we are also below his notice," Bellor said. "We are merely humble servants of the Earth Father," he glanced at Bree, "and the Winged Goddess."

"This is not the time for any of you to be humble," Barius said. "Be proud, for tomorrow you will kill two false gods, and the Mephitian people will be free of their tyranny for the first time in over five hundred years."

516

LXXXVIII

Prepare a path for me, for I will face an evil foe this night.
—from the Sacred Scrolls of Amar'isis

Dabarius finished enchanting the last of the urns at midnight, afraid that his spells had all failed, and that his father would be even more disappointed in him than he already was. He would not know until they tested them, and he feared more than anything to look like a worse fool. He had promised his father that he and his friends could defeat the brother gods, but now he wasn't so certain. He had never been very religious, but for hours he had prayed to Amar'isis to help him.

Feeling the power of the Goddess channeled through him, as cool and eternal as his own magic was sudden and fiery, he knew that the beginnings of faith had been planted within him. Finally, when he felt the magic would hold fast, he carefully carried the urns, individually wrapped in thick towels inside a padded basket up the stairs and out into the courtyard where Bellor, Thor, and his father waited.

Gurion kept watch from the third story window, ready with a birdcall to announce that someone was coming. Bellor had advised him to keep watch on the sky, as Draglûne was the only one who could see them while inside the courtyard. Not wanting to take any chances, the two Drobin kept under the house's awning, while Barius stood under the light of the moon. He stood before a large ceramic tub filled with water up to its brim.

Dabarius looked at the two dwarves.

Bellor motioned toward the tub. "We have blessed all of the water in there, one bowl at a time. It is holy, sanctified in name of the Earth Father. It holds the deep echoes of the world's very birth, and will scald the unnatural like molten metal."

The still water reflected the giant silvery moon above, and Dabarius prayed once again that this would work. He knelt in front of the water and put his hands beneath the surface, cupping the rippling moon. He spoke the archaic Mephitian words of the spell exactly as he remembered them while saying the words of power in his mind in counterpoint to what he spoke aloud: "O hail, Moon Goddess of the night sky, who rises on the back of your mother. May you, Amar'isis, give power and might in vindication, and come forth as a living soul to see your children. Descend from your Soul-mansion and infuse this water with your light. Shine into this water with your magic. Light my way in the darkness. Prepare a path for me, for I will face an evil foe this night."

He recited the verse again, while in his mind he said the words of power that could never be uttered aloud, though fumbled them slightly, and blamed the mental fogginess he'd felt ever since the wyvern's ambush. He had learned the power words in Oberon's book of spells and learned new and more potent ones in the Sacred Scrolls of Amar'isis. His mind could barely hold them all now, but with tremendous intention he said them, and recited the sacred words out loud.

The ancient incantation had been used to free those who were possessed by evil spirits in centuries past. Tubs of water were empowered with moonlight, and the afflicted person would be submerged in them, instantly casting out the demon or the ghost possessing them. Surely this water would affect the undead God King Ra'menek and force his spirit out of his five-hundred year old body. Bellor and Thor had forced out the wingataur demon spirit in the cavern inside Mount Kheb with holy water, and combining Lorak's blessing with the power of the moonlight spell of Amar'isis would give them victory. Dabarius willed it to be so.

Dabarius said the spell over and over, repeating it for a quarter of an hour though he sensed no effect. He did not want to admit defeat, and prayed to Amar'isis harder than he ever had before, then said the spell one last time and allowed the words of power to run together in his mind. When he said, "Prepare a path for me, for I will face an evil foe this night." The water glowed with a faint silver light and the scent of lotus blossoms filled the air.

"Now," Dabarius said with relief, "it must be now." He removed one of the urns from the basket and held it above the tub. His father used a funnel and a pitcher to pour the water into the urn. One full pitcher disappeared inside. Then a second and third and on until the urn contained over twenty times its capacity. It weighed what it had after one and Dabarius put a stopper in it and brought up the second. His father filled four urns that should have held a half-gallon of water, but they held ten or more. Dabarius brought out one more vessel. This was a small votive bottle made of red clay and painted with flowers, meant to hold an offering of incense. It was two fingers wide and shorter than his hand. His father used the funnel and poured its capacity at least thirty times over before it finally overflowed.

The tub had a lot more water in it, but Dabarius had no more vessels to fill. Dabarius looked at his father who gave him an approving nod. They finished their tasks inside the house, and with the help of Gurion, Bellor and Thor, they sealed the urns with perfectly sized lids and hot wax, then used strong twine that held a second lid in place. Then they wrapped the holy water jars in thick towels and hid them in a pantry with the carrying baskets rigged with strong shoulder straps the dwarves had made.

"We should get some sleep," Barius said. "Tomorrow will start early, and it may go very late."

The dwarves went off to their room after Bellor put a blanket on Gurion, who slept on the floor using a rug for a pillow.

Father and son stopped in a shadowy hallway, Barius planning to stay downstairs and Dabarius going up.

"I have prayed for years for a way to defeat my enemies,"

519

Barius said, "but I never thought my own son would be the spear in my hand."

"If I knew you were here, I would have come long ago," Dabarius said, wanting to believe his own words.

"I envy you, son. I want to go with you and your friends tomorrow. I want to see Ra'menek and Draglûne killed. They must pay for all the lost loved ones, all the lost years."

Dabarius thought about his last memory of his mother and sisters. He remembered his sister Allaya's head exploding in front of him as she was murdered, and his mother screaming for him to run as she leapt from their house flames burning her dress. He remembered his father taking him north and holding him when he cried for his mother on those lonely nights in the desert. Dabarius had always preferred his gentle mother to his almost always absent father, and remembered their strained relationship on the long trip north. Lord Barius, Wizard of Isyrin, did not have time for a frightened little boy who wanted his mother and sisters to be alive, and did not understand why his father, the great wizard could not make them come alive again.

Lord Barius could not have lived with that constant reminder of his limitations reflected in his son's eyes. Barius needed someone else to raise him, and Oberon and Noah happened to be two of the best fathers anyone could ever have.

No, this had all worked out for the best, though Dabarius was grateful to meet his birth father now, and know how strong he was.

His father reached a hand forward and they grasped each other's muscled forearms. Barius fixed a hard gaze on him, and Dabarius returned it. They stood locked together for some time, neither wanting to break their grasp first.

"If I had kept you with me," Barius said, "you would have seen things a boy should not see."

Dabarius nodded. "I already had."

LXXXIX

The trunks of some trees are hollow, but the branches live, reaching for the sky. Without love, we are hollow trunks with no branches. Without hope, the sky above us clots with clouds, and day is much the same as night.

—passage from the Goddess Scrolls

The polite knock on her cell door startled Jaena. The guard had already delivered her dinner and the Lord Marshal only came to visit her during the day, so who might this be? Her jailers always knocked, and waited for her permission to enter her tower room, but she had a bad feeling about the timing of this.

"Come in," she said after she stood up from the couch where she had been reading from the Goddess Scrolls using the light of the glowstone.

Lord Marshal Gunther Krohgstaad bowed as he entered with a fat bulldog on a leash. The light brown and white dog seemed very winded from the stairs and Jaena smiled, telling herself there was not bad news if Gunther brought a dog to see her. It was also the first time the Lord Marshal was not dressed in his uniform. He wore casual clothing, a sweater and trousers of a high quality, but what she would expect a Drobin of his station to wear when he was at home curled up in a chair by his hearth.

"This is Odo," he said. "He needs to walk more, and I knew you liked dogs."

Odo tugged on his leash, his tail wagging, as he tried to get to Jaena. She knelt beside him, rubbed his head, and scratched behind his ears. He reminded her of the bullmastiffs of Cliffton, and knew that Drobin bulldogs and Nexan mastiffs had been the origin of the dogs of her village.

521

She offered the Lord Marshal the leather armchair he always sat in and Jaena returned to her couch with Odo, who lay on her feet, exhausted from the climb up the stairs. She missed having a dog around. It had been so lonely in the tower, and she wished Priestess Nayla would have let Kraig bring along his two dogs. She didn't want to think about any of that now, and returned her attention to her Drobin guest.

"I wish that tonight I had come for social reasons," he said. "Please forgive my late visit." The bleak tone of his voice made her forget how to breathe, and the dog glanced up at her, sensing her distress. It was bad news. Very bad. She tried to calm herself, and took a deep breath.

"Lord Marshal, I am always pleased when you visit."

His uncomfortable and grim demeanor terrified her.

"I received an order signed by the seven surviving members of the High Council of Lorak this evening," he said. "They have decided that tomorrow will be the day."

Jaena felt the blood drain from her face and she could not even blink. He had assured her that her execution would not take place while so many Nexans were in the city demanding her release. Villagers from all over the Nexan Plateau, and many city dwellers, had rioted and marched every day for a week now. Almost all of the Nexans had refused to work for any Drobin, and a worker strike had paralyzed the city, which was dependent on Nexan labor. More angry Amaryllians streamed into the capital every day according to what the Lord Marshal had told her. This would be the worst possible moment for them to behead Jaena in the square.

"Please, I don't ask this for myself," Jaena said, "but for all of the lives that will be lost if I am . . . put to death, now. Please, delay this. Wait."

He rubbed his temples with one of his large hands, his expression one of consternation. "I have just spoken to the most senior High Priest on the council in his home, a dwarf I've known for over a century. He has changed much in recent days. I don't know what madness he and many of the other council members are suffering from, but this is deliberate inflammatory sabotage. It must be the assassination of two of their fellows and the fact that none of the killers have been caught."

"I'm so sorry," she said, and was almost certain it had been Rill, Lyal, Holten, or Emmit. The dwarves had been shot with poisoned crossbow bolts.

"I failed to protect them," he said.

"You warned them," she said. "It's not your fault."

"It *is* my fault," he said. "If the three who were slain had been alive today, this would be delayed. They would not have made this rash decision."

"What did they say? Don't they know what's going to happen?"

"They feel that tomorrow is an 'auspicious day,'" the Lord Marshal said, "and this will send the Nexans a message to go back to work."

She tried to control her now ragged breathing. She had sensed that tomorrow as an important day as well. That very morning, before she woke up, the connection she had with Bree was strong and she felt that the next morning, Drake and his companions would face Draglûne. It might have been her imagination, but it felt very real to her.

How had her execution day coincided with the day the man she loved was going to face Draglûne? Her intuition—or perhaps knowledge from the astral world—told her that this was no random event. Draglûne himself would be watching when she died, all his attention focused on her, and not Drake and his friends. Who could have possibly set this up? One of Draglûne's enemies? Or the gods themselves? Jaena could not fathom any of it, but then she wondered if Draglûne would be waiting for her when she passed to the other side. He would try to enslave her and sever the golden cord connecting her to Drake. Would he use her against Drake when they fought?

Would this evil dragon hold her soul hostage somehow? A tear rolled down her cheek.

"I'm sorry," the Lord Marshal said. "I don't want to do this."

"I know," she said, and wiped her face.

Odo whined and nuzzled her leg.

"When will you come for me?" Jaena asked.

"In the morning. Those are my orders. I could try to delay."

She shook her head. "No, the morning will do. Thank you for telling me and for visiting me tonight. My prayers tonight would have been much different had you not come."

"I can have a sleeping draught delivered if you like," he said, "so you are not awake all night long."

"No, thank you. You have already done so much for me. I am grateful."

He knelt before her, kissed her hand, and then rested his forehead on her knee. When he finally stood, he was unable to look at her.

"Please guard yourself well, tomorrow, Lord Marshal," she said. "I do not want anything to happen to you when the fighting begins."

He stared at her, speechless for a moment. "There have been many individuals imprisoned in this keep during my years here, but none have had as much moral character as you, Jaena of Cliffton. I know you are not my enemy. I am very sad for this divide between the Amaryllians and the Drobin. I wish I could talk some sense into the High Council members."

Odo did not want to go, but the Lord Marshal guided the dog away after Jaena pet him and said goodbye. She wanted to ask him to leave Odo so she wouldn't be alone that night, but a whisper from her intuition told her to let the dog go.

Before they left, Lord Gunther put her small journal on the table by the door with a box of writing tools. "I thought you might like to write in it, one last time."

524

"Thank you."

He left and she read through her old entries. The hardest to read were the ones about Drake. She also read the last few she had written while she traveled with Emmit and Priestess Nayla. The more she had thought about the woman over the past days the more questions she had. Nayla was known to the Lord Marshal and he had asked many questions about her. No one knew where she came from, only that she had appeared on the Nexus Plateau two years past and spread sedition among the villages and in Nexus City where she worked with an underground group of revolutionaries. She had almost been captured a number of times and how she escaped could not be fathomed by the Drobin marshals. Jaena did not want to believe it, but the Lord Marshal said Nayla had set Jaena up as a sacrifice to incite the Nexan people.

It didn't seem possible, but when Jaena read her own journal entries, she realized how skewed her thinking had been during those weeks in the villages. She would write how she was going to confront Nayla, and then the next day she would fail to do so after having a change of heart while speaking with the woman. What had been wrong with Jaena? She did not regret all of the people that she helped, but she wondered if the woman who had convinced her to leave Cliffton had been the one to betray her to the Drobin marshals. The man who had delivered the information detailing when and where Jaena could be apprehended had escaped custody, but the vague description reminded Jaena of Emmit, Nayla's devoted Guardian.

She didn't want to think any more about her failures, and how stupid she had been. Jaena felt ashamed, and wanted to tell her mother that she should have listened to her and never left Cliffton.

Much later that night, when her tears had run out, Jaena decided she would visit Drake one last time in her spirit body. She had told herself she would stay away, but she was so desperate for the comfort only he could give her.

It took her a long time to calm herself enough, but she entered the spirit world and found herself with Bree'alla, who dozed on a bed in a large stone house. Drake was awake, working downstairs. The connection between the two women was strong, and they were drawn together. Bree sensed her presence immediately and they both floated together in the place between waking and dreaming.

"Jaena, why are you so sad?" Bree asked, her concern genuine and heartfelt. Like a sister's or one's best friend.

"Forgive me and this intrusion," Jaena said. "I couldn't stay away tonight."

"What's happened?" Bree asked.

"I've come to say goodbye. To you, and to Drake. Tonight will be my last opportunity. Tomorrow, I am to be put to death."

Red spikes of fury erupted from Bree's spirit body. "This is not justice for them to kill a woman such as you."

"I'm sorry to burden you with this. Please, don't tell Drake. It won't help him."

"I will continue to do as you ask," Bree said. Keeping secrets was what she was good at. "I only wish I could do more."

Their spirit bodies embraced. She felt love and concern, but it wasn't like when Drake held her.

"You want to see him tonight," Bree said, reading Jaena's thoughts. "You want him to hold you and comfort you. To love you as only he can."

"This is my last chance to know him in this world before I'm gone," Jaena said. "Our spirits shared each other once, but I want his arms around me, and I know I can't have that ever again."

"Tomorrow he and I, and the others, will go into Draglûne's lair," Bree said, "tonight may be our last chance to be together as well."

"You have not . . . ?"

"No. He is an honorable man," Bree said. "He wants us to be man and wife, and for our task to be over before we give ourselves to each other."

"I will pray for you both to survive," Jaena said.

"Thank you."

Jaena could read Bree's aura. She wanted very much to lay with him as his lover and she had for some time. She envied Bree so much at that moment because even if they didn't make love, they would hold each other. Perhaps more.

"He will not," Bree said. "He has already refused more than once."

"He's strong," Jaena said. "We never lay with each other, not once, back in Cliffton."

"Never?" Bree was shocked. "Then he has never been with a woman?"

"No," Jaena said. "I wish he and I had married before he left. I wish he had never gone away. I regret not having the life that we could have had, and shared what we could have."

"I have many regrets as well," Bree said. "I have done things I am ashamed of."

"Don't be ashamed tonight," Jaena said. "Love him. Give him all that you can. I don't want you to have regrets like I have."

"You won't," Bree said. "Not after tonight."

Jaena understood what she meant, but how could she share such a private moment. She couldn't do it.

"You can," Bree said. "Linger in this part of my mind like I know you are able. I will not let you have control, and this will be the only time I make this offer. You must accept. Your time is short."

"I don't know if I can do this," Jaena said.

"I will tell him to come to me, and that I will not be refused tonight," Bree said. "He will listen to me, and we will all have one night of love before tomorrow. No more regrets."

XC

We shall eat, and drink, and laugh, and sing, for tomorrow we face our greatest enemy. I know that not all, if any, will survive. None but Lorak can say who will fall, but we shall celebrate our friendship tonight, and every dwarf and every Priest of Kheb who has traveled with us will hear his name honored by the others. We shall have no regrets for we have lived boldly and done all in our power to do what was right.

—Bölak Blackhammer, from the Khoram Journal

While Dabarius, Bellor, and Thor worked downstairs, Drake put the dogs in front of the stout door on the second floor of Barius's home. "Sit. Guard."

Temus wagged his tail and Jep groaned before sitting down and giving him the "sad eyes."

Drake gave them some bones to chew on, patted them both on the head, then went inside and bolted the door. Bree had been very clear about what she expected tonight, and he still had not thought of a way to refuse. He didn't want to, but he should, and leaned against the door, facing the room lit by three flickering lamps. A soft glow illuminated a bed of piled blankets and pillows. The sweet scent of lotus blossoms filled the room.

Bree lounged on the bed, wearing nothing except the blue tattoos spiraling up her thigh and decorating her lower back, a sheer sheet covering only one foot. She rose slowly, deliberately, and stepped toward him, his dark eyes locked on her alluring green ones, outlined with a thin layer of kohl. She kissed him on the mouth and their lips pressed hungrily together. He loved the way she kissed him and knew that if this continued they couldn't stop like they had so many times before.

Bree touched his waist and unclasped his belt, letting it fall heavily. She put his strong hands on her hips and pressed against him.

He fought the primal urge to be with her and shook his head, then rested his forehead against hers. "*Tonight . . .*" he said, searching for the words.

"This is all we have left," she whispered, "*Tonight.*"

He stood in silence, thinking of the promise he had made to Bree in Shahan that they would not lay together unless they were married. But how could he stop himself or deny her this moment that she—and he—wanted so much? For the first time in forever, Drake could think of nothing but being with her. All thoughts of Draglûne, of the God King, his friends, were gone. There was only the burning desire to hold Bree, and run his hands over her skin.

Jaena drifted in the dreamy place inside Bree'alla's mind where both their consciousnesses mingled together. She could feel what Bree felt, and knew her frightened thoughts about facing Draglûne, and her carnal needs for the handsome foreigner from the Thornclaw who had saved her life and her soul so many times. Without him, she would have died in the desert, and he loved her like no man ever had before. He believed in her, trusted her, and he did not take. He gave everything he could. This was a man above all the others she had ever met. He forgave her weaknesses and her mistakes, and her past. He loved her for who she was, and did not judge her for her failures. He would die for her, and she would never—could never—let that happen. He deserved to live and before she passed from this life, she would show him how much she loved him. The desperation Bree and Jaena both felt intensified because tomorrow both of them were probably going to die.

Not Drake.

No, he must live, but Bree was going to fall in battle defending the man she loved. She would cut down their enemies, and if her sword broke she would scratch out their eyes and shield him with her body until the last drop of blood flowed from her wounds. Then she would linger as a spirit and guard him however she could manage. Not even death would keep her away from him.

Bree's fear of failing was overwhelming, and Jaena could feel some of the confidence that Bree'alla relied upon as a warrior slipping away. Was some of this fatalism because of Jaena's own way of thinking? Tomorrow, Jaena truly was going to perish. She would be executed in front of tens of thousands of people. Made an example of for what she had done to teach those who prayed to the Goddess a lesson. The humans could pray to Amaryllis, but no Priestesses were allowed to practice their magic with them. Death was the penalty all Amaryllian Priestesses would face if captured by the Drobin, but why did Bree feel so certain she was going to die after all that they had survived so far?

Jaena's dreaming body shuddered as she lay on her bed in the tower cell of the Marshal's Keep. She knew the truth of it and never should have made contact with Bree'alla tonight. Jaena's belief about her immediate future had influenced Bree'alla's belief about hers. Guilt for what she was doing to Bree made Jaena want to pull away, and retreat to her prison where she could cry all night for the decades of life she had lost with Drake. She would never marry him, never lay with him, never bear his children, or grow old with him in the most beautiful village on all of the plateaus. Their love would endure in the next world, but in this one, they would have had only the briefest moment together. Never could she express her most sincere desires and share herself with him as his wife and soul mate.

Regret and anguish gnawed at her for all that she was losing, and she could not face being alone, even if it was for only one more night. She needed him to hold her, and comfort her now, for on the morrow she would face the axe.

Jaena lost herself in Bree's senses, feeling Drake's body and his arms around her, the delicious smell of his skin. This was how it should be, and this would be the last time she would ever be connected to him in this world. With that thought she let go of all her doubts and became one with Bree'alla, filling the space where fear and doubt plagued the Mephitian swordswoman. They shared one body and one mind, united in their love and their desire.

Jaena's lips trembled with excitement and she gasped, mirroring Bree'alla's reactions. She wanted him so much and nothing would keep her from him now.

Drake blinked, then looked again into Bree's eyes. For an instant he thought her eyes became sapphire blue like Jaena's, and her face changed. The set of her mouth, the way she looked at him reminded him of Shahan when Jaena had taken control of Bree and saved them. It seemed like a dream.

Then it was Bree again, her smoldering green eyes staring at him.

"Are you all right?" Drake asked.

Bree nodded, then whispered. "She loves you, and she knows you don't want to hurt her."

He jerked back, his hands on her shoulders thinking of Jaena. "What?"

"She's been connected to me ever since Shahan, since before that, but she's with us tonight. Her spirit."

Drake glanced around the room, fear, hope, and confusion bundling together. "Where is she?"

531

"Here," Bree said, pointing to her head. "In my mind," she touched the place between her breasts, "in my heart."

Drake stepped back. "She knows what we're doing?"

Bree nodded. "She knows, and she thinks that she is never going to see you again." Her eyes closed as if Bree was deep in thought. "This is the last time she will ever be close to you. She wants this. I've allowed her to be here. Only tonight. Never again."

Awkwardness and shame made him want to stop and leave, find another room to sleep in. "No, we can't. This isn't how it should be."

"I love you," Bree said, clinging to him, "and so does Jaena. That is never going to change. How else could it ever be?"

He stood there, his love for them both so intense that he knew he couldn't bear losing either of them.

"Love me," she said, and Drake heard both of their voices.

"I do," he said, and pulled her against him, kissing her hard and running his hands over her skin. She helped him pull off his clothes and they admired each other, eyes wandering. Then he picked her up, Bree's strong legs wrapping around his hips as he carried her to the bed and gently lay her down. She tried to pull him on top of her, but he resisted and gazed down, wanting to burn in his memory her beauty in this perfect moment.

Her fingertips explored a scar on his chest and he brushed the red line *Wingblade's* tip had left on her side. Wantonly, they lost themselves in a passionate embrace, his chest on hers, kissing until their bodies came together at last. Nothing mattered except for the feeling of utter bliss. They made love holding each other tightly as if they could be torn apart at any moment.

He felt their three spirits swirling together like three leaves in an autumn wind that burst into flame when they blew into a raging fire. Months of pent up desire and frustration fueled their lovemaking as the passion climbed again and again to the highest mountain, then stopped for delicious moments when they stared at each other, hands entwined, only to start again as Drake's desire kept flaring back to life.

They didn't want it to end, and Jaena's sad tears flowed from Bree's eyes, though Drake kissed them away. Long after midnight, they lay utterly spent, and fell into a perfect, blissful sleep, wrapped in each other's warm embrace, their bodies and spirits forever connected by the love they shared.

XCI

The day has come. Soon we will know if our preparation and dedication will give us the victory we have prayed for these past decades. I only wish Bellor were here with us today. It seems sad that the greatest living *Dracken Viergur* won't be with us when we face the beast.

—Bölak Blackhammer, from the Khoram Journal

Drake's bleary eyes popped open at the loud sound. He and Bree leaped from their bed reaching for their weapons as someone pounded on the door to the room where they had been sleeping. Gurion's excited voice made a lengthy announcement. Drake wondered what the hour was since it was still dark outside. "What did he say?" he asked Bree, who stood beside the bed holding her sword and wearing nothing.

"The first battle of Lesh'heb is over." Bree put the sword down and kissed him. "We've won."

"I know," he said smiling, then pulled her into the bed with him, enjoying the feel of her lithe body atop his.

She grinned and let her hair fall into his face. "Don't you want to know what else he said?"

"No," he drew her closer, ready for more.

Bree shook her head. "Master Barius has given us an order. We must be ready to leave as soon as we are able, and there is food downstairs waiting. The gatehouse of Lesh'heb is captured, as is the town. They attack the library school next, and we cannot be delayed. Sunrise is too late. *Get dressed.*"

They were ready to leave shortly and ate as much warm and oily bread covered in bean paste as they could and washed it down with cool water before following Barius, Dabarius, Bellor and Thor out the door. The dogs came along last licking their lips after their own big breakfast.

As they marched away, Drake decided he would remember the moment before they left the house forever. He tried to fix it into his mind, recalling every detail. Bree had braided her dark red hair and tied it off her neck. She was so efficient and meticulous. No enemy would find her hair a convenient dangling handhold to grab. She also picked over the table of weapons and carried extra knives supplied by Barius, attaching a matched pair to her belt. He had never seen her wear armor before, but she chose a small bronze shield and strapped it to her left forearm, and put a metal wrist guard on her right. She buckled *Wingblade* around her waist at the very last, and smiled at him so warmly he was almost embarrassed that the others would see. They didn't, and even in the pre-dawn light Bree'alla had an aura of joy about her. He felt the same way.

Bellor had ordered Bree to keep him safe no matter what, and Drake had to accept it. Her prowess as a warrior, and her toughness would keep him alive, and he vowed that he would protect her as well, no matter what happened. He just wished she had become a *Dracken Viergur* and gained a rune mark, like he and the others had branded onto their souls. Without it, she was vulnerable to Draglûne's ability to read minds, but Bellor was counting on that and had a devious plan to defeat the wyrm.

The companions gathered behind Barius in a grove of trees less than a stone's throw south of Lesh'heb village and waited. Drake cocked his upper crossbow as quietly as he could with the ticking krannekin and put in a bolt as two men armed with maces, shields, and javelins jogged from a house and entered the trees with them. They reported to Barius, calling him "General Ben'ahmi."

Dabarius and Bree handled the translation, whispering to the companions as the men spoke. The situation was as it had been an hour before when Barius led the attack. The gatehouse and wall were still secure and all of the warrior Priests left to guard the village were dead.

535

Barius ordered the two men to keep the gates barred for now and prepare to demolish the first section of the elevated and covered bridge-road as they had planned, leaving only one central arch beam connecting the village of Lesh'heb to the God King's Road. Fifteen men were to remain in the village on the wall, and the other sixty-five warriors would proceed to the Library School, a half-mile further south as soon as they were all assembled.

Both men bowed and went back into the village. A moment later a man burst from a doorway and sprinted south along the gravel road passing right by them. Barius ran out onto the road, and yelled for him to stop, or at least that's what Drake thought he heard as he followed Dabarius and his father.

"Should I shoot him?" Drake asked, his crossbow raised as he took aim. The man was almost forty yards away now.

"No," Barius said in Mephitian, holding up his hand.

"We can't let anyone warn the Priests at the school," Bellor said. "Surprise is all we have."

Dabarius and his father spoke tersely to each as the distance grew much greater, and Drake almost lost sight of him. Moonlight illuminated his linen kilt and Drake's eyes focused on his back. He didn't turn and ran in a perfectly straight line away from them.

"He won't make it," Dabarius finally said, trying to calm Bellor and Thor. "There are men in the canyon down there."

"He might get past them," Thor said.

"Shoot him, Drake," Bellor ordered.

The sprinting man was almost a hundred yards away and Drake had already switched out the heavy bolt for a lighter one with better fletchings. He aimed high, the bolt would drop significantly over that distance. He thought about where he wanted to hit the man and squeezed the trigger. The pop and recoil of the bolt release echoed a little in the canyon, and his friends held their breath watching the arc of his shot.

536

The fleeing man suddenly fell and rolled, a shaft protruding from the middle of his back. Relief and some nausea washed over Drake, as he hoped this wasn't a mistake, and the man innocent, perhaps one of Barius's messengers? The dying man crawled a few feet before six men came out of the shadowy trees on either side of the road. One of them clubbed the now motionless man in the head, and the others dragged the body into the palm trees. Relief overcame the sickness. It was an enemy, and that was the longest shot he'd ever made against a moving target.

Barius pushed Drake's crossbow down angrily, stopping him from reloading. Then Barius glanced at his men as they removed the body from the road. "I am the commander here," Barius said through his son, who translated the same harsh tone. "You will do as I say."

"Forgive me," Bellor said, stepping forward. "I told him to shoot."

Drake did not back down in the face of the tall and angry general. Today was not the day.

"He never would have gotten through my men," Barius explained, then said more words, but Dabarius didn't translate.

Father and son exchanged heated words of their own.

"What are they saying?" Bellor asked.

"Barius says he can't trust us," Bree said. "He doesn't want us with him if we won't follow his orders."

"What'll he do, then?" Drake asked.

"We'll find out when they're done arguing," Bree said, as Barius poked son in the chest with pointed finger.

XCII

We shall be Priests of Kheb, disguised as our allies. We shall enter at night to perform rituals in a funeral chapel for the dead. The Eternal God King Ra'menek will not know who we are until we have killed his ally. Then we shall escape this place.

—Bölak Blackhammer, from the Khoram Journal

Dabarius blamed Bellor for getting them banished to the quarry master's house while the battle for the library school raged, Barius leading the attack. Gurion was glad to see them, and seemed quite frightened to have been left behind.

Drake left the dogs guarding the front door, and they accompanied Gurion to the third floor where they watched through small windows as groups of men in Barius's little army crept south along the road as the first hints of sunrise filled the eastern horizon. None of the warriors on the road spoke and their discipline impressed Drake. All of the men seemed very lightly armed and carried hunting bows, spears, clubs, and only a handful bore shields or wore leather helms. The sound was nothing like when the Storm and Solar Priests left Lesh'heb the day before.

When the last group of men disappeared in the south where the canyon curved, Drake had counted nearly seventy. "How many will they face in the school?" he asked Dabarius.

"A handful who will fight," the wizard said. "The rest are old men and young boys."

"Those old men trained the assassins and warriors," Bellor said. "Don't discount them."

"We should be fighting alongside the brave villagers," Thor said.

"No," Bellor said, "we follow the General's order this time."

Dabarius let out a sigh.

"Anything can happen in close quarter fighting," Bellor said. "None of us needs risk a wound or worse this early in the day."

The companions paced and waited until less than an hour later when a runner arrived to escort them to the library school.

"It's time," the white-bearded dwarf said as the sun streamed in the windows. He seemed so old in the light.

"I wish we hadn't missed the battle," Thor said.

"These people suffered under those Priests," Bree said. "This was their moment. Let them have it."

Gurion begged to come along when they left the house, and the boy promised to follow no matter what. Bellor did not stop him, and in the end they all marched south quickly along the road. They each carried an urn of the blessed water enchanted with the power of Amar'isis in a padded basket inside a small pack.

They walked at the edge of the roadside where the trees and lush bushes grew right up against the slate gray walls of the jagged canyon, which curved and climbed to over three hundred feet in places. Pinnacles of rock and some areas much lower in elevation, perhaps fifty feet or less of scalloped impassable curtains went off into the distance for what seemed to be miles. The very tips of bushy green trees poked out here or there, and Drake imagined there were thousands of narrow slot canyons, or grykes as the dwarves had called them.

Drake kept thinking that Draglûne would fly low and appear suddenly over them. He would burn them to death as Bellor had not warded them with fire protection magic yet. Or perhaps he would attack the village first. A counter attack was sure to come, but when? He wiped the sweat off his brow and asked Dabarius, "What's going to happen to the people of Lesh'heb?"

"None will stay," Dabarius said. "The women and children are leaving this morning. My father said they're going somewhere safe, but he didn't say where. I don't think he wants us to know."

"He is a prudent man," Bellor said. "Your father told me the Brother Gods have punished the people of Lesh'heb before. Forty years ago. So we must not fail."

Drake kept his attention on the sky, and with the height of the canyons he wouldn't see the dragon until it was right on them anyway, but he had two wyrm-kin-slaying bolts loaded in case Draglûne attacked. At this range, even if his bolts hit home, it wouldn't keep the dragon from savaging them. His size and momentum would crush them, even if he fell to earth with a pierced heart.

Drake shook his head, and made his mind go elsewhere. He pictured Bree, her eyes wavering between green and blue as they lay together in the soft light on the bed. Jaena had always said that love shined a light that conquered any darkness, and he guessed that she was right. He caught Bree's eye and nodded to her.

Bree nodded grimly to him, and he knew she was ready for whatever happened. No evil, not even the gods, could take back what had already happened, and he would fight for last night to be a beginning, not an end.

Moments later they rounded a bend and faced the twenty-foot tall Wall of Jackals. Huge stone blocks of gray stone halted any advance on foot through the now forty-paces-wide canyon, and he imagined it also served as dam to block any flooding. Sharp-nosed dog statues leered from all along the length of the wall and the only way through was a reinforced bronze gate with sun discs all over it. Five men carrying spears and shields guarded the way, but their escort led the companions through without a problem. The men bowed low to Thor and Bellor, and then backed away from Jep and Temus, though both of the bullmastiffs seemed oblivious to their menacing presence.

On the other side, a promenade of pillars and arches followed a smooth road south deeper into the canyon. Stone benches lined the way where spectators could watch a funeral procession advance toward the Tunnel of Tombs, which had to be nearby.

Oved met them and directed them toward the right and the western side of the canyon, following a well-defined road lined with rectangular blocks of stone that rose flat on each side, but their tips had been carved to look like mountain peaks. Mephitian picture symbols, etched in the stone and painted dark black covered the surfaces. An impressive doorway waited at the end of the short road. The cliff side had been carved into an elaborate façade over a hundred feet tall. Two levels of pillars, awnings, rooftops, statues of dragons—which seemed newer than everything else—adorned the rock wall. The giant statue of a man holding a glowing sun in his hand stood over the doorway. The sun sphere appeared to be the only object that was not stone, and shone brightly, some magic inside it the apparent source of the glow.

"This used to be the entrance to the tomb of the Eternal God King Ra'menek's father," Gurion said. "Now it is the entrance to the school."

A lookout watched the sky as a handful of wounded men were being treated on the steps leading up to the tall rectangular doorway that led to blackness. Three bodies lay covered by a single blanket at the top of the stairs. A distressed man with a graying beard stood guard over them. He eyed the bodies of seven men piled haphazardly nearby. Flies swarmed in their wounds, mostly grisly gashes on their heads and chests.

Barius walked slowly out of the doorway, his lip swollen and his left arm bruised and scraped. He regarded them with a firm resolve, and nodded at his son, motioning for him to stand beside him.

"The library and archives, the school, the living quarters, and all of the temples are ours," Barius said, and Dabarius translated. "Only Three dead, more wounded. We had people on the inside who opened the gates and let us in, but we've failed to find the God King's son, Ahken'mose. We're still searching for him, as he may be hiding somewhere within. There is one chamber we have not breached where a few Shenahrians have barricaded themselves. We'll get in eventually, and likely find him there, but we have all the other children, safe in their dormitories, and the teachers locked away."

"What of the Vessel of Night, the dragon's blood?" Bellor asked.

"I shall take you to it in a few moments," Barius said. He conferred with his captains, giving orders and listening to their reports. A large group of at least three-dozen teenage girls and some adult women filtered out of the front entrance and Drake watched tearful reunions between them and some of Barius's warriors.

"Who are they?" Drake asked.

Bree asked Oved, who replied with obvious distaste.

"He says they are servants of the Priests," Bree said. "Some are daughters of the people of Lesh'heb, and others are slaves."

Dabarius's father organized squads of men to escort the women and girls back to Lesh'heb, and he sent most of his warriors with them to help with the evacuation. Then Barius led the companions past the tall metal gates and into the library school. A dozen heavily armed men with shields and helmets formed their bodyguard, with two in the front and back, and four on their flanks. Oved was with them, and his helmet seemed too small for his head, and his shield too large.

"The fighting is not finished here," Drake whispered to Bree.

"If I were holding a place such as this," she said, "I would have a safe hiding place and a plan to take my attackers one by one from the shadows."

A great hallway led deeper and many doorways went off into passages lit by ever-glowing torches that cast off a pale yellow light. There must have been hundreds or thousands of other rooms inside, but Barius kept them in the main passage.

After they passed a circular chamber with a domed ceiling painted to look like storm clouds with lightning behind them—and lit by some magic that would dim and brighten quickly—simulating lightning, they followed a smaller tunnel and exited into bright sunlight again, which hurt Drake's eyes.

Barius led them across the center of what appeared to a be an athletic practice ground with fighting circles, archery ranges, running tracks, outdoor classrooms, some covered with awnings, and an amphitheater cut into the rock that could hold at least five hundred and faced the east.

They approached the entrance of what had to be temple of Shenahr. The carved façade was covered with clouds, lightning, and dragons. Drake noticed that a pair of wingataurs carved in bas-relief flanked the dragon statue above the lintel.

Four men guarded the doorway and opened it as Barius approached. They bowed respectfully to him and gawked as he led the companions inside. The dark hall beyond was filled with several dozen pillars painted to look like what Drake thought were sentinel trees, though he had not seen a single tree of that type since they left the Thornclaw months ago. It reminded him of the temple of Amar'isis in Isyrin. At the far side of the room a light filtering out of a room beckoned them onward.

The warriors guarding them closed ranks around "General Ben'ahmi" as they entered the hall. All of were on their highest level of alertness now, and Drake did not like all of the shadowy places around them. Bree drew her sword.

"Is this place not safe?" Bellor asked, raising his axe.

"Only Priests of Shenahr were permitted to enter here," Barius said. "My men fear a curse from the Storm God, and they fear that one of the Shenahrians may be hiding here. We are not certain who stayed and who left. Not everyone is accounted for yet."

Bree kept her sword ready.

They crossed the hall of pillars and entered the inner sanctum, a small room with murals decorating the walls and magical lights glowing from the ceiling. An iron statue of a dragon sat on a pedestal. It seemed so small to Drake, but very lifelike.

"We should tear it down and smash it to bits," Thor said.

"I would help you," Dabarius said, "but I fear this is not the time."

"We will study it first," Bellor said, approaching it.

"The relics are back here," Barius said, motioning to a doorway in the rear of the room. "The Vessel of Night is there."

A bright light flashed, and a boom thundered through the chamber as the two guards ahead of Barius fell writhing to the ground. The smell of burned meat filled the room as Barius's remaining bodyguards raised their shields around him.

A raspy voice echoed from the hallway where the magic had come from.

"It's Elder Priest Tzadok," Barius said. "He will not let us have any of the relics of Shenahr."

"We shall see about that," Thor said, setting down his pack and pushing one of the bodyguards out of the way and taking a step toward the hallway. The dwarf stopped when an old man, at least sixty or more, in a white kilt and wearing an elaborate necklace of lapis lazuli, golden bracers and greaves appeared under the archway. He also wore a serpent crown that ringed his bald head. Tzadok lifted his hands and touched his thumbs together, aiming at Thor.

Drake pulled both triggers on his crossbow and the bolts streaked over Thor's head and right toward the Shenahrian. Impossibly, Tzadok warded off both of the missiles like he was brushing away flies.

Everyone paused, glaring at each other, as Drake tried to recover from the shock of seeing his bolts turned aside.

"You don't have to die, Tzadok," Barius said, stepping between Thor and Tzadok. "Surrender and I shall spare you."

Bree'alla translated for the companions, keeping herself in front of Drake who began reloading, as Dabarius removed his pack and whispered a spell, using his father's bodyguards to screen his actions.

"Ben'ahmi, you traitorous bastard," Tzadok said. "I will not believe anything you say now. I knew you were not what you seemed, always so friendly to the slaves and teaching them battle touch on the pretense of giving our students better sport. I should have known you were just a greedy commoner. Now you want the treasure of our god."

"He was never my god," Barius said, stepping forward again. "All of the treasure will be returned to the tombs when this is over."

"Over? You think you can sweep aside the Brother Gods like you've swept aside the few guardians here? There is no rebellion in the north!"

"There will be," Barius said.

"And both of the Brother Gods will be dead before sunset," Dabarius said, stepping next to his father.

"Who is this fool?" Tzadok asked.

"I am his son," Dabarius said, as he held his father back.

"You are his dead son," Tzadok said, then raised his hands sending a bolt of white-hot electricity arcing forward. It struck Dabarius in the chest, the flash of light, momentarily blinding Drake.

When he could see again, Dabarius and the old man fought hand-to-hand under the archway. Tzadok blocked and turned aside Dabarius's blows. Obviously the Shenahrian was a master of *Teha Khet*, but the taller and much stronger young man overpowered Tzadok and threw him against the wall, locking his arms behind his back.

Barius joined the fray and pinned Tzadok with his son's help, pushing the old man's face against the stone. Tzadok struggled for a moment, then listened as Barius whispered in his ear. The Shenahrian smiled and nodded, saying something back.

Unceremoniously, Barius ripped off the necklace and crown, then forced the old man to the ground where he inserted a slender knife into the base of his skull, burying it to the hilt. He left the blade there, and waved for the companions to follow him down the hallway and through the open door.

"Are you all right?" Bellor asked Dabarius.

"The Shield of Amar'isis defended me," the wizard said. "Another spell from the Sacred Scrolls."

"We may all need her shield before the end of today," Bellor said.

"And you shall have it," Dabarius promised.

The relics and treasures of the Storm God filled many rooms, though they found the Vessel of Night and the key to the Tunnel of Tombs displayed prominently in the front chamber, each enclosed in their own alcove and lit by a soft golden light.

The dragon's blood was in a golden urn in the shape of a dragon's head, though it was only the size of a human skull. Bellor shook it gently, then unscrewed the lid and sniffed inside. He wrinkled his nose and nodded. Then put the blade of his axe over it. *Wyrmslayer* reacted instantly and glowed with a crimson light. A wild look crossed the old Priest's face, the hand that held his axe tightening until the knuckles cracked. The hackles rose on Jep and Temus' necks, and they backed away from Bellor, growling, their heads low.

Bellor grit his teeth and backed away, his composure returning. "It is dragon's blood," he said. "Some magic has kept it as a liquid. We must have at least a full cup of it here. Enough to enchant every bolt that we have and more to spare. Dabarius, tell your father that this alone was worth the noble sacrifice of his men."

Thor clapped Bellor on the shoulder. "The anger of the father still rages, doesn't it? If you listen hard, you can still hear Mograwn's death roar."

"Let us . . . not speak of that, Thor," the old War Priest said. "I am not as strong as I once was, but Wyrmslayer is as vicious as ever."

Drake felt the pressure of what he had to do when he faced the Dragon King. He could not miss. Tzadok's casual disregard of his bolts had unnerved him. He had never dreamed of such a thing. It hardly seemed possible. The speed of his missiles, especially at a scant four paces, should never have allowed such a feat. *It must be some magic of Shenahr combined with his Teha Khet skill,* he told himself. If the Elder Priest had it, what of the Dragon of Darkness and Ra'menek? Drake spun the krannekin back and loaded two more cruelly-tipped bolts. He could only shoot. What happened next was in the hands of fate.

The key was a bronze staff, six feet long, topped with a sun sphere, and adorned with many Mephitian symbols. When the sun was twisted a half-dozen metal fins extended from the base of the staff in four directions, then slipped back inside the shaft when the head was twisted the other way. Dabarius carried it and Drake could tell it weighed a lot.

Thor and Bellor glanced at some of the other treasures of gold, alabaster, and jewels. They examined the looted artifacts of dead Mephitian royals and nobles with obvious indifference, faulting the human artisans for their inept craftsmanship. Drake saw only fabulous beauty and assumed that the amount of wealth contained in the treasury would be enough for every person in Lesh'heb to live like a king or queen for the rest of their lives, though Barius said no one would take the looted treasure.

"What good are gold and gems to the dead?" Drake asked Bree.

"It is . . . complicated," she said. "What belongs to the God Kings and their ilk, belongs to them forever. If their bodies have fallen to dust, they still own all they held. Things that sit in these tombs are not for anyone to remove. This wealth is not meant to be passed on or inherited. I have never managed a way to truly make a Nexan or a Drobin understand it."

Drake took a breath, about to say that he wasn't Nexan, but he let it pass. Just as he couldn't understand the purpose of letting wealth linger in a dark tomb, Bree couldn't really grasp the difference between being an Amaryllian, a rebel, and living under the iron heel of the Drobin Empire.

"Look at this!" Thor said, lifting a black metal steel spear point from a small dais on a shelf. The tip was designed for penetrating deep and looked to be very sharp. The wooden shaft was missing and the spear point did not look like it belonged at all beside the wondrous treasures.

"A Drobin spear tip," Bellor said, "and it's got blood on it."

Bellor put *Wyrmslayer* over it and the axe glowed faintly.

"This is from one of my uncle's hunters," Thor said reverently.

"They carried spears?" Drake asked. He had it in his mind that they carried crossbows and weapons similar to Bellor and Thor, but he did remember spears being mentioned in the lessons.

"At least seven of them had spears at one time or another," Bellor said, "and I know that several of them carried a spear point."

"It's a lot easier to find a shaft before the battle than lug a twelve-foot spear across a desert," Thor said as he wrapped the tip in a cloth and put it inside his pack with the urn of blessed water.

"Dabarius," Bellor said, "please have your father take us to the temple of Kheb. We have work to do."

Thor broke down the door into the long shuttered temple of the Mephitian Earth Father. No one could find the key and they couldn't waste any more time. The small door was in the center of the large hallway near the main entrance to the school and was not as decorated as it once had been. Sloppy plaster and bricks had walled off carvings outside the holy place and gray paint made it all blend in.

"This was done forty years ago," Barius told them, "after the Khebian Priesthood was thrown out of Lesh'heb."

Thor and Bellor marched right into the dusty temple, past the huge pillars, which grew up in the shape of mountains to the ceiling. They found an altar in a small inner sanctum and after Thor made certain the room was safe they went about their work. Drake laid out all of his crossbow bolts and the dwarves added theirs as well. Between them they had over twenty, and Drake berated himself for the two that broke when Tzadok knocked them aside. Both of the shafts had broken against the wall. At least he had the tips, which he asked Bellor to enchant.

The Drobin Priests prayed near the toppled stone statue of Kheb that had been knocked from its dais. Great Kheb not surprisingly, was a short and squat, wide-shouldered, bald, and bearded man, who looked very much like a dwarf.

"Sons of Kheb indeed," Drake said as he examined the broken statue. The more he explored the world, the more he thought that there were only a few gods, but with many faces.

Bellor dipped each bolt into the urn filled with Draglûne's blood and then prayed over them with Thor. *Wyrmslayer* was put well away from them to allow Bellor to concentrate properly. It took the better part of an hour, and when they were almost done, Drake put his and Ethan's thorn bolt in front of them. They dutifully prayed over them and the job was done, they had to wait until the blood was dry and considered taking them outside into the sun.

Thor's grin said it all. Each of the bolts would be lethal to Draglûne if shot in a vital area, as the blood had been turned into a toxic poison enhanced by magic. Each one would be lethal to Draglûne specifically, though powerful against any true dragon. To wingataurs and other wyrm-kin, the bolts would be deadly, as any wyrm spawn would be greatly affected by the power of the magic combined with pure dragon blood, and Bellor was certain that's what they had.

They had more than enough and both of the dwarves poured the blood into small copper vials they carried with them. Bellor whispered to Drake as they were leaving. "If we fall, don't bury the vials with us. Keep them. They're too valuable to waste in a grave."

Barius accepted the vessel with the small remainder of the dragon blood and promised to keep it somewhere safe. They marched toward the entrance to the school and once outside found the guards in a panic as they swarmed around a lone messenger shouting questions at him.

Bree and Dabarius looked at each other with fear in their eyes as Barius shouted for the men to be silent. The messenger came forward and bowed to him, then rattled off what sounded like a dire warning.

"What is it?" Drake asked, his pulse pounding in his ears.

Dabarius translated the ominous warning. "The Storm and Solar Priests have returned. They are outside Lesh'heb attacking the gate. The bridge is still intact and there are too many to hold off for long. Most of the women and children are fleeing the village with all the food and seed they can carry and are taking the secret way through the razor rocks."

"Why did the Priests come back?" Drake asked. "How did they know what was happening here?"

"The messenger doesn't know," Dabarius said. "The Priests don't care that we have hostages either. They will not negotiate."

"The Crystal Eye," Bellor said. "Draglûne must have seen what's happening."

"Or Ra'menek," Dabarius said.

Barius sent most of the men running back to the town and ordered Gurion to carry a message to the few guards watching the children inside the school, as well as the men besieging the last few Shenahrians. Barius whispered parting words to his son, then bowed to the companions. "We will hold them as long as we can at the wall of Lesh'heb, if it hasn't fallen already when I get there. Then we will fall back to the Jackal Gate here. My friends, in case your task inside the tombs takes very long, you must shut the gates so the Storm Priests can't come in behind you. Finish this as quickly as you can and then I shall meet you outside the tombs. Even if I am not there, someone will be waiting to guide you away from this canyon."

Bellor tried to thank him, but Barius hugged his son, then ran after his men. He had the look of a man going to his doom.

Drake wanted to run along with him, fight the enemy at the wall, but instead he turned south and started marching. Jep and Temus followed on his heels. Bree'alla came next with Dabarius. Bellor and Thor caught up next, unflinching determination on their faces.

No one said anything as they fell in step with Drake.

XCIII

What dark magic has this long dead king used to cling to life? What has it done to his mind that he must model and shape the Mephitian people to such a small degree? He makes them into soulless creatures who care nothing for life? Their people starve as their Priests constantly bring offerings of food to the dead. Why do they not see that this undead king is destroying them? His Solar Priests are corrupt and cater to his whims and the Storm Priests have no moral restraint. When Draglûne is gone we shall find a way to defeat this Ra'menek and stop his reign of tyranny.

—Bölak Blackhammer, from the Khoram Journal

The Eternal God King Ra'menek sat on his limestone throne atop the highest pinnacle of rock above his impenetrable fortress. His Crystal Eye sat beside him locked in a bronze tripod, mist swirling inside the perfect sphere. It was never far from his side, as it was his greatest treasure, and needed be protected at all times. His pet, Draglûne, would try to take it if he left it un-warded. The wyrm was so much like a hungry dog, such a slave to his base impulses and he could never really be trusted.

At least the day was a beautiful one, and the sun shone through a clear blue sky with only a few clouds in the east. The Void mist was already retreating from the labyrinth of canyons and spiny ridges sprawling around him. He hated days when the mist covered his fortress or when clouds blocked the sun, delaying his daily renewal.

Ra'menek opened and closed his hands, letting the sunlight revitalize him after the long dark night. The gray pallor was almost gone now as the sun healed him. He enjoyed the bright rays striking him in the face, and his heart suddenly beat stronger, and faster, after lying dormant all night long. He had slept in his black and silent tomb for almost five hours last night, then spent the rest of the dark hours in the archives, reading the clay tablets from the three-hundred-and-forty-fifth through forty-sixth years of his reign. Reading them kept his mind off the accelerated rotting process his body underwent every night, and he loved to read his own thoughts, even the old ones from when he was not very enlightened. Every time it was like discovering something new and important.

But lo, the tablets had been so entertaining last night. He had been very eloquent then, though the Mephitian language was cumbersome and not suited to beauty or the expression of such complex thoughts as he had. He had revised it as much as he could in the years since, but he knew the common folk did not follow the new rules he created and arbitrarily invented their own. They spoke as they needed, and did not care how they mangled the ancient tongue or befuddled him with their strange ways of speaking when he watched them in his Crystal Eye.

At least the Priests in his school did as they were told and spoke as he intended. They enforced his rules of grammar and pronunciation, but his evolved language was not for common speech, and was more suited for the discourses of learned men, or grand poetry. Today he would be sure to inscribe all of his thoughts, as unlike most days, noteworthy events were transpiring in the very heart of his kingdom.

His view of Lesh'heb was limited, but he could see the dam he had engineered over five-hundred years before, and the bridge connecting it to his road. Loyal Storm and Solar Priests had just arrived and he watched them inside his Crystal Eye throwing themselves against the gate, fighting for him with little concern for their lives. He had relayed the message to Elder Priest Ev'karum as soon as he realized that his enemies were taking over Lesh'heb and attacking the school. How long had it been since the last time they had dared to do this? Fifty years? No less. Forty. He would consult the archives as soon as he was rejuvenated. He hated that he could not remember exactly how long ago it was. His mind was still sharp after all these centuries, sharper than when he had been a mortal man, but the years built up so fast he had trouble differentiating them now. So many were the same and time was irrelevant when you had eternity.

He watched the fight at the gatehouse in Lesh'heb. A javelin pierced the neck of one of his loyal Storm Priest warriors, a brute of a man who had shown promise in the fighting circle. The big man had nearly made it to the top of the gatehouse in Lesh'heb, though he would have been too large to climb through the window. Perhaps he was a fool. His body fell and spasmed on the bridge below. For mortals, it was such a thin veil between life and death. They perished in a moment. Untidy, impermanent things. They were fortunate that their god took such an interest in their actions, that he expended great energy and consideration on their behalf. Ra'menek had felt this, these dramatic tidings, like whispers on the wind.

Dramatic things always happened when the world was about to change. He'd seen it many times. Even dead men twitched after their death, something with their nerves, which he had studied extensively on fresh human cadavers and rarely on live subjects. He never understood why the dead didn't have the sense to be still. No matter.

Ra'menek knew his loyal Priests would get back into the village soon. The rebels would be killed as he had ordered, and the sources of this disturbance thoroughly investigated then executed most painfully. His library school was quiet now, at least, which he saw in his Crystal Eye. The children were unharmed and he wondered if the men guarding them would have the courage to kill them all before the Shenahrian Priests returned to free them. Doubtful. He cared little for the fifty children cowering in their beds, but this was not the time for any of his most educated subjects to be slain. Part of a generation would be ruined and could set back his plans to some degree, though he was certain it wouldn't be much. He would run a calculation later when he had more time to devote to the arithmetic. For one such as himself, failure was not the concern, only the length of the endeavor.

He did worry that when the world changed he would not have enough appropriately trained subjects to administer over his new realm. He had culled out as many of the deficient candidates as he could, and it was likely that at least a quarter of the child hostages would be found lacking and be eliminated. Still, he would much rather expunge them himself than have the rebels kill them all. They would likely kill the students with no rationale, and that would yield unpredictable results. No, it was no good. If students were to be killed, only his own skilled hand could be trusted with the task.

It was of little consequence, however. Their parents would undoubtedly breed again to replace the losses to their line. That's what he would have done. It would simply take a few more years, Ra'menek told himself. They were far from irreplaceable as the children of the noble families had a much lower level of required performance. If he judged them as he judged his own line's strengths, he would have to eliminate at least three out of four. He had done just that with the offspring of the detestable Mortal King Ahken'ra. His first three sons were so petulant and disrespectful that they had to be killed. They could not follow simple commands and did not understand the gifts Ra'menek was bestowing upon them or appreciate the hours of instruction he provided.

It was better that they were gone and their youngest brother served as his chosen heir to the Solar Throne in Mephitep. Their father could wear the crown for a little longer, perhaps three years at most. Ahken'mose would be a much better ruler and was so precise in his thinking. Where was the boy? He hadn't seen him in days. Was he back in the school now or had Ra'menek left him in the dark archives again?

Ah, there he was. Safe and protected. Of all, Ahken'mose was the most difficult puzzle piece to re-fashion. Preserving the line of the Mortal Kings had become tiresome of late. Few of them had even the minimum levels of aptitude required to perform their function.

Ahken'mose would be a strong leader, however. He might live to see the new kingdom of Mephitia stretch back across the plateaus all the way to Nexus City. The once-ascendant Drobin would soon suffer their first real blow in hundreds of years and the Nexan people would start their climb to the top after being under the Drobin's grasp for so long. He would use them and manipulate them as he had controlled his own people. Religion was an easy device and the Nexans wanted their precious Goddess very desperately. He would give them Amar'isis back, or Amaryllis, as they liked to call her.

Draglûne's servants in the north were doing well with their schemes, no thanks to Draglûne himself. The dolt would have accomplished nothing without Zultaan, his most competent advisor. Whatever fragment that was left of the essence of Shenahr that resided in Draglûne made a negligible contribution. Mograwn had not given it all up for some reason, and Ra'menek had never learned why or what had happened. Drobin had killed the wounded king in the end, he knew.

At least King Priest Zultaan of the Wingataurs had all the guile and intelligence of the best Dragon Kings of old. Draglûne would be lost without him, no doubt. Ra'menek had done what he could to educate the brutish Draglûne, but the dragon's cup could only hold so much. His father, Mograwn, had been much more subtle and a much better tactician. If Draglûne had not staged a coup at the worst possible moment Ra'menek's plans would have been further along by decades. But what was fifty years or so? Nothing really, and it would be two hundred and fifty years, perhaps three hundred, before the humans on the plateaus all spoke Mephitian and worshipped the gods as they were supposed to be worshipped. They would not speak the common Mephitian language of today, but an elevated version that his Solar Priests would teach them. The language would unite his realm.

Ra'menek would care for the Nexan people much better than the Drobin ever had. Priestesses of the Goddess would minister to them and his Priests would educate them, once the Drobin were exiled to their mountain halls in the Dark Spire Mountains. It would take at least five hundred years, or even one thousand for the last of the fast-breeding dwarves to be exterminated, but he had no doubt that the Giergun folk would be up to the task once the Nexans abandoned the Drobin King and refused to fight in his armies any longer.

Draglûne would help, if he were still alive that long, which Ra'menek doubted. Dragon-kind were relics of a distant age. Their time was over and the last of their line was an example of a failed bloodline that had once held sway over the plateaus. He appreciated their contributions to his own family line in millennia past, but all things ended, except for his blessed existence.

Draglûne's offspring were all half-breeds and abominations at best. Ra'menek would rid himself of the dragon when the time was right, but not yet. Among other reasons, he had spent far too much time teaching Draglûne the ancient magic of his draconic forefathers to let him be killed now. He would care for him just as a craftsman cares for a simple tool. Dull as he was, the dragon was a hammer that could be used for certain rough tasks. He was also a convenient object of hatred for the humans, a fiery brand that caught the eye and held the attention of the horde.

Ra'menek could act in the North through Draglûne's Iron Brotherhood, thereby allowing him to remain unknown. If the common folk on the wide plateaus ever knew of him, it would be in rumor, as a shadow within the darkness. He would rule them in secret, his orders moving at such deep levels that none could see how he shaped everything in their lives. He would be their secret emperor, and his reign would never end.

The God King glanced at the Crystal Eye once more, bringing up images from the school and the pitched battle at the gates. He understood that much of this strife had been the work of just a handful of ambitious individuals. Agents of change and tribulation. He had seen these so-called heroes come and go for centuries. They were of interest to him, shining brighter candle flames than the rest. The group of three humans and two dwarves had come a long way, but their journey to kill Draglûne was at an end.

Ra'menek watched them in his Crystal Eye from very high above the canyon. Some Drobin magic that prevented him from scrying on them up close, but he could see them nonetheless. Pity he could not hear what they said to each other. They must be very brave and determined to have come this far. He looked forward to meeting them and learning how they made it so far from home. They must have followed after the Drobin that came here once before to slay Draglûne. History repeated itself again, as it always did.

Would this group try to sneak past him disguised as Priests of Kheb as the last Drobin had done? Those had been a crafty lot indeed and more subtle than this bunch who must have had some hand in the insurrection in Lesh'heb. If not for that, he may not have known what was happening until they entered his fortress.

These few shortsighted individuals who approached his home would not be allowed to change his plans. It bemused him that they thought they could. He was Ra'menek, the Eternal God King. What were heroes to him? Momentary diversions.

Nothing would jeopardize his plans to reclaim the lost glory of the Mephitian Empire, which would be far grander than before the dragons had come millennia ago. The first dragon wars had almost destroyed everything, except for a tiny enclave in Far Khoram. His ancestors had ruled well and then befriended the Dragon Kings' of old, and learned their arcane secrets and inherited their divine essence when no suitable heirs remained in the draconic line after the last wars ended.

His bloodline truly was magnificently prescient, as they must have seen his own rise. Now the Drobin Empire would fall, the Nexans would rule, and then the Mephitian people would come to power again following the pattern of all things.

Ra'menek's hands felt so alive now and he wanted to get his thoughts down as soon as he could. He wiggled his fingers, and their color was a rich golden brown, no gray remaining at all. He could move his tongue freely, as it no longer stuck to the bottom of his recently desiccated mouth.

He should make his way down the steps and into his fortress. Perhaps he had time to visit the archives and read the tablets he had wondered about before the group of five visitors arrived at his doorstep.

No, he should not be late for them. He might become engrossed in a tablet and read for hours. That would not do. He should go straight to the Gate of the Sun and wait patiently. The visitors must have the key, but if not, he would open the gates for them. It would be entertaining to speak with them and he did wonder who they were and how they had made it so far. They must hate Draglûne so much and it proved that his plans were working perfectly.

When Ra'menek killed the imbecilic dragon at last, the people would all love him for it. When would that be? A hundred years? Perhaps more, but it would come at the right time when Draglûne was no more of use, and this certainly was not the right time.

Ra'menek released the spell locking his Crystal Eye in its tripod and picked up the sphere, holding it delicately with his very strong and now acutely sensitive fingers. He would deposit it in a safe place and then wait for his guests. As he descended the first of the six-hundred and twenty-four steps that led down to the bottom of the tombs he already had in mind how he would start the brilliant record of his thoughts of the day. He would make time to inscribe them on a clay tablet before the visitors arrived.

XCIV

Lo, today is most auspicious. My plans have stirred up enemies from distant lands once again, and miraculously they have arrived at my Great House. It is a sign of the grand success of my designs. I am assured that my absolute vision will come to pass.

—God King Ra'menek, Son of Ah'usar, Eternal Father of the People, from a clay tablet inscribed on the 246th day of the 507th year of his reign

Drake and his companions hurried down the road toward the tombs of the ancient God Kings. The fractured and vine-covered walls of the canyon pressed in close as the cliffs rose to over three-hundred feet or higher. Pinnacles of rock towered in the distance, rising from where the tomb complex had to be. Drake thought he saw a flash of light on the highest towering peak. "Did you see that?" he asked.

No one had, but he suspected they were being watched. Was Draglûne watching them from the heights? The dragon had to know they were coming, or at least Ra'menek knew as the Priests had known to return to Lesh'heb.

The entrance to the tunnel of tombs, the Gate of the Sun, was less than a mile past the library school, and in a matter of a few moments they would come face to face with Draglûne, and most likely the undead king, Ra'menek.

All the miles they had traveled across the desert, months of pain, and hardship had come down to a few more steps. They would confront the most dangerous dragon in all of Ae'leron, and a Mephitian king that had died centuries before.

This was no time to go forward meekly. Drake had two dragon-killing bolts loaded in *Heartseeker*, and if Draglûne appeared right now both of them would find their mark. He had no doubt.

560

The dogs recognized Drake's sense of calm and both walked more confidently, un-tucking their tails from between their legs and raising their shoulders a bit.

They passed several side branches to the main canyon, and saw the façades of ancient tombs, the intricate carvings stained black and covered with creeping vines. The roots of trees that perched on the side of the cliffs, and thorny bushes blocked many of the entrances. Drake prepared for an ambush out of the side canyons, and looked for any sign of imminent attack.

They turned around a wide bend in the canyon and got their first look at the gigantic statue of the Eternal God King Ra'menek seated on a throne and looking north. The mountain of rock had been carved in his image according to what Barius had told them. Ra'menek sat in front of a pyramid shape with his hands on his thighs, a stern look on his face. Beside him a large sphere, carved of white stone rested on a huge bronze tripod.

"The Crystal Eye of Ah'usar," Dabarius said, "my father didn't mention there was a sculpture of it here."

The entrance to the tombs, the Gateway of the Sun, was a pair of tall bronze doors covered in sun disks. The doors stood in between Ra'menek's ankles, and were very small compared to the titanic statue, though they must be over twenty feet tall.

Ten male sculptures with animal's heads lined the way forward, a set of five on each side of the roadway. The figures had the heads of cobras, jackals, lions, and griffins. The last two at the end of the canyon had the heads of dragons. The draconic visages looked extremely new, compared to the other statues.

The river that had once flowed into the limestone mountain must have entered through a large cave mouth, but tremendous blocks of stone and the statue of Ra'menek erased any hint of the original opening.

The sun rose a little higher as they approached and its radiance hit the metal gates, reflecting the light with a brilliant flash, dazing Drake. To regain his vision, he guided his friends away from the glare and into a shadow at the base of a jackal headed statue.

The companions all looked at each other, squinting and blinking.

Bellor protected them with fire warding magic and Dabarius cast the Shield of Amar'isis on them all. They all looked at each other, single-minded and grim.

"Let's open the gate," Thor said.

Dabarius marched forward with the heavy staff of bronze and found the perfectly round hole at the inside edge of the left gate. Before he slipped the long shaft into the lock, he twisted the sun sphere, and watched the fins extend from the surface of the bottom of the staff. He twisted them back into place and slid the staff into the hole. It went about two feet before stopping against something solid. Dabarius made sure the sun disk was "facing the sky," as his father had instructed. He turned the sphere and a loud clicking sound echoed from inside the gates.

Thor and Bellor pushed against the left gate, while Bree and Drake heaved against the other. They couldn't budge the doors until Dabarius put one hand on each and pushed with a strength that must have come from his wizardly powers. The Gates of the Sun slowly opened as a harsh metallic grating sound came from the massive hinges. They fought against a malodorous breeze that rushed out of the passage, bringing the scent of mold, decay, and something worse.

Drake smelled the foul cloud of rotten sulfur, and brimstone smoke, the stench that always accompanied a true dragon. The odors wafted over them and the dogs growled, ears up. Drake stared into the huge tunnel, which was at least forty paces wide and almost as high as the head of the statue of Ra'menek. Daylight streamed inside revealing a smooth, water-hewn passage that disappeared into darkness. A wide road of flat stone went into the gloom, though the sides of the road were covered in gravel and strewn with large and small boulders. All of the rocks had smooth and rounded edges, as would be expected along a riverbed. Some of the larger rocks had been lifted upright and set into the ground to line the way. Images of gods and many glyphs covered the rocks. The road itself had been carved like the standing stones beside it, and the surface was covered with geometric patterns and symbols.

At the edges, in the shadows, dozens of Mephitian statues of regal looking men and women on thrones were carved into the walls on a grand scale on both sides, though they were half as tall as the great statue of Ra'menek outside.

Dabarius removed the staff from the lock. "My father said to close the gates. Shall we?"

"Can we open them from this side?" Thor asked.

"Yes, look." Dabarius found a wheel that could be turned to open the lock on the backside of the left gate.

"We close it," Bellor said, "and protect our backs."

Drake didn't like cutting off their only escape route, but when the gates shut and they were in the darkness with only the glowstones illuminating their way, he had even more reason to focus on finishing the job.

They stood there, letting their eyes adjust to the shadows and Bellor considered the way forward. The gravel would crunch under their feet and Drake wondered if it would be wiser to keep on the road. They could jump off it and take cover behind the standing stones if necessary. He looked at Bellor who motioned for them to walk on the road, all of them staying on the right side. Thor led the way, a glowstone hanging around his neck, and another set into the center of his shield. Bellor had already distributed the glowing rocks to each of them, and the companions wore one or more around their necks on strong leather cords. A circle of leather topped the glowstones on the necklaces, to prevent the light from fouling their vision.

The darkness around them was still vast, and their small lights could not even penetrate to the ceiling, where Draglûne could be hiding, ready to drop on them from above.

Just be ready, Drake told himself. Bellor followed Thor, then Dabarius, and Drake with the dogs flanking him. Bree watched their backs, *Wingblade* unsheathed.

Before they had gone twenty steps down the tunnel, Drake heard gravel crunching underfoot as something or someone moved toward them out of the darkness.

XCV

We retreated to a stronger position to face the Giergun. The men think we are defeated, but my dwarves know that now we have won. Still, I must make all of them believe.

—Bölak Blackhammer, journal from the Eleventh Giergun War

Barius entered the gatehouse of Lesh'heb after running all the way from the Jackal Gate. He caught his breath and surveyed the situation, wondering how long they could hold. His men, led by stalwart Gha'brel, shot arrows, dropped stones, and threw javelins at the tightly packed Shenahrian Priests who attacked the gate with axes. The enemy had formed a protective shield wall over the heads of their men, and chopped at the wooden doors. The Lesh'hebians were having little success stopping them, as any Shenahrian injured or killed had ten replacements ready to fight.

Barius realized that if the enemy had had a ram, they would already be through the gate, which had not been designed to withstand a concentrated attack. Ra'menek had never wanted the defenses strengthened, perhaps for this very reason, as a rebellion by the villagers was always a possibility, especially since the purging of the Khebian Priesthood.

The enemy screamed for blood and threw themselves at the gate, which would not hold up much longer. Barius needed more time before all of the women and children were safely away in the canyons and on their way to a sanctuary where the Shenahrians would never find them. The trail had to be covered well, then his men could fall back to the Wall of Jackals or retreat altogether and lead their enemies into the slot canyons where they would harass and ambush them mercilessly, while leading them in the wrong direction. If only the bridge itself had been dismantled as he planned. Two days would have been enough time to remove a large section, but not a few hours.

As the fighting raged below inside the enclosed roadway, Gha'brel, Oved, and Ja'den, Barius's most trusted captains, and leaders of the village work gangs, presented themselves to him for orders.

"You have done well," Barius told Gha'brel. "Keep dropping the rocks, but have only our best archers shoot arrows. We can't afford to waste shafts here. Target any of Elder Priests or warriors who are vulnerable. Drop rocks on them to keep them back, for we shall not run out of them. Ja'den, focus on piling as much flammable wood and stone as you can behind the gates. Oved, lead twenty men and bring as much lamp oil as you can from the village to me here. We're going to burn the gate and retreat. The fire will stop them for a while and the smoke will force them to fall back."

"We don't have enough time," Gha'brel said. "They're breaking through."

"I'll give you the time," Barius said, "hold them for a few moments more."

"It shall be done," Gha'brel promised, then he and the others ran off to execute his orders. Barius looked through a tiny window at the bunched up Shenahrian warriors in the covered roadway, then ran down the steps and sat cross-legged, his palms flat on the ground, three paces back from of the splintering gate as his men braced it with timbers.

Axe blades fell repeatedly in a deadly rhythm, the tips of the blades poking through several cracks. The shouting of the enemy was deafening and his brave men battled them through the holes in the gate jabbing at them with spears.

Barius closed his eyes and touched the surface of the road, and spoke the words of power he learned in the temple of Kheb in Mephitep. He felt the feet of dozens of the enemy where they stood on the road on the other side of the gate. He extended his power as far as he could, nearly sixty feet beyond the failing gateway.

A spear penetrated through a crack and stabbed a man

bracing the gate in the face. He stumbled back and fell in front of Barius.

Blood wet his hand, but he did not lose focus. He unleashed the spell and the stone roadway ceased to exist for two heartbeats. The Shenahrians massed in front of the gate and in a wide swath over sixty feet beyond fell through the floor which disappeared for an instant revealing the muddy waters of the lake below them. Dozens of men plummeted fifty feet down and splashed into the lake in front of Lesh'heb's dam.

A few managed to hold on to the side of the enclosed road, but their legs dangled through the floor, and when it materialized again they were fused in the rock. The hideous screams echoed in the enclosed bridge.

The attackers right outside the gate and far beyond were almost totally eliminated, and Barius prepared to use the magic again when more rushed forward, but the Solar Priests held the reinforcements back. He could sense them countering his magic and they threw back his power, preventing him from using any spells on the roadway. There were so many of them he could not hope to defeat them, but he fought hard and gave his men time to reinforce the gate, pile wood, and bring up the lamp oil. He hung on for a few precious minutes until the barricade was finished.

The enemy attacked again and Barius helped pour the newly arrived lamp oil on the barricade behind the gate. It would become a huge impassable bonfire when the time was right.

The fighting raged for some time, and when the gate was about to fall, Barius had Gha'brel's men pour the rest of the oil on the attackers deploying it with clay funnels. The tightly packed men on the bridge outside were soaked, and Barius threw the first of many torches that followed.

The fire exploded and the screams of the immolated filled the smoky air, which choked many of the others in the bridge-tunnel. The fire raged and Barius sent gusts of wind through

567

the windows in the tunnel, making the fire flare up and burn hotter like a bellows in a forge. The men of Lesh'heb cheered as their oppressors for so many years burned.

The Storm Priests used their magic to stop the wind and they filled the air with moisture and dampened the blaze. Barius could not counter so many of them and the fire burned out as moist fog formed in and around the gatehouse.

The Shenahrians broke through the gate a short time later, but were faced with a tall and thick barricade of piled wood. The first few of them who crawled through were slain by spears, but the gates were pulled down and a large group forced their way through leading with their shields. As they climbed over the debris, Barius had more torches dropped, and the oil in the barricade came to life, setting many of the enemy on fire despite the fog.

The gate of Lesh'heb was lost and Barius led the defenders away, using the smoke and the fire to cover their retreat. He had at most ninety men under his command, and it appeared all of the Priests of Shenahr and Ah'usar had returned. At least four-hundred and fifty strong and armed for battle, minus those who had just perished or were wounded.

There would be no victory, but he could delay them and give his son time to finish the job in the tombs. Barius might hold out for weeks or more in the library school behind its thick gates, but that was not the goal. The fact that he held hostages did not matter to his enemy. No student at the school mattered, not even the son of the Mortal King, Ahken'mose, who may still be in hiding.

Barius would lead the people away to freedom, and abandon Lesh'heb as they had always planned, but before that, the men of Lesh'heb would fight. The vile Priests of Shenahr and the Solar Priests who ordered them around would pay for all of the misery they had caused, and there would be far fewer of them left when the hunt for the women and children of Lesh'heb began.

XCVI

Lo, I have suffered assassins in my Great House. The Khebian Priests and the foolish king Ahken'ra will pay for this treachery. I shall destroy the Priesthood of Kheb, and the young king Ahken'ra, a boy I personally trained for years and showed much favor, will be taught a harsh lesson. If he had a legitimate heir I would have Ahken'ra brought to me and I would watch him strangled with his own entrails. I shall curse him in other ways and when I have trained an heir, I shall delight in Ahken'ra's passing, for he will be buried here and I will turn him into a wraith to serve me. The delights of the Afterworld will be denied him for eternity.

—God King Ra'menek, Son of Ah'usar, Eternal Father of the People, Ruler of the Empire of Mephitia, Head of the Great House of Lesh'heb, from a clay tablet dated the 54th day of the 467th year of his reign

Ra'menek stepped off the gravel and onto the road of the dead. His visitors heard him and paused, though they could not see him yet as he wrapped himself in pure shadow. He relished how their faces filled with fear and anticipation. The moment of his arrival must be perfect and he willed the glyphs on the standing stones flanking the road to glow faintly with a pale golden light. Mist coalesced in the air, seeping up from the cracks in the road and forming a ring around them.

Dozens of his ghostly servants appeared in the fog, taking the shapes they had in life of his bodyguards, ministers, craftsmen, and some of his favorite wives, but Ra'menek kept them away, chastising them for wanting to drain away the life force of these visitors to his home. He did not want to share.

To further impress the mortals, he manifested the sweet and slightly lemon and conifer smell of the olibanum tree, as Frankincense was the scent of the gods, though he could barely smell it, or the dragon odor his Priests so often complained about.

Ra'menek made certain his *nemes* crown of gold and black striped cloth was straight on his head, and the flaps hung perfectly in front of his shoulders. He straightened the sun disk diadem that held the cloth crown in place and willed for his pleated crisp white linen kilt to be free of all dust and grime so prevalent in the tombs. All the golden jewelry on his wrists, upper arms, ankles, fingers, and on his belt instantly sparkled as if polished a moment before by dutiful slaves. The brightly colored stone and glass beads of his thick collar necklace would dazzle, and so Ra'menek called for his Solar Eye to appear in the ceiling. A soft light, like a sunrise on a winter morning, shone from the upper reaches of the cavern, penetrating the mist and illuminating a circle on the road of the dead.

The God King Ra'menek, Son of Ah'usar and Carrier of the Divine Essence, Eternal Father of the People, Ruler of the Empire of Mephitia, Head of the Great House of Lesh'heb, stepped into the ring of light with his ceremonial flail in one hand an ebony shepherds crook in the other. He let the warmth invigorate him and let the visitors tremble as he changed the angle of the light to be more in their faces.

He waited for their reaction as they carried weapons openly. Would they be foolish enough to attack him? The tallest of their party, a young man, perhaps half of Ra'menek's apparent physical age, and almost as tall as the Eternal God King, had the handsome look of the old Mephitian nobility. He bent a knee in homage, and lowered his eyes.

Splendid, at least this one was not an uncouth foreigner.

The Sons of Kheb also bent their knees, the gray beard going before the younger brown beard, who did not want to bow judging by his irritated look. They all placed their weapons on the ground, though they rudely kept a hand on them. The attractive half-breed Mephitian-Nexan woman knelt beside her lover—their connection was obvious—and Ra'menek could sense the Goddess Amar'isis in her. She was a Wing Guardian and all of them carried trust scarabs of Isyrin. He could sense the protection of the Goddess and Kheb on them, even on the large dogs, which he wanted to kill and press into his service as guardian wraiths. The pair of them would be perfect for such a role and would terrify so many of the Priests and young boys who visited him in his archives.

It was most undesirable that all of the visitors had such strong protection magic on them, and he wished he had the ability to penetrate their thoughts as easily as a dragon could. Dragonkind had that advantage over him, but he had studied humans and dwarves for so long he could read them without much effort.

"Great King, may you live eternally, prosper and be healthy," the noble said, "We insignificant slaves to your divine will are honored to be in your glorious presence, and we apologize for our unannounced arrival. If it pleases your Radiant Magnificence, I, Dabarius, Emissary of Queen Khelen'dara of Isyrin, will explain our imposition in your great house."

Ra'menek was impressed at the man's diction and pronunciation. He had the unpleasing accent of Isyrin, but he was schooled in the proper forms of addressing one of the highest station at least. He was obviously arrogant and somewhat disingenuous, but that was to be expected, and Ra'menek would have thought him not of noble birth had Dabarius, definitely his real name, been any other way. He certainly could be an emissary of the Isyrin Queen, but Ra'menek could sense a coming deception.

"Emissary Dabarius," Ra'menek said, "I will be pleased to hear who you all are and what reason you will give for coming into my house without an invitation. You and your entourage are bold and determined to have come so far."

"What's he saying?" the old dwarf whispered to the woman in Nexan.

She began to whisper a wildly abbreviated translation of Ra'menek's words and this irritated him to no end.

"I am insulted that your entourage does not speak Mephitian," Ra'menek said in perfect Nexan, using the northern accent of the line of the Alaric named kings, and not the colloquial dialect that the backwoodsman carrying the Drobin crossbow no doubt spoke. "It would have shown your sincerity if they had all learned the Father Tongue before meeting with me."

That surprised them.

"Great King, forgive us," Emissary Dabarius said, then bowed so low that the out of place urn filled with liquid hanging from his chest nearly touched the floor. "Not all of my companions are astute enough to master such a complex language."

Ra'menek smiled, showing them his perfectly white teeth, and giving a generous compliment for such cheap humor that did have the ring of truth. Against his instincts, he liked this man, though he would not trust him under any circumstances. "I shall not forget this lack of respect that some of your companions have shown, but I will be content to converse in the Nexan tongue, as it amuses me to speak the language that none of my human subjects on this plateau are fluent."

"Great King," Dabarius said in Nexan now, "We are honored, and my companions are eager to understand your every word."

Ra'menek nodded once and waved his flail, the sign for the emissary to proceed.

"Great King, I wish to present my companions: Master Bellor of the *Dracken Viergur* Order; Thor his apprentice and nephew; Wing Guardian Bree'alla of Isyrin, and Drake of the Forest Men. We have come to your great house to request the opportunity to kill your servant, the iron Dragon King, Draglûne. More importantly we are here to present a letter from the Queen of Isyrin, and offer a stronger alliance between Isyrin and you splendid kingdom."

"Queen Khelen'dara sent you to make this offer?"

572

"Great King, allow me to respond. Queen Khelen'dara did request us to bring the offer I mentioned." Dabarius produced a small letter. "This missive is a peace offering from Queen Khelen'dara. Though it does not state it in the letter, she has asked us to slay the wyrm, Draglûne, as his followers have committed many crimes in her land and she believes he is the cause. She does not fault your Magnificent Radiance for anything Draglûne's followers, mainly the Priests of Shenahr, have done, and requests your forgiveness if this was at all perceived. Great King, I humbly present you with Queen Khelen'dara's letter."

Ra'menek wished it and the letter glided to his hand. He approved of Khelen'dara's signature, but did not approve the liberties her scribe had taken with the glyphs used to represent the title of God King or the structure of the letter as it was not in accordance with the ancient forms. It was most offensive and not a true treaty, but a poorly conceived letter of introduction that only a poorly educated scribe relegated to the duties of a border guard might find compelling. The letter burned into ash and drifted away into the mist, which was now swirling with the hungry wraiths, as they sensed Ra'menek's displeasure.

"I accept the peace terms of Queen Khelen'dara. The treaty will be sanctioned as soon as she invades Arayden with all of her army. I also reject your request to slay my servant, Draglûne. I have use of him, and it does not please me to have assassins in my home."

Dabarius and Bellor exchanged nervous glances. The others closed their grips on their weapons and Ra'menek sensed the ending of this exchange would be sooner than he expected.

"Great King, we accept your answer and will be pleased to carry it to Queen Khelen'dara, though if I may impose upon you, there are a few other matters which I am compelled to discuss."

Ra'menek waved his flail indifferently. Now he would see

how brave and foolish this man really was. It had been some time since Ra'menek had felt such interest, but he knew this man was preparing for words he knew would be foolish to utter.

"Great King, I am a humble student of *Teha Khet*, and was informed that you, Radiance, are the original teacher of the discipline."

"That is common knowledge."

"Yes, Great King. Forgive my impudence, but I wondered if you would consent to giving me a lesson. It would be the most meaningful experience of my life if we could face each other in a contest, and I would like to make a wager on the outcome."

"A wager?" Ra'menek was insulted, but also intrigued by this insane young man. With ten more possessing Dabarius's courage he could conquer the plateaus in fifty years.

"Yes, Great King. I will wager my life, and this jug,"—he tapped the urn hanging in front of him. "If I fail to defeat you, Radiance, my life, and this jug are yours."

"Defeat me? You mention the impossible. I would take your life, but do not insult me with mention of a common *jug*."

"Great King, forgive me, but this is no common jug. This contains a fresh batch of *haunqt* from the best brew-woman in your village of Lesh'heb. I watched the woman squeeze the golden liquid from a thick loaf of fresh barley bread. It has been fermented perfectly and when you are truly gone and dead, I shall drink from this jug in your honor, and pass it to my friends. I have looked forward to drinking this for many hours now and it is no small thing that I refrained."

"Dabarius, you've gone mad," Bellor said, and glanced nervously at Ra'menek.

"You will wager your life and that jug of barley alcohol?" Ra'menek asked, refusing to take the bait for his trap and react angrily. "Your death is a simple thing and I have no need of any sustenance now. Surely, there is something more of value you can offer me than that jug and your pitiful life."

"Forgive me Great King, I shall, but there is more I would ask of you," Dabarius said. "I have been informed that Queen Khelen'dara was married to the bearer of the divine essence of Ah'usar when she came of age."

"She is the eighth wife I have had and have never met," Ra'menek said, though he suspected she might be the seventh. No matter. He would check the archives later as he kept track of all the Queens of Isyrin since the sundering of the empire, and long before that.

"Quite so, Great King. I am pleased to say that Queen Khelen'dara informed me that only if I personally carried the divine essence of Ah'usar could I marry her, and I wish to have that essence so that she will become my wife."

"You *have* gone mad," the younger dwarf said, raising his shield and standing up now, as all of the visitors had.

Ra'menek raised an eyebrow. This was very amusing. He would spend hours recording this later on several tablets.

"Great King," Dabarius said, "I wish for you to make me your heir so that when I kill you, the divine spark of the Sun God will pass to me."

"And once I'm gone *you* will be the God King of Mephitia?"

"Yes, Great King," Dabarius said, "and I will dedicate myself to destroying your legacy. Even now the scrolls in your library school are being burned and the tablets broken. All the pieces will be ground into dust under a millstone. I am told you have the original copies of all of them here, and they too will be shattered and ground into dust. This I swear in the name of Great Kheb and the Goddess Amar'isis."

Ra'menek smiled. This man was bold and fearless. Even the uncouth lout Draglûne had never dared speak such open threats. Such entertainment as this was most uncommon. Ra'menek considered instituting some policy that would allow a hero such as this to enter his home, perhaps once a year, to render similar amusement. He would have to write it down.

The visitors tensed, their feeble eyes struggling with the glaring light.

"Great King," Dabarius smiled broadly and assumed the fighting stance Ra'menek had invented, "if you seek motivation or are afraid that your failing memory of *Teha Khet* is lacking after not fighting for over five centuries, think of your reward. You will drink from a fresh jug of *haunqt*, though you may have to wait until after you've dispatched my companions, as they will certainly try to kill you if I fall. If such an outcome does occur, I hope that this," he stroked the urn lovingly, "will taste like sour piss in your rotting mouth."

Ra'menek knew what was coming. His five visitors tensed for battle and raised their weapons. The crossbowman's finger touched the trigger as he took aim, but it was as if they all moved at the pace of sap running down the trunk of an olibanum tree, and he moved as a ray of sunlight. The Eternal God King Ra'menek sprang forward to kill Dabarius with his bare hands and simultaneously unleashed his most powerful spell, the *Tuu'ahk'naa*.

The bright light behind him pulsed and solar rays struck the visitors and their two dogs, who sadly could not be saved now.

All of those in the glare of the light would be blind, deaf, paralyzed, and dying as their organs cooked and exploded inside their bodies. They would all be dead as soon as they hit the ground, except Dabarius. He would keep him alive just a heartbeat longer, as he wanted to look into the man's eyes as he died and send him to the Afterworld with a chain that Ra'menek could pull whenever he wanted.

In less than a quarter blink of an eye, Ra'menek crossed the distance and seized Dabarius by the throat, and attached a dark cord of energy to the brave man's soul, and two more to the dogs.

Oddly, he did not feel the intense heat in Dabarius's skin that he should have, and realized that the protection magic of Amar'isis he had disregarded earlier had somehow—impossibly!—shielded Dabarius from the *Tuu'ahk'naa*.

It had been centuries since Ra'menek had been truly surprised, but this was one of those moments. Still, he blocked the punch Dabarius launched at his head, and the feeble one aimed at his gut, his hands clamping on the man's wrists and holding him fast.

"Shoot!" Dabarius shouted to the blind crossbowman only two steps to his right. The man, who should have been dead from the spell, released a shaft, which sailed past Ra'menek's shoulder. He watched it go by for a moment and realized it would not have hurt him very badly if it had struck, though his flesh could heal from any wound.

The younger dwarf attacked, but Ra'menek kicked the center of his shield and sent him tumbling backward. How was the dwarf not blind like all the others were?

"Drake!" Dabarius yelled as a second bolt streaked toward the God King. Astonishingly, the shaft flew straight at Ra'menek's side. It was a simple thing for him to flick his arm, and deflect the tip of the strangely shaped missile. He would avoid it piercing his body, but as his upper arm bracelet impacted with the ceramic head of the bolt—why a ceramic head?—the clay exploded in a white spray of water that covered Ra'menek's arm, shoulder, neck, and face in an impossible amount of water. The instant the first few drops touched him he knew what it was, and pulled away trying to avoid the rest, but Dabarius held onto him now, using a simple reversal hold all novice *Teha Khet* students would master, and this simple move, perfected by Ra'menek himself, delayed him for the briefest of instants.

The water, somehow empowered by concentrated moonlight, and another force antithetical to the undead nature that had kept Ra'menek in this world for so long, burned and stunned him to inaction. He could barely control his limbs now, when before he could move as fast as a hummingbird's wings. He was powerless as Dabarius grinned and smashed his knuckles against the jug dangling in front of his chest. The ceramic urn shattered and impossible gallons of the water that glowed silver and drenched Ra'menek, burning and melting his flesh.

The white-hot pain was like the moment when he had first come back from the dead, except this time he was nearly paralyzed and fell onto his back. Then and now every part of his body was on fire. He remembered the excruciating misery as he felt the burning of every one of his body cavities, which been scraped out and filled with natron salts. He writhed in torment until he had broken out of his sarcophagus and crawled out of the tomb and into the sunlight, which had calmed and rejuvenated him.

He had vomited and defecated the natron and the other preservatives put in him by the Khebian embalmers for hours. The wonderful sunlight had re-grown his organs and his brain, which had been scraped out from his nose with a wire hook. None of the Priests had believed his words, that after he drank the elixir of dragon's blood, various poisons, and other more secret ingredients he would come back from the Afterworld and become the Eternal God King. They were sorry to see him and his revenge had been terrible.

Now he was dying again, wailing in agony as the cruel men poured blessed water on him, and placed holy stones on his chest and abdomen. All of it made Ra'menek recall the terrible moment of his rebirth. He could do nothing to stop them aside from scream and struggle weakly, like a skeleton of a man deprived of food for a month. Ra'menek could feel his flesh and bones melting away now and the agony was like a raging waterfall crashing down his throat.

The terror of fading to nothingness made him fight to survive, but his spells would not work. None of his servants would obey. His eyes still worked, though he could not move or focus enough to use the power bestowed upon him by the essence of Ah'usar. The Sun God had abandoned him, as had his servants. Scores of ghosts and wraiths watched him being tormented, as his immortal spirit was paralyzed and his flesh disintegrated. These ephemeral souls, his captives and slaves for so long, did not look unhappy at this turn of events.

The younger dwarf loomed over him, a satisfied grin behind his brown beard as he poured an endless stream of water from an urn marked with a Khebian Mountain symbol.

Ra'menek's feet, legs, his genitals, everything dissolved under the assault from moonlight acid water.

Dabarius leaned down, and still blind, felt for Ra'menek's mouth. He held another urn to his lips—*oh Ah'usar, please no!*

"Great King," Dabarius said, "drink this and you will be free at last." The evil man poured the water down Ra'menek's throat as the Drobin prayed and chanted to Kheb.

"*Grusslig boren,* we cast you out!" the dwarves shouted as more water was poured onto the small amount of flesh that remained on his shriveled body. He was bones and marrow, a skull with no flesh. A pile of jewels and soaked linen. He fought them and resisted as much as he could with this stumps, but the burning water robbed him of his strength and he could not move, or see, or hear. His spirit fragmented and slipped further and further toward the dark place where the ghosts he had tormented—some for centuries—waited to greet him with cold fingers and smothering embraces. They ringed him, his very servants who had protected him and done his bidding. They floated above the slivers of bone and skin that had been his body. Only some finger bones lay on the road of the dead where he had been slain, tricked by a devious man, an assassin of Amar'isis and the Queen of Isyrin who had finally gotten her revenge for what his assassins had done to her family in the past.

The mist evaporated and the glowing glyphs on the rocks

faded as the light in the cavern ceiling went out, the Solar Eye extinguished.

The essence of Ah'usar, the powerful spark that had been the source of his magic and power flitted away to its new heir, a young man who was not ready for the gift he never should have inherited. What an incomprehensible tragedy for the world! All Ra'menek's glorious plans had not yet come to pass. Now they never would and he would be . . . gone. The realization was the worst pain his disembodied spirit could endure.

Ra'menek shrieked and flailed as the vengeful ghosts he had once chained to himself descended on him with frigid claws and dragged him to a place of darkness and despair where he would never see the sun again.

XCVII

We weep for our Khebian friends. Many are dead, others will pass soon. They have stood with us in our hour of need, and they have paid the price. The Drobin hierarchy in the North would not be so quick to dismiss humans if they had seen firsthand the courage and strength of will that I have.

—Bölak Blackhammer, from the Khoram Journal

Barius stood atop the Wall of Jackals and faced the hundred men who had volunteered to stay behind and fight. They would hold the wall until their families were much further away from Lesh'heb, and then they would all retreat to the library school and shut the nearly impenetrable metal gates designed to repel Draglûne himself. The enemy would take days trying to break in, if they even could, and most of the men would escape into the canyons, climbing and crossing the spiny curtains of rock, using the secret ways known only to a few, and rejoining their families very far away in a new village where their enemies would never find them, especially if Draglûne and Ra'menek were dead.

A handful of brave young men would remain behind to look after the child hostages, guard the gate until it fell, and delay any pursuit or attempts to cross the stone ridges and sneak in from the rear. This would divert the enemy and give the women and children all the time they needed to get away. It would also give Dabarius and his friends more time to accomplish their task.

Barius stood above the Jackal Gate wearing a breastplate emblazoned with the mountain symbol of Kheb and a helmet with the Earth Father's mark on it as well. He had found both in the forsaken temple inside the school. Seeing the toppled the statue of the Earth Father angered him greatly, for he had studied in the temple of Kheb when he first came to

Mephitep. Old, blind, and handless Priests had taught him the most powerful spells of the earth. He would honor them today and would honor Great Kheb.

"Men of Lesh'heb," Barius spoke from the fighting ledge on the Wall of Jackals, "many of you know that my son has joined our fight. He, along with two of the Sons of Kheb—"

"Praise Kheb!" the men cheered and shouted the name of the god they worshiped in secret and more fervently than any other as their families had for many generations.

"My son and the Sons of Kheb have gone to the Tunnel of Tombs to slay the false gods. Before this day is over we will all be free of the Dragon of Darkness and the Abomination King Ra'menek at last!"

The men cheered, raising their weapons, which were more numerous and deadly now that they had raided the armory in the fighting school. Many of them had helms and leather breastplates as well. Most of them were strong from working in the quarry, or from building tombs, and all of them had sparred with the assassin Priests of Shenahr in the fighting circles since they were boys. Several had already shown their mettle today and others were eager to fight.

"You men are workers, not soldiers," Barius said, "but you are all warriors, tested and blooded in this very school where the false Priests made you endure indignities no man should suffer. When you were defeated by them, they would punish you, and when you bested them, they would torture and humiliate you."

The men shouted curses at the Sun and Storm Priests. Barius hated them as well. He had been forced to associate with them, but he duped the Shenahrians into thinking he was one of them, and under the guise of loyal quarry master and Priest Ben'ahmi, he had taught the men of Lesh'heb *Teha Khet*, as he had explained to the assassin masters that "the battle touch would give better sport to the Shenahrian warrior students."

582

He waited for the shouts to die down. "Finally, you can fight and do more than try to protect yourselves from being beaten senseless by gangs of angry young nobles trying to impress their teachers."

More cheers and insults against the Shenahrians.

"You will avenge the maltreatment these vile men have visited upon your mothers, wives, and daughters condemned to work in the school. You will have revenge after generations of cruelty that has been inflicted upon the long suffering people of Lesh'heb."

The roar was deafening.

"We let them have the burning gate at the village," Barius said, "but we will fight them here, and when we have spilled enough of their blood, we will leave this place forever."

Loud cheers and oaths.

"They will never forget the lesson we will give them today!"

The final roar and cheer echoed into the canyons and Barius knew that the only way his men would suffer defeat today was if Draglûne himself attacked from the sky. He was afraid of that, but the dragon was his son's task and the ranks of Sun and Storm warriors and assassins marching toward the Wall of Jackals was his.

He watched his enemies march forward. The black banner of Shenahr with a gray dragon head on it was partially burned, but they waved it high, rallying their warriors. The men shouted for vengeance for what had happened at the gatehouse, pounding their chests and pointing to the sky as they made oaths to the Storm God. Many of their number had been wounded or killed, and over a hundred appeared missing, but at least three hundred remained.

Barius noticed they had brought a simple battering ram made from a tree trunk and had brought the old and rotten ladders he had left piled in the village for them. Did they not realize that they would barely hold one man's weight? All of the good ladders had been burned in the bonfire or sent with the women and children to ease their passage, or saved for his men's eventual escape into the razor canyons.

"General Ben'ahmi," Gha'brel said, "what are your orders?"

Gha'brel, Oved, and Ja'den listened carefully and then sprang into action. Gurion had also come from inside the school to speak with him.

"What is it?" Barius asked.

"General, some of the boys don't want to be left behind. They are afraid of what will happen when the Storm Priests return."

Barius understood completely why the boys would want to leave this school of depravity and death. "They are too young to make that important of a decision. We shall not kidnap children and take them into the wild." Dabarius had grown up apart from him, and he would not keep these boys away from their families.

"Many of them have been here a year of two," Gurion said. "They know what's in store for them. They're afraid."

"No, they will stay when we leave," Barius said. "Return to your post and keep watch." He glanced up at the plateau of scalloped rock that formed the roof of the school two hundred feet above them.

Gurion ran off and Barius rethought his decision to refuse the boys. He knew all too well about the initiation rites, and the atrocities they would face, but he could not steal away other people's children, even if so many of them would be killed during their training.

He busied himself with a review of the men on the wall. He deployed all but a reserve force of a dozen men atop the fighting ledge, instructing them to hide behind the ramparts and the jackal statues. The defenses would hold for some time, especially the Jackal Gate, which now had huge stone blocks behind it. His men knew how to move stone and had blocked up the archway in record time. The battering ram would do almost nothing against the bronze gate, which had been designed to hold back a strong attack. With the bracing behind it, even if the hinges broke, the enemy would need chisels to get through.

The Priests of the school feared the men of Lesh'heb and always posted guards night and day at the Jackal Gate. Barius found it very satisfying to use their defenses against them.

The Solar Priests sent their banner forward, a red sun on a golden field, and many warriors flocked around it. When they came close enough, Barius unleashed a surprise volley of arrows, which hit several of the enemy. The blood was bright red as it stained the white kilts and robes of the enemy.

The men of Lesh'heb cheered as the banner of Ah'usar withdrew beyond arrow range. Barius watched as they argued about how best to proceed. The Solar Priests were in charge, and unfortunately kept the Storm Priests from attacking in a disorganized fashion. They came in tightly packed squads with shields in front and above their heads. Their first wave struck the gate with the battering ram while groups of Shenahrians tried the ladders, which broke apart when two men climbed up them.

Arrows and stones harassed all who came under the wall, but one Storm Priest made it up a ladder and reached the top. He threw down two defenders before he was stabbed with a spear in his back, but he fought on until Oved drove a spear through his side and pushed him off the ledge.

No other enemies gained the wall, and the men of Lesh'heb threw back the opening assault. The Solar Priests watched from the distance, gauging the strength of the defenders. The ram had no effect and the men on the ladders were slaughtered.

Two more tries at the gate convinced them to withdraw to a safe distance and lick their wounds. Barius led the men in a loud cheer, but ominous thunder in the distance dampened their celebration a moment later. Dark clouds blew in from the

585

southeast on a sudden wind.

"They've called a storm," Gha'brel said, making the sign against evil. Most of the men followed their captain's gesture, splaying four fingers and passing them in front of their eyes.

Barius had not thought of what so many Storm Priests could do if they worked together. He should have foreseen this, and felt doubt about holding the wall.

The rain began a few moments later and the defenders murmured prayers as the wind lashed them and the sky darkened. Barius considered having them get down from the wall and hide at the base of it, but he was too late.

Forked white lightning flashed, blinding and deafening Barius as it struck right next to him. When he regained his sight he smelled burned flesh and saw the four men to his left had been killed, some thrown from the ramparts. Another forked bolt struck an instant later and the six men over the gate screamed in agony. Two more died convulsing on the ledge as the smell of burned hair filled the air. He called for everyone else to get down and take cover below. He had been a fool to think they could hold the wall for so long.

Barius crouched low, using a jackal statue as cover and invoked the protection of Shenahr, saying the spell as he had been taught by the Elder Priests in the school of Lesh'heb. He stood up and a bolt of lightning streaked down from above and turned aside the instant before it would have hit him. More bolts struck the top of the wall, now empty of defenders.

"You will not take this wall!" Barius screamed down at his enemies. He threw a stone, then a javelin.

Rain pelted him and Shenahrian warriors with shields on their backs and short swords in their belts climbed up and over the ramparts. He blocked a man's attack with his wrist, then threw him to the side, cracking his head against the sharp ear of the jackal statue. He blocked another attacker's sword thrust, and forced the blade back at him, stabbing him in the eye.

586

Two Shenahrian assassins wearing large dragon head necklaces arrived on either side of him. They attacked with swords at the same moment. Barius used a discarded shield to block the killing blow from the man behind him then hit the assassin in the face with the sharpened edge of the shield.

An arrow sprouted from the other assassin's chest and Barius threw him off the wall and finished the stunned man behind him. Gha'brel and two archers came up the stairs desperate to reach their leader. Three bolts of lightning hit the wall in rapid succession. Half-blind and deaf, Barius waved his men down. He looked out and dozens of Shenahrians were forming human pyramids and climbing up each other to reach the ramparts on the left flank.

Barius used the storm they had provided him and called down lightning of his own. The bolt struck the man on top of a pyramid and the electricity spread to every man below him, killing them all. He sent two more bolts and killed many more before the storm refused to obey him. The Shenahrians blocked his magic, and he could feel them trying to kill him now, as they willed his heart to stop beating. He sank to his knees, his strength fading as the enemy attacked and reformed their pyramids.

Barius felt his life slipping away as he crouched behind the rampart. He could not fight so many Priests, though his training as a wizard gave him some protection and he said the words of power and tried to throw off the curse that killing him.

One enemy gained the wall beside him, but fell back with an arrow in his chest. Another took his place, and he too was shot. A third man blocked an arrow with his shield and landed beside Barius, who was so weak that all he could do was gasp for air. The Shenahrian raised his sword to cut off Barius's head, but Gha'brel and Ja'den charged up the stairs and blocked the blow, then dispatched the warrior. Gha'brel helped Barius stand and they looked down to see the enemy massing below them.

Barius prayed for a miracle and stones rained from the sky splitting men's heads open. Dozens of melon sized rocks fell all at once from the clouds above crushing and maiming the Shenahrians and breaking up their human towers.

"Shenahr curses you all!" Barius shouted and the enemy broke and ran away from the hail of sharp rocks. Then Barius saw the source of the attack. Atop the heights of the library school young boys flung the stones down on the attackers. It had to be Gurion and the captive boys who must have been watching the battle and decided to join in when all was lost. The boys hated the men who called themselves teachers, and who had abused them or killed their friends. This was their chance to get revenge.

More lightning struck the wall and Barius stumbled, disoriented and blind. Strong hands pulled him and he staggered down the steps. When he could hear again, Gha'brel was pulling him along as they retreated toward the entrance to the school.

"I can't go in," Barius said.

"You must," Gha'brel said. "We need you."

"I promised my son I would wait for him outside the tombs," Barius said, regaining his senses as his hearing started to return. "Take command and leave as soon as you can. Do not linger in this place as we discussed before, and promise me you will take with you all of the children who threw the stones, and any others who wish to go. Get everyone as far away as fast as you can. Promise me."

"Ben, I swear it on my life," Gha'brel said.

"May the Great Earth Father protect you." Barius shook forearms with Gha'brel, then ran south down the road and into the canyon. He had failed to hold the Wall of Jackals, and soon his son would be trapped inside the tunnel of tombs by an angry army of Storm Priests.

XCVIII

Hezekiah is the only Khebian left. After we pray one last time, we will go forward again, pressing our final attack.

     —Bölak Blackhammer, from the Khoram Journal

Blind, Drake knelt down and kept his arms around Jep and Temus, consoling them as the God King's ear-piercing screams echoed in the Tunnel of Tombs. All he could see was a corona of bright light no matter where he looked. His eyes hurt as if they were burned with a torch, and Drake worried that he might be permanently blind.

"Drake!" Bree shouted over the screeching of the God King's death throes.

"Here!" he said, and at last they found each other. One of Bree's strong and calloused hands grabbed his arm and he pulled her in close.

"My eyes," she said, huddling against him, and the whimpering dogs.

"It'll be all right," he said, getting a good hold on her and trying to sound confident.

Thor and Bellor prayed loudly, trying to cast out the horror born God King.

A spreading pool of water soaked Drake's knee. He could hear it sizzling as it was poured onto their enemy's body, but the water touching him was cold.

The two Drobin War Priests tried to break the bond Ra'menek's spirit had with his flesh and shouted prayers and admonitions.

"Can we help?" Bree asked.

"No," Thor said, interrupting his prayer as Bellor continued the words. "Stay there and stay down and—"

The wailing of the dying man drowned out Thor. The terrible inhuman sound made Drake want to run and escape the cold miasma of fear that was tightening around him and Bree. He hugged her and tried to keep the dogs close, though now they were edging away from the expanding pool of water.

A frigid hand, lightly pressed on his shoulder kept Drake steady. He thought he heard Ethan in his mind, telling him it was better that he did not see, and that he should stay there and pray to Amaryllis for protection. He did and had the feeling that Bree was also praying. His prayers kept him from going mad and running away, but he kept thinking what would happen if Draglûne or some wingataurs attacked them right now. They would all be dead and would never see the blow that killed them.

He could tell that Bree wanted to run, but he kept his hand tightly around hers, reassuring her while hoping and praying that a blow would not fall. Bellor said Draglûne would attack at their weakest moment, and wasn't this it?

Finally, the screaming stopped, though the Drobin still prayed and poured water on whatever was left of Ra'menek's body.

"Thor, are you keeping watch?" Drake asked.

"I am, perhaps you should reload," Thor suggested.

Drake managed to find his discarded crossbow and it was not that difficult to blindly span the weapon. The krannekin did all the work, and he randomly selected two bolts and slipped them into the tracks.

"Be ready to shoot," Thor said.

"Thor, read my lips . . . *I can't see*," Drake said inaudibly, in case Draglûne or his minions were listening, or worse, watching.

"Good, keep your eyes on the tunnel," Thor said. Then he moved Drake and pointed him in a direction. "Shoot anything you see."

"Bree, you and dogs stay behind me," Drake said, and he made Jep and Temus lay down, finding a dray place for them nearby. Bree put her back to his and they sat on the floor, waiting for the attack.

Drake focused on his hearing as the dwarves continued their prayers.

It felt like an hour had gone by when Thor finally announced, "It's done."

"He's gone?" Drake asked.

"The horror born monster is forever banished from this world," Bellor said. "Thank you, Father Lorak."

"Thor, can anyone besides you . . . ?" Bree let the question linger.

"No," Dabarius said.

"No," Bellor said.

Their plan had worked, though Drake had never imagined that all of them but Thor would be blind at the end of it.

"This will pass," Dabarius said. "Wait, Drake, you shot him without being able to . . . ?"

"Ah, Emissary Dabarius," Thor said, "I see your powers of reasoning haven't left you entirely after being choked by a God."

"Shut up," Dabarius said.

"I missed the first shot," Drake said. He had hoped to hear the bolt hit and when it didn't he knew he had gone wide. "I heard him choking you, and when you spoke again I adjusted my aim."

"It was a good shot," Thor said.

"He never suspected what we were planning," Dabarius said.

"He did not die easily," Thor said, and took a deep breath. "There were things in the fog . . . watching us."

"I felt them," Bellor said. "They're gone now. All of them."

Drake sensed that Ethan was close by. Their connection still strong.

It took at least half an hour before the bright light in Drake's eyes started to fade. He began to see shapes and what

591

he recognized as Bree's face right in front of his own. She blinked and they embraced.

"We've given Draglûne too much time to prepare for us now," Bellor said, his vision returning as he glanced at the others.

A short while later they could all see again, though bright halos surrounded everything for Drake unless he squinted.

"It would have been the right moment for Draglûne to attack us," Drake said. "We were sitting targets."

"Perhaps he is away," Thor said.

"He knows we're here now," Bellor said. "If he has a Crystal Eye he can see us in it now. The *Dracken Viergur* protection magic won't work as well here."

"Then he'll be coming soon," Drake said, as he checked his crossbow for damage. He made certain the pair of wyrm-killing bolts sat perfectly into the double tracks and tried to blink away the continued distortion in his eyes.

"Do you hear that?" Dabarius asked.

Drake didn't hear anything, but Jep and Temus both growled low and deep, like they had before.

"He's coming now," Thor said, raising his shield.

Drake aimed down the tunnel, ready to do his part, though his vision was so blurry.

"*Wingataur hooves. A scout?*" Dabarius whispered, and Drake suspected his friend had augmented his hearing. "There." The wizard pointed and the dogs looked in the same direction down the tunnel.

"*Goss velleg?*" Bellor said in the *Dracken Viergur* battle tongue. *Willing to cast?*

Drake nodded and raised his crossbow. He aimed down the tunnel, though he could see only shadows and blackness beyond the immediate radius of their glowstones, and the three Thor had cast ahead to give them a larger perimeter. His eyes felt heavy and swollen. Blinking did not help.

Thor removed an extra glowstone from a thick black leather pouch filled with them and cocked his arm, aiming where the dogs were looking with their ears pricked up.

"*Goss*," Drake said—*cast*—and Thor pitched the stone as far as he could. It flew and then bounced and skipped along the edge of the cavern past a black tunnel entrance. For an instant—half a heartbeat—the bouncing light revealed a bull-headed demon stretching its wings in preparation to fly. It held something in its clawed hands.

Drake pulled one trigger and heard the shaft crack and skip along the wall. He'd shot too late, his aim had been off because of his vision. He held the second shot, not wanting to waste a good shaft.

The rapid flapping of wings echoed as the demon escaped as fast as it could, abandoning any attempt at being stealthy. Thor cocked his arm to throw another glowstone.

Bellor stopped him.

"Too far now," Bellor said. "Drake, reload."

The crossbowman worked his krannekin as fast as he could and pulled back the top bow of his spring-steel weapon.

"Did you see what it carried?" Dabarius asked.

"No," Bree said, and they all shook their heads.

"It had a Crystal Eye and a tripod," Dabarius said.

"Are you certain?" Bellor asked.

"I am. It must have been Ra'menek's," Dabarius said. "We've given Draglûne a gift that he has wanted for a long time."

"What will happen?" Bree asked. "He must have three of them now."

"He must," Dabarius said, "but I don't know what three will do for him."

"We shouldn't linger here any longer," Bellor said. "Can you all . . . well, are you ready to go?"

They all mumbled their ascent and Drake wondered if the time they had just taken to recover had doomed them somehow. Drake felt numb, like he had already missed the killing shot and he would never have another chance.

Thor led the way, tossing square glowstones ahead of them and then picking them up as they moved forward. Drake's senses were on the highest possible alert as they crept forward, ready for an ambush or attack at any moment. Both Bellor and Thor did what they never had before in Drake's memory. They loaded their crossbows and kept them slung over their shoulders, but cocked, the safety cog in place, protecting from an accidental release.

Draglûne or some wingataurs could be waiting in a large side passage, or up in the ceiling, ready to drop on top of them from a black crevasse.

Thor always kept at least two stones farther ahead in the endless tunnel that wended its way like a snake through the limestone mountain. The road followed the bed of the dry river, and they continued on the right side, advancing carefully.

They moved from one of the standing stones embedded in the road to the next one, staying behind cover whenever they could. The rounded river boulders began to increase in size the further they went. At first they were no taller than a dwarf, but now they were huge monoliths with large geometric shapes or Mephitian glyphs covering them. Wingataurs could easily hide behind the stones or inside any number of the dozens of unsealed tombs or large and small tunnel entrances on both sides of the wide tunnel.

Drake watched the dogs carefully for any sign that demons lurked in ambush. Many tomb entrances had been broken open long ago, judging by the amount of dust and mold growth on the burial artifacts and debris that was often scattered about outside. He looked for tracks, and let Jep and Temus listen and sniff the air before they passed them, in case a wingataur hid inside, waiting for them to pass.

Drake kept expecting an ambush from an open tomb or

when Thor stepped around the corner of a huge stone.

"Wait, listen," Dabarius said. He turned back north, the way they had come from.

The dogs' ears pricked up, and they looked behind them.

"The Gate of the Sun may have just opened," Dabarius said. "I thought I heard hinges squeaking."

It was too far back for them to see any light, and they waited for a while, listening, but Drake heard nothing more and the dogs fixed their attention on the tunnel ahead.

"The entrance has to be a mile behind us," Thor said, "you couldn't have heard it open."

"Who would open it?" Bree asked.

"I worry more about who will come inside it if it's open," Bellor said. "If the Storm Priests break through Barius's men . . ."

"We'll have an army on our arses," Thor said. "No offense to your father," he glanced at Dabarius. "He's a good man."

Dabarius and Thor regarded each other with respect for a moment, and in the lull as they all stood there considering what may or may not be coming after them from behind, Drake imagined Draglûne's fiery breath exploding around them, then his claws tearing them apart. Why couldn't Dabarius hear what was ahead of them? Bellor had said that dragons knew magic that hid the sound of their movements. He turned his attention back down the tunnel. After a few more steps Jep and Temus tensed up, their shoulders tight and their teeth bared, tails up.

"Something's coming," Drake said, gesturing at the dogs with his non-trigger hand. The stench of dragon increased so much that the sulfur and brimstone scent burned his nose.

Five gigantic obelisks that looked like head stones rose from the flat road covered with arcane Mephitian symbols and glyphs. The standing stones with rounded tops were roughly the same size as the arched Gate of the Sun entrance to the Tunnel of Tombs. They were spaced as two pairs, and then one large blue gray obelisk, shaped like two standing stones were trying to split apart at the top, rose from the center of the road. It was the very first time one of the obelisks had been placed in the center of the road. This must be the end of the path, and Void mist clung to the walls and swirled around the rocks. They were near the end of the tunnel where the river had poured into the Underworld.

"We will face him here," Bellor said, slipping his crossbow off his shoulder. Thor tossed out four glowstones all around them to light the battlefield and held his own crossbow, then glanced back to where Bellor was pointing, not wanting to take his eyes off the tunnel ahead. "Look at these marks."

Thor noticed them, and his eyes widened. "Drobin runes and Mephitian script," Thor said. "A battle marker. *Names of the Drobin dead.*"

"This is where Bölak and the Viergur faced Draglûne," Bellor said.

Drake, Dabarius, Bree and the dwarves stared at the markings for a long moment. They had followed the trail of Thor's uncle for so long and now they stood in the place where he and his hunters had all died according to the list of ten names. Perhaps this was not the place they should make their stand.

Jep and Temus barked loudly at something in front of them, and the decision was made.

"Demons wings," Dabarius shouted, and the leathery wings were right on top of them.

"Step back, now!" Drake shouted leading his friends several steps back behind the obelisk rather than to the side of it and they put their backs against the vertical stone.

Sparks exploded from the space where they had just been standing as several invisible and heavy creatures landed with a thunderous crash. If Drake had not pulled them back they would have all been crushed under iron-strong hooves.

Dabarius shouted something, and a distortion like a bubble of air in water, exploded outward revealing seven-foot-tall wingataur demons landing all around them. Ten or more of the brutish monsters hemmed them in, and attacked with long serrated swords, clawed hammers, two-handed axes of black-steel, and clubs with iron spikes flanging out at many different angles.

Bree narrowly missed getting hit in the head by sharp hoof. She sliced upward, cutting deeply into the demon's groin, which sent blood spurting onto the stone where the demon crashed. She stabbed it through the back of the neck, and *Wingblade* erupted from its windpipe in a spray of blood.

Drake released both his bolts before two of the wingataurs near him even hit the ground. The wyrm-killing bolts ended their lives the instant they penetrated their chests. The pair of demons died on the right side of the obelisk where Bree, Drake and the dogs held their ground. The momentum of the two Drake shot carried them forward. They crashed and rolled, getting in the way of two more demons trying to attack Bree. She parried and dodged their attacks, keeping them away from her and Drake.

On the left side of the obelisk, the dwarves shot the demons in front of them at point blank range, then discarded their crossbows. Thor raised his hammer and Bellor his glowing crimson axe as three wingataurs swung their large weapons at the Drobin, trying to smash them into the ground.

Jep, Temus and Bree held off a pair of demons while Drake reloaded faster than he ever had before.

Bellor chopped through the knee-cap of his opponent with *Wyrmslayer* and the axe raged, the crimson light expanding. Dabarius sent a bolt of white electricity into the same wingataur's face and it was so stunned and blind that Bellor hacked off one of its hooves, and brought it down to the ground where he made quick work with a chop to its throat. The old dwarf moved with shocking speed, the weight of centuries fading in the heat of battle.

Thor dove between his two opponents, forcing them to

turn away from Bellor and face him. He blocked a slash from a sword and dodged an axe swing that would have split him from skull to stomach. He kept their attention until Bellor chopped one demon's spine in half, and it went limp from the waist down. Dark blood splashed across his beard as he yanked the axe free. He roared something in Drobin that Drake couldn't understand, *Wyrmslayer* rising and falling in a blur.

Bree slashed and blocked, trying to keep the pair of wingataurs from killing the snarling and snapping dogs while Drake reloaded. They had spread apart making it nearly impossible for Bree to keep both of them away from Drake.

Jep was about to be killed by an axe when Drake slipped the first bolt into the track and then the second.

"Look up!" Dabarius shouted at Drake.

A wingataur must have been perched on the obelisk and it dropped straight down with a spear pointed at Bree's back, while aiming its hooves at Drake's head.

She spun and turned, her eyes on the wingataur plummeting toward Drake. The demons kicked the snapping dogs out of their way and raised their axes to chop Bree apart. She ignored their raised weapons and tried to push Drake out of the way, and also raise her sword to ward off the demon falling on him. The axe-wielding monsters behind her were a heartbeat from striking her down as she pushed him back onto the corpse of a demon.

Drake shot both of the wingataurs menacing Bree through the chest as he stumbled backwards and landed on his shoulder. She blocked the spear tip and thrust *Wingblade* straight upwards, impaling the demon through the gut, but it crushed her to the ground with its bulk, one bent knee on either side of her small body, trapping her completely and leaving her helpless as blood from its gut wound spilled into her face. She could not move her arms to reach any of the knives in her belt as it raised the spear, preparing to pierce her through her open mouth.

She looked at Drake, their eyes met. Everything they had been through came down to this moment. He would not let her die. He screamed and hooked the double bows of his empty crossbow around the shaft of the spear and yanked as hard as he could. The tip descended and scratched along the stone beside Bree's head. The monster turned as Drake pulled his Kierka blade and attacked.

"No!" Bree screamed as black blood drained into her face.

The wingataur changed its thrust and aimed the butt of the spear at Drake's chest while it closed a clawed hand around Bree's throat and squeezed. The blow caught him in the left shoulder, but his right arm carried through with his swing and he chopped into the side of the demon's neck, cutting through red meat and severing arteries. The bull-demon swung its long horns at him and dropped its spear, but strangled the life out of the woman he loved.

Drake grabbed hold of one horn and held the head still as he chopped over and over with his Kierka knife, but the dying demon kept squeezing her throat, refusing to yield her life for its own.

Thunderous hooves and the war shouts of more wingataurs barely registered in Drake's mind as he tried to pull the demon off Bree's body.

"Drake!" Dabarius shouted and tried to drag him out of the way as two more wingataurs became visible in the unmasking circle and attacked. They charged Drake with huge hammers raised over their heads, ready to crush him into pulp.

Jep and Temus limped forward, and tore at the monsters' legs, trying to defend their master. Temus tripped one demon with his body, but the stomping hooves smashed the yelping dog hard to the ground. Jep attached himself to the other wingataur's leg, but failed to slow the demon, and it swung its hammer down toward Drake's skull.

XCIX

Dear Lord Marshal Gunter, Thank you for everything that you have done for me. When I have passed into the Afterworld, I shall remember your example. The kindness that you showed gives me hope that the wound between the Amaryllians and Lorakians can be healed. I know that you did everything you could to spare my life, and I do not fault you in any way. Mourn me as you will, but do not worry for my soul. I go to be with my Goddess in a place of light and love.

—Priestess Jaena Whitestar, from her personal journal

Jaena watched the crowd gathering from her tower cell window. How many of them were going to die today when the violence began after her execution? It chilled her to the core, and she kept turning away from the window, wishing that this was not happening and that her wonderful dreamlike night had never ended.

The people had already begun filling Father's Square, the name of the plaza in front of the Temple of Lorak. She suspected some had slept there the night before and it appeared to her that every human in Nexus City was coming to see her put to death. They had been arriving in a constant stream ever since the sunrise and tens of thousands had already gathered.

The Drobin army began assembling as well, forming a line of heavily armed and armored dwarves five or six ranks deep and blocking every side to the small square building called the Red Block where she would be killed. It was more of a twenty-foot tall platform made of gray granite at the edge of the plaza. A blood red banner flew from a flagstaff atop the building.

The wide steps that led up to the Temple of Lorak loomed over the stone platform on the north side, and a long line of Drobin soldiers waited halfway up the steps blocking any humans from getting to the high ground in front of the temple.

600

The three large tunnel openings that cut into the steps and provided underground passage from the square to the temple were also blocked by heavily armored dwarves.

The soldiers looked to be a strong force, all wearing helms, plate armor, and carrying tall shields, but they could not number more than five or six hundred, perhaps less, and most of them were in front of the temple.

The crowd of humans had to be fifty thousand and was growing rapidly. She went back to her bed and lay face down, putting her hands over her ears and trying to think about the night before and not the nightmare of today.

Jaena could still feel Drake's hands on her skin. She had held him, kissed him, felt everything that Bree felt. They had made love, going again and again, until Bree had fallen into a blissful sleep with his arms around her.

A few short hours later, just before dawn, Jaena had woken up in her tower cell, completely alone. Perhaps what she had done was wrong, but she loved him, and was so thankful to have seen him and said goodbye. It wasn't just Drake now. Jaena could clearly feel herself connected to Bree. They had shared something so personal, so deep that words couldn't explain it. If what her mother had always taught her was right, and that a person's worth was measured in the number of golden cords, the close bonds of love she carried, then Jaena was richer by one this morning. She wasn't ready to die, but she told herself that now she could face what was coming. If Drake and Bree could find the courage to face Draglûne, she would find her courage to do this.

Jaena wondered if she would see Drake in the Afterworld today, then immediately chastised herself for such a thought. She knelt on the soft rug at the foot of her bed and prayed to Amaryllis, begging the Goddess to look after him and all his friends, especially Bree. He needed her, and Bree would look after him. Perhaps some tiny fragment of her would stay and live on inside of the Wing Guardian. In that way, perhaps she

601

would always be there with them, even after what would soon come to pass.

She was praying when the knock came at the door. "Breakfast, if you please," the guard said.

The thought of food made her made her sick to her stomach. "No, thank you."

He left and she dressed herself. She kept thinking that this was the last time she would braid her hair, or put on her shoes, or wash her face. She refused to shed any more tears, and knelt back down and prayed harder for Drake and Bree, and the others. Her task today was easy. Kneel, hold still. That was all.

Bree and Drake would need a miracle. With force of arms, and strength purpose, Drake and his comrades had a chance to bring a terrible monster to account and change the world for the better.

It hurt her, that in death, she would sow discord and bloodshed, when all she had ever wanted to do was ease the suffering of others. Life happened all too fast, and she found herself so far from understanding, though she had spent her years trying to accumulate wisdom. It seemed that the only lesson she'd ever really learned was how little she really knew.

"Goddess, I have tried, and will never stop trying to act as your eyes and hands and heart, until my body is broken and my eyes go dark," she whispered, finally levering herself up and sitting quietly on her narrow mattress.

The next knock did not scare her. She had been waiting for it, but she could not speak at first, and a respectful moment later, the knock came again.

"Please enter," Jaena said.

The young dwarf in the doorway wore the gray and dark green trimmed uniform with the copper buttons of a marshal, but she did not recognize him as one of her usual guards. Where was the Lord Marshal Gunther? He had told her he would escort her personally. Had something happened to him?

"It is my honor to meet you, Priestess Jaena," he said. "My father has told me much about you. I am Marshal Wilke Krohgstaad, his fourth son. He sent a message to me this morning, asking me to escort you, in case he was . . . delayed."

"I'm pleased to meet you Marshal Wilke," Jaena said, bowing. "Will your father be meeting us later?"

"Yes, he will," Wilke said. "He wishes to see you before the . . . "

"Before the end," Jaena said. "You don't need to put padding around it for me, sir."

He walked closer to her, his face apologetic and very grave. "If it pleases you, I have a tonic that will calm your nerves. I can mix it with water, or wine."

"No thank you, Marshal Wilke," she said, "but will you please do something trifling for me?"

"I shall do anything that is within my power," he said.

"Please give this to your father." Jaena handed him her journal.

"It will be my privilege."

"I also have a message for him."

"I swear to you that he will hear it word for word," Wilke said.

"Tell him that I am glad that he read it," she said. "I know he had to, and tell him that I've made a few other entries. He must read them after I'm gone. I've also written a note to him personally."

"My father will be greatly honored by this," Wilke said. "Thank you."

Per Wilke's instructions, Jaena wrapped her braided hair around her head and covered it with a white scarf so that it was all off her neck, save for a few blond wisps. She wore the green dress that the Lord Marshal had given her and her traveling boots that had been made in Cliffton.

They descended the long staircase side by side, but in silence, with two guards in front and behind them. They did not

603

exit into a courtyard and instead went deeper underground until Jaena assumed they were below the level of Father's Square. They entered a large dry tunnel supported by arches and lit by glowstones that went perfectly straight into the distance. A carriage pulled by a lone elderly vroxen waited for her.

Wilke delayed for several moments, expecting his father to arrive, but instead of the Lord Marshal coming out of the staircase, a sharp-featured dwarf wearing expensive gray and red-fringed robes with an axe insignia on the lapel emerged with eight soldiers.

"Who's that?" Jaena asked, as the dwarf eyed her like she was a vile creature.

"Aksel Reinheld, Defender of the Faith," Wilke said. "He's the leader of the Father's Paladins."

Jaena had heard of them. They were the most zealous of the religious warriors who served Lorak and the High Council, notorious fundamentalists who may have been the ones who burned alive Gwynedd the Kind and her Sacred Grove.

Wilke and Defender Aksel spoke tersely in Drobin to each other for a moment. The four marshals with Wilke eyed the eight soldiers. Wilke pointed in some direction, his brows furrowed, and began to speak louder. Aksel gave a short but unyielding retort. The argument between Wilke and Aksel escalated and the Paladin pushed Wilke against the carriage.

The four marshals pulled their war hammers from their belts and the soldiers raised axes and shields.

"Stop this!" Jaena shouted, and stood between the opposing sides. "Put your weapons away and tell me what's the matter."

"We are going to wait for my father," Wilke said in Nexan, but the Paladin's expression was uncompromising.

"No, we are taking the prisoner right now," Defender Aksel said.

"We wait," Wilke said.

"She gets in the carriage now, or we spill your blood, Marshal. I have orders from the Lorakian High Council and they will not tolerate this insolence."

Marshal Wilke stepped in front of Jaena and though he did not draw the hammer from his belt, he looked as if he meant to fight for her to the death.

Jaena bypassed him and got into the carriage and sat down. "Marshal Wilke, I'm ready. If it pleases you, will you sit beside me?"

He stared at her, the surprise in his face changing to high-esteem. He did sit beside her and his marshals rode on the sideboards. The angry Paladin and the soldiers followed along easily as the driver did not rush the pace.

The tunnel went on for at least half a mile with a few gradual turns. Jaena looked down the many branches all lit by sporadic golden light stones. The underground road system seemed extensive. Only a handful of Drobin hustled about, but those that did appeared to be on urgent errands and many pulled handcarts loaded with supplies.

Wilke noticed Jaena's questioning expression. "The Drobin populace knows what's going to happen and are stockpiling food and supplies."

"Everyone knows what's going to happen?" she asked.

"The Nexans have been on strike for a week," Wilke said. "There have been many riots already, and fighting. Everyone thinks war is coming to Nexus City. The human king has fled, and taken the road to Drobin City. There aren't enough dwarven soldiers to defeat all of the people who have come from the countryside and the locals. It's going to be a slaughter and both sides will lose in the end. My father is so worried. He blames himself."

"I don't blame him, please . . . tell him that," she said.

"I will."

"I knew the law when I put my feet upon this road. I have never agreed with it, nor will I, but I never intended anything

605

more than to care for my people, and to share the joy that knowing the Goddess has brought me. We are a gentle hand, and this . . . this pains me deeply."

Wilke looked at her for a long moment, clearly wishing to say something, but remained silent. He reached out his broad hand and gently gripped her wrist. From afar, it was easy to hate the Drobin, but even as she rode to her demise, Jaena could see that there was much good in them, and far more kindness than she had imagined.

The vroxen groaned as the driver pulled tight on the reigns.

Jaena looked around them, noticed the door against the wall held open by a soldier and the blood red square painted over it.

She stepped out of the carriage slowly.

Aksel and his guards surrounded Jaena, and their stern faces made her wilt inside. Wilke bristled.

"She must be bound," the Paladin said and produced a length of coarse rope.

"Not with that," Wilke said. He retrieved a soft cord from his pocket. "I will do it."

She nodded and allowed Wilke to bind her hands behind her back. He made sure it was not painful to her. They entered the doorway and a room with a staircase that seemed to go up for a long way, and what appeared to be a small lift room. A young dwarf attendant waited, ready to work the levers and controls.

"We'll take the lift," Wilke said, ushering Jaena inside. His four marshals accompanied them, barring the Paladin and the soldiers from entering. Defender Aksel glanced at the stairs, but waited until the half-door was shut and the attendant had called up through the speaking tube ordering six barrels of sand to be used as counter weights before he sent his dwarves ahead on the stairs. He waited until the lift had begun to slowly rise before he hurried toward the staircase.

Jaena felt enclosed in the small lift-room, and her heart fluttered. The walls pressed in tightly and her stoicism fell away when the door shut tightly. The sounds of gears and pulleys terrified her. She'd never ridden a lift before, but then she had the realization that right above them was the place where she would die.

"Let me hold your arm," Wilke said, and put a reassuring hand on her. "What can I do to help?"

"I don't know," she said, then realized that not knowing what would happen on top of the small building called Red Block was terrifying her. Perhaps if she knew, her nerves would calm down. "Please, tell me exactly what will happen now. Please."

"This will carry us only to the level of plaza," Wilke said, "then we shall walk up some stairs to the roof of a small square building. I will bring you to a rectangular table . . . and will use leather straps to tie you down. Your head would dangle off the edge giving the executioner space to wield the axe."

Jaena had the terrible thought that they would tie her face up and she would see the axe coming toward her throat. That was not at all what she imagined while waiting in her cell. "Face up?"

"No, no, no," Wilke said soothingly. "You will be face down, and a blindfold will be provided if you want. Two of my marshals will guide you to the table. The top of it will slide off and they will strap you to the board, face down. Your sentence will be read by a herald, and you will not be allowed to speak to the crowd. A Lorakian Priest will carry out the sentence with an axe. It will be quick."

C

Here the Ten Sons of Kheb fought the Dragon of Darkness and his bull demons. They died with honor.

—Priest Hezekiah of Kheb, from the Sacred Obelisk

Barius stood alone waiting to face an army of his enemies. Sharp pinnacles of rock surrounded him on both sides of the narrow canyon south of the library school. A light rain helped wash away the blood of his enemies from his skin, but the stains on his clothes seemed worse as they got wet. At least there was no thunder, as the storm that the Priests of Shenahr had summoned was over now, and left behind only a soft patter that would turn the dirt to mud, and do little else.

The library school had to be under siege, and if Gha'brel had followed orders he was escaping into the razor canyons. Barius prayed for him, and the men, and the young boys who wanted to go with them rather than face death, torture, and humiliation as a Priest of Shenahr or Ah'usar. The boys would rather leave the school and risk never seeing their families again instead of subjecting themselves to the sanctioned abuses by the Priests of Lesh'heb.

Why did the Storm and Solar Priests think they were so righteous? The power given them by their class and Ra'menek had destroyed any good in them long ago. He wondered what information they must have been given to make them return to Lesh'heb. Did they come back only wanting to save their precious God King, and the Dragon of Darkness? Did they even think about the boys in the school? Would all of them who had returned come down the canyon to defend the brother gods? He hoped all of them would come, but not just yet.

Barius continued kneeling in the warm mud, the humid air preventing any chill from the rain. He had reached through the thin brown muck and placed his hands on the bedrock of the canyon. For a long time he had prayed, his mind finding all the masses of stone around him as Kheb's magic guided his mind. He followed the fracture lines, examined the layers of rock, and noted the most unstable faults making a map in his head.

Moments later he heard the Shenahrians coming and strengthened his connection to the earth, sending out roots of energy along the fault lines and the weakest fracture points. He put all of himself into the magic, willing the power to flow and build up until he thought his head was going to explode. Then he released the magic, letting it expand and follow the fracture lines, radiating outward over and over again, like a wave getting higher and higher. He felt the power pressing against the rocks, the energy like a torrent of water about to rupture a gigantic dam. He could feel the cracks forming, the layers about to slip and break.

There was nothing more he could do, but wait until they came, letting the spell work and loosen the rock. Then he would send the last bit of his power into the ground and hope it was enough.

He didn't wait long.

No less than two hundred men, mostly Solar Priests, but quite a number of heavily armed Shenahrian warriors and assassins, walked toward him in disorganized mobs.

At first, a lone man kneeling in the mud during the rain did not raise any alarm, but then someone recognized him and the front group stopped.

A grizzled veteran named Teshup, who was past his fighting prime came forward. "Ben'ahmi, the traitor. You are the turn-cloak who led the rabble."

"You are wrong," Barius said. "Ben'ahmi is not my name. I am the wizard Barius of Isyrin."

"You are far from Isyrin, lying fool," Teshup said. "You will pay for abandoning your vows."

"Vows to a false god do not bind me," Barius said. "I came here to destroy your order, and those are the vows that I kept."

"How shall we kill you, Barius of Isyrin?" Teshup asked.

"You shall not, for I have already chosen the manner of my death. I will have vengeance and justice for the evil planned and perpetrated by the Priests of Lesh'heb." Barius released a final blast of force into the ground that spread cracks in the fabric of the stone all around him. The energy he had set in motion burst forth like a stuck door finally forced open by one hard push. He had chosen this particular place because of the weak rock walls and the precarious pinnacles, and he thought it a beautiful place for his grave.

The ground rumbled. Cracks opened in the ground in front of Barius and sucked down the water and mud. A pair of wide fissures raced left and right from where he stood and hit the canyon walls like a hammer striking a ceramic plate. Then cracks went horizontal and vertical in both directions for over two hundred feet.

"Run!" Teshup shouted, but the men did not know whether to run forward or back. The falling walls and tumbling boulders found them all just the same as they shouted in panic, trying in vain to escape. Precarious boulders perched on the edge of the canyon cliffs fell and killed the Priests as great slabs of limestone slid into the canyon grinding soft fleshy bodies into mush.

Barius knelt reverently as boulders fell all around him. The army was being pulverized by the falling debris, and Barius would die knowing he had taken hundreds of his enemies with him in death. These men, trained to intimidate, murder, or fool others would not sow any more chaos in Mephitia or beyond. Nor would they torture and abuse children in the school, or attack his son his companions.

Dabarius would help end the lives of the Brother Gods and the people of Mephitia would be free to choose their own destiny once again. His bones would return to the earth, and

Barius smiled as a slab of rock pinned him down. A huge boulder bounced toward him and he welcomed the end. It would be a good death.

CI

The Dragon of Darkness assailed the Sons of Kheb with fire and claw, demon bulls, and foul magic that broke their spells.

—Priest Hezekiah of Kheb, from the Sacred Obelisk

Bree woke up with the rotten egg taste of wingataur blood in her mouth. She choked and spat, coughing as she tried to breathe. Her shoulders and back ached, and she remembered being pinned under the wingataur demon, helpless as it wrapped a clawed hand around her neck. Drake tried to save her, then he was attacked by more of the bull-demons. What had happened to him? She shot up, "Drake?!"

Bellor's strong and gentle hands held her as she came to her senses. The obelisk where they made their stand loomed in front of her. She had been dragged out from under the demon, and more than a dozen bloody—and some burning—bodies of wingataurs lay strewn in front of her. The ground was slick and covered with gore. She realized her friends had dragged her out of the carnage to a clean patch of roadway.

Thor kept watch, wiping blood off his forehead as it trickled from his scalp. He kept looking at the tunnel ahead, which was filling with Void mist. Dabarius stood beside him, and they glanced back at her, but neither would meet her eyes.

"Where's Drake?" Bree asked, her voice a whisper.

Bellor hesitated, glanced down, then with a bleak expression, the dwarf motioned behind her with his chin.

Jep lay beside Drake's body, partially screening him. The dog's tan coat was covered with blood spatter, and the bullmastiff looked beaten and sad. Temus stood over them both. Forlornly, the dog glanced at Thor and Dabarius, then at his fallen master.

Bright red blood saturated Drake's chest. A thin linen scarf covered his face and head, also covered in blood, as was a makeshift pillow under his head.

Bree's face scrunched together and a cold numbness spread over her entire body.

Bellor interposed himself between her and Drake.

"Is he . . ?" she whispered, her voice catching in her throat.

Bellor nodded, his eyes blank. "He's gone."

"No," she said, wanting to crawl to Drake, hold him, tell him she loved him. "Bellor, heal him, please."

"The ground is tainted by evil," Bellor said. "I cannot."

She tried to get to Drake. A high-pitched and grief stricken scream that did not sound like her came from her throat.

The old dwarf held Bree tightly, comforting her. "Don't look at him now, lass. Not like this."

"*Bellor*," Thor said, shaking his head angrily.

The old dwarf ignored him, and stayed with Bree, letting her mourn.

"I have to see him," she said, as hot tears fell from her eyes and Bellor embraced her.

"You will, but not now," the War Priest said.

"Bellor, we need to decide if we're going to run and hide in one of the tombs," Dabarius called back to them, though she didn't think he wanted to retreat. He wanted to fight, and so did she.

Bellor put the sticky handle of *Wingblade* in her hand. "We can't kill Draglûne without Drake, but we're not going to run." He helped Bree stand up and he faced down the tunnel. "We're going to fight you, wyrm!" Bellor shouted, daring Draglûne to come.

The *Dracken Viergur* Master guided Bree, Thor, and Dabarius to the other side of the roadway where they would make their last stand. The place where they had been was too slippery, and there were too many corpses that might trip them.

Near the center of the road, and behind them now, Drake's body remained with Jep and Temus flanking him. Bree wanted to stand in front of him, guard him and face Draglûne in the very center of the road. She would wait until the wyrm was close, about to bite, then she would stab *Wingblade* through his eye.

For now, they remained behind the cover of a standing stone, peeking around the side of it and down the center of the road. Thor and Bellor held their crossbows and aimed into the gathering mist, which was much thicker now.

A slight tremor shook the ground, but it was gone in an instant.

"What was that?" Bree asked.

"It came from behind us," Bellor said. "It's not the dragon."

"Earthquake?" Thor asked.

"A sign from Lorak," Bellor said. "The Earth Father favors us."

"We'll need all the help we can get," Thor said, touching the mountain-shaped medallion around his neck.

Bree prayed to Amar'isis, Kheb, Lorak, and any god who would listen. She wanted to trade her life for Drake's. He should not be dead. It should be her. She had failed to protect him, but now she offered herself to the gods, a willing sacrifice to bring him back. She would pay any price.

Bellor tapped Thor on the shoulder, and the younger dwarf shouted, "Come, wyrm! We may die, but we will die fighting you!" his deep voice reverberated off the cavern walls.

Dabarius mumbled a spell, and she could see blue sparks arcing between his fingers. The wizard's body was almost vibrating with power and she could feel a buzzing cloud radiating from him that irritated her skin even from five feet away.

Boom! Boom!

The ground shook as something massive struck the road and the echo blasted through the tunnel of tombs. It wasn't very far away.

Boom! Boom!

"Draglûne strikes the ground with his tail," Bellor said. "He will not frighten us with such tricks."

Thunderous hoof beats echoed the dragon's *booms* as many wingataurs stomped on the stone with iron-shod hooves. They had to be right beyond the large split-topped monolith in the center of the road. Bree heard their snorts and could smell their musky odor.

"Now we know why he delayed," Thor said. "He's summoned an entire tribe."

"He's afraid of us," Dabarius said. The wizard's muscles surged until his clothing hardly fit. "As well he should be."

"How many?" Bree asked, glancing at the fourteen bodies of the demons they had already slain. It had been incredible luck that only Drake had fallen in the first attack. They would not all survive this next one, as Drake had perished after he had personally killed five of the demons.

The wingataurs stomped and snorted, roaring now as they prepared to charge.

"*How many?*" Bree asked more urgently.

"Thirty or more," Bellor said.

Boom! Boom! Boom! The stench of dragon increased tenfold as a damp wind brought the nauseating scent of wyrm and wingataur musk into Bree's nostrils.

The two glowstones that lay furthest down the tunnel went out.

Many leathery wings flapped hard as wingataurs took to the air, while even more stampeded forward, their hooves like thunder.

Bree knew she should see them now coming right at her as they flew and charged down the center of the road, but they were all cloaked in draconic sorcery.

Dabarius stepped forward and blue sparks of electricity crackled from his hands. He raised his arms and his entire

615

body was cloaked in blue sparks, which surged away from him and formed a glowing web of energy that ascended from the floor to the cavern ceiling directly in front of the charging wingataurs. Three-dozen demons became visible as they passed through the lightning wall, their bodies burning as they went into convulsive seizures. Charging wingataurs fell and slid on the floor while flying demons dropped out of the air or fell hard to the ground, their horns scraping against the rock as frothy mucous foamed from their mouths.

Not a single wingataur survived Dabarius's huge electricity spell. The wizard collapsed to his knees, but somehow kept the lightning wall in place. A few other bull demons tried to cross it, but died writhing on the ground. Dabarius's face was ashen gray, his whole body trembling, but his eyes were exultant.

Everything went quiet for a moment. Bree wondered what was coming next. More wingataurs or . . .

The swirling Void mist and the foul smoke from electrocuted wingataurs blew into Bree's face as a massive creature leaped from the darkness behind the central standing stone. With wings spread, the dragon landed in the center of the road. The tremendous crash knocked Bree, Thor, Dabarius, and Bellor onto their backsides as the limestone road rose and fell like a wave.

As they tried to stand, Draglûne glared at them with unrelenting hate. The lightning wall collapsed in on itself and the electricity was attracted to the Iron Dragon King, making his gray armor shine blue as the lightning streaked across his scales.

"Eyes!" Bellor shouted as Draglûne spewed a hellish gout of flame, engulfing them all in a firestorm that went around the obelisk. Bree pressed her lids shut and huddled into a ball, but the pain did not come, and the flames relented. She could see and hear, but could not get a breath of air.

Bellor's magic had protected her from being incinerated, but she could not see how her sword would hurt the gigan-

616

tic dragon. She crawled toward the standing stone looking for cover. Up until that moment, she had always been brave enough, but the enormity of the dragon shook her to the core. Without Drake, what could they really hope to do?

"Clan Blackhammer!" Thor and Bellor shouted, and she knew they charged at Draglûne with no hope of survival.

She wanted to turn and look over her shoulder at them, and see how bravely they were going to die, but movement caught her eye, and she could not believe what she was seeing.

Drake sprang up from his bloody pillow and aimed his crossbow at Draglûne.

CII

The first two of the Ten Sons of Kheb who died facing the Dragon of Darkness gave their lives to slow his charge and give their brethren a chance to defeat him.
—Hezekiah, Priest of Kheb, from the Sacred Obelisk

The worst moment for Drake came when Bree had broken down and screamed his name in despair. He could see her the whole time through the linen scarf, and almost sat up then. He had let someone who loved him think he was dead, and he hated himself for it. Bellor's plan to make Draglûne believe their most potent warrior was dead had worked, though, and that was the only thing that mattered.

Drake sprang into a shooting stance while Draglûne's attention was focused on the dwarves and their suicidal charge. As he aimed, he did not think about how he had deceived Bree'alla. He did not think about anything except that moment. He aimed not with his mind, but with his entirety of who he was. He would not get another chance. There were no words in his mind, but there was a "Way."

Drake released the two bolts from *Heartseeker*. The crossbow and the two shafts had become part of his body, and they were him as they sped toward Draglûne's chest.

The Iron Dragon King carried the essence of the Storm God and had heightened senses, but he did not see the bolts approaching, as his attention was focused on Thor and Bellor's valiant charge.

The wyrm-killing missiles struck Draglûne in the chest near his sideways s-shaped birthmark, puncturing the iron scales and burying themselves inside him up to the end of the fletchings.

Bellor's enchantments and Dabarius's seeking magic helped them burrow through his chest like two glowing hot

618

lances. The wyrm bellowed in agony, clutching at his wounds. The holes in his iron scales flashed with a white light as Drake's bolts penetrated Draglûne's evil heart.

Bellor and Thor stopped their bluff charge and watched the wyrm tremble and gasp. Draglûne's head dipped down and Thor threw his hammer, using every bit of strength he could muster. The dragon's head pitched backwards as the flying hammer struck one of the two longest upper teeth at the front of his mouth. The huge tooth shattered and tumbled down, bouncing on the stone with Thor's hammer.

Steaming blood poured from the chest wounds, and Draglûne roared so loud Drake felt his bones rattle. The sound stunned the dwarves who were so close to Draglûne now, and the wyrm reached for Bellor and Thor with his black claws.

Dabarius grabbed both the dwarves by the back of their chainmail shirts and dragged them to the ground, just outside of the dragon's reach. Claws as long as swords gouged the floor, then Draglûne drew backward, clutching at his bloody wounds.

"We shall finish you!" Bellor shouted and lifted *Wyrmslayer*, the axe blade glowing crimson. The old War Priest struggled against Dabarius, fighting to escape his friend's grasp and attack.

I AM A GOD! YOU WILL NOT SLAY ME!

The words in Drake's mind felt like a blast of scalding air from a furnace.

"I cut off your father's head with this axe," Bellor said, "and I shall cut off yours just the same." With a final surge, he broke free of the wizard's grasp and sprinted toward Draglûne like a dwarf possessed.

NEVER!

Draglûne swept his immense wings forward. The gust of wind lifted Bellor, Thor, Dabarius, Bree, Drake, and the dogs into the air and flung them backwards. They rolled and scraped along the floor, blinded by dust.

619

When Drake finally stopped rolling he wiped his eyes and saw the huge wyrm dragging itself away. Mortally wounded, Draglûne moved quickly, though he staggered a bit and seemed uncoordinated.

Drake had seen vrelk shot through both lungs and their heart run for a mile uphill before dying. How long could a dragon run?

Drake grabbed Bree's hand and dragged her to her feet. "Come on!" he shouted and ran after the dragon.

"You are not getting away!" Thor shouted and ran after Draglûne who limped into the darkness behind the last standing stone.

The dwarf snatched up his hammer, and the large tooth he had knocked out without missing a stride.

The wyrm left a vast blood trail as he fled and the dogs barked loudly running faster than all of the companions.

Draglûne covered large distances in one stride, though blood leaked out of him in great spurts. He managed to increase his lead and almost faded from view, though they could hear his bulk scraping along and the pounding of his clawed feet.

Drake reloaded as they ran and noticed Bellor lagging far behind, his face pale and as he sucked in his breath. The light of his axe had faded, and much of his strength had gone with it.

"Come on!" Drake yelled to Bellor.

"Go!" Bellor said, as he stumbled and leaned against the wall, trying to catch his breath in a section of the tunnel with a giant dirt pit that had to be Draglûne's nest.

"Dabarius!" The disembodied voice of what sounded like an old man came from a glowing white sphere filled with mist. Drake had heard it before.

"I'll help Bellor," Dabarius said, slapping Drake on the back.

620

Bellor waved for the others to keep going and Bree, Drake, Thor, Jep, and Temus chased the wounded dragon who fled down the tunnel toward a spot of bright daylight not very far away.

CIII

I hope I am strong enough to see this to the end.
—Bellor Fardelver, from the Desert Journal

Dabarius stared into the perfectly round ball of clear crystal filled with Void mist. The clouds swirled and Dabarius saw an old man standing in a foggy realm. "Oberon?"

The old man looked out, eyes wide. "Dabarius! I'm trapped in this accursed place."

"How do I get you out?"

"Touch the crystal and use a summoning spell that can connect with pocket dimensions," Oberon said.

Dabarius remembered the spell in his master's book. He would have to use it when they had time, which was not now.

"Go on without me," Bellor wheezed and fell to his hands and knees, coughing hard.

Oberon's image faded, but another one appeared. The swirling mist showed him the canyon that approached the Gate of the Sun outside the tunnel of tombs. Piles of boulders and rubble had crushed a large number of Storm and Solar Priests. A few survivors moved aimlessly over the rocks trying to dig their brethren out. Then Dabarius saw his father's face peeking out from under a large rock. He was dead.

Dreadful sadness made Dabarius turn away from the Crystal Eye. The very moment he had found his adoptive father, he had lost his real one who had sacrificed himself in the canyon to stop the advancing warriors.

"Take it and go," Bellor said, defeated as he collapsed on the floor.

Dabarius tried to lift the sphere, but it wouldn't budge from the tripod, which was firmly attached, clearly with magic of some sort.

The Crystal Eye could wait.

Dabarius didn't want Drake and the others to get too far ahead. He couldn't wait for Bellor to catch his breath. Instead, he lifted the old dwarf over his shoulders and ran down the tunnel using every bit of strength and magic he had left. Bellor would see Draglûne die today. He deserved that much.

CIV

Wounded from the battle with the Sons of Kheb, the Dragon of Darkness fled the House of Lesh'heb in defeat, his armor torn and his blood flowing like a dark river upon the stones.

—Hezekiah, Priest of Kheb from the Sacred Obelisk

Drake saw daylight in the tunnel ahead and a burst of speed propelled him forward. Draglûne had slowed, his tail dragging on the ground in a straight line as his strength faded at last. Jep and Temus barked loudly in close pursuit, though both of them could barely run after their injuries from the wingataurs.

Drake had to end this chase, and end it now. It was a straight shot and there was plenty of light. The tail was moving and he would time it right or the spiny appendage would block a leg shot. Draglûne kept his long neck down making a head shot impossible.

Just shoot, a voice in his mind said. Drake stopped, coming to a landing on both feet. He let out his breath, and pulled the first trigger. The bolt struck the back of Draglûne's left foot, but it didn't slow the wyrm much. Drake saved the last shot and sprinted after Bree and the dogs who were gaining ground. If they got too close the tail might crush them. Drake was about to yell for the dogs to come back to him, but it was too late.

The Dragon King slapped Temus and sent him rolling against the cavern wall. The dog yelped and went limp.

Bree'alla sprinted with everything she had left and slashed the back of Draglûne's right leg, which fell out from under him as she rolled forward.

Momentum and his front legs powered him still, and an instant later Draglûne reached the daylight, and jumped off the plateau. The dragon soared over the white clouds.

"No!" Bree screamed.

624

Jep tried to stop at the edge of the cliff and skidded forward, his feet slipping on the mist-slicked rock where a waterfall had once been. The dog would have gone over the brink, but Bree grabbed his tail and stopped his slide.

A powerful blast of wind hit Drake in the face a few strides later when he made it to the edge and teetered on the brink. Draglûne was below them and his wings caught a draft, which blew him upwards, and a little backwards as he glided south. Spires of striated gray and white rock poked out of the cloudy abyss in the near distance reminding Drake of the Lily Pad Rocks.

Draglûne gained more altitude, but was barely flying above the swirling fog, which churned in the high wind. Large vortexes that looked like mouths spun below the wyrm whose blood fell like red mist.

"Shoot him!" Bree yelled.

The winds were too strong. He could never hit the dragon in these conditions.

Take the shot, Ethan's voice commanded him.

Drake took out the shaft, and replaced it with Ethan's thorn bolt. It all happened so fast, in the span of a breath, and it seemed so right.

The wyrm was ascending, a gust blowing him backwards, and Drake took aim at his left wing joint where the wing bone connected to his shoulder. If he could hit the joint the dragon could not fly.

Let me go, brother, no more regrets, Ethan said.

For you, Ethan. The Bloodstone mantra was suddenly in his head like it had been so many other times. In that moment, Drake realized that he rarely said the words alone. Another voice had often said them with him. The voice had been there to help him and guide him, and reassure him when he needed it. Now it was time to let Ethan go. He felt a spirit leave his body and enter the thorn bolt.

Drake pulled the trigger and the shaft sailed into the wind, rising and then falling like it was climbing a mountain and dropping into a valley then climbing again. The bolt flew so far, and then dove at an incredible speed toward the wyrm.

The bolt hit Draglûne in the center of his wing joint, a shot that Ethan had guided all the way.

The dragon's wing locked up instantly, and Draglûne could barely maneuver, and started to fall. Desperate, he crashed toward one of the spires of rock. He reached out with both front claws and smashed into the vertical cliff. He wrapped his tail around it, hugging the stone that went skyward like a bulbous tower built on top of the clouds.

One wing lay useless behind the dying Dragon King as he climbed the cliff, smearing his dark blood all over its chalky surface. His injured rear legs were mostly ineffective as he tried to climb, but he used his tail to wrap around the rock and stabilize himself while dragging his tremendous weight up the vertical surface. Finally, Draglûne reached the top. He pulled his bulk onto the blasted and slanted surface, barely large enough to hold a third of his length. His long neck and tail both drooped over the edge.

A stream of bright red blood poured out of his chest, staining the tower of stone as Draglûne clung to life.

Drake watched his enemy settle into what had to be his final resting place.

The wind picked up even more making it almost impossible for a bolt to reach him now.

"Die!" Drake shouted into the wind, and raised his crossbow.

"Die!" Bellor, Thor, Dabarius and Bree repeated his shout, their voices echoed as the wind carried the word aloft and repeated it back to them.

Blood poured down the grayish-white stone.

All movement ceased in the wyrm, whose body remained on the rocky island poking out of the Void.

Thor, Bellor and Dabarius held onto each other grinning.

Jep, and a limping Temus, nuzzled up against Drake as Bree took the Clifftoner's hand in hers and squeezed.

A smile creased Drake's face as a huge weight lifted from his shoulders. They had done it. All of their sacrifices, all of the pain had been worth it. They were alive and their duty was done. Drake glanced at his friends, and then back at Draglûne's corpse. Relief and pride, and a feeling of triumph swelled inside him.

"He's dead!" Drake shouted into the Void as loud as he could, and he hoped his words traveled all the way to the bottom of the Underworld.

CV

I wish I could see all the people I love one more time. I would tell them that I love them, and that I would see them again in the Afterworld. I take comfort from that, but do not think I am perfect like the Goddess. I have the desires of the flesh and I will carry many regrets with me. Twenty years is not long enough, and I know my life was not lived fully. My greatest regrets are that I will not be Drake's wife, or the mother of his children. I will not be a teacher or a healer to the people of my village or those of the Nexus Plateau. Instead, I will be a martyr slain because of my beliefs. I am afraid of what will come after I'm gone. There will be bloodshed in my name, and that is the worst legacy I can imagine. I have failed to stop the war that is coming, but I pray that my death will someday bring peace.

—Priestess Jaena Whitestar, from her personal journal

Jaena was in a daze as the lift stopped and the door opened into a room packed with Drobin soldiers in heavy armor. Wilke escorted her with his hand on her arm, and the warriors made a path for her. She could not understand the roaring sound in her ears. Then she realized the people outside were yelling, screaming, and chanting. The small building they were inside had a few tiny windows near the ceiling, but she could not see out. Agitated Drobin soldiers and officers of higher rank with fancy helmets gave terse orders and looked out the two doorways that exited the building on opposite sides.

She ascended a steep winding stone staircase, and would have tripped, but Wilke caught her and another marshal flanked her now, supporting her other arm. The light coming from down the open staircase made her blink and the sound outside was twice as loud now. Right before she made it to the top she saw the flagpole with the blood red banner streaming in the wind.

Head down, she emerged onto the little rooftop, no more than twenty feet on a side with only a tiny lip. The middle of the stone roof had been blackened by fire, and she wondered how many Priestesses had been burned atop this building. Her fate would be different, and she saw the table with the leather straps and a basket filled with rags where her head would fall. The basket sat on a bloodstained block of gray stone. A dwarf wearing a full helmet and carrying a large axe with a long tapered blade sat on a stool near the staircase. She could not see his eyes, but she knew that he watched her. His eyes on her made her blood go cold.

She turned away from him, and in all directions a sea of people filled Father's Square. She was stunned as the crowd had doubled since she last looked out her window in the tower. A hundred thousand pairs of eyes fixed on her, and Jaena began to tremble.

When the people saw her they roared even louder, and continued chanting, "Free Jaena! Free Jaena!" over and over again. Many of the closest people in the crowd surged against the line of Drobin soldiers surrounding the tiny building.

Jaena knew with certainty that all of the soldiers would be killed and the crowd would storm the Red Block, and probably take it apart piece by piece. Afterward, they would attack the Temple of Lorak behind her, and burn the city. The Drobin soldiers guarding the sweeping stairs in front of the temple would not stop the crowd who howled her name, and fervently cried for Drobin blood. Many of them were armed and thrust weapons in the air. Clubs, daggers, axes, scythes, hammers, and for an instant she thought she saw a pair of Kierka knives raised by young men she knew. She lost sight of them, but it looked like Blayne and Kraig.

In a daze she walked with Wilke supporting one of her bound arms and another marshal on her other side. She glanced up at the gigantic Temple of Lorak for the first time. The colossal head of Father Lorak was carved into the ridge

629

behind the blocky temple and he stared down menacingly at her. From her tower cell, Lorak appeared to be looking at the horizon, but from this angle he was looking down on the whole city as if he were judging it. How must he look to the assembled crowds? He must be a harsh figure of stark condemnation, a symbol of their oppression that never took his eyes off them.

She turned away, not wanting to imagine the scale of butchery that was to follow her death. Jaena bit her lip, and felt the urge to shrink in on herself. Then she stared out at the crowds, and thought about Drake. These people, and the man she loved, were all so brave.

They gave her courage, and she told herself that this wasn't the end. She would see Amaryllis today, and her father, whom she had never met.

Jaena stood tall and people roared for her.

A dwarf in front of her tried to get her attention and finally reached up and grabbed her shoulders making her look down at him. Lord Marshal Gunther Krohgstaad shouted her name, trying to make her hear him above the cacophonous din around them. He was haggard, and his eyes bloodshot as if he had been up all night. The Lord Marshal said something to Wilke, who sprang into action. Wilke and his four marshals drew their weapons, and guarded the top of the stairs they had just ascended, keeping a group of angry soldiers and the Defender Aksel penned below.

"Gunther, what's happening?"

He smiled at her.

She realized she had used his first name. "Please, forgive me," Jaena said, having to shout, "Lord Marshal, what's happening?"

"It's all right," he said, smiling. "You are *pardoned*."

She did not think she heard him right. "What?"

"You are pardoned!" he shouted, and pulled her closer to him.

630

Jaena did not believe it, but Gunther cut her bonds, and told her, "I spent all night trying to get the Priests of the High Council to meet again, and discuss this," Gunther said. "I went with the Priests I gathered first to the homes of the others, and found that three of them were dead, along with their servants, and some of their family."

"That's horrible," Jaena said. "I'm so sorry. I wanted to prevent them from being killed."

"Listen," Gunther said, "The Priests and the others had all been dead at least a week."

She did not understand.

"The council members who voted for your death *yesterday* had been dead for a week. We would have never known, but I had my dog, Odo with me. He bit one of the Priests when he opened his door. The dwarf fled when I tried to follow him and apologize for Odo, but the Priest disappeared. We searched for him, and Odo found decomposing bodies in a locked cellar room. We found the Priest's corpse—the dwarf we had all just seen!—among them. We found the same thing in two more houses. We had all spoken to these Priests over the past days, and we found three of them had been murdered for a week or more."

He paused and she tried to comprehend what had happened. Had shapeshifter imposters—demons—infiltrated the Lorakian High Council?

"The four surviving Elder Priests voted to pardon you and stop this madness, but we need your help to end this. You must speak to this crowd, get them to stop the riots, return to work, stop attacking the Drobin in the city."

Wilke took down the blood red banner and affixed a golden banner to the rope and began hoisting it up.

Defender Aksel Reinheld confronted Gunther. "Lord Marshal, are you pleased with yourself? You've weakened the empire today. You've given in to a rioting mob and freed a cult leader whose followers advocate armed resistance. What

631

about Drobin law, which you are charged to uphold? I shall have you stripped of your post. I vow to Father Lorak that this pardon will not stand." He stormed off down the stairs, and the Lord Marshal shook his head.

"He is wrong," Gunther said. "The pardon will stand, but we need your help."

Jaena stared at the people who were already attacking the Drobin soldiers and throwing stones. This would not be easy. "What did the council offer the people?"

"Terms?" he asked. "You are to be exiled to the Thornclaw Forest, and pardoned. There were no other terms."

Jaena knew that would not stop the crowd. "That's not good enough. The council must give the people something more."

"More?" he asked.

"They want to be able to practice their religion, and have Priestesses of Amaryllis serve them without fear of arrest and death."

"I can't make these promises," he said.

"You don't have to," Jaena said, "but the council must meet with the Nexan people, and discuss the terms of the peace. I will help."

"First we must stop this," he said. "Will you speak to the crowed now?"

"I will."

The golden banner, meaning "pardon," had made the crowd murmur with confusion and some stopped attacking. Jaena stood beside the Lord Marshal who used a brass speaking trumpet, his voice booming out over the crowd. Some magic must have augmented it, as he was very loud, but how could the tens of thousands all hear him?

"Pardoned! Jaena is pardoned!" he shouted. "Smile, raise, your arms," he told her.

She did. She was going to live. The relief and triumph were the best feelings she'd ever had.

"By order of the High Council of Lorak, this woman known as Priestess Jaena, is pardoned of all crimes. She is pardoned! Pardoned!"

He faced each of the four directions and repeated his message again and again until the crowd understood. Jaena's smiles and waves helped them comprehend and the roar of euphoric joy was deafening. She waved and smiled, still in shock at what had just happened.

She accepted the speaking trumpet, and thanked the crowd repeatedly. They roared and shouted her name, until finally they began to quiet themselves as she asked them to. She didn't know what she was going to say, but she would say it from her heart. When the volume had gone down so she could hear individual voices shouting to her she began facing south, away from the Temple of Lorak to begin her speech. "People of Nexus City, people of the villages, and beyond, the Great Goddess Amaryllis has heard you!" She took the scarf off her head and let her long blond braids fall across her neck and down her back.

The people roared and she waited for them to quiet before continuing, and turned toward another direction.

"Thank you, Great Goddess, for the clear sky today."

They roared again and she learned how to wait between each sentence before continuing.

"Please, put down the stones, lower your weapons, do not harm the Drobin soldiers any more today. Please, hear me speak. No more stones. Not today."

Most complied, but not all.

"I have been pardoned because of you. Thank you!" She noticed that all of the dwarves except Gunther, Wilke, and the four marshals had left the rooftop. She was glad not to see the executioner any longer, and was still in shock at the turn of events.

"I am alive because of Lord Marshal Gunther Krohgstaad of the Kingshield clan." She raised his arm beside her. The crowd's reaction was mixed. "He saved my life, and he is what is good in the Drobin."

The people cheered for the Lord Marshal, and shouted his praises. Jaena realized he was known to many of them, and must have a reputation that echoed how he had treated her.

"This day is not about my life, it's about our wish to live with more freedom to love the Goddess, and her Priestesses, as we want. We will have more freedom, and it will not take any more bloodshed."

Jaena knew what to say now and it poured out of her. "The Goddess teaches we must be tolerant and peaceful. But this does not mean we are weak. The Lorakian High council will meet with us because we are strong."

She glanced at the Lord Marshal, and he nodded to her, some fear in his eyes.

She faced the people. "Because of today, because of what you've done, your lives will be better. Some of you will ac-company me when I leave today, and we will choose a few to represent the others, and we will speak to the representatives of the High Council of Lorak. We will demand that Amaryl-lian Priestesses be allowed to live and work in the open on the Nexus Plateau."

The crowd cheered and Jaena looked at the soldiers on the steps of Lorak's Temple, retreating into the tunnels, and into the temple itself. She would force their leaders to act.

"I thank you all for your love, and for your sacrifices, but now there must be peace. We must have a new calm as we speak to the Drobin leaders, and our own who have turned their backs on us.

"I ask you, Priestess Jaena asks you, to return your weapons to your homes and leave them there. We may need them in the future, but not now."

Jaena saw Blayne and Kraig at the front of the crowd right in front of her, and nodded at them.

"My friends, people of the Nexus Plateau, I want you to go back to the fields and to your families, and to your work. The Drobin know how strong we are now. We have proven they cannot oppress us any longer. Let us now prove that we are worthy of their trust, and that our two peoples can live together without one being servant and the other master. As brave as you've been today, I need you to be wise as the sun sets. Take heart in our victory and look to the future with hope.

"Thank you all, and thank the Goddess Amaryllis for your blessings. May the sky be clear!"

"May the sky be clear!" the crowd roared and Jaena knew that her new life had begun. She may never be able to leave these people who looked up to her. They needed her here, and she doubted if she would ever return to Clifton again.

After several minutes of waving in all four directions to the adoring people, Jaena allowed Lord Marshal Gunther to escort her down the steps. She would go out into the crowd now, and find Blayne and Kraig.

At the bottom of the narrow steps a crowd of Drobin soldiers stood waiting, smiles on their faces. She had saved their lives today, and she waved at them as they cheered her.

A demonic voice stunned her and whispered inside her mind.

This war must happen.

A young Drobin soldier standing in front of Jaena suddenly reacted with shock, his eyes bulging as he reached for something behind her at the edge of the staircase. In that horror-filled breath, Jaena glanced over her shoulder as a collective gasp erupted from the soldiers. The executioner in his full helm stood behind her, and Jaena knew it was a shapeshifter demon in dwarven flesh. She was hemmed in with no room to avoid what was coming. The long tapered axe blade hung in the air the instant before it descended toward her forehead.

CVI

The Dragon of Darkness flew south over the clouds of the Under-world, escaping the House of Lesh'heb. Such were his wounds that a single arrow or spear–thrust would have spelled his demise, but the essence of the Storm God preserved his life.

—Hezekiah Priest of Kheb, from the Sacred Obelisk

Thor stood with his friends at the edge of the Void. He stared at the unmoving dragon, searching for any sign that Draglûne was still alive. The blood had stopped flowing from his wounds, and judging by the amount of it they had passed on the cavern floor, the wyrm may have bled his last drop.

Seeing Draglûne dead brought him no elation now, only a sense of tremendous liberation as his Sacred Duty had been accomplished after so many years, and so many trials. The wind blew in his face, causing moisture to form and run from his eyes.

Jep and Temus rubbed against him, offering him their sup-port. He scratched both of the dogs on the neck. How they had survived the last few months and today without anything more than some big bruises and a few cuts was proof that Lorak had a fondness for big, ugly, smelly dogs that were the most loyal and unselfish friends any dwarf could ever have. They were, of course, far too tall, but he had forgiven them for their short-comings long since.

"Are you all right?" Dabarius asked.

"It's only the wind and this bright daylight," Thor said, wiping his eyes.

Dabarius put his hand on his friend's shoulder.

"You fought well today," Thor said. "No man or dwarf has ever killed an entire tribe of wingataurs by himself."

"You could have taken at least a dozen of them," Dabarius said.

"Not likely," Thor said. "Four, maybe five, but you . . . " Thor whistled. The wall of lightning had astounded him, and he knew that Draglûne had tried to break Bellor's fire protection spell, but the Shield of Amar'isis had defended them perfectly, and Draglûne's fire breath had no effect. "I want you to have this," Thor said, and he handed Dabarius the ten-inch long tooth he had knocked from Draglûne's mouth.

"Thank you," Dabarius said, drying it off a bit. "I don't have a gift for you."

"Carrying Master Bellor the last of it, and giving me my life is gift enough," Thor said. He grinned. "That, and revenge, of course."

Dabarius smiled and walked out of the wind, sat down, and took out his book of spells.

Thor wiped his eyes again. He wanted to go back into the tunnel of tombs and look at the obelisk where they had seen the list of names, and the grave marker rune symbol above them. All of the names were there, including Bölak's, but Thor still refused to believe they were all dead. Who had made the rune marks? A Khebian Priest? Until he saw his uncle's body, he would consider him still alive. Thor's mother would want him to assume that, and to keep looking for her favorite brother. The Blackhammer clan had many brave and famous members, but Thor was most proud of his uncle and his mother. She had shielded him with her own body when Draglûne had treacherously attacked decades before. She had finally been avenged, and Thor felt like he belonged among the renowned members of his clan.

Now that his Sacred Duty had been accomplished he did not know what he would do. He had planned to die today in glorious fashion, but Bellor's plan had worked too well, and Drake had done the impossible. He and Master Bellor could not go back to Drobin lands. They were wanted by the Lorakian Priesthood as heretics, and would spend the rest of their days in a dark cell, unless they were executed.

No, he would not risk that. The Mephitians in Isyrin were quite hospitable when they were not in the process of trying to kill him or trick him into being cooked in the deep desert. Maybe he would settle there? Bellor would have to decide, as he would stay by Bellor's side until the end. He looked at his friend who was also having trouble with the wind in his eyes. Thor embraced Bellor, and silently thanked Lorak for keeping the most important member of his family alive. He imagined that it could be said that Bellor was the greatest *Dracken Viergur* to ever live, having played a part in the deaths of two dragon kings. He was proud just to have known him, though he didn't have the words to express it.

Tears of joy streamed from Bellor's eyes. None of his friends had been slain, and Draglûne was dead. His plan had worked. He had spent almost three centuries perfecting his craft. The amassed skill, magic, and the luck he had earned with hard work and bitter lessons, had combined to defeat the carriers of the essence of the Sun and the Storm God. And his companions were all still alive. A miracle. Perhaps three.

Draglûne had taken far too long to expire, but Bellor suspected the essence of Shenahr must have had something to do with it. Drake had delivered the bolts to his heart as if it had been the simplest of shots, and the enchanted shafts should have killed him almost instantly. Not almost five minutes later after Bellor thought he might get away. The sprint after Draglûne had almost killed the old dwarf, not the small horde of wingataurs.

The exertions of the day had made Bellor's chest ache fiercely, and he still had trouble catching his air. Perhaps his heart was giving out after *Wyrmslayer* accepted its toll for making him nigh unstoppable when the first wave of wingataurs attacked. It fed on blood and rage, but it pushed Bellor beyond his limits and now he wouldn't blame his heart for failing. He was ready if the moment came, but he did want to speak to Bree'alla. He took her hand and said, "Please forgive me, lass, and don't blame Drake. I forced him to keep my plan secret from you, as I knew Draglûne would read your thoughts. Your despair convinced him to attack, and I am so sorry for the pain I caused in you."

"It's all right," Bree said. "I've kept many secrets from you." She hugged Bellor. "Drake's alive, and it worked."

The old dwarf kissed her hand, and faced the young man who had no equal. "Master Drake, it has been my honor to travel with you. Thank you for your skill, your friendship, and your trust. This is your victory."

"Our victory," Drake said, and hugged Bellor, who finally had to excuse himself and wipe his eyes. He needed to write in his journal and he also needed to copy down the names and whatever else was on the grave marker in Mephitian.

Funeral prayers must be said and he would see if the ghosts of any dwarves lingered in the tunnel of tombs. He hadn't seen any dwarf spirits, but there had been many others here. Once that was all settled, he would see how he felt about clinging to this mortal life before he made the journey to the Earth Father. Perhaps he had another ten years in him? Thor was a *Dracken Viergur* Master now. He would carry on and teach the next generation, but where would the school be, Isyrin?

The details would sort themselves out. For now he would be content to read aloud the ten Drobin names on the grave marker, a final act of remembrance for the ten fallen *Viergur* who had come forty years before and perished. If not for his young friends, especially Dabarius, and Drake, they all would have died today, just like Bölak and his hunters.

Bellor sat down out of the wind and began to write in his journal. He immediately fell asleep. His dreams, for the first time in years, held no blood, or fire, or death.

Bree stood next to Drake, squeezing his hand as she leaned against him as they watched the body of Draglûne. The dragon was gone, and Drake was alive. That was all that mattered now. Somehow, they would escape this awful place and get back to Isyrin. They would make a home there, and get married in a sacred palm grove. They would have children and raise them in a home surrounded by trees and flowers. She could work at the temple of Amar'isis and become a teacher of language, the sword, whatever they wanted of her. Her father, Ben'syn, who had died defending his people, and the Scrolls of Amar'isis, which had made all the difference in their fight, would be proud. She would cleanse herself of all the blood she had shed in the service of the Goddess.

The wyvern-dragon, Verkahna, who killed her father was dead, and now Verkahna's own father shared that same fate. The line of the Dragon Kings was much diminished, if not gone entirely. Bree would personally lead a hunt for the dragonling spawn of Verkahna at the Mouth of the Underworld. Drake would go with her, maybe even the dwarves and Dabarius would accompany them. One more hunt and it would all be done, Draglûne's known line exterminated, as they should be.

Bree'alla quickly reconsidered her blood wish. Maybe some others would do that deed and kill the dragonling. Her companions had risked their lives enough, and Bree could not bear it if anything happened to Drake. She felt such love for him, and it had grown ever since Jaena had been inside of her body at Seb'most, and last night.

Poor Jaena. Was she still alive or had she been executed?

Bree closed her eyes and thought of Jaena. Today—of all days!—was to be the day of her death. How could that have been a coincidence? She had some vague notion that Jaena's execution had been arranged to happen today by an evil connected to Draglûne.

The bond between Bree and Jaena was still there, not as strong as it had been the night before when she and Drake had made love for the first time, but it was present on some other level. Jaena must be dead. She had had one last moment with the man she loved, but it was over. He was Bree's man, only hers now, and he would live in Mephitia. Queen Khelen'dara would never let him leave, even though he had a trust scarab. He knew too much, and had traveled too far.

Bree glanced away from the hideous dragon on the rock tower, and up at Drake's handsome face still smeared with blood. She noticed a small stream of water dripping off the cliff where the great river of Lesh'heb had once flowed. She wet her scarf in the sweet water, not at all fouled by the dragon, and she washed out her mouth ridding herself from the lingering taste of wingataur blood. Then she wiped away the blood from Drake's face, though he would not stop looking at Draglûne's body.

He was so quiet most of the time and said nothing now. She liked his quietness, his tenderness, and especially his kindness. She knew that someday he would be an excellent father, and that their children, and grandchildren would be loved and protected. He would not have to worry so much about aevian threats like he did in the North. He would learn to love the desert.

Drake wanted to take his eyes off Draglûne's body. He wanted to turn away and look at Bree, but he couldn't. Not yet. The dragon had been motionless for a long time now, and yet Drake still worried that he was alive. If Draglûne truly did have a god inside him, could it bring him back to life? What had happened to the essence of the Storm God? Did it pass on to an heir? He would have to ask Dabarius and Bellor about these things. For now he would watch, and wait.

Why couldn't he let go of his worry? His friends had, and he envied their relief and calm.

Draglûne looked dead. Ethan's spirit-guided thorn bolt had stopped the dragon from going somewhere, and now they could see his body, and know he was dead for certain. If only they could reach the top of the tower and cut off his head, then Drake would stop worrying. It would be good if the corpse was in the Void before sunset as well. That would trap the dragon's spirit there for all time. Drake shook his head, irritated that he wanted to believe in Amaryllian superstitions when it was convenient for him.

If Jaena could hear his thoughts, what would she think? He missed her and he loved her, but he would never see her again. He would never forget her, but he had learned that the promises naïve young people made to each other don't always come to pass. Grand events, like war caused by truly evil creatures like Draglûne and Ra'menek, had to be dealt with. Sometimes young men had to leave home and fight for what they loved, though they may never return, and be able to enjoy what it was they fought for. How could he go home after all of this?

Even if they escaped back across to New Mephitia the Queen of Isyrin would not let him go, even if he wanted to. How would he fit in Cliffton? He would have more in common with Old Man Laetham than anyone close to his age. Now he understood why the Elders acted the way they did sometimes. They knew.

He would like to see real forests again, and the Wind Walker Mountains, and his hammock under his family's cover tree, and juicy vrelk steaks which were far better than any food he had eaten in Mephitia.

Though he did have something else now.

Blue skies.

Clear skies.

His conscience was lighter. He had let go of Ethan at last, though his adopted brother had picked the exact moment to depart. Drake wondered how often Ethan had been the strong one in their haunted friendship over the past five years? How would Drake cope with things now?

He knew how. He would cope by having Bree at his side. He loved her, and he would never hurt her, or make her feel like she had today when he pretended to be dead. Her scream was imprinted in his mind, and he knew he would hear it for a long time to come. He wanted to tell her how he felt, ask her to become his wife, but he still couldn't look away from the dragon. She wiped the wingataur blood off his face and smiled at him, trying to get him to turn.

"Look at me," she whispered, one finger stroking his nose.

He resisted, then smiled and turned. Her green eyes sparkled mischievously. He felt like he barely knew her, and yet he knew so much about her that no one else ever would because of what they'd been through. She was the toughest, bravest, most hot-blooded woman he had ever met. Their life together would be anything but predictable.

He kissed her, and when they had finally peeled apart and stood nose to nose, Bree glanced around at their stark surroundings, then back at him. "We need to get out of here," she said. "This is not where we're going to spend the night."

Dabarius read over the summoning spell Oberon had mentioned as fast as he could. It was a complicated spell, but he would read it right from the page and use the power words as Oberon had taught him. Dabarius was exhausted from the magic he had already used today, but he had a little bit of stamina left, and that was all it would take. He would free Master Oberon, unlock the Crystal Eye from its location and they would get out of the tombs and search for his father's body. From what Dabarius saw, the chance Barius had survived was slim, but he had a faint hope. He would hold his grief until after he knew. Then he would have to decide what course of action to take. The Khebians in Mephitep might be able to handle themselves and depose the Mortal King Ahken'ra. The villagers of Lesh'heb had already decided where they were going to start their new lives out in the wild, but it felt wrong to leave his father's mission undone. Should Dabarius stay and help bring down the false Storm Priests, and the sycophantic Solar Priests who had done Ra'menek's bidding for so long?

Master Oberon would give him good council when he was free. He would primarily have to look after the elderly man, and he would not risk his life unnecessarily after going through all of this to save him. Oberon and Noah had done so much for him, and he owed them everything. Now they would be able to talk openly, as both of them wore binding scarabs from Isyrin.

The master wizard could perhaps help with the affairs in Old and New Mephitia. After that, Dabarius would help resettle Oberon and Noah back in Isyrin where he could look after them. Khelen'dara would allow Noah to come south, he hoped. The city would be safe once the unfinished business with General Reu'ven was taken care of, though Queen Khelen'dara may have already handled that by now. How long would it take before Dabarius got to see Dara again? Was she was carrying his child?

Gods he missed her, and how she would laugh when he told her about what he had said to Ra'menek as he tried to become the heir of Ah'usar. Who was the true heir? Probably Ahken'ra, the God King in the capital. It would be a matter sorted out later.

Half an hour after Draglûne had died, Dabarius figured out the nuances of the summoning spell. Drake and Bree were kissing again and staring into each other's eyes, Bellor scribbled furiously in his journal having woken from his nap, and the wind still seemed to be giving Thor's eyes some trouble.

Dabarius cleared his throat. No one paid attention to him. "I've figured out how to get Oberon out of the Crystal Eye."

"Good," Bellor said. "How long will it take?"

"A few minutes, perhaps less," Dabarius said.

"Well, you can't go alone in there," Bellor said. "Wingataurs might still be around."

No, I killed them all, Dabarius thought to himself.

"Take the dogs with you," Bellor said, "and Thor."

The younger dwarf sniffled and tried to pull himself together.

"Jep, Temus, go with him." Bellor pointed down the tunnel, and the dogs limped after the wizard obediently, glancing back at Thor and Drake as if they'd done something bad and were being punished.

"I'll be along in a moment," Thor said.

Temus whimpered in pain and limped, and Jep's hips seemed incredibly sore.

"Poor dogs," Dabarius pet them on the head and wished he had some food for them. They studiously avoided the dragon blood on the floor, and he paid attention to how Jep and Temus reacted when they passed side tunnels or alcoves where a wingataur might be hiding. The dogs did not sense any danger, and he trusted their senses far more than any of the others. They would also be quiet and wouldn't ask questions that might disturb his concentration during the spell casting. Hopefully Thor wouldn't catch up until after he freed Master Oberon.

Dabarius arrived in the dragon's sleeping chamber and stared across the dirt pit, shining his glowstone, then he stopped dead in his tracks. The Crystal Eye was gone.

CVII

Draglûne is dead. After all these years we have brought him low. Our Sacred Duty is achieved. Lorak's will is done. All of my companions are alive. Thor, Drake, Dabarius, Bree'alla, and the dogs, Jep and Temus. Our plan has worked. I am so thankful. My body is so tired. Soon I will rest, passing from this world, and my mantle will go to Thor.

—Bellor Fardelver, from the Desert Journal.

Draglûne's body coiled around the pinnacle of stone, his head and chest balanced on the very peak of the tower. Sunlight flashed off his iron scales, and his white belly covered with blood blended with the red-stained rock. Over half an hour had passed since the wyrm had died, and Drake was certain the body had not moved.

The wind had gotten worse, so Bree, Bellor, and Drake had stepped away from the ledge in case an errant gust blew them off the cliff. As capricious as the Storm God had been to them so far, and the fact that they had just killed his mortal vessel, Drake wanted to take no chances with a gusty wind.

Suddenly, and very slowly, one of Draglûne's wings lifted up from his body.

Drake stood in shock as the wing rose into the air. He had just convinced himself that the wyrm was dead and now . . . the hulking body began to move. Drake and Bree held onto each other shaking their heads in disbelief.

"It's the wind," Bellor said patting them. "Calm yourselves."

Drake's moment of sickening dread changed to indescribable relief as he realized the truth of Bellor's words. Sustained high wind continued to lift the dragon's leathery wing into the air like a giant sail. The body of the beast unbalanced. The tail, which had been coiled tightly began to loosen, and the upper body of the dragon inched toward the edge of the rock.

A powerful gust raised the wing even higher, causing Draglûne's corpse to hang precariously on the edge.

Then the dragon's head rolled off the stone, and like an anchor, dragged the rest of the body with it.

The aversion Drake had once experienced when anything fell into the Void was gone. He did not turn away as Draglûne plummeted toward the swirling vortexes in the clouds below. The dead wyrm returned to where he belonged, the Underworld where his spirit would be condemned for eternity.

The mists almost parted as the dragon cut through the haze. Drake caught a glimpse of gray stone, just the side of the tower of rock. He didn't see the bottom, but miles down in the depths was where the Dragon King would fall.

A feeling of profound peace came over Drake. He put his arm on Bellor's shoulder and hugged him, then he took Bree's hand, and they walked away from the Void, never looking back.

THE END OF BOOK THREE

Coming soon:

BOOK FOUR: THE CRYSTAL EYE

BOOK FIVE: THE IRON BROTHERHOOD (the finale)

ABOUT THE AUTHOR

A toy castle is what sent fantasy author and editor Paul Genesse over the edge and into madness. Dragons and castles gave him reason to live from elementary school through college where he loved his English classes, but pursued his other passion by earning a bachelor's degree in nursing science in 1996. He is a registered nurse on a cardiac unit in Salt Lake City, Utah, where he works the night shift keeping the forces of darkness away from his patients.

Paul lives with his incredibly supportive wife, Tammy, and their collection of well-behaved frogs and moderately scary dragons. When he's not at the hospital working, or crafting novels in his basement, Paul enjoys speaking at schools to students about writing. He's also worked as a computer game consultant, a copyeditor, and as a proofreader for a small press publisher.

He is the author of several short stories featured in *Fellowship Fantastic*, *The Dimension Next Door*, *Furry Fantastic*, *Imaginary Friends*, *Catopolis*, *Terribly Twisted Tales*, *Pirates of the Blue*

Kingdoms featuring *The Pirate Witch, Steampunk'd* and more. He is also the editor of several volumes of the demon-themed *Crimson Pact* anthology series, which you can learn more about at thecrimsonpact.com.

His first book, *The Golden Cord Book One of the Iron Dragon Series* released in 2008 as a hardcover and has become the best-selling fantasy novel Five Star Books has ever had. *The Golden Cord,* and book two, *The Dragon Hunters,* and *The Secret Empire* are out now as trade paperback and eBooks; book four, *The Crystal Eye*; and the finale, *The Iron Brotherhood* are coming soon.

Learn more about the *Iron Dragon Series,* check out some awesome maps, listen to podcasts, see original art, and watch videos, at paulgenesse.com. For the latest news visit his blog, paulgenesse.blogspot.com or friend him on Facebook.

Made in the USA
Charleston, SC
24 January 2012